"SAVILLE. . . .
IT THROBS WITH LIFE."
Boston Globe

"A recklessly honest portrayal of a decent man
who cannot resist the powerful forces
that shape his destiny. . . . The images are haunting
in their simplicity. . . . No one should be
unmoved by this novel."
Chicago Tribune

"Take it to the beach,
lie on the sand, and let yourself be caught
up in a book that you will not
forget for a long time."
Baltimore News American

DAVID STOREY is the only three-time winner of the New York Drama Critics Circle Award. SAVILLE, his newest novel, has garnered the Booker Award, Britain's most prestigious literary prize.

Saville

DAVID STOREY

AVON
PUBLISHERS OF BARD, CAMELOT AND DISCUS BOOKS

AVON BOOKS
A division of
The Hearst Corporation
959 Eighth Avenue
New York, New York 10019

Copyright © 1976 by David Storey
Published by arrangement with Harper & Row, Publishers, Inc.
Library of Congress Catalog Card Number: 76-50169
ISBN: 0-380-01889-6

First Avon Printing, June, 1978

AVON TRADEMARK REG. U.S. PAT. OFF. AND IN
OTHER COUNTRIES, MARCA REGISTRADA,
HECHO EN U.S.A.

Printed in the U.S.A.

Saville

PART ONE

PART ONE

1

Towards the end of the third decade of the present century a coal haulier's cart, pulled by a large, dirt-grey horse, came into the narrow streets of the village of Saxton, a small mining community in the low hill-land of south Yorkshire. By the side of the haulier sat a dark-haired woman with phlegmatic features and dark-brown eyes. She wore a long reddish coat which covered the whole of her, except for her ankles, and a small, smooth-crowned hat which fitted her head rather like a shell and beneath which her hair showed in a single, upturned curl. In her arms, wrapped in a grey blanket, sat a child, scarcely more than a year old, with fair hair and light-blue eyes, who, as the cart pulled into a street several hundred yards from the village centre, where the houses gave way to farm fields, gazed about it in a blinded fashion, its attention suddenly distracted from the swaying of the horse in front.

On the back of the cart were piled numerous items of household furniture; numerous that is in the context of the cart, for it was plainly not designed to carry such a multifarious cargo. There were a square wooden table with four wooden chairs, two upholstered chairs in a dilapidated condition, a double bed with wooden headboards and a metal-sprung base, various pots and pans and boxes, a cupboard, a chest of drawers and a tall, brown-painted wardrobe, the door of which was lined with a narrow mirror.

Riding uncomfortably on top of this load was a small, fair-haired man with light-blue eyes. He wore a loose, unbuttoned jacket, a collarless shirt and, unlike the woman, was gazing around him with evident pleasure. As the cart came to a turning of small terrace houses leading

3

directly towards the fields he called out to the driver, who, clicking his tongue, turned the horse and, to the fair-haired man's instructions, pulled up finally outside a small, stone-built house, the centre one of a terrace of five. A door and a window occupied the ground-floor of the building, and two single windows the first-floor, the roof itself topped by large, uneven stone-slab slates.

The fair-haired man sprang down; he opened the tiny gate that led across a garden scarcely six feet broad and, taking a key from his jacket pocket, unlocked the dull brown door and disappeared inside. A few moments later he came out again; he signalled to the cart and after a moment's hesitation the child was lifted down. No sooner was it on its feet, however, than it set off with unsteady steps, not towards the open gate, but away from it, back along the street the way they'd come.

"Nay, Andrew," the man called and, after helping down the woman, he turned and went after the baby, finally catching him up in his hands and laughing. "And where's thy off to, then?" he said, delighted with the child's robustness. "Off back home, then, are you?" turning the baby's head towards the house. "This is thy home from now on," he added. "This is where thy's barn to live," and called to the woman who stood apprehensively now at the open gate, "Here, then, Ellen, you can take him in."

The furniture was lifted down, and the haulier and the fair-haired man carried it inside: the bed, in pieces, was set down in the tiny room at the front upstairs; a cot, little more than a mattress in a wooden box, was set beside it —with that and the wardrobe there was scarcely any space to move at all. The chest of drawers was squeezed into one of the two rooms overlooking the rear of the house: one room was scarcely the width of a cupboard, the other was square-shaped, its narrow window looking down on to the communal backs and, beyond those, the strips of garden exclusive to each house, which ran down to the fenced field and were enclosed by the houses the other side.

The remainder of the furniture was set in the kitchen and the front room downstairs.

"Well, fancy we mu'n celebrate," the fair-haired man said when the job was done. He hunted through the various boxes and produced finally three cups; from a shopping bag he took out a bottle. He looked round for somewhere to remove the top and finally edged it off against the square-shaped sink which stood beneath a single tap in the corner of the kitchen. A high, mantelshelfed cooking range and a pair of inset cupboards occupied the remainder of the wall.

"None for me," the mother said, still holding the baby to her and looking round at the room. "I can't stomach beer."

"Just what you want after a job like this." The fair-haired man drank his undismayed.

"Well, here's to it, Mr. Saville," the haulier said. "Good luck and happiness in your new home." He raised his cup to the dark-haired woman, who, until now, had removed neither her coat nor her hat, and added, "May all your troubles be little ones."

The woman glanced away; the fair-haired man had laughed. "Aye, here's to it," he said, quickly filling his cup again and offering the remainder to the driver.

Finally, when the cart had gone, the front door was closed and Saville and his wife began to arrange the furniture in the tiny room. A fire was lit, they made some tea and sat looking at the bare interior of the kitchen; the stains and the smells of the previous tenant were evident all around. The woodwork of the back door, which opened directly to the yard, was scratched through to the other side. There were cavities in the floorboards beneath which were visible odd pieces of paper and items of refuse which finally, disbelieving, Saville got down on his knees to examine.

"Would you believe it? They've shoved their tea-leaves down here, tha knows."

The baby had wandered off upstairs, they heard its steps on the floor above.

"You'll have to watch it," the mother said. "It's not used to stairs." Previously they'd lived in a room in a flat: it was the first home they had had entirely to themselves.

"I s'll have to make a gate," the father said, yet going to the stairs and looking up them proudly. "Well, this is a grand place. We'll soon have it in shape," he added, seeing through the kitchen door his wife's despairing glance and, with something of a laugh, going quickly to her and endeavouring to hold her.

"No," she said, holding to the chair in which she was sitting, her gaze turned disconsolately towards the fire. "No hot water but what we heat, and the lavatory across the yard."

"It could have been worse. We could have been sharing it," the father said.

"Yes," she said with no belief. "I suppose so," and adding, rising to her feet, "We'd better start."

"Nay, we can leave it for one day at least," her husband said.

"*I* couldn't leave it. I couldn't bear to sleep here, let alone cook and eat, with all this dirt around."

So, on that first day, the Savilles cleaned the house: they worked into the night; the gas flare from their lamps spread out into the yard long after the houses on either side were dark. The baby slept in its cot upstairs, undisturbed by the scrubbing and brushing. Towards dawn the man slept for two hours then, finally, as the light broke, he got up for work.

"I shall see you this afternoon," he said, standing at the door. "I'll come back on the bike: I'll bring the last things over." He gazed in a moment at the room in which the fire still burned, then, turning, set off across the yard. His wife watched him: on parting at the door she'd kissed his cheek and now, in the faint light spreading directly over the field before them, and over the houses opposite, the isolation of her new home was suddenly apparent. She called after the man and he, turning finally at the end of the deserted yard to glance back, waved cheerily as if this were for him the beginning of but one of many similar departures and disappeared, still waving, towards the road outside.

The woman stood alone for a while. With the door closed, the fire still glowing, she gazed round her at the room: there was nothing there to reassure her, simply the table, the four chairs, a cupboard, and the pots they'd mounded in the sink for washing. She sank down finally by the hearth and cried.

The Savilles had been married eighteen months when they

came to Saxton. Before that they had shared a room in a flat with another couple. Then, finally, had come the chance of a farm-labourer's cottage in a neighbouring village: an old man had lived there, a widower, and it was the smell of his dog and his cat they were most aware of in the days following their arrival, and the odour of the food he'd pushed down beneath the floor.

Not having had time to prepare the house they spent the first few days scrubbing the floors, washing down the walls and woodwork, and filling in the holes which the dog, with its scratching, had dug in the various doors and the plaster. They repaired the ceilings, and replaced the crumbled boards in the floor; finally they distempered the walls, painted the outside woodwork and, in the evenings, when Saville had slept from his morning shift, at a colliery some six miles distance, he dug the garden, turning over the thickly matted weeds between the narrow barrier of fences.

Later, in the evenings, he would take the child out and sit in the yard: he had built a wooden bench from disproportionate bits of timber, and here, the child on his knee, he would smoke his pipe, the baby snatching at the clouds of smoke, Saville wafting them away and laughing.

Soon there was a routine in the mother's care of the house: on Mondays she did the washing, on Tuesdays completed the drying and started the ironing. On Wednesdays she did her midweek shopping, finished the ironing and, if she had time baked bread—large, tea-cake-shaped loaves which fitted one to each shelf in the tiny oven, and smaller, oblong-shaped loaves, the dough of which she raised in a large porcelain bowl in front of the fire. The boy, sitting in his chair or on the floor, would watch her, eager at times to use the dough himself, watching her drawing it out and shaping it in the tins or on the black, greased oven-plates, occasionally, if a fragment were over, rolling a piece himself and laying it on grease-proof paper, first in the hearth, where the flames shone and flickered on its surface, then sliding it beside the tins inside the oven and waiting impatiently, while his mother adjusted the tiny, chromium ventilator and stoked the fire, then, finally looking at the clock on the tall man-

7

telshelf, she'd stoop to the door, a piece of hessian in her hand and, if the bread were ready, lift his out first. "There, what do you think of that?" she'd ask him absent-mindedly, her attention solely on the loaves and the tea-cakes she'd baked herself. Yet there was an alertness in her son which belied his age, even a dexterity with his tiny hands so that at times, although she helped him, she would be astonished at the way he took the bread and was able to connect the various stages—the mixing, the leavening, the shaping out, the final raising and then the sliding of the plates and tins inside the oven. "He mu'n be a baker," Saville would say, coming home to see the tiny, irregular-shaped loaf the boy had baked himself, breaking a piece off, at Andrew's insistence, putting on jam and then, watched raptly by his son, chewing it carefully and with evident pleasure: "Nay, I mu'n come to his thouse again. They know how to treat a hungry man."

On Thursdays she cleaned the house upstairs, first the front bedroom, the only room apart from the kitchen to have linoleum on the floor, which she washed and polished, then the two rear rooms and finally the stairs. On Fridays she swept and cleaned the kitchen, washing the floor, and swept out and scrubbed the tiny room at the front: here the two easy chairs stood before an empty, black-enamelled fireplace. This she polished as she did the black enamel on the stove in the kitchen: on Friday evening the house smelled of polish and the gas light glowed, flaring, against all the shiny surfaces. Saville, taking the baby, would bath him in front of the fire, laying out sheets of paper and standing the metal tub in front of the hearth. Andrew would flap his arms and shout, the water would hiss against the coal, the mother would call at the damage done to her recently polished floor. Saville himself would laugh, sometimes singing, leaning back on his heels as he knelt to the tub, the child finally gazing up at him with a look of wonder, his pale eyes bright, transfixed, as his father, his face flushed, his teeth gleaming in the light from the fire, sang long and lustily for his amusement.

"By go, just see his little legs, Ellen," he'd say as he stood the child in the bowl, feeling the mound of muscle and fat, his own hand, gnarled and knotted and stained beneath the skin with tiny filaments of coal, incongruous against the smoothness and pinkness of Andrew's flesh. He'd lift him, still wet, above him in the air, the child's arms and legs flung out, dangling below him, calling, shrieking as he shook him by the fire, the flames sizzling once again, and the mother shouting, "Wash him, for goodness' sake, without all that mess."

Ellen frequently went back to visit her parents. They lived in a village four miles away, their house one of a pair, backing on to a paddock in which they kept geese and hens and, in sheds, at the farthest end, a number of pigs. She would take the boy with her, preparing him thoroughly for the journey, in his best clothes, his face bright and gleaming, his hair brushed neatly and parted at the side. He would sit beside her in the bus, gazing out at the fields with the same look of perplexity which characterized his features whenever his mother chastised his father, his expression vaguely disconcerted, yet as if in a curious way their quarrel had scarcely anything to do with him at all.

Mrs. Saville's mother was a small woman; she had had seven children in all, two of whom had died, and had long since relinquished her domestic responsibilities to these surviving offspring, one of whom visited her almost every day. So it was, whenever Ellen brought Andrew, she was obliged at some point of her visit to pull on an apron, roll up her sleeves and wash a floor, or clean the windows, wash the clothes, or prepare a meal. Her father, a tall, silent man who had been out of work for much of his later life, and who scratched a living from the weed-strewn acres at the back of the house, would leave the women of the house to their own devices, for, despite her good intentions, quarrels were frequently the outcome of Ellen's visits home. The keynote of her mother's resentment was her marriage to Saville—Ellen herself being the youngest of her mother's children and destined traditionally for several years at least to combine the services of a daughter and a domestic servant; an expectation which had been terminated by her marriage and further compounded by the birth of Andrew.

The boy would sit between the warring women, immaculate in his child's suit, with his gleaming hair and bright, robust face, open, frank and blue-eyed, vaguely aware of the animosity that passed between the adult figures and relating it conceivably to the animosity of a not dissimilar nature, a rancour and a bitterness, that passed between his mother and father at home, and which, usually, had preceded if not occasioned this visit to his round-faced, red-cheeked, dark-eyed grandmother. His playing in the dust of the yard at the back of the house was rigidly supervised by his mother. Occasionally, if he were allowed into the paddock at the back of the house, it was with instructions never to let go of his grandfather's hand —an injunction which the tall, elderly man with large, soft brown eyes and an almost inaudible voice, so self-effacing was his manner, adhered to as conscientiously and as unremittingly as Andrew did himself. "Sithee, then, what dost think to Jackie?" he would say, holding him to the pigs' pen and, if he couldn't see through the wooden lathes, lifting him to the top of the wall to peer over: the mud and the mess there would fascinate them both, and they would still be gazing at the pink and whitish bodies splashing through it when Ellen's voice would call from the house, "Dad, bring him away from there."

"Nay, muck never did no man any harm," the old man would say when they got back to the house.

"No," Ellen would say with the same vehemence as she did at home. "You don't have to wash and clean him."

"Nay, I've washed and cleaned seven of them. And thy's been one of them."

"*Who* have you washed and cleaned?" the little old grandmother would say and the father would turn away, silent, leaving these squabbles as he always did to the peculiar moralizing passion of the women.

Yet Andrew enjoyed these visits to his grandparents' house. For one thing, he enjoyed being out of his home: even going into the village with his mother he appreciated, as well as those longer journeys with his father that took him to the Park, on the slope that overlooked the village, or even farther afield than that where, some two miles away, the river came round in a vast dark curve from the distant towns.

On the journey back from his grandparents' house his mother would frequently set him on her knee, so that his head was raised to the bus window and he gazed out at

10

the fields from between her arms—a gesture she seldom made on their journey to the house when her thoughts, seemingly, were on the chastisement that lay ahead. "Well, then, there's a horse," she would say to him on the journey back, pointing out objects that caught her attention as if the relief of going home, and the peculiar victory she had won—for survival in her family atmosphere was sufficient of a victory to satisfy Ellen—were scarcely more than she could bear. These moments of companionability were the deepest that Andrew and his mother shared, as if he himself were both a trophy and a burden, she the successful recipient and the suffering host.

2

When Andrew was three the Savilles moved house. They moved up the street to one of the miners' houses which had a lower rent. As it was, their first cottage was old, and despite their renovations water came in through the roof in winter and soaked in in huge patches through the walls. Shortly after they left the four other tenants of the block moved out and the terrace was demolished, the stone taken away in carts and the timber burnt. A little later the miners' row was extended to take in the newer ground.

Shortly after they moved Andrew ran away from home. Saville, coming in from work, was met by his wife at the door. Pale, almost speechless, she came out with him to search the streets, he wheeling his bike beside her. At odd corners she would wait and Saville would pedal off, looking in yards, in odd fields and alleys; finally, as they were returning to the house, the boy appeared, escorted by a neighbour. He had been found several miles away, walking steadily along the road to a neighbouring village: he was quiet and composed: Ellen sat with him by the fire; he scarcely seemed conscious of having gone away.

Perhaps the warmth that greeted his return persuaded him to leave again: he was brought back a second time from the pit by Mr. Shaw, a miner who lived in the house next door. Saville saw him carrying Andrew along the street, the boy's face pale, earnest, gazing steadily before him, uncertain of the other man's grasp.

"Why, where's he been?" Saville asked him.

"We found him in the engine-house, curled up by the boiler," Shaw had said. "How he got in we'll never know. The engine-man found him, tha knows, by chance."

12

Finally on a third occasion, he was spotted by a tradesman on the same road leading out of the village.

"But where were you going?" Saville asked him.

"I don't know," the boy had said.

"Aren't you happy here?" he said.

"Yes." Andrew nodded.

"Don't you know it's dangerous?"

He shook his head.

"I shall have to smack you. You'll have to know it's wrong," he said.

Andrew stayed home. It was almost a year before he began to wander off again, his eyes wide, startled, whenever he was brought back, the blueness burning so that, having beaten him, Saville would go to the lavatory outside and sit on the seat, smoking, his hands shaking, like on those first occasions in his marriage when he had quarrelled with his wife.

She too seemed numbed. There was almost a ritual now; the boy's wildness a quiet, almost systematic thing, so that the father no longer felt alarmed or frightened by his going, as if he sensed the boy's immunity to danger in much the same way that he sensed his own down the pit, a carelessness, almost an indifference. He spent longer hours in bed; he bought a dog. He would take the dog up to a deserted colliery to the south of the village where the small black and white animal ran to and fro amongst the overgrown pit-heaps chasing rabbits or digging at their burrows.

Andrew started school. He was as much trouble there as he was at home. One day, coming home from one of his walks, Saville saw his son in the road ahead. He was, perhaps because of his mother's close attention, curiously well-mannered; the trouble came from these almost inadvertent gestures, the same absent-minded movement which, at school, might result in the knocking over of a desk, or the breaking of a window, and which at home led to his constant wanderings off.

He was kicking a stone in the middle of the road, and as Saville began to catch him up the stone flew up, glancing off another boy's head, the boy himself stooping down and crying. Saville saw the look of consternation on Andrew's face, the rigidity which gripped his body, a

13

helplessness which overcame him whenever he discovered he'd done something wrong. A moment later he'd crossed the road but the boy, his hands clutched against his face, ran off, crying. For a while Andrew watched him, disconsolate, standing in the road; then, with strange, stiff gestures, his face flushed, he stepped back on the pavement and with the same strange, stiff strides, set off towards the house.

He wondered even then why he hadn't intervened, and wondered what it was that held him back, as appalled by this as he was by Andrew's grief, that strange remorse which gripped them both, the son walking on ahead, unknowing, the father walking on behind, half-raging. When he finally reached the house he saw Andrew playing in the yard, on his own, digging at the soil between his feet, his face red, glistening, as if recently he'd been crying.

One morning he came home from work to find the boy was ill.

His wife was three months' pregnant. Saville stayed home that night to nurse them both. In the morning his wife was feeling better. Andrew, however, had a hacking cough, slow, half-delirious, fevered.

"Don't worry, it'll soon pass," he told his wife, and gave the boy a powder, going to bed himself in the afternoon, ready to go to work that evening.

When he got up the boy was worse.

"Don't worry," he said. "If he doesn't get better I s'll fetch the doctor." He gave Andrew another powder now to sweat it out: he put another blanket on the bed. "Will you be all right on your own?" he asked his wife.

"I don't know," she said and shook her head. She was pale, sick herself, moving round the house in a daze, unsure of what was happening.

"I can't miss another night," he said. "There'll be all hell to pay, I can tell you."

"We'll be all right," she said. "You go. I can always ask Mrs. Shaw."

"Nay," he said, determined. "I'm damned if I can't look after my own."

He stayed at home. In the night the boy got worse. He started crying out and then, a little later, could scarcely catch his breath, his body arched, rising in its struggle.

Saville got out his bike and set off in the night to fetch the doctor.

The one he called at in the village was already out. He was given the address of a young doctor who was setting up in practice. The doctor was even younger than himself and had no car: he got out his bike and cycled back with him.

Ellen was sitting by the fire in the kitchen when they reached the house.

"How is he? How's he been?" he said, surprised to find her out of bed.

"He's just the same," she said looking up, still dazed, her face paler than before.

He saw she was heating milk on the fire.

"Which way up is it?" the doctor asked.

They followed him up, putting on the light.

For a while he stooped over Andrew, half-crouched, running his hands across his chest.

"How long is it since you looked at him?" he said.

"Ten minutes. Maybe less," his wife had said.

"There's nothing I can do," the doctor said, and a moment later, still gazing at them, he added, "It seems I've come too late. I'm sorry."

"Why? What's the matter with him?" Saville said.

"I'm sorry," he said. "I'm afraid he's dead."

Even then Saville doubted what the doctor said. He stepped past him, looking down, gazing at the boy. His night-shirt had been drawn up above his legs. His head had sunk back against the pillows, his eyes half-open.

"I'm sorry," the doctor said again.

"Nay, he's never gone," he said.

"I should come down," the doctor said.

"Nay, he's never gone," he said, his wife standing back, her eyes blank, vacant. "He's never gone," he said, gazing at the shadow beneath the half-shut eyes.

"I should come down," the doctor said again, turning to his wife and taking her arm.

At the door, downstairs, he said, "No fee. No charge," fastening his bag on to the rack behind the saddle.

A few days later, when the boy was buried, his wife went back to her parents. Saville fended for himself, cooking his own meals, cleaning up the house, cycling to work. When his wife came back a week later she was silent. He helped more in the house, leaving a little later for work and, by cycling harder, getting home a little sooner, cooking, cleaning, helping with the washing. His wife was no longer sick each morning, yet it was as if the pregnancy had fatally weakened her. In the evenings when he left she would be lying prostrate by the fire, exhausted, pale, her dark eyes lifeless, dazed. He asked Shaw's wife to keep an eye on her. "Don't worry," she said. "I'll sit by her." Sometimes too, on a morning, she cooked his breakfast. "She'll soon be over the worst of it," she said.

His own life in some strange way was cancelled out. He got rid of Andrew's toys, unable to bear the sight of anything that reminded him of the boy and of what they might have done together. Weeds grew in the garden and the holes that the boy had dug there he filled in. Occasionally he set off for walks but seldom got beyond the end of the street. Soon he was falling asleep at work, and was called up by the manager.

He almost gave up work. He felt ashamed, denying what he was, unable to break the hold, the feeling of contempt. He talked to his wife but saw there a distress he didn't know how to approach, blank, blinded, uncomplaining. In the mornings when he went to bed he would find the pillow damp from her crying, and when he got up in the afternoon he would find her wandering, lifeless, round the house, a duster in her hand, a broom, unable to put it to any use.

"Nay, we s'll have to do summat," he said. "It can't go on. It can't. I s'll kill myself. I shall. Nowt that happens could be worse than this."

One morning he came home later than usual, unlocking the back door with his key to find the fire already lit, his wife kneeling in front of it, her head bowed, stiffened.

Only as he neared her did he see the knife, the blade gleaming in the light, and only as he caught her hand did he stop the movement. "No," he said. "Whatever," taking her against him, feeling the resignation. "Nay, for God's sake," he said, his hand still on her. "What is it? Whatever are you doing, then?"

She cried against him and he felt his own grief breaking, pouring out, a sudden devastation, calling out, unable to see or hear. "Whatever shall we do?" he asked her. "That's no way out. We've got another one to think of now," he said.

"Why did he go? Why did he go?" she asked him.

"Nay, let's think of the other one," he said.

"Why did he die?"

"Nay, we mu'n never think of that," he said.

Some nights now, before he left for work, he prayed with her. The first time he'd seen her had been in a church, with a friend of hers, standing in the porch after an evening service. It had been raining and he'd had an umbrella, borrowed from his father, and he went up and offered it to her, taking her home that evening, and taking her out again a week later. To begin with all their meetings had started at the church. But for the wedding, and the funeral, they had never been again. Now, however, before he left for work he knelt with her by the fire, prayed "Our Father," and then, on her behalf, prayed for the new baby. "May it be a good child, may it live and not die," he said, while at the back of his mind he prayed, unknown to her, "Give us something back. For Christ's sake, give me something back," taking it with him as he cycled through the dark, looking back at the village, at the coke ovens glowing, wondering how she was, if she were sleeping, whether it might be a boy or, better still, a girl. And though all his new hope was on the baby, he felt the dead weight of the other pulling at his back.

Shortly before the child was born his wife went to a hospital in a near-by town. On two afternoons a week he caught a bus there, taking her fruit, or a change of clothing, sitting on the upper deck, smoking, anxious, yet somehow relieved she was away and he helpless now to intervene. It was two weeks before the child was born, a boy, and when she came back he'd been almost six weeks on his own, his meals occasionally cooked by Mrs. Shaw.

The boy was dark-haired, with dark eyes, like his wife, but with something of his own features, the broad face and the wide mouth, a little larger at birth than Andrew.

It was a strange child. His wife gave it all her attention. It never cried. Its silence astonished him, its gravity, an almost melancholic thing. After the noise and spirit of the other child, its quietness frightened him.

"Do you think it'll be all right?" he said.

"Why not?" she asked him. She'd seemed confident about it from the start, from the moment he first saw them both together. It was as if her grief had come out of her and was now lying there, to hold. He would watch the baby with a smile, not sure what it represented, half-afraid, reluctant to hold it unless his wife were willing, she suddenly amused by his uncertainty, restored, almost contemptuous of the way he drew back, letting her the whole time go before him. "No, no, you see to it," he'd say whenever she suggested he should feed or change it, which he'd done often with the other boy.

They called it Colin. It was the name of her mother's father, the only member of her family she'd ever admired, a sailor, who was seldom home and who, whenever he returned, was always giving her sweets. Her memories of him were very faint, but for his uniform, the sweets, and the beard which covered her face whenever he embraced her. She had a yellowed photograph of him which she kept with one of her parents and one of their marriage in a folder in the wardrobe by the bed.

He felt a little helpless with the boy, and only relieved when he could make him laugh, or turn and move at some distraction. In the summer he would sit over him in the garden and wave a leaf to and fro above the pram, the tiny hand reaching up and snatching, the face smiling, the look half-curious, aroused. It scarcely seemed a child. The only time it cried was when she lifted it from the bath, beside the fire, suckling it then, the sobs dying down, shuddering through its shoulders, its tiny hands clutching, reaching out.

"That'll be a strange 'un, then," he said. "That's soon contented."

"Yes," she said, gazing down, stroking its head.

"Can't make head nor tail of it," he said.

It was like a part of her, never leaving, growing, so that he saw the quietness growing in her, a calmness, the other women in the street peering down, uncertain, as bemused by the child's passivity as he was himself.

"It's as good as gold. A little angel," Mrs. Shaw told

him, flushing, smiling, whenever she was allowed to pick him up.

"See, he'll go to anybody, then," he told her.

"If he'll come to me, he'll come to anybody, then," she said, and laughed.

When it was walking it seldom left the garden, and then only if he called it from the field, or from a neighbouring yard, shouting across the backs as it forced its way between the fence, coming over, blindly, taking his hand while whoever it was he was talking to would gaze down at it, smiling, and shake their heads.

"He's going to be a boxer, then," they said, looking at his hands, his arms. He had the same muscular confidence as Saville himself, his limbs already thickening out. "Aye, he s'll soon have you down, Harry," they told him and laughed whenever, for their amusement, he got the boy to skip about.

Usually he was shy and wouldn't be moved, standing by the father's side and gazing up at the other men with a slight frown, his brows knitted, his eyes dark and listening.

"Here, do you want half-a-crown, then, Colin?" they'd ask him and laugh when he refused to put his hand out. "He'll not be bought off," they told Saville. "A dark horse. We'd better all watch out."

He took the boy for walks like he'd taken Andrew, sometimes carrying him on his back, but more often walking. He sometimes took him out of the village, to the north and east, beyond the farm fields, to where the road led down towards the river. Its water was dark, its surface flecked by wads of foam and broken up here and there by clumps of timber. Barges passed bearing bales of wool, red and orange, blue and yellow, the bright colours glowing out against the darkness of the bank. There was a coal-slip farther up where the lorries from the colliery tipped their loads, the black dust sliding down the chute into the holds of the barges waiting in the stream below. A small tug with a red funnel pulled each of the barges off, a long slow train that swung from bank to bank, the men calling at the rudders, the bright funnel visible miles away, across the fields, unsupported, and belching out black clouds of smoke.

He bought another dog when the first dog died, and in

the evenings, before he went to work, he would take it and the boy with him to the old colliery site at the farthest end of the village. He'd come here often before, on his own, and now he would lie in the grass and watch the boy digging with a stick, or following the dog about aimlessly, calling after it, "Billy! Billy!" falling down, then coming back to tell him it had gone.

"Nay, it'll soon come back," he said "It knows where its dinner comes from. Just you see," laughing when the dog re-appeared, its snout muddied from digging at the holes. "You'll see, one of these days it'll catch us both a rabbit."

It was as if, looking back, Andrew's death and the boy's birth were part of the same event, the paying off of a debt, the receipt of a sudden, bewitching recompense. As time passed he never quite got used to it, sensing in his wife an almost mystical interpretation of what had happened, as if she saw the two boys as elements of the same being, Andrew the transgressed, the new boy a figure of atonement: the same element and spirit was in them both, like a rod put in the fire and brought out cleansed and glistening. Almost for these reasons he would attack the boy, half-joking, afraid of him being moulded, afraid of the way he cancelled the first child out. He would fight him on their walks, at the colliery site, rolling on his back while the boy grappled with his arms and legs, aroused, half-laughing, the dog barking at their heels. "Nay, you s'll half-kill me," he said panting, the boy moving round, out of reach, his arms extended, before he made another attack. He would laugh at the boy's strength and the strange ferocity that drove him. "Nay, half a chance, half a chance," he'd tell him, rolling off, the dog barking, the boy jumping at his legs, bouncing on him, up and down, laughing. He came to a strange life the moment he was roused, so that at times it was as if Andrew were there again, calling out and shouting, the mood passing into that even stranger silence when, walking back, he'd glance down to see the face quite still and calm, the dark eyes abstracted, solemn, shadowed by a frown.

3

The summer after the boy had started school they went away on holiday.

Colin had never seen the sea before; Saville had told him, during the weeks before they left, about its blueness, its size; about the sand, the gulls, the boats; about light-houses, even about smugglers. He'd heard about a lodging from a man at work; his wife had written; they'd sent a deposit. The day they left he got up early to find the boy already in the kitchen, cleaning his shoes, his clothes laid out on a chair by the empty grate, the two suitcases which they'd packed the night before already standing by the door.

"You're up early," he said. "Do you think they've got the train out yet? Yon engine, I think'll be having its breakfast."

The boy had scarcely smiled; already there was that dull, almost sombre earnestness about him, melancholic, contained, as if it were some battle they were about to fight.

"Could you do mine up as well?" the father asked him.

Saville got his own shoes out, then got the breakfast, his wife still making the beds upstairs.

Later, when they set off, the boy had tried to lift the cases.

"Nay, you'll not shift those," the father said. From the moment the boy had finished the shoes he'd been finding jobs, clearing the grate, emptying the ashes, helping to finish the washing-up, following his mother round as she inspected all the rooms, turning off the gas, checking the taps, making sure the window catches had been fastened tightly. They bolted and locked the back door then carried

21

the cases to the front. Saville had set them in the garden, the patch of ground between the front door and the gate, and as he locked the door and tested it, and looked up at the windows, the boy had lifted first one case then the other then, finally, gasping, had put them down.

"Better let me carry those," Saville said. He'd laughed. He gave his wife the key. "Though I don't know why we're locking up. There's nought in there to pinch."

Even then, with nothing to do but follow them, the boy's mood had scarcely changed; he held his mother's hand, looking over at his father, waiting impatiently, half-turned, while Saville rested, or switched the cases, trying one in one hand then the other.

"We've enough in here for a couple of months," he told her. "I mu'n have got a handcart if I'd known they were as heavy as this."

It was still early. The streets were empty; the sky overhead was dark and grey. Earlier, looking out of the window, he'd said, "Sithee, when it sees we're off on holiday, it'll start to brighten." Yet, though they were now in the street and moving down, slowly, towards the station, it showed no sign of changing: if anything, the clouds had thickened.

"I should say no more about the weather," his wife had said. "The more you talk about the sun the less we'll see."

"Don't worry. When it sees us on our way it'll start to brighten." He glanced over at the boy. "It likes to see people enjoying themselves," he added.

At the end of each street Saville rested; at one point he lit a cigarette but soon abandoned it. Occasionally, as they passed the houses, they saw people stirring, curtains being drawn, fires lit; one or two people came to the doors.

"Off away, then, Harry?"

"Aye," Saville said. "I think for good."

"Weight thy's carrying tha mu'n be a month in travelling."

"A month I should think," Saville said, "at least."

A milkman came down the street with a horse and cart; he brought the jugs from each of the doorsteps to the back of the cart and ladled the milk out from the shiny, oval can. At the back of the cart hung a row of scoops, some with long handles, some like metal jugs.

22

He called and waved.

"I could do with that this morning," Saville said.

He gestured at the cart.

"How far are you going?" the milkman said.

"Down to the station."

"I'll give you a lift," he said, "if you like."

His wife wasn't certain; she looked at the cans of milk; there was scarcely any room inside.

"Thy mu'n take the cases," Saville said. "We can easy walk."

"I'll take you all, old lad," the milkman said. "I won't be a jiffy."

He wore a black bowler hat and brown smock; they waited while he finished at the doors.

"Off to the coast, then, are you?" he asked them as he came back down the street.

"That's where we're off," Saville said, looking at the boy.

"First time, is it?" the milkman said.

"That's right. First time."

"I wish I wa' going with you."

The milkman had red cheeks; his eyes, light blue, gazed out at them from under the brim of his hat.

"Jump in," he said. "I'll load your cases."

His wife climbed up first, holding on to the flat, curved spar that served as a mudguard. She stood on one side, Saville on the other.

The boy, when the milkman lifted him in last, stood at the front, where the reins came into the cart over a metal bar.

The two cases, finally, were set in the middle, up-ended between the tall cans of milk.

"Now, then," he said. "We'll see if she can shift us."

He took the reins, clicked his tongue, and the brown horse, darker even than the milkman's smock, started forward.

"Not too good weather yet," the milkman said. He gestured overhead.

"It'll start to brighten," Saville said. "I've not known one day it's shone the day we left."

"Start black: end bright. Best way to go about it," the milkman said.

23

The horse clattered through the village. The cart, like a see-saw, swayed to and fro.

"They mu'n be wondering where I've got to." The milkman gestured back. "Usually on time, tha knows, within a couple of minutes."

"It was good of you to bother," Saville said.

"Nay, I wish I wa' coming with you. What's a hoss for if it can't be used?"

Colin clung to the metal bar in front; it was looped and curved: the reins came through a narrow eyelet. His head was scarcely higher than the horse's back.

Saville saw the way the boy's legs had tensed, the whiteness of his knuckles as he clutched the bar. He glanced over at his wife. She was standing sideways, pale-faced, her eyes wide, half-startled, clutching to the wooden rail with one hand and to the side of the cart with the other; she had on a hat the same colour as her coat, reddish brown, brimless, sweeping down below her ears.

The last of the houses gave way to fields; Saville could smell the freshness of the air. A lark was singing: he could see its dark speck against the cloud. Behind them the colliery chimney filtered out a stream of smoke, thin, blackish; there were sheep in one of the fields, and cattle. In another, by itself, stood a horse. He pointed it out, calling to the boy.

Colin nodded. He stood by the milkman's much larger figure, looking round, not releasing the metal rail, his head twisted: Saville could see the redness of his cheeks, the same sombre, startled look that had overcome him as he was lifted in the cart.

"Thy mu'n say goodbye to them, tha knows," he said. "Tell 'em we're off on holiday."

The milkman laughed.

"They'll have seen nothing as strange," he added to his wife. "Off on holiday on the back of a milkman's cart."

The road dipped down to the station; the single track divided and went off in two deep cuttings across the fields.

The milkman turned the cart into the station yard; he got down first, helping Mrs. Saville then the boy, then taking the cases as Saville held them out.

Saville got down himself. He dusted his coat.

"That's been very good of you," his wife had said.

24

"Aye, it's helped us a lot. I don't know how long it'd have taken me to carry that lot." Saville gestured back the way they'd come. "We'd be still up yonder, I should think, for one thing; and for another, my arms might have easily dropped off after all that carrying." He glanced over at the boy: he was gazing at the horse, then at the cart.

"Well, I wish you a good holiday, then," the milkman said. He climbed into the cart and took the reins. "Get back to me round afore they've noticed."

"It's been very good of you," his wife had said again.

They watched him turn the cart: he waved; the horse trotted out to the road then disappeared across the bridge.

"Well, that was a damn good turn. I suppose we shall have to wait though. It's put us thirty minutes early," Saville said.

He took the cases over to the booking-hall. There was no one there. The bare wooden floor was dusty.

A planked walk took them through to a metal bridge: as they crossed over it they could see the rails below. A flight of stone steps, steep and narrow, took them down to the platform the other side.

He set the two cases down by a wooden seat.

"I'll go back up," he said, "and get the tickets."

Looking back from the booking-hall, he could see his wife and the boy standing by the cases; after one or two moments his wife sat down. The boy wandered over to the edge of the platform; he gazed down at the single track, looked up briefly towards the booking-hall, then turned and crossed the platform.

A goods train came slowly through the station; the bridge for a moment was hidden by smoke. The station itself had vanished; when the smoke had cleared his wife and the boy were standing at the edge of the platform watching the row of wagons pass.

The booking-clerk came through from an office at the rear: Saville paid for the tickets and, having re-crossed the bridge, went down the narrow steps and joined them.

The town had been built in the angle of a shallow bay. To the north, overlooking the houses, stood a ruined castle. It had been built on a peninsula of ochreish-looking rock which swung round, like a long arm, above the red-tiled

25

roofs of the town itself; all that remained of the castle was a long, sprawling wall, and the dismembered section of a large, square-shaped keep. Around the foot of the headland formed by this peninsula ran a wide road, below which the sea boiled and frothed; even in calm weather it came up against the wall below the road in a heavy swell, following its sharply curved contour round to the shelter of the harbour on one side and to a broader, somewhat deeper bay to the north.

When the tide was out there were wide, sandy beaches. The house where they were staying lay to the south of the castle, near the harbour; from the upper windows they could see into the bay: they could see the white, glistening pleasure-boats as they churned in and out on their trips along the coast, and the fishing-smacks that lay in droves against the harbour wall, one fastened to another, and the crowds of people on the beach itself.

Saville had worked two weeks' overtime for his two weeks' holiday; instead of an eight-hour shift each day he'd worked sixteen hours, coming home exhausted to snatch a few hours' sleep. He still felt the tiredness now, an emptiness, as if his limbs and his mind had been hollowed out: it was a hulk that he took down to the beach each morning; it was a hulk that was slowly filled with the smell of the sea, with the smell of the fish on the harbour quay, of the sand. Even the sun, once they'd got there, had begun to shine. He felt a new life opening out before him, full of change; it was inconceivable to him now that he'd ever work beneath the ground again.

He watched the boy; he would sit with his wife, in deck-chairs, the boy digging at their feet, immersed in the sand, wading in the sea, bringing his bucket back, afraid at times of the waves which, away from the protection of the harbour, crashed up against the beach.

There were donkeys on the sand; a man came round each morning and gave a Punch and Judy Show; there was a roundabout cranked by hand. They went on one of the pleasure-boats; it was like setting out to sea, clearing the headland, turning along the coast—the town now, with its castle, little more than a cluster of rocks at the water's edge, the tall cliffs beyond like the shallow bank at the edge of a lake.

There was an orchestra aboard; a man in a sailor's hat sang songs. The boy watched it all with wonder. There was a sudden alertness about him: when he got up on a morning Saville always found him waiting, sitting in the narrow hall downstairs where, beneath a hat-stand, his bucket and spade were kept—gazing through to the dining-room, anxious for his breakfast, or already at the door, the spade in his hand, ready to be off.

"Nay, you mu'n hold on for some of us old 'uns," he told him. They would go down to the harbour before his wife was up; the trawlers would come in, unloading fish, seagulls drifting over in vast clouds above their decks, screeching, swooping to the water. The boy, in watching, would grow quite still: it was like some cupboard door that had suddenly been opened, a curtain drawn aside to reveal things he'd never encountered or ever imagined could exist before. On the beach, the first morning, the boy had gazed at the sea, abstracted, half in fear, reluctant to go near it, watching it fold over in waves against the shore, the white spume, the suction of the water against the sand; and had finally gone down with Saville, holding tightly to his hand, gasping as he felt his bare foot against the cold, stepping back, laughing, half-amazed, as he saw the children splashing through the waves. Its vastness had amazed him, the lightness, the buoyancy of the boats, the hugeness of the cliffs that towered above it.

Then, almost overnight, the mystery had vanished; he would dig at the sand with scarcely a look towards the sea, gouging out a hole, building a castle wall, building turrets, Saville stooping to the hole beside him, the boy running off to the water's edge, collecting water in his bucket, running back undisturbed, the waves pounding beyond him.

Yet, as though within himself, Saville sensed a new life spreading through the boy, slow, half-thoughtful, confusing, drawing him to the vastness of the sea, as if, in some strange way, their life in the past had been cancelled out, the smallness, the tiny house, the tower of the colliery belching out its smoke and steam. Now there was nothing to contain them: they could grow as large and be as unpredictable as they liked, eat what they wanted, sleep only when they were tired, stand in the sea, dig the beach, ride

27

on donkeys, sail on the water. There was nothing now to hold them back: they were free at last.

His wife too, he noticed, had something of the boy's nature; he'd never seen her out of the context of the home before. Now, seeing them together in a fresh place, without any associations, he saw how alike they were, the slowness, the heaviness, the strange, scarcely imagined inner life they both possessed, so that at times it was as if, casually, they shared the same expression, the same mood, the same slow look, the same transformation from a dull, brooding, almost melancholic awareness to a lighter, brighter, more accessible, scarcely conscious expectancy and alertness. He would see her laughing along the beach, running with the boy, or holding his hand as they stepped across the waves, running back from the larger ones, screaming, the boy and she joined in a way he knew he could never share himself. His own approaches to the boy were always sharp and heavy, sideways, almost ponderous, speculative, afraid that the boy himself might not react; he entrusted his loneliness to the boy, looking to him to give him something of a link beyond himself. The blackness of the mine had always brought him back, now, with the sea, he felt them all advancing, in lightness, almost gentle.

His wife had bought a hat; it had a broad brim, bevelled, sweeping down across her eyes. It was made of straw; a broad pink ribbon was fastened round the crown, its ends fluttering out across the brim. She would walk in the sea with the wind tugging at the ribbon, holding one end of her light-coloured dress, her other hand holding the boy's, walking to and fro in front of the spot where they had their deck-chairs. She was like a girl, or a woman just grown, light, uncaring; he scarcely recognized her from a distance. The other men, he noticed, watched her too; it was as if she were taller, slimmer, unconscious now of the things that lay behind them, careless, untouched. He couldn't relate her in any way to the woman that he knew.

A war was imminent. There were men in uniform lying on the beach, or walking on the promenade above. One of them he recognized one morning, a man from the village. He had a sergeant's stripes and had called out to them as they went to the beach, coming over, nodding, leaning on the rail, the boy and his wife going on down to the beach below.

"Why don't you join up?" the man had said. He had a broad figure, and since he'd last seen him as a miner in the village, he'd grown a short moustache. "If you join now you'll get preferment. I could get you your stripes within a month."

"Will we join in the war do you think?" he said. Until then, glimpsed vaguely in the papers, he'd scarcely any notion of what the war might mean.

"We'll be in it, in the thick of it in no time," the miner said. "If you join up now you'll have a choice, of what you do and where you're sent. If you wait till you're called up they'll send you wherever they want to. Join up now and the world's your ticket." He slapped his back.

Saville gazed down at the figure of his wife; she was stooping to a chair, unfolding its legs, propping it against the sand. The boy was helping her with another; they seemed contained, one unit, bound up in themselves, with no need of anyone else. The soldier's offer sent a dull surge along his arms and legs; he felt a slow heat inside his chest: it was a glimpse of a horizon like the one before him, open, fathomless, full of light.

He saw his wife look up; uncertain for a moment where he was, she scanned the row of figures leaning on the rail, her gaze finally pausing as she came to his. He saw her wave, the face lit-up, smiling.

"Nay, I mu'n stay where I am," he said. He looked at the soldier. "They'll be needing miners. To dig coal. They can't fight wars without," he added.

"Take it or leave it," the soldier said. "But if you decided now I could fix it up."

Saville glanced back towards his wife; she was sitting in the chair, opening a paper. He could see the word "War" emblazoned in the headline; she turned it over and read inside.

"Nay, I better stay." He gestured to the sands. "I've got a lad."

"So have I. They'll be all right at home," the soldier said.

"Nay, I mu'n stay with them, I suppose," he said.

He saw the glow in the soldier's eyes; there was a boldness there that frightened him, a certainty of where he was going and who he was. It filled him with dismay. He felt it was cowardice that held him back.

He gazed over at his wife.

"Think it over," the soldier said. "I'll be down again tomorrow."

When he went back to the chairs he felt the warmth of the holiday drain away, the coldness and the dampness of the colliery coming back.

"What did he want?" his wife had said.

"Oh, nothing," he said. He shook his head.

"He seemed improved a lot," she said, "since we last knew him. Do you remember that slouch he had? And the way he never washed."

"It's done a lot for him, I suppose," he said.

He gazed over at the sea; he felt cut off. The boy dug at his hole; his wife, reading the paper, sat beside him.

They didn't go down to the same beach again: each morning they took a bus round the promontory of the castle and found a spot in the bay to the north; the wind was slightly fresher here, the sand less crowded. There were still the donkeys, and the Punch and Judy, and the roundabout, and they could still see the boats sailing from the harbour. Above them, more sternly, loomed the castle; it was all a good preparation, he felt, for going back.

4

Shortly after returning from the holiday, Colin came home from school one afternoon and found his father digging at the end of the garden. Saville had cut off the grass into neat sods which he had rolled up and stacked to one side. Underneath, in the grey soil, he had begun to dig a hole.

It was quite large, the sides measured out with pieces of string fastened to pegs in the ground. The soil he threw carefully away from the sides of the hole, mounding it up in smooth piles, occasionally climbing out of the hole to shovel back the edge.

A little lower down the soil had turned to clay. It was pale yellow and came out in great clods which Saville slapped down on the pile with a great deal of groaning, shaking the spade from side to side to loosen its hold. Sometimes, his face red and streaming, he climbed out to slide the clay off with his foot. As the hole grew deeper the clay darkened. It was occasionally flecked with orange and stuck to the father's boots and his clothes. Now when he came home from school in the afternoon all he would see were his father's head and shoulders, occasionally stooping and disappearing, the spade flying up behind him in the air.

Later there would be nothing there at all. He only knew if his father was in the hole when a piece of clay came flying out, landing sometimes on the pile, sometimes on the beds of cabbages and peas the other side. When he stood at the edge and looked down his father would be an almost diminutive figure stooping to the spade, pushing it in with his foot, forcing down the handle, tugging it free then flinging up the clay above his head. His face would be crimson, his eyes shrunken, and every few minutes he would wipe

31

the sleeve of his shirt against his forehead. A little ladder
had been propped up against the side to enable him to
climb in and out.

Sometimes when he looked in he would find his father
resting on the spade, leaning back against the side of the
hole, smoking, his eyes fixed on the bottom or the opposite
side as if, despite its depth and width, he were planning
some further extension. "When it comes it'll come," he
would say whenever a neighbour leaned over the fence or
came, smiling, to examine the hole, peering down on to
the top of his head.

The neighbour would look up then, at his own garden,
at his house, and nod, frowning.

The sides of the hole were very clean and neat, the separate blows of the spade clearly imprinted. At the bottom
pools of water had formed and the clay itself had turned to
a dull crimson.

In the end, the hole itself had got too deep: he had to
shout for someone to come and help him over the edge
from the top of the ladder.

The next morning he brought home several pieces of
wood from work. They were long and flat. He wheeled
them home roped to his bike. With them, too, he brought
strips of conveyor belt, pieces of webbing and piles of nails
which, the moment he came in, he unloaded from his
pockets on to the table. They lay there amongst the cups
and plates, glistening, the fresh smell of wood and rubber
mingling with the more familiar smell of coal from his
clothes and the even more familiar smell of cooking.

"You've never walked all that way?" the mother said.

"I have," Saville said, sitting down at the table, his eyes
reddened and still black with dust. "It's surprising what
you see when you're not riding. I must have pushed that
lot up every hill in sight." He indicated the pile of wood
which he'd stacked up in the yard outside. "I go like the
wind down the other side."

An image of his father came to Colin's mind, of him
pushing the bike up the winding lanes that lay between
the village and the colliery, and of him sitting astride the
wood strapped to the cross-bar and riding down the other
side, his flat cap pulled over his eyes, his short legs dangling above the roadway, his coat tails flapping out behind.

He could even imagine the sound of the wind in his father's ears, and the soft hissing of the tyres under their heavy load.

"I'll break my neck one morning," Saville said, laughing, his mouth red and glistening as he lay back. "I s'll. Don't any of you be surprised."

He brought the wood home each morning, staining it with creosote then nailing it together.

He built four walls, kneeling on the timber as he hammered the pieces together, the sole of his boots turned up, the studs shining, the nails hanging from his mouth like teeth.

Sometimes he hit his thumb, which was thick and curled, and for a while he would lean on his heels, his head turned up, his eyes closed, his mouth full of nails, grimacing.

When he had built the walls he lowered them into the hole, the two long walls held in by the shorter ends. Then he nailed several beams across the top to fasten them together.

In the mornings now he brought back other shapes roped to his bike. There were pieces of tarpaulin, black and smelling of tar, and bricks.

He brought the bricks in a pannier fastened to the back of his saddle, in his knapsack and, once or twice, in his overcoat pockets until they tore at the weight. In the evenings, when he set off for his night shift, he would string his knapsack with his tin of food and his bottle of tea over one shoulder and an empty knapsack for the bricks over the other, setting off with a wave, his red light visible to Colin and his mother long after he himself had disappeared.

He built a roof over the hole, wedging the wooden beams into the earth on either side, and across them nailing planks of wood.

Over the planks he laid the tarpaulin, tacking it down and covering it with blocks of clay. Over the clay he threw the grey soil and on top the grass sods, yellowing now, which had originally covered the spot. "It'll be invisible from the air," he said, "don't worry," as if, when the bombing started, this was the one place where the enemy would come and look.

33

He built a flight of steps down one side of the hole, each step supported by a wedge of timber and neatly paved with bricks. Inside the hole itself he laid a floor of bricks, mixing the cement and the mortar in the street outside and carrying it in buckets through the house along a line of newspapers laid down from the front door to the back, disappearing down the steps into the hole from where, reddened and sweating, he would emerge a little later, hurrying back.

He worked with the aid of a miner's lamp which, like everything else, he had brought with him from the pit. A small, shell-like case, it hung with its pool of yellow light from one of the beams in the ceiling.

With the remaining timber he built four bunks. He built them in pairs, one on top of the other, nailing them together. Across the bed of each bunk he wove the strips of webbing and the bits of conveyor belt, which he cut into strands like thick bandages, nailing them down, so that each bunk looked like a huge, ill-fashioned net.

The last thing he brought home was a tin of grey paint. He painted the bunks with it and the wooden door, which was the last thing he made. It had two bolts on the inside and a lock on the outside. When he had painted it he hung a sign over it which said, "Wet Paint. No Entry." A week later he took it down and let them look inside.

They went down one afternoon, just after Colin had come home from school and his father had woken from his day-long sleep. The lock too he had brought with him from the colliery and the strange, square, stubby key. "Mind the steps," he said as they climbed down and he unlocked the door. "I'll just light the lamp."

Saville stepped into the darkness beyond, feeling with his foot, then went down the steps inside which led into the well of the shelter. For a moment there came the sound of his heavy breathing, then a match was struck. There was a brief glimmer of light, then it went out. "God damn and blast," he said.

"Oh, now," the mother said. "There's no hurry."

There was a second flare of light which faded then, after a moment, expanded.

A dull yellow glow lit up the interior of the shelter and

Saville said, "Watch the steps, then. You can come inside."

The hole smelled of tar from the wood, of oil, and of the clay. Saville stood in the middle of the pool of light, his head stooped slightly from fear of the ceiling.

Ellen stood with her arms clenched to her, her eyes shining in the light, gazing round.

"It should be safe," she said.

"As safe as houses," Saville said.

"Yes." She gazed up at the bunks.

"And water-tight," he said.

"Yes." She nodded her head.

The lamp swung slowly on the nail which held it to the beam. To Colin his mother and father appeared to be moving, the shadows on their faces swaying in time to the larger shadows which swung behind them on the walls. Their faces dissolved then re-appeared, their eyes glinting with the light one moment then buried in shadow the next.

"We'll have the bottom bunks," his father said. "The lad can have the one up yonder."

The whole interior rocked to and fro, like a ship, as if they were floating.

"Let's hope we won't have to use it," his mother said.

"Oh, yes," Saville said. "Well, I suppose we s'll have to, but let's hope we don't."

As they climbed out he added, "I'll look round for a little stove. We might have to live for days down there, you know."

"Mrs. Shaw," his mother said, referring to their neighbour, "says they'll go down the pit if there's any bombing."

"Oh, will they?" Saville said. "And how many can they get down there, and how fast, once it starts," And as they came out of the hole and waited for him to extinguish the lamp, he called up, "And what if they bomb the shaft, then? How will they get out?"

"I hadn't thought of that," the mother said.

"No," Saville said. "I'm the only one round here who has."

The day the war started Colin had gone out into the garden in the evening and looked up at the sky. It was grey and cloudy, the sun visible only to the west, above the

colliery, through narrow gaps. Behind the clouds, he imagined, aircraft were already waiting. Yet they gave no sign.
It was as if the houses, the clouds, the pit, the village
had been changed now, re-fashioned, the brick no longer
brick, the cloud no longer cloud, merely elements of some
new and incomprehensible presence stretching all around.

He watched the sky the next day and the next and yet,
despite these changes, nothing happened. It wasn't until
the following spring that anything occurred. Then, at the
station less than a mile away, soldiers disembarked from
long, blacked-out trains and marched up in small groups
to the village. They were tired, some were only half-
dressed with overcoats thrown over their vests and shirts.
Some had no rifles, others carried packs. When they
reached the village they sat down on the pavements, smoking, sitting in the coal-dust, scarcely troubling to look
around.

One of them came to stay in the house. He had the only
other room, next to the boy's—a small, cupboard-like
space that looked out on to the backs. He was a tall, well-
built man like Colin had always imagined soldiers were,
towering over his father, standing in front of the fire in his
khaki shirt and his rough khaki trousers or, more usually,
lying on the bed in his room, staring at the ceiling, smoking, and sometimes singing songs in a light tenor voice.

He brought his rifle with him. It stood leaning by his
room door. In the narrow space between the single bed
and the wall he laid out his equipment. All of it was tar-
nished with salt and all the clothes in his pack were damp
when he unrolled it.

Most of the space in his pack was taken up by three
large tins. Two were full of sugar which he gave to his
mother, who put them in the cupboard by the fire to dry.
The third was full of medals, metal buttons, and money.

In the evening when the soldier came back from the pub
he would sit at the kitchen table and count the money out,
arranging it in neat piles, silver and copper-coloured, then
laughing, and leaning back and saying, "If I was a Jerry
I'd be a rich man now."

He often sat by the fire, gazing at the blaze, and sometimes he would take the boy on his knee and from his
breast pocket, where he kept a wallet, take out a photo-

graph of a woman and three children, pointing at each one with his finger, which was thick and nicotine-stained, and tell him their names and what they were doing when he last saw them. He came from some other part of the country and had an accent which at times Colin found hard to understand. "Oh, don't worry about the way I talk, boy," the soldier would say, laughing, looking up at Saville. "I come from a place where they go about with nothing on."

He would often go for walks with his father and sometimes his father would take him to look at the shelter, unlocking the door and letting him go inside, lighting the lamp, the soldier gazing round, trying the bunks at his father's insistence, lying sprawled out, his head cradled in his hands.

"It's as safe as houses," his father said.

"More," the soldier would say, laughing, "if I had a guess."

When they went for walks the two men would go off down the street with their hands in their pockets, coming back hours later with a bunch of flowers or chewing a piece of grass. "Oh, don't worry about me," the soldier would say if they were late and the meal spoilt. "By all rights I should be dead, so anything'll do for me. Just cough it up."

Each morning he went into the street and with the other soldiers marched up and down. Children followed them on the pavements. On Sundays the soldiers walked in groups in the fields or down the road to the station, where they would sit on a wall by the bridge, gazing at the lines and smoking.

One day the soldier called Colin into his room and from his pack brought out several bullets. There were five of them, fastened together at the base. The cartridges were copper-coloured, the bullets silver. "Go on," he said. "You have them. I've a lot more here." He brought out several more, laying them on the bed. "You can have the gun as well," he said. "I don't want it."

He reached across for it by the door, pulled back the bolt and showed him how to slip in the bullets. "There now," he said. "You can shoot anybody you want."

He laughed, watching Colin hold it, unaccustomed to the weight.

"Nay, don't point it at me," he said. "I'm your friend." When he went down his mother stood back across the kitchen, one hand raised to her cheek frowning.

"You've never given him that?" she said.

"I have," the soldier said. "Why not? I don't want it."

"Well," she said. "We'll have to see when his father comes."

And his father too, when he came, looked at it and, in much the same manner, said, "You can't give it away, can you?" the soldier laughing and nodding his head.

"I've lost it," he said. "It's yours."

"Well," his father said. "I'll put it away. It's no good for Colin." Yet, although he locked it in the wardrobe in their bedroom, on an evening he would take it out, after the soldier had gone, and ram the bolt to and fro, put in and take out the bullets, and sight it at various objects outside the window. In the end, however, he gave it to the police and said that he had found it under a hedge.

"Don't you want to fight?" he would ask the soldier, frowning.

"I have been fighting," the soldier said.

"But to fight again," his father said.

"What for?" the soldier asked him. He would lie back easily in a chair or stand in his stockinged feet in front of the fire, smiling down at his father and nodding his head.

"To defend your country," his father said. "To defend freedom. To keep your wife and children from being captured."

"Nay, it'll not make much difference," the soldier said. "Whoever's here we'll live much the same, one way or another. There'll be the rich and the poor, and one or two lucky ones," he went on, "between."

"Nay, I can't make any sense of it," his father would say, rubbing his head, shy in the face of the soldier, suddenly uncertain. "Don't you believe in anything?"

"Not you could put your finger on," the soldier would say, smiling and lighting—if he hadn't got one lit already —another cigarette.

"He was nearly drowned. In the sea," his father said when the soldier had gone. "They picked him up in a small boat as he was going under for the third time," he added.

"For the third tin, more likely," his mother said. "With all that sugar it's a wonder he came up at all."

"Still, he's given it all away," his father said.

"Yes," she said. "I'm not surprised. Nearly everything he's got is stolen."

Yet long after the soldier had gone they continued to use the sugar, to sweeten tea and finally to make some jam.

When he left, marching off to the station in a long column, his father went with him, walking along the side of the road, across the fields. When he came back he sat by the fire, looking up at the buttons and the medals the soldier had left on the shelf. Then, after a while, he went up to the soldier's room and tidied up the bed.

One evening, a short while later, Colin woke to the sound of the sirens and lay for a moment listening for the roar of planes and the crashing of bombs. But beyond the wailing there was no other noise at all.

Then he heard his father's feet pounding on the stairs.

"Come on, lad," his father said. "We're all ready."

"Are they the sirens?" he said.

"They are."

"Have they started bombing?"

"Nay, if we wait to see we'll never get there at all," his father said.

His mother was already wrapped in her coat and had his own coat ready.

"Come on. Come on." His father danced at the door. He'd already switched off the light and, in the silence as the sirens faded, other voices could be heard along the terrace.

"Nay, we'll wrap up warm," his mother said. "They'll give us a minute, surely, before they start."

"A minute?" His father had lit the lamp at the door, shielding one side with his hand. "They don't give any minutes. Don't worry. It'll be down on our heads before we can start."

They went out across the garden in single file, his father waiting impatiently while his mother locked the door. "We'd look well sitting there," she said, "and the entire house burgled."

"Burgled?" his father said. "You think they'll have time for that?"

"I can't hear any planes."

"You won't hear them. Don't worry. Not till they're overhead." Grumbling, he led the way across the yard, the lamp lighting up the ground around his feet. "They'll all be coming in now," he said. "Now they see what it's all about."

A voice had called across the backs and he'd paused, holding up the lamp.

"What is it?" he said.

"Can you take our lads?" a man had said.

"Aye," his father said. "They'll be safe with me."

A small knot of figures emerged from the darkness, stumbling over the fences that separated the yards. They were four brothers, older than Colin, from a family farther down the terrace. Behind them came the figure of their father.

"How many have you got room for, Harry?" the man had said.

"Oh," his father said. "We'll squash a few in." He looked up at the sky. "We better be getting in," he added.

"Can you take the missus?" the man had said.

"Oh, you'll be all right with us," Saville said. "There's room for you as well."

They collected, then, around the steps, Saville fumbling in his pocket then stooping to the lamp and taking out his key.

Across the yard other figures had begun to converge on the shelter: Colin could make them out, vaguely, silhouetted against the sky, climbing fences, calling out in low voices towards the houses.

"Mind the steps," his father said. "I'll just unlock it."

"Which way will they come?" someone said and the heads turned up towards the sky.

"They could come any way," Saville said. He was at the bottom of the steps, below them, his figure stooped to the door, the lamp lighting up his face. The lock clicked, then the bolt was drawn back. "I'll go in first," he added, "and light the other lamp."

He opened the door, paused, then stepped inside.

"Women and children first," a man had called behind.

From below them came a splash. It was followed a moment later by Saville's shout, then the light inside the shelter was suddenly extinguished.

"God damn and blast," the father said.

The splashing continued a little longer then, as someone switched on a torch, Saville re-appeared at the door below, his hair matted to his skull, his clothes clinging to his body.

"The place is flooded," he said. In his hand he still held the miner's lamp.

"What's that, Harry?" someone said.

"The shelter," he said.

"You're flooded out?" he said.

"It's all that rain we've had," he said. "I should have watched it."

"Well, then," the mother said. "We better get back to the house."

"It's catch us death of cold in theer, or a bomb under t'kitchen table," someone said and somewhere, at the back of the crowd, someone else had laughed.

Colin followed his father back to the house. "I can't understand it," Saville said. "It shouldn't have been flooded." He stood shivering, his teeth chattering, as he waited for his mother to unlock the door. "Come on, come on," he said. "Can't you open it any faster?"

"I can't see," she said.

"Where's the lamp?" he said, then realized he was holding it, sodden, in his hand.

Across the backs other voices were calling out and in a doorway someone else had begun to laugh.

"Well, that was a quick raid," the mother said. "Let's hope the all-clear goes soon."

"That water," Saville said. "I can't understand it."

"All that work," the mother said. "For nothing."

"Oh, don't worry," Saville said. "We'll be as safe as houses."

"Where? In here?"

"No." He shook his head, shivering, and pointed towards the shelter. "When I've drained it."

"Drained it?" she said. "Tonight?"

"Not tonight," he said. "Tomorrow."

"It'll be too late tomorrow."

Saville shook his head, standing in his wet pants and

vest before the fire. "Don't worry," he said. "There'll be no bombing tonight. I'll have it drained by the time it starts."

A few days later he brought a pump home from work. It was shaped rather like a pudding basin, and was made of heavy metal. Colin could only lift it with his father's help. From one end ran a metal tube perhaps a yard long. It was this his father rested in the water. Then, panting, his face flushing at the exertion, he worked a little handle at the side. It was made of wood and as he jerked it to and fro there was a sucking noise inside the metal basin and out of a long rubber hose attached to the other side emerged a jet of water.

It came out in little spasms and starts, draining off across the garden.

His father worked it for an hour.

"Is it empty, then?" his mother said when they went in.

"Empty?" His father sat at the table, spreading out his arms. "It hasn't shifted an inch."

"I told you buckets would do it faster."

"Buckets," he said and banged the table with his fist.

At the end of the week, however, Colin was helping to carry the buckets himself, his father kneeling by the door and stooping inside the shelter to fill them and he carrying them, half-spilling, across the yard to empty in the drain the other side. "Don't empty them in the garden," his father said the first time he did so. "It'll drain straight back. God damn and blast, it'll be weeks before we've finished."

The next raid, when the sirens went, they spent in a cupboard beneath the stairs. As on the previous raid they heard no sound at all. After a while his father got up to go to work. "No," he said, "don't come out. You wait there until you hear the all-clear," shutting the door quietly and moving on tiptoe across the kitchen, breathing heavily as he wheeled his bike out into the yard. They heard the rasp of the tyres on the ashes, then the sound of his boot as he pushed himself off. Then, for a while, they sat in silence.

At last the mother got up. "Well, then," she said. "I'm not waiting here any longer," opening the cupboard door but turning back when he followed her and adding, "No, you stay there, Colin. I'll tell you when to come out."

He sat alone then with the lamp re-trimmed, heating up

the tiny space, staring at the white walls of the cupboard, the odd boxes, the spare tyre from his father's bike, the ribbed, zinc tub out of the top of which poked the week's washing.

Outside he could hear his mother moving about, lighting the gas and, a little later, catching her foot against a chair.

"Would you like a cup of tea?" she said through the door.

"Yes," he said.

He heard the clinking of the cups and the water being poured into the pot.

When his mother opened the door he said, "Can I come out?" before taking the cup.

"No, you better stay there," she said. "If anything happens I can rush inside."

When the door had closed again he watched the steam rising from the cup in the lamplight and saw the waves of heat distorting the shape of the tyre as they came out of the little holes round the top of the lamp.

When the all-clear sounded his mother opened the door. She stood listening, her head to one side, gazing at the ceiling, then said, "Well, then, it should be all right." He climbed back up to bed with the smell of the washing still about him, and the smell of the burning oil from the lamp.

Eventually they dispensed with the cupboard. When the sirens sounded he would go down to the kitchen and sit with his mother and with his father if he were home from work, the door of the cupboard open and sometimes the lamp lit in readiness inside.

Finally, when the bombing started in earnest, his father would take him out on to the step to watch.

The planes came from the east, flying high above the houses, with just the dull throbbing of their engines to indicate their passage, like some low moaning inside the head. Almost every night the sky to the west would be lit by flames, silhouetting the houses of the village, lifeless but for the odd whispered cries from the other doors and windows. It was as if the horizon burned, a dull, aching redness flung against the sky. Across it, intermittently, waved the beams of searchlights and occasionally came the crackle of gunfire, like some vague tapping overhead.

One day his father took Colin with him on a bus to the city. It took them almost an hour to get there, making detours up narrow lanes to tiny farms and hamlets, the bus cresting a hill finally to reveal the city still some distance off perched on a steep and rocky outcrop, its various spires and towers shining in the sun.

Only when they'd passed through the suburbs and crossed the river did they see the damage. The factories were still there, the mill chimneys: it was the houses alone that had been hit, street after street of rubble, the bus occasionally brought to a halt while gangs of men dug with shovels or signalled it through some narrow gap.

Smoke rose from the debris: small crowds of people stood about gazing at the fractured beams and the gutted windows of what had once been their homes.

In the centre of the city the cathedral and the old brick buildings surrounding it were still intact. The tall, black spire stood at the very summit of the escarpment, open on every side. Only its stonework, however, had been chipped, the soot-encrusted surface laid open to the yellowish texture underneath. It was as if it suffered from some huge infection, yellow spots gaping from the black. Some of its windows had been broken. Inside several women were picking up the glass.

"That'll never be hit," his father said. "It's as safe as houses. They need have no worry over that."

Colin followed his father through the crowds, Saville stopping here and there, before a guttered shop or house, talking to the people, nodding his head, his small, stocky figure swelling with indignation.

"By God, when it comes to bombing women and children it's come to something. It has that."

"Ah, well, there's no providence in bombs, one way or another," a man had said. He had, it seemed, been bombed out already. "The place they put me in got bombed out the night I was sent. They're chasing me from one hole to another."

When they reached home his father sat at the table, drinking his tea, describing what he had seen to his mother. "One row of houses we saw: perfect. Not a stick out of place. The only thing was that not one of them had a window. Blast: it had removed every bit of glass."

"They say there are ten thousand homeless," his mother said.

"More," Saville said, "if I had a guess."

Sometimes, on a morning, Colin would tie a magnet to a piece of string and pull it through the gutters of the village. He seldom found anything but old bolts and nails. Once, however, he picked up a piece of greyish metal, torn at the edges, like paper, and slightly burned. He put it in a box, along with the war medals, the foreign coins, the cartridges, and the .303 bullets.

5

There were two parts to the village. The older part stood
on a ridge a little to the north. It was made up of several
old stone houses, still inhabited, an old manor house, deserted and falling into ruin, and the stone church which
had once belonged to the manor. Two or three old farms
stood here, back to back, their fields stretching out on
every side, a system of mud lanes joining them together.

The more recent part of the village fell away on the
lower ground to the south. At its centre stood the colliery
with its twin headgears and its dykes and pyramids of
slag, the terraced streets built for the miners strewn out on
three sides like the spokes of a wheel: on the fourth side
the slag ran off towards the country, the grey mounds of
ash and rubble tumbling down finally at the edges of
the nearest wood, one arm running off at the side of a little wagon track before it petered out amongst the fields.

The streets were numbered from one to five: they started
with First Avenue, which stood in the shadow of the colliery, and ran round through ninety degrees to Fifth Avenue; here the streets had been named after trees, Beech,
Holly, Laburnun, Willow. Once he had collected all the
names and numbers in a book, along with the numbers of
several cars which he had seen passing through the village
on their way to the town, and the numbers of several
railway engines he had seen passing through the station
on the road to the south. Between the village and the station were strung out the various amenities of the village
itself, the shops, a prefabricated Catholic Church, a Wes-
leyan Chapel, a greyhound track and, in a dip in the
road, a small gas-works and a string of sewage beds. They

46

stood amidst marshes and pools of stagnant water and the place was known locally as the Dell.

The surrounding countryside was given over entirely to farms, their hedged fields strewn out to the near, hilly horizon where, beyond a frieze of woodland or the silhouette of the fields themselves, a cloud of smoke or the tip of a slag heap would betray the presence of the other collieries stretching all around.

Shortly after the bombing began his mother went away to hospital and he went to sleep at Mrs. Shaw's house next door. She had no children and her husband worked in the colliery in the village. The house was cleaner and neater than their own, and his bedroom had linoleum on the floor. On all the walls, on the stairs as well as in the rooms, were hung pieces of brass, small reliefs and plates, and medallions with figures. Almost every day Mrs. Shaw cleaned them with a rag, breathing on them, or rubbing on a white liquid from a tin, the brasses laid out around her, on a table, in neat rows. At lunch-time he stayed at school for dinner and at tea-time he would go back to see his father, who had usually got out of bed. He would be getting ready to go and see his mother on his way to work, getting his things together, the fire unlit, the place itself untidy, the sink full of plates and pans he had never washed, the curtains in most of the rooms still drawn. "I'll be glad when she's back," his father would say. "How are you liking Mrs. Shaw's?"

"Can't I stay here?" he asked him.

"Nay," his father said. "You can't sleep in the house by yourself."

"I wouldn't mind."

His father looked down at him then with a half-smile. His face was grey, his eyes reddened.

"You're better off where you are, Colin," he said. "Your mother'll be back home before long, then we'll be all right."

He would dress for work then and wheel his bike out into the yard.

"Come on, then, out you come," he would say. "I mu'n lock the door."

Sometimes Colin stood in the yard holding the bike

while his father locked the door, turning the key then stooping down to fasten on his cycle clips, folding his trousers round the tops of his boots. Sometimes too, as he waited, he pumped up the air in the tyres, his father waiting then, groaning, and saying, "Come on. Come on. I'll be here all night. You need a drop of meat in that arm."

Usually he went out into the street to watch him cycle off. His father wore a long overcoat, his flat cap pulled well down over his eyes. In the pannier behind the seat he would put the parcel he had made up to take to his mother, some fruit or a change of clothes which he'd carefully washed and ironed himself. "You be a good lad, now," he would say. "I'll see you tomorrow."

"Good night, Dad," he would tell him.

"Good night, lad," his father would say and push off his bike with one foot, riding on the pedal then, as it gained momentum, lifting his leg over the seat.

Mrs. Shaw was a tall, thin woman. She had a large jaw and large, staring eyes, dark and full of liquid. Her cheekbones stuck out sharply on either side. She had little to do with the other neighbours. Often she would stand with her arms folded beneath her apron staring out into the street.

Her husband was a small man with light, gingerish hair and a freckled face. He went to work early in the morning and came back home while Colin was still at school. At night he would come into his room, sometimes with a book, and tell him a story, his wife listening to the radio downstairs. Often, however, as he listened to Mr. Shaw reading Colin would begin to cry, covering his face with his hands.

"Why, what is it?" Mr. Shaw would say. "What's the matter?"

He would shake his head.

"Your mother will soon be back," Mr. Shaw would say. "And what will your dad say when I tell him you've been roaring?"

"I don't know," he'd say and shake his head.

" 'Why,' he'll say. 'Not my lad, surely?' "

"Yes," he said.

"Well, then," Mr. Shaw would say, and add, "Shall I fetch you up a chocolate?"

48

Sometimes he would accept one and, after Mr. Shaw had gone, kissing him good night, he would lie sucking it in the darkness, the taste of the sweet and of the salt from his crying inextricably mixed up inside his mouth.

Before he went to school each morning, Mrs. Shaw would brush his hair. She would look in his ears in much the same fashion as his father would look at his bike when he couldn't find what was wrong with it. Sometimes she would take him back to the sink in the kitchen and wash his ears again, pushing his head forward and rubbing round the back of his neck. "You'll never get clean," she said. "You'd think you worked down a pit yourself."

At the end of the week, on the Friday evening, she set out a bath in front of the fire. Around it she lay down sheets of newspaper to collect the drips.

"I don't think he wants to get in it," Mr. Shaw said the first time it appeared.

"I've changed the sheets," she said. "He'll have to."

"I want to get bathed at home," he said.

"Nay, this is your home," she said. "And your dad's gone to work in any case and locked the door."

"I'll get bathed tomorrow night, then," he said.

"You can't," she said. "I've changed the sheets and I'm not getting the old ones out of the wash."

Her eyes expanded, her cheekbones flushing.

"Now don't be such a silly," she said.

In the end he got undressed and got into the bath. Mr. Shaw had gone into the other room.

He sat perfectly still in the water, his toes curled up against the zinc bottom.

"Well, then," Mrs. Shaw said. "You better stand up. You'll never get washed cramped up like that."

She'd already washed his face and neck, his back and his shoulders.

"I can wash myself," he said.

"I know," she said. "I've seen it. Black ring left everywhere you've been." She put her hand under his arm. "Now, then. Up you get."

He stood gazing down at the fire as she washed him. It was full of pieces of coal that had already caught alight.

49

"Well, then. That wasn't so bad," she said when she'd finished.

She knelt back on her heels by the bath, the apron damp between her knees.

"You can get out now," she said, "and dry yourself."

"Stand on the paper," she added, and gave him the towel.

He rubbed himself up and down, turned to the fire.

"Now then. You see, that's not dry," she said.

She took the towel from him and rubbed him, his body shaking at the force. She held him with one hand and rubbed him with the other.

"Getting into dry pyjamas you want to be dry all over."

Mr. Shaw came in and picked up the bath. He opened the back door and carried it outside, emptying it down the grate.

Then he came in and picked up the damp sheets of paper, putting the bath away beneath the sink.

"Now then, he looks as bright as a new pin," his wife said.

Mr. Shaw nodded, gazing down at him.

"Would you like a chocolate?" he said.

He went up to bed and lay down in the clean sheets. They were like strips of ice. No matter how tightly he curled they burned him all over.

Sometimes at night, when he couldn't sleep, he got out of bed and looked down into the garden next door, at the shelter, its black square mound at the end of the garden, at the rows of vegetables covered now, since his father's absence, in weeds. It was all changed, as if it had been set down in a different place entirely. In the early mornings he could hear Mr. Shaw get up and plod his way through the house, sometimes one of the brasses jangling as he caught it with his arm, his boots finally beating out across the yard and fading with the sound of other boots towards the colliery.

Each morning his father came in the kitchen, just back from work, ducking his head awkwardly in the doorway and smiling, Mrs. Shaw sometimes offering him a cup of tea which he always refused. "Nay, you're doing enough for me," he'd say. "I don't want to put you to any more trouble."

"Ah, yes," she'd say as if she understood.

"And how is he, then?" he would ask, standing still in the doorway, his cap in his hand.

"Oh, he's no trouble at all," she said.

"Is he eating, then?"

"More than enough."

"See, Colin," his father would add. "I've fetched thee some chocolate." He would step in and lay it on the table, stepping back to the door.

"Well, then," Mrs. Shaw would say. "Aren't you going to say thank you?"

"Yes," he'd say and looking up he would see his father smiling, nodding his head.

"Thank you," he said.

"Oh, that's all right, then," his father would add, flushing.

He preferred in the end not to see his father at all, or to go into the house next door when he knew he could see him alone. Yet, whenever he looked in the house before going to school, he would find his father already asleep, lying in a chair, the fire unlit, full of dead ashes, the curtains drawn, the pots from the meals still unwashed on the table.

It was as if everything had moved away. At school he found himself suddenly cut off.

One day he had begun to cry, covering his face with his hand.

"Why, Colin. What is it?" the teacher asked him.

"I don't know," he said.

"Now then," she said. "It can't be that bad, surely."

"No," he said.

She held his head a moment against her smock.

He smelled the chalk there, and the dust from the cloth she used to clean the board.

"Well then," she said. "Are you feeling better?"

"Yes," he said, afraid to look up and see the other children.

Finally she took him to the teachers' room. He sat there on a chair by the window, the book she had given him open on his knee.

He stared out at the colliery which backed on to the school across a lane. A column of white steam, thicker

than a cloud, coiled slowly in the air. A little engine
pulled a line of trucks in and out of the yard.

Every now and then another teacher came in, collected
a book, glancing at him, smiling, then going out and
closing the door. He sat quite still, watching the engine,
looking up, flushing, whenever anyone came in to find
him there.

Eventually the teacher came back and filled up a kettle,
setting it on a gas ring by the door. "Are you all right?"
she said.

"Yes." He nodded his head.

"Well, then," she said. "You better run along. In five
minutes it'll be time for play."

One morning he saw his father standing by the school
railings, gripping the spikes and gazing over at the children.

The yard was full, everyone waiting to go in. When he
ran over he saw his eyes lighten, their blueness suddenly blazing then, just as quickly, fading away.

He seemed shy to find him there, like picking out a
stranger.

"I came looking for you," he said. "I might not see you
tonight when I get back. I'm going to see your mother
early."

"Can I come?" he said.

"They won't let children in the hospital," he said.
"Otherwise you could. Don't worry."

"When shall I see you?" he said.

"I'll look in tomorrow morning. You'll be all right."

"All right," he said.

His father gazed over the railings a little longer.

"Shall I give you a kiss?" he said.

"Yes," he said, and put up his face, holding the railings.
His father leaned down, stooping over.

"You'll be all right, then, won't you?" he said.

"Yes." He nodded.

Though his father had washed, the coal-dust was still
imprinted round his eyes.

"Well, then," his father said. "I'll be off."

He turned away and walked down the road to where his
cycle was propped up at the kerb. At the corner, where it
turned off between the school and the pit yard, he waved,

his hand touching the neb of his flat cap before his bike swung away.

When he came home at tea-time Mrs. Shaw was standing in the door, her arms folded beneath her apron, gazing down the street. His tea was already on the table. There was a piece of cake beside his plate.

"Now, then," she said. "I bet you're hungry."

He ate all the tea she put before him. Some of it was sandwiches with meat inside. It was like setting out on a journey: he felt he might as well get all he could inside.

"Would you like another piece of cake?" she said and brought the tin out from the pantry, lifting the cake out on a plate and cutting off another slice, and raking all the crumbs together with the knife.

As he ate it Mr. Shaw came down. He had just got out of bed: his braces hung round his trousers and he hadn't tucked in the tail of his shirt. His hair stood up around his head like grass.

"Well, then, he's eaten all that, has he?" he said. "When we take them off we'll find his boots are full of bread."

Mrs. Shaw came in later to tuck him into bed. "Well, then, sleep tight," she said and kissed him. It was the first time she had tried and he saw her eyes close as she stooped towards him. "Well, then," she said, tucking in the sheets.

For some time he lay awake, listening for sounds of his father next door. But, as on every other night, it was silent. Vague voices came through the wall from the house the other side.

In the morning he heard Mr. Shaw going to work, the kettle being filled in the kitchen below as he made some tea.

He heard his boots finally clack out across the yard and some time later the pit hooter. It would be another two hours or more before his father came home from work. He imagined him coming out of the cage, blackened, crossing the yard to give in his lamp, going to the locker, washing, putting on his coat, getting his bike from the rack; then he tried to imagine the ride back through the lightening countryside, the hills, up some of which his father pushed the bike, the bends, the level-crossing which occurred at some point on the route, the bridge across a railway.

He fell asleep, saw, vaguely, his mother lying in a bed, unfamiliar, her face round and curiously shining, like glass; then found himself riding his father's bike, flying across the hedges and walls that blocked his path.

It was Mrs. Shaw's movements on the stairs that finally woke him and he immediately sat up, listening for any sounds next door.

When he went down Mrs. Shaw was lighting the fire.

She was kneeling by the grate and looked up, her long face half-hidden by her shoulder.

"Well, then, we'll soon have this lit and breakfast on," she said.

"Has my dad come back?" he asked her.

"No," she said. "I don't think so. Would you like me to take you to school?"

"No," he said, and shook his head.

He went out into the garden. It was still early, the sun scarcely risen: long shadows ran out from the edge of the terrace.

He played in Mrs. Shaw's garden, emptied the bucket of ashes and filled it up with coal, looking back at his house, at the window of his bedroom. He looked over at the shelter, at the weed-covered vegetables: it looked more abandoned and neglected now than ever, something he had left behind a long time ago.

He climbed over the fence eventually and knocked on the back door. He tried the handle then went to the window and looked inside. The curtains were still drawn as his father had left them.

He walked down through the other yards, past kitchen windows where other women were lighting fires and cooking breakfast, and round into the street the other side. He walked down to the corner; he looked down the lane that led out towards the fields and along which his father normally returned.

He sat down finally and waited, saw the newspaper boy go by, then the milkman with his horse and trap.

"Now, then, lad," he said. "You're up early. Any news from your dad?"

He shook his head.

As the milkman neared the other end of the street Mrs. Shaw came to the door and called him.

"I wondered where you were," she said. "I couldn't find you in the yard."

She watched him, waiting, while he washed his hands.

He saw his father as he was setting off for school. He was pushing his bike along the lane that led into the village. His head was bowed so that only the top of his cap was visible, and he was pushing the bike as if he had walked a long way, his short legs thrust out behind him, his arms straight and stiff.

He had to call out and run to him before he looked up.

"I'm just off to school," he said.

"Aye," his father said. "I was hoping to catch you. How have you been?"

"Oh," he said. "I'm all right."

His father's eyes were red, the lashes coated with black, his cheeks drawn as if he had nipped them inside. "I called in to see your mother on my way from work."

"Is she all right?"

"Yes," he said. "Champion." He stared at him a minute longer. "You better get off to school."

He stooped down then, as if reminded, and kissed his cheek.

"Will I see you tonight?" he said.

"Aye, well," he said. "You'll be all right with Mrs. Shaw. I might have to go off to the hospital again when I've had a bath."

"Can I come with you?"

"Nay, what'll they think at school? Any road, they won't let you take children." He looked away, across the fields, the way he'd come. "Don't worry, you'll be all right at school."

"Can't I come to the door?"

"Nay, they won't let you past the gate, you see."

He put his foot on the pedal and began to push the bike along.

"Now, you be a good lad," he added.

At school the teacher sat him by her desk, giving him special tasks. He got out the paper, gave out the books, collected the pencils and rulers. In the playground he stood by the fence, gazing out over the colliery to the rows of chimneys beyond. At tea-time he ran all the way home but his father had already left.

His mother was away for six weeks. In the end he decided she wasn't coming back and at night, in bed, he tried to invent a life for himself with Mrs. Shaw. One day he offered to clean her brasses and she sat by him at the table, anxiously watching each one, taking it from him when he had finished and polishing it a little harder herself. He dug Mr. Shaw's garden and planted some seeds, gazing over at his own garden, at the house now almost always silent, his father at the hospital nearly all the time. At school the other children told him his mother was dying and once an older boy told him she was dead, watching his expression, stooping down to look into his eyes.

When, finally, they went to fetch his mother he felt frozen all over. It was as if everything had been numbed. He sat with his hands clenched on his knees, staring out of the bus window, past his father's shoulder. He couldn't remember what his mother looked like, or what kind of person she was.

He had on his suit, and before they had left his father had washed him. He had tidied the house, pushing most of the rubbish into piles, setting a chair in front of it. He had put on his own suit and his cheeks were bright red where he had shaved.

"Ah, we'll be all right now, when we have her back," he said.

Colin nodded, gazing at the fields. In one some pit ponies had been let out to graze, their heads still blinkered against the light. "See, now," his father said. "They've been let up on holiday," turning in his seat to watch them pass.

At the hospital he waited in a small lodge at the gates. Wooden chairs were set against a wall and behind a glass shutter in the wall a man in uniform sat reading a newspaper, occasionally looking out into the drive.

He didn't see his mother come down the drive. A door at the end of the room opened and she appeared wearing her coat, her cheeks flushed, her eyes shining, almost shy, as if she had been away on holiday. In her arms she carried a bundle wrapped up in a white shawl.

"Oh, now," she said, "and how are you, Colin?" turning to his father who put down the case he was carrying.

She stooped down then and said, "Now then, love. Have you missed me?"

He nodded his head and as she leant against him he began to cry.

"Now then, I'm coming home. We'll be all right."

"Yes," he said, hiding his face against her arm.

"Are you having a taxi?" the man in the uniform said. He had come out from behind the glass partition and stood with his newspaper in his hand by the door.

"Aye," his father said. "Ring us a taxi, will you?"

He was smiling, almost laughing, nodding his head as he gazed at the man.

"Here, now," his mother said. "Have a look at him if you like."

"Yes," he said, and looked down at a tiny face sticking out at one end of the bundle.

It was sleeping, its eyes closed, a tiny fist clenched by its cheek, the thumb nail showing, almost white.

"What shall we call him?" his mother said.

"I don't know." He shook his head, gazing at the face.

"We've thought of Steven. But you choose one. We'll think of one when we get home."

When the taxi came his mother's case was put into the boot and the driver held the rear door for her to climb in with the baby. Colin sat beside her and his father got in front with the driver.

"Where to?" the driver said.

"The bus stop," his father said.

"Nay," the driver said. "That's less than two hundred yards."

"I can't afford any more," his father said. "It's six miles to where we live."

The driver looked up a moment, his eyes closed, and said, "I can do that for ten bob."

"Ten bob," his father said. "Do you know how many hours I work for that?"

They got out at the bus stop and the driver stayed behind the wheel. They had to get the case out themselves; Colin held the door for his mother.

"We ought to have paid it," she said. "This once."

David Storey

"I would have done," he said. "I didn't like him, that's all. I'm damned if I'm going to pay all that to somebody like him. I'll walk back if you like and get another."

"No," she said. "We'll get the bus."

She held the baby to her, occasionally looking down into its face, shielded by a fold of the shawl.

"We should have had that ambulance," his father said. "I pay all that every week into the Hospital Fund and we can't even get an ambulance."

"Oh, you don't know," his mother said. "I've been looking forward to the ride."

In the bus he sat behind his mother and father, his mother's case in the locker by the door.

Occasionally they turned round to glance at him. "Are you all right?" his father said.

He nodded, his hands clenched in his pockets.

"You ask Mrs. Shaw: he's been a good lad while you've been away," he said.

The other passengers in the bus turned round to smile, stooping down whenever they got off to look under the fold of the shawl.

"He's a lovely one," the women said. "What is he, then, a girl or a boy?"

"A boy," his father told them, looking down at the face himself.

"He makes enough row, I suppose, for a lad."

"Oh, enough," his father said, "to be going on with."

When they reached the village his father sprang off the bus, whistling, lifting down the case, calling out to the conductress and looking round.

As they walked down the street the women came to the doors and his mother stopped, pulling back the shawl from the baby's face.

"He's after his dinner," the women said. "We better not keep him."

"Aye, another bloody mouth," his father said.

Colin walked behind them to the door, carrying the case, setting it down when they stopped, looking off down the street, still feeling strange at having his best suit on on a week-day.

At the door his father said, "You mu'n never mind

58

the mess," putting the key in the lock. "Just sit yourself down and I'll make some tea."

He put the kettle on the fire which he had stoked up before they left. On the table he began to get out the pots and the tea-pot.

"I can't tell you," his mother said. "It's so good to be back."

She sat gazing round at the kitchen, her eyes shining, her cheeks still flushed.

"I better get this seen to," she said, talking to the baby, making sounds into its face then taking off its shawl. Its legs were tiny and curled up, red like its face from crying. "Now then, what do you think to your new home?" she asked it.

Its colour deepened and it cried more loudly, its face disappearing in folds and wrinkles. His father had taken it from her while his mother took off her coat. She sat down then by the fire and took the baby back, calling to it, and began to unfasten her dress.

"Here," his father said, "run down to the shops and fetch us some cigarettes."

"He doesn't have to go," his mother said.

"Nay," he said. "I've run out and I'm dying for a smoke. You can buy a bar of chocolate for yourself."

Colin went out with the half-crown his father had given him clutched in his hand. It was still hot from his father's pocket.

It was almost lunch-time. The street was deserted. From the colliery came the soft panting of the winding engine and the voice of a tradesman calling from a cart.

His shoes squeaked in the silence and in the window of the shop at the next corner he caught a glimpse of his figure, the dark suit, its trousers ending at his knees, his stockings pulled up beneath his knee-caps and folded over, his neatly brushed hair.

"How's it feel, then, to have a baby in the house?" the man in the shop had said. He was cutting up a piece of cheese with a wire, his tongue sticking out between his teeth.

"Thy'll have to teach it a trick or two. How to stand up and brush its hair."

"Yes," he said, taking the cigarettes.

"Nay, have it on me," the man said as he made to pay for the chocolate. "It's not every day it happens."

He walked back slowly along the street, eating the chocolate, then putting most of it away in his pocket. He wondered if they would want him back so soon and for a while stood on the kerb kicking his shoe in the dust.

From the school he heard the bell ring for lunch and a moment later, from behind the houses, came the roar of voices of those children who were going home.

He waited until they crossed the end of the street, running and shouting, then he went on towards his door.

Mrs. Shaw was leaving the house as he entered.

"You must be feeling proud," she said. "A lad like that in the family."

"Yes," he said.

His father was in the kitchen, pouring out some tea.

"It'll make all his waiting seem worthwhile," Mrs. Shaw said from the door.

"It will that." His father nodded.

She ruffled his hair and said, "We'll miss having him, I can tell you. It's been like having one of your own."

"Aye," his father said. "We're very grateful to you."

"What with the garden dug and him cleaning my brasses."

His father nodded, laughing.

"He can get stuck into our garden now," he said. "These last few weeks it's gone to ruin."

"Ah, well," she said. "You're all back now, thank God, and a re-united family."

"Aye," his father said. "We've a lot to thank Him for."

When Mrs. Shaw had gone his father put one of the cups of tea on a saucer with a biscuit and went to the stairs.

"I'll just take this up," he said. "Then we'll see what we have for dinner."

"Is my mother coming down?" he said.

"Aye," his father said. "When she's finished."

He sat in the kitchen, gazing out at the overgrown garden and the shelter. Overhead he heard his father's steps then his voice followed by his mother's.

At the colliery a buzzer sounded.

He put the cigarettes on the table. At the end of the

garden, between it and the back yards of the next street, was a narrow field. It opened out on one side on to farm fields and at the other was enclosed by the converging houses. Several children were playing, waiting for their dinners, jumping in and out of a hole.

When he went out he shouted to them, trying to avoid the patches of clay and soil either side of the path.

"Hey," he said from the fence. "We've got a baby."

"What's that?" they said.

He indicated the house behind.

"What is it?" they said.

"A boy."

They jumped back into the hole, disappearing a moment then suddenly climbing out, running off down the field then back again, their arms stretched out. Every now and again they made a stuttering noise in their throats.

He stood watching them for a while, holding the railings.

Then, his hands in his pockets, he turned back to the house.

Across the yards a woman was hanging out washing. She stood on her toes, reaching up to the line.

"Is your mother back?" she said.

"Yes," he said and nodded.

"What colour's its eyes?"

"Blue," he said.

"Well," she said. "Just like his father's."

When he went in his father was stoking up the fire.

"Now, then, let's see about some dinner," he said, stooping down and setting the pans against the flames.

PART TWO

6

The boys he played with were slightly older than himself. Some of them already wore long flannels. Their leader, when he wasn't in hospital or didn't feel too tired to come out, was a boy called Batty. He was very tall and had bright red hair. It was because of his height that he was always having trouble with his feet. They stuck out sideways and when he ran his legs were flicked out sideways too, his knees knocking against one another and causing him such discomfort that usually when he was out playing he spent most of his time calling to the others, "Hey, come on. Let's walk." He was sometimes called Walkie-Talkie, other times Lolly, though usually Batty seemed to do.

He came from a large family farther along the terrace: there were seven brothers, all with red hair. "Our kids'll bash you," Batty would say whenever his authority was questioned and he would indicate the windows of his crowded home.

The centre of Batty's life was the hut he had built in the Dell, half a mile away. It stood between the high, fenced walls of the gasworks on one side and the sewage beds on the other.

After the birth of the baby Colin spent a lot of his time in the hut. He would go down there after school, or in the dinner hour. Sometimes, getting up early and hearing his mother feeding the baby in the bedroom, he would get dressed and go out, taking a piece of bread with him. His mother would sometimes call out and when he went in she would be sitting up in bed, the baby held over her shoulder. She would ask him if he would like some tea, straighten his tie with her free hand and look at his ears and neck. His father worked mornings now and got up like Mr. Shaw next door, though an hour sooner because of the ride. Sometimes when he came home from school he found his mother in bed, white-faced, her cheeks sunken, his father busy in the kitchen with a brush, or washing-up.

"It's all this getting up at night to feed him," he would say. "She'll be all right once he settles."

"Can I go out?" he would ask him.

"Yes," he'd say. "Just clear this bit up first."

In the hut, when Batty wasn't there, he usually found Stringer. He was Batty's deputy: he was small and squat with black hair, and whenever they were alone he would sit in the armchair normally reserved for Batty and bite his nails, gazing with an abstracted look at the glow of an old oil lamp, which stood on a table immediately inside the door and, on hearing the slightest noise outside, rushing for his gun which he always brought with him.

It was an air-gun Batty himself had given him and which, once he was in the hut, he fired at anything that moved. One night by mistake he had fired at his own father, who had come to fetch him, a man as squat and as black as Stringer himself. Mr. Stringer had taken the gun from his son, bent it in two, first one way then the other, then finally wrenched the halves apart. The next day, however, Batty had provided Stringer with another. "I'm glad he broke it," Stringer said. "That o'd 'un wasn't any good." Outside the door he would hang up the birds he had shot, their feet strung up to a rafter, the blood collecting in beads around their beaks and eyes.

Stringer didn't like the hut a great deal. But for Batty he would gladly have moved it to another spot. There was always the smell of the gasworks lying there, mingling with the smell of the sewage pens. "The pong's all right," Batty told him whenever he complained. "I picked it because of that. It's a good defence." Beyond the sewage pens were the swamps. Tall reeds obliterated the view in every direction. If anyone entered they had to walk on the piles of bricks and sods of earth that at some time in the past Batty had placed there. Amongst the bulrushes were still, brown pools about which Batty had invented stories. Into them bodies had fallen never to be retrieved.

They had no bottoms. They opened out directly into the centre of the earth. It was here that Stringer hunted for rats, hanging them up by their tails along with the birds he had shot.

Once or twice, when Stringer was busy elsewhere, Colin would be left on his own in the hut. He would light the lamp and sit in Batty's chair, the door barred, one of the windows which were normally shuttered open so that he could see anyone approaching along the path.

There was a small stove in the hut on which Batty made cocoa or cooked chips in a broken pan. On the walls hung bows and arrows, the arrows tipped with rusty wire. There was also a cupboard which Batty kept locked and inside which he kept his secret possessions —a rope with a noose on the end, a tin called his 'In-it' tin, for no one knew what was inside, and a hammer.

It gave Colin a dull ache to sit alone in the hut, looking round at the wooden walls and the weapons, listening anxiously for any sound or signal from outside. Often he was glad even to see Stringer.

"What do you come down here for?" Stringer would ask him: there were two or three years difference between their ages.

"To look after it," he would tell him.

"I mean," Stringer would say, "why do you come so much?"

"I don't mind," he said.

"Not even the pong?"

"No," he said.

Sometimes he would add, "In any case, there might be an attack."

"Aye," Stringer would say, looking at him slyly.

An attack was what Batty most longed for. It was in anticipation of an attack that all his weapons and the various booby traps outside had been prepared. The latter were a series of deep holes covered by grass that they had to walk around when they arrived.

The attack too would bring a light to Stringer's eyes and invariably, when it was mentioned, he would check his gun, pushing in a pellet if by some rare chance it was unloaded, and go to the window, narrowing his eyes to peer out. A pair of binoculars, another of Batty's possessions, facilitated his watch.

Yet the attacks never came; the only intruders who approached the hut were miners from the Club and Institute who came to relieve themselves behind the wall as they struggled home at night.

His father was a little sceptical of the time he spent with Batty. "Nearly all their lads have been in prison," he said. "You don't want to get mixed up with that. What do you do in that hut, anyway?"

"Oh," he said. "Play around."

"If he asks you to go thieving you better tell me straight away."

"Yes," he said.

"We've enough worries with your mother being unwell, without us adding another."

Yet in the evening his father would go into the field at the back of the house with Batty's father and some of his sons, and sometimes Stringer's father and Mr. Shaw, and play cricket. The women would come out into the yards to watch, their arms folded under their aprons.

The men would set up two sticks for a wicket, Batty's father—who was tall like Batty and almost completely bald—swearing at his sons whenever he was out, his own father laughing, standing with his hands on his hips, his head thrust back, or sometimes bowling, running up with a slow, stiff stride and flicking the ball out of the back of his hand. Whenever one of the men hit the ball towards the houses they would call out, as if a tree were falling, and if a window were broken they would run off and hide behind the fences and in the doorways before coming back, laughing, to hand out the money. Later, as the sun set, they would lie in the grass by the worn wicket, talking, their wives calling from the doorsteps as it grew dark.

"Toil and trouble," his father would say, getting up, although his mother never called him. "Come on, Colin," he would tell him. "Time for bed."

"How's thy young 'un going?" they'd ask him.

"Oh, fair and away," he'd say.

He'd built a cradle for the baby from an orange box and painted it grey, like the bunks in the shelter, with colliery paint. It stood in their bedroom on a wooden chair. The box had been hexagonal in shape and his father had removed three of the sides, the baby lying inside on a pillow and rocked slightly, whenever it cried, from side to side.

It was as if the baby represented a subtraction from his mother's life, a piece of her that had been taken away, without anything to replace it. She was so much thinner, and gave all her attention to the child. Sometimes when he went in to see her in the morning she would call out, "Is that you, Colin?" even when she knew they were alone in the house and he would stand at the door waiting until she added, "It's all right now, love. You can come in."

She would be holding the baby across her shoulder and patting its back. Whenever he looked at it its eyes were closed, its cheeks bloated, its lips pouting slightly and covered in greyish milk.

On Sundays, when she had fed it, he would take it for walks in the pram. "We all have to do our bit," his father said. Often now his father did the cooking himself, standing at the kitchen table, whistling, his hands covered in flour. "I don't need a book," he said whenever his mother opened her cookery book for him on the table. "If you haven't the touch you might as well not try." He took as much trouble over the cooking as he had over the shelter and he seldom got anything wrong, laying out the cakes he had made on a tray by the windows so that Mrs. Shaw or whoever passed by could inspect them. He bought himself a small sewing machine which, like the pram, he had seen advertised in the local paper, and in the evenings, before he went to bed, he would sit by the fire, his head stooped to the light, sewing curtains, his eyes glowing, his heavy fingers drawing out the thread. "You get your strength up," he said to the mother. "I'll see to this for a while."

On Sundays, when Colin pushed the pram out, he would walk past Batty's house and when he whistled Batty would come out, usually with a plank of wood or a piece of metal, and they would put it across the sides of the pram, the baby asleep underneath, and push it down to the Dell.

The pram was a high, carriage-like shape, with a curled handle and with large spoked wheels that overlapped at the sides. When his mother noticed the mud collected on the wheels and discovered where the baby spent its morning, lying beneath the rows of rats and birds outside the hut, she told his father, who, baking at the time, wiped his hands of flour and took him upstairs, looking in his bedroom for his belt.

He seldom beat him, but when he did it was with his belt, laying him over the arm of a chair or over his bed, his father, afterwards, going out to the lavatories, where he would sit smoking a cigarette, his head in his hand, his mother standing in the kitchen, her hands clenched, gazing at the fire.

The following Sunday she watched him walk off in the opposite direction, towards the centre of the village and, beyond, the colliery and the Park.

Every Sunday his father put on his best suit and walked out in the same direction, past the Park, to the manor house. Here, at the back, an outbuilding had been designated as the headquarters of a local defence volunteer force. The building had stone walls and a padlock on its metal-studded door, and inside there was an old desk and several canvas chairs. In some respects it was a bit like Batty's hut.

The men assembled here at eleven o'clock just as the bell in the church across the manor grounds was sounding for morning service. Some of the men wore uniforms, but most of them had suits. They marched up and down on the paved yard of the manor, swinging left at each corner and coming to a halt when the sergeant in charge called out. He came in a small army truck which, once they had finished marching, some of the men took turns in driving round the yard, calling out and laughing, crashing the gears.

After a while the man in the truck brought several rifles with him. His father at this time was one of the few men without a uniform, because of his small size, and he would march at the back of the column, the rifle held almost horizontally over his shoulders, his head thrust back, his eyes glaring, his left hand swinging stiffly at his side.

When they had finished drilling they would line up and load the rifles with imaginary bullets and fire them at imaginary targets at the end of the manor yard. Occasionally they would charge across the yard, fling themselves down on a grass bank the other side and fire at the bushes. A piece of hessian and a sack were laid down where his father and another man had to fall because of their best suits, and when they reached it they would pull up the knees of their trousers before getting down.

One Sunday the sergeant brought several bayonets in addition to the rifles, and on each subsequent Sunday the men would attach them to the ends of the rifles and run with them, screaming, across the yard, and stick them in a sack hanging from the branch of a tree the other side.

Colin, pushing his brother in the pram, occasionally accompanied his father to the manor. He would climb up into the house while the men drilled in the yard. A flight of narrow stone steps led up to the first floor, and from there a broad wooden staircase led up to the floor above. Few of the ceilings of the house remained; birds nested in the rafters; most of the windows had been removed. Through the gaps he could gaze down into the grounds, at the church and the Park, the colliery and the village lying beyond. He could pick out figures moving in the streets or on the colliery heap and, on a clear day, could make out the trees by the river almost two miles away. From below would come the shouts of the sergeant, the screaming of the men as they ran with the bayonets, and the barking of the caretaker's dog, fastened up at the side of the building.

From the rear windows he could look down on the men in the yard below, sprawled out on the bank if they were firing at the bushes, or marching up and down if the session had just begun, his father, smaller and neater from this perspective, marching stiffly behind.

His face was quite severe when he drilled, his chin tucked in, his chest pulled out, his eyes having a glaring, slightly strained expression. Often when they had left

71

were walking home, he would say, "Come
ow. Pick 'em up. Pick 'em up," in much the
as the sergeant, marching along, his head
ns swinging, and looking down now and again
to m re that, despite pushing the pram, he kept in
step.

One Sunday the men marched through the village.
They were joined by a unit from another village and by
a band. At first, his father had refused to go because
he had no uniform. "You go," his mother said. "It's
the spirit that counts. And in any case, you'll have a
rifle."

"You'd think they'd have made one my size by now,"
he said. "I wouldn't even mind one a bit bigger."

Yet he went in the end and on this occasion had been
set near the front, the taller men at the rear. At the
front itself marched an officer with a cane, an elderly
man with silver hair and a row of coloured ribbons
on his chest. His father came only a few steps behind.
They marched through the village one way, past the colliery, then the other way, their route the shape of a cross.
When they came back once again to the centre, where
the road from the station and the south met the road
leading to the west and the city, they drew up in a long
column, marking time, his father's knees rising high in
the legs of his best trousers but, because of the newness of
the cloth, not as high as the rest.

Afterwards, as the men drank outside the pub, his
father stood back from the rest, nodding his head but
scarcely talking, the men who had joined much later than
him leaning in their uniforms against the pub wall, laughing and calling, some already with stripes on their arms.

"I'm going to have no suit left," he said as they
walked home. "What do you think? I nearly asked that
officer for one himself."

Yet when his uniform finally came he was unable, as
a result of a serious accident, to wear it: it hung for a
while from a hook on the wall, his father, his legs encased
in plaster, gazing at it in frustration from across the room.

He had been coming home from work one morning,
while it was still dark, riding down one of the many

lanes that led from the pit to the village, when he had
seen the lights of two cyclists coming towards him and had
already turned tiredly to ride between them before he realized they were the heavily shaded headlights of a car.

He had hit the bonnet in the middle and had been flung
over the top of the car, crashing down on the boot before
being flung off into the road.

The driver of the car took him to hospital in a near-by
village, and a few hours later, after his mother had tele-
phoned the colliery to find out where he was, a policeman
came with the news of the accident and she went out again,
leaving Steven and himself with Mrs. Shaw, to telephone
the hospital and find out how seriously he was hurt.

He came home a few days later in an ambulance. He
had broken both his legs, an arm, and had damaged
several ribs. He seemed, as he got out of the ambulance,
more cheerful than he had been for a long time, particularly since his trouble with his uniform. He was carried
in on a stretcher and put straight to bed.

He only stayed there a few days. The plasters on his
legs had been made in such a way that they could support
his weight: they passed down in iron rings under his feet
so that he appeared, suddenly, several inches taller. With
the aid of these and a stick he walked down the stairs.

It was his ribs that caused him most discomfort. He
would lie in the chair by the fire, holding his chest and
groaning, breathing slowly in and out.

"You don't have to tell me," he said whenever his
mother complained. "I'm lucky to be alive," adding, "but
then, lying in that bed I might as well be dead."

Other times he would lie back, his eyes searching the
ceiling, wild, half-tormented, and say, "The number
of times the roof's broken and I've been nearly buried,
my back broke and God knows what else, and then when
it really comes where am I? On an open road wi' nothing
else in sight."

The baby was crawling now and he would give it rides
on his pot leg like a rocking horse, stooping forward,
stiffly, to hold Steven's hand, bouncing him up and down.

Sometimes too he would stand at the window, balancing on the hoops, staring out at the backs, sometimes holding to a cupboard and hitting the pot on his legs with his

stick. He had, over the year, been trying to save ten pounds for a holiday and now it had all gone. He would beat the wall with his fist while his mother looked on, her hands clasped together.

"The thing to do now is get you better," she said. "Not complain."

"Complain?" he said. "With my life draining away."

"It's not draining away by the sounds of it."

"Isn't it? Isn't it?" He would throw the stick on the floor, trying to break it only, a moment later, having to ask her to pick it up because he couldn't move without it. "Last time I broke my leg, you know, I damn near lost my job," he said.

"Yes," she said. "But now there's a war, and everybody's wanted."

"Everybody's wanted. And what have I got? Two pot legs."

Earlier in his life, just before he had got married, he had lost his job when it was impossible to get a job at all. He had been helping to sink the shaft at the colliery where he now worked when, at the bottom of the shaft, while it was still being dug, he had fallen out of the cage and twisted his leg.

It was only as he cycled home that it had begun to swell, particularly around his ankle. He bandaged it up and went to work for another week, afraid to have his leg examined in case it might be more seriously injured than he thought. At the end of the week he could scarcely bear to put his foot to the ground and it took him almost two hours to push his bike to work. Finally, he collapsed one morning in the lane leading to the pit and lay in the road groaning, his bike fallen over him.

The foreman of the site sent him to hospital on the back of a coal cart. He was in for three weeks.

"Another day and they'd have had to take off my leg. They couldn't understand how I'd managed."

"How did you manage?" Colin said. Each day now, when he came home from school, his father would tell him some different incident from this episode, or from others not unlike it.

"If you had my job you'd know how," his father said, laughing. "As soon as I came out I went straight back and reported for work. 'I thought you were dead, Harry,' the foreman said. 'We've given your job to another man now.' 'What man?' I said. 'Why, that man,' he said. 'The one that told us you were dead.' Would you believe it? He had him brought up in the cage. An Irishman he was, as big as a house."

"What did he say?" Colin asked him.

"What could he?" his father said. " 'There's two of you and only one job,' the foreman said. 'I'll give you five minutes to settle it between you.' " His father paused. "We went round the back of the foreman's hut and after five minutes only one of us came back." His eyes lighted, smiling, as he watched his face.

"And which one was that?"

"I'm not saying," his father said, laughing. "But I've worked there ever since!" He burst out laughing once again, with his mother, watching his expression.

His father was always having fights as a young man, and he was often drunk. He never lost a fight and he was never so drunk as to lose out on any situation.

"Oh, he was a devil when I met him," his mother said. "When people heard his name they used to rush in their houses and lock the doors."

"How do you mean?" his father said. "I could always look after myself. I mayn't be very big, but the thing was I could move very fast."

"Yes," his mother said. "Particularly when he saw trouble coming."

His father would smack his stick on the table, his face reddening. "I've never run away from nought. Never."

"No. No. I know," she'd add, leaning down to kiss him.

His father was often angry, but just as easily appeased.

Perhaps it was the accident that made him decide to leave the pit where he was and go to the one in the village.

Colin had never really thought of his father working underground at all. He had never even seen the colliery where he worked, though he had heard him describe it many times and the men who worked there, Walters, Shawcroft, Pickersgill, Thomas; each one of them brought some particular image to his mind, large men who in some way, because of their strength, submitted to his father's authority whenever there was a crisis or a situation they didn't understand.

"I'm surprised that that pit's still working while you're away," his mother said when, after a week or so, she began to grow tired of his stories. She would hold Steven over one shoulder while she changed his nappy, kneeling to the hearth then to lay him down and looking at his father with the pins in her mouth. Since his accident she had grown much stronger, and now Steven slept virtually the whole night through.

His father would get up at these moments and go to the window, rocking on the irons with the aid of his stick. Perhaps it hurt him that the battles he had fought at work, the roofs collapsing, the men he had saved, the instinct that had led him one way rather than another whenever a rock fell, that none of this could be reported to her other than by himself: Walters, Shawcroft, Pickersgill and Thomas all lived in other villages. It might have been this that finally decided him, so that Mr. Stringer and Mr. Shaw, and perhaps even Mr. Batty could report to her the things which, one way or another, he did to save life and increase production almost every day at the pit.

A few doors down the terrace lived Mr. Reagan. He worked in the office at the colliery, and every day went to work in a dark suit, wearing yellow gloves and a bowler hat and carrying a rolled umbrella. He was a tall man with a red face, and had a light Irish accent. His wife would hold open the front door every morning when he left for work, standing there with her arms folded, gazing after him until he reached the corner of the street and disappeared. He never waved nor looked back, yet she never moved until he had gone. Shortly before he came home again in the evening she would re-appear at the door very much as if, in the interval, she hadn't stirred at all, holding the door for him to enter, which he did at the precise moment that he removed his bowler hat. They had one son. He was called Michael and played the violin. He was built like Mrs. Reagan, with a large head which jutted out at the back, a narrow body and thin legs. His father, Mr. Reagan, would have nothing to do with him. In the evenings, whenever the men were playing cricket in the field, he would stand by the fence at the end of his garden, his waistcoat open, his white collar removed, and shout, *"Hit it, for Christ's sake! Hit it harder,"* while behind him, from the open window, would come the sound of the violin.

His father was very attracted by Mr. Reagan. He was the only man in the street who didn't work shifts, who had regular hours, who dressed like a gentleman and who never seemed to care about his wife. On a Saturday night he would go to the Institute dressed in his suit, with his bowler hat and gloves, and stand at the bar never showing, despite the quantities of liquor he consumed, the least discomfort. The miners at the pit stood a little in awe of him: he made up their wages, was responsible for explaining their stoppages, and knew what every man in the village earned. In addition, he would fight any man by whom, for one reason or another, he felt he'd been abused.

His father would describe Mr. Reagan's fights in some detail, and they frequently followed the same pattern. In most instances they took place at the bar of the Institute, and invariably began with some comment on Mr. Reagan's appearance, on the hat he never took off, except at the office, or as he entered his front door, on the yellow gloves which, similarly, he never removed, or on the rolled umbrella which he never opened, even when it rained.

Mr. Reagan himself, in fact, would give no indication to begin with that anything untoward had occurred. He would continue whatever it was he was doing, talking, smiling, gazing benevolently around until, at a point determined entirely by himself, he would put his glass down, resting it a moment on the counter as if he suspected very much that, out of his grasp, it might disappear for good, then, with the same gravity, remove first his hat which he would lay beside his glass, then his right glove which he would lay on the hat, then his left which he would lay on the right; then, finally, he would hoist up his cuffs.

"Would it be you," he would say, turning slowly to the person in question, "who passed a comment upon my appearance a moment ago?"

The man, quite frequently, would look round puzzled, the moment for him, at least, having passed.

"If so," Mr. Reagan would say, "you're on the very point of having your teeth pushed down your throat."

Occasionally the man would deny all knowledge of having made any comment on Mr. Reagan's appearance, or indeed on anything at all.

Other times, however, he might nod his head, smiling, and say, "Oh, and who's going to do that for you?"

"Why," Mr. Reagan would say, "I have the feller here just ready for the job."

According to his father, who watched over Mr. Reagan's fights with an almost envangelical passion, Mr. Reagan seldom hit his opponents more than once, so fast and so hard was his initial blow. If more were required he provided them, if not he turned with the same casual momentum to the bar, pulled down his cuffs, replaced his gloves, then his hat, tilting it to the angle he favoured best, and picked up his glass. Raising it, he would empty its contents at a single swallow.

His father, when he felt strong enough to go outside, spent much of his time now with Mr. Reagan. He would stand at the window at tea-time and wait for him to come down the road from the colliery office, then he would come into the kitchen, wait impatiently for fifteen minutes while Mr. Reagan had time to consume his tea and glance at the paper, then go out along the backs, rocking on his rings and swaying on his walking stick, and tap on Mr. Reagan's back window calling, "Are you in there, Bryan? Don't tell me they've let you out already?"

Sometimes Mr. Reagan would return along the backs with him and putting down a folded newspaper sit on the doorstep, his collar and waistcoat undone, his braces showing at the back when he leaned forward.

His father would argue with him about his work. "If I worked the hours you did, and did nought but lick envelopes and fill in forms and count out other people's money, I'd fall asleep before ever I started."

"Ah, well," Mr. Reagan would say. "I know the feeling well. But then, any silly fellow can heave a pick and shovel. It takes a man with brains to sit on his backside all day and get paid for it."

His father would nod and laugh, looking in at Colin and his mother inside the kitchen as if this were just the answer he wanted them to hear.

"In any case," Mr. Reagan would say, "you don't do so much yourself. Two pot legs and a pot arm: it's a wonder there aren't more at it."

"Aye," his father would say, sadly. "I'm lying around like any old woman."

"Oh, now," Mr. Reagan would say, "I wouldn't say it was as bad as that."

Whenever his mother protested Mr. Reagan would add, his accent thickening, and bowing his head, "Oh, now, Mrs. Saville, not counting yourself." And then, tipping his head in the direction of his own house he would add, "But there are some, you know, who go round flicking dusters all day till you can't put your foot down without breaking your neck, who dress their lads up like lasses and have them scraping cat-gut all evening till you don't know where you are from one minute to the next."

Yet Mr. Reagan himself seemed either too indifferent or too lazy to do anything about it. He would sit on the step, or stand by the fence, shouting at the cricketers, the colour of his face slowly thickening, but in the end, his arms swinging loosely, he would turn back to the house. Occasionally he would come out into the yard with a violin and chop it into pieces. "I'll tell you what I'll do with it," he would shout. "And I'll tell you what I'll do with him too in a minute." Sometimes he would do the same with his son's clothes, which his wife made specially for him, little suits and bright blouses, standing in the yard ripping them up and stamping on the pieces, his face so red it seemed it would burst.

"And yet why do I do it?" he would say to his father. "I have to pay for all the damned things in the end."

Whenever his father asked Mr. Reagan about working at the pit he would look up, surprised, and say, "Why, you're better off where you are, Harry. If I told you some of the things that went on there you'd never walk past the place."

"Oh," his father said. "One pit's much the same as another."

"Aye," Mr. Reagan would say. "That's why I'd stick with what I'd got."

Perhaps Mr. Reagan did put in a word with the management. Yet when his father went to see them, shortly after the pots on his arm and legs had been removed, he came back looking pale and discouraged. Colin saw him walk up the street, his legs straddled slightly as he tried to walk without the stick, and go into the house without as much as glancing in his direction. When he went in his father was sitting at the table, his arms laid out before him, his back stooped.

"They want you where you are," his mother was saying. "They know how valuable you are."

"Valuable? I'm not valuable. I could be killed tomorrow and there'd be somebody to take my place."

"It's not what you always say," she told him.

"Say?" he said. "What do I say?"

"How valuable you are. Where you work at the moment."

"Aye." He nodded his head, not looking up from the table. "I have to say that. If I don't, what am I? Just another piece of muck."

In the end he went back to his old pit. Even when he could walk without the stick, and had long lost his limp, there was a slowness in his movements as if some part of his life had been arrested.

7

He started Sunday School. He went with a boy called Blctchley who lived in the house next door.

His mother until then had had little relationship with Mrs. Bletchley: she was not unlike Mrs. Shaw, who lived the other side. Though no brasses hung on her walls, her floors were covered in rugs and carpets, lace curtains hung in the windows, and in the front window stood a plant with flat, green leaves that never flowered or seemed to grow. Mr. Bletchley was one of the few men in the terrace who didn't work at the colliery. He was employed at the station and occasionally when Colin went there he would catch sight of Mr. Bletchley carrying a large pole and supervising the shunting of the trucks in the siding, or walking to and fro across the lines. He was a small man, with sallow cheeks, and seldom spoke to anyone at all.

Mrs. Bletchley was small too and was always smiling. Her main dealings were with a Mrs. McCormack who lived the other side. Mrs. McCormack would stand with her broad arms folded, nodding her head whenever Mrs. Bletchley called from her step, unable to resist the attentions of the other woman, for whenever Mrs. Bletchley failed to come out, on a morning or in the evening, she would go and knock on her door and stand there, still as silent as ever, listening to Mrs. Bletchley speak.

The Bletchleys' son was called Ian. He was fat; his mother made all his clothes. His trousers were of grey flannel and ended just below his knees, which popped out

beneath them as he walked. He had little interest in anything and would stand in the back door sucking his thumb
and staring out at the children in the field.

In addition to his fat body he had a very large head;
his features were gathered together in a straight line
down the centre of his face, folds of fat drawing out the
contours disproportionately on either side. His legs were
too fat; they were flat at the back and flat at the front,
the sides vaguely curved. The skin on the inside of
his knees was inflamed: it was at this point that his legs
rubbed together and each morning, before he went to
school, Mrs. Bletchley would rub them with cream.

On alternate Saturday mornings, if the weather were
fine, she would set out a wooden chair in the yard and
Mr. Bletchley would sit on the step while his son sat on
the chair and Mrs. Bletchley cut his hair, snipping behind
his ears with a comb and scissors. He often cried. Colin
would hear him crying on a morning, and in the evening,
and when he had his hair cut he would often scream, rising in his chair and attempting, unsuccessfully, to kick
his mother. "You've cut me, you've cut me," he would
shout.

"No, dear," Mrs. Bletchley would tell him. "I don't
think I have."

"You have. I can feel it."

"I don't think so, dear. Let me have a look."

"I'm not."

"I can't cut it unless I see it."

"I'm not letting you cut me any more."

He would run off into the house, his knees already
reddened from their chafing on the chair, Mr. Bletchley
standing up to let him by and occasionally going to the
chair himself.

"Oh, we'll give him a minute, dear," his wife would
say and stand waiting, occasionally sweeping up the bits
she had cut into a pile.

"If he was my lad," Colin's father would say, watching
from the step or the window, "I'd boot his backside."

"Well, you're not his father," his mother said.

"I would. From morning till night."

Once, when his father was working in the garden, he

had called out to Mrs. Bletchley, "You're as daft as a boat-hoss, missis."

"What?" Mrs. Bletchley had asked him.

"You want to clout his backside."

Mr. Bletchley himself had looked away.

"Oh, well," she said. "You've got to be patient."

"Aye," he said, shaking his head. "But not for long."

It was his mother's idea that he should go to church with Bletchley. She had seen him several Sunday afternoons setting off for church, his legs creamed, dressed in a grey-flannel suit and a red-striped tie, and in the evening she had said, "Well, whatever you say about Ian, he's always tidy."

"So's a pig-sty," his father said, "if it's never put to use."

"Well," she said, "going to church won't do you any harm."

"Who?" his father said. "Him or me?"

"Colin," she said.

They had both glanced at him. Then, just as quickly, they looked away.

"I don't want to go," he said.

"No," his father said. "I suppose not. But then, you don't want to do a lot of things."

"It'll do you a lot of good," his mother said. "You could go with Ian. I'll ask his mother."

Two Sundays later he set off with Bletchley, in his own best suit, which he had scarcely worn since the birth of Steven.

Bletchley was silent for most of the way. There was the soft rubbing of his legs as he walked, the faint drag of one trouser leg against the other. He breathed heavily the whole time, occasionally snorting down his nose as if it were blocked and walking a little distance ahead as if reluctant to be seen with anyone else. In much the same way he walked in the street with his parents.

When, prior to setting off, Colin had appeared on the doorstep, Bletchley had regarded him with a great deal of surprise, his eyes, buried in folds of fat, gazing out at him with a surly distaste. Only as they neared the church, having passed the colliery and started up the slope, past the Park, towards the upper part of the village, did he turn round and say, panting slightly, "You believe in God?"

"Yes," he said, nodding his head.

"What's He look like?" Bletchley said, stopping and gazing at him.

In the Park, little more than a field stretching down at the side of the road, Batty was swinging on one of the swings in the recreation ground, pushing himself to and fro with one foot, and kicking Stringer, who was sitting in the next swing, with the other.

"Like an old man," he said.

Bletchley examined him for a moment and said, "Have you seen Him?"

"No," he said.

"If you don't believe in God they won't let you in the door."

"Yes," he said, and added, "Well, I'll tell them I do."

"They send you to see the vicar and he gets it out of you."

Bletchley watched him a moment longer, then turned and, in much the same silence, continued up the slope.

From the swings Stringer had shouted, "Where're you going?"

"Church," he called.

Stringer nodded, glancing at Batty, but added nothing further.

The Sunday School was split into two groups. The Crusaders, who were eleven and over, sat in the church itself behind a row of banners clipped to the end of the pews, each bearing the emblem of a saint or an apostle: a bird for St. Francis and a pair of fish with large eye-balls for St. Peter. The Juniors met in the Church Hall, a small stone structure to the rear of the church, which at one time had been a barn. The floor was of bare wood and the walls were unplastered. A large fire at one end kept the place heated and throughout the meeting a small woman with red eyes would shovel on pieces of coke, sending up little puffs of smoke, wiping her eyes then her nose on her handkerchief as if she were crying.

The children sat on small wooden chairs arranged in

circles. Each circle was supervised by a teacher, a young man or woman, they themselves overlooked by the vicar's wife, a small, fat woman, in shape not unlike Bletchley himself, her eyes hidden behind a pair of thick glasses. Their own teacher was a man called Mr. Morrison. He was tall and thin, with a long thin neck and a long thin face. On either cheek was a clump of bright red spots. He had a prayer book and a Bible which Bletchley, sitting on his right, held for him, handing them to him whenever they were required, his own face serious and extremely grave. They sang a hymn first under the supervision of the vicar's wife, then they put their hands together and said several prayers, some of which the children knew by heart. They sang another hymn, then they sat down and Mr. Morrison told them a story about a man who went fishing.

The teachers in the other groups were telling stories too, some of the children looking across at Colin, others sitting on their hands, gazing at the walls or ceiling.

In the roof were visible the timbers of the barn, old and gnarled as if they'd been taken straight off a tree, and here and there pieces of string hung down as if at one time they had held decorations. Periodically one or two of the children went out to the lavatory, coming back to sit down again, folding their arms and staring at the roof. Everyone had on their best suit or dress, and clean shoes.

Bletchley listened carefully to Mr. Morrison, his head turned stiffly from his tight collar so that he could watch Mr. Morrison's mouth. Whenever Mr. Morrison asked a question Bletchley would put up his hand, and though for a while Mr. Morrison might ignore it, despite Bletchley whispering, "Sir, sir," in his ear, in the end he would turn towards him with a slight nod, his eyes avoiding Bletchley altogether, who, in turn, would lower his arm, coughing slightly, and direct the answer specifically at the circle of faces before him.

When Mr. Morrison had finished speaking he glanced at his watch and looked over at the vicar's wife talking to her group by the fire, then took the Bible from

Bletchley, opened it at a piece he had already marked, and handed it back to Bletchley to read.

Bletchley stooped forward to read, resting the Bible on his inflamed knees and following the print with his chubby finger. Whenever he faltered on a word he would bow his head several times in rapid succession then, having got it out, would look up at Mr. Morrison with a smile.

Finally, at the end of the room, the vicar's wife stood up. A last hymn was announced, Bletchley wandering round the group sorting out the pages for those who couldn't read and stabbing his finger at the number. Mr. Morrison stood by his seat blowing his nose, dabbing at the spots on his cheek then looking at his handkerchief to see if they had left a mark.

When the piano began to play Bletchley sang with a loud voice, almost shouting, his head turned conspicuously away from the page to indicate that he knew it by heart. Those who couldn't read and didn't know the hymn simply stared at the book, occasionally opening their mouths and making a humming sound in time with the music.

At the end of the hymn a moment was allowed for everyone to put down their books. Bletchley had already closed his before the last verse and had turned, while everyone else was singing, and laid his book on the seat, turning back, still singing, to finish the hymn with his eyes half-closed, gazing vacantly towards the ceiling.

A final prayer was said, the vicar's wife waiting until everyone had closed their eyes and put their hands together, then a blessing was given and as the woman at the piano began to play a slow tune each child picked up their chair and carried it to the side of the room. Bletchley, with one or two of the older children, had begun to collect the hymn books and the Bibles, the teachers themselves standing together at the end of the room with their backs to the fire, rubbing their hands.

When Colin went out the sun was shining and the wind blowing across the fields towards the church. The children either went and stood in the church porch to wait for their elder brothers and sisters, picking up the piles of confetti dropped there from the weddings the previous day, or ran off down the slope, past the Park, towards the village.

Batty was still sitting on the swings when Colin went past. Stringer was standing behind him, pushing him to and fro.

"Hey," Batty shouted and he went in the gates. One or two children from the Sunday School had already run in before him and were standing by the swings and the roundabout waiting for Batty's permission to climb on. "Hey," Batty said. "How often you go there?"

"It's the first time," he said.

"Who sent you? Your old man?"

"No," he said.

Batty nodded and said, "All right, Stringer, catch me," and Stringer caught the chains, bringing the swing to a halt.

Batty jumped off the swing and sat down, taking off one of his boots and pushing his hand inside. The sole of his foot, just below his big toe, was covered in blood.

"What d'you do, then?" Batty said. "Talk about God?"

"Yes," he said.

"My old man," Batty said, watching him intensely, "believes in God." He examined him a moment longer then, adding nothing further to confirm this, said to the children waiting the other side, "You wanna ride?"

"Yes," they said.

"All right," he said. "Five minutes."

Stringer had put back his boot and removed the other one. On a seat the other side of the Park the Keeper, a retired miner with a wooden leg, sat with his leg up on a bench, reading a paper.

"Hey, Fatty," Batty shouted, catching sight of Bletchley in the road. He was walking down the hill with Mr. Morrison, carrying his Bible. Beside him walked the woman with the red eyes.

Bletchley didn't look up, his gaze turned towards Mr. Morrison and the woman the other side.

"Hey, Stringer," Batty said. "You want to bash Fatty Bletchley."

"Yes," Stringer said, wincing, as he drew on his boot. Colin's Sundays now were very full. His father's uniform had arrived while he still had his legs in pot and though he had conveyed to his mother at the time something of the irony of it appearing when he could no longer wear it—laying it out on the kitchen table and stroking it very much as if it were a dog—now, once again walking freely and with no longer the trace of a limp, he would march through the village on a Sunday morning, in khaki and with the one stripe which, perhaps because of his accident, he had recently been given, Colin walking beside him, or sometimes a little behind, pushing the pram and combining with this duty the two undoubted pleasures of watching his father drilling and exploring the old house. In the afternoons he went to Sunday School and it wasn't until tea-time that he was free.

He took little notice of the baby: it had begun to sit up now, so that when he took it walking, it would invariably be looking round, its blue eyes large, impassive, occasionally waving its arms. In the house it sat on the floor turning over the toys it was given, reaching over, making tentative efforts to move but only in the end falling over, lying on its stomach then and beginning to cry. His mother was now trying to make it hold a spoon, and each morning there was the ceremony of holding it over a pot.

His father, since his return to work, had grown quieter and more detached. In the evenings, though he still went out into the field to play cricket, he would, more often, sit at the table in the kitchen, drawing.

He had brought home a large pad of squared notepaper, a black pencil, a wooden ruler and a piece of rubber. Whenever he had spread the sheets out on the kitchen table and begun to draw his cheeks would swell out and redden, and no more so than when he had made a mistake and, with his tongue sticking out between his teeth, he rubbed it out, fanning away the crumbs of the rubber with the side of his hand.

At first it was difficult to make out what the subjects of his drawings were. Whenever he had finished for the evening he put them away in a drawer at the end of the table, reminding his mother that no one was to look at them in his absence. After a while, however, when it seemed that the rubbing out had passed its peak and he had begun to write on the drawings, occasionally asking for words to be spelt and sketching large arrows from one side to the other, he told them that the drawings were to do with an invention he had thought up at work. He stood with his head held slightly to one side as he regarded the various sheets, his eyes half-closed, his tongue slowly licking his lower lip: then, having spread out the sheets on the table top, he leaned carefully over them and in the top left-hand corners numbered them from one to six.

The first drawing was of an aeroplane. It was a bomber, standing on the ground, with a single engine drawn in carefully on either wing. Underneath the aeroplane lay a large bomb and beside it, coiled in a heap, a metal chain.

The second drawing was of the same aeroplane taking off. Heavy strokes of the pencil around the edges of the paper indicated it was night, and amongst the pencil strokes several stars and a large crescent moon like a half-closed eye had been carefully interspersed. His father had no particular skill at drawing: one wing of the aeroplane rose rather helplessly from the top of the fuselage, despite numerous half-rubbed-out efforts to correct it, and on one of the engines the whirling propeller was almost as large as the wing itself.

In the third drawing a group of aeroplanes were shown flying together. A swastika had been carefully inscribed on each wing, on each fuselage and on each tail. This group was confined almost exclusively to the right-hand side of the picture and a trail of black dots beyond them suggested that there were still many more to come. To the left of the picture, and by far the largest shape in it, was the bomber. It was flying, as a large, shaded-in arrow indicated, at a height a little above that of the aircraft approaching from the right. The round emblem of the Royal Air Force had been inscribed on its tail, on its fuselage and on both wings, while, from the bottom edge of the paper, the beams of numerous searchlights stood up like blades of grass.

Beneath the aircraft itself was slung the bomb, dangling on the end of the chain, on its side too the round emblem of the Royal Air Force and a message which said in capital letters, "THIS IS FOR YOU, ADOLF." A series of notes and arrows indicated that it had been lowered to the precise height of the approaching aerocraft.

The fourth drawing suffered more than any of the others from corrections, the bomb itself having been drawn in various positions before it had arrived at its final situation almost touching the nose of the nearest aircraft from which the faces of several Germans, each wearing a swastika on his arm, could be seen anxiously peering out.

The fifth drawing was taken up entirely by the subsequent explosion. Flames and jagged pieces of metal had been flung in every direction, while around the edges of the conflagration sections of tails and wings and disembodied pieces of fuselage could be seen falling to the ground. Several notes in the margin confirmed the effectiveness of the explosion, indicating not only the number of aircraft destroyed but the number of enemy airmen killed and the number of bombs exploded in the bombbays. The last drawing provided additional confirmation of this for from a clear sky a dozen or more aircraft could be seen hurtling towards the earth, flames licking at every surface, black plumes of smoke spiralling from their shattered frames in an elaborate pattern of swirls, curls and volutes. Flying above, close to the upper edge of the picture, was the solitary bomber responsible for all this destruction, bearing the insignia of the Royal Air Force on its fuselage and tail, the chain still dangling beneath it, while from its cockpit had emerged a hand, as large as the tailplane itself, with its forefinger and second finger upraised, amidst numerous erasures, in the signal of the Victory V.

His father sent off the drawings in a brown envelope with the address printed in the same black crayon on both sides. At the top of the envelope he wrote the word "Private" then, shortly before he took it into the village to post, he crossed it out and wrote instead "Of Utmost Concern," practising the words first on a piece of paper.

A little later, when he had given up hope of any reply

and had begun to copy out the drawings again with a bigger bomb and even more aircraft falling, the envelope already prepared and marked in red ink "Urgent!!," he received a letter with an official address printed across the top and a typed message underneath indicating that the drawings were receiving attention.

For several days running he took the letter to work, bringing it back each morning a little dirtier and more heavily creased, in the evenings taking it along the backs with various copies of the drawings, stopping at the doors and explaining to Mr. Shaw, to Mr. Stringer, to Mr. Reagan and Mr. Bletchley, and even on one occasion to Mr. Batty, the principles on which his invention worked. The following week he brought home a fresh pad of paper from the pit office and began to draw a second invention, suspending in this instance not one bomb but several beneath the aircraft, at varying height, like bait swinging from a row of hooks.

The culmination of this design was a drawing which occupied the entire surface of the kitchen table. Several squared sheets had been glued end to end, their edges crinkly and embellished with thumb prints, and on the single sheet, with a great deal of groaning, his face flushed, his tongue almost permanently protruding, he drew a flotilla of aircraft with an assortment of bombs strung out beneath them, some of the bombs, because of their size, carried by two or more aircraft with "THIS IS FOR YOU, FRITZ," printed on the side.

After he had posted it, folded in a neat parcel and sealed with red wax, he turned his attention to several other designs which this recognition of his efforts had suddenly encouraged. As time passed and no news of his inventions reached the papers, these grew in complexity and profusion, culminating in the design for a bullet which, according to his calculations, could be fired round corners. It was shaped like a ball and was flung out of a grooved barrel in such a way that it curved in flight, eventually, if it was provided with sufficient velocity, returning to the point at which it had started.

"Won't it kill," his mother said, "the person who fires it?"

"How can it?" he said, irritated whenever he had to explain his inventions unduly. "There's bound to be something in the way. And in any case, you can shorten the range by reducing the size of the cartridge."

"I see," she said, nodding her head and gazing down at the numerous figures, firing round house corners, that his father had drawn.

Occasionally, as the flow of inventions faltered, he would get up from the table, put his pencil down, stretch for a while before the fire, his head back, his hands clenched into fists above his head, then, making sure that his work things were ready for the evening, his shirt warming in the hearth beside his socks and his boots, his trousers and his coat hanging on a nail beside them, he would wander out on to the doorstep and light a cigarette.

From there it was only a few steps down the garden to the field where the men were playing football. And there, by the fence, he would stand smoking, his hands in his pockets, occasionally calling out, finally glancing back at the house and climbing the fence and offering a kick at the ball as it came in his direction.

Within a short while he would be standing in the centre of the field, waving his arms, calling, the cigarette still in his mouth until that moment when, laughing, the ball at his feet, he flung the cigarette out, running one way then another towards the nearest goal, shooting then calling out, "Goal! Goal! What did I tell you?" His legs were slightly bowed when he ran, and they kicked out wildly whenever he lost control or the ball was taken from him, his voice calling "Foul! Foul!" distinguishable from all the rest by its tone of belligerence and complaint.

Later, as it grew dark, the men would crouch down in the middle of the field. Finally, when the light faded, all that was visible was the glow from their cigarettes and the occasional flare of a match. The low murmur of their voices came through the quietness. His mother would go on to the step and call into the darkness, scarcely loud enough to hear, "Harry. Harry. You'll be late for work."

He would come in complaining, his eyes still dazed from the darkness, his elbows and knees stained green, his figure stooping impatiently by the fire as he drew on his work clothes and fastened his boots: "I must be a madman, going to work at this time," taking his bottle of tea and his tin of sandwiches which his mother had already packed in his knapsack and getting out his bike, feeling the tyres, switching on the dynamo for his lights, then calling out to the men still gathered in the darkness as he rode away.

8

Mr. Reagan's son Michael had joined Bletchley and Colin at Sunday School. He was a tall boy with a long thin face and a long thin nose. His eyes were pale blue like Mr. Reagan's. When Bletchley and he walked down the road together people laughed, the one so fat, the other so thin, Reagan apparently unnoticing but Bletchley himself walking more quickly, his knees reddening as his agitation grew. When they returned from Sunday School Reagan walked on one side of Mr. Morrison and Bletchley on the other, the woman with reddened eyes walking slightly ahead or behind.

On the third Sunday Reagan brought his violin. It was at the invitation of the vicar's wife, who announced the presence of the instrument at the beginning of the service, Reagan stepping out from behind his chair with the case so that the vicar's wife could hold it up. The violin itself was like a large shiny nut, reddish brown, lying in a bed of green baize. He had, the previous two weeks, been practising a hymn tune and when the last hymn was announced he went to stand by the piano and took the violin out.

The children watched him in silence. He folded a white handkerchief beneath his chin, bending his head towards it to keep it in place, then sliding in the violin.

Bletchley stared across at him intensely. He had, on the way to Sunday School, kicked the case at one point, saying, "The vicar'll take it off you. They don't let you have things like that inside."

"Mrs. Andrews asked me to bring it," Reagan said, mentioning the vicar's wife.

94

"She's not the vicar," Bletchley said. "In any case, if she doesn't do what *she's* told he knocks her about."

Now, however, Bletchley regarded him with a smile. He winced, screwing up his eyes, glanced at Mr. Morrison, and winced again, gazing at the roof.

Reagan's eyes expanded as he played, squinting slightly as he tried to watch the bow crossing the strings, pausing, his body shuddering, his eyes closing whenever his notes failed to correspond with those from the piano, the sound fading when the children, and Bletchley in particular, began to sing.

Bletchley sang with his eyes closed, turned in the direction of the violin, his head raised as if he were addressing Reagan directly.

When they walked home after the service he kicked the case again. "You'll be getting it broken, bringing it out like this," he said. "In any case, I bet you can't play the piano."

"No," Reagan said.

"My cousin can," Bletchley said.

A few days later Colin noticed Bletchley and Reagan playing in the field at the back of the house. Reagan was carrying Bletchley on his back, his thin figure stooped under the load, his head bent almost double. Bletchley was hitting his legs with a stick, saying, "Go on, boy! Go on!" and clicking his tongue. They wandered round a hole, the sides of which had fallen in.

A little later Mr. Reagan appeared in his garden. He had just returned from work and was in fact wearing his yellow gloves and his bowler hat, his jacket alone unbuttoned as an indication that he had, at last, arrived home. "Hey," he shouted, and when Bletchley looked up added, "Get off his back."

"What?" Bletchley said.

"Get off his back," Mr. Reagan shouted.

Bletchley got down. He stood for a moment gazing across at Mr. Reagan.

"Michael," Mr. Reagan shouted. "Get on his back."

Reagan had stooped down to rub his legs, inflamed from Bletchley's stick.

"Get on his back," Mr. Reagan shouted.

Bletchley stood still, frozen, his eyes never leaving Mr.

Reagan as Reagan himself grasped his shoulder and tried, unsuccessfully, to climb on his back.

"Get down," Mr. Reagan shouted, waving his arm.

"What?" Bletchley said.

"Bend down."

Bletchley stooped slightly, his eyes still fixed on Mr. Reagan, and Reagan himself slowly clawed his way on to Bletchley's back. Bletchley stood swaying for a moment, his hands clamped behind him on Reagan's legs.

"Give him the stick," Mr. Reagan shouted and when Bletchley did so he shouted again, "Start walking."

Bletchley stumbled, hoisted the weight on his back and, his legs trembling as he struggled to keep his balance, began to walk round in circles.

"Hit him," Mr. Reagan said.

Reagan had looked up, his eyes wide and staring as when he had played the violin.

"Hit him."

Reagan did so, fanning the stick beneath him at Bletchley's legs.

"Ow," Bletchley said, screwing up his face.

"Faster," Mr. Reagan shouted.

"I can't," Bletchley said, beginning to cry.

"Faster. Or I'll come out there myself."

Bletchley tried to run, his cheeks trembling, his knees rubbing together.

"Ow," he said each time Mr. Reagan called out, his shouts growing louder as he tried to attract the attention of someone in his house.

"Faster," Mr. Reagan said. His face inflamed now as when he watched the cricket, his thumbs tucked into his waistcoat pockets. "Faster, or I'll fan you myself."

Bletchley had fallen.

He gave a loud groan and collapsed on his side, his eyes closed, his mouth open.

He lay moaning for a while, clutching his ankle, Reagan standing over him scratching his head. "Oh," Bletchley said. "I've broken my ankle."

"I'll break the other one if I catch you again," Mr. Reagan said. "Get up now, or I'll lift you myself."

Bletchley stood up. He groaned again, his eyes closed, his face turned up. "I'm going home," he said, adding something which Mr. Reagan couldn't hear, glancing round however in case he had been mistaken and with several groans and grimaces limping his way back to his fence, his arms flung out either side to retain his balance.

"I'll give you a leathering myself," Mr. Reagan said to Reagan, "if I catch you again. If he hits you with a stick hit him back."

"Yes, Dad," Reagan said.

Bletchley was attempting to lift his legs over the fence farther down the field retaining at the same time all the effects of his injury, his groans and sighs, his tortured expression, limping up his garden to his door. "Mam! Mam!" he shouted as he neared it, "Mam!" almost screaming and, as the door opened, collapsing on the step.

And yet, after that, it was unusual to see Bletchley and Reagan apart. They went to school together each morning, walking at the same slow pace, each wearing an identical satchel in which they carried an apple, a bottle of ink, which often got broken, and a pen. Occasionally their respective mothers stood talking in the street, or passed across the fronts of the houses to one another's doors. Finally, a little later, the two women began to go to church together, attending the Sunday morning service, occasionally accompanied by Mr. Bletchley dressed in a brown suit, and a little later by Bletchley himself and Reagan. Mr. Reagan could occasionally be heard shouting to them from the bedroom as they passed the door.

"They've gone to church, Harry," he would say, coming across the backs to where his father sat at the back door reading the paper. "She has that lad kneeling down every night by the bed."

"Kneeling?" his father said.

"Praying."

"Ah, well," his father said. "Praying never did any harm."

"Nor any good," Mr. Reagan said. "She's going to make him as silly as she is."

"Ah, well," his father said again, still gazing at the paper and, in this instance at least, refusing to be disturbed. "You can never tell."

"That's what I mean," Mr. Reagan said. "The same happens whether you do or you don't."

On Sundays Mr. Reagan wore his suit without the jacket, the waistcoat unbuttoned save for the bottom, a stiff collar and around it the tie of his old school. A thin gold chain ran from the top button of his waistcoat to the top pocket on the left hand side. "Though it's fastened to nought but a lump of stone," his father said. "I know that for a fact."

Since his disappointment over getting a job at the local pit his regard for Mr. Reagan had slightly faded.

"Oh, Reagan's all right," he'd say. "But if he's got all these complaints why doesn't he do something about it?"

"He's frightened of his wife," his mother said. "In fact, he's frightened of women in general."

"Of women?" His father had laughed, gazing at his mother in amazement. "If he was frightened of women," he said, still laughing, "he'd be on his knees afore any man. And he's never been that. Not as long as I've known him."

His mother nodded but answered nothing back.

In fact, having heard this excuse, his father's regard for Reagan was momentarily restored: he even went across the backs to talk to him on a Sunday morning after Mrs. Reagan and Michael had gone off to church, sitting in the porch and laughing at the various things they read in the paper, occasionally joined by Mr. Batty or Mr. Stringer and a little later setting off for the Institute in a noisy group.

It was from Mr. Reagan that the idea sprang that Colin should sit for the examinations. The opportunity to go to the grammar school in the city came the following year, and if he failed the examination a second opportunity occurred the year after. If he failed again he would go to the secondary-modern school at the other end of the village, from which the pit recruited most of its miners.

"It's as Reagan says," his father told them. "Do you want him to be like me or like Reagan, getting paid for sitting on his backside all day? I know what I'd do."

"Mr. Reagan works," his mother said. "Sitting down is a different kind of work, that's all."

"Ah, well," his father said. "You're the one that knows about education." His mother, unlike his father, had stayed at school until she was fifteen. In a cupboard upstairs was a certificate carefully filled in with copper-plate script testifying to her efficiency at English, nature study and domestic science.

It was his father, however, who set him his homework, coming round the table whenever his mother had suggested some subject he might do, saying, "He'll never learn nought from that," taking the pencil and setting his own small, square hand, bruised, its nails blackened with coal, firmly in the middle of the paper and across the top, with much snorting and panting, printing in capital letters the subject of a composition: "A FOOTBALL MATCH," "SUNDAY SCHOOL," "A RIDE ON A BUS." Sometimes he would stand by the chair, waiting for him to start, stooping forward slightly to follow the words as he began, sometimes stepping back, whistling through his teeth until, finally, he called out, "If you take all that time to begin, by God, the exam'll be over before you start."

"He has to think it out," his mother would tell him. "In any case, standing over him won't be any help."

"And what if I don't stand over him? He'll never get done at all." Yet he would step back then, perhaps pick Steven up, who was walking now and swing him over his head, saying, "When you get started we'll see the sparks fly. You wait, we'll show them. By God, I'm sure of that."

Steven had blue eyes, like his father, but his face was like his mother's, round and smooth, with the same turned-up nose. He had much the same expression as his mother, as if inside there were a shy, almost silent person peering out. He'd begun to speak and his mother, whenever she handed him an object, would repeat its name several times, nodding her head at each one. Occasionally when Steven was out of the house and playing in the yard with the younger children from down the terrace he would talk quite freely, running to and fro on his short, slightly bowed legs, shouting, "It's mine. It's mine," or, to some much older boy, "Stop it. Stop it."

"Can you say Colin?" his mother would ask him.

"Colin," he would say, looking up with a frown.

His father usually had to get ready for work as Colin was finishing the essays, looking over his shoulder while he pulled on his trousers or his shirt to see how much of the page he had covered with his slow, careful scrawl, or if he had turned over to the other side. "Two sides," he'd say. "They won't give any marks for half a dozen lines."

"Leave him alone," his mother would tell him.

"Don't worry," his father said. "You won't educate anybody by leaving them alone."

He'd brought a red pencil home from the pit office to mark the essays and as he waited he would sharpen it impatiently over the fire, turning round then and saying, "Are you ready? I've to be off to work in half an hour," looking over Colin's shoulder then at the clock to say, "I should leave it there, then. End of the sentence will do," sitting down in the chair as soon as Colin himself had stood up and adding, "Don't go away. I want you to take notice of these mistakes." He screwed up his eyes slightly to read, his mouth pulled down at one side as he puzzled over the spelling, occasionally looking up and saying, "How do you spell 'fair,' Ellen?" and when his mother had told him, scarcely looking up from her own tasks, her ironing, or her washing-up, he would say, "Isn't there an 'e' in it somewhere?" adding impatiently when she explained, "All right, then. All right. I only asked. I don't want a lecture."

"Do you want to get it right or not?" she'd ask him.

"All right, then," he would say, pressing the point of his red pencil more firmly into the paper, going carefully over each of the words he had written himself and at the end of each sentence, if he approved of it, giving it a little tick. "That's right. And that's right," he would say to himself.

He took a great pleasure in marking the paper with the red crayon and when he had finished he would write in the space at the bottom some comment he thought appropriate: "Excellent," "Could do better," "Attention not on your work," or, "Will have to work harder for examinations." Beside it he would add some mark out of ten. On principle he never gave him less than three and seldom more than seven. Finally, when all this had been completed, he would draw in a large tick, beginning it at the bottom left-hand corner and stretching it across almost as far as the top right, and beside it printing, with something of a flourish, his full initials, "H. R. S.," Harry Richard Saville.

Later, when he had grown tired of reading Colin's stories and compositions, he brought home several mathematics books borrowed from a man at work. Inside the front cover of each one was printed in pencil, "Sam Turner HIS book," and beside it, in one or two instances, the figure of a woman which his father had tried unsuccessfully to rub out.

The books dealt with subjects he had scarcely touched on at school, fractions and decimals, figures split up on the page into little parts, and since his father didn't understand them either he would read the book first himself, sitting in the easy chair by the fire, a piece of paper on his knee, copying out figures over which he coughed and dropped the ash of his cigarette, rubbing them out and groaning, and quite frequently stamping his foot, slamming it against the floor and rubbing his head in exasperation.

"Here, let me have a look," his mother would tell him.

"Damn it all, woman," he would say, covering the book up or snatching it away. "Am I supposed to be doing it or aren't I?"

"Well, you're supposed to be," she'd say.

"Well, then let me get on with it and stop shoving in."

She would go back to her work and he would continue to groan and stamp his feet, finally getting up and coming round the table to set out the figures on the squared colliery paper on which, much earlier, he had drawn out his inventions, scratching his head over each one as if, even as he wrote them, he wondered if they might have any resolution.

He would then copy down the same problem himself and take it back across the table, working it out as quickly as he could, whispering under his breath, rubbing out, groaning, looking up to ask Colin if he had finished and going back to his own with relief when he told him he hadn't. When he came round to mark the sums he always stood beside him, never asking to sit down, as if at any moment he expected himself to be corrected, stooping over his shoulder or occasionally going back to his own version on the other side of the table to stare down at the figures before coming back yet again to mark down a tick or a cross.

As the problems increased in complexity and his father's patience slowly ran out, and as Colin's own tiredness after a day at school grew more apparent, his mother would begin to complain. Often when he had gone to bed, the problems, still unsolved, racing round his head, he would hear their voices raised in the kitchen, his father saying, "Nay, I won't bother, then. We'll send him down the pit like all the rest. After all, why should he be different?"

And when he came down in the morning his mother would be saying as soon as his father came in from work, "There's no reason at all why he should go down the pit."

"And where else will he go in this place, then?"

"I don't know," she would say as he clattered about the kitchen, taking off his boots, picking up his red pencil and beginning again with the problems where he had left off the night before, even occasionally bringing out the solution from his waistcoat pocket, written down for him by someone at work. "It's no good forcing him," she would add, "into something he can't do."

"He can do them," he would say. "The reason he doesn't do them is because you're for ever hanging over him."

"He can't do them," she said, "because he's tired," picking up Steven, who invariably cried when they quarrelled, pulling at his mother's skirt and asking to be lifted.

"It's better that he's tired now than he should have my job and be tired like I am, later."

"Well," she said, "you should give him time and not press him."

"Press him," he would say, stamping his stockinged feet and, getting no effect from that, banging his fist on the table so that all the cups and saucers rattled. "I'm damned," he would add, "if I'm going to be beat by a decimal point and a couple of fractions."

In the mornings too when Colin came down his father would look up from his breakfast, the pit dirt still black on his lashes, and say, "What's two point five multiplied by seven? Quick now, in your head," gazing down and saying, "That's right," when he had answered and adding, "How do you spell 'geography'? Quick, now. Isn't it with a 'j'?" shaking his head in frustration if his mother corrected him and saying, "I was only testing him out," beating the table in rage.

In the end his father was quickly distracted. On the road leading out of the village to the south, past the Institute and the Dell, a field had been divided up into allotments. Each plot of land was twenty or thirty yards square and in the evenings and on Sunday mornings the men would go down there, carrying their spades and forks, to turn over the hard, tufted turf of what had once been a cow pasture. His father had been given a plot close to the road so that as the men came into the field or left he could always call out to them and frequently, having carried the spade down for him, Colin would be left digging on his own while his father sat in the hedge bottom smoking and talking to Mr. Stringer or Mr. Batty or Mr. Shaw. "Nay, dig a straight line," he would call out and add to the men, "The war'll be ovver afore we've grown ought here."

He bought plants on the way home from work and set them out in neat rows: cabbages with pale-green leaves on yellow stalks, cauliflowers and sprouts. While Colin dug back the grass on one side, turning it over and breaking it up in the earth, his father would rake out the rows, sifting the soil and drawing the stones and larger pieces away. Crouching down at the end of each row he would take out the gaily coloured packets of seed from his waistcoat pocket, tearing off a corner and tapping a few of the seeds into his hand. With his fist clenched he would waft them out on to the soil like a man shaking dice, crouching down or stooping, and covering the seeds up with the edge of his boot as soon as they were scattered. When he had reached the end of the row he would look for a stick, pierce the empty packet, and set it in the ground. In this way he planted carrots and beetroot, while peas and beans he carried in large packets in his coat, sticking his finger in the soil if it was soft and setting one bean or one pea at the bottom of each hole. Finally, when all the seeds were planted, he cut sticks out from the hedge at the end of the allotment and set them over the rows like a net, occasionally breaking off to cross over to where Colin was digging and say, "Here, let's have a go: we'll be here till midnight," digging in the spade and turning over the heavy sods. "You'd have thought they'd have ploughed it over for us, for a start. It's like trying to dig a mountain."

With the proximity of the Institute many of the men spent their time there, bringing their tools down in the early morning only, once the Institute was open, to disappear up the road, coming back at lunch-time to retrieve their spades or forks or, in the case of Batty's father, lying down on the grass mounds between the plots to sleep, his mouth wide open, snoring, his arms stretched out at his sides.

"I don't mind drinking," his father would say. "But I don't go for a man who doesn't know when he's had a drop." Yet whenever he spoke to Mr. Batty he would stand by him, looking up almost shyly at his red face, saying, "That's right, Trevor, lad," laughing with his hands held to his side.

His father took a great deal of trouble with the allotment. He paid the same sort of attention to it that he did to his sewing, or to the cooking when his mother was ill. Whenever the milkman's cart had passed the door and left some manure in the street, he would say, "Up you get and let's have it in," and in the evening Colin would carry it in a bucket to the allotment and spread it over the rows, his father wandering off to one of the other plots to talk to Mr. Batty or Mr. Shaw, and adding, "You might pull out a few of those weeds while you're at it. I don't know. They come up as soon as you look."

Though he hadn't troubled to take a plot himself Mr. Reagan often came down on a Sunday or, extending his stroll beyond the Institute, on an evening, carrying the cane which he always affected whenever he intended going beyond the end of the street or the colliery yard and, standing by the hedge in his bowler, leaning on his stick, he would say, "No, no, I won't come in," indicating his shoes which were always shiny, and adding, "I wouldn't like to put the old lady to any great trouble cleaning these."

If he had arrived unobserved he would call over the hedge to his father, laying the leaves aside with his cane, saying, "Why, Harry, that's a fine job you're making there," or, later in the year, when the beetroot had come up in dark clumps above the soil, and the carrots were shining bright orange beneath the ferny leaves, he would call, "Why, Harry, that's a very fine showing you have there," adding, if his father took one out of the soil to show him, "Why, Harry, I wouldn't mind having a few of those on the table tomorrow lunch-time," shaking his head in surprise whenever his father pulled a few out. "Why, Harry, that's very decent of you. That's very decent of you, indeed," leaning over the hedge to take them or coming to the gap, holding them well away from his suit, by the tip of their leaves, as he walked away.

"Aye, well, we can't eat them all ourselves, can we?" his father would say and invariably would also pull up a few vegetables for Mrs. Bletchley next door.

A little while earlier Mr. Bletchley had been called up. Unlike the men who worked in the mine his job had no priority and in fact, shortly after he left, from the same station, carrying a little suitcase and with Bletchley on one side and Mrs. Bletchley on the other, both crying, a woman in faded blue overalls took over his job of carrying the long pole between the trucks and, after a brief visit home, in uniform, looking strangely tanned and contented, Mr. Bletchley wasn't seen again. The only contact they had with him was through Bletchley himself, who, on the way to school with Reagan, would describe the number of men his father had killed the previous week, the number he had captured, and the extent of the terrain which Mr. Bletchley personally had overrun. "How many has he killed?" Batty would ask him and when he'd been told would gaze at Bletchley with a slightly dazed expression, saying, "What's he do it with?"

"His bare hands," Stringer would say. "It'd take half an army to kill as many as that."

"Not with a machine gun," Batty would tell him, rushing strangely to Bletchley's defence whenever his figures and exploits were questioned.

Some Sundays they went walking, usually for about an hour before tea. They spent some time getting ready. His father would clean his own shoes and his mother's, rubbing at them with a brush and then with a duster as if he wished to rub them away, Colin cleaning his own shoes and Steven's. Then they got washed and while his mother dressed Steven in a pair of grey shorts and a jacket Colin would put on his suit, his father coming down in his own, his face red and glistening, stopping over him while he inspected his ears and neck and then his hands. There would be several minutes waiting then while his mother went upstairs to get dressed, his father standing in the kitchen in front of the mirror, spreading cream in his hands from a small white bottle then rubbing it on his hair, combing it down with a parting at one side, the fringe neatly turned back on top, calling out over his shoulder, "Now, look. Stand still. Keep clean. Don't move."

When finally his mother came down in her best coat, dark brown and hanging almost to her ankles, she would bolt and lock the back door on the inside and put the key in his father's pocket saying, "Have you got your handkerchief? Have you got any money?" never troubling to look at herself in the mirror at which, although he had repeatedly combed his hair, his father still cast frequent glances. They would then all go through to the front door.

It was the only time the front door was used to come in and go out of and his father, conscious of the windows across the street, would lock it carefully behind him, test it, then put the key in his pocket with the other one. "I never know why we lock it," he would tell her. "What have we to pinch?"

"It's surprising what people find once they get inside," his mother said and, looking up at the windows to make sure that they too were secure, they would set off down the street.

Colin always walked in front, holding Steven's hand, his mother following behind with her arm linked in his father's. Occasionally they would call out, "Pick your feet up. Don't drag them. Take your hands out of your pockets. Your hair needs cutting. No wonder those shoes are worn out," or, if they were trying to walk with some care, "Come on, now. Walk a bit faster. We're going to be treading on your heels."

Invariably they walked through the village to the Park, his father, whenever they passed someone they recognized, whether he knew them or not, calling out, "Afternoon, Jack. Afternoon, Mick," the men often glancing across, uncertain, nodding their heads. "They had that chap up last week for carrying matches," he would tell his mother and she would say, "That one? I don't think it can be him. He drives a lorry."

"No, no," he would say. "He's down the pit. I know him well," glancing back to make sure but seldom arguing further.

In the Park they would walk slowly round the paths that took them by the swings and the ornamental pool. Other families, often pushing prams, would be walking up and down or, if the day were dry, sitting on the grass, the men lying back asleep, the women sitting upright, knitting, talking across to one another, the children playing on the swings. "No going on swings on Sunday," his father said whenever Steven showed signs of wandering in that direction, "keep to the path and keep your shoes clean."

Usually on the way back Steven would ask to be carried, and though he often cried, tugging at his father's hand and saying, "Dad, I want to," his father would say, "You're walking. How can you get any exercise if you're being carried about? And in any case, if I was going to carry you I wouldn't have put on my suit," sometimes taking his hand however so that Steven could swing between him and his mother, Colin himself walking on ahead or, if he were feeling tired, following behind, his father occasionally turning and calling, "Come on. Don't lag," and adding to his mother, "It's like trying to drag a horse."

Finally, when they reached the house, his father would unlock the door, his mother would go inside before him and, picking up the kettle, would set it on the fire before she removed her coat, his father mending the dying ashes with pieces of coal before he too removed his coat, and turning to the table—which was set already with cups and saucers—he would help to get the tea.

9

The air-raids began again in the following winter and his grandfather came to live with them. He was a small, slight man with a straight back and thick white hair which, like his father's, was still cut in a boyish fringe. His eyes too were light blue and the skin around them creased up in a half-smile. "This is a big lad you've got here, Harry," he would say, grasping Colin's arm, standing him between his knees, feeling his biceps, or, when he had lifted Steven up, he would sing in a light voice, "Follow my leader, follow me do: I've got a penny here for you."

"Which pocket is it in?" Steven would say, feeling round him.

"Nay, Steve," he would say. "You're as quick as your dad."

He had been living with his father's brother for some time but now the brother had been called up and he had come to live with them. He had only two teeth, one at the top and one at the bottom, and shortly after he arrived Colin's mother took him to the dentist.

"Last time I went they near tore my mouth to pieces," he said. When he came back he had no teeth at all. "They'll be ready in a fortnight," he told Colin's father. "What have I to do till then?"

"You'll be all right, Dad," his father said. "We'll fill you up with beer."

"Beer," he said. "Beer did no good to any man. I've lived long enough to tell you that."

Whenever the air-raid sirens sounded he sat under the table, smoking his pipe. The shelter had been dug up in the back garden and replaced by a metal one, of corrugated iron: each of the houses had one but many of

108

them were full of water and refuse and none of them were used. "They'll not frighten me," he said whenever his father tried to coax him out into the cupboard beneath the stairs. "I'm not frightened of any bombs."

He would sit under the table with his legs stretched out, smoking his pipe, his head stooped forward. Or sometimes, if Colin's father and his mother tried to coax him out together, he would crouch on all fours or lie on his side with his hands wrapped round one of the legs. "You get in," he would tell them. "I'll be safe enough here. It's not me they're after." And later, when he had got his new teeth, he would crouch under the table with his pipe clenched between them as if they had been fixed, perpetually, in a grin.

The teeth were large and very white and he often sat in the doorway so that he could see Mr. Shaw or Mrs. Shaw or Mrs. Bletchley, smiling whenever they appeared so that they would say, "Why, you look twenty years younger, Mr. Saville."

"I don't know about younger," he would say, sitting there again the next day, and the next.

In the evenings he would take the teeth out and brush them under the tap, then drop them into a jar full of water, taking them up to his room and standing them on a chair facing him by the bed. He slept in the same room that the soldier had slept in and on the same bed, and Steven, who had had the room for a little while, moved in with Colin.

His grandfather always wore his suit, which was dark blue and slightly too large for him, the sleeves hanging over his hands, the trousers drooping over his ankles. Each evening he hung it up on a coat-hanger, the trousers underneath and the coat on top, sometimes calling to his mother as he got into bed, "Ellen. Ellen. Come and hang up my suit," standing about impatiently until she had come and hung it up on a hook on the wall.

"It wouldn't do it any harm to fold it over a chair," Colin could hear her say through the wall.

"Nay, I've had that over twenty year, Ellen."

"You bought it two years ago," she would tell him.

"No, no," he would say. "It was longer than that."

He had a special regard, perhaps because of the suit,

for Mr. Reagan, and Mr. Reagan had a similar regard for him. "A good suit is a good suit," Mr. Reagan would say. "And there's nothing in this world quite with which to compare it." And when his grandfather had asked Mr. Reagan to inspect his teeth, smiling for him or even, on some occasions, taking them out, Mr. Reagan would say, "I always say a good set of teeth make up for any deficiency of face. And that, mind you," he would add, "I'm saying to someone whose face, if you'll pardon the expression, doesn't come into that category at all." On other occasions, when they had been out for a walk together, to the Institute or down to the allotment to see Colin and his father digging, he would say, "There's many a restraint I've to put on the women, Harry, now that your father's walking through the place." And when his father laughed he would add, "Oh, now. He'll be coming back from his walk one of these days a married man."

His grandmother had died long before Colin was born and his grandfather had been a widower for many years. "He always says twenty years about everything," his mother told him, "because that's when his wife died."

"Aye," his grandfather would say. "She was a fine woman. They don't make them like that any more."

He saw too, occasionally, at this time his mother's father and mother. They lived in the next village, four miles away, and on some Saturdays he would go with his mother and Steven on a bus to visit them. They lived in a row of little houses built specially for old people. Each house consisted of a single room from which an alcove opened out on one side, and in which, behind a curtain, stood a metal double bed, and on the other a small alcove which was used as a pantry. A door led directly into the house from a footpath at the front, and at the back a porch led to a lavatory and a tiny walled-in opening in which they kept coal. Sometimes at week-ends his father filled a sack of coal and having roped it to his bike, laying it across the pedals, he and Colin between them would push it the four miles to the next village and tip the coal into the little opening. "I get it at reduced rates," his father would say. "It's cheaper than them buying it," or when they got back, riding on the bike, Colin sitting sideways on the cross-bar

110

between his father's arms, his father would say, "Has your mother told you what her father was when I met her?"

"He was a farmer," his mother would say.

"A small-holder, a small-holder," his father would tell him, almost shouting. "He kept pigs. He was a pig-breeder. You had to be in love, I can tell you, to step inside that house."

His father would sit laughing in his chair while his mother complained, then he would add, "Ah, lass, you know I love you. I married you all the same."

"We kept other things as well," his mother would tell him, ignoring his father, her face flushing, her eyes large.

"Aye, but pigs is all you smelled!" His father would lie back in his chair laughing and slapping his knee with his hand or, if he were smoking, sit choking on his cigarette. "Pat us me back, pat us me back," he would say. "I forgive you."

His mother's father and mother were perhaps even older than his grandfather. They were called Swanson; the name was embroidered on a piece of cloth which was framed and hanging over the high mantelpiece of their room: "To Edith and Thomas Swanson on their Golden Wedding," beneath which was the date and, in smaller lettering, "From the Old People's Guild," the writing itself surrounded by a border of pink flowers and small bluebirds swooping in between.

Grandfather Swanson would either be sitting by the fire, which was set in a high range on the wall at the level of his knees, or lying on a couch at the back of the room. He very seldom moved when they were there, only his head rising occasionally when they came in, after knocking, and his grandmother had said, "Ellen's come to see us, Tom," his dark eyes turning slowly in their direction before his head sank back on the couch or the chair. His grandmother had a small, very round face as if, all the time, she were puffing out her cheeks. They were always bright red, particularly in winter, and her eyes which were greyish were very narrow so that when she smiled they almost disappeared. She often got Colin's name mixed up with Steven's and with the name of some other grandson he had never met, so that she would often say, "Would you like a sweet, Barry, or an apple?" then look up when

111

he didn't answer. "Now," she would say, the grey eyes shining, "I don't know which one it is."

Sometimes his mother came away from his grandmother's crying. Some time after they had arrived his grandmother would say, "You'd think you'd get more help from your own daughters as you grow older," and his mother would say, "I do help you, Mother. Harry brings you coal, and I come over and do your washing." Sometimes, too, his mother would do the cleaning. While his grandfather and his grandmother sat by the fire she would put on an apron she'd brought with her, fill a bucket at the sink in the corner, then scrub the floor. Outside she would scrub the front step and the paving stone below it and scone it with a yellow stone so that when it had dried it glowed a dull yellow. She would do the same with the back door and then make the big double bed with its brass rails and brass head-piece, and clean the small, heavily curtained windows, borrowing a pair of steps from a woman next door. The washing she did in a shed built at the back of the houses. Colin never went there, for his mother, ashamed to be seen working in these conditions, with pumped water and where the washing was beaten against a stone, refused to let him inside. He would play on a piece of bare ground between the shed and the houses while he waited, or sit with his grandmother by the fire. When his mother came in from hanging the clothes up she would say, "You can ask Mrs. Turner to get them in, Mother, when they're dry."

"Oh, we'll be all right," his grandmother would say.

"I've to get back for Harry's supper. He'll be off to work," his mother would add.

"Don't worry," his grandmother said. "We'll manage somehow."

And when they got back home and his father could see that she had been crying he said, "Take no notice. They're like that. Just do as you see fit."

"I never get any thanks. Ever," she said.

"Then don't go expecting any," he told her.

"If I did nothing at all she'd have some right to complain."

"Aye. She'd be in a right mess all right." His father would look away, uncomfortable when she cried.

Sometimes on the bus back the conductor said, "Are you all right, love?" leaning over her, his hand on the back of the seat.

She would wipe her eyes then blow her nose and try to see the money in her purse.

"People are like that when they grow old," she said, and other times she would say, "Never expect anything of people then you'll never get hurt."

However, at Christmas or on their birthdays she would take over a present or even a special cake that she had baked herself. "There's a time for forgiving," she would say whenever his father complained and he would turn away saying, "Let them find out what it's like on their own. They'll soon come begging." On their birthdays, or sometimes on the Saturdays when she went over, she would cook them a meal, grandfather Swanson lying on the couch gazing at the ceiling, his white hair falling in thin wisps over his cheeks, his grandmother sitting in a rocking chair by the fire saying, "Two potatoes will be enough," or, "If you use all that cabbage, Ellen, we'll be without for the rest of the week."

"I'll buy you some more, Mother," his mother would say, "before I go."

"If you have the money you can always manage."

Sometimes she stood over the pans with her eyes full of tears, wiping them away on the back of her hand, his grandmother taking no notice.

"I've no patience with you, I haven't," his father said when she got back, enraged himself and banging the table with his hand. Yet he would add, "No, no, sit down. I'll make you a pot of tea before I go to work."

Grandfather Saville had fought in the First World War. He would sit looking at the newspaper through a pair of heavy black-rimmed spectacles perched on the end of his nose, his head held back, studying the pictures but never the text. "Look at this, Colin," he would tell him, holding the paper up so that he could see the picture of a burnt-out building or a tank with its turret broken open or slumped down in a hole without its tracks. "They don't fight wars now like they used to. In those days it was man to man. Now they think nothing of bombing women and children, or shelling people miles away they never see."

In the evenings when Colin was ready for bed and had changed into his pyjamas, and his mother had looked in his ears and at his neck, his grandfather would say, "Sit down, lad, for five minutes," and when his mother complained, saying, "He hasn't even said his prayers yet, he's going to be late into bed," he would answer, "What I have to tell him, Ellen, won't take more than a nod of your head."

Or when he was already in bed and had put out the light his grandfather would come in and say, "Are you awake, lad? They've sent me up to bed as well. Sitting down there listening to the wireless. They'll listen to ought, people nowadays. In one ear, out the next."

His grandfather had been to Russia. He would sometimes call to Mr. Reagan in the street or in the backs saying, "Come in, come in. The missis will make us a cup of tea," and when Mr. Reagan had come in and, carefully easing up his trousers, taken a seat at the table, he would say, "Did I tell you the time I was in Russia?" and when Mr. Reagan had answered, "Yes, I believe you did," he would say, "We went in to save the Czar. Would you believe it? A socialist all my life and when they call me up they send me to shoot the workers."

"War's an unpleasant thing," Mr. Reagan said, "even at the best of times." He was himself only a year ahead of the latest drafting and would sit at the table when his grandfather had finished, saying, "A colliery official like myself is as important to the pit as any miner, perhaps more so. Yet do I get deferment? I do not. Why, only the other day one of the owners came up to me and said, 'We shall have to get someone out of retirement to take your place, Reagan, or one of the women out of the offices.' Why, it's taken years of training to get where I am."

"Have you ever seen snow?" his grandfather would ask him.

"Snow?" Mr. Reagan said.

"Marching for days with it up to here."

"Oh, a biscuit would go very well with it," Mr. Reagan said whenever his mother put down his cup of tea. "That's very kind of you indeed. Ah, ginger. A favourite."

114

"Moscow," his grandfather said. "Landed at Sebastopol in the Crimea and marched four hundred miles and all the way back again. Wolves? We fought everything. We even fought women."

"Women?" Mr. Reagan said, sipping his tea.

"They come in at night when you're asleep, with sticks and shovels, and try and take your food," his grandfather said. "Why, one woman could take ten men apart in a matter of seconds."

"I can well believe it," Mr. Reagan said. "If they left wars to women they'd be over in half the time. Perhaps even sooner."

"When we left we were shelled."

Mr. Reagan nodded and bit his biscuit.

"Came down on you from every side. The Heights of Sebastopol," his grandfather said. "We threw everything off the ship that we could and filled the hold full of women and children. Aristocrats. Hundreds of them. When we reached Istanbul they wouldn't let them out until we'd de-loused them."

"Istanbul? Now, isn't that in Turkey?" Mr. Reagan said.

"Filled the holds with disinfectant and they had to swim around for hours. When I came ashore a woman offered me a gold necklace to marry her so that she could come back to England."

"That sounds a very tempting offer," Mr. Reagan said, re-crossing his legs.

"They were all at it. You could have anything you wanted," his grandfather said. "There was nowt they wouldn't do, given half the chance."

"Here, Colin," his mother would say. "Will you take the bucket and fill it up with coal?"

"It won't do the lad any harm, missis," his grandfather said, "to hear where his forebears came from."

"The Irish Revolution," Mr. Reagan said, "was very much the same."

"You fought there, then, Mr. Reagan?" his grandfather said.

"No, no. But I had an uncle who was killed in Belfast."

"The Black and Tans," his grandfather said.

"Ah, yes," Mr. Reagan said, and shook his head.

If his father came in and found them talking he would say to Mr. Reagan, "Has my dad told you about the harem in Constantinople?" and when Mr. Reagan said, "No, no, I don't believe he has, Harry, that's the one thing he hasn't mentioned," and winked at his father, he would add, "Show us your leg, Dad," and his grandfather would pull up his trouser to reveal a long white scar running the length of his calf. "There," his father said. "The guards caught him one as he was nipping over the wall."

"On the way out," his grandfather said, smiling with his new teeth.

"On his way out, Mr. Reagan," his father said.

"It's a miracle I've still got a leg at all," his grandfather said, laughing, his father getting up then as he choked to tap his back.

At night he said two prayers that his mother had taught him since starting Sunday School, kneeling by the bed, his head pressed against his hands. "God bless Mother, Father and little Steve, and make Colin a good boy. Amen," and "Lord keep us safe this night, secure from all our fears, may angels guard us while we sleep, till morning light appears." Then he said, "Please God, let me pass the examination. Amen," and pressing his head against the blankets repeated it three times before climbing into bed.

His uncle called at the house. He was small like his father, with the same light-coloured hair and blue eyes and even the same moustache, though he was younger, and would come into the house without knocking, saying, "Ellen, and how's our favourite lass?"

His mother's temples reddened and she would turn away to the fire, to the kettle, and put on a pot of tea as if his appearance caused her no surprise at all, saying, "Don't you knock before you come in?" and he would say, "Not when I'm visiting my favourite sister."

"Sister-in-law," she would tell him and he would answer, "Well, then, aren't I going to have a kiss?"

He had been called up into the Air Force and usually came in his uniform, his cap tucked into the lapel on his shoulder, parking a blue-painted lorry with an R.A.F. insignia on its cabin on a piece of waste ground at the end of the road. When he had kissed his mother on the cheek and hugged her a moment he would stand with his back to the fire clapping his hands together and saying, "Well, then, who wants a round?" shadow-boxing for a while then adding, if no one responded, "Aren't we going to have a cup of tea?" and then, "Here you are, Steven. Here you are, Colin. See what I have in my pocket."

He usually brought a bar of chocolate or, failing that, would bring out a coin and press it into their hands saying, "Don't tell your mother where you got it or she'll want it back," and adding in a louder voice still, "Now, then, make sure she doesn't hear."

When his father came in he was always serious, saying, "How are you, Jack?" shaking his hand before sitting down at the table and perhaps adding, "Have they given you a cup of tea?"

"It's on the boil, Harry," he'd tell him, clapping his hands again and looking over at his mother. "I wish I was a miner and that's for sure. Fighting on the Home Front. There's nothing to beat it."

"Oh, I'll swop you any time," his father told him. "Riding around in a lorry. You never risk ought but a bloody puncture."

"Don't worry. The Jerries are over our station every night," his uncle said.

"He doesn't look as though he's worried, does he, Dad?" his father said and his grandfather shook his head and added, "Have you brought us ought, Jack? What's in the back of your lorry?"

They walked down sometimes and looked inside and sometimes his uncle would say, "Come on, Colin. Jump up inside," and they would sit together in the large seat, smelling of oil and petrol, Steven sitting between Colin's legs, while his mother would say, "Don't take them far, Jack, I want them back for dinner."

"Just round the town," his uncle would shout over the roar of the engine, which he revved up for some time before they began, attracting the attention of the people in the other houses.

He drove, always, very fast. They started with a jerk, the tyres squealing, and ended with one. Because he was a small man his uncle's head was scarcely visible from outside and he would sit on a cushion, occasionally half-standing to see ahead, pulling himself up on the wheel

117

and saying, "Now, then, what happens here?" whenever they came to a bend. If someone got in the way he would shout out, "Just look at that. They don't know how to use a road let alone a vehicle."

"Mad Jack they used to call him," his father said when they got back. "And Mad Jack he still is."

"Mad as a hatter, me," his uncle said and if his father had come down from his afternoon sleep before going off on the night shift he would say, "Don't you keep proper hours in this house? I keep coming here hoping to find you at work and my lovely sister-in-law all on her own."

"It's a good job I do work nights," his father would say, sitting down at the table and looking up, blinking his eyes, at his brother.

For several weeks before the examination Colin had returned to doing his nightly essays and his nightly sums while his father sat across the table correcting them, occasionally, if he had to go to work, leaving them on the sideboard to correct when he came home in the morning. "What's the decimal for three-tenths?" he said when he came down on a morning. "They won't give you any longer than that. How do you spell hippopotamus?"

The day before the exams he and the other children who were taking them were given a new pen, a new pencil and a new ruler at school to bring home with them. In the evening Colin had gone to bed early, his mother coming up to tuck in the blankets and his father coming up before he got ready for work. "Think of something nice," he said, "like your holidays, and you'll soon be asleep. An extra hour's sleep before midnight is as good as half a dozen next morning." And after he had gone out his grandfather came in and said, "Are you asleep, lad? Spend this on ought you like," putting a coin in his hand. When the door had closed he put on the light and saw that it was half-a-crown.

He seemed to be awake all night. He heard his father go to work, wheeling his bike out into the yard, calling out to Mrs. Shaw as she came out of her door to get some coal. Then, only a few minutes later it seemed, he heard his grandfather climbing into bed and singing as he often did now, "Rock of Ages, cleft for me," his voice trailing off into a vague murmuring and moaning. Then, later, he heard his mother raking the fire and bolting the back door, coming up the stairs to her room, saying something to Steven, who for that night was sleeping with her, then going back down to bring him a drink. All night he lay awake turning fifths into decimals, decimals of a pound into shillings and pence, spelling circumference, ostrich and those words that his father had made him learn by heart. He was still struggling to convert a fraction of a yard into feet and inches when he felt his mother holding his shoulder and saying, "It's time to get up, Colin. I'll warm some water for your wash." When he went down his clothes were lying over the arm of the chair by the fire, his trousers pressed, his socks just mended, his shoes freshly polished in the hearth. His mother had been up early to iron his shirt and it was stretched on a clothes horse in front of the fire. "I cleaned your shoes then you won't get polish on your hands," she said. The bowl of water stood steaming in the sink.

A little later his father came back from work, wheeling in his bike, the shoulders of his overcoat and the top of his flat cap wet, the wheels of the bike leaving a wet track on the floor. "It's just started," he said. "Cold enough to snow," shaking his coat as he took it off. "Have you got a bit of spare paper," he added, "to put in your pocket? It's just what you'll need for working things out." He washed his hands at the sink, then tore a sheet from the colliery pad and folded it up ready for him to take. "Is his ruler and his pen out?" he asked his mother, and took them down off the mantelpiece to examine the nib, saying, "This isn't very strong. One good bit of writing and it'll break in two. Haven't we got one he can take with him, Ellen?"

"They'll have all that there," she said. "I should just leave him to get on."

"Aye, he'll be all right," his father said, standing by the table, rubbing his hand along the back of the chair, gazing down at him, then at his mother, then staring helplessly about the room. "Remember what I've told you," he said. "Before you write ought down think. They'll not go much by somebody who's always crossing out."

119

When Steven came down his father lifted him up and said, "Now, then. Are we going to have another scholar in the house?" Steven struggling to get down to the table where his bowl of porridge was waiting. "If he does his sums as well as he eats we'll be all right," his father added. "We'll none of us have to worry."

When his grandfather came down still in his pyjamas he said, "Where's my tea? Nobody brought me up my tea this morning, missis," and when his mother said, "Oh, we've got more important things to think about," he looked down at the table and said, "Porridge, now that's going to fill out his brains."

"Aren't you going to eat it, Colin?" his mother asked him.

"No," he said. "I don't feel hungry."

"You want something. You'll do nothing with an empty stomach," she said.

"It's nerves," his father said. "I get the same feeling when I'm going down at night."

"He can take an apple," his mother said, gazing down at him, her hands clasped together. "He'll soon fill up when it's over."

When he was ready he picked up the ruler and the pen and pencil and put the piece of paper in his pocket with the apple his mother gave him in the other. He pulled on his black gabardine raincoat and his cap, and his mother said, "Nay, not out of the back. You can go out of the front today."

She'd already gone to fetch her coat, saying, "I'll come down to the bus stop with you," and he'd said, "No, I'd better go on my own."

"Well, if you're sure," she said.

She held the door open, holding Steven in her arms and saying, "Are you going to kiss him for luck, then, Steve?"

Steven shook his head, kicking his legs against her and turning away, and his father said, "Well, good luck, lad. And remember what I've told you."

"Yes," Colin said and shook his father's hand as he held it out, shyly, half-flushing.

It was still quite dark. The rain fell in a fine drizzle. Farther down the street Mrs. Bletchley and Mrs. Reagan were walking towards the bus stop with Bletchley and Michael Reagan, the bright orange pens and pencils sticking from their satchels.

"Have you got everything, then?" his mother said. "Your money for your dinner?"

"Yes." He didn't look up.

"Remember last night," his grandfather said. "There's more where that came from."

When he reached the corner and looked back his mother was still standing in the door. When she waved he waved back, then turned the corner and walked quickly to the stop.

There was a crowd of children and mothers already there, clustered together in the half-darkness, and one or two men with pit dirt still on their faces. Everywhere there were the bright orange rulers and pens and pencils.

"Have you got a rubber?" Bletchley said.

"No," he said.

"You have to have a rubber." Bletchley took one out of his pocket. "That's for rubbing out pencil and that's for rubbing out ink," he said, indicating either end. "Got any blotting-paper?"

"No." He shook his head.

Bletchley opened his satchel and took out a sheet folded in two. Reagan had a similar piece in his satchel and an identical rubber. Inside too were a bag of sweets, a bar of chocolate, an orange and an apple, and a bottle of ink.

"Haven't you got any ink?" Bletchley said. "You won't be able to write anything, will you?"

When the bus came, with its shaded lights glowing in the damp road, Bletchley was the first to get on. He kissed his mother, who then stood in the doorway until he had got up the steps. There were twelve children and when they were all on the mothers and the two or three miners stood at the windows, the women on tiptoe, waving. A teacher sat down at the front. The bus started.

The fine drizzle fell against the panes as the day lightened, and the lights with their blue-painted bulbs were switched off. The hedges on either side were drooped down with damp, the cattle herded together in the corners of the fields. The windows soon steamed up, and after a while, except by rubbing against them, little of the countryside could be seen. Bletchley sat near the front with his satchel on his knees, the inside of his legs still covered in the white cream that hadn't yet been rubbed off. Reagan, who had sat farther back in the bus, had begun to cry, his thin face screwed up, his forehead a peculiar white, his cheeks crimson.

The teacher got up finally and came up the gangway to stoop over him, and when they stopped at the next village and another group of children climbed on, their coats wet with rain, the teacher got off and went to fetch Reagan a cup of water from a house. When they set off again he sat sobbing in his seat, his chest shuddering with strange, sudden spasms, the air rattling in his throat, his satchel still strapped around his body.

"His dad says he has to pass or he'll get a good hiding," Bletchley said coming up the bus to sit with Colin. "If they see you crying they knock ten marks off. They watch you all the time. Did you know that?" leaning across to say to Reagan, "They've probably failed you already, Mic."

The school they arrived at was a brick building with tall, green-painted windows and a tarmac yard: it stood beside a row of arches carrying a railway across a shallow cutting, and at the other side of the yard ran a stream full of oil drums, pieces of bedding and mounds of rusted metal.

Several groups of children were already waiting in the lee of the building, out of the drizzle, each of them clutching the familiar orange pens and rulers. The doors of the school were still closed: numerous muddy footprints marked the lower panels.

Another bus stopped at the gate and several more children came into the yard, looking vaguely about them, at the school, at the arches across which occasionally an engine hauled a line of trucks, sending clouds of white steam and black smoke billowing into the yard.

"Why did they pick this place?" Bletchley said and Reagan shook his head.

"Every school," someone said, "takes its turn. Next year it might be yours, then you don't get an advantage."

122

"I wouldn't call this an advantage," Bletchley said. "Not even to anyone who lived here."

The boy who had spoken had fair hair, cut short and brushed into a neat parting at one side. He wore, too, a clean white shirt and a woollen tie with red and blue stripes. He had a fountain-pen clipped in the top pocket of his blazer and beneath it was the badge of his school, a red rose on a white background with "En Dieu Es Tout" written underneath on a scroll.

Bletchley, who had stared at the silver clip of the fountain-pen for some time, said, "You've been here before, then, have you?" scarcely troubling to look at the boy's face.

"Not here," he said. "I've taken the exam before. This is my last chance." He laughed and put his hands in his pockets.

"What's it like?" Bletchley said, Reagan too looking up, his chest still shaken intermittently by sobs.

"It's not the exams," he said. "It's just there are so many taking it. It's just a question of luck."

"Luck?" Bletchley said, nodding his head as if, in this respect, he possessed an undeniable advantage. His face began to swell and his eyes expanded.

Behind them one of the green doors had opened and a woman appeared carrying a bell. She looked up at the sky, at the viaduct then began to ring the bell just as another teacher began to do the same at a second door. "Boys in this door, girls in the other," she said. "Go to the classroom with your initials on."

The school was set out in a square with classrooms along each side. He entered the classroom with "Surnames S-Y" inscribed on the door. Several boys were already there, one from his own school whom he scarcely knew, standing in the space between the blackboard and the desks. A small, gray-haired woman said, "You'll find your names and your examination number pinned to your desk. Find it, sit down, fold your arms and don't talk." A notice which said "No talking" was chalked on the blackboard behind her.

His own name and number were pinned to a desk at the front by the door. A piece of pink blotting-paper was already laid there and the ink-well, set inside a metal disc, had recently been filled. He lifted the lid, looked inside the desk, then set out his ruler, the pen and the pencil on the top and folded his arms.

Across the room the boy with fair hair had sat down, unscrewed the top of his fountain-pen, examined the nib, screwed the top back on and placed it in the rack on the desk. Beyond him three large windows looked out on to the yard and, beyond that, the line of arches. Thin lines of moisture had begun to run down the panes.

The teacher called a register, ticking off each name, then came round the room collecting the letters which stated they could sit for the examination and which in his case had been signed by his father.

Returning to her desk she read out the rules of the examination from a printed paper. A boy came in carrying a pile of ruled paper; when a piece was placed on his desk he saw that it was folded like a book with a notice printed on the front which said, "Do not write your name. Fill in your examination number and leave the rest of this page blank."

The room grew quiet. Later, the only sounds that came in were the movement of milk bottles in the corridor outside, and the noise of lorries passing in the road. Occasionally an engine and trucks passed across the viaduct.

Some boys wrote quickly, scarcely looking up, their heads bowed to the desk, almost touching the paper, others gazing up at the ceiling then at the figures around them, dipping their pens repeatedly in the inkwells, tapping the nib dry, then beginning to write slowly only, a moment later, to look up again and stare at the window.

Across the room the boy with fair hair wrote with his chair pushed well back from his desk, his arm stretched out casually before him as if at any moment he might push the desk away, get up and walk out. He wrote with his left hand, his head slightly inclined to his right, glancing at the question paper without moving his head then writing out the answer with his fountain-pen, its cap fastened on the top, its bright clip glinting in the light from the window. He pursed his lips slightly as he wrote as if he were chewing the inside of his cheek.

The boy next to him was writing his name on his blotting-paper, stooped over the desk, his cheek laid against the desk top, dipping the nib in the ink-well then printing the letters in rows of little blots. Occasionally he half-raised his head to glance at the effect, then laid his cheek down on the desk top again and began to surround his name with an elaborate scroll.

After a while the teacher said, "There is now half an hour left. By this time you should have reached question eight or nine."

Question nine comprised an entire sheet of the examination paper. He had to copy out the description of a shipwreck and put in the correct punctuation and the correct spelling. The very last question on the paper simply said, "How many words can you make from 'Conversation'?"

Several of the boys had put down their pens and were sitting with their arms folded, gazing at the teacher.

"If you have finished already," the teacher said, "don't waste the time. Read through your paper again and see if you have made any mistakes. I'm sure some of you have."

Finally she said, "In two minutes I shall ask you to put your pens down. Finish off the sentence you are writing and make sure that your ink is dry."

When they had put their pens down she said, "I want no one to speak until I have collected the papers. You will remain in your places until I tell you to leave."

When he went out in the playground the boy with fair hair came across and said, "How many did you do?"

"Nearly all of them," he said.

"I just about finished," the boy said. "I thought it was harder than last year. It doesn't matter, I suppose."

Across the playground Reagan was eating an orange and Bletchley an apple, Reagan with his satchel still fastened across his back.

"What's your name?" the boy said.

"Saville," he said.

"Mine's Stafford," he said. "Both S's!"

When Bletchley came across he said, "How many words did you get for 'conversation'?" and when he said, "Nineteen," Bletchley said, "Is that all? I got twenty-seven. Did you get onion?"

"No," he said.

"I got thirty-four," Stafford said.

"Thirty-four," Bletchley said, his face reddening round his cheeks and nose. "Did you get notes?"

"Yes," Stafford said, his hands in his pockets. "And nation."

"Nation," Bletchley said, flushing more deeply. "I got that one too."

When they went back a mathematics paper had been given out.

Whenever Colin looked up he saw Stafford sitting in exactly the same position as before, his arm stretched out casually to the desk as if it were something he touched with only the greatest reluctance, his head resting just as casually to one side, occasionally glancing up at some point immediately in front of him, above the blackboard, and frowning slightly before returning to his figures, which he wrote out very quickly. Whenever he crossed anything out he did so with a slick flick of his wrist, as though he were pushing something aside, his head stooped forward very briefly before returning to its position.

The time passed more quickly than before. Several of the questions involved the conversion of decimals to fractions, and fractions to decimals, of the kind that he had practised at home, and when he had finished he had time to go over the paper once again before the teacher said, "Pens down—Sit up. Arms folded. Leave your papers in front of you for me to collect."

When the papers had been collected she added, "Those of you who are staying to dinner form a queue at the end of the corridor, those who are going home for lunch must leave by the main entrance."

"Are you any good at sums?" Stafford said as they waited in the queue.

"Not really," he said.

"Decimals," Stafford said. "We've only just started them at school. Last year they weren't as difficult as this."

Bletchley was already sitting at one of the tables in the hall when they went in, writing something on a piece of paper for the benefit of the boy sitting beside him, then slowly shaking his head and pointing at the paper with his fork. Reagan, with his satchel round his shoulders, stood at the back of the queue searching in his pockets for money, then came to the woman at the door and shook his head. Finally his name was taken and he was allowed in.

"Intelligence after dinner," Stafford said. "Last year one was, 'What has a face, a pair of hands, a figure but not often any legs?' Can you guess?"

"No," he said.

"A clock." Stafford laughed, leaning back on the bench where they were eating. He ate in much the same way that he wrote, sitting well back from the table.

"Did you finish all the sums?" Bletchley said as he went past.

"Yes," he said.

"I finished half an hour early. But they wouldn't let me out. Did you get eighty-four for number nine?"

"No," he said.

"You've got it wrong, then," he said and glancing at Stafford went on to the door.

After lunch, when he returned from a walk, the yard was full of children. Reagan was sitting in the porch eating an apple. Bletchley was standing, leaning against the wall beside him, eating an orange.

When they went in the teacher, who was aready standing by her desk, had said, "Some boys have been writing on their blotting-paper. This is not allowed. All the blotting-paper that has been written on has been changed and anyone caught writing on it, or printing anything on it whatsoever, will find themselves in serious trouble."

The examination paper was given out. It was a small book with a space left for an answer beside each question.

The woman teacher put her handbag on the desk and took her watch from her wrist and laid it on the lid before her. After a certain shuffling of chairs and the occasional groan or gasp which greeted the first reading of the paper, the room fell silent. A dog began barking in the yard outside, and on the viaduct another engine passed. A cloud of steam, caught by a gust of wind, condensed against the windows.

The first question was, "Complete the following sequence of figures: 7 11 19 35—." The second was: "If a man in the desert walks north north east for five miles, south south east for five miles, east south east for five miles, west south west for five miles, south south west for five miles, north north west for five miles, west north west for five miles, east north east for five miles; (i) at what point will he have arrived? (ii) Describe *but do not draw* the shape his footprints will have left in the sand."

Perhaps it was this question he saw Stafford answering, for he was drawing with his pen on the back of his wrist, occasionally looking up at the teacher behind the desk then licking his finger and rubbing it out. Another question was, "Which is the odd one out and why: a rectangle, a parallelogram, a circle, a rhomboid, a triangle, a square?"

The boy sitting next to him had laid his cheek again on the desk and with his pen was inking in a shape on the desk top, his tongue sticking out between his teeth, his eyes distorted. Beyond him, in the next row, a boy had screwed up his face, bringing his eyebrows down over the bridge of his nose, and from beneath this was gazing fixedly at the teacher.

Finally, when the teacher said, "There are twenty minutes left. You should now be on question eighteen or nineteen if you are doing them in order," a heavy groan came up from the back of the room and a moment later someone else had laughed.

When the papers had been collected they were allowed outside.

"Do you know what the boy next to me wrote?" Stafford said. "For that question about the man in the desert who walks all the way round the compass?" He walked beside Colin, his hands in his pockets, kicking his feet against the ground. "Where it said 'at what point will he have arrived?' he wrote, 'potty.' I saw it as they collected them up."

A wind had sprung up since lunch-time and clouds of paper were blown across the yard, drifting up against the wall of the building then swirling round.

"I've run out of ink," Stafford said. "I'll have to fill up with this school ink. It rots the rubber." He unscrewed the pen to show him. "Do you want a sweet?" he added. "They're to give you energy. I've forgotten them until now." He ran off across the playground, taking out a piece of paper and standing with a group of boys in the door, comparing answers.

Reagan was standing against the school wall with his

satchel still strung round him, his hands in his pockets, his shoulders hunched up against the wind. When Bletchley came across he said, "Did you get number seven? Half of them have written rhomboid because they didn't know what it was."

"What was it?" he said.

"A circle," Bletchley said. "It's the only one that hasn't got a straight line." His face was flushed, his eyes watering slightly from the wind. From his satchel, which he carried under his arm, he took out a piece of chocolate. "One boy in our room got disqualified," he said. "He'd written down the answers on a piece of paper to pass to somebody else. Did you hear the shouting?"

"No," he said.

"That's him over there."

Bletchley pointed him out but he couldn't see him. When they went back in fresh sheets of paper had been given out and the woman behind the desk was smoking a cigarette which, the moment they came in, she put out.

Later, when they came out, Stafford said, "Which subject did you write about?"

"The war," he said.

"I wrote about the pit hooter 'blaring out the emergency signal.' I've never seen a disaster. Have you?"

"No," he said.

"What else did you write about?"

"My favourite hobby."

"I wrote about an historical character. King Canute."

"Do you know anything about him?" he said.

"No," he said. "Not much." When they reached the buses standing in the street outside he said, "Which one are you on?" and when he pointed it out he added, "I'm on the one behind. I'll see you. Good luck," standing outside however with several boys until Colin had climbed on.

As he sat down Bletchley, who was in the seat behind, leaned over and said, "You know what Reagan's done? In the essay he wrote about the nurse, writing home to her parents," continuing to lean forward slightly while he laughed in his ear.

Reagan, who was sitting beside him, his satchel on his knee, smiled slightly, gazing across at him then out at the school and the yard where, in the faint light, several boys were playing football.

"There are male nurses," a boy said who was standing up in his seat behind Bletchley.

"Male nurses," Bletchley said, glancing at Reagan then, falling back in his seat, slapping his knee. He winced then, slightly, drawing down his brows, frowning. His knees were reddened from the wind and he held them apart.

The bus moved out of the village. Gusts of wind swept under the door, swirling the tickets between the seats. It was growing dark and the sky had begun to fade against the mass of fields and trees outside. Inside the bus itself the dull blue lights came on.

Low grey clouds scudded across the sky. Someone at the back of the bus had begun to sing.

When they reached the village Mrs. Bletchley was waiting at the bus stop with Mrs. Reagan. "You've been a long time, mister," she said to the driver.

"Nay, missis," he said, "you can't drive fast down these lanes," lighting a cigarette then and laying his hands on the radiator cap to warm them, stamping his feet in the road.

"How did you get on, Ian?" she asked Bletchley, pulling his scarf more tightly round his neck and fastening the top button of his coat. "You'll catch your death of cold. How was it?"

"Easy," he said. "Michael wrote a composition about nurses."

"About a nurse," Reagan said to his mother in case she might complain.

"Oh, well. That's very good," Mrs. Bletchley said. "We better get home for a hot meal."

They walked down the street together, Bletchley getting out one of his examination papers from his satchel and showing the questions to his mother in the dark. She flashed a torch on to the paper, not troubling to read it, but saying "Ian, you've done very well, I can see."

Mrs. Reagan had taken Reagan's satchel, holding it in one hand and holding Reagan with the other.

"You'd think they'd have an easier way than this for sitting the scholarship," she said.

"You would," Mrs. Bletchley said, clapping Bletchley's gloved hand between her own to keep them warm.

When they reached their respective front doors they called good night and went in. Colin went round the back assuming that now the day was over the privilege of using the front door had probably expired.

When he went in his father's bike was standing upside down on a sheet of newspaper in the kitchen, his father kneeling beside it, the chain hanging down from the rear wheel. His grandfather was sitting by the fire asleep.

"How did you get on?" his father said, looking up. "We were just thinking of coming down to the bus stop to find you."

"All right," he said.

"What were the papers like?"

"Oh," he said. "All right," and shrugged.

His father watched him intently for a moment then glanced away. "My chain's broken," he said. "And I'm off to work in an hour. You haven't seen a spare link, have you, lying on the floor?"

"No," he said.

"I meant this morning."

"No," he said, and shook his head.

His father looked around a little longer on the floor, under the cupboards and the table, then stood up. "Well, then," he said. "Let's see what they're like."

He took the papers out of his pocket and put them on the table. Then he took off his coat.

"Is there any tea?" he said.

"There is. There is," his father said, stooping over the table and trying to examine the papers without actually touching them with his blackened hands. "See," he said. "Just turn this one over. Thirty-four. That looks right to me."

His mother came down, calling behind her to Steven, whom she had just put to bed, then closing the door and saying, "Well, then, I thought I heard you. How did it go?" going to the kettle, filling it and putting it on the fire.

"He's one or two right here," his father said, nodding his head now, almost laughing. By the fire his grandfather opened his eyes, which were red and watery, gazing blankly at the ceiling a moment. Then, groaning, he leaned forward and ran his hand across his face.

"By," he said. "You need some coal on that fire, Ellen. It's freezing," looking up to add, "Well, then, did you get any of the answers?"

"What did you get here, then, for number twelve?" his father said. He brought a piece of paper and his red pencil to the table and, still keeping his greasy hands off the cloth, began to work it out.

"I don't know," he said, looking over his shoulder.

"One pound, three and sixpence," his father said, staring at the paper, then crossing the sum out and starting again. "There's a catch in that somewhere. I hope you were watching out."

"Now, let's have the table and get him some tea," his mother said.

When the time came for his father to set off for work he hadn't mended the chain. He went next door to borrow Mr. Shaw's bike and when he came back he said, "Don't move any of those papers. I'll work it out in the morning." The table was covered in calculations, some screwed up. "If it's not thirty yards for number eleven," he said, "I'm not sure what it can be. I'll ask Turner. He'll know."

When he went up to bed and drew his curtains he saw that it had begun to snow. It drifted down from the darkness in large flakes, driven up against the window. Already a thin layer covered the garden, outlining the declivities of the soil and leaving a dark space by the railings at the far end.

When his father came back in the morning the snow was plastered to his coat and his cap. It fell off in frozen crusts, sizzling in the hearth and melting in little pools on the floor. "Now, then," he said. "Where have you put the sums?" slapping his hands together in his khaki gloves and rubbing his stockinged feet in the rug. The snow had frozen on his eyebrows and lay in a thin crust around his mouth.

10

The snow lasted for several days. Only the tips of the fences and the mounds of the air-raid shelters were visible in the yards.

Colin's father came home the second morning an hour late. Across his back were roped several pieces of timber and two metal rails. "See here, I took these off a wagon," he said, unfastening the wood in the open door.

The snow was plastered to his boots, which he knocked against the outside wall, and to his trousers as far as his knees. It had been driven up and frozen on to the back of his coat. "I've pushed that," he said, "through some stuff," banging the bike against the wall so that the snow, matted together between the spokes, fell off. The wood had been sawn into even lengths. Holes too had been drilled through the rusty rails. "I had Harris joiner it at work," he said. "It won't take more than a minute to put together."

When Colin came home from school at lunch-time a sledge was standing half-completed against the kitchen wall. It was long and flat. In the hearth were the two metal rails and a hammer. One of the rails was bent at one end. "He's been trying to curve those to fit underneath it," his mother said, indicating the thin rib of wood where the runner would have to be screwed.

"I've never heard so much swearing," his grandfather said. "Not in one house, by one man, in one morning. It's a wonder this place hasn't turned bright red."

When he came home at tea-time the sledge was finished. Pieces of wood still lay about the floor, the sledge itself turned upside down, his father polishing the runners. "This'll go," he said. "You'll have to keep your eyes skinned I think to catch it."

Two holes had been burned through the wood at the front. A piece of rope had been knotted through. "Have your tea," he said, "then we're off."

His father dressed Steven to take with them, pushing the sledge up and down outside, wearing the rust off the runners. When they set off it left two brown tracks in the snow behind.

"No, no, you sit on," his father said, setting Steven between Colin's legs. "The more weight on we have the better."

His father looped the rope around his shoulders and strode along in front, stooped forward to their weight, the studs of his pit boots shining underneath, the snow collecting in the insteps then falling off: it crunched beneath the runners, the woodwork rattling over the bumps. It had already begun to grow dark and as they passed the windows his father would call out, tapping on some, saying, "Get him out. Get him out. Let him have some fresh air, then, missis."

When they reached the hill running up to the Park his father added, "Nay, Colin, you'll have to jump off," and as they started up the slope, "Don't you want a pull? It's light as a feather with Steven on."

In the Park, on the slope of the hill, several figures were silhouetted against the snow and as they got nearer he recognized Batty and Stringer and Stringer's father. Batty was half-way down the slope pulling up a sledge on the back of which Stringer was sitting, kicking his legs.

"What've you got there, then, Harry?" Mr. Stringer said.

"This is a toboggan," his father said.

"A toboggan, is it?" He came across. "It'll not last five minutes," Mr. Stringer said.

"It'll beat anything of thine," his father said.

"Right," Mr. Stringer said. "You're on."

In the faint light the flattened snow could be seen curving away between the flower beds and the ornamental pond.

"Ay go, our Malcolm," Mr. Stringer said. "Hurry up wi' yon sled', we're barn t'have a gamble."

Mr. Stringer was dressed as he always was in a sleeveless shirt with its collar undone. His trousers were tucked into his socks: on his feet were a thin pair of shoes.

"Are you coming down with me, Colin?" his father said. He sat on the sledge with Steven between his legs. "When I give you a nod," he added, "give us a shove and when we've got going jump on behind."

Mr. Stringer had already sat down on the other sledge. It was slightly higher than his father's and had a piece of carpet to sit on, wet now, however, and crusted with snow. He began to shout through his cupped hands to the figures below, "Ay up. Move over," adding, "We s'll have killed somebody afore we've done. How much do you want on, then? Half a dollar?"

"We'll give it a go first," his father said.

"Right," Mr. Stringer said. "When I say off." He shouted down the slope once more, waved his arm, then said, "Give us a good shove. Hold on. Are you ready? Right. We're off!"

They began to shout as they pushed the sledges down the top of the slope. "Faster," Mr. Stringer said. "Faster. God damn it, I'll get off here and push it myself." He went off first down the slope, Stringer and Batty jumping on behind.

As their own sledge gathered speed his father shouted, "Jump on, Colin. You'll have us over." The distance between them, however, increased.

Colin held on to his father's neck, his father kicking his legs to one side then the other. "Nay, you'll have us over," he shouted, laughing, the sledge, half-way down the slope, plunging suddenly to one side, dipping down into a drift of snow and flinging them off.

His father lay beneath him, kicking up his boots. The front of the sledge was buried in snow. From lower down the slope came Mr. Stringer's shouts followed by his cries as he guided his sledge between the swings.

"That was short and quick," his father said, adding as Steven, his face covered in snow, had begun to cry, "A bit of snow won't hurt you, love."

"I want to go home, Dad," Steven said.

"Nay, we'll have one more go at least," his father said.

When Mr. Stringer came to the top he said, "How much was that, then? Ten bob?

"Ten nothing," his father said. "We've had no practice."

"You'll need no practice with that," Mr. Stringer said. "You'll never get it to go, not if you put it on wheels and fasten on a motor."

"I'll ride it down myself," his father said. He pushed the sledge to the top of the slope.

"How much start do you want?" Mr. Stringer said.

"None," his father said. "We'll go together."

Mr. Stringer sat upright and was pushed off by Batty. "Go on, Dad," Stringer shouted. "Faster."

Colin's father however ran behind the sledge, pushing it, then, when it had gained momentum, flinging himself on top, kicking out his legs to steer.

"Get over," Mr. Stringer shouted down the slope. He caught hold of his father's sledge and pulled it across. "Get it off. Get over," he shouted, his small figure upright as if, silhouetted against the snow, he were sitting on nothing at all.

The sledges ran off into the snow to one side. A little later Mr. Stringer could be seen standing up, dusting the snow from his head and his shoulders saying, "I was going to overtake you there, then, Harry."

"He had hold of my legs," his father said when they finally came up. "I'd have beaten him to the bottom by a mile. I had him beat."

"A mile," Mr. Stringer said. "Why, I had to hold on in case he fell o'er."

His father picked up Steven and said, "Come on down and have a ride."

"I want to go home, Dad," Steven said. He shrank against his father as Mr. Stringer said, "I'll warm you up. Have a go on my back, then, love."

"He's a bit frightened," his father said. "He hasn't been on a sledge, tha knows, afore."

Several other people had arrived and set off down the slope. Shouts echoed up from the swings below.

"I'll have one more go," his father said. "Then I'll take him back." And as he put Steven down he said, "Give him a ride round, Colin." And when it seemed he wouldn't be pacified he said, "Come on, then. We'll all go down together."

But Steven refused either to sit on the sledge between

his father's knees or on his back, and when Mr. Stringer took him and set him down on his own sledge he called out even louder.

Already his father was pushing off.

"A gill to nought, then, Harry," Mr. Stringer said.

Colin pushed against his father then jumped on top. His father gasped. As they came to each bump his father gasped again. Behind them they could hear Mr. Stringer's shouts.

The snow shot up against Colin's face. Beneath him his father twisted, his legs kicking, as he turned the sledge. They slid between the posts of the metal swings.

"Hold on. Hold on," his father said as Colin clung more tightly to his back, his head pressed down against his father's neck.

The snow crunched beneath the runners, his father flinging his legs from side to side, the sledge running out into the unmarked snow at the foot of the hill. They turned in a wide arc and came to a halt beneath the hedge.

"That was a run," his father said. "A run and a half." He lay on the sledge for a while, groaning, after Colin got up. "By go, you're a ton weight," he said. "I wouldn't be surprised if I've broken my back."

Mr. Stringer was waiting farther up the track. "I thought you were off home theer and none of us'd see you again," he said. "I'll stand you a gill and a half for that."

"I thought I better pull in," his father said. He lifted Steven on to his back and said, "I better be getting this one home. He's not enjoying himself a bit."

"I'll come back with you," Mr. Stringer said. "They've been open an hour." He rubbed his hand across his arms and then his chest. "Sithee, it's running out of me like water."

Colin could see them a little later as they reached the Park gates, his father—with Steven on his back—pausing as he lit a cigarette then held the match for Mr. Stringer. They disappeared down the road towards the village.

Later, he was left alone on the track. When he went down all he could hear was the scudding of the snow beneath the runners. No sound came from the Park at all.

The sky had cleared. Ice ran beneath the sledge to the foot of the slope.

He went sledging each evening as soon as he came home from school. Occasionally Batty and Stringer came with him, and sometimes only Batty: he would slide down the slope in his large boots, then, having got tired of pulling the sledge, he'd go back home. Only on the second night did Colin's father come with him: his interest in the sledge expired with its making. He stood at the top of the slope smoking after the first ride down saying, "You go, lad. I'm getting too old for this," finally turning back up the slope and adding, "I better be getting ready for work. Your mother gets worried, you know, if I'm late."

Often he was last on the slope, waiting for the others to grow tired and leave, pulling their sledges slowly up to the gate, their voices fading down the road. Sometimes, when he had come down the track, he lay on the sledge, his cheek on the snow that had frozen to the wood, his breath rising in a thin mist past his face, the hill silent, glowing faintly, the odd calls, the barking of a dog and the shutting of doors coming from the houses beyond. A moon had risen on the second night: it shone as a bright disc, the track like a strip of metal running between the smooth mounds on either side. Towards the town, as the night settled, there was the faint probing of searchlights, moving like stiff fingers, slowly waving to and fro.

Each morning when he came home his father brought news of fresh disasters he had seen: a lorry driven over a banking, a car skidding into a wall, a factory so frozen up that no one could work in it, a chimney that had collapsed through the ice breaking up the stone. "It's a wonder I've got home at all," he would say if there had been a fresh fall in the night. "It's not often it comes so late in the year. There were buds on the branches a week ago. Now look at it. Antarctica. I s'll come home one morning a penguin and you'll wonder who I am."

His father built a snowman in the garden almost as tall as himself, setting on top of it his flat cap and underneath a pair of eyes, a nose, a moustache and a large mouth, each feature made up from bits of coal. Bletchley, who had built a snowman in his own yard, threw stones at theirs in the early mornings, removing first its head then various pieces of its body, the buttons, the fingers and the dividing of the legs, all of which his father had fashioned from pieces of wood. Finally the snowman toppled in the yard. Its body, freckled with soot, still lay there, dismembered, when the rest of the snow in the gardens and the backs had melted.

The last night Colin took the sledge to the Park the runners grated against the pavement. The track was worn through in dull brown patches.

In the spring his grandfather left. He went back to his uncle's. "I'll be back," he said the day he left. "That's the motto of my life: 'Keep moving'." He bent down to kiss him. "Look after them, Colin. Keep an eye on them. They need somebody, tha knows, round here." When his suitcase had been put on the bus he sat by the window at the front, smoking, winking at them with nods of his head.

The next day his father said, "It looks as though we shall have another young 'un in the house, then, Colin."

"When is it coming?" he said.

"Oh, not for a few months yet." He grasped his shoulder and laughed. "Don't worry," he said. "You and Steve can look after him all right."

Colin played with Steven now a great deal. His brother had something of his father's build, broad and fair-haired, his blue eyes slightly pained, and puzzled, preoccupied, so that when they were crossing the field or had gone to play on the wasteland at the end of the street, or, as spring came, in the Park, his sole preoccupation would be on where he was walking, stumbling over holes or protuberances, his arms stretched out, awkwardly, scarcely looking up from the ground by his feet. The other children called him Flipper. "He's like a seal," Batty said. "Are we supposed to wait for him or summat?" Frequently Colin would be left behind, waiting for Steven, taking his hand or finally lifting him up and carrying him on his back.

"Don't ever leave him on his own," his mother said. "If he's any trouble, wait. He's more important than any of them."

Once he took Steven to the river; they went on bikes, taking it in turns to ride. Some of the children rode on the cross-bars, some on the seats; the others ran behind. It took them the whole of the afternoon to get there: they played on the metal coal-slip used to load the barges, and beyond, on the supports beneath a metal bridge. It was almost dark by the time they got home.

His mother was standing at the door.

"Wherever have you been?" she said.

He was carrying Steven, who was almost asleep. They were covered in coal dust from the metal chute.

"Your father's out looking for you. He's been all over." She took his arm. "Is Steve all right?"

"I've been carrying him," he told her.

"Just look at him," she said. "Where on earth have you had him?"

When his father came back he took him upstairs.

"Supposing Steven fell in?" he said. "And you couldn't get out."

Colin felt the strap against his legs. The pain tugged at his stomach.

Afterwards he stayed upstairs. He heard Steven go to bed, his mother's voice in the other room, then her steps outside the door. She paused. A moment later he heard her voice.

"Are you all right?" she said.

"Yes," he said.

"I hope you've learnt your lesson."

"Yes," he said.

She put her head round the door, peered in a moment, then closed it quietly and went on down the stairs.

In the summer the results of the examinations had been announced. It was three months since he'd sat them. He was standing at the back of the hall, in morning prayers, when he heard his name read out. It was the last to be announced. Bletchley's name came first: he was going to a co-educational school in a near-by village. His own name was included in the list of boys being sent to a grammar school located in the city. When the successful candidates were let out early he ran off home, rushing in the door. There was no one in the kitchen. He could hear his mother in a room upstairs: she came out on the landing.

She stood there for a moment, looking down.

"I've passed," he said. "I'm going to the grammar."

140

"Well," she said.

She started slowly down.

"Is my dad in, then?"

"He's gone down to the shop. He won't be a minute."

"Bletchley's passed as well."

"Has he?"

"He's going to Melsham Manor."

"That's a good school."

"Reagan hasn't passed."

"Well," she said. "I'm not surprised."

They waited for his father.

When she heard his step she stooped to the fireplace, setting on the kettle.

His father, his head bowed, rubbed his feet on the mat, looking up suddenly to see his mother.

"What's got into you?" he said.

"He's heard the result," his mother said. "Of the examination."

"Nay, then." His father slowed. He gazed at him with a kind of anger, as if suddenly afraid he might be hurt.

"I've passed," he said.

"Have you? Have you?"

"To the grammar."

"By God, then, lad."

His face had flushed.

"Sithee, are you sure?" he said.

"It was announced. Those who passed they've let out early."

"Sithee, I better sit down," his father said.

He rested in a chair, leaning to the table.

"I knew you could do it. What did I tell you?" he asked his mother.

"Yes," she said. "We knew he could."

"It'll mean a lot of expense," he said. "They wear a uniform," he added.

"I suppose we'll manage," she said, and laughed.

"Aye. I suppose we will," he said. He shook his head. "I can't believe it's happened."

Steven came in from playing in the yard. His mother picked him up.

"And what's your brother gone and done?" she said.

141

"Nowt but show," his father added, "that he's just about the brightest on this road."

"Wait till Steven gets started, then."

"Aye, we'll have two of 'em," his father said.

"If not a third," his mother said.

"Aye."

His father laughed for a moment, then clapped his hands.

"Wait till I tell them at work," he added.

11

Colin went with his mother to the town to buy the clothes. He'd only been to the town on one or two occasions, most memorable for him when the bombing started. There were still signs of damage. But no bombs had fallen for over a year. They crossed the river and started up the hill the other side. The shop where the clothes for the school were sold stood opposite the cathedral, in the city centre. They gazed in the window at the uniform before they entered: it hung on the bright pink dummy of a boy with blue eyes and red lips and cheeks, a dark-blue cloth with a gold-coloured ribbon. The badge of the school, a coat-of-arms, was almost as large as the breast pocket of the blazer.

"There, then: what do you think of that?"

A boy came out of the shop: he had on the cap; beneath his raincoat Colin glimpsed the blazer.

"I suppose we better go in," his mother said.

It took them an hour for his mother to choose the clothes. Everything she bought was too large for him; the blazer itself, and the trousers, were particularly large.

"He'll need room to grow into them," she told the assistant.

"On the other hand," the man had said, ticking off their name in a list of pupils, "by the time he fits them they may have worn out."

"Aren't they good quality, then?" his mother had said.

"Oh, they're good quality," the assistant said. "But boys will be boys," he added with a smile.

"If they're good quality he'll look after them," she said.

Colin stood in front of a mirror in the gold-ribboned blazer. The man, after trying several sizes, finally put a

143

large peaked cap on his head. Gold ribbing ran down from the button at the top. "His head's not likely to grow," he said when his mother inquired if he might have a larger one.

The raincoat he brought came to below his knees. It reached almost to his ankles.

"There's a good three or four years' growth there," the assistant said. He fastened the belt. It was large enough to encompass a figure twice his size. The tongue of the belt was fastened round his back.

"Well, I think that should do him," his mother said, yet gazing at the next size on the peg.

"Oh, I think that's large enough for all eventualities," the man had said.

He totted up the bill.

"Will that be a cheque or cash?" he said.

"Oh, cash," his mother said, and flushed.

Each of the notes she had folded into four; she lay them down on the counter one by one, and added, "I've got the change," rooting in the narrow purse and taking out the coins. She'd worked out the sum exactly at home, allowing even for the larger sizes.

"Would you like to wear them, or shall I make a parcel?" the assistant said. He was an elderly man with greying hair; he wore the kind of suit Colin had only seen Mr. Reagan wear before.

"If you could make a parcel," his mother said.

Colin put his old clothes on. His mother, after watching him put on his coat, pulled out his collar. She straightened his tie as they waited by the counter.

The man came back with the clothes in a parcel.

"If there's anything we can do in the future, Mrs. Saville," he said, "you only have to ask." He smiled across the counter as he handed Colin the parcel and added, "I suppose you'll carry it, young man," and as he held the door of the shop he said, "And good luck at the grammar."

Outside the shop his mother paused. She looked at the bill, checked the items, checked the money remaining in her purse, then looked round her in a blinded fashion.

"The bus doesn't go for an hour," she said. She looked

over the roofs to the cathedral clock. "I suppose we could go on the train, only I've gone and got returns."

They stood by the window; he could see their two figures reflected in the pane, his mother in her long brown coat, ending just above the ankles, he in his short raincoat which he'd had for several years. The town stretched back, immense, beyond them: the shop fronts, the crowds, the passing traffic.

"We could go and look at the school," she said.

She'd made this suggestion before they left; his father for this reason, had wanted to come with them. His mother, however, had put him off. "We're only getting his clothes," she said. "We can see the school another time." And when his father had persisted, she had added, "When I'm buying his clothes I'm *not* to be hurried."

"I suppose we ought to have the time," his mother said. She stopped a man in the street and asked the way.

An arched alleyway ran beneath an old timber-framed building opening off the city centre. It was broad enough to take a car, its surface roughly cobbled; on one side stood a baker's shop, on the other a café with wooden beams and panelled walls. Beyond, the alleyway opened on to a narrow street; it was overlooked by shops on either side and farther on broadened into a main thoroughfare which ran back, diagonally, towards the city centre. Trees overhung the pavements, and the shops themselves gave way to houses, low, brick-built and black with soot. Tall brick chimneys projected from low, large slabbed roofs.

"Well, this is an interesting part. I don't think I've been up here before," his mother said.

She gazed over at the houses on either side; some had shallow, tree-filled gardens; others opened directly on to the road—they could see into sitting-rooms, and here and there, through an open door, into a narrow hall.

"I bet it costs a lot to live in those. See how old they are." She paused at a doorway and read the date inscribed on the stone above the porch. "Seventeen nineteen. And some are older if I'm not mistaken."

The school itself stood back from the road. It was a long, low building with tall mullioned windows. It had two turrets at the centre, battlemented, and a wing, going back from the road, at either end. It was built of stone; a broad stretch of lawn led up to a pair of metal-studded doors.

Both the grass itself and the doors were evidently unused. A gravel drive ran up to either end of the building: twin metal gates, set between black gate-posts, were standing open; one or two figures in the now-familiar school uniform flitted between the main building and a taller, narrower building, also of stone, standing farther back from the road.

"They even go on Saturdays," his mother said.

They stood at the gates looking up at the low, stone mass.

"Saturdays as well?"

"Saturday mornings, the letter says. Though they have Tuesday and Thursday afternoons for sport."

A boy came down the drive. He put on his cap, pulled a satchel across his shoulder, and ran off behind them, across the road.

"See how clean they are," his mother added.

They set off back towards the city centre. A bus swept past. It was the first time he'd been aware of how large the city was. In the past the place itself had been a name, a vague memory of towers and domes, the single steeple glimpsed from the bus across the valley: now it was narrow streets and looming buildings, and roads amongst which he felt already lost.

"Oh, you'll get used to it in a week," his mother said.

They waited at the bus-stop, below the cathedral.

"We'll get in touch with the Connors' boy. He goes," she added. "He'll know the way."

He sat silent on the bus when it finally came. He watched the outskirts of the city pass, the river, then the fields, the woods, a stretch of heath.

"Shall I have to stay for dinner?" he said.

"Lunch," his mother said. She added. "You can't really come back, then, all this way." She eased the parcel against her knee. "As it is, you'll set off early. And you'll not get back until quite late. Then there's homework, of course. That takes an hour. An hour and a half, I think they said."

When they got back home the clothes were unpacked.

He went upstairs, at his father's insistence, and put them on.

Colin came back down; he saw his father's look—he gazed at the blazer, at the large badge, the coat-of-arms, worked in gold thread on the breast pocket, at the gold ribbon that followed the edge of the blazer as far as the collar, at the cap, with its gold ribbing running from the button, the badge set at the front, the broad, projecting peak; he looked at the stockings with their twin gold lines around the turned-down tops; his lips had parted; he began to smile.

"Sithee. I wouldn't have known him then."

"Now he looks something like," his mother said.

Steven sat across the room, not stirring.

"Sithee, and what does that mean, then?" his father said.

He ran his fingers beneath the badge.

" 'Labor Ipse Voluptas,' " he read aloud.

"I don't know," Colin said. He shook his head.

"Didn't you ask at the shop?" his father said.

"No." His mother touched the badge herself: she ran her finger around the yellow thread.

"Labour something," his father said. "Dost think they're all socialists, then?" he added.

"I don't think it can be that," his mother said.

"It's one of the oldest schools in the country. I hope you realize that," his father added.

His smile had faded: he shook his head.

"I never thought we'd do it. Come up from nowt, and now see where we are," he said.

He went over to the Connors's house one evening. They lived across the village on a small estate of private bungalows. Connors was a tall boy, solemn, fair-haired: he was half-way through the school. His father had offered him his rugby shirt, gold and blue striped and worn slightly at the collar, and a pair of worn-down rugby boots. Connors himself, too, had offered on the first day to take him to the school, and arranged to meet him at the bus-stop.

When Colin got to the door Connors had come after him.

"I better warn thee, I suppose," he said. "My faither says I should."

"What about?" he said.

"They collar new lads, first day theer, and duck 'em in the toilet."

He gazed up at Connors's face: it was dull and heavy, the cheeks flushed, as if he were talking to him from a long way away.

"What do they do?"

"They pull the chain."

He pictured it for a moment, then shook his head.

"Do they do anything else?" he said.

"Well, sometimes," he said, "they shove you in the basins. Full of water. And count ten slowly before they let you up."

The vision haunted him throughout the summer, first the toilet, then the basin. He practised holding his head under water and counting up to ten, slowly. His mother came in one morning to find him with his head submerged, the sink spilling over on to the floor of the kitchen.

"What on earth are you doing?" she said.

"Nothing," he said, and added, "Washing." He practised holding his breath in bed at night. He thought, in the end, he would be able to manage, if not, he'd decided, he would have to drown.

Occasionally on week-days Bletchley wore the uniform of the new school he was going to. It was more austere and simpler than his own, the blazer decorated merely by a badge, his cap the same. He wore it to Sunday School, wore it to the shops, or whenever he went out walking with his mother. He'd bought a new satchel; he would sit on his step, taking out his ruler, his pen, his set of instruments for geometry and science, showing them to Reagan, who, not having passed the examination, regarded them with a dazed expression, gazing off, after having been shown them, across the yard. Bletchley had also been bought a present for passing, a red-painted bicycle with white celluloid mudguards and swept-down handlebars which he rode up and down the street each evening.

"We'd have bought you summat, don't worry," his

father said. "If it hadn't have been the expense. What with that and a new brother or sister on the way, we've not much left."

There was talk now of sending him to his uncle, his father's younger brother, who lived in the town.

"Nay, we mu'n keep you at home if we can. Both of you," his father said. "I hope to get on days when the baby's due, then we can all of us sleep at home together."

He played in the street, watched Bletchley on his bike, played cricket with Stringer and Batty, and several of Batty's brothers. He watched the others go back to school. The grammar school didn't start until two weeks later; he wandered through the village on his own. Occasionally he caught sight of Connors on a bike, and of one of the other boys who'd passed to the grammar school; apart from the long holiday they had nothing in common. He practised holding his head under water for longer spells.

When the day came his mother offered to go with him to the stop. It was barely seven o'clock; the streets of the village were still deserted. He stood at the door, conspicuous in his uniform, while his mother pulled on her coat.

"I want to go on my own," he said.

"What if Connors isn't there?" she said.

"I'll still catch the bus."

"And what happens at the other end?"

"I can always ask the way."

She stood in the door with her coat unbuttoned and watched him walk off along the street. When he reached the corner he didn't wave; he glanced back, sharply, then went on towards the stop.

He was twenty minutes early. The stop was opposite a public house in the centre of the village. There was no one else about. He carried his raincoat over his arm, his satchel, an old one, over his shoulder. There was nothing in it. He'd thought of taking the football shirt and the pair of worn-down rugby-boots, but, despite his mother's insistence, had decided finally he wouldn't.

A lorry went past. Through the windows of the pub he could see the vague shape of a clock set up against the wall. He couldn't see its face.

149

A miner came down from the direction of the colliery and sat down in the gutter. He sat with his hands between his legs. Another came down; one or two other men appeared. Their voices came in a quiet murmur as he himself stood farther down the road against the window of a shop.

Finally, from the direction of the nearest houses, Connors and another boy appeared. Connors didn't wear his cap; apart from a worn satchel which he carried beneath his arm, there was no indication he was going to school at all. He wore long trousers; his school blazer, if he wore one, was concealed beneath a greyish raincoat.

He scarcely glanced up as he reached the stop; he nodded his head then went on talking to the other boy. They stood against the wall of the pub, between the miners, Connors kicking the wall behind him with his heel.

The other boy was older; he carried a small suitcase, dented and fastened by a leather strap. The cap of some other school was screwed up and set inside his jacket pocket.

Colin waited. One or two of the miners had looked across: they glanced at the brightness of the jacket, at the gold ribbon, which glistened in the sun, at the cap, at the new raincoat folded on his arm. One of them nodded to the others; there was a burst of laughter.

He glanced the other way. The stop was opposite the junction of the two roads that met at the centre of the village. The principal road swept through from east to west; the road from the south, and the station, crossed it, between halt signs, and continued past the Park and the manor, northwards, narrowing slightly as it crested the hill.

It was from this direction, careering downwards, that the bus would come. Twice he heard the roar of an engine, and twice a lorry appeared, rattling down the hill in a cloud of dust.

He heard a second burst of laughter; he glanced in the window of the shop behind—he could see his reflection, the high-peaked profile of his cap, the neat outline of the blazer. The shop was full of clothes—skirts, blouses, stockings, and women's underwear. He studied the houses opposite, where the slope dipped down from the shop-lined crossing. He thought of his mother at home, and Steve.

The bus appeared: it ran rattling down the hill, its windows glinting in the sun. It paused at the corner; the miners crouching against the wall stood up.

He waited for Connors. He and the other boy, still talking, leant against the wall.

Colin got on. He sat downstairs.

One or two other people appeared, a man in a raincoat, a woman with a basket. Their feet shuffled on the roof above his head; then, but for the murmur of the miners and the occasional slur of a match, the bus was silent.

Connors had taken out a book and was turning the pages; the other boy took the book from him and pushed back against the wall. The conductor came round. The driver got in. The engine started. Only when the conductor pressed the bell did Connors make a move: he closed the book in the other boy's hand, put it in his satchel, made some remark to the boy, then, waving, stepped up on the platform. As the bus gathered speed he glanced over at Colin, nodded, and without making any remark went quickly up the stairs.

There were only two other people sitting downstairs, both miners, both black-faced and laughing as the conductor called out to them in recognition. He saw the redness of their lips, the white eyes and teeth, and smelled the dust from their clothes as the draught came back from the door.

He waited; there was no sound of Connors coming down again.

The conductor took his fare. He sat with his satchel across his knees, his raincoat laid on top.

They passed the end of the lane leading to the pit; he could see the roof of the school across the yard and nearer the plume of smoke and steam from the colliery engine. A miner was running down the lane; he waved his arm, but the bus passed on.

From where he was sitting, leaning backwards, he could see the last houses of the village as they disappeared. Soon all that was visible behind were the hedged fields, the top of the pit chimney, and the outline of the colliery stack.

Another boy, wearing a new uniform like himself, got on; he was accompanied by his mother.

The passed a large stone mansion, set back beyond a line of trees; the bus swept over a hump-backed bridge; he glimpsed a lily-padded lake. Beyond, the road rose steeply to a row of houses; a group of girls got on. They wore light-blue dresses and yellow straw hats: he could hear Connors's voice as they climbed upstairs. The bus was full: at the crest of a rise he caught a distant glimpse of the town, a silhouette of towers and the single steeple.

They emerged finally beside the river: barges were moored above a concrete weir. The single spire and the towers of the town were visible once more above stone-slabbed roofs. A hill appeared: the bus shuddered slowly to its summit.

"All off. All change," the conductor called.

The walls of the cathedral were visible across the road.

Colin caught a glimpse of Connors as he came off the bus—talking to the girls in the yellow straw hats, he set off in the direction of the city centre.

There were other groups descending from the crowded buses at the top of the slope. He followed the largest group, which made its way through the narrow, cobbled alley into the thoroughfare of shops beyond.

It was half-past eight. Other groups joined those emerging from the alley: a mass of dark-blue figures moved slowly along each pavement.

The doors to the school itself were closed. A flight of stone steps led down to a field. Blazered figures walked to and fro. Immediately behind the building itself a wooden fence divided the field from a pebbled yard.

A bell was rung: the mass of uniformed figures divided into two and moved off towards either end of the dark stone building.

He went back up the steps. Boys with tasselled caps were standing at the door. They called out to the boys as they rushed inside.

Connors was standing immediately inside.

"I wondered where you'd got to," he said. "I've been looking in the field."

152

He took his arm.

"Have you got your health certificate?" he added.

He took out the piece of paper he'd been given before he left. It had been signed at the bottom, first by his mother and then, after an argument, by his father.

"Three A. You'll have old Hodges," Connors said.

"When do they do the ducking?" he said.

"Haven't they collared you already?"

He shook his head. He wondered if he'd been abandoned because of his build, or overlooked.

"They'll probably have you in at break, then," Connors said. He released his arm. "If you have any trouble I'll see you around."

The corridor itself was full of figures; the walls were lined by framed photographs of football teams. Stone steps went up to the floor above.

Connors had left him at a panelled door. The room inside was tall: so high, in fact that the ceiling went up into the roof of the building. The windows, mullioned, with diamond panes, took up the greater part of the outside wall. The other three walls were completely bare. The desks themselves were large and stood in four rows the length of the room. The spaces between the rows were full of boys—mostly like himself, in new blazers, some still wearing caps, they stood gazing up at the ceiling, at the height of the windows, at the massive, square-shaped desks and the empty walls.

A man came in. He wore the white collar of a clergyman. His clothes were dark, his face red, a line of white hair receding across his scalp and growing out in two broad tufts at the back of his head.

"Caps off! Caps off! Do you wear caps inside a building? What manners have you been taught? Caps off, caps off inside a building."

The few caps still on were taken off.

"Sit down. Don't stand around," the man had said.

He went to a large desk at the end of the room.

"What are you doing, boy?" he shouted.

Several of the boys, following his command, were already sitting.

"Do you sit down before a master?"

"No, sir," one of the boys had said.

"Wait till I'm seated." He raised his head. "Then you sit down, when I'm sat down."

The boys got up. The master sat down. He wore a long black gown over his dark-blue suit.

"Now please be seated, gentlemen," he said.

Colin found a chair at the back of the room. Most of the desks were already taken.

"First things first," the master said. "I'll call your names. Have you got that clear?"

"Yes, sir," some of the boys had said.

"When I call your name you come up here, hand me your certificate, your *health* certificate, and go back to your place."

He wanted for an answer.

"Yes, sir," most of the boys had said.

"Sit up straight. I want no loafers in 3A."

The names were called. The master ticked them off inside a register.

"Not here. Not here," he began to shout at one point. "You're in 3 Upper, boy, not here. In with the brainy lot, not these first-year duffers."

The boy went out.

Colin went up when his name was called. He gave in the certificate: it was opened out, straightened, put on the pile, and he went back to his chair.

"All present. All correct," the master said. He screwed back the top of his pen, took off the pair of glasses he'd put on to mark the register, and glanced slowly round the room. The murmur of voices faded.

"My name is Hodges," he said. "Not Bodges. Or Codges. Or even Dodges. *Mister Hodges.*" He gazed round at them again for several seconds. "I'll be your form-master for the whole of the year. And woe betide," he added, "any boy who gets himself into any kind of trouble. I don't like trouble. I have an aversion to trouble. Trouble and I have never got on well together. You'll see that now by the colour of my face. You'll see it going slightly red. It gets even redder when trouble actually appears. It becomes positively scarlet, and woe betide anyone who comes in front of me when my face is scarlet. I do all sorts of unimaginable and horrible things when my face is scarlet. I do pretty terrible things when it's even red, but when it's scarlet I can't tell you the things I'm capable of. So trouble is something I don't wish to hear even mentioned in this room: not in my own classes, that is, or anyone else's."

He waited for the colour to subside.

"Now there's a lot to do today. At times, to some of you, it may seem extremely tedious. Whenever it does I want you to gaze, not at me, nor at your neighbour, nor at the floor, nor at your desk, but at the ceiling. If you gaze at the ceiling it's my opinion you won't come to any harm. I want you, whenever you feel boredom coming on, to gaze in a vertical direction and silently, so no one anywhere can possibly hear, recite to yourself your multiplication tables. I want you to recite the two times, the three times, right through to your twelve times. I shall test you on those tables at the end of the morning and woe betide anyone who gets one wrong. I have a strong aversion to boys who get things wrong; particularly to boys who've had all morning to get things right." He waited. "You, boy: *what's twelve times seven?*"

A boy near the front put up his hand.

One or two other hands went up.

The boy who had been asked had gone bright red.

"Twelves times seven." He waited. "You'll be one of the boys whose head I'll expect to see gazing for quite lengthy intervals in a vertical direction. What is it? What is it? What is it, boy?"

"Seventy-two, sir," one of the boys had said.

"Seventy *what?*"

"Eighty-four!" several boys called out.

"My goodness. The procedure for admitting boys to this school deteriorates visibly every year. I expect a seven-year-old boy to tell me that. How old are you?"

The boy with the red face had murmured his age.

"What? What? What's that?"

"Twelve, sir."

"Twelve? Twelve what? Weeks? Months? Hours? *Rabbits?*"

"Years, sir."

"Years."

He waited, nodding.

"I can see we've got a great deal of work before us here. A great deal."

He waited once again, still looking round.

"I was going to add, if there are any clever-dicks here who think they know their tables backwards I would like them by a similar process—namely, the head inclined in a respectful manner towards the ceiling—to memorize and familiarize themselves with a favourite hymn. It may be a Jewish hymn, a Catholic hymn, a Methodist hymn, or an Anglican hymn, or, indeed, a Buddhist hymn if they so desire. But whatever its source, a paean of praise directed to the Divine Presence who overlooks us all. Has that been understood?"

He waited.

"I shall, after the multiplication tables have been thoroughly tested, turn to the hymns and call forth from amongst you, ad hoc . . . What does ad hoc mean, boy?"

Another boy's face turned red.

He waited.

No one, however, had raised their hands.

"Ad hoc. Ad hoc. What language can it be, I wonder? German? Dutch? *Double*-Dutch."

He waited.

"Anybody heard of Latin?"

Several hands went up.

"I wonder: can ad hoc be Latin."

"Yes, sir," someone said.

"There's a bright boy. Latin. Latin." He waited once again. "Ad hoc is Latin for "specifically for this purpose." In other words, I shall ask certain individuals specifically to give evidence of their silent—and I repeat emphatically silent—memorizing of their favourite paean of praise to God Almighty. And may God Almighty come to your rescue if you haven't got one ready." He paused. He examined each of their faces in turn. "What a miserable looking lot. What a clump of sour-faced duffers. Here I am, sitting in front of forty white-faced puddings, while you have the privilege of sitting in front of me." He paused. He looked up, speculatively, towards the ceiling. Arched supports ran across it from the walls on either side. He contemplated these for several seconds. "I shall expect," he said, "to see not only forty studious faces memorizing

156

their tables as well as their favourite hymnal text, but forty cheerful faces, forty smiling faces—not grinning, *smiling*—not laughing, not baring teeth and fangs, but *joyful* faces, not dismal faces, but faces which will be a welcome distraction whenever I happen to raise my head."

He examined his watch. He removed it from his waist-coat beneath his gown, placed it on the desk in front of him, then opened the register once again. He replaced his glasses.

"Now, then, boys," he said. "Begin."

Several additional desks were brought in later. Piles of books were carried in. Paper parcels were opened and exercise books, brightly coloured, revealed inside. Several of the boys were moved around: "You, that big lump, I think I'll have you sitting here by me. I can keep an eye on you if we both move closer, the mountain cometh to Mahomet." Finally they had all been given desks.

Colin sat near the back. A hot-water pipe ran along the wall immediately below his elbow: through a hole in the floor came a smell of cooking. He was too low to see out of the window.

Books were given out. Most of them were old and battered. At one point a bell rang and they lined up by the desks and were marched out to the corridor; columns of boys were moving down the tunnel-like interior towards a pair of glass-panelled doors at the opposite end. Older boys directed them to follow.

They came out in a hall. It was taller than the classroom, its ceiling vaulted. A large mullioned window almost as broad as the room occupied the wall at one end. Immediately beneath it stood a wooden stage, with a lectern, a tall, narrow desk, and several chairs. The body of the hall was full of benches; at the rear a spiral staircase ran up to a narrow gallery in the centre of which stood an organ, its pipes set up on the wall on either side. Benches too had been arranged here were already full of boys.

Hodges appeared on the platform; several other gowned figures filtered through the hall. Their own class had been set at the front: rows of boys were sitting on the floor. The chairs on the stage were slowly filled. Finally, the hall itself grew quiet; an odd voice called out, intoning a name. Then, to Colin's right, a figure appeared in a mortar-board and gown: the face beneath was sharp and thin, the mouth broad, thin-lipped, the eyes narrow. Without any expression it moved down the hall and mounted the platform. After a quick look round, the mortar-board was taken off and slotted in a shelf beneath the desk.

"Morning, school," the figure said.

A murmur of acknowledgment came from the hall behind. The room was packed. The heat rose with the dust through the beams of light which came in diagonally through the mullioned window.

"That's Trudger." He heard the whisper to one side, saw other heads turn, then immediately above him a hymn was announced. From the platform, beyond the headmaster's figure, Hodges gazed down in their direction.

The hymn was sung: the boys sat down. A tall boy wearing a blazer stepped up to the platform, mounted the lectern, and read the Bible. His legs trembled as he read, his voice faltering finally when he closed the book.

"Let us pray," the headmaster said.

Hodges continued to gaze round even while the prayers were said; his face, if anything, had begun to darken, glowing red against the whiteness of his clerical collar.

The other masters were of a similar age; there were three women, also wearing gowns, their handbags set on the floor beside their feet.

Finally, when the prayers were over, the boys sat down.

"I'd like to welcome all the new boys at the beginning of our school year," the figure at the desk had said. "I'm sure they'll grow familiar with the routine of the school by the end of the day. If they have any inquiries they can ask the master in charge of their form. And, of course, I welcome back the rest of the school." He took out his mortar-board from his desk and with a slight acknowledgment of the figures behind stepped down from the platform.

The masters and the mistresses on the platform, having stood up for the headmaster leaving, slowly filtered out of the door on the opposite side.

They went back to the classroom.

Hodges came in. He strode to the desk, sat down and waited until the last shuffle in the room had died.

"Someone in this class," he said, "prays to the Almighty with his eyes wide open."

He waited.

"They also pray with their hands stuck in their pockets."

He put on his glasses, and set his watch in front of him again.

"On future occasions, at morning assembly, I shall keep a watchful eye on the praying habits of this evidently dissolute class and woe betide anyone who doesn't show the respect appropriate to such occasions. Eyes closed, hands together, and mind fixed resolutely on the true essentials: heaven, redemption, and the alternative prospect of a long sojourn in hell."

He waited. He looked around.

"Now, then. I'll give you your time-table for the week."

A small, rectangular notebook was given out to each of the class; it was like a diary. "Record Book" was printed in black on the cover and inside were pages divided into columns for the days of the week.

"This is the most important document you're likely to possess," the master said. "Keep it with you at all times. On suitable occasions, in addition to your time-table, certain masters will inscribe *commendations* or, conversely—though in this class I'm sure it won't apply— *reprimands* in the space given over to their respective lessons. At the end of each term the total of good records—or, conversely, bad records—will be added up. Those with a certain number of the former will be invited to visit Mr. Walker in his study; those with a certain number of the latter will also be invited to visit Mr. Walker in his study—but with quite a different purpose in mind; quite a different purpose. Those in the latter category will be invited to make the acquaintance of, if I may use the phrase, a certain piece of vegetation— known affectionately in these environs, though not by those with whom it comes into the closest contact, as 'Whacker.' 'Whacker,' I might add, takes a very *stern* view of boys who mount up records of a reprehensible nature, a very *stern* view, I might add, indeed." He paused, adjusted his glasses, glanced round, then, getting up from the desk, turned to the blackboard and began to write down the time-table for the boys to copy.

More books, later, were given out. At one point, referring to the register, Hodges had said, "Saville? Who is Saville?"

Colin stood up.

"Your name is Saville, boy?"

"Yes, sir." Heads at the front of the class had quickly turned.

"Is that with one 'l,' boy, or two?"

"Two l's, sir," he said.

"Two l's. There are two l's in your name, not one l?"

"Yes, sir."

Several of the boys had laughed.

"Why is it that I have one l in the register?" he said.

"I don't know, sir." Colin shook his head.

"There's one l on your certificate, boy." He held up the certificate still on his desk.

"It's always been two l's, sir," he said.

"Come here, boy," Hodges said.

He got up from the desk. The room was silent. His feet echoed as he walked down the room to the master's desk.

"Is that one l, or two?" the master said. He pointed a narrow finger at his father's signature. It was something Colin had noticed occasionally in the past, that his father signed his name differently on different occasions, sometimes with two l's, sometimes with one.

"One, sir."

"One, sir." The master gazed at him over the top of his glasses. "You'll admit I'm not mistaken, then?"

"No, sir."

"Very well, Saville double l, go back to your desk." The class had laughed. He walked back to his place.

"Now, then, Saville double l, either your father can't spell his name correctly"—laughter—"or I have entered it incorrectly on my list." He examined the register once again. " 'Father's occupation.' " He wrote something down on a piece of paper. "Now 'colliery worker' means that he works at a coal-mine. Is that correct?"

"Yes," he said.

"Yes, *what?*"

"Yes, sir," he said.

"Now there are any number of people who might legitimately say they work at a *coal*-mine. The *manager* of a *coal*-mine might say he works at a *coal*-mine."

He waited for an answer.

"Yes," he said, then added, "Sir."

"I take it, of course, he's no such thing."

Colin waited, unsure of what to add.

"He's not the manager, Saville?"

"No." He shook his head.

"No, what?"

"No, sir," he said.

"He's not the deputy-manager, either, I imagine."

"No," he said.

"Does he work on top or, as they have it, underneath?"

"Underneath."

"Does he superintend the men down there, or does he actually hew the coal itself?"

"He hews the coal," he said.

" 'E' ews the coal."

"Yes, sir."

The class had laughed.

"In other words, Saville, he's a miner?"

"Yes, sir."

"Then why couldn't he put that on the form?"

He bowed his head and wrote in the register for several seconds.

"Well, Saville double l, have you got an answer?"

"No, sir." He shook his head.

"What's the meaning of those words written on your jacket?"

He glanced down at the badge.

"I take it you're aware there are words written on your jacket?"

At first he wasn't sure what the master meant.

"Beneath that rather decorative emblem, placed symbolically above your heart, are written three words. I assume you've read them?"

"Yes," he said. He bowed his head.

"And I suppose," the master added, "you're familiar with their meaning?"

He didn't answer.

"Are you familiar with them, or are you not?"

"No," he said.

"Am I to assume you don't know what your school motto means, then, boy?"

He didn't answer.

"Do you think they're there for decoration?"

"No." He shook his head.

The master paused.

"Where do you come from, Saville?"

"Saxton, sir," he said.

"And Saxton, I take it, is located somewhere in these regions?"

"Yes, sir."

"How old are you, Saville?"

"Ten, sir."

"And are you able to read?"

"Yes, sir."

"In that case, would you mind reading those three words out?"

He couldn't see them clearly: he twisted his head.

"Labour ips voluptas," he said.

"Good God, man, do you realize what you're saying?"

He gave up offering any answer: he saw Hodges's face now through a sudden haze.

"Lab*or*, Lab*or*, Lab*or*," Hodges said, "Ip*se*, Ip*se*, Ip*se*," he added. He gestured round. "Wolupt*ass*, Wolupt*ass*, boy." He groaned. "Sit down, Saville, I believe I'm ill."

He took out a handkerchief and wiped his brow.

" 'Labor Ipse Voluptas'," he said. "Does anyone know what the phrase might mean?"

Several hands went up.

"Yes, boy? Yes, boy?" He waited. "Don't give me the wrong answer, boy. If you're not sure of your answer better confess to it, like Saville. Well, then, boy?"

"Work is pleasure, sir," a boy had said.

"Work is a pleasure. Correct, correct." He wiped his brow again. "Work is pleasure, Saville. Have you got that? Have you heard?"

"Yes, sir." He stood up at his desk.

"Work is pleasure, Saville, which to revert to our original point, is a concise and unambiguous statement."

"Yes, sir," he said.

"Whereas 'colliery-worker,' as the definition of some-one's occupation, is not an unambiguous statement, Saville. I'd say, as a definition, it might cover, quite easily, a multitude of sins."

"Yes," he said.

"Whereas miner, and, in particular, *coal*-miner, as a description of someone's occupation, is unlikely to cause misapprehension on anyone's part. If someone tells me he is a *coal*-miner I am immediately aware of the sort of job he does, even if," he added, wiping his brow again, "I am not aware of the actual way he goes about it. Does he work with a pick, for instance, or has he got a machine?"

He waited.

"Does he use a pick, then, Saville?"

"Yes, sir," he said, and added, "sometimes."

"I see." He gazed across at him for several seconds. "I think we have the seeds of a rebel in the class." He paused. "I sense a certain degree of rebelliousness in Saville's nature, a resistance to instruction." He paused again. "I shall keep my eye on Saville. And on one or two other people whose behaviour over the past two hours has not escaped my notice." He glanced round. "Sit down, Saville. I shall look forward to hearing your answers to our arithmetical test, as well as to your no doubt individual hymnal contribution."

More books were given out. Names and subject-matter and the class were inscribed on the covers. The bell sounded once again.

"The bell is for my benefit, not yours," Hodges said as several heads turned round. "You've fifteen minutes' break, to be spent in the field behind the school and not, I might remind you, on the steps. No one stays inside. Milk, for those who take it, will be found in the cloisters beneath the school. When you've drunk it, straight into the field."

They were dismissed in rows.

The cloisters comprised a row of filled-in arches facing on to the field at the back of the school. The central arch stood open: it was here the milk was stacked. Crowds of boys milled round in the yard outside. Inside, within the darkness of the building, he made out several doors and the flickering, intermittent glow of boilers.

"So you got here after all, then," someone said.

He turned from the crates and saw a fair-haired figure leaning up against the cloister wall drinking from a bottle.

"What form are you in, then?" Stafford said.

"Three A."

"Three Upper."

"Where's that?"

"Across the corridor from you."

Stafford smiled.

"How do you like it, then?" he added.

"All right."

"You passed your exam all right?"

He nodded.

"I failed."

"How did you get here, then?" he said.

"Paying fees." Stafford shrugged. But for the blazer he looked no different. A silver-coloured pen was clipped to his pocket.

"What's the difference between Three A and Three Upper?" he said.

"I think we do Greek, as well as Latin," Stafford said. "You just do Latin." He smiled again. "Finished your milk? We can go into the field," he added.

They walked up and down.

"Have they ducked you in the toilets?" Stafford said.

"No." He shook his head.

"I don't believe they do. It's one of the things they tell you, but it never happens. I know three people who started here last year and all three of them say it never happens."

Groups of boys ran past. One took hold of him a moment, spun him round, shouted to someone behind, then, still shouting, ran quickly on. Air-raid shelters, like low, windowless houses, lined one side of the field. Metal railings, set on a low brick wall, cut off the end of the field from a road beyond. To one side of the field stood a yellow brick house.

"That's where Trudger lives. And one or two boarders,"

Stafford said. Its large windows looked down directly to the field. "He's not supposed to be keen on teaching," Stafford added.

"Why not?"

"I don't know. They say when he canes anybody he begins to cry."

Colin looked at the house. He could see a figure standing at a window, but from this distance it was impossible to see whether it was a man or a woman.

"He's got two daughters who're worth looking at," Stafford added.

A bell rang. The games of football were broken up. The crowd of dark-blazered figures turned back towards the school.

"Staying for lunch, then?" Stafford said.

"Yes," he said.

"See you later, then."

Stafford slapped his back and ran off, calling someone's name, towards the steps.

The day passed slowly. He didn't see Stafford at lunch. They ate in a narrow room converted from one half of the cloisters, rows of tables and wooden benches set out behind the windowed arches. Afterwards, in the field, he saw Connors playing football, jogging up and down, the tail of his shirt hanging out beneath his jacket. For a while he stood with several other boys at the edge of the field, avoiding going to the toilets as long as he could. Finally, when he went there he found them empty. There were the usual cubicles and row of basins, but going by their colour they could never have been used.

The afternoon, like the morning, was divided into two. Lessons started. Hodges, deliberately or otherwise, had forgotten about the tables; he'd forgotten about the hymn as well. After dismissing them for lunch they only saw him briefly at the beginning of the afternoon when he came into the room to mark the register and to announce that lessons were to start forthwith. "Mr. Platt, who is coming in shortly to take your English, makes me, gentlemen, sound like a veritable angel. I should pay the utmost heed to everything he says, and woe betide any boy who doesn't do immediately everything he tells you."

He went out quickly with a swirl of his gown, removing his glasses and brushing his hand across his head.

For a while the room was silent. Then one or two voices had murmured from the front. Someone laughed; they heard a surge of voices in the corridor outside; someone called; the voices died.

The murmuring in the room began again. Throughout the morning, when they'd finished writing out their time-table in the record books, or writing their names on the fronts of the exercise books, or inside the covers of the text-books, the heads of most of the boys had been turned towards the ceiling. Several heads were turned up now, the eyes held wide and vacant, the noses below the eyes distended, the lips below the noses moving.

A man had appeared at the back of the room. He was short and squat, with thick black hair. He wore glasses; the eyes behind them were invisible because of the reflection of the light. The lenses were thick, the features beneath the glasses heavy, the nose short like the man himself, the mouth full-lipped and broad, the jaw projecting sharply.

He waited until his presence had been acknowledged by the boys at the front. Then, in silence, he walked the length of the room, placed a pile of books on the teacher's desk, cleared his throat, wiped his mouth with his handkerchief, then, glancing round the room, sat down.

"My name," he said, "is Mr. Platt."

He continued his inspection of the class for several seconds.

"Your names I don't know but quite shortly," he said, "I suppose, I shall."

He allowed the silence to continue a little longer.

"You'll have been given a green-backed text-book this morning with the title *Principles of English Grammar*. I'd like you when I give the order, quietly to take that green-backed text-book out. I'd also, when I give the order, like you to take out your blue-coloured exercise book, marked 'English Grammar.' " He paused. "Two books, a pen, a ruler. The ink, I believe, for those without fountain-pens, is already in the ink-wells. I give the order now: take out."

Colin remembered little of the lesson. A drowsiness, induced by the heat of the room as well as by the smell of food still coming through the hole in the floor, caused him at one point to lean his head against the wall. He felt the coolness of the wood against his cheek, and was aware of little else until a bell rang to mark the end of the lesson.

There was no play-time in the afternoon: the black-robed figure of Mr. Platt went out and was replaced a few moments later by a tall, fair-haired figure in a sports-coat and flannels who introduced himself as Mr. Wells. He taught French. They recited vowels. Wells had a narrow mouth; his eyes were blue, his nose long and thin. He caused laughter round the class as he pronounced the vowels, pulling back his mouth to shape the e, elongating his face to shape the o, pouting his lips grotesquely to shape the u.

The class repeated the sounds together: they wrote down simple words. One or two stood up at Wells's command and sounded the vowels singly: there was a suppressed air of laughter in the room of which Wells himself appeared to be unaware. He stood red-faced by the teacher's desk almost as if he were alone, practising the sounds in front of a mirror. The lesson, like the one before it, had lasted three-quarters of an hour. A feeling of excitement crept over the room as the prospect of the bell grew near. When it actually sounded a murmur swept the class.

The lesson continued. The boys grew silent. They could hear shouts and cries from the corridor outside, the banging of doors, the shuffle of feet. Shouts came clearly from the street beyond.

Wells continued: words had been written on the board; they were copied down. Finally, looking up, the master turned his head to the noise outside.

"Was that the bell?" He gestured around.

"Yes, sir," nearly everyone had said.

"Homework," he said. "I take you, I believe, tomorrow morning."

Instructions for learning certain words were given out.

Wells picked up his books; with the same absent-minded expression with which he'd entered the room he wandered out. Before he'd reached the door several boys had gone out before him.

He didn't see Connors on the way to the stop; by the time he reached the bus he found a queue had formed. He stood for the first few miles. It was six o'clock by the time he got back home; he'd been away from the house for over ten hours.

His father came down; he sat at the table, listening, while his mother prepared his tea.

"You've started work already, then?"

"French," he said. He mentioned the English.

"Have they set you homework?"

"I've an hour to do tonight."

"Nay, tha mu'n better get started, then," his father said.

"You'll let him get his tea first. *And* have a rest," his mother said.

They watched him eat.

"What are the teachers like?" his father said.

"They call them masters."

"Masters. Masters. What're the *masters* like?"

"They're very strict."

"Nay, they'll have to be, I suppose, to get things done." He took out his Record Book.

His father glanced through it; he flicked the pages.

"What're these for, then?" he said.

"Good work and bad work. They mark it down."

"I can see they believe in work," his father said.

"That's the motto. Work is pleasure." He pointed to the blazer.

His father laughed.

"Sithee, not where I work, then," he said. "The one who wrote that has never been down yon."

He read the time-table, stooping to the page.

"Latin, I see. Chemistry. Physics. That's a lot of work inside a week. Four mathematics. Four English. *Five* English," he added, running his finger across the page.

His father went to work a little later. He stood in the yard, fiddling with his saddle.

"Thy football's on tomorrow, then."

"Yes," he said.

"Give as good as you get," he added.

"Yes," he said.

His father glanced across.

"They're not stuck up or ought, then, are they?"

168

"No," he said.

"You don't feel out of place?"

"No." He shook his head.

"It's a damn good school."

"Nay, get on," his mother said. "It's as good as he deserves and nothing less."

"Aye, I suppose you're right," his father said.

He set off down the yard.

"Good luck tomorrow, if I don't see you before I leave," he said.

Colin stood in the yard and watched him go. He went up to his room a little later. He sat on the bed, pronouncing vowels, learning the list of words the master had set.

His mother came up at the end of an hour.

"Nay, love, you ought to be getting in. It's after your bed-time, you know, already."

"I haven't learnt them all," he said.

"Well, you've done as long as you should," she said.

"I still haven't learnt them, though," he said.

"Well, I'll write them a note saying you've learnt them long enough," she said.

He got ready for bed. He could see Batty and Stringer playing in the field outside. Before he got into bed he went back down.

"You needn't write a note," he said. "I'll tell him myself."

"Don't worry, I'll write him one. You've done the work, after all," his mother said.

"I'll tell him myself," he said. "You needn't bother."

She watched him go. He could hear her from his bedroom moving round the kitchen; he heard Steven stirring in his bed through the wall. Finally the doors were bolted, the windows shut: the sound of his mother's feet came slowly from the stairs.

She went into Steven's room. He heard her creak the bed as she tucked in his blanket; she opened the door of his room.

He waited; a moment later the door was closed.

The sun hadn't set; daylight came in beneath the curtain. He fell asleep with Batty's and Stringer's voices still ringing in his head.

PART THREE

12

A narrow footpath wound behind the backs of several large, brick-built houses, coming out finally at the edge of a field. Other fields, hedged, swept up to a low horizon of trees and houses.

In the centre of the principal field stood a cricket pitch, marked off behind a barrier of rope. A brick-built pavilion adjoined the opening of the path on to the field itself, beside it a smaller one, painted green and built of wood. It was in the second, slightly decaying structure, the base of its woodwork beginning to rot, that boys of his own age were already changing.

The two dimly lit rooms inside were crowded; at one point he found his clothes removed from a peg and finally he folded them up inside his satchel and, waiting until the others had gone, hung that on a peg already occupied inside the door.

The youngest boys had been called over to a pitch at the farthest side of the field. Two masters were standing there, one of them Platt, short and squat, and one he hadn't seen before. He too was a small man, and slightly built; he had thin grey hair which, with a slow, hesitant gesture, he would fold across his head. His eyes were dark and moist; he nodded at the boys, checking their names with a list in his hand.

Groups of boys ran up and down on the remaining pitches; names were being called and whistles blown while, on the largest pitch of all, with tall, broad-based goal-posts painted in the school colours of dark blue and gold, boys the size of men had begun a game.

"What boys have played rugby union before?" Platt had said. He blew the whistle. "Will you pay attention," he shouted, "to what's being said."

173

Colin jumped up and down. His boots were worn over at the outer edges; the football shirt itself was far too large. He'd rolled up the sleeves and tucked the bottom of the shirt between his legs. He could feel it flap out behind him when he ran.

"Those who've played rugby union," the second master said, "can stand over here."

He formed a group around him beneath the posts.

"What boys have played rugby league, then?" Platt said.

One or two boys put up their hands.

"We don't want any rugby league players here." He gave a laugh. "We'll reserve *judgment* on those who have played the game," he added.

.̣.̣ɛ glanced around.

"There are three sports played in this area at this time of the year," Platt said. "One is soccer, a game which, in my opinion, might, with profit, have been reserved for girls; one is rugby league, which is played very largely by people for money; and the third is rugby union, a fair and equitable game, played at our oldest universities as well as by all our major public schools. It is a game conceived by and therefore, quite naturally, played by gentlemen, and gentlemanly shall be the conduct of those who play the game under Mr. Hepworth's and my supervision." He gestured to the slight figure standing beneath the posts. "We wish to choose a team, of course. One to represent the school at Junior level. All of you present will have an opportunity to compete for places, bearing in mind, particularly those who have played under the *professional* code, that gentlemanly conduct and playing to the rules *at all times* are the qualities both Mr. Hepworth and I are looking for. Fisticuffs, bad temper and inconsiderate running with the ball—characteristic, I might tell you, of the professional code—are *not* required at King Edward's. I can tell you that for nothing." He gazed round at the jerseyed figures for several seconds. "Now, then: *names*. When I call them out you'll line up here."

Several boys were later dismissed. They went off slowly, kicking their heels, some indifferent, calling later from the pavilion as they dashed out from a shower.

By the end of the afternoon only half the boys were

left. Colin ran up and down. He had never played the game before. The first time the ball came to him he passed it on, wildly, to a boy much larger than himself.

"You, you there. Haven't you ever passed a ball, boy?" Platt had said.

He took the oval ball and held it by his chest.

"Laces in the direction you want the ball to go. Ball vertical. Now: have a try yourself."

He passed the ball.

Platt shook his head.

"Stand on the side for a bit," he said.

He stood with several other boys, waiting to be dismissed. Groups from the other pitches were already drifting off. The older boys alone were running up and down.

"You. You there, boy," Platt had called.

He ran back on the pitch.

"Do you know how to form a scrum, boy?" Platt had said.

He put his head down and linked his arm to the boy beside him. They put their heads between the hips of the boys in front. He saw the ball tossed into the mass of players, and saw it go out between his legs.

The game went on. The ball came loose between his feet. He picked it up and began to run.

He ran round one boy then, with a sickening crunch, ran into several others.

He fell between their legs, saw feet kicking round his head, released the ball and rolled away.

"Well played, boy. That's the method," Platt had said.

He ran with the ball again; he pulled another boy down. He felt a dull pleasure as the game progressed. He did nothing to draw attention to himself.

Names were read out at the end of the match. "Nichols, Beresford, Jones, Saville." He completed the list. "Those not read out will report to Mr. Hodges at the Spion Kop field next games afternoon," Platt said.

The two masters walked away. One or two boys walked with them. Others drifted over to the senior pitch. Names were mentioned and players pointed out. "Swallow. Tranter. Smith Major. Cornforth." The ground shook as the players pounded past. Weals were left in the grass at each of the tackles.

David Storey

He went back to the pavilion; his arms and legs had begun to ache. There was a basin to wash in at the back of the room: most of the boys hadn't bothered, they put their clothes on over the mud and stains.

By the time he set off for the bus he could scarcely walk; his feet were sore from the boots, his shoulders ached from the weight of the bag. When he got on the bus he fell asleep, waking briefly when it lurched across the hump-backed bridge and only finally roused himself when it descended, rattling, towards the village.

He stayed up even later that night. In addition to the French he had Math and Latin. The Latin, however much he tried, he couldn't get right.

"You've been three hours on it," his mother said. "It's after *my* bedtime, never mind yours."

"I've got to get it right," he said.

"Let me write in the book," she said. "I'll tell him that you tried."

He held the book from her.

"For goodness' sake," she said, "if you work like this you'll be worn out completely by the end of the week."

He went to bed with the work unfinished. He was late for the bus the following morning, catching one that came almost half an hour later.

Assembly had started. He stood outside with several other boys, allowed in finally after the prayers were finished. His name was taken down.

"What's this? One boy late this morning?" Hodges said as he marked the register for the afternoon. "Not Saville double l, then, is it? Not finding out, I suppose, how to spell his name correctly."

"No, sir," he said.

He'd already given the Latin in.

"Distinguished himself, I gather, on the rugger field. So Mr. Platt and Mr. Hepworth tell me." He gazed at him from his desk over the top of his glasses. "Rugger doesn't entitle you to privileges, boy. However well you play. Do you understand that, Saville double l?"

"Yes," he said.

"Well, double l, I don't expect to see another late mark

176

against your name." He removed his glasses. "Let me see your record book."

He took it down to the desk.

"I shall mark it on this occasion, double l, as a warning not only to you but to all the rest." He glanced around him and drew out his pen. "A bad record at this point of the term is a very bad thing indeed. It sets a tone for the book which it is very difficcult to eradicate, particularly for a boy just starting and for a master looking at it to see what sort of lad he is."

"I was late for the bus," he said.

"We're all late for the bus, double l, if we all *get* up late for the bus," he said.

He blotted the record, which he'd written in red ink, and handed him the book.

"Let that be a lesson to anyone else who feels inclined to miss the bus," he said. "Back to your place, then, double l."

When he got back to his desk he looked at the book. "Late for his third morning at school. J.T.H.," had been written in the column.

He put up his hand.

"What is it, double l? Is anything the matter?"

"What you've written here isn't correct," he said.

"What's that, Saville?"

He saw the eyes tighten behind Hodges's glasses. The colour deepened swiftly in his face.

"What you've written in my record book," he said.

"What's that, boy?"

He waited.

"Do you know how to address a master, Saville?"

"Yes, sir," he said.

"That's the first 'sir' I've heard, Saville, from the moment you stood up."

"The bad record you've given me, sir, makes it sound as though I've been late for three mornings running."

He waited once again.

"Read to me what's written, Saville."

" 'Late for his third morning at school,' " he read aloud.

Hodges waited.

"I think that's perfectly clear."

He took out his pen. "Bring your book to me again, then, Saville."

He went down through the class to the teacher's desk. The bell had already sounded for the afternoon lesson.

"I shall give you a second bad record, Saville, for insurbordination. I needn't tell you how serious two bad records in one day can be. Three in one week and it's my duty to report you to Mr. Walker. At this time on Friday I shall require you to bring me this book again. If any other master has found it necessary to endorse my opinion of your behaviour the matter will be out of my hands completely."

He wrote again in the book with the same red ink. He blotted it carefully and handed it back. The door had already opened and a master appeared.

"Is that understood, then, Saville?"

"Yes," he said and went back to his desk.

"It's seldom been my duty to give two bad records on the one occasion," the master added, looking at the class. "I'm sure Mr. Hepworth will agree that it's a singular disappointment to any master to have to perform such a duty in respect of a member of his own class. I can't tell you with what regret I look upon this incident. I hope, now that it has occurred, that it makes our positions clear, and that nothing remotely like it will happen again. Take out your books for Mr. Hepworth's lesson. I shan't, if I can help it, refer to this incident again."

He went out, removing his glasses, and, in total silence, closed the door.

Hepworth said nothing for several seconds. He stood at the back of the class; then, pushing his hand across his head, he walked slowly down to the desk at the front.

"Please open your atlases at page thirty-one," he said.

Colin waited outside the staff-room at the end of the afternoon. He didn't see Hodges.

He waited in the drive.

Finally Platt came out, walking to the gate; he went across to him and touched his cap.

"What is it, boy? Out with it," Platt had said. He had a brief-case in his hand, a hat on his head, his overcoat unbuttoned, and was plainly in a hurry.

"Has Mr. Hodges come out of the staff-room, sir?" he said.

"Hodges? Free period last period. He goes home early. What did you want to see him about?"

"I wanted to make a complaint," he said.

"See him in the morning if it's anything important. Otherwise leave a message in the office, boy," he said.

He was almost in tears when he reached the bus.

"Why, what is it? Whatever's happened?" his father said when he got to the house.

He showed him the book.

He saw the whiteness rise to his father's face.

"By God, I s'll come to school in the morning."

"No," he said. "You'll make it worse."

"I'll not make it worse than this, don't worry."

"I'll talk to him on my own," he said.

"Don't worry, lad. I'll set it straight."

"You can't set it straight. It's written in."

"I'll have it written out," his father said.

"But you can't do anything," he said, "but make it worse."

"Don't worry, lad. I'll sort it out."

His father went the following day. Colin was called to the headmaster's study after the break-bell went. The headmaster himself was sitting at a desk; books lined the walls; a window looked down on to the crowded field below. There were framed photographs on the wall and in the corner, on a wooden pedestal, stood a massive globe.

A face in profile, like a mast, was set in a frame above a wooden mantelpiece. Its eyes were closed; it echoed, in its features, something of the headmaster's narrow face. Pale-blue eyes looked out from beneath bushy brows.

"Your father came to see me this morning. About this incident with Mr. Hodges," the headmaster said.

"Yes, sir." He nodded. "He said he would."

"It seems you were late on your third morning at school, and complained at the way Mr. Hodges had phrased the remarks in your record book. He said your manner was insolent and amounted, in his view, to insubordination."

"Yes, sir."

"It's a master's privilege to make judgments on your

179

conduct, Saville. Not only is it his privilege, but it's also, in Mr. Hodges's case, his particular duty. Not only is he a master with great experience, but with a great deal of feeling and sympathy for boys your age. If this is his judgment, then this judgment is correct; it's one I trust. I take a very dim view of boys who, when they get themselves into trouble, see no other resort but to complain to their parents, who come to the school with a wholly distorted view of the entire affair."

"I asked my father not to come here, sir." He gazed past the thinly featured face to the field below.

"He says you've had trouble with your homework, Saville."

"Yes, sir."

"If at the end of an hour and half it's not completed, it's better to make a note in your book to this effect and report your difficulties to the appropriate master—not stay up so late that you're too tired in the morning to catch your bus."

"Yes, sir."

He glanced down at the desk. "I'm sorry this has happened so early in your career in the school. Mr. Hodges, to make his own feelings quite clear, has offered to erase the two records from your book and has suggested I issue you with a new one. I'm afraid, despite his recommendation, that that is something I won't and can't allow. The record book is there for all to see, and is the most important document you'll carry through the school. I hope from the incident you'll learn a useful lesson: that the masters and the mistresses are here not to punish you for misdemeanors, but to instruct and guide, and, whenever in their view it is necessary, to reprimand. I hope you'll learn from this to trust their judgment. I'd like you to report to me at the end of the term, with your record book complete, and we'll see, from looking at it, precisely where you stand."

He went out to the office. A grey-haired secretary with a red, sunburnt face was working at a desk; she glanced up, smiling, and said, "Was there any message?"

"No." He shook his head.

"That'll be all, then, Saville," she said.

He went through to the corridor, then, since the bell

marking the end of the break hadn't sounded, down to the field.

He stood by the wooden fence. He looked up at the headmaster's window. The school's coat-of-arms with its motto, which he hadn't noticed while he was in the room, was set in the middle of the diamond-shaped panes in coloured glass.

His father, when he got home that evening, had been subdued.

"I'll give you that he's fair," he said. "I'll give you that. And Hodges. I spoke to both of them," he added.

It was the first time he'd seen his father back down from something he believed.

"They said it wouldn't influence them in any way. I mean, about your work," he added.

"At least it's over and settled," his mother said.

"Aye, it's cleared the air," his father said. "Though tha mu'n never miss that bus again," he added.

In the second week, at football, Stafford appeared. Saville had spoken to him occasionally in the field at the back of the school, and had walked down with him one afternoon into town, parting at the narrow opening which, he'd discovered earlier, led down towards the station. On the Thursday afternoon Stafford was standing on the pitch when Colin arrived for football, his hands on his hips, apparently unconcerned by all the activity going on around. He dug his heel against the grass, glancing round at the other pitches, then smoothing down his hair with slow, almost conscious gestures as if anxious to move away to something less demanding.

He played amongst the backs. He had a slender, almost delicate physique; he stood around a great deal, his arms folded, chewing grass, always anxious to talk to the other players, sometimes picking up stones or clods of earth from the pitch and throwing them off on either side. He ran with the ball; he moved so slowly that it seemed impossible then that he wouldn't be caught; he slipped away, half-gliding, turning slowly, almost lethargically between the outstretched arms, avoiding one group of figures and then another and finally, when he appeared to be bored by the ease with which he eluded his opponents, he threw the ball away to another boy, who was immediately tackled.

"More effort, Stafford. More effort," Platt said. He wrote on his list and nodded to Hepworth.

In all, thirty boys had been left in the game; occasionally they changed sides, swapping jerseys. The rest of the boys had been sent away. The remainder, on the whole, were in the third year, some in the second; Stafford, Colin himself and two other boys were all that remained from the first.

At half-time they were called in a loose circle in the centre of the pitch.

"Now all you boys," Platt said, "will come here every Tuesday and Thursday. You'll form the nucleus of our Under 13 Team. Is that understood, then, Stafford?"

Stafford, after joining in the circle, had lain down in the grass. He lay with his head in his hands, gazing at the sky. His eyes, when Colin glanced over, appeared to be closed.

At Platt's inquiry he raised his head.

"Yes, sir," he said.

"That's not going to be too inconvenient for you, Stafford?" Platt had said.

"No, sir." Stafford sat up slowly, pushing his hand across his head. "I was feeling tired."

"That's all right, Stafford," Platt had said.

As he continued talking to the boys Platt moved slowly round the circle, gesturing, calling names, offering advice, outlining the team's plans for the coming season, ending up finally only a few inches from where Stafford was sitting. "Harrison will be captain," he said, indicating a large, bulky boy with fattish legs and hair almost as fair as Stafford's. "This will be his third year in the team and I want you to listen to any advice he has to give." He half-lifted Stafford with one hand as he got to his feet. "You'll go on Harrison's side, Stafford. And I want more effort in this second half."

At one point in the middle of the game Stafford got the ball almost directly in front of where Colin was standing; he went to him, intending to drag him down. He saw the half-awareness in Stafford's eyes, the strange flexing of his back as he moved aside and a moment later when it seemed he had no way to go, Stafford moved past him,

casually, his figure tensing to meet those moving up behind. He ran to one side of the pitch, slipped past two
boys, avoiding a third, then, to Platt's and Hepworth's
shouts, put the ball down between the posts.

He walked back slowly, his cheeks flushed, his eyes
gleaming, as if he'd been driven to something he hadn't
wished to do.

"Stafford, you might have gone straighter," Platt had
said. "Straight down the middle is the quickest way."

"Yes, sir," Stafford said. He stood with his hands on his
hips. The redness of his cheeks had scarcely faded.

Finally, a few moments later, when the kick had been
taken, the whistle went.

Stafford had already left the pitch; he jogged off slowly.
As Colin changed he saw him coming back from the senior
pavilion where he'd had a shower; later, setting off down
the ginnel, he heard someone coming up behind him and,
turning, saw Stafford smiling now and waving.

"Platt's a bit of a stickler," he said. "What do you
think?"

"He doesn't seem to miss much, I suppose," Colin told
him.

Stafford's hair was neatly combed; he hadn't, as yet,
put on his cap.

"Where were you last week?" Colin asked him.

"I played at Spion Kop. They sent me up here."

There was no sense of achievement or even pride in
Stafford; more, it was an inconvenience he was stressing,
something which, in the near future, he intended to set
right.

"It seems you'll be in the team," Colin said.

"Do you think so?" He'd already forgotten about the
game: he was looking down at his jacket, checking the
buttons, feeling in his pockets. He carried a neat canvas
hold-all in his other hand.

"If Harrison's the captain, and you're playing on his
side."

"He's a bit of a lump. Did you see the way he moved
around?"

He walked on quickly, as if anxious to get away from
the field. "I thought of getting a letter."

Colin looked across.

David Storey

"From a doctor." They came out from the ginnel. "If you get a letter saying you're not supposed to be playing games you get two afternoons off free. What do you think? We could spend them at the pictures."

"I couldn't get a letter," he said.

"I can get one for you. No bother at all." They were passing by the school. Stafford paid it no attention. At one point, glancing in a shop window lower down the street, he took out a comb and, pausing, combed his hair.

Colin waited.

"You don't enjoy all that, then, do you?" Stafford said.

"All what?"

Stafford shrugged.

"Running round that field. And having that big fat lump jump on top of you."

"No," he said.

"Tell me your christian name and I'll get a letter. If two of us do it, it looks better than one."

"It's Colin."

"Okay, Col. Leave it to me."

He went off down the narrow opening leading to the station.

Colin watched him: he didn't look back.

He never saw the letter. He never discovered whether Stafford had even got one; despite his mentioning it on one occasion Stafford never referred to it again. He avoided walking with him whenever he could; Colin would see his friend hurrying to the ginnel with the other boys, or, if he himself were already in front, walking behind slowly, waiting for someone else to catch him up. In school itself they scarcely met; he could be seen occasionally lounging against the wall at the end of the field, or against the fence, his hands in his pockets, his back rounded as he slowly kicked the grass, laughing, calling to other boys who invariably came up and whom, characteristically, he never approached.

Once, on a Tuesday afternoon, Colin caught him up.

"You played well this afternoon," he said.

Stafford glanced up. He'd been walking by himself, along the ginnel, his canvas bag beneath his arm.

"Oh, that. Platt seems pleased enough. I've been picked

184

for the team next Saturday. At least, that's what Hepworth says."

"What position are you playing?"

"Stand-off half."

Stafford kicked the ground, slowly, as he walked along. "They've made me vice-captain as well it seems."

"Who told you?"

"Platty told me."

When they reached the turning to the station Stafford glanced across.

"How do you get to school?" he said.

"By bus."

"Don't you ever come by train?"

"No," Colin said.

"Where do you come from?" Stafford said.

"Saxton."

"The train I come on comes through there. It goes back that way as well. It's twice as quick as coming by bus."

"It costs more on the train," Colin said.

"You could easily cough it up."

"I shouldn't think so.'" He shook his head.

"Hasn't your father enough money even for that?"

"He prefers to use it on other things," he said.

Stafford looked at him slowly; his eyes had lightened.

"I'll see you tomorrow, then," he said.

He went off whistling, his bag now dangling from his hand.

He was made a reserve the following week; he struggled with Latin. Between waking and sleeping was a continual movement: rising, running for the bus, the hour-long journey through the villages, the approach to the city, the walk to school, assembly, lessons, break-time, lunch. After lunch came the smell of cooking from the cloisters below, the distant droning of the master's voice, a brief interlude of tiredness, a slow lethargy induced by the underventilated room. Only after the middle of the afternoon had passed did a lightness return; the briskness of the final lesson, the hasty collecting of books, the walk through the narrow streets of the town to the stop immediately below the walls of the black cathedral.

In the evening he sometimes played in the field at the back of the house; the rest of the time he spent on homework. The village involved him less and less; it was more of an inconvenience, its distance and remoteness. He seldom saw his father: sometimes he would have left on a morning before his father came home from work, or, if he were working afternoons, he'd be in bed by the time his father got back; only when he worked a morning shift would they be at home together, in the evening—occasions now that he'd learnt to dread, the examination of his books, the marks.

"Nay, they aren't so good, then, are they? C minus. What's C stand for?"

"Gamma," he said.

"And what's Gamma when it's at home?" his father said. He explained the system of marking.

"Nay, that's one out of ten." He looked at him with a sudden fury, the familiar whiteness spreading round his eyes.

"There's Delta," he said. "They give that too."

"Do they? And what's Delta when it's at home?" he said.

"Less than Gamma minus."

"Nay, Delta must be nought," he said. "I can't understand why they don't put it into English. Ten out of ten, one out of ten. I can't see the point of all these words."

He'd go through each of the books quite slowly, examining the marks, the ticks, the crosses, the smallest correction.

"Sithee, even I could do that. Thy's not been paying attention."

"Oh, let him be when he's at home," his mother said.

"Let him be what? Slovenly and lazy? Content to do things he knows with a bit of effort, he can do much better?"

"Let him have a bit of peace when he comes back home," she'd tell him.

"Just look at the stuff," he'd say. He'd push the book beneath her face. " 'Conclusion': he could spell that three years ago."

"Well how *do* you spell conclusion, then?" she'd say.

"Nay, damn it all, he's the one at school," he'd tell her. "I'm the ignorant one round here."

Colin could hear his parents from his room at night, either arguing in the kitchen, where, he knew from the way his books had been disturbed, they went through his work together; or, later, if his father was working mornings or afternoons, from their bedroom at the front.

"All right. He isn't good at physics. Then he can get good at physics. Same with Latin. They're not that difficult. If six hundred other children can do them, I can't see why he should be an exception."

He would start going through the work with Colin at night; by the time the first term was almost over his father had learnt how to conjugate Latin verbs; he'd learnt how to construct a simple Latin phrase; how to work out algebraic equations, how to distinguish between compounds and oxides, alkalis and acids, how to tell the difference on maps between deciduous and coniferous vegetation. During those weeks when his father worked nights or afternoons, he would find notes left for him, the correction of some work he'd done the previous evening, or some revised account of work his father had come across in one of his books, elaborating, usually in a clumsy manner, suggestions in the margins by dissatisfied teachers.

One Saturday afternoon he was chosen to play in the football team against another school. His father came to watch.

There were two games being played, a second-team match, and the junior match; his father, unfamiliar with the field, had wandered over to the senior pitch. He was still standing there when the junior game began, and only came over after fifteen minutes. Small, wearing an overcoat against the briskness of the late autumn weather, he was the only other adult there apart from Platt and Hepworth. His shouts had filled the field. "Go on! Go on! Run with it! Grab him!" while Platt and Hepworth, glancing across at him, called more quietly, "Feet, school, feet," and, "Back up your captain, Edward's."

"Grab him! Grab him!" his father called.

"Feet, Edward's," Platt had called, his voice fading at the violence of his father's cries.

At half-time oranges were brought on to the field.

Platt, who'd brought them on a tray and given them out, took Colin aside once they'd all been eaten.

"Is that your only jersey, Saville?"

"Yes," he said.

"I've sent Hopkins over to the groundsman to get another." He indicated one of the reserves who was already coming back. "For one thing the shirt's too large, for another the colours of the school have faded."

"I haven't got another," he said.

"Then you'll have to buy another. If you want to play in the school team you won't be allowed, I'm afraid, to play in that."

He moved on, casually, to the other boys.

"Come on, King Edward's," his father called. "Get stuck in this second half." His face flushed, his hands fisted, he paced briskly up and down at the side of the pitch.

"Whose father is that, then?" Stafford said.

"I don't know," Harrison said. He shook his head.

"He wouldn't shout like that if he had to play."

"He wouldn't shout at all," Harrison said, "if he had any sense."

The game now was more bewildering than any he'd played in. The other side on the whole were bigger; he found himself lost amidst a morass of arms and legs, his head banged down against the frosted ground, his knees torn, his elbows bruised. Twice he ran with the ball and twice he felt it taken from his hands, his arms wrenched back, his fingers bent, his hands crushed beneath stamping boots.

"Stafford, hold the ball. Hold the ball, Stafford," Platt began to shout.

Yet Stafford, aware of the figures waiting, or rushing up as he took the ball, would pass it away carefully to either side. There was an earnestness in the way he played, as if he were judging which parts of the game he might avoid.

"Hold it, Stafford. Go through the middle," Platt had called.

Colin took the ball; he passed to Stafford. He saw the look of surprise on Stafford's face, the tensing of the eyes, and saw the quick look round for one of his side.

There was no one near. He began to run, slowly, still looking round; he avoided one boy and then another, casual, still slow, almost insolent, waiting for someone to come towards him. No one came; each of the school's team was hanging back.

He ran to one side; there was an instinct in the team that Stafford should run: he stepped aside, avoiding another boy and then effortlessly, half-pausing, looking for no one now, waited as players from the other team came up, stepping aside, slowly, an inflection of his body sending one group of players one way while he went another.

He crossed the line. Platt and Hepworth and his father threw up their arms. Stafford put down the ball, glanced round, then, the ball beneath his arm, walked back.

"I'll kick it," he said as Harrison came to take it from him.

The ball was held from the ground; he stepped back a pace, swung his leg and, as the opponents ran up, the ball curved over their heads between the posts.

His hands on his hips, his cheeks white, his eyes blazing, he walked slowly back.

At the end of the game Stafford came up to him as they left the pitch.

"Don't pass to me like that again."

"There was no one else to pass it to," he said.

"Then do what I do. Bend down, or pretend to be looking the other way."

His father, he noticed, had walked away. He stood at the gate of the field, by the opening to the ginnel, his face red, his hands pushed deeply into the pockets of his coat. He stamped his feet against the cold.

They went into the showers.

His father was still waiting at the gate as he left the field.

"We've to go into tea with the other team," he said.

"That's all right," he said. "You enjoy yourself in theer. I'll wait out here."

"Why don't you come in as well?" he said. The room occupied the basement of the groundsman's house. He could see where the games equipment had been pushed to one side: a wooden table had been set in the middle.

"No, no. You go in. I'll be all right out here." He added, "Teams and officials in theer, you know."

Plates of sandwiches and cakes had been set out on the table. At the end of the room, by the door, a broad window looked out to a yard and, beyond the yard, to the field. The goal-posts were visible above a hedge.

Platt came in, followed by Hepworth and two masters from the other school. The other team came in. Stafford, his hair combed, his clipped pens showing in his blazer pocket, sat alone: he glanced up briefly as Hepworth tapped his back, but got up when the first boys began to leave. He picked up his canvas bag from the door and went out to the yard.

When Colin followed he saw his father talking to Stafford at the mouth of the ginnel. He'd evidently stopped him and, gesturing behind him, was talking about the match.

"Oh, here's Colin," he said. "Which way do you go, then, lad?"

"I'm going to the station," Stafford said, looking back at him, surprised.

"We'll go down with you. We catch a bus in town," his father said.

They walked through the ginnel.

"Thy's got a good future there, if you put your back into it," his father said.

"Oh, it's too rough a game for me, Mr. Saville," Stafford said.

His father laughed, looking at Stafford in some surprise.

"Rough? I can't see there's much rough about it," his father said.

"Oh, I don't know," Stafford said. "If you're playing out there you'd think it was rough. Particularly when they kick you instead of the ball." A certain neatness had come into his movements; even his voice was clipped, the accent sharp.

His father, intrigued, had glanced across.

"There are rougher things than that," he said. "Give me football every time, tha knows."

"If there are, then I hope to keep away from them. It seems silly to go seeking roughness," Stafford said.

He left them at the opening leading to the station.

"You go that way, then?" his father said.

"If I rush now I might just catch an early train," Stafford said. He put out his hand. "It's been nice meeting you, Mr. Saville." He swung his bag, as he turned, beneath his arm.

"Well played, then, lad," his father said.

He watched him cross the road to the alley.

"Well, that's a bright 'un, then," his father said. "He could have won that match, tha knows, himself."

Still talking of Stafford, they walked down to the stop.

"And who was that feller with the jet black hair?" his father said.

"Platt," he said.

"He came up to me and asked me who I was waiting for."

"What did you tell him?" Colin said.

"I said I was waiting for thee." He laughed. " 'Didn't you hear me cheering?' I said."

He laughed again.

"He said I needed a new shirt. If I wanted to go on playing," Colin said.

"And where do we conjure new shirts from?" his father asked.

On the bus, however, he added, "Well, then, I suppose we might," and a moment later, "I wish he'd mentioned a shirt to me. By God, I'd have shirted Mr. Platt all right. I've a damn good mind to write him a letter."

"I shouldn't write to him," he said.

"Nay, I mu'n think about it though," he said.

Towards the end of that month his mother went away, to hospital, and in the mornings he and Steven went to Mrs. Shaw's for breakfast. His father was working mornings and got home each day in the afternoon. He was there to put Steven to bed at night but would come into Colin's room each morning at five, whispering, laying the alarm clock beside his bed.

"I'll be off now. Tha mu'n not sleep in."

Half-woken, he would gaze up blearily at his father's face.

"Sithee, then, I'm off. Mrs. Shaw'll look after Steve. Don't be late for the bus," he'd add.

He'd hear his father's feet go down through the house, the back door close, the key turned in the lock then slipped back through the letter box. Scarcely would he have fallen asleep it seemed than the alarm clock went. One morning he'd slept on to be woken by Mrs. Shaw banging on the door downstairs.

He was more tired now than at any time since he'd started at the school; coming home in the bus each evening, watching the fields and villages pass, the colliery heaps, the distant glimpses of ponds and lakes he felt, at the thought of his father in the house, a kind of dread: grey-faced, red-eyed, washing dishes or turning, wearily, to cook the food, it was as if he and Steven and himself had been left behind.

He'd even, one Sunday morning, gone into Mrs. Shaw's to clean her brasses; other memories of his mother flooded back. Neither he nor Steven could go and visit her; he would watch his father wheel out his bike each evening, the saddle-bag bulging with a parcel, clean clothes or fruit, sometimes a book he'd borrowed from work, and be waiting for him, two hours later when, with an exhausted eagerness and anxiety, he came cycling back.

"Sithee, aren't you in bed then, yet?"

He'd be fingering his homework, or reading a book by the light of the fire.

"Tha mu'n go to bed," his father would add, "I've got a key," yet glad, beneath his anxiety, that he hadn't gone yet.

They'd sit by the fire while his father brewed some tea.

"She's champion. She's looking well," he'd tell him. "She won't be long in theer, don't worry."

He'd talk to him, then, about his work, the pit, about Fernley, Roberts, Hopkirk and Marshall, new names and old names, about accidents at the face itself, a roof collapsing, a machine being stuck, about a man being caught beneath a rock.

His father had no one else to talk to now. It would be two hours or more after his bed-time frequently before Colin went to bed; his father would follow him. "Now you get to sleep. I'll put out the light. I'll set thy alarm for seven o'clock."

It was always half-past six when the alarm clock went;

at the last minute, as if loath to let him sleep in, he'd set it earlier. "Think on. As soon as it rings, get up. If Mrs. Shaw sleeps in tha'll be in trouble."

He often had the feeling that his father wanted him to get up as well, to see him off to work; he would often cough in the kitchen below as he got on his clothes, or trim his lamp in the yard outside, flashing a light against the window. Later, when Colin got up, he would have to waken his brother, pull back his covers, get him dressed; he was four years old, yet, with the absence of his mother, he would often cry.

"Mam?" he would call, anxious, listening, as if overnight she'd come back to her room.

"She won't be long," he'd tell him.

"Mam?" his brother would call.

He would pull on his clothes, which Steven could do himself but always resisted now. Sometimes he would lie in bed, moaning, his head to the pillow, and he himself would sit on the edge, his energy gone, waiting. Only the clock and the thought of being late would finally drag him back to his brother and the bed.

"Steve? She'll have us breakfast ready."

"Mam? I want my Mam."

"Don't you want any breakfast, then?" he'd ask him.

"I want me Mam. *Mam?*" he would call again.

Sometimes, still crying, he left him at Mrs. Shaw's.

"Oh, he'll be all right with me. I'll have him clean my brasses. And I take him to the swings in the afternoon."

She would sit him on her knee, her gaunt figure upright, Steven, pale-faced, leaning apprehensively against her.

"Don't worry. He'll be all right. You get off to school. Don't fret. His father'll be home in two or three hours. "Not *my* Steve? Not *our* Steve?" he'll say. "He's never *worried!*" "

There was a coldness about the school; he felt nothing from the moment he walked between the gates to the moment he came out. Only on the bus would the nagging return, a slow tugging, as if he were being brought down inside.

His mother gave birth to a son. His father was waiting

193

for him when he came home one day, smiling, dressed in his suit. He'd just come back from seeing her.

"He's a beauty, lad. As big as a tree. What do you think we mu'n call it? Your mother's thought of Richard, then."

"Yes," he said.

"Do you like it, then?"

"Yes."

Steven came in.

"Now, then," his father said. He picked him up. "What dost think to a brother, then?" He held out his arm. "Sithee, his leg's no thicker than that." He wiggled his finger. "By God, but I'm feeling glad."

His mother came home. His father and Steven had gone to fetch her. "Can't I have a day off school?" he said. "You could write a letter."

"Nay, they'd never let you off for that. She mu'n be here when thy comes back home, tha knows." He laughed at his dismay and rubbed his head. "Just think on: thy'll have *two* brothers waiting for you, then, at tea."

He'd felt the excitement then all day. While his mother had been away she'd written him letters: he'd taken them with him in his bag to school. For days he waited for some meaning to emerge, reading them again, uncertain of what the phrases meant. "How much I miss you." "I hope, Colin, you're looking after Steve." "I hope your work is going well." "Don't forget to get up on time." "All my love." There'd been a row of kisses at the foot of each: his mother seldom if ever kissed him in any case.

In the end he'd left the letters on the kitchen table.

"Have you finished with these?" his father said and when he nodded his head he dropped them in the fire.

Now, coming back on the bus from school, he sat at the front as if he expected his mother to materialize in the road ahead.

When he reached the village he ran to the house.

There was no one in.

He ran upstairs: he looked in his parents' room; he looked in his own and then in Steve's.

He went back down; he glanced out at the yard. He

194

went through to the room at the front and looked in there. The house was silent.

He went through to the kitchen, stood at the door; he gazed along the terrace. Already, with the early evening, it was growing dark. A vast cloud of steam whirled up from the colliery yard.

He went down the terrace to Mrs. Shaw's. He could hear his mother's voice inside: he heard her laughter, then Mr. Shaw's.

His knock at first had gone unheard. He knocked again. A moment later he heard his father call.

"Sithee, then, there's someone at the door."

He heard his mother's laughter, high, shrill, then the latch was lifted and the door pulled back.

"It's thy Colin, then. Come in, lad." Mr. Shaw, still laughing, had stepped aside. "Come in, then, Colin, and see your brother."

His mother was standing directly beneath the electric light in the middle of the kitchen: one side of her was lit up by the light from the fire. In her arms, wrapped in a white shawl, she was holding a baby; she'd just taken it from Mrs. Shaw, who was leaning across, one finger extended to stroke its cheek.

"Why, Colin, love," she said. "You've got back quick."

His father stood by the fire; he held a glass in his hand. Steven, eating a biscuit, was sitting at the table.

"Why, how are you, love?" his mother said. She leaned down, with one free hand; she pressed her lips against his cheek.

"Look at your brother. Who do you think he looks like, then?"

She held the baby down; a red, tightly wrinkled face gazed up from inside the shawl.

He looked at the face, then shook his head.

"Dost think he looks like me?" his father said. His face was flushed; he leant back, glancing at Mr. Shaw, and laughed. "Or dost think he looks like the postman, then?"

"Nay, whatever will he think?" Mrs. Shaw had said. A bottle and several empty glasses stood by an empty plate.

"Nay, round here," his father said, "you mu'n never tell." Mrs. Shaw had laughed again.

195

David Storey

"Get on with you, Harry," Mrs. Shaw had said. She turned to the baby and stroked its head.

"He's been a damn good brother has Colin," Mr. Shaw had said. "He's looked to that lad like a father would."

"Is there anything in for tea?" he said.

"Tea, sithee. And thy's only just got home," Mr. Shaw had said.

He laughed again.

"Well, here's to t'third 'un," his father said. He emptied the glass. "Another mouth to feed," he added.

"Aye. Thy better be going careful, Harry." Mr. Shaw had laughed again. "Thy'll be needing a new house as well as a pram."

"Nay, this is t'last, as far as I'm concerned," his father said. "There mu'n be no more, then, after this." He smacked his lips then laughed again. "Sithee, it's not every day we've summat to celebrate," he added.

"Thy mu'n find summat afore long, though, Harry," Mr. Shaw had said.

They laughed again.

"There's two lads ready for food if I'm not mistaken," Mrs. Shaw had said. "And one of em's not just come home for the first time either." She stroked the baby's face again. "Nay, but he's like you, Ellen," she added.

"Let's hope, though, he grows up to look like me," his father said.

Colin went to the door.

"Mind the blackout," Mr. Shaw had said.

The light went out: his mother came to the door, stooping, the baby in her arms, looking for the step.

"Two down, then, love," Mrs. Shaw had said.

They crossed the yard; he could hear his father, still standing in the kitchen.

"Nay, I can't leave here wi' one or two drops still left," he said.

Mr. Shaw had laughed.

Steven's voice had called. His father's voice echoed from the yard.

"Put the light on, love," his mother said. "Never mind the door," she added.

196

She came in, the baby held upright, its head against her arm.

"There, now. There, then, love," she said.

She laid it on a chair.

"Can you get me a nappy?" she said, her back towards him now. "You'll find it in the cupboard."

He opened the cupboard door beside the fire. He took out the nappy.

The baby, behind him, had begun to cry.

"He's just had his feed. So he can't be hungry yet," she said.

Its legs were thrust out in tiny spasms. Its hands, fisted, waved to and fro before its face.

"Well, then. I'll just take him up for a bit," she said.

She went to the stairs; he could hear her a moment later in the bedroom at the front.

The kitchen door had opened. His father came in.

"Sithee, has she taken him up? Has she taken him up to bed for cheers?" he said.

He took off his jacket. His face was flushed, his collar undone.

"There, then. Did'st see thy brother, then?"

"Yes," he said.

"What did I tell you, lad? She's come home in the end."

His father went to the fire, swaying, then loosened his tie.

"By go, old Shaw had a bottle, then." He belched, slowly, then held his chest. "I mu'n get off to bed. I haven't had a sleep, tha knows, today. I mu'n be off again at five. Thy'll know that, then, o' course," he added. "Thy's been here long enough, then, an't 'a?"

He sat down in a chair; his eyes were closed. Steven came in; he held another biscuit.

"Is my mother here?" he said.

His mother came down. Like his father, her face too was flushed.

"He might sleep for an hour," she said. "Though all that noise, I think, has wakened him for good."

She looked over to the table.

"What are you doing, then, love?" she said.

"My homework," he said. He bent to the book.

"Nay, can't you give it a miss for once?" she said.

"No," he said. He shook his head.

"He's worked like a Trojan, has Colin," his father said. "He's looked after this house as good as a woman. He's had it cleaned a time or two, floors polished, pots washed. And lit that fire for when I come back in," he added.

His head sank over, slowly; a few moments later he began to snore.

"See, then: your father's drunk too much," his mother said. "He always lets it go to his head," she added.

"I'll go in the other room to work," he said.

He picked up the book.

"Will you, love? That's good of you. I wouldn't want to disturb him," his mother said. "And I'll get your tea ready for you," she called after him, "in a couple of minutes."

He went in the other room and drew the curtains. The room was cold. A fire hadn't been lit in the room for several weeks.

He put on the light and began to read; through the wall, intermittently, came his mother's voice and then, more rhythmically, his father's snores.

13

"How far can you bend it?" Batty said.

He was holding the branch against his chest. In his other hand he held the gun.

"Pull it right back, then fasten it with the string."

Colin fastened off the branch, then cut the remnant of string with Batty's knife.

From farther back, near the hut, came Steven's shout.

"Thy wants to leave him at home, thy young 'un," Batty said. "He mu'n give it away, where we have the hut."

Batty had grown much taller in recent months; his figure had narrowed, the legs drawn out, the thin, red-thatched head set on top of a limb-like neck. He was taller now than any of his brothers; even his father looked up to him whenever they spoke, and his mother's head came scarcely to his chest.

Now, having set the branch, they went back to the hut: it was Stringer, he discovered, who was playing with Steven. He was riding him up and down, upright, on his back. Steven clutched at the twigs as they passed above his head, startled, wide-eyed, uncertain of Stringer's mood. Frequently, even when Colin was there, they would set his brother to some ill-considered task, urging him to climb a dangerous tree, to mend the fragile roof, to walk along a sunken path with brackish pools on either side, to wade into a part of the swamp where they hadn't been before, Steven sinking to his knees before they hauled him out. There was an imperturbability about his brother which nothing disturbed.

"Here, Stringer," Batty called. "We've set another."

"Tha mu'n catch *us* coming through if tha sets any more, then, Lolly," Stringer said.

He lifted Steven from his shoulders and set him down; blue-eyed, his face flushed, Steven ran off inside the hut.

"What mu'n thy do theer, then, Tongey?" Batty said.

"Do wheer, then, Lolly?" Stringer said.

"At Tongey's school, then," Batty said.

Stringer took his gun which Batty had borrowed.

"We mu'n go theer one day. We mu'n wave to him," Stringer said, "between the bars."

Stringer laughed. He sighted the gun. He sat down on an upturned box beside the wooden door.

From inside the hut came the sound of Steven poking the fire.

"Dost sit in a room, then," Batty said, "or dost thy have to move around?"

"For some lessons we move. Though most of them," Colin said, "we stay where we are."

"Which ones do you move for?" Batty said.

He examined Colin for a moment with narrowed eyes.

"Chemistry," he said.

"It's a big place, then."

"I suppose it is."

"I suppose they have cleaners in, an' all, at night."

"They come as we're leaving," Colin said.

"I bet they have some cleaning up."

"I suppose they have," he said. "Though we put the chairs up," he added, "before we leave."

"Up wheer?"

"On top of the desks."

Batty looked up from the corner of his eye.

"Wheer dost t'headmaster keep all his books and equipment, then?"

"In the stock-room," he said.

"Wheer's that, then?"

"Next to the secretary's office."

"I suppose thy's been in a time or two. Getting new books, tha knows, and things."

"No," he said.

Batty looked away, then said, "If thy has two afternoons up on yon playing field laking footer I suppose there's nobody left," and added, "In the school, I mean."

"There might be one or two."

"Oh, aye?"

"Thy knows what Lolly's after, dost 'a?" Stringer said.

"Tha mu'n shut thy mouth afore I put summat in it," Batty said.

He turned to the hut.

"What's thy young 'un cooking, then?"

They went inside.

"Thy knows what Batty Industries are, then, do you?" Stringer said.

Batty took the pan from Steven and looked inside.

"Biggest industrial combine in Saxton," Stringer said.

"And thy'll have t'biggest thick ear in Saxton if thy doesn't shut it up, then," Batty said.

"Bloody field-marshal, tha knows, is Loll."

Batty stirred the pan; he'd taken out his knife, unfolding the blade.

"Their two kids are up in court this week."

"I've telled thee," Batty said. He waved the knife.

Steven, laughing, put up his hand.

"Work afternoons down t'pit and half the neet, then, somewhere else."

Batty leapt across; Stringer, already, had sprung aside.

Steven, still laughing, ran over to the door; Stringer was running off across the swamp.

"I mu'n cop him one day," Batty said. He cleaned the blade of the knife against his sleeve. "And when I do he mu'n get the feel of this."

He went back to the pan.

"I better be getting Steven home," he said.

"Aren't you having some of this, then?" Batty said.

"I better be getting him back," he said.

"Can't I have some, Colin?" Steven said.

There were beans in the pan, and bits of bread.

"It's past your bed-time now," he said.

"Thy have some afore thy leaves, then," Batty said.

He set the pan down.

"Sithee, thy can have first taste."

He held out the beans on the tip of the knife.

"Theer, then, young 'un. Dost fancy that?"

It was over an hour later before they reached the road. His father was coming down the slope from the village, pushing his bike, looking over the hedge towards the pens.

"There you are. I've been looking for you, you know, for hours." He mounted the bike. "I'm going to be late for work," he added. "Go on. Get off. You mu'n tell your mother where a f'und you."

He watched his father cycle off; to walk more quickly he set Steven on his back. He was still carrying him when they reached the house.

"What do you call this?" his mother said. "Your father's out looking for you. He'll be late for work."

"We saw him. Down by the sewage pens," he said.

"You've not been playing there?" she said.

She'd been stooping to the fire where she'd been baking bread: the loaves, rising, were standing in the hearth.

"You've never had Steven there?" she said.

Before he could answer she had struck his head.

"Get those clothes off before you come in here. Just look at them," she said.

She took Steven to the sink in the corner and washed his legs; she washed his hands and arms, and then his face.

Upstairs, a moment later, the baby cried.

"Just look at his neck: he must have been soaking in the stuff," she said. "Just smell his clothes." She held them to his face. "And yours."

He went to bed; he lay listening to his mother as she took Richard from his cot. He and Steven now slept together; already, despite his crying, his younger brother had fallen asleep.

He turned in the bed; he held his hand against his cheek: the skin still throbbed. With the smell of sewage around him he fell asleep.

"Back up. Back up, School," Platt had said.

He stood on the touch-line, his collar up, a scarf wound round his neck, his hands thrust down, heavily, into his overcoat pockets.

"Back up, School! Feet! Feet!"

Snow lay in odd patches round the edges of the pitch.

Colin took the ball; he ran against a line of figures: his arm swung out.

The whistle blew. He went on running: his collar was caught and then his arm; his legs were swept away. He fell down; snow was crushed up against his cheek.

The whistle blew again.

"Free kick against King Edward's," the referee had said.

He pointed Colin out.

"If you use your fist again I'm afraid I'll have to send you off," he said.

Platt, red-faced, was standing still.

The players fell back. The kick was taken.

"Just watch how you play, Saville," Harrison said. His face, too, was turning red.

He could scarcely feel his fingers; the cold had numbed his feet. He ran for the ball, felt it bounce away and got down, stooping, ready for the scrum.

Stafford took the ball; he kicked: it soared down the field and floated into touch.

"Well kicked, Stafford," Platt had called.

Stafford did a great deal of kicking now. It was more positive than passing and had none of the disadvantages of trying to run: his clothes at the end of a match were almost as clean as when he began. He folded back his hair and with a slight raising of his shoulders jogged after the ball.

At the edge of the field stood a stone pavilion: white-painted windows echoed the whiteness of the snow that had collected in odd ridges around the eaves and ornamental chimneys.

Beyond, in the faint haze, lay a line of wooded hills; snow-covered fields ran up to silhouetted copses. The sky overhead was clear; a frost had fallen.

"Harder, Edward's! Harder!" Platt had called.

Before the match, arriving early in a coach, they'd been shown around the school: dormitories with rows of beds; studies, with casement windows, shelves of books and fires; a library, a gymnasium with a gleaming, spotless floor; a tennis court indoors; a science room from whose tall windows they'd gazed out, briefly, to the distant line of hills and woods.

Trees overlooked the school; they screened the pitch so that as the sun descended vague shadows, like ribs, spread out across the grass.

Steam rose from the scrum; the boys' breath rose in clouds as they waited for the ball then ran, slow-limbed, as Stafford casually kicked it into touch. There was an air of desolation about the place: Platt's voice echoed now and the referee's whistle or the calling of the boys lingered on, faintly, beneath the trees.

"On, School! On, School!" Platt had said.

They ran to and fro.

The field darkened.

"Just look at my fingers, I think they're swelling," Hopkins said. "They'll hardly move."

A large boy, with broad features, he was the one Colin got down with in the scrum. Though smaller than Harrison, he had much the same build, lumbering, almost careless. His knees were reddened with cold. His teeth chattered as they leant down. He gave a whimper: blood ran down from his cheek and round his mouth.

"Do you want to go off, then?" Colin said.

"They won't let you," Hopkins said. "In any case," he added, darkening, "we've got to win."

Colin ran aimlessly towards the ball; he ran so slowly that the ball, continuously, moved away. There was a pointlessness to sport which he'd never sensed before: a plodding after things which, even if they should occur, were over in a second.

"Feet, School! Feet, School!" Platt had said.

Rooks rose slowly from the trees; wheeling, they climbed then, as the game ended, descended once again.

"Three cheers for Edward's. Hip hip."

"Hooray."

"Hip, hip."

"Hooray."

"Hip, hip."

"Three cheers for St. Benedict's," Harrison said.

The sound faded as they crossed the field.

"I shan't consider you for the next match, Saville."

Platt, his hands still in his pockets, walked beside him; but for the fact that he'd heard the voice he would have doubted that he'd even spoken.

"Yes."

"Foul play is something I particularly take objection to. It lets down the individual, but more important, it lets down the school."

"Yes."

"It'll be a long time before I forget today."

204

"Yes."

He waited; already the other players had gone ahead.

Platt, as if nothing had occurred, had turned aside. He called out cheerily to the referee.

Colin took off his boots; his feet were sore. He walked on slowly to where the steam already rose from the pavilion doors.

He sat alone on the bus on the journey back.

Stafford sat at the back with Harrison and Hopkins, singing; most of the players had gathered round, gazing backwards, kneeling on the seats.

Platt sat at the front beside the driver; occasionally he glanced round and smiled.

The sun had set. The bus ran on in virtual darkness. Colin caught a brief glimpse of trees outside, of hills silhouetted against a lightless sky. In the window opposite he saw his face, the bulk of the seat behind, the pallid shape, the dark shadow beneath his eyes, his hair, uncombed, still wet from the showers.

"Not singing?" Stafford said. He slumped down beside him in the seat.

"No."

"Come and sit at the back."

"No thanks."

"I'm not keen on sitting there, either. I suppose you have to on a thing like this."

"A good game today, Stafford," Platt said, calling from the seat in front.

"I think it went our way, sir," Stafford said.

Platt had smiled, nodded; he turned his head.

"I better get back, then," Stafford said.

"Okay," he said.

The figure beside him rose, pulling on the seat in front, then turning to the aisle.

"See you."

"See you," Colin said.

The singing continued; it had scarcely faded when they reached the town.

His parents were in bed when he got back home.

"Wherever have you been till this time?" his mother said.

205

"Playing," he said. "It was farther than I thought."

"I've been down to the bus stop twice."

"We went on a coach."

"If you went in a coach couldn't you get back before this time, then?"

He turned to the stairs.

"And don't wake Richard when you get undressed."

Moments later, however, after he'd reached his room, he heard the familiar wail from beyond the wall.

"God Almighty, isn't there any peace for anyone?" his father said, calling, from the darkness of their room.

"In decimals everything is measured in tenths, whereas in this country we have the privilege of measuring everything in twelfths, boy," Hodges said.

He leant his arm against the desk.

"What instances are there of the use of tenths in the monetary system, Saville?" he added.

"A ten shilling note." He shook his head.

"Do I hear a suffix to that remark?" he said.

"Sir," he said.

"A ten shilling note, then. Anything else?"

"A ten pound note."

"A ten pound note."

"Twenty shillings in the pound," he said.

"Walker: have you any examples you're eager to give?"

Small, light-haired, with a bright red nose, Walker, after a moment's hesitation, had shaken his head.

"No further examples forthcoming, then?"

Walker, once again, had shaken his head.

"What about the use of twelfths, then, Walker?" Hodges said.

"Twelve pennies in a shilling, sir," he said.

"Twelve pennies in a shilling. Brilliant. Anything else?"

"No, sir," Walker said.

"What about half-pennies, Walker?" Hodges said.

Twenty-four half-pennies in the shilling, sir," Walker said.

"Brilliant, Walker. Anything else?"

"No, sir."

"Are you quite sure, Walker?" Hodges said.

"Forty-eight farthings in a shilling, sir," he said.

"Walker, I can see, is coming out, very slowly, from his habitual coma," Hodges said. "What are you doing, Walker?"

"I'm coming out from my habitual coma," Walker said.

"And what word do we use to distinguish our system from the so-called metric system, Saville?"

"I don't know," he said. He shook his head.

"Did I not hear the suffix once again?" he said.

"Sir," he said.

"Saville doesn't know. Does anyone else? Walker, I suppose, this is far above your head?"

"What, sir?" Walker said.

"What do we call the system that uses twelfths instead of tenths?" he said.

"The Imperial system," someone said.

"Why Imperial, Walker?" Hodges said.

"Has it something to do with the king, sir?" Walker said.

"It might. Indeed, it might very easily, Walker," Hodges said.

He looked around.

"It comes, need I mention it to a class steeped already in the subject, from the Latin what?"

He paused.

"From imperialis. From imperialis. Meaning?"

"To do with kings, sir," someone said.

"Not to do with kings precisely. To do with authority, Stephens. *Command.*"

He took off his glasses and wiped them on his gown.

"Imperium: command, dominion. In other words, a system that, in this instance, has to do with empire."

"Yes, sir," Walker said.

"Certain unfortunate nations may use the decimal system because they have nothing better to fall back on, Stephens."

Stephens had nodded his head.

"Whereas we, in this country, and in those lands that constitute our empire, and our dominions, Stephens, use a measure which, for better or worse, is peculiar to ourselves. Peculiar, that is, to an imperial nation. Imperialis, imperium. To a nation which is used to authority, to dominion, Stephens. How many pennies in a pound?"

Stephens paused; he raised his hand. Then, finally, he lowered it and shook his head.

He was a pale, thin-featured boy; he sat immediately in front of Colin. His hair was thin and long, hanging in greasy strands across his narrow head. His back was bowed by some malformation. His legs were swollen round the knees as if in some peculiar way the upper and the lower parts had been bracketed together by artificial means.

"Two hundred and forty." Colin whispered behind his hand to the back of Stephens' head.

"What was that, Saville?" Hodges said.

Stephens' head had begun to tremble.

"Were you telling him the answer, Saville?" Hodges said.

"Yes," he said.

"Will you stand up, Saville?"

The class had turned.

"Your name is Saville, I take it?"

"Yes," he said.

"I haven't been deceived into assuming it was Saville, with or without a double 1, when all the time it was really Stephens?"

"No," he said.

"How many pennies in a pound, then, Stephens?"

"I don't know, sir," Stephens said and shook his head.

"You don't know, boy? For God's sake, how did you get into this school? A five-year-old child could tell me that."

Stephens bowed his head; he began to cry.

"Don't *blub*, Stephens," Hodges said. "I'm asking you a reasonable question. There's not one person in this class who couldn't answer it."

Several hands went up.

"Saville: can I have your record book?" he said.

He got out the book from his inside pocket, saw that Hodges expected him to walk down to his desk, and stepped out in the aisle.

"In your own time, Saville, of course. I can hardly expect your efforts to be directed to the convenience of someone else." He glanced at Stephens. "While I'm inscribing Saville's record for impertinence it will give you,

Stephens, several vital seconds in which to work out a suitable answer. And by suitable I mean of course, since our subject, I believe, is mathematics, a correct one. Have you understood that, Stephens?"

"Yes, sir," Stephens said. He bowed his head.

"The principle of learning, Saville, isn't that one should learn on behalf of someone else, but that one should do such learning as is required, in this establishment at least, on a wholly personal basis. How is one to learn anything if there is someone sitting behind you who is content to do it for you?" He opened the book. "I see you have a good record here. Geography, from Mr. Hepworth. That's hardly a credible first term's work." He wrote in red in the opposite column, the gesture exaggerated slightly to demonstrate his displeasure to the class. He blotted the book and then, not glancing at him but holding it out sideways and gazing absorbedly at Stephens, added, "And what conclusion have you come to, Stephens?"

Only after a moment was Hodges aware of the book still in his hand.

Stephens gave his answer, repeated it louder at Hodges's insistence, then the master said, "You may have your book back now, Saville."

"Thank you, sir," he said.

"Saville: would you come back here, boy," Hodges said.

Colin turned in the aisle, saw the redness rising, slowly, round Hodges's eyes, and went back to the desk.

"I've noticed my blandishments, Saville, carry very little weight. I detect an insolence in your manner which, the more I attempt to accommodate it, grows, it seems to me, from day to day. I shall ask the headmaster to speak to you. For one day at least I've had enough of your face. You'll put your work away and go and stand outside the door."

He replaced his books inside his desk, closed the lid and, without glancing at the others, crossed to the classroom door, opened it and stepped outside. The corridor was empty. He closed the door behind him.

He leant against the wall. An older boy went past. He glanced back at him down the length of the corridor, then, still gazing back, went on up the stairs at the opposite end.

The drone of a master's voice came from the classroom opposite. He could hear Hodges's voice coming quietly from behind, the occasional voice of a boy answering a question, the scraping of a chair, a desk. Other voices drifted down from adjacent rooms. He could hear the roar of a lorry passing in the road outside.

The door to the office opened; the secretary came out: her face reddened, almost cheerful, she started down the corridor past him. She carried several papers beneath her arm.

"Have you been sent out?" she said.

"Yes," he said.

"Is that Mr. Hodges's class?" she said.

"Yes."

She nodded, adjusted the papers beneath her arm, and went on down the corridor to the masters' common-room at the opposite end.

She re-appeared a few moments later, walking past without a gesture, her shoes echoing on the stone-flagged floor.

She went back inside her room and closed the door.

The school was silent. He could hear, from the farthest distance, the sound of a master's voice raised in anger, the calling of a name.

Laughter came from the room behind, then the sharp, hissing call of, "Sir, sir!" as Hodges waited for an answer.

Some further laughter came a moment later.

The door opened; a boy came out, glanced across, then went on down the corridor and out of the school door.

He came back a few moments later and went back in.

Colin waited. He tapped his feet slowly against the stone-flagged floor; he pushed himself gently against the wall.

The sound of footsteps descending came from the stairs at the nearest end.

A tall, gowned figure appeared in the corridor, silhouetted for a moment against the light. A face came into view, thickboned, large-featured; the hair above was short and dark: it stood on end and projected forwards over a massive brow. A heavy, broad-knuckled hand gripped several books.

Colin moved back to the door and stood beside it, his hands behind his back.

"What are you doing here?" the master said. He smelled of tobacco; his teeth were large and irregularly set inside his mouth.

"I've been sent out. For insolence," he said.

"What's your name?"

"Saville."

"What class is it?"

"Arithmetic," he said.

"That's Mr. Hodges's, I suppose," he said.

"Yes."

The man had paused.

"And what insolence is it, Saville?"

"For telling someone else an answer."

The master gazed down at him for a while, then shook his head.

"We don't care for insolence here," he said. "It gets you nowhere, and if you're missing a class you're missing out on work as well."

"Yes."

The man had frowned.

"Stand up from that wall," he said.

He stepped past him quickly and opened the door.

Hodges, caught in the midst of some appeal, had paused.

"There's a boy out here who says he's been sent out for insolence," he said. There was silence in the room beyond.

"That's perfectly correct, Mr. Gannen," Hodges said, his voice instructional, as if he were speaking on behalf of everyone in the room as well.

"I'd like to add to that, Mr. Hodges, loutish behaviour," the master said. "I find him standing here as if he'd been sent out specifically to prop up the building." He turned to Colin. "Shoulders back, chin in, hands behind your back," he called.

"I expect one or two people are going to see him standing there, Mr. Gannen," Hodges said. "I'm glad you've brought an additional impertinence to my notice."

"I'll be passing along again in one or two seconds," the master said. "I'll keep my eye on him and anyone else, for that matter, who thinks it's for wholly recreational purposes that he's sent outside."

He closed the door.

A murmur came from the room behind.

"One foot from the wall," the master said.

He adjusted the books beneath his arm and, without glancing back, went down to the common-room at the opposite end. The door was closed.

The room behind fell silent; faintly came the drone of Hodges's voice.

The door to the office suddenly opened.

The headmaster came out, glanced down the corridor, then went out of the door at the nearest end.

The door slammed shut.

Another boy went past.

A desk lid was banged in the room behind.

His shoulders ached.

A boy came out of the classroom opposite the office, went into the office, then came out with a bell.

He came along the corridor to ring it.

There was a shuffling of feet in the room behind. A door down the corridor suddenly opened: figures hurried out.

Hodges appeared at the door behind.

His head erect, he appeared on the point of walking past him.

"I've decided, Saville, to postpone any reference of your behaviour to Mr. Walker. Since Mr. Gannen is now acquainted with it, and since Mr. Gannen, as you are probably aware, is the deputy-head, I shall leave the situation for the present precisely where it is; namely, that I and Mr. Gannen have taken note of your insolent behaviour and any further expression of it will leave me with no alternative but to carry out my original intent. Have you understood that, Saville?"

"Yes," he said.

"You have my permission to go to your desk and collect your books for what I hope will be a singularly amicable lesson."

"Yes," he said.

Hodges swung away; his figure was caught up in those surging from the classrooms on either side.

He went back in the classroom and opened his desk.

"What did he say to you?" Stephens said.

"Nothing, really," Colin said.

"See here. Your school's been broken into," his father said.

He folded the paper up and ran his finger across the lines.

"Two hundred and forty pounds' worth of stuff's been stolen."

He read the paper intently for a while.

"They got in at the side through a broken window. They think it's somebody local, then."

"They'll break into anything, these days," his mother said. "No counting how much good they're doing. Hospitals, churches: you see it all the time."

"There's not many banks get broken into," his father said.

"No. Don't worry. They take trouble there."

"Can I go out now?" Colin said.

"Sithee, hast done all thy errands?" his father said.

"I think he has," his mother said.

"What about his homework, then?"

"I can do that tomorrow afternoon," he said.

"Thy's Sunday School tomorrow," his father said.

"Nay, let him go," his mother said.

She was worn and faded; since the birth of Richard there'd been a greyness in her face. When they went out to the shops she would say, "You'll have to take the basket, Colin. I can't bear lifting anything now." On washdays she would wait for him to come home from school and they'd spend an evening together in the kitchen, he lifting the water to the metal tub, plying the peggy stick up and down, sliding the tub to the grate outside. Other times, white-faced, she'd be sitting at the fire, the clothes half-washed, or standing at the sink, round-shouldered, the water cold, trying to wash the clothes by hand.

"Are you sure there's nothing he can do?" his father said.

"Nay, he's done enough for now," she said.

Colin went out to the backs; Steven, with one or two other children, was playing in the field.

"Now don't be late for your dinner," his mother said.

He went to the Dell. Smoke from the colliery hung close to the village.

It was beginning to rain. A stream of thick brown water ran along the beck; a cloud of black smoke drifted from the gas-works chimney. The metal container, full, loomed up mistily beyond the hedge.

The shed was locked. He loosened a panel and climbed inside; he lit a candle. Two black objects slid out beneath the door.

The stove was hot; he put on wood: flames licked up around the metal pipe.

There was a steady drumming, like fingers tapping, on the metal roof.

Then, from the direction of the sewage pens, came a low-pitched scream.

He picked up a stick.

A second scream sounded from the pens and then, moments later, he heard the sound of movements in the mud outside.

A key was turned in a lock, a chain removed; a metal bar was raised and the door pushed back.

Batty stood there, a box in his arms, gazing in.

"I've never locked you in, then, have I, Col?"

"I got in under the wall," he said.

"What wall?"

Batty looked round him at the hut.

"Nay, thy's never, then," He put down the box. "Dost make a habit of breaking in?"

"I'll mend it for you, if you like," he said.

"Nay, tha'll never."

Batty bent to the wood. He replaced the panel.

"Thy mu'n stay if thy wants to, I suppose," he said.

Colin sat by the fire.

"Thy mu'n stay and have some dinner."

"What dinner?" Colin said.

"I've got some grub." He gestured at the box.

"I'll have to get home for it," he said.

"I've got some other stuff, an' all." He gestured at the box again.

"What sort of stuff?"

Batty opened the box. He took out a piece of newspaper, unwrapped it and showed him a piece of meat.

"I wa' going to save it, tha knows. Until to-neet. Stringer's coming, and one or two more."

He took out a bottle.

"Gin," Batty said. "One drop o' this and tha's out like a leet."

"I'll try and get down tonight," he said.

"Tha can have a sup now, tha knows, if you like."

He began to unscrew the bottle.

"I'd better be getting back," he said.

He went to the door. Batty, the bottle in his hand, had followed him out.

"Sithee, then: here's to it," Batty said.

He raised the bottle, drank briefly, and began to cough.

"I'll see you later," Colin said.

"Tha's not running off just 'cos I've come in, then?" Batty said.

"No," he said.

He set off through the drizzles; a steady pattering came from the swamp. Smoke from the hut's fire hung in thin wreaths around the bushes. His feet were wet by the time he reached the road.

"You're back early. Dinner's not for another hour," his mother said.

"I thought I'd come back," he said, "to help."

"Help. Two mysteries in one morning," his mother said.

"Move up! Move up, boy," Gannen said.

Colin closed his eyes; he judged the curve of the track and ran more quickly. When he opened his eyes he found he was last: the remaining runners were strung out in a line ahead. Following Stafford's example in the previous race he ran quickly enough at the finish to get fifth place. "Bad luck, Saville," Macready said. A tall, thin man with a gingerish moustache, he stood by the finish writing names. "If you'd come up sooner you'd have got a place. First four go through, you know, to Saturday's final."

He walked away; he could see Gannen making towards him across the field.

"Saville." He waved his arm.

Colin turned towards him, making some display of the effort he'd made.

"You're a slacker, Saville. You could have come in easily second or third."

"I ran as fast as I could," he said.

"You ran as fast as you wanted. You're a slacker. You'll come to no good. What other events are you entered in?"

"The long-jump, sir," he said.

"I'll come and watch you in the long-jump, Saville. Do you understand that, boy?"

"Yes," he said.

"Aren't you in the relay, too?"

"No." He shook his head.

"You've got out of that as well, then, have you?" He took out a book and wrote inside. "I've put you back in the relay, and if you don't run as fast as you can you'll feel the weight of my foot behind you. Do you understand that, Saville?"

"Yes," he said.

"Two-thirty, Saturday."

Colin walked over to the pavilion. Stafford, his canvas bag beneath his arm, was coming out.

"What did Gannen want?" he said.

"He thought I didn't run fast enough," he said.

"What you've got to do is run as fast as you can," Stafford said, "but with a shorter stride. It's surprising how slow it makes you go."

He took out a comb and smoothed his hair.

"Are you running in anything on Saturday?" Colin said.

"Nothing," Stafford said. "I've got out of it all."

Calling to some boys he ran off, alertly, towards the ginnel.

Colin watched him go, then turned into the pavilion to find his clothes.

"That's more like it, Saville."

Colin went back to where he'd left his blazer and put it on.

"You've jumped well there, Colin," his father said. The remaining jumpers ran off in turn.

"Which is your mark?" his father added, straining between the figures in front to look at the wooden pegs driven in at the edge of the pit.

The masters stooped down; the crowd had drifted off.

"We mu'n stay and see where you've come in," his father said.

Gannen had turned.

A boy came past.

"You've come in third, Walters. And you've come in second, Saville," Gannen said.

"Second," his father said and, almost involuntarily, shook his hand. "What else are you racing in?" he added.

"The relay," he said for a second time, for he'd already explained the events at home.

"Sithee, then: you mu'n run well in that."

He went back with his father across the field.

They sat on a bank beneath a hedge. Other events had already begun. Immediately beneath them was the finishing line. Across the centre of the field lay a sprinting track, and to their right, by the pavilion, a high-jump pit.

A master with a loudspeaker announced each event.

"You mu'n tell me who everybody is," his father said.

Colin pointed out Gannen, who, a pencil in his hand and a sheaf of papers, was still standing by the jumping pit; he pointed out Platt, whom his father already knew, and then Hodges in his clerical collar, holding the tape on the running track with Macready.

"I suppose I know him, an' all," his father said.

Boys in white vests jogged slowly to and fro. Odd groups, at irregular intervals, set off around the track. Whistles blew; on a blackboard in the centre of the field numbers were chalked up and rubbed off again.

When the relay was announced he went down to the track. He ran from one corner of the field to the one adjacent to the finish. His team came second.

He went to the pavilion and got changed quickly; when he came out a little later his father was waiting at the gate. They walked together along the ginnel.

"Where's that other lad today?" his father said. "The one that doesn't like trying ought."

"He was eliminated earlier on," he said.

"Aye. I mu'n expect he was," his father said. "As bright as a new pin and twice as sharp."

When they reached the stop they stood in a queue of shoppers; boys from the school with their parents drifted past.

"It's a good school, all right," his father said.

"Why's that?"

"You can tell by the way they dress." He paused. "And the way they organize things," he added.

Colin waited.

"They get the best out of you, I can tell you that."

"Yes," he said.

"Not like where I wuk." His father laughed. "Where I wuk their number one aim is to put you under."

The bus drew up. They climbed upstairs. His father sank down in the seat beside him.

"Thy being at that school means everything to me. Whatever happens, I want you to know that, lad," he added.

14

There were pieces of machinery inside the shed, a work bench, a tyre from the tractor, a number of shovels and spades, a cluster of forks, and, leaning against the wall, the only unspoiled object there, a motor-bike.

"You're up bright and early," the foreman said. "Quarter to eight, I make it." He took out a watch from his waistcoat pocket. "Got your snap, then, have you?"

"Did you see the farmer?" he said.

"He said I could take you on." He added, "He'll be coming down here himself today."

"How much do I get?" he said. He'd been down the previous day to ask for a job.

"Nay, you mu'n not ask me, old lad." He put back his watch. "I'm t'on'y foreman here, tha knows. The me'ster'll tell you that himself."

Colin sat down on a pile of sacking at the door of the shed. The tractor stood in the rutted yard outside; a binder stood beneath an overhanging roof beyond. The sheds formed a tiny cluster in the middle of the fields, their roofs supported by baulks of timber—so low that when entering even he had to bow his head. Only where the binder stood were the roof beams any higher.

The foreman, having removed his jacket, had gone out to the tractor. He lit a piece of rag, put it in a hole at the front, and began to swing the handle.

Colin got up and went across.

"Nay, stand back," the foreman said. "This thing can give a kick when it begins to fire."

He swung the handle.

"It takes time to get warmed up, tha knows."

He swung again.

219

There was a low sucking sound from inside the engine. The foreman pulled out the piece of rag, stamped on it, then lit another. He flicked a lighter from his waistcoat pocket, put the blazing rag inside the hole, then quickly swung the handle, swung again, then stepped back sharply as the engine fired.

It puffed up a cloud of smoke from its vertical exhaust; a few moments later, after listening to the engine, he slowed it down and, wiping his hands on a cloth, came back across the yard.

"Is this a regular job, or just your holidays?" he said.

"The holidays."

"Tha's not been lakin' truant, then?"

"No."

"Here's Jack," he said as a man in overalls rode into the yard. He got off his bike and pushed it to the shed. "Yon rabbit's turned up: the one that came looking for a job," the foreman said. He added, "Mention work round here and you don't see many folk for dust."

The man had a long, thin face, with bony hands and arms; his hair was thin and cropped closely to his head. When he'd put his bike inside the shed he took off his jacket and opened a carrier bag hanging on the handle.

"I mu'n have me breakfast. I never had time this morning," he said.

He took out a sandwich, coming to sit by Colin on the pile of sacks.

The foreman had brought out a scythe from the back of the shed; its blade was wrapped in sacking bound on with lengths of string. He slowly unfastened it, drawing out the blade.

A third man had arrived; he was short, thick-limbed with bowed legs, and older than the other two. He came walking along the path that led off, by a hedge, across the fields. He too wore a cap and carried a small brown bag, fastened with string across his shoulder.

"Here's Gordon: better late than never," the second man had said. He finished his sandwich and put the remainder inside his carrier bag.

"We mu'n get yon binder oiled up, afore the me'ster comes down, Jack," the foreman said. He placed the blade of the scythe against the sacks and went back once more inside the shed; he came out with the binder's saw-toothed blade, wrapped, like the scythe had been, in sacking.

"I see yon young 'un's come," the bow-legged man had said.

He took off his cap and wiped his brow.

"By God, we mu'n see the corn dry early today."

He looked from the fields to Colin and back again.

"It mu'n be too early to go in yet," the foreman said. In addition to the binder's blade he'd brought out a small hand scythe which, sharpening on a stone, he brought over to the sacks.

"Dost know how to use one of these?" he said.

"Yes," he said.

"Then I've got just the job for thee."

He led the way across the yard. The tractor, puffing out its smoke, trembled on its massive tyres.

The foreman crossed the rutted track beyond the yard; they climbed a fence. A large field stretched down to a railway embankment; the grass was long; clumps of trees stood up in scattered copses. All across the field, in broad stretches, grew mounds of nettles.

Several horses were grazing by the fence.

"I want you to cut them down," he said, indicating the nettles. "You know how to use a scythe, I take it?"

"Yes," he said.

"Always cut away. Never cut towards."

The grass was damp; his feet, in walking from the fence, were already wet.

The foreman disappeared towards the yard.

He worked quickly; he looked round at the immensity of the field, counted the nearest clumps, and worked more quickly still.

The sun was hot. A thin mist which had lain over the fields when he'd first set off had faded; the heat came down from a cloudless sky.

The horses, as he worked near them, raised their heads; he fed one or two with clumps of grass.

A car came up the track; it went past the opening to the yard and continued along the track to a distant house.

A train went past; the horses raised their heads: one

221

of them began to gallop. It circuited the field: he could feel the ground tremble as it galloped past.

The car came back; he saw a fair-haired figure gazing out, then it turned into the road and disappeared.

Mounds of thistles and nettles were strewn out behind him now across the field; he switched the scythe to his other hand. The horses, their tails flicking at the heat, had moved into the shade beneath the trees.

The thumping of the tractor faded.

The foreman disappeared towards the yard.

He'd been working for about an hour when the foreman re-appeared. He called from the fence and waved.

When Colin reached the yard the bow-legged man was sharpening a scythe. The foreman was sharpening another; the binder and the tractor had disappeared. The second man was still sitting on the sacks. "Wheerst thy been, then?" he said, finishing a sandwich.

"Are you ready, Jack?" the foreman said.

"Aye, we're ready, Tom," the second man said. "I've been waiting here for hours."

They set off along a rutted track that ran round the back of the sheds. It followed the edge of a field, a metal fence on one side, marking off the grounds of a large stone house, wheat growing on the other. The crop had been blown down and flattened; as they walked along the foreman would stoop into the field and lift the stalks with the end of the scythe. Some of the heads were blackened.

"He'll not be pleased, will Smithy, when he s'es he's got black rot."

The other two men however took little notice as they walked along. The bow-legged man, the scythe on his shoulder, hung behind, talking to the bony man, who was still eating a sandwich, his carrier in his hand.

They came out on to a broad field which flowed off in an even wave to a near horizon; on the opposite side, at its lowest end, it ran up against a field of pasture, divided from it by a hawthorn hedge and by a copse of stunted, windswept trees.

"Here's the starting line, then, Gordon," the foreman said. "Up hill or down, whichever you choose."

"Am I having Jack, or the young 'un?" the bow-legged man had said.

"Nay, I'll have him with me to begin with," the foreman said.

"Then we'll have downhill." The bony man laughed, setting his bag and his jacket beneath the hedge.

They set off, then, in opposite directions, cutting at the corn. The bow-legged man scythed a track down the edge of the field, the taller man, stooping behind, binding up the corn in sheaves and propping them against the hedge. The foreman started up the slope, working for a while with casual strokes as if, absent-mindedly, he were sweeping a room.

After cutting several feet along the edge of the corn he came back to where Colin was picking up the strands.

He made one sheaf secure, then fastened another.

"Theer, then, have you got the hang of it?" he said.

He went back to the scythe.

To the weals and swellings on the backs of his hands were now added the cuts from the straw: thistles grew in clumps, threaded through with strands of wheat. Like the tall, bony man behind him, he leant the sheaves up against the hedge.

The heat had increased; they worked slowly up the hill.

"Soft hands, have you?" At intervals the foreman paused. "Shove 'em in salt water when you get home tonight."

The sun rose higher; soon the other two men were tiny dots at the foot of the field. Beyond, in the pasture, cows moved slowly against the hedge: a narrow lane wound off towards a distant line of houses, large, built of brick and shrouded by trees. In the farthest distance, beyond other corn fields, stood the long, broken-backed outline of a colliery heap, a column of smoke drifting off in a vast, black seepage overhead. Intermittently, clouds of steam shot up, as large as hills.

A car came along the track from the sheds; it raised a cloud of dust at the entrance to the field.

A man got out, red-faced, burly; he took off a trilby hat and wiped his brow, gazing up to where Colin and the foreman worked.

"Keep working. That's Smithy," the foreman said.

The figure, examining the sheaves, came along the hedge. Colin went on working until a voice called out behind.

"How's it going, Tom?"

"I think it's going all right," the foreman said. "We'll have it opened out, I think, tonight."

"Tha mu'n get round here in a day at least. This weather'll never last." The man had pale-blue eyes; his legs were jodhpured. He glanced at Colin and shook his head. "What's this twopence ha'pennyworth o' nowt?"

"This is Colin," the foreman said.

"How old are you, lad?" the farmer said.

"Eleven," Colin said.

"Tha mu'n be fo'teen if anyone asks." He looked to the foreman. "And how's he been working, then?"

"Oh, he's been all right," the foreman said. He winked to the farmer and nodded his head. "He's been cutting yon thistles. He's got half on 'em, I reckon, i' the back of his hands."

"He's not teking 'em home for fodder, is he?"

"Aye," the foreman said. "I reckon he shall."

"And how's that suit you?" the farmer said.

"Yes," he said.

"How long are you going to be with us, then?" he said. "Not here today and gone tomorrow?"

"I can stay till the middle of September," he said.

"Two months you can give us, then?" He glanced, half-smiling, at the other man. "We've gotten us a full-time workman, Tom."

"Aye, he mu'n see us in with the harvest," the foreman said.

The farmer glanced down at Colin's hands.

"Where do you live, then, lad?" he said.

"Saxton."

"By go, tha's got a long ride to get here, then." He looked down the field to the other men. "And what's thy surname?"

"Saville."

"Saville from Saxton. Well, I mu'n remember that." He turned to the foreman. "I'll drop in tomorrow and see you start."

He went down slowly, to the other men, examining the heads of the corn. He talked to the men for a while, then returned to the car.

They worked till lunch-time; covered in dust, they went back to the shed.

The foreman sat apart to eat his food; the bow-legged man and the tall, bony man sat across the yard. They talked between themselves, lying in the shade beneath a tree, the older man scarcely speaking yet laughing frequently at what the other one had said.

Colin sat on the sacks by the door of the shed. He drank the bottle of cold tea his mother had given him and ate the dried-egg sandwiches she'd made.

The foreman drew out his watch at one o'clock.

"Jack. Gordon." He got up slowly, lifting his scythe. He'd brought a thermos which he propped up by his bike. There was a smell of straw and grease from inside the shed.

The two men lay back beneath the tree.

"No rest for the wicked," the taller one had said.

They set off to the field. Clouds of dust rose from their feet as they walked along. They climbed the field.

By mid-afternoon, working slowly, they'd reached the top.

"There'll be an hour or two of overtime tonight," the foreman said. He took out his watch which, since he'd removed his waistcoat, he'd transferred to the waistband of his trousers. "Are you all right for an hour or two?" he said.

"Yes," he said. "As long as you like."

The foreman, throughout the day, had spoken little; when his back wasn't stooped to the scythe he was sharpening the blade, or, his gaze half-abstracted, he'd be staring back, watching the sheaf he was fastening, then nodding his head.

Colin, as he worked, was adding up the money he'd earn. Eight hours on the first day would be seventy-two pence. Seventy-two pence were six shillings. If he worked overtime for an hour he'd make another ninepence, plus fourpence halfpenny; if he worked overtime for two hours he'd make two shillings and threepence, bringing his wage for the day to over eight shillings. Even without overtime he'd calculated he could earn thirty-three shillings in a single week; it gave him a fresh energy the more he worked it out. He felt now he could work until it grew dark; once the mid-afternoon was passed the rest of the day had seemed downhill.

They worked till seven. It had taken them six hours of the afternoon and three hours of the morning to open up the field. He could hardly mount the bike when he got back to the sheds.

"Eight o'clock tomorrow," the foreman said.

"Don't come too early, now," the bow-legged man had said. He and the bony man had laughed. They stood talking by the sheds while the foreman locked the door. Finally the older of the two set off across the fields and the other rode off on his bike towards the track.

Colin cycled after him. As he reached the wooden gate which opened to the road the foreman went past on his motor-bike: he waved to the bony man and set off towards the distant houses.

At each of the hills Colin got off to walk. It was well after eight when he got back home. He'd been away from the house for over thirteen hours. He leant the bike against the wall and staggered in.

Steven, in his pyjamas, was standing by the fire; his mother, with a pair of scissors, was cutting his nails.

"Wherever have you been?" she said, her mouth opening then as she saw his state.

He caught a glimpse of his face in the mirror above the sink, red, almost crimson, streaked with sweat; his hair and eyebrows were white with dust.

"I'll be all right when I've had a wash," he said.

"But where have you been?"

"We worked overtime," he said.

The touch of the water against his hands began to fade. He rubbed the soap against his arms; he rubbed his face; he rinsed his head beneath the tap.

"Your meal's been waiting for hours," his mother said.

"Just put it on the table, then," he said.

"Well," his mother said. "Are you going to be home at this time every night?"

"Oh, I'll be all right," he said. "Once I've worked in I'll easily manage."

They cut the field the following day. The foreman drove the tractor, Gordon, the bow-legged man, sitting on the binder with its tall metal lever, watching the cutting of the blade, the binding of the sheaves, their slow, rhythmical ejection from the side of the machine. Colin and the tall, bony man stooked behind. They covered six rows of sheaves between them, carrying them in pairs and setting them in the stooks, eight pairs to each, angled slightly inwards to prevent them falling.

"Do you know what I'd do if I was in charge of this war?" the bony man had said. "I'd get a lot of animals, infect them with cholera, rabies, dysentery, beriberi, and drop them all over Germany every night. You wouldn't have to drop bombs, or anything, or have a thousand planes. You could go through the entire country in a week dropping down rats and mice on parachutes. Drop them near large towns, near rivers, and near farms, tha knows, at harvest-time."

He gazed round him as if imagining some such incident taking place in the surrounding fields.

"You could overrun the country inside a week. Tha'd have no opposition, tha knows, at all. They'd all be in hospital, or at home in bed. Hitler. There'd not be one of them fit to stand."

Later, when they reached the corner of the field, he lit a cigarette.

"Another thing I'd do, with these submarines. I'd drop an electric cable round their harbours at night, fastened up to the electricity, tha knows, with electric wires. And whenever one of them came out, or touched it, I'd switch it on. You'd see the buggers jump; they'd come up like freshboiled fish, tha knows: alive."

The bony man worked slowly. Frequently he would pause, gazing round, looking over to the tractor and binder as it cut against the wall of corn, stooping casually, despite his height, to hoist the sheaves, bending and straightening, the movement scarcely perceptible.

"You don't want to work too hard, tha knows. They'll still have to pay us if we're here at ten tonight."

They reached the bottom of the field: he could see into the copse. A pool of water lay in the shadow of the windblown trees; branches curled down beneath its surface. A dry dust rose from the sharp, cut-off stalks as they trudged between the rows of sheaves. A single row of stooks ran, parallel with the hedge, down one long side of the field.

They turned at the bottom. The tractor puffed slowly up the slope above them, stopping occasionally while the bow-legged man got down, cleared some obstruction from the teeth of the cutters, or rooted out some unfastened sheaf. Sometimes when the binder stopped all they could hear was the distant barking of a dog or the calling of some voice in the large house beyond the trees. It was usually at these moments that the bony man sat down in the shade of the hedge, lighting a cigarette, appearing for a moment to fall asleep, the cigarette smoking in his mouth, Colin working on, stooking the man's sheaves as well his own, the bony man rising as the tractor started or re-appeared over the crest of the slope.

A broad swathe now had been cut round the contour of the field. "How long to dinner, dost think?" the bony man said. He had no watch; he'd brought his carrier bag to the field and intermittently, after they'd advanced some distance, he'd go back to retrieve it from beneath the hedge and place it some little distance farther on. "I make it thirty-five minutes," he added, "by the sun. And I bet I'm correct within one or two minutes." He was continually watching the tractor now; each time it paused he raised his head, a sheaf in his hand, seeing whether the foreman was breaking off for lunch.

"He'll work through till one o'clock, will Tom. He doesn't much care for time, tha knows. I hope old Gordon reminds him, or we'll be stuck down here for hours."

And yet, only moments later, the tractor stopped. The clatter subsided: the puffs of blue smoke had disappeared.

The bow-legged man was already moving off across the field; the foreman himself was stooping to the binder.

"That's it! That's dinner!" the bony man said.

He retrieved his carrier bag and, half-running, half-walking, started off towards the track.

Colin, more slowly, followed on behind. By the time he reached the yard the bow-legged man and the bony man were already stretched out beneath the tree. It was some twenty minutes later before the foreman appeared along the track, going into the shed, with a spanner in his hand, comparing it with several others, coming out, his canvas bag across his shoulder, setting himself down in the open door, the shape of his motor-bike gleaming in the dark behind.

"I think I've fixed it now, then, Jack."

"I told you them nuts were on too tight."

They called across the yard for a little while.

"And how's your stooking going, kipper, then?"

"All right," Colin said.

"Not going too fast for yon loafer, then?"

"Who's a loafer?" the bony man had said.

"Don't set him up, Jack," the foreman said, "with any bad ideas."

"Nay, Jack doesn't have any ideas, Tom," the bow-legged man had said.

"I might get one or two from yon college-boy," the bony man had said.

They laughed.

At the end of the hour they went back to the field. The day was hotter than the one before. They worked uphill now, stooping to the slope. At one point the tractor halted and for an hour or more the foreman and the bow-legged man stooked the sheaves themselves.

"They won't be doing that for long," the bony man had said. "Get sat on that tractor and they don't like shifting off again."

The tractor re-started after a little while.

"Sithee: what did I tell thee?" The bony man sat determinedly in the bottom of the hedge while Colin worked on alone.

The farmer appeared in the middle of the afternoon. There were two other figures with him, a girl and a man in jodhpurs who carried a gun. The man with the gun and the girl strolled round the diminishing area of un-cut wheat, following the binder.

"After rabbits," the bony man had said. "They'll come out like flies when they get down to the last bit o' corn. I was hoping for one or two, tha knows, mesen."

The farmer, as he waited for the binder to come round, checked on some of the stooks himself, re-setting sheaves, lifting one or two up and adding them on.

"It's a good place to work, is this," the bony man said. "He's got two or three farms and he never stops for long. We're t'farthest away from t'farm itself. That's why he relies so much on Tom."

The gun went off; a puff of smoke rose up.

"He couldn't hit a rabbit if it sat on t'end on his barrel. That's Smithy's son. And that's his daughter. There might be summat theer for you." He laughed across. "Bit of all right, tha knows, is yon."

A little later when the two figures of the jodhpured man and the girl came closer Colin glanced across; he saw a fresh, red-cheeked face and fairish, auburn hair, and turned back to the sheaves, not looking up again until they'd passed.

After a little while the farmer left, the car with its three occupants bouncing off along the rutted track.

The day grew hotter.

They stooked a single row now, half-way up the slope: a side and a half and they would have circuited the field. They met the unfinished row the foreman and the bow-legged man had started, and went to work then across the top of the field.

"It'd be too much to reckon that he'd bring summat for us all to drink," the bony man had said. "Last farm I worked at the farmer's wife wa're out all day: glasses of ale, and ginger pop. It was a pleasure to work, I can tell you that."

The indications of a tennis court were visible amongst the distant gardens: white-clad figures moved to and fro; the faint noise of a ball being hit came floating to the field.

Several aircraft passed overhead; they were too high in the sky to see. A vapour trail had formed, and then another: a thin striation of white marks, like veins, faded against the blueness overhead.

He worked with a regular rhythm now; the lightness he'd felt in the morning had already gone, replaced by a cautious calculation of how many hours of the day were left. They worked without speaking, the bony man taking fewer rests, crouching, when he did so, in the shade of a stook, or lying sprawled out in the shade of the hedge, calling out then, half-mockingly, if Colin paused.

"Nay, don't let him see you resting, lad. I'm the gaffer, tha knows, down here."

The farmer came back: the three figures got out of the car. It was growing late.

The tractor paused on the upward slope and the foreman got down from the seat, the three figures then standing by the binder.

"He'll not keep us on overtime," the bony man said. "He'll just keep Tom and Gordon back. He'll send us two off packing."

And a little later, with the band of uncut corn now like a narrow path down the centre of the field, the farmer, waving, had signalled them across.

"That's us done for. We could have had two hours, at least."

At the far end of the field the younger man with the gun had given a shout.

A rabbit, its legs kicking, was bowled over as it ran.

A second rabbit broke away: a small bundle of fur darting away across the low-cut stalks.

The young man fired again: the ball of fur flew up, kicking, then, with a sudden convulsion, fell over on its side.

"You two can get off now. It's just after five," the farmer said. "We'll finish cutting tonight and start stooking first thing tomorrow morning. There'll be too much dew to start cutting then."

He was holding the rabbit by its ears; a stream of blood ran from its mouth.

"And how're you making out, young man? Got the hang of it, have you, or is Jack here having to do it all for you?"

"Oh, he does one or two bits and pieces, Mr. Smith," the bony man had said.

The girl, her face reddened by the sun, had glanced across; she was standing half-way to the car, looking down the field towards her brother.

She pulled back the hair from her eyes, calling, and pointing down to the uncut corn.

The younger man had fired again.

"We mu'n have us a good bag today," the farmer said. Jack, his carrier beneath his arm, had gone ahead.

He'd already reached the track and was dusting off his clothes as he walked along. He lit a cigarette as he reached the trees, cupping his hand; a breeze, light, blowing in faint gusts, had suddenly sprung up.

The young man, sighting the gun, had fired again; the bow-legged man on the binder was pointing to the corn. A dog in the back of the car had begun to bark.

The girl, hearing it, turned back.

"Don't let it out, Audrey," the farmer said. "We mu'n keep it till we're down to the last few yards."

Colin reached the track. The girl, flushed by the heat, was standing by the car, holding the door and talking to the dog.

She glanced up as he passed.

"What kind of dog is it, then?" he said.

"A collie."

She glanced up again, quickly, then called sharply to the dog.

She had a thin rash around her neck: it showed on her arms below the short-cut sleeve of her blouse.

"Is he good for rabbiting?" he said.

"Not really. No."

She opened the car door and caught the dog's collar as it tried to rush out.

Half-stooping, still holding the dog, she walked back across the field.

Colin turned to the track. He could see into the car: cartridges, a flask, several metal mugs and a white cloth wrapped round what looked like sandwiches.

He went on, dusting down his clothes, towards the sheds.

The field had been cut when they got back the following day, the sheaves strewn in rows across the contour of the hill. Colin worked with the foreman at the bottom of the field. The stooks stood up like little houses, the tyre-marks of the tractor leaving silver-coloured streaks across the stubble.

"How many rabbits did you get last night?" he said.

"Four." The foreman laughed. "Though going by the commotion you'd have thought it wa' nearer twenty."

"How many hours' overtime did you get?" he said.

232

"And what's that to do with you?" The foreman laughed again. "Eager for more work, then, are you?"

Yet later, as they walked back to the sheds, he added, "As it is, we could have done with you staying on last night. We've another field, tha knows, to cut tomorrow. We mu'n stay behind and oppen out."

Yet after lunch Colin and the bony man were working in the field alone: the foreman and Gordon had set off to the second field. Relieved of supervision, the bony man spent longer spells beneath the hedge, stepping out of its shade at intervals, quickening the pace when he saw the comparatively few that, working alone, Colin himself had done.

"They'll expect us, you know, to get more on than this."

The intervals of moving up and down the field got shorter; more than half of it was stooked. The heat, in the centre, was greater than it was on the track or working round the edge, the ground dustier, the scent of the straw more overpowering. His clothes were sodden now with sweat. After their first hardening, his hands had begun to bleed again.

A group of boys had come to play in the copse at the foot of the hill. He'd seen them earlier, coming down the track from the direction of the house beyond the trees; they were carrying a dinghy which, after they'd raised it over the hedge at the bottom of the field, they lowered on to the pond. For an hour he heard their cries, seeing the flashing of the water: splashed columns of it were sprayed up at intervals beneath the trees. Finally, when he and the bony man had reached the hedge, he glanced across.

A small island stood in the centre of the pond: it was overgrown with brambles. A large nest was built near the water's edge. There was a smell of decay from the copse itself.

The boys were paddling the dinghy towards the island; there were three of them, two in costumes, one of whom, as Colin watched, plunged into the water and, to the shouts of the other two, began to push the dinghy vigorously before him, spraying the two still in the boat.

One of them, in shirt sleeves and shorts, he recognized as Stafford; he was standing in the middle of the dinghy

233

directing the other boy who, bare-chested, was fanning the oar ineffectually at the water.

"To your left. Left," Stafford called to the boy, who was spraying them with his feet behind.

They scrambled ashore as the dinghy reached the bank, Stafford leaning up to grasp a branch. He held the boat while the other boy climbed out. The third figure, still in the water, was slowly clambering to his feet: black mud stains marked his shoulders.

Stafford, releasing the branch and taking the paddle, pushed off the dinghy into the middle of the pond.

"Ay! Neville," the other two had said. "*Ay, Neville*," they called, "come back."

Stafford leaned on the oar, still standing. His laughter echoed beneath the branches of the copse.

"Ay! You rotter," the two boys called.

The whiteness of their legs and bodies showed up against the darkness of the trees behind.

"Ay, Neville. Bring it back."

Stafford pushed the oar into the pond, found the bottom, and pushed the dinghy on.

"Ay, Neville."

The boat rocked with the momentum of Stafford's laughter. The two boys began flinging spray across.

"Ay, Nev. Bring it back."

Stafford shook his head, kneeling in the boat, still laughing.

"It's too muddy to get back," the boys had said.

"Swim, then," Stafford said.

"It's too shallow," one of the boys had said.

Stafford got up; he wiped his eyes.

"Go on, you rotter: bring it back."

"Come and fetch it."

"Go on, Nev: be a sport," they said.

"How much is it worth?" he said.

"How much do you want?"

"How much have you got?"

"Go on: we've got nothing." They gestured at their trunks.

Stafford, having reached the bank, had sat down by the boat.

"Go on, Nev. Be a sport."

Perhaps Colin had moved, or one of the two boys on the island had glanced across.

Stafford turned: for a moment he gazed up, confused. He shielded his eyes.

"Hi," Colin said. He nodded his head.

Still confused, Stafford got up; the two boys on the island had called again.

"Who is it, Nev? Come on, then, bring it back."

"Oh, it's you, then," Stafford said, his voice quiet now and suddenly flat. "What're you doing here?" he added.

"I'm working," he said. He gestured to the field behind.

"What at?"

He gestured to the field again.

"Stooking," he said.

"What for?"

"Money."

Stafford turned to the boat; he scarcely glanced at the field at all.

"Are you working, then?"

He nodded his head.

"I'll see you, then." He climbed into the boat. He pushed it off.

From the field, the bony man had called: the car, in a cloud of dust, was bouncing along the track from the direction of the sheds.

He went back across the field and was already stooking, stooping to the sheaves, by the time the car pulled up and the farmer, with the foreman and the bow-legged man, climbed out.

They worked into the evening; the farmer stooked as well. At six o'clock he went to the car and got out a flask of tea. They sat in the shade of the hedges, drinking the tea from metal mugs and eating sandwiches which he'd also brought.

Earlier, shortly after the arrival of the car, Stafford and the two boys had emerged from the edge of the copse, carrying the boat between them. They'd glanced over to where he and the four men worked, Stafford walking some distance ahead, the two boys gazing over, Stafford scarcely glancing once he'd reached the track. He disappeared beneath the trees in the direction of the house, the two boys, white-skinned against the shadows, labouring to lift the boat across the fence. "Nev? Nev," he heard them call.

It was growing dark by the time he got back home. The bike had no lamp; he cycled in the coolness, his eyes half-closed. A new momentum had taken over his life. All he could think of now were the lines of stooks, the glimpse he'd had, in the half-darkness, of the field they would work the following day, the stooking of the first field now completed; having washed off the sweat and dust, he went to bed, brushing aside his mother's complaints, his father's questions.

He sank down in a daze and fell asleep.

He worked for seven weeks at the farm; eight fields were opened up, cut, stooked: men from another farm came with a red-painted thresher driven by a tractor with a fly-wheel as large as the rear wheels themselves. Once he saw the two boys who'd been wearing costumes cycling along the track that led from the large house past the sheds to the near-by road; they gave no sign; both had auburn hair and whistled cheerfully to one another as they pedalled past. On other days occasionally, he could hear their shouts coming from beyond the trees that surrounded the house.

The corn was threshed; at the end of the seventh week, late on Saturday after working overtime, the farmer told him he wouldn't be needed again.

"Not that I couldn't use you, mind. But I've no more fields to cut round here."

He gave him his money as he left the field.

The following day he set off on the bike again; he visited the farms he'd been to before. He found new ones farther afield, but late that evening, cycling home, he'd passed a field only a few miles from the village where a tractor and binder were working with no one stooking, and he had gone to the farm building a few hundred yards away and got a job to start the following day.

The farm stood at the foot of a hill; a stream ran past its door; a footbridge led across the stream to the farm-house itself: the farmer's name was also Smith.

"Tha mu'n be on thy own," he said, "unless I can get som'body in by tomorrow. I've two fields cutting and nob'dy to stook," and yet, the next morning, when he started work, two men in dark brown uniforms were standing by the gate: one was tall and thin, with long, black hair, the other small and broad-shouldered, with blond hair cut short, and colourless eyes.

"This is Fritz," the farmer said, indicating the shorter of the two, "and this is Luigi," he added. He indicated the other man, who stooped down and shook his hand. "They're prisoners of war, so if they try to escape you'll let me know." The farmer laughed, the two strangely contrasted prisoners laughing with him. "They've to be back in camp, tha knows, by six, so if there's any hanky-panky tha mu'n march 'em to the gate." He turned with a wink, thickening his accent. "They're all right," he added, "I've had 'em afore: but tek no notice of the way they wuk."

He spent the next two weeks working with the Italian and the German. The former had been a soldier, captured in the desert, the other a pilot shot down in southern England. They spoke, in his presence, a made-up language of signs and gestures, but whenever he was alone with either one they spoke English fluently with a slight, half-mocking, thickened accent.

His father had cycled past the field one day. Colin saw him leaning by the hedge, his bike propped up against the gate.

He went across, slowly, wiping his face.

"This is where you work, then, is it?"

The field was up the road from the farm, on the lower slope of an adjoining hill. In the farthest distance, in a clear day, were visible the buildings of the town, the cathedral spire, the wedge-shaped tower of the town-hall. Now, with the day overcast, all that was visible was the broad sweep of the field itself.

"That's thy two prisoners, is it?" His father gazed down the field, between the stooks, to where the tall Italian and the stocky German were lifting sheaves, arguing, flinging them down. Sometimes they'd dismantle a stook in fear that one of their own sheaves had been incorporated by the other; they always worked separately, but never far apart.

Even as his father watched they had begun to quarrel. "You no good."

237

"*You* no good."

"You bad."

"*You* bad."

"*Schweinhund.*"

"*Bastard.*"

They started fighting, their gestures as stylized as their conversation.

His father laughed: he watched them with a slow amazement, the tall, boneless figure of the Italian coiling and uncoiling around the squat, muscular outline of the fair-haired German. "Sithee, then." He wiped his eyes. "It's a wonder they do any work at all," he said.

"I do nearly all of it," Colin said. It was really the stooks he wanted his father to see, the straightness of the rows, the way they ran down the profile of the field. His father smiled.

"I can see they've got their heads screwed on," he said.

The two figures now were rolling on the ground: they disappeared behind the sheaves, re-appeared for a moment, the German on top, then, a moment later, the Italian.

"Don't they ever have a guard?" his father said.

"I've never seen one," Colin said.

"They mu'n escape, tha knows, if they don't watch out."

"I don't think they want to," he said, and shook his head.

The prisoners' camp was a mile up the road. He'd cycled past it one evening, on his way to Saxton: rows of wooden huts ran back from the road, surrounded by barbed wire and overgrown hedges. Only one soldier was visible, stooping down by a car, in his shirt-sleeves, examining its engine.

"Do they spend all day doing that?" his father said.

"They work sometimes, I suppose," he said. "I don't suppose they have any need to, though," he added.

"Nay, they've been caught fighting this country, lad. I hope thy's not forgotten it," his father said.

The two men now were standing up; one was dusting down the other's clothes; then, as a final gesture, ceremoniously bowing to one another, they both shook hands.

"They might be all right on a stage, but this is a war-effort they're supposed to be helping." His father gestured to the fields around. "Every bit done here leaves space in a ship."

He gripped the gate between his hands.

"If they mu'n not help the ones who're looking after them they mu'n lock 'em up: that's my view," his father said. A sudden smile, nervous, half-expectant, crossed his face as the two men, seeing him by the gate, called to Colin and came across.

"This is my father," Colin said, and added, almost as a provocation, "He's come to see you work."

"Work?" The broad, tanned face of the German turned to gaze up at the long, mournful face of the Italian beside him.

"Work?" the Italian said, imitating the German's accent.

"We leave all the work to Colin, Mr. Saville," the German said, his accent now so casual that his father looked at him in some alarm, almost as if, mentally, he'd stood to attention and begun to salute.

"Aye, he works very hard," his father said, glancing at the field. On numerous occasions since his first week of work, his father had said, "They're paying you a boy's wages for a man's work: I know what bargains these farmers get." Now he added, "The only trouble is people take advantage of how hard he works," and repeated "advantage" as if uncertain that the German had understood his meaning.

"Oh, we help him all we can," the German said, and added, "We help Colin all we can, Luigi. Help."

"Help," the Italian said, bowing slowly to his father, his dark eyes examining him now in some confusion.

"Back to work, Luigi," the German said, and added, "Work."

The Italian bowed; he examined his father a moment longer then turned back slowly towards the field.

"I suppose you have to make allowances," his father said. "If we were prisoners on the other side I don't suppose we'd work too hard. They do summat, I suppose," he added.

He turned to the bike.

"I'll leave you to it, then," he said.

Colin watched his father ride off along the lane; he could

see him some time later, riding along the road that led off across the fields, his small figure stooping to the bike, unaware perhaps that he was still visible from the field for he never looked back.

"Your father is a farmer, too?" the German said when he went back to the sheaves.

"A miner."

"A miner?" He added, "He's not a farmer, Luigi. He works underneath the ground." He made a shovelling motion with his hand, pointing down, then fanning his hands out slowly either side.

"Ah," the tall man said. He spoke in Italian for several seconds.

"Luigi says: does he dig for gold?"

"For coal," he said.

"Coal," the German said. He added, "Carbon."

"Ah," the Italian said again and with a mournful gesture shook his head.

"And when you grow older, will you become a miner, too?" the German said.

"No."

"What will you become?" His light-blue eyes gazed steadily at him.

"I haven't decided yet," he said.

"A farmer?"

"No," he said.

"A soldier?"

He shook his head.

"Will you leave your beautiful land? Will you travel the world?" he said.

"I don't know," he said.

"Never go to Italy. Italy bad," the German said.

"Germany bad," the Italian said.

"Go to the Mediterranean," the German said. "Blue seas, blue skies." He gestured around. "Nothing at all like you have it here. Go to Africa. Go to *Greece*. But not to Italy. Italy bad."

"Germany bad," the Italian said and, as Colin stooped to the sheaves, the two men fought again.

He worked at the second farm until two days before he started school. He called at the farmhouse in the evening to collect his wage. The door to the kitchen had been standing open; the farmer's wife was baking at a stove inside.

She was a small, stoutish women, her face inflamed from the heat of the fire. On some evenings, when they were working overtime, she'd come to the field with tea and scones, bringing the tea in a metal jug. Already sweetened and mixed with milk. Now she came across with a large round cake.

"I've baked this for you, love. Just something to remember us by."

"He lives on fresh air, this lad," the farmer said. "Just look at his muscles. He's grown a foot with us at least."

The cake was slipped into a paper bag. He put it in his own bag, along with the wage.

"And he's kept a guard on them prisoners an' all," the farmer added.

"Has he?" The farmer's wife came to the door to see him off.

"He's been a right good officer," the farmer called, half-hidden in the shadow of the kitchen.

From the footbridge he glanced back at the farm: the farmer himself had appeared at the door.

"If thy ever wants a job you must come back here again," and still stood there, waving, when he reached the road.

15

"How much did they pay you?" Stafford said.

He told him about the farm, and then the prisoners.

"I don't do much work during the holidays," Stafford said. He added, "I was over there, you know, for the day. I know the Thorntons. They live in that house beyond the trees."

He walked beside him, his canvas bag hitched up beneath his arm. He whistled for a moment between his teeth.

"Are you playing football this term?" Colin asked him.

"I've been injured this week." Stafford shook his head. "I'll probably come in later. It hasn't been arranged."

When they reached the turning to the station, Stafford had added, "I'll come down to the bus stop, if you like. I'll be catching the later train tonight."

They walked through the narrow alley and into the town-centre. Crowds of boys were moving down from the direction of the school, joined by groups of uniformed schoolgirls.

Stafford had called across at one point; two girls, on the opposite side of the street, had waved. One girl had called out, pointing back in the direction of the station.

Stafford smiled and shook his head.

"Look at that," he said. He indicated a shop window, catching Colin's arm. "What do you think?"

A wooden plaque of the school's coat-of-arms was set in the centre of the window, beside it a tray of coloured scarves.

"Some of those look pretty nifty." Stafford leaned to the window, gazing in, his head against the glass.

He moved to the door, holding it open.

242

An elderly shopkeeper inside had already looked up; he appeared to recognize Stafford for he came out quickly from behind the counter.

"And what can I do for you?" he said as Colin followed Stafford in.

"We'd like to look at the scarves," Stafford said. "The ones in the window." And when the shopkeeper brought them over, sliding the glass panel at the back of the window and lifting them out, Stafford had added, "Not the school's, Mr. Wainwright: those civilian ones," laughing then at his own expression.

"The civilian ones," the shopkeeper said, beginning to smile himself.

They were made of silk; he spread them on the counter.

"And have you got your coupons, sir?" he said.

"Do you need coupons for one of these, then?" Stafford said.

"I'm afraid so." The shopkeeper shook his head.

"What have you got without coupons?" Stafford said.

"Well, any number of things," the shopkeeper said. "Tie-clips, for instance. Do you fancy those? I take it," he added, "it's for a present."

"Yes," Stafford said, and glanced across.

A tray of tie-pins was laid before him.

"What do you think to that one?" Stafford said.

He picked it out.

It was a silver-coloured tie-pin shaped like a feather. Its image, Colin saw, was that of a quill. A tiny nib was fashioned one end.

"Do you like it?"

"Yes," he said, impatient now to get to the stop.

"I'll take that one, Wainwright," Stafford said and from his inside pocket drew out a wallet.

"That's rather an expensive one," the shopkeeper said.

"I thought it might be," Stafford said.

He laid out the money.

"Could you wrap it up?" he said. "Decently, I mean. In a sort of box."

Outside the shop Stafford glanced at his watch and added, "Are we late for your bus? What time does it leave?"

"If I hurry," he said.

"We'll run for it in that case," Stafford said.

They ran through the centre; at one point, for a while, they ran on the road, Stafford dodging the traffic and keeping abreast.

"Keep running: I'll keep up," he said.

The bus was waiting when they reached the stop. Stafford stood beside Colin as the queue climbed on.

Then, close to the door, he said, "Here you are, then. I hope you can use it."

He thrust the parcel into Colin's hand.

"Go on. Take it. You'll never get on."

And when he hesitated he thrust it to his hand again.

"See you tomorrow," Stafford called, already moving off along the pavement.

He saw Stafford's head, its fair hair conspicuous amongst the crowd, moving swiftly up the hill, back towards the city centre: he watched a moment longer then, as the crowd moved on, the fair-haired figure disappeared.

He opened the parcel when he got back home.

"That's beautiful. Wherever did you get that?" his mother said.

"It was a present," he said, and added, "From a friend at school."

"It isn't your birthday yet," she said.

"I know," he said. He shook his head.

"Do they give presents to you, then, like that?"

"Yes," he said. "I suppose they do."

"Have you bought him one, in that case, then?" she said.

"No," he said. "I suppose I shall."

"Well, love," she'd added, "make sure you do."

He didn't see Stafford at school the following day; he went to his classroom at the afternoon bell: everyone had left. He walked down to the station: there was no sign of Stafford on the platform.

On the Monday he only saw Stafford briefly, from a distance, leaving the field at the end of break; he didn't run after him or call across. The next time they met was on the Tuesday afternoon: Stafford was coming out of the pavilion, already changed. He waved across, calling, and trotted casually across the field.

He never mentioned the present again. Colin scarcely wore it; he clipped it on to his tie occasionally on Sundays; he went to the Crusaders now in the afternoon, still with Bletchley, and less frequently with Reagan, who, since his failure in the exam, had been often ill.

Bletchley wore a suit on Sundays; over the previous year he had worn his school uniform to church but as it faded it had been replaced by a suit of dark-grey cloth with long trousers and a double-breasted jacket. Both he and Bletchley as well as Reagan were in the same Crusader group; a banner with the device of a fish was clipped to the end of their pew. The vicar took the service: small, portly, with thick-lensed glasses, he spoke with his head inclined towards the ceiling, waiting for each word to echo before he called the next: "I . . . *I*—shall . . . *shall*—wait . . . *wait*—here . . . *here*—for . . . *for*—si . . . *si*—lence . . . *lence*. He sang loudly, standing by the pulpit, sometimes disappearing behind the varnished pews to the organ, where, through an angled mirror, he could watch the groups below.

With no Mr. Morrison to talk to Bletchley would frequently fall asleep; he would prop his arm on the end of the pew, immediately beneath the banner, and with his head against his hand, his face shielded, he would assume an attitude of rapt attention; in the shadows of the church, and beneath the extended shield of his hand, it was impossible to tell that he wasn't listening; even when the vicar called for the answer to some question he would put up his hand, slowly, instinctively, half-dazed, having to be roused, cautiously, if he was asked specifically to answer.

Reagan had grown taller over the previous year; he too, in response to Bletchley's challenge, had taken to wearing long trousers; they emphasized his now almost skeletal figure with its massive, bulbous head. Occasionally he could be seen walking across the backs, his hands in his pockets, glancing in windows and open doors and recoiling abruptly whenever someone called. He had been moved to a private school in the city, and each morning his mother took him to the station to catch the train, waiting for him on the platform of the village station each evening and walking back up to the village with him, hand in hand.

"They mu'n be getting married soon," his father said whenever he saw them pass the window. "Reagan's not got a look-in where yon lad's concerned."

"It's because he's sensitive," his mother said. "He's always been sensitive, even as a baby. She's always had to look after him," she added.

"He'd be less sensitive if he'd had a boot up his backside," his father said. "I'd de-sensitize him inside a week if I had him in this house."

"Oh, we know how sensitive you are," his mother would add.

"Sensitive? I'm sensitive to ought," his father said. "I'm more sensitive than yon streak o' whitewash."

"Yes: and we know that, Colin, don't we, love? We know how sensitive your father is," she'd tell him.

"I'm sensitive enough to work in that pit," he'd add.

"Are you?"

"And give you a decent living."

"Do you?"

"And you can't get more sensitive," he'd say, "than that."

Steven had started school. He spent a lot of his time now out of the house, coming in at meal-times. But for the fact that they slept together Colin would scarcely have seen him. His brother had a pale, feather-like existence: built broadly like himself, he floated from one interest to another, running constantly from one demand to another, from one group of boys to another, his laughter frequently, whenever he was excited, filling the backs, a loud, harsh, almost hen-like cackle.

The baby he scarcely noticed. It was almost standing, prematurely, straight-backed, its tiny legs thrust out, its eyes light blue; it had a ferocious, almost obsessive energy; if it wasn't watched it would crawl out to the yard, and once in the street, finding its way to the street, on some occasions to the Battys' kitchen, on others across the field to the street the other side. His mother would endlessly be endeavouring to restrain it, her cries of vexation ringing round the house while Colin in his room would be trying to do his work, calling down to her in the end, "Mother, I can't work if you go on shouting."

"And what am I suppose to do? Talk to it in sign language?" she'd call from the stairs.

"I just can't work with all that noise."

"Richard, come here!" she'd shout, distracted immediately by the child again.

He took it for walks occasionally on Sunday mornings. Sometimes, if he had nothing better to do, Bletchley came with him; they would go to the Park.

"The Park and nothing else," his mother would say. "I might be walking out that way and I'll be popping in to have a look."

"You could take him in that case, then," he'd say.

"Harry," his mother would call, "can you hear the way he talks?"

"Just hold your tongue when you talk to your mother," his father would add.

"It's that I feel silly pushing out the pram," he said.

"And you'd feel silly doing some of the things I've had to do," his father would call, invariably, during these incidents, preoccupied in some other room of the house.

"Why can't we just leave him in the yard?" he would ask his mother.

"Because he never stays in the yard," his mother said. "In any case, I would have thought you'd have been proud to take your brother out."

"Well, I'm not," he said, yet beneath his breath, afraid of the retribution this sentiment might bring.

"I don't know why you have to bring him," Bletchley would add, kicking the wheels of the pram as they walked along.

Yet, despite his resentment, he and Bletchley and Richard, and sometimes even Steven, continued to go to the Park on Sunday mornings. Groups of other children would be wandering there, girls from Bletchley's school with whom Bletchley himself exchanged insults and occasionally, whenever he could get near them, blows. It was the prospect of seeing the girls from the school which took them there and which, later, sustained them during the tedious hour and a half of Sunday School; afterwards, freed of the pram, they would wander round the paths of the Park, and occasionally along the tracks that led across the fields beyond, following diminutive, skirted figures who, to Bletchley's taunts and jeers, would frequently, turning, call insults of their own: "Fatty," and "Belcher," and "Who's your friend, then, Belch? Hasn't he got his pram?"

Bletchley gave him glowing accounts of his life at school, of episodes in the bushes which surrounded the building, a converted manor, and of even more lurid incidents which took place in the actual rooms. It was a long way from King Edward Grammar, and even farther from the impression he got of Bletchley himself, who, by reputation, was as actively despised at school as he was in the village; he felt a strange loyalty to his friend, his portly figure, and felt drawn to defend him whenever, in Bletchley's presence, he was ridiculed or attacked.

"Belcher's all right," he would say to Batty who, whenever he saw the gargantuan figure, would immediately run after him shouting, "Show us your knee-caps, Belch," or, "Lend us half your suit."

"He's all right: he's all right as an advertisement for plum-puddings," Batty would tell him, adding on one occasion, "Do you want a fight or something? If I want to shout after Belch I bloody shall."

They'd fought then for half an hour; the fight had drifted from the street: they fought in the yard of a house and then the field. He fought Batty as if he had been preparing for it now for years; he felt calm, preoccupied, self-possessed, hitting Batty strongly, refusing to be bound up in his looping arms. Blood came out on Batty's face; he was aware of Batty's brothers coming to the field, and of other figures standing in the yard and along the fences. Reagan's voice called out: "Hit him, hit him harder," his waistcoated figure collarless, red-faced, standing by the fence.

Batty finally had pinned him to the floor, beating him about his eyes and mouth: he flung his fists up at the reddened figure but Batty knelt casually above him, out of reach.

"Go on, go on, our kid," his brother called.

Batty got up. Aware of his brothers' shouts he paused. He wiped his mouth on the back of his hand.

"Go on, bash him," his brothers called.

Batty turned aside; he glanced back at Colin briefly as he got to his feet, then went on towards his house.

"Go on, bash him," his brothers callel.

"Nay, he mu'n have fought him fair." His father had come out from the house and stood by the fence.

Reagan had already turned towards his door.

"He fought fair: you can't say better than that," his father called.

Farther along the terrace he saw Batty climbing the fence.

"Thy ought to have beaten him," his father said. "Go under his guard, not try and stand outside. With fellers like that you've to go beneath."

"I suppose you're satisfied," his mother said, standing at the door as they reached the house. "And what was it all about?" she added.

"Nothing," he said.

"It looks like nothing. Just look at your eyes: they're almost closed."

"Nay, they'll come up like two beauties," his father said.

"And look at your mouth," his mother cried.

"He'll not be speaking tomorrow either." His father laughed. "See nowt, and say nowt: we mu'n have a bit o' peace at last."

Yet later he'd added, before he went to work, stooping to his boots to pull them on, "You must go under his guard when you've somebody big. Take my word for it, I ought to know. Hitting up you can hit much stronger."

He got up in his work clothes and, despite his pit boots, began to dance around. "Left, left, then right. One, two, then bring it over. If you'd have taken a bit more notice you'd have been all right."

He was still talking about the fight when he went to work, pedalling off slowly across the yard.

"All wind," his mother said. "Don't take any notice of your father in your fights."

He heard his father's voice then his mother's, then Steven's feet as he ran through the passage. A moment later, as if antagonized by the commotion, the baby began to cry.

He went through to his parents' bedroom and looked down at the street. A red-painted bicycle with white mudguards was propped against the fence; it had a dynamo and electric lights, its handlebars curved down with rubber grips.

He heard his father's strange, half-strangled tone in the passage below, then his mother's almost formal accompanying tone, then, in response to some remark or gesture on their visitor's part, a sudden burst of laughter.

"Come in. Come in, lad," his father said and almost at the same moment he had added, calling, "Colin. There's someone here to see you, then."

When he went downstairs his father was standing awkwardly in front of the fire, smiling, his mother by the table, her hands clenched together, Steven by a chair uncertain now whether he might sit down; the baby was crawling across the floor, pacified for the moment by a piece of bread.

Stafford appeared to be unaware that anything unusual had occurred; he lay stretched out in a chair, pulling off a pair of gloves then, casually, raising one leg and removing a cycle clip that held his trousers.

"It was farther than I thought," he said. "I missed the bus so I came on the bike. I looked up the trains: there's not one through till after tea, and not one back until late tonight." He showed no curiosity in the room, or its inhabitants; it might have been a place he'd been coming into regularly for several years. Having removed his clips he dropped them on the table, his gloves beside them, and began to unfasten the buttons of his jacket. "You've some terrible hills round here," he added. "If I hadn't a three-speed I couldn't have managed."

"Oh, you need a bit of muscle to live round here," his father said. "None of your three-speed namby-pambies in a place like this."

"I can see that. I s'll have to get into training," Stafford said, thickening his accent then and smiling.

The baby, suddenly conscious of his strangeness, stood up by a chair and began to cry.

"Now, then. Now, then," his mother said, lifting it

quickly. "It's only a young man who's come to see you. We don't need any more of that, then, do we?"

"And this is Steven, Colin's brother," his father said.

Stafford nodded; he scarcely glanced in Steven's direction, loosening his jacket then smoothing down his hair.

"Would you like a cup o' tea, or summat?" his father said.

"I wouldn't mind. Or just a drink of water," Stafford said.

He looked up at Colin for the first time since he'd come into the room.

"Hi," he said. "I've got here, then."

"Oh, it'll be tea, don't worry," his father said. "You're not coming here to sup us watter."

"Water," his mother said.

"Water. Watter," his father said. "Dost think when you're thirsty it makes any difference?"

They went out a little later to show Stafford round the village. "He won't have seen a place like this afore," his father said. "You know, where people work."

"Oh, it's not all that different from where I live," Stafford said. At his father's insistence he'd got up to wheel his bike through to the yard behind.

"And where's that, then?" his father said.

"It's over at Spennymoor," Stafford said.

"Oh, I know that well." His father laughed. "They have that big mill theer. What's its name?"

"Stafford's. My family own it," Stafford said.

His father's face had paled. He looked as if, at that moment, he might have fallen down.

"Oh, thy's *that* Stafford," his father said, glancing quickly at his mother.

Now, as they moved away from the house, Stafford had clapped his hands.

"That gave your father a shock," he said. "Didn't he know, do you think, or did he put it on?"

"I shouldn't think he knew," he said and shook his head.

"People are funny about things like that. Money, I mean. As if it matters."

"I suppose if they haven't got any," he said, "it probably does."

"What difference does money make?" Stafford said. He gazed over for a moment then shook his head. They were walking along the backs, Colin's habitual path to get to the street outside. When he didn't answer Stafford glanced about him, freshly; he gazed in at the open doors, at the dark, fire-lit kitchens. "If you have less money you have fewer worries," he added, as if quoting something he'd heard before.

They came to the street.

"What would you like to see?" he said.

"What do you usually do on Sundays?" Stafford said.

"Go to Sunday School." He gestured off, vaguely, in the direction of the church.

"No, honestly?" Stafford said. He gazed off, with fresh curiosity, along the street. "I suppose it's too late to go," he added.

"We could go to the Park, if you like," he said.

Stafford looked around him at the houses. "Have you always lived here, or did you live somewhere else?" he said.

"I've always lived here," he said.

"I come through the station on the way to school, but you can't see up to the village," he said as if he'd wondered at the curiosity of this on his journeys through.

They reached the centre of the village and turned up the hill towards the Park.

Stringer and Batty were coming down the road, Batty with a stick which he flicked in the bushes on either side. When he saw Colin approaching he called to Stringer, who, without his gun, picked up a stone which he weighed, reflectively, in either hand.

"Who's your friend, Tongey?" Batty said.

"He's from our school," he said, and added, "This is Lolly, and that's Stringer." Stafford, his hands in his pockets, nodding, about to go on up the road.

"Who says tha mu'n go up theer, then?" Stringer said.

"Up where?" Stafford said and shook his head.

"Up theer," Stringer said, suddenly dismayed by Stafford's accent.

"I don't see that anyone mu'n say I have to go up theer or not, then," Stafford said, imitating Stringer's accent.

"Thy mu'n want thy nose knocking in, then?" Stringer said. He put up his fist in Stafford's face.

"I mu'n not want anything knocking in, then," Stafford said, his voice faltering for a moment as he regarded Stringer's fist.

"Tha mu'n feel this, then," Stringer said, "if thy goes up theer. Nobody goes up theer without permission."

"Have we got permission, Colin?" Stafford said. He looked half alarmed at Batty, then, almost reluctantly, glanced at Colin.

Stringer, turning his attention now to Colin, raised his fist again, waving it to and fro in front of his face.

Assuming Batty wouldn't do anything, he hit Stringer as hard as he could on the end of his nose.

Stringer stepped back and covered his face.

"Watch it. Watch it, Tongey," Batty said.

He came over with the stick, tapping the end of it now in his other hand.

"Watch it," he said. He tapped the stick more slowly, glancing at Stringer and then at Stafford, not sure, of the two of them, which to go to first.

"We'll go on up, then," Colin said. It was as if then, for a moment, nothing had happened; as he turned from Stringer Colin saw him swing his arm. Stringer lunged at him with his boot and then his fist and before he could give an answer ran off calling to the foot of the hill.

Batty, deserted, stood gazing up the hill, his legs astride, the stick still in his hand.

"Thy mu'n cop it when thy comes back down," he said. "I s'll fetch our kid."

He walked backwards, then turned, still tapping the stick against his hand.

"Thy look out, then, when you come back down."

"Aye: thy look out," Stringer called from the foot of the hill.

"Who are those two?" Stafford said.

"I suppose they own the village," Colin said. Yet he felt a strange resentment now, as if Stafford had forced him to something he hadn't wished.

"All bluster I suppose, then," Stafford said.

"Something like that," he said and turned off the hill to the gates of the Park, which, like the railings to the school playground, had been removed.

Odd couples were walking along the paths inside, groups of children playing on the metal roundabout and swings.

The afternoon was overcast; grey clouds mounded over the horizon beyond the pit: a light wind blew in from across the fields.

"That looks good fun, then," Stafford said and with a sudden lightness ran down the hill, clambering on the box-like rocking-horse and calling out.

Colin went down slowly; Stafford was standing on the side of the rocking horse, swinging it violently up and down.

"I say, get on the end," he said.

Colin clambered up the other side.

Another boy climbed on and Stafford laughed; he flung the rocking-horse from side to side, the metal arms knocking underneath, the boy who'd climbed on last holding to a handle, calling out.

"Come on: rock it, Colin," Stafford said.

Almost mechanically now he followed Stafford's movements; the head of the rocking-horse, hard, with beady eyes and flaring, metal nostrils, flew up and down by Stafford's head.

A strange carelessness had come into Stafford's movements; his coat flew up behind him, his face reddening, his eyes starting with a strange intentness.

"Keep it going, Col," he said.

The boy sitting on the rocking-horse half stood up.

"Keep it going," Stafford said.

The boy got off; the rocking-horse slowed.

Before its swinging motion had finally stopped Stafford had sprung down and run across to the roundabout. Several children already were swinging it round: they dropped off quickly as they felt his weight.

"Come and give it a push," he called.

Another, larger boy got on. He ran at the side of the platform, pushing it round then, his legs swinging, he clambered on.

Colin watched. Stafford climbed up the metal rigging, standing spread-eagled with his feet on a spar.

"Shove it. Shove it faster," he called to the boy.

The boy swung off; large, heavy, with studded boots and a torn jacket he pounded round the concrete track, the metal cusp of the roundabout clanging as it cracked against the top of the metal pole.

"Sithee: 'od on tight," he said.

Stafford called out, his figure flattened against the metal spars. The roundabout clanged to and fro, swaying, the metal framework spinning round.

"Jump on. Jump on, Col," Stafford called, laughing now, his head bowed, his hair flung out. His jacket billowed up behind.

Yet only moments later he was climbing down, the roundabout slowing, the boy pounding the concrete track again.

Stafford leapt off, the roundabout swaying up.

"Why didn't you jump on, then, Col?" he said. Without waiting for an answer he moved over to the swings.

Figures rose slowly, swaying on the chairs.

Colin sat on the concrete seat beside the playground; Stafford, as the swing swept out from the metal stanchions, laughed and, tugging at the chains, called out.

"Come on. Grab one, Col. It's going free."

Stafford's hair flew up as the swing swept back.

He was rising higher, crouching at the back of the swing then hanging poised, his head thrust back.

"Col!"

He thought, then, he might have fallen, the chains falling slack, the wood seat swaying sideways, Stafford, unsure of his balance, crouching there before, with a half-nervous gesture, he carefully sat down.

He let the swing rise and fall, his legs swaying to its slow momentum, then, as the swing slowed further, finally jumped down.

"I say, aren't you going to have a go?" He slumped down on the seat. He tapped his chest, sighing, and glanced around.

A group of girls, familiar to Colin from his walks in the Park with Bletchley, came slowly past. One of them called.

"Where's Belcher today?" she said.

"Who's that, then?" Stafford said. He ran his hand across his head, leaning forward. He smoothed his hair.

"They're from the Manor," Colin said.

Stafford got up from the bench.

"Come on. We might as well go this way, then," he said.

He set off along the side of the path, kicking at the grass edges as he walked along. As he reached the girls he called across. Colin heard them laugh, one of them shrieking, tossing back her head.

Stafford, shrugging, laughed himself.

When Colin reached him he was walking in front of the girls, turning then and walking backward, still laughing and then adding, "Do you know a girl called Berenice, then?"

"Not Berenice *Hartley?*"

"I believe that is her name," he said.

The girls had laughed again, as intrigued by Stafford's accent as they were by this inquiry.

"Your name isn't Henderson?" one of them said.

"Jones," Stafford said and began to laugh.

"Jones the butcher, or Jones the baker?"

"Jones the lover," Stafford said.

"Oh, listen to him. Honestly," another of the girls said.

"Honestly, do you know Berenice Hartley?" another said.

"As well as I know anyone, my darling," Stafford said.

"Honestly, just listen to him."

"I think he's deeply in love," another girl had said.

"I'm deeply in love with two or three girls at the moment," Stafford said.

"Honestly, just *listen* to him," another of the girls had said.

"I think *all* the girls at that school are pretty attractive," Stafford said.

"And what school do you go to, glamour-britches?" one of the girls had said.

They laughed, linking arms and leaning their heads against each other.

"I've left school. We don't go there any longer, do we, Colin?" Stafford said.

"Tongey goes to school. Don't you, Tarzan?" one of the girls had said.

"Why do you call him Tarzan?" Stafford said.

"That's Belcher's name for him. Isn't it, Tarzan?" one of the girls had said.

"He says he's so *strong*, does Belcher," another girl had said.

They laughed.

"You're too young not to be at school, in any case," they added.

"Well, I may drop in odd days, of course, my darling," Stafford said. "When the mood is on me, so to speak."

"Honestly, just listen to him, then," they said.

"Isn't there any room in there for me, then?" Stafford said, indicating that a space might be made somewhere in the middle.

"We wouldn't let you walk with us, then, would we?" one of the girls had said.

"Not somebody who knows Berenice *Hartley*," another girl had said.

They wandered on.

Stafford, smoothing down his hair, had let them past.

"They're a load of scrubbers. I don't think much of those," he said. He began to whistle, his hands in his pockets, looking round idly and kicking the grass.

"Are there any shops open in the village? We could get a bite to eat. I'm feeling pretty ravenous," he said.

"We could go back," Colin said, "and get some tea."

"I don't want to put your people out. I mean, they've enough to do, I suppose," he said.

"They're expecting you to stay, in any case," he said.

"I suppose we could go back," he said. He looked up the hill; figures were drifting down from the direction of the church: odd groups of girls in brightly coloured coats and boys who, walking behind them, climbed along the walls.

Bletchley was walking along with Reagan in the middle of the road; whereas Bletchley was broad and fat, fitting with some difficulty into his long-trousered suit, Reagan, tall and thin, appeared scarcely to inhabit his clothes at all, his dark, long-trousered suit exaggerating the extraordinary movements of his gangly body.

257

David Storey

"I shouldn't let Mr. Trubshaw see you," Bletchley said, referring to the vicar. "He asked where you were this afternoon and I told him you were sick." He glanced uneasily at Stafford.

Reagan was wearing a bright red tie; he had a long brass tie-pin clipped to it, beneath which hung a thin, brass-coloured chain. His eyes were large and staring, his long thin features, since he had grown much taller, more pronounced, the massive swelling of his head at the back disguised now by longish hair which he allowed to hang down towards his collar. He fingered his tie nervously as he glanced at Stafford.

Colin introduced him; Bletchley nodded. "Weren't you at the scholarship exams?" he said.

"Which ones were those?" Stafford said.

"The ones where you sit for the scholarship," Bletchley said.

"I can remember going to something of that sort," Stafford said.

"Which school are you at, then?" Bletchley said.

"Oh, I don't go to school very often," Stafford said. He stood with his hands in his pockets, looking round. He glanced at Reagan. "Which school do you go to, then?" he added.

"He goes to St. Dominic's," Bletchley said. "You have to pay fees. He didn't pass the scholarships," he added.

"Oh, those are the best schools," Stafford said. "I wish I'd gone there now myself."

Bletchley's neck reddened.

Mr. Morrison walked past, with the woman with the red eyes who played the piano. Bletchley touched his school cap and gave a smile as he gestured at Colin. "He'll tell Trubshaw and you'll catch it, I suppose," he said. He called out to two girls passing in the road. "Where's your boy-friends today?" he shouted.

"What's it to do with you, then, Belch?" they said.

Bletchley laughed; he pulled down at the peak of his cap and glanced at Stafford nervously, he began to kick his feet against the road.

"You'll be late for your violin class," Bletchley said.

"I don't have it on Sunday afternoons, now," Reagan said.

"Mic plays the violin. He's a virtuoso," Bletchley said. He laughed again, slowly, still watching Stafford. "You should hear him play. It's like a cat being cut in two."

"Who do you have lessons with?" Stafford said.

"I go to somebody in town. You won't have heard of them, I reckon," Reagan said. His face had darkened. Faint white marks, like smears of paint, showed at his temples.

Bletchley's neck had begun to swell; the red flush spread slowly upwards towards his cheeks.

"Not Mr. Prendergast?" Stafford said.

"Do you know him?" Reagan said.

"I go there twice a week myself."

"Honestly? Not the violin?" he said.

"I do the piano," Stafford said.

"Honestly," Reagan said, gazing at Stafford in admiration.

"I did violin about two years ago. I go on Wednesdays and Fridays, after school."

"I go Tuesdays," Reagan said.

"I had piano lessons, and violin lessons, but I go to elocution now, though," Bletchley said. " 'The rain in Spain stays mainly on the plain.' 'Tea for two is good for you.' 'How soon will you be finished with your spoon?' "

He quoted the phrases carefully to Stafford.

"Weren't we going to your place?" Stafford said, looking up at Colin. He glanced down sharply then towards the village.

"We're going in the Park," Bletchley said, indicating Reagan. He glanced over once again at Stafford. "Why don't you come? There are one or two tarts I know from school."

"We've just been down," Stafford said. He turned towards the hill. "Are you coming?" he added to Colin.

Bletchley turned to the Park, holding Reagan's arm as if afraid for a moment that Reagan might be inclined to follow.

"See you, Tarzan," he said.

"They look like Laurel and Hardy," Stafford said. "Just look at them," he added, glancing back.

The two figures, the one inflated like a large balloon,

the other tall and willowy, like some misshapen stick, were moving slowly along the path towards the slope leading to the recreation ground. Bletchley was already calling out, waving to a line of girls who, as they passed, had all glanced back, their laughter floating up across the hill.

"Belcher," he could hear them calling out, the sound echoing a moment later beneath the trees. Perhaps they'd called to Bletchley a second time; though still holding to Reagan's arm he appeared for a moment as if he might run across, the girls screaming then and moving off. They ran separately across the grass, coming together slowly, laughing, some distance down the hill.

"A village Romeo," Stafford said and for the first time that afternoon laughed, lightly, without any intention of provoking Colin.

There was no sign of Batty or Stringer at the foot of the hill; the miners were sitting in rows outside the pub, crouching in the gutter and along the walls, calling out suddenly to Stafford as he passed, attracted by the fairness of his hair, and the strange freshness of his manner.

"Dost fancy yon, then, Jack?" they said. "Wheerst tha come from, lad? Ar't'a sure he's not a lass?"

The laughter from the crouched rows and the odd, isolated figures standing in the road followed them down towards the house.

"What's the matter with them?" Stafford said. "Haven't they seen somebody dressed decently before?"

"They're always like that," he said, "with strangers. Suspicious of anything or anyone they haven't seen before."

"I'm surprised anyone comes here, in any case," Stafford said. "I mean, the place hasn't got many attractions at the best of times," he added.

"I never knew you played the piano," Colin said.

"Oh, I don't do it much. Sometimes I skip the lessons as a matter of fact. Prendergast, who takes me, doesn't mind. If he makes a fuss I'll be taken away, and he'd lose whatever fees he gets."

He began whistling slowly to himself, walking along with his hands in his pockets, kicking at the kerb.

"You ought to come to our place," he said, as they

260

reached the house. "We could have some fun. It's different to this." He shrugged his shoulders. "Well, not much
different, I suppose," he added.

The table was already laid when they went into the
kitchen. Walking along the backs Stafford had glanced
with the same intentness as before into the open doors
and windows; now, standing in the door of the house itself, he appeared dismayed by the sight of the table, as if
the identity of the room itself had changed, or he'd
come into the wrong room entirely; then, seeing Saville
sitting in a chair beside the fire, the Sunday paper open
awkwardly on his knee, he stepped inside, ducking his
head slightly then smoothing down his hair.

"You've seen all we have to see, then?" his father
said, folding the paper and standing up. "There mu'n not
be much around here, I suppose," he added.

"We went to the Park, Mr. Saville," Stafford said, sinking into the chair opposite his father, and mentioning the
Park now as if it were a place of some significance.

"Aye, well: it's a bit of a dump, is yon," his father
said. He put the paper down. "There's not much to see
up there, tha knows. Though there's one or two nice walks
around the village."

"Don't let him take you down to the Dell, at least," his
mother said. "That's been his favourite haunt these last
few years."

"Where's that, then?" Stafford asked him, looking up.

"Down by the sewage works," his father said.

"And the gas-works," his mother added.

"Thy hasn't to breathe too deeply when thy passes
there." His father laughed.

The baby, attracted by Stafford's presence, had pulled
itself up against a chair. Stafford put out his hands.

"Sithee, yon's too shy for ought, unless it's asking to be
fed," his father said. "We've just stuffed him up to keep
him quiet."

"Now, you know that's not true, not true at all," his
mother said.

She was opening a tin of fruit on the draining-board beside the sink; glancing at Stafford she brought it over in a
bowl to the table, standing there a moment uncertain
whether, before the meal, she ought to serve it out.

David Storey

"Do you like fruit, then, Neville?" she said, hesitating slightly as she mentioned Stafford's name.

"Any amount of it, Mrs. Saville," Stafford said, turning in the chair.

"It's tinned fruit," she said, still holding to the bowl.

"Tinned fruit all the better," Stafford said, turning once more to face the baby.

"We alus have tinned fruit, tha knows, on Sundays," his father said, then added, "Well, some Sundays, tha knows, when visitors are here."

The baby got down from the chair and crawled across the floor; it stood up finally by the door, which Stafford had left open, and began to stumble out.

"And where's thy off to?" his father said, his movements stiff now, his voice uncertain. Something about Stafford's presence had affected him immensely; he seemed uncertain where to put himself, picking up the baby, then putting it down, closing the door behind him, then standing once more beside the table, straightening the plates and spoons, and pulling out a chair.

A kettle was simmering on the fire.

"Well, I think it's ready," his mother said.

They sat at the table. His mother served the fruit. No one was sure whether to eat it first, or the bread and jam which stood—the thinly buttered slices on one plate, the jam in a bowl beside it—in the centre of the table. Finally they took their lead from Stafford, who started on the fruit, his mother offering him a slice of bread and asking him if he'd like to eat it with it.

"That's very kind. Thank you," Stafford said, evidently unused to eating tinned fruit and bread together.

"When we have a meal in this house we have one. Don't you worry," his father said.

Steven came in. His face was marked with grease, his knees were cut.

"Wherever have you been? And on Sunday, Steven," his mother said.

She got up from the table and took him to the sink. There was a moment's pause at the table; his father, with a loud sucking noise, began to drink his tea.

The tap ran in the sink; Steven's face was bent towards it; his hands were scrubbed, his knees were washed. Red-faced from stooping, his mother led him to the table.

"Start on your fruit," she said when Steven reached across to take the jam.

"Why have we got it in a bowl?" he said. "What's happened to the jar?"

"We don't always have it in a jar," his mother said, glancing uneasily at Stafford.

"I've never seen it in a bowl afore, then," Steven said.

"*Before*, not *a*fore," his mother said.

Steven had already finished his fruit; he looked expectantly around the table.

"Can I take your dish, then, Neville?" his mother said.

She got up from her place, leaning across to take Stafford's bowl. Her own fruit, as yet, she'd scarcely touched.

"Shall I pour your tea out now?" she added.

Stafford held out his cup; his father watched with an air of concern, nodding his head, half-smiling, encouraging Stafford now to take something else.

"How about some jam?" he said.

"I'd love some jam, Mr. Saville," Stafford said.

When the fruit was finished, and the bread had been consumed, the plates were removed and a plate of jam tarts and a sandwich roll were placed on the table.

"By go, where've we been saving this, then?" his father said.

"Now don't go embarrassing us, Father," his mother said. "Neville'll think we don't always have this," she added.

"We don't!" his father said, and laughed, crumbs spraying from his mouth. "By go," he said, stooping to the table. "Thy mu'n come every week at this rate, Nev."

The plates were handed round; his mother, red-faced, stooped to the table, short-sightedly, and cut the roll into even slices.

Stafford ate a piece; he ate a tart.

"Have one more," his mother had said, offering him the plate. There was one tart for each person, and one piece of roll.

"I'll never get home if I have any more, Mrs. Saville,"

263

Stafford said. "That's the best tea I've had, you know, for a very long time. We don't often have it, you see, at home."

"Not have tea?" his mother said as if she suspected some deprivation now in Stafford's background.

"We usually have dinner, you see, at about seven o'clock. And if I have a big tea I don't have the appetite at seven," Stafford said.

"Oh. Dinner. I see," his mother said. She looked away. "Won't you get into trouble, then? Eating all this at this time, then?"

"Oh, we have dinner later on Sundays," Stafford said. "We usually have visitors in the evening and nobody likes to eat until after eight."

"Oh, you should be all right, then," his mother said, distantly, as if this absolved her of all blame for Stafford's condition.

"Well, if nobody wants it, I'll have the extra tart," his father said.

"Well, it was my tart, actually," his mother said.

"Oh, I didn't know that, my dear," his father said.

"I didn't mind, if Neville would have liked another," his mother said.

"No, no, you go ahead, love," his father said. "It's yours by right." He looked fiercely at Steven, who had shown signs of laying claims on it himself.

His mother ate it in silence. The baby, fastened to a chair by a scarf, having spent most of the meal consuming a biscuit, began to moan quietly, making signs that it wanted a drink.

Colin leaned across and held the handleless cup it drank from against its lips; it bit against the edge, swallowing, its arms waving to and fro on either side.

"Well, that was a meal to be proud of," his father said, sighing now and finishing his tea. "I don't care who they are, or where they come from, they couldn't have a better tea than that, tha knows."

"Oh, I don't know," his mother said. "If it wasn't for rationing it might be better."

"Rationing or no rationing," his father said. "You

couldn't make much improvement, I'm telling you." He got out a cigarette and struck a match.

"You don't mind if Mr. Saville smokes?" his mother said.

"No. No. That's all right, Mrs. Saville," Stafford said. His father, hastily, had blown out his match.

"You can get up from the table if you like," his mother said.

"Aye, we mu'n give you a hand with the washing-up, Mother," his father said.

"Nay, I'd much prefer to do it on my own," she said, and added, "You could take Neville into the front room, Colin, if you like."

"Aye. I've lit a fire in theer," his father said.

Colin glanced at Stafford; having got up from the table he seemed uncertain where to turn; he'd grasped his chair as if to remove it from the table but, after glancing around, could see no other place to set it.

"We'll clear up in here," his father added. "It's not the visitor's job, tha knows, isn't that."

They went through to the other room. Despite the fire the air was cold. There was a smell of dampness in the room. Stafford glanced out to the street at the front.

"I suppose, really," he said, "I ought to go. It'll take me an hour to cycle back."

He held the curtain, stooping to the glass, then, releasing the curtain, glanced round quickly at the room itself. Because of the curtains and the size of the window, and with no outer door to supplement the light, it was darker than the kitchen.

"Where's this place your mother mentioned?"

"It's not far away," he said. "It's where those two hang out. The two that stopped us in the road."

"I don't mind meeting them again." Stafford raised his head, gazing across, his eyes quite bright. "Shall we go down on the bike, or walk?" he added.

"We could walk down. There's nowhere," he added, "to leave the bike."

He called out to his mother in the kitchen.

"Don't leave it too late for Neville getting back," she said, coming into the passage as he opened the door.

The cloud had thinned since the afternoon; a desultory light shone through the gaps. In the Dell the gas-works chimney was filtering out a stream of smoke, the cylinder of the storage tank sunk down, within its metal supports, almost to the ground.

Stafford had fashioned a stick from the hedge; he whipped it at the grass and the weeds at the side of the road, glancing round, his gestures those of someone who'd been to the place already: he was scarcely interested in where they were going.

The path wound off between the brick-built pens: it faded out amongst the swampland the other side.

Colin led the way between the reeds; on the site of the disused colliery figures were running to and fro between the trees, a dog barking, and from the direction of the road itself came the sound of a car engine as it started at the hill.

Birds flew off from the shrubs; the smell of the mud from the brackish pools replaced the smell of gas. Stafford walked along with a half-expectant air, startled, gazing at the banks of reeds, at the strange pools that opened out intermittently on either side. He grew self-absorbed, his shoulders hunched, Colin waiting for him at each of the difficult stretches. Finally, at the edge of the clearing, its chimney smoking, appeared Batty's hut.

Stringer was standing at the door, his gun raised, aiming it vaguely in their direction.

"I heard you, Tongey. Don't come closer, then," he said.

"Is that one of them, Colin?" Stafford said.

"It's the one I hit on the nose," he said.

A smear of blood could be seen on Stringer's face.

"Is he likely to fire it?" Stafford said.

Something ripped through the leaves above their heads.

Immediately, stooping, Stringer snapped the gun; he fumbled with the barrel, loaded it, straightened, then raised it quickly in their direction. He fired again.

"We better get under cover," Stafford said.

He'd half-raised his arm to cover his face.

Stringer, re-loading the gun, had backed inside the hut. The shutters on the window closed. A moment later an arm reached out and the door, at the end of a piece of string, was pulled quickly to.

Stafford stood at the edge of the clearing uncertain whether to cross.

"Is Lolly there, then?" Colin called.

"There's a lot of us in here, Tongey," Stringer said. His voice came faintly from inside the door.

Colin crossed over to the wall of the hut. The gun, from inside the window, was fired again.

He waited for a moment in the shelter of the door; Stafford, across the clearing, was waving his arm.

"Are you in there, Lolly?" Colin said.

"We're all in here, Tongey," Stringer said.

He could hear the table being moved against the door; a chain began to rattle the other side. When he pressed against the door it yielded.

"If you come in, Tongey," Stringer said, "I'll fire."

"We only want to look," he said.

"I mu'n fire if you come any farther," Stringer said.

Colin opened the door and glanced inside. The stove was lit. A candle burnt against the wall.

Stringer stood with his head stooped to the barrel of the gun.

"Don't say I didn't warn you, Tonge," he said.

"We only want to look," he said again, and added, "Lolly isn't here. I thought he was."

"He's coming. He'll be coming any time. He's bringing their kid down with him," Stringer said.

"I should put the gun down," he said, and stepped inside.

He stood with his back to Stringer and felt the stove.

"If Lolly's coming," he said, "I'll wait."

He went to the door and waved to Stafford.

"You can come in," he said. "It's only Stringer."

Stafford crossed slowly from the trees and looked inside.

"I say, what a super place." He glanced at Stringer then quickly at the hut. "Is this where you cook stuff, then?" He bent to the stove.

"Lolly'll be on to you," Stringer said. "If I let you go thy mu'n have a chance."

Stafford, having examined the stove, glanced uneasily at the table behind the door, at the wooden chairs and cupboard, and finally once more at Stringer.

"Do you want to stay, then?" Colin said.

"I don't mind," Stafford said. He looked round him at the hut again.

"He's fetching their kid down, is Lolly," Stringer said. He moved towards the door.

"Let's have a go with your gun, then," Stafford said.

"You mu'n have a go: but it'll be me who's firing it," Stringer said. He raised it slowly to Stafford's head.

Stafford stooped to the stove; he felt it with his hand.

"You want to put more wood on," Colin said.

"You mu'n not touch that wood, then," Stringer said.

Stafford lifted up a piece; he lifted the lid of the stove and dropped it in.

"Tha mu'n not touch it," Stringer said.

Stafford crossed over to the cupboard door; it was secured by a lock and a metal bar: he pulled back the shutter on the window, gazing out.

"I could bring a gun as well," he said. He gestured at Stringer. "It's newer than that."

"Tha mu'n not come here again, then," Stringer said and turned quickly at a sound outside.

Batty was standing at the door; he had the stick in his hand that he'd had before.

"Here, quick, Lolly, fetch thy kid, then," Stringer said. "Tongey's here and that mate of his."

Batty gazed in for a moment, then stepped inside.

"Who gave you permission to come in here?" He glanced at Colin and then, less certainly, at Stafford.

"He forced his way in, Loll," Stringer said.

Colin sat down on one of the chairs.

"We just came in to have a look," he said.

"Tha mu'n have a look and go, then," Batty said. He stood by the stove himself now, gazing round. "Tha mu'n go. Go on. Or I'll chuck you out."

Stafford went to the door; he passed Stringer, stooped to the doorway slightly, and stepped outside.

"Go on," Batty said. "And thee an' all."

Colin got up from the chair.

"And don't come again. I've told you now."

Stringer laughed; he lifted the gun again and aimed it vaguely at Colin's head.

He went outside; Stafford, the switch in his hand, was flicking at the mud around the hut; he glanced up at its roof, its metal chimney, and called to Batty, "It's quite a good place you've got, you know."

"We mu'n keep it that way an' all, then," Batty said. He stood in the doorway of the hut, the barrel of the air-gun poking out behind.

"It's a bit of a dump really," Stafford said as they came away. "What a terrible pong." He held out his arms, throwing the stick away, to keep his balance as they crossed the swamp. "I don't know how they stand it. What a dump."

Something clipped through the leaves above Colin's head.

"I suppose you don't notice it after you've been here a while. I suppose you get used to it," he said. He led the way, holding back the bushes until Stafford caught him up.

They reached the road.

Stafford glanced up towards the village.

"I ought to be getting back," he said. He scraped off the mud at the side of the road. "Honestly, what a pong."

"I suppose it's a good place to build a den, though," Colin said.

Stafford shrugged.

"When you come to our place I'll show you mine. You don't have to wade through all that mud."

They walked up the road towards the village. The light, showing in odd patches of the sky, had begun to fade. Far away, across the plain, rain had begun to fall, a vague blurring in the sky that sloped at an angle towards the fields.

"What time have you to be back home, then?" Colin said.

"Depends. They don't usually mind if I'm late, though," Stafford said.

He scraped his shoes against the road, occasionally crossing to the verges and wiping the mud off against the grass.

"Honestly, it really sticks on. You can't get rid of it," he added.

A thin shower of rain began to fall; they began to run. Bletchley was standing at the door of Reagan's house.

"Hey, where've you been? You should have stayed with us," he said. Reagan, in his shirt-sleeves, was standing in the door. "We're off back later, you know, tonight."

"Where?" Stafford said. He raised his head.

Bletchley flicked his head as if he didn't care to say the word. He glanced behind him at the passage, past Reagan's figure, to the kitchen at the other end.

"The Park. Do you want to come?" He called out louder, "We might go up to church as well."

Colin waited; Stafford had paused, uncertain; then, slowly, he came to the door.

"I better be getting back, I suppose," he said.

The kitchen had been cleared when they went inside; his father was listening to the wireless. Stafford's bike had been wheeled inside: it leant with his father's against the sideboard. Steven was playing on the floor in front of the fire.

"We brought your bike in. We thought it looked like rain," his father said.

"Oh, there's no need for that, Mr. Saville," Stafford said. "It's quite used, you know, to getting wet."

He took out his clips, stooped down, and put them on.

"You're off now, then, Neville?" his father said.

"I think I'd better, Mr. Saville," Stafford said.

He looked for his gloves which he'd left behind.

"Gloves, gloves," his father said, opening a drawer and taking them out. "I put them in here, you see, in case one of this lot picked them up. You can't keep ought in this house, tha knows, for long."

He went to the stairs.

"Ellen! Ellen. Neville's leaving, then," he said.

"I won't be a minute," his mother called, faintly, half-whispering, from overhead.

"She's putting the baby to bed," his father said.

He took the bike from Stafford and wheeled it out.

"Out of the front today," he said when Stafford, initially, had turned it to the yard.

He wheeled it down the passage, opened the front

door, stooping, then half-carried it to the street beyond.

Stafford, his jacket fastened, his collar up, with one glove on and the other in his hand, followed him down the passage, turning then, his hand out, as his mother appeared at the foot of the stairs.

"Goodbye, Mrs. Saville. And thank you so much for giving me tea," he said.

"It's been a pleasure having you. I hope you'll come again," his mother said.

"Next time I might try the train, then," Stafford said.

"A Saturday might be better," his mother said.

Steven followed them out to the street. Stafford mounted his bike. The thin rain now had strengthened.

"Sithee: you'll need your lights on soon," his father said.

Bletchley, still standing in Reagan's door, had waved. Reagan appeared beside him after a moment, their two strangely contrasted figures pressed together.

"I'll see you tomorrow, then," Stafford said and, stooping to the low handlebars, pushed off from the kerb.

Steven ran after him, waving, pausing finally some distance down the street and watching Stafford as he pedalled out of sight.

His mother had turned back inside the door; his father waited while Steven came back in.

"Did you enjoy himself?" he said.

"I think so," Colin said. "I can't see why he shouldn't."

"He'll not be used, I suppose, to the likes of us."

"I can't see why not," he said and shook his head.

"I never knew he was a Stafford, then."

"Are they that more important, then?" he said.

"Nay, they're the biggest family, tha knows, round here. You can ask your mother: her father worked for them. Years ago: afore we married."

"Oh, they're an important family all right," his mother said. "Though I don't suppose he'll want to come down here again."

"I don't see why not," he said.

"Nay, lad: thy's a lot to learn," his father said. "Though I like him well enough, mysen."

He got his books and went upstairs.

He could hear them talking, as he worked, in the room

271

below, his father's voice half-wearied, slow, getting on his clothes for work, his mother's querulous, half-complaining. He only went down, finally, when Steven came up to go to bed.

16

Miss Woodson sharpened her pencil slowly. The waste-paper basket into which she fed the shavings stood immediately by the fire, itself now a mass of smoking coke. No one in the classroom stirred; they watched the small, sharp blade of the penknife, which she'd removed moments before from her large black handbag, cut into the now sharply pointed piece of wood and waited while the last thin shaving had floated down into the large straw orifice below.

"Two-thirds, expressed as a decimal, is what?"

Stephens, the boy with the misshapen back, had raised his hand. It was a speculative gesture: Miss Woodson, inevitably, would ask one of those whose hands were lowered.

"Two-thirds expressed as a decimal."

The large black eyes came up; the black, bushy eyebrows were slowly raised. The spectacles were hitched up, slowly, on to the broad, projecting platform of Miss Woodson's nose.

Walker's hand went up; the hands of almost the entire class, in a communal gesture, were raised as well.

"I'm glad to see so many hands."

The small, silvery-coloured blade was folded; the ivory-handled penknife was returned to the large black bag.

"Two-thirds."

The bag, having been placed on the desk top, was lowered on to the floor beside it. Miss Woodson's figure, small, compact, surmounted by a crest of jet-black hair, sank down into the round-backed chair behind the desk itself.

"Two-thirds."

"Miss, *Miss!*" one or two had said.

"Two-thirds."

Her large eyes moved slowly along one side of the room, across the back, then returned along the opposite side until they came to rest on Stephens.

His eyes, fixed on hers, huge, startled, were suddenly lowered.

"Stephens."

"Point . . ." Stephens said, his hand still raised, almost pinned there, as if fastened to the wall itself.

"Nought point, Stephens," she said, and paused.

"Nought point," Stephens said, then added, "Six."

"Six." She glanced around, briefly; her gaze, finally, came back to Stephens. "Any advance on six?"

"Miss, *Miss!*" several of the boys had said.

"Two-thirds expressed as a decimal, is what?"

She waited.

"Walker?"

Walker's hand, judiciously, had been lowered to a less conspicuous place behind his desk; nevertheless, his red nose, if nothing else, had caught Miss Woodson's attention.

"I don't know, Miss," he said and shook his head.

"Walker doesn't know. I wonder," she added, "if the same is true . . . ," she paused, "of everyone else."

"Miss, Miss!" nearly all the boys had said.

"Saville."

"Nought point six, six," he said, "recurring."

"Now, then," she said. "I hope we all heard that." The thick-framed glasses were slowly lowered. "Walker?"

"Nought point six, six recurring," Walker said.

The arms were lowered.

"And what would *one*-third be, expressed as a decimal, Walker?"

"Point three, three recurring," Walker said.

"And if I asked you to give me two-thirds of one pound, Walker, how much would you give me?"

"Two-thirds, Miss?" he said. His eyes expanded; the redness around his nose had deepened. A sudden agitated movement took place beneath his desk.

"Two-thirds, Walker," Miss Woodson said.

"Two-thirds of one pound would be . . ." Walker

said, his fingers entwined, working frantically together.
"Two-thirds . . ."

"Stephens."

"Yes, Miss?"

"Don't 'Yes, Miss' me. Two-thirds of one pound,
Stephens, in shillings and pence."

Stephens's head had begun to shake; a look of terror
lit his features; even his hair had begun to tremble, his
habitual stoop suddenly pronounced as if he intended to
hide beneath the desk.

"Miss, Miss," two or three boys had said.

Again, with a communal, self-protective gesture, nearly
every hand in the class was raised.

"Two-thirds of one pound, Stephens."

Stephens's eyes wandered slowly from Miss Woodson's
gaze to the door behind; from there they drifted helplessly
across the wall until, half-way down the side of the class
they came to the low, rectangular-shaped window which
looked out to the basement wall of the drive. All that was
visible, beyond the wire-netting shielding the window, was
the ancient, eroded stonework of the wall itself.

"Twelve shillings, roughly, Miss," he said.

"Twelve shillings roughly, Stephens," Miss Woodson
said. Her lips slid back; two rows of large, uneven teeth
were suddenly revealed. "If twelve shillings represent
two-thirds of a pound, what does the remainder represent?" she said.

"Miss, Miss," several boys had said.

"Eight shillings, Miss Woodson," Stephens said.

His lips, too, had begun to tremble. Tears welled up
around his eyes.

"Represents, Stephens. Represents. If twelve shillings
represents two-thirds, what does the remainder represent?"

"One-third, Miss."

"And one-third, by your reckoning, is equivalent to
eight shillings, Stephens. And that being so, what would
three-thirds represent?"

"Miss!" several boys had said.

"Twenty-four shillings," Stephens said.

"And how many shillings are there in one pound,
Stephens?"

"Twenty shillings, Miss," he said.

"How many shillings and pence are represented by two-thirds of a pound, then, Walker?"

"Me, Miss?" Walker said.

"Don't 'Me, Miss?' me, Walker. Am I talking to the wall?" she said. "Out with an answer before I thrash you."

She got up slowly from the desk; she came down the aisle between the desks, gazing towards the window at the end of the room; it opened out directly to the field; a small, black dog crossed between the brick-built shelters.

"I don't know, Miss," Walker said.

"Out to the front, Walker," Miss Woodson said.

Walker got up; his head held slightly to one side, he stepped carefully between Miss Woodson and his desk.

"Stand facing the blackboard, Walker," Miss Woodson said.

He stood with his hands behind him, his legs astride.

"Pick up the piece of chalk before you."

Walker picked up the chalk from a wooden tray beneath the board.

"Write down one pound on the blackboard, Walker."

Walker wrote one pound, reaching over.

"Now divide one pound, Walker," Miss Woodson said, "by three. Do it clearly. We all want to see your ignorance," she added.

"Three into one won't go, Miss," Walker said. He stood with his hand half-poised, the stick of white chalk clenched tightly in it.

"Oh, dear. And what shall we do now, then, Walker?" Miss Woodson said.

She'd taken up a position at the back of the room, gazing down to Walker and the blackboard at the opposite end.

"Change it into shillings, Miss Woodson," Walker said.

"Let's see the machinations of your brilliant logic, Walker. Twenty shillings divided into three," she said.

"Threes into twenty go six," Walker said. "With two left over."

"Two what, Walker? Legs, arms, feet?"

"Shillings, Miss."

"And what do we divide those by, Walker?" Miss Woodson said.

"Change them into pence and divide by three, Miss," Walker said.

276

"And the answer, according to this mathematical genius, then, is what?"

"Eightpence, Miss."

"So, one-third of one pound is how much, Walker?"

"Six shillings and eightpence, Miss Woodson," Walker said.

"Go back to your desk, genius," Miss Woodson said.

She came slowly down the room again.

"I want to see no hand down when I ask you this. Two-thirds of one pound is what, then, class?"

Everyone's hand except Stephens went quickly up.

"Two-thirds of one pound is what, then, Stephens?"

He was writing quickly, with his finger, on the top of the desk.

"Are you washing that desk, Stephens?" Miss Woodson said. "Or endeavouring in some way to improve its surface?"

"No, Miss," Stephens said and shook his head.

Several boys had quickly laughed.

"I shan't give you another second, Stephens. Two-thirds of one pound: answer quick."

"Sixteen shillings and eightpence, Miss."

Miss Woodson took off her glasses. With a sudden, uncharacteristic violence, she struck the desk with the flat of her hand. "What was that answer, Stephens?" she said, gazing now into Stephens's eyes.

The dark-haired boy had shaken his head. It was as if the two figures were preoccupied in some private conversation, stooped together, Stephens bowed, Miss Woodson bending, scarcely inches now between them.

"Two-thirds of one pound is what, then, Stephens?"

"I don't know, Miss," Stephens said and once again he shook his head. His voice had faded off into a moan; he buried his head between his hands, banging it down against the desk.

For a moment Miss Woodson gazed down on to Stephens's hair; then, with something of a groan herself, an ecstatic, choking wail, she slowly straightened.

"What boy in this room does not know what two-thirds of one pound is?" she said.

Every hand was raised.

"Two-thirds of one pound," she said again, almost chanting out the phrase.

"Miss! Miss!" nearly everyone had said.

"Well, Walker?"

"Thirteen shillings and fourpence, Miss," he said.

"Thirteen and fourpence," Miss Woodson said. "And what decimal of a pound is that?"

"Nought point six, six recurring, Miss," he said.

"And what decimal of six shillings and eightpence, then?"

"Nought point three, three recurring," Walker said.

"What is it, now, class, all together?"

"Nought point three, three recurring," the class had said.

"And what fraction of a pound is nought point three, three recurring, then?"

"One-third of a pound, Miss Woodson," the class had said.

She sank down in her chair again. Stephens, his head between his hands, moaned quietly against his desk, his back, misshapen, thrust up, reproachfully, towards the class.

"Does anyone know of an opening as a kitchen maid?" Miss Woodson said.

"Left, left. Left," Carter said. "Left, boy. Left. Left. Right up then, boy, against your cheek. You're leaving yourself wide open."

He crossed over with his right into Colin's face.

"Higher, higher. Up against your chin, boy," Carter said.

Having raised his glove to his chin he felt an even harder blow against his ribs; though not much taller than himself Carter appeared, suddenly, to have acquired a longer reach: he felt a left from Carter against his face, another right beneath his ribs, and the next moment his back was against the rope and the room, or that aspect of it which he could see from a horizontal position, was revolving slowly above his head.

"On your feet, Saville," Carter said. "You're not hurt yet."

Cold water was splashed down on to the top of his head;

other figures, farther off, were dancing up and down, white-vested, with the large, brown-coloured, bulbous gloves at the ends of their arms. The gym-master half-lifted him beneath the rope then called over another boy and ducked back into the ring.

He sat on a bench at the side of the ring and waited for his turn again.

Carter wore the red trousers of a track-suit; on top he wore a vest. He was a small, almost daintily featured man, with doll-like eyes and a tiny nose; his hair was long and brushed smoothly back across his head, the end flapping up each time he swung a blow.

He was boxing with one of the senior boys, his left hand held straight out.

"Don't wait when you come in, Thompson," Carter said. "Come in with your left and, if you're going to do nothing else, step out. Don't hang around to see what's going to happen."

He demonstrated Thompson's move again.

"Let's have young Saville in again," he said. "He can show you how not to do it, if nothing else."

Colin climbed in beneath the rope.

He kneaded each glove against his palm. The master, having called the senior boys across, wiped his neck and arms on a towel; he wiped his face and chest. Finally he hung the towel across the rope: it ran round, a single strand, along the tops of the padded posts.

"Watch my counter, Saville. It might come up; it might go down—I might counter with my left if it comes to that. Don't do what Thompson does: bang one in then hang around."

Colin took up his guard. Carter crouched down; he raised his head each time he intended to throw an in-structional blow, but now, his forehead furrowed, he gazed keenly at him across his gloves: it was like fighting an ape, or a grizzled monkey, the thin face thrust menacingly down.

Colin struck out with his left hand and moved away; he struck out with his left again, both times failing even to make contact with Carter's bobbing head. Each time he put out his hand that tiny head had slipped away; he put out his right, missed, then once again, measuring the distance, put out the left: something of a smile crossed Carter's face.

Colin moved forward; he had some vague notion of keeping so close that, no matter how quickly Carter moved, he could muffle the blow. From one corner of the ring he drove him to another; from there he drove him to the next; he threw his left out continuously now, feeling it at one point crack comfortably against the master's face, saw, briefly, his look of consternation, then, his own head bowed, his right hand tucked up against his cheek, bore in with his shoulder, releasing his right as he came in close. With his left he banged at Carter's head. He stepped back, measured the distance to the master's chin, pulled back his right and felt, almost simultaneously, a sharp, needle-like pain in the middle of his chest. A flicker of colour shot across his eyes; for a moment he wasn't aware of anything at all, a vague redness, then a blueness, and a moment later he was gazing up at the metal, rivet-studded beams that crossed the ceiling.

"The first rule of boxing," Carter said, "is never lose your head."

Voices echoed from across the gym; there was the familiar rattle of the punch-bag against a metal frame. One or two figures outside the ring were leaping up and down. Perhaps, after all, they thought he'd slipped.

He got slowly to his feet. He felt a towel thrust into his hand, smelt its odour of dust and sweat and, when he finally looked up, saw Carter in the ring with one of the senior boys, parrying blows, calling, then parrying again.

"You can get changed, then, Saville," the master said, casually, calling across his shoulder almost at the same moment as he spoke to the other boy.

He hung the towel on the rope, crossed the gym, and went into the changing-room beyond. A single light, shielded by wire-netting, shone down on the dusty floor.

Carter came in as he finished changing. The towel now he'd hung around his neck, his jet-black hair brushed freshly back: it lay like a textureless lacquer across the top of his head.

"There's no point in trying to get one over on me," he said. "I'm here to teach. I'm not paid to be, and I've no intention of becoming, a punch-bag. Do I make my meaning clear?"

"Yes," he said, and added, "Sir."

"You can brawl all you want in the field outside; you can brawl all you want, if it comes to that, at home. When you step inside that ring it's with the purpose of learning something, not much, but a little bit about boxing. Do I make my meaning clear?"

"Yes," he said.

"If you fancy coming again I'd be glad to see you. If not, no hard feelings." He put out his hand.

After a moment's hesitation Colin took it.

As he was leaving he glanced through the sliding doors into the interior of the gym; sunlight, diffused by the frosted glass, fell in a broad panel across the floor. Dancing in and out of the shadows were the white-vested figures of the senior boys, ducking, weaving, their breathing staccato, irregular, following him out to the gymnasium door.

It was early evening. The first offices had begun to empty, a thin trickle of figures moving down the narrow streets towards the city centre; there were odd groups of girls in the winter uniform of dark-blue skirts and white blouses, the dark-blue coats hanging almost to their ankles: now, instead of the straw hats, they wore berets. Groups of older boys from the school had joined them; they stood on the pavements around the city centre, in front of the windows of the large hotel, leaning against the walls, one leg hitched up, or feet astride, hands in pockets, their caps pushed carelessly to the backs of their heads.

The bus was full. He sat upstairs. The windows, all closed, had begun to steam up. Fields flew past, figures rose; others came up the narrow stairs beside him. When he reached the village he could scarcely stand.

The air was cold. The sun had gone. He walked through the narrow streets with a strange feeling of physical suspension.

"The war'll be over before another year is out. Don't have any doubts of that," his father said.

He sat with Mr. Reagan in the porch, their backs to

the kitchen, the afternoon shadows spread out before
them.

They'd sat there for an hour, Mr. Reagan's voice drifting in, faintly, to where Colin sat at the kitchen table;
occasionally Mr. Reagan glanced back to make some
remark, half-laughing, nodding his head: "There's an
object lesson to us all: there's a boy who's not going to
be fastened up for long. There's a boy with prospects,
Harry," his father laughing and glancing in, half-serious,
to watch him at his work. "Go in the front room if you
want to concentrate," he told him and Colin, glancing
up, had shaken his head, reluctant at times like this,
when his mother was out, as on this occasion, visiting her
parents, to lock himself up in some room of the house.

"Once it is over you'll see things change," Mr. Reagan
said. "There'll be none of this living like paupers, fastened up beneath a stone, scratting a living like a rat in
a hole."

"Nay, I suppose things won't change much," his father
said, glancing into the kitchen once again, at the worn
coverings on the floor, at the dilapidated furniture.
"Things were hard enough afore the war, I don't think
they'll get much easier after."

A certain quietness had come over his father during
the previous year; he no longer read the newspapers as
avidly as before, nor silenced the family so vehemently
to hear each bulletin on the wireless. It was if some
issue with which he was passionately concerned had been
decided, and he was now looking round for other things
to fight; as if the emotions which engaged him when he
read a paper, or listened on the wireless to the account
of the battle, of miles advanced, of enemy equipment
taken, were looking for some other exploit, some other
turmoil, to focus on. His main part-time duty now was
that of warden; the house was the principal fire-point for
the street: a pump, brass-coloured and with a wooden
handle, was stored with a length of narrow hosepipe in
the cupboard beneath the stairs. A large, decaying house,
adjacent to the colliery yard, had been taken over as an
air-raid post, two rooms made habitable, and groups of
men worked shifts, making tea, sleeping there, or leaning
up against the walls outside, smoking and gazing vacantly

to the colliery yard, keeping a lookout whenever the sirens went. There were few raids now on the surrounding towns; one night two planes had bombed the town and Colin on his way to school the following morning had seen from the bus window a house with its outside walls peeled off standing amidst a pile of rubble.

"There'll be no more unemployment," Mr. Reagan said. "It'll not be like the last time. Officers selling laces: no jobs to go to, and no homes to go to, too."

His braces showed whenever he leaned forward; he'd come without his jacket but on top of his waistcoat had put on a knitted cardigan. Small loops were attached to each end of the braces, the tops of his underpants showing underneath.

"I can't see as there'll be much difference," his father said. "Those that had the money afore have still got it, and those that haven't it are still without."

"Oh, there'll be a big shake-up when this is over," Mr. Reagan said. He was smoking a pipe, a recent acquisition, and the smell of it drifted into the back of the room. The films of smoke, like gossamer, hung in the air outside the door. "There's been too many killed, and too many countries affected for it to be the same as it was before."

"Aye, I suppose we'll see one or two improvements," his father said, sighing, and with no conviction in his voice at all.

There were steps across the yard.

Mrs. Shaw came into view.

"And what problems of the world have you been straightening out?" she said. "What shape is it in now, after your cogitations?"

"Oh, we've rounded it up, Mrs. Shaw," Mr. Reagan said. "Taken off the edges."

"Nay, well, I didn't know we had any," Mrs. Shaw said.

"You can be sure it's in better shape, any road," his father said. "Two words from Reagan over any problem and you mu'n wonder where it wa' afore he came."

"Oh, now, I don't claim any great philosophical virtues, Harry," Mr. Reagan said, standing to Mrs. Shaw at first with something of a bow. The ends of his braces with their little white tapes had re-appeared. "I have but the general view of things, namely that things themselves are getting better."

"Well, they couldn't get worse," Mrs. Shaw had said.

"Oh, now, what a doleful yard we have this evening," Mr. Reagan said. Having offered his seat in the porch to Mrs. Shaw, and having seen it gracefully refused, he sat down again, hitching up the knees of his pin-stripe trousers. "Spring on its way, if I'm not mistaken, when a young man's fancy turns to love. And a young woman's, too, if I'm not mistaken."

"I don't notice any young men round here. Nor young women come to that," Mrs. Shaw had said. She gave a scream which broke into a laugh. "And what do you think, Mrs. Bletchley?" she'd called across.

Mrs. Bletchley's voice came floating back.

"Oh, I'd keep my distance from those two romancers, Mrs. Shaw. Especially when they gang together."

"Now, would we gang together, ladies?" Mr. Reagan said. He'd risen from the step again, this time presumably to bow to Mrs. Bletchley, who remained hidden beyond the angle of the door. "In the presence of two such charming members of the opposite sex would a man like myself, or a man like Mr. Saville, think, even if we were overwhelmed entirely, of ganging up? Each man for himself in this world, Mrs. Bletchley."

"Oh, now, just listen to him," Mrs. Bletchley said, her voice, like Mrs. Shaw's, breaking into a scream and then, less violently, a laugh. "He's got a tongue like a spoon of sugar. All sorts of things go past before you've even noticed. It's a good job he lives two doors away, and not next door," she added, "or I think we'd have come trouble."

"Would I let a brick wall, let alone a window or a door, come between me and the ones that I admire, Mrs. Bletchley?" Mr. Reagan said.

Both women had laughed again; a high-pitched wail came beseechingly from either side of the open door.

"Just listen to the man," Mrs. Shaw had said.

"Oh, beauty can be admired from a distance, over any number of years, Mrs. Bletchley," Mr. Reagan said. "The most carefree of us have passions that it might astonish

the closest of our friends to hear. Isn't that so, Harry?"
Reagan added.

"Nay, *he* mu'n have summat *he* never confesses to," his
father said, glancing uneasily behind, as if this aspect of
Mr. Reagan's neighbourly existence wasn't one he was
particularly anxious for Colin to hear.

"Ah, what secrets the most inconspicuous of us harbour
in our bosoms, Mrs. Bletchley," Mr. Reagan added, his
large head turning casually from one side to the other, his
thin neck reddening as if in measure of the feelings that
the sight of these two women had suddenly inspired.
"Might each one go about his labour, but he doesn't at
some point lift his head and glimpse in some distant door
or window a head, a face, a pretty hand or ear, that catches
a secret fancy, Mrs. Bletchley. Who's to say, now, whose
pretty hand or whose pretty ear, whose face or figure, et
cetera, is not the one to inspire him; and who's to say who
the person is who keeps such longings wrapped secretly
up inside his bosom?"

"More sugar, more sugar," Mrs. Bletchley said, breaking into a laugh, if anything, even wilder.

"If I were a few years younger I might very well be leaping yon wooden fence and giving your heart a little flutter,"
Mr. Reagan said, half-rising from the steps.

"Mr. Reagan," Mrs. Bletchley said, "it's a good job Mr.
Shaw isn't here or Mr. Bletchley, now," she added.

"Who's to say what he might get up to if there wasn't
someone to keep an eye on him," Mrs. Shaw had said.

The two women's laughter came once more, alternately
screeching, from either side of the open door.

"If Mr. Bletchley were here," Mr. Reagan said,
"wouldn't I be the one to remind him of what a treasure
he's left behind. While he fights for King and Country,
would I, now, be the one to make demands upon his wife."

"I'm sure I don't know what you might do, if I gave you
even half a chance," Mrs. Bletchley said, her voice raised
higher now beyond the door and fading off into another
laugh.

"Is that an invitation or merely a speculation, Mrs.
Bletchley?" Mr. Reagan asked. He stood up on the step,
his arms poised as if he'd leap the fence from where he
was standing.

"Oh," Mrs. Bletchley said and gave a screech, which was immediately echoed from the other side.

"Restrain me, Harry. Restrain me," Mr. Reagan said, putting his hand down now to his father's shoulder. "But the woman's a provocation, I haven't a doubt."

"Oh," Mrs. Bletchley said again, her voice sounding farther from the door.

"And would you barricade your door, now, Mrs. Bletchley, with a handsome feller like meself without?" Mr. Reagan said, raising one leg in addition to one arm as if he were flying across the fence already.

Another screech of laughter came from the adjoining door, then the sound of Mrs. McCormack's voice calling from the other side.

"It's Mr. Reagan up to his tricks, Mrs. McCormack," Mrs. Bletchley said. "Saying I won't be safe," she added, "not even inside the house."

Several words of advice were called from the other side and Mr. Reagan, as if pacified, lowered his leg, lowered his arm and, though still leaning on his father, sat slowly down.

"Outnumbered, three to one. Who am I to deny that women have the best of everything?" he said.

A communal screech came up from across the yard.

"And since when has a woman had the best of anything, Mr. Reagan?" Mrs. Shaw had said.

"The best of anything?" Mr. Reagan said. "Why, there's not one thing she doesn't have the best of, Mrs. Shaw," he added. "The best of us," he tapped his chest, "in the prime of life. The best of our wages on a Friday night. The best part of the day entirely to themselves, feet up on a cushion, a box of chocolates by their side. What woman would you find, now, down a mine? And what woman would you find up at the front line, defending her country?"

"You're a one to talk," Mrs. Bletchley said. "A fine office to go to every morning, with a coal fire burning in the hearth, and the nearest line you've ever been near is the one where Mrs. Reagan hangs her washing."

"To God, but did a man ever get the better of a woman?" Mr. Reagan said. His hand still clutched to his father's shoulder he glanced into the kitchen behind.

"Take notice of these Valkyries, boy," he added. "Witches. Every one."

"Oh, we'll witch you all right, don't worry," Mrs. Bletchley said. "With his airs and graces, and his carnation button-hole."

"To God, but they're at me every side," Mr. Reagan said. "We better retire to the kitchen," he added. "But a man can't find a drop of peace once he steps outside his house."

"Nor a lady, either, once she finds you and that other gigolo around," Mrs. Bletchley said, screeching with laughter.

"To God, Harry, but they're after you too," Mr. Reagan said, getting up quickly as if, suddenly, it had begun to rain. He rarely, if ever, came inside the house, and now, instead of stepping into the door, he pulled down his waistcoat and woollen cardigan more securely and, with a discreet bow, first in the direction of Mrs. Bletchley, then Mrs. Shaw, retreated, still bowing, across the yard.

"He's a great gabbler, is Reagan," his father said, getting up slowly and coming inside the door. "If he could work half as hard as he talked he'd be a rich man now, not sitting on a doorstep and filling in his time."

He went to the fire and put on the kettle. His face was still flushed, however, from the conversation on the step outside. He folded a piece of paper and reached into the fire, drawing his head away quickly then lighting a cigarette.

"Though Mrs. Bletchley when she has a mind can match him. It's best not to listen to half the things they say," he added.

It was as if in some way he'd been put out by the flow of Mr. Reagan's conversation, secretly elated yet anxious not to show it.

"Your mother hasn't much time for it," he added. "I can tell you that," as if the conversation might, if he wasn't careful, be reported back. "They've a tongue at times where their brain belongs."

He stood aimlessly for a moment beside the table, gazing at the books. He turned to the fire.

"Dost set much store by living here?" he said. He stood with one hand raised to the mantelpiece, glancing around when he didn't answer. The kettle, set against the flames, had begun to simmer.

"Living in this house?" he said.

"This house. This village. I thought we might move out," he said.

"Where would we move to?" he said.

"Nay, I've no idea." He shook his head. It was as if the conversation at the door had roused him to the thought. "Away from here, at any road," he said.

"We couldn't move far, in any case," he said. "You'd have your work to go to still."

"Nay, I mu'n give that up, an' all."

"What sort of job could you get?" he said.

"Nay, not much, I suppose." He shook his head. "I'm only good for shovelling. That's the sum total of my life," he added.

He went to the sink, emptied the tea-pot, rinsed it beneath the tap, then took it to the kettle.

"We mu'n move into town, or summat like that. You'd be nearer school, for a start." He crouched by the fire, poured water from the kettle into the pot, took it to the sink and rinsed it out.

He put in the tea. He waited then for the kettle to boil.

"Just think on it, any road," he said. "I don't want to do ought if you mu'n think it wrong. I've mentioned it to your mother, but she's no idea. She's one for sticking in a place," and a few moments later, as if summoned to the room by his father's thought, his mother's step came from the yard outside.

"Well," she said, looking in, pale-faced, the baby in her arms, Steven dragging at her coat, "what have you two been up to, then?"

They lay, like two stone effigies, on either side of the double bed. The bed itself, with its metal bars at either end and its large brass-coloured balls on each of the bedposts, stood in the curtained-off alcove in the corner of the room. The curtain itself, on its wooden rail, had been drawn aside; a slow, stentorian breathing, like the gasping of an engine, filled the room.

Their heads were small, shrunken against the bulk of

the single pillow; he remembered seeing them before, his grandmother's red, cherubic face, her small, short-fingered hands and stubby nails, and his grandfather's long, angular frame, with its dark, melancholic eyes and seemingly disjointed limbs. Nothing joined them now but the single bolster beneath their heads, and the patchwork cover which gave scarcely any indication of their figures underneath; their skin was yellow, their mouths open, their eyelids bulbous, their cheeks drawn in.

"They're sleeping now," his mother said, standing at the foot of the bed, as if some long-drawn-out battle had been fought before his arrival. He'd come down directly to the place from school, travelling on unfamiliar buses, in response to some wish of his mother's that he should see his grandparents before they died. He hardly connected them with anything living; there was something vague, inanimate, past recognition in their faces now: almost ghostly, the colour of their skin glowed eerily, like paper, from the shadows of the room. He saw the strange stoop of his mother's shoulders, a weariness verging on regret, nearer bewilderment he would have guessed; she gazed at the two heads as she might have examined some mysterious object inside a box, puzzling, uncertain, prompting her to some memory she couldn't recall. "At least it's something," she added, "that they'll go together. My sister's coming in an hour, then we can both go home."

A bucket of water stood by the hearth; in the top of it floated a wooden scrubbing-brush. The carpet had been rolled up in front of the fire and the stone floor between there and the door opening to the yard scrubbed clean. There was a smell of soap in the room, overlain by the musty, almost stifling odour which came from the bed. One of the curtains had been drawn across leaving a faint strip of light to fall through the remaining single pane on to the chair where his grandmother in the past had usually sat and on to the sofa with its leaking horsehair at the back of the room where silently, smoking his pipe, his grandfather normally reclined.

"They haven't eaten anything all day," his mother said, still gazing at the figures as if some huge puzzle in her life were suddenly complete, all the pieces drawn together, yet leaving her more confused than ever. Her hands were red from scrubbing, her arms bare, the sleeves of her dress, which came down to just above her elbow, damp. She wore an apron which she'd brought, strangely unfamiliar in these surroundings. There was a certain helplessness about her which he'd never seen before: even as he watched she began to weep, drawing a handkerchief from the pocket of her apron. She wiped her eyes, lifting her glasses. "They've had a terrible life, they have. They've never had anything," she added. "And I've brought them nothing else but worry."

She waited for some comment of his own; he gazed back to the bed. Nothing but horror filled him now, the strange, seemingly identical heads, like the two heads of a single body, united by the bolster, by the strange, waving symmetry of the patchwork quilt.

"They'd have liked to have seen so much more of you, Colin," she said, speaking now on their behalf; while all he remembered were the strange, half-querulous looks. "They were so proud of the scholarship," she added, gazing at the heads as though at any moment one of them might rise, confirm it, peeling back those bulbous lids, peer at him a moment and then, with a cry of approval or acclamation, sink back down to that slow, irregular, stentorian breathing. It was as if there were some blockage in their throats; as if, beneath the patchwork cover, some hand invisibly had gripped their bodies and were pressing out their life.

"Poor mother," his mother said, and he, thinking it so strange to hear his mother refer to some mother of her own, had glanced at her again.

A red flush, slowly, had spread across her face; her eyes, distended, glistened with tears, glancing down in turn at him almost as if, now, she were expecting him to protect her from the figures on the bed.

"Well, then, we can't go on like this," she said. She wiped her eyes on her handkerchief again. "Would you like something to eat?" she added, almost casually, as if he'd just come into the room at home. She turned to the gas ring beside the fire.

"No," he said. He shook his head.

"Have you had something to eat?" she said.

"No," he said again.

It was some aspect of his mother's life he no longer wished to see. He watched her then as she finished the scrubbing, the torn stockings, the torn dress, and the inflamed, seemingly blistered arms, the hands covered in soap, the slow, angular motion of the brush across the floor.

"Shall I finish it, Mother?" he said.

"Nay," she said. "You've got your school-clothes on."

He sat on an upright chair beside the door. His mother drew the curtain in the corner: only a faint, muffled panting now was audible behind it. The ticking of a clock on the mantelpiece began once again to dominate the room.

For a while his mother forgot him; he watched her back, its round, amorphous shape, her stooped head, and saw, as she knelt across the room, that the soles of her shoes were worn through to the welts beneath. In the middle of each hole he could see the darkness where the hole went through to the foot.

A fresh weariness, then, had flooded through the room; his one thought now was to get up and leave, to take his mother with him, and never come back. Beyond the curtain, that breathing would go on for ever, an element of the room as integral as the ticking of the clock, the crackle of the fire, the slow swirling of the brush as it spread the white suds across the floor.

"Shall I go for a walk?" he said.

"What, love?" His mother glanced back, startled, as if surprised to find him there.

"I thought I'd go for a walk," he said.

"Nay, love, you've only just come." He could see the appeal in her face, whether he'd only just come or not, not to leave her in the room alone.

"I just wondered if you wanted me out. I mean, while you were washing the floor," he added.

"Nay, love, I've washed that part of it," she said. She turned back to the scrubbing, then, a moment later, glanced back at him again. It was like someone gazing down a road; there was even the look of a girl about her, reluctant, half-ashamed. "They've had a hard life," she added, her eyes flooding once again with tears. "You can't imagine how hard life could be in those days."

He glanced down from the tear-streaked face to his

mother's worn-out shoes, her torn stockings, the frayed
edges of her dress. It was like some child now, a sister,
making some last appeal, some desperate demand before
it disappeared.

"He was out of work for nearly three years. We had
hardly anything to live on. He could have done so much
if he'd had a chance. As it was, it never came. It's not
like nowadays, love," she added. "If you have anything
about you now there'll always be someone who'll be glad
to take you. In those days nobody wanted you, no matter
how good you might have been, no matter how hard you
were prepared to work."

She turned away; he could hear her sobbing: her grief
echoed the dull breathing from the alcove, and the sharp
ticking of the clock.

He gazed beyond her head to the tall rectangular pictures on the wall above the horsehair sofa: cows standing
knee-deep at the edge of a river with purplish mountains,
topped with snow; a cottage with a thatched roof standing
amidst a sea of flowers, the branches of an oak flung out
in a bulbous angularity above.

She went back to the scrubbing; it was like some childhood task, the slow drawing of the brush across the floor,
the dull moaning, half-resentful, sobbing, a grief he'd
never heard before, melancholic, resigned, prompted by
some discontent that could never be appeased. It was a
strange, unknown figure now that knelt before him, someone in a passage, anonymous, caught up in a task he
couldn't understand.

His aunt came later. He scarcely knew her; he'd visited
her home on one occasion, years before, a tiny terrace
house in some back street of a town, and had met her
with his mother in this same room when his grandparents
were, seemingly, both well. She was built more stoutly
than his mother, her hair already grey, her face chubbier,
the features more pronounced: unaffected by the two
figures lying on the bed, she pulled back the curtain, gazing in like someone who had been called in to clean the
house; she set a shopping-bag down on the narrow table,
put a kettle on the fire and began generally to tidy up the
room, straightening the furniture and the carpet which
his mother had disturbed.

"And how's your school? Are they teaching you to be a professor or what?" she said. "Just look at his cap. And sithee, Ellen, just look at his blazer. Anybody would think he was at a university already." She scarcely glanced in his direction, taking note of his appearance out of the corner of his eye, disappearing at one point into the alcove, where he could hear the cover of the bed drawn back, a faint sigh, and a certain grunting and groaning before she re-emerged, a sheet beneath her arm. "Are those his books? Just look at his satchel. If our Eric or Gordon were here they'd be green with envy. They hardly see a book from what I can make out from one day to the next." She went on talking from the yard outside, taking out the sheet, re-appearing, a bucket in her hand. "You've scrubbed the floor, then? That'll save some trouble. I was wondering when I'd get to that. Though they'll both be left, of course, next year. Be factory fodder for a year then in the forces. You can't expect much, I suppose. They've never put their backs into anything," she added.

His mother sat on a chair. At his aunt's appearance inside the door she'd picked up her coat, about to leave, looking for her bag, then finally sitting down, the bag by her feet, her coat pulled on but still unbuttoned, gazing abstractedly through the uncurtained half of the tiny window. His aunt, unaware of the atmosphere, had pulled back the half-drawn curtain and let in something of the evening light.

"We better go for the bus," his mother said, yet continuing to sit, round-shouldered, on the straight-backed chair. She was turned sideways to the table, her face in profile, one arm on the table, gazing, now the curtain had been drawn, at the fireplace and the fire.

"Won't you have some tea before you go, then, Ellen?" his aunt had said. She didn't wait for an answer; she didn't even glance up to ask the question, her broad figure disappearing once again inside the alcove from where a moment later came another, deeper sigh and a further series of grunts and groans.

His mother, startled, had suddenly turned round.

"Here, I'll help you, love," she said.

She disappeared beyond the curtain, drawing it to behind her. The springs creaked on the double bed and briefly it seemed the bed itself was moved; he could hear the heavy breathing from his aunt, his mother's fainter gasps, and the interrupted, slower breathing of the two figures on the bed.

"There, then," his aunt said, re-appearing. "Though the sooner they take them off the better. Nobody can nurse them properly in a house like this."

"Will you be all right on your own?" his mother said, faintly, coming out from behind the curtain. "Would you like us to stay a little longer?"

"Oh, our Reg and David'll be dropping in later," his aunt had said. "You get off now, while you have the chance."

His mother picked up her bag again; she buttoned up her coat. She looked round, helplessly, at the tiny room, thought of going to the alcove once again, then said, "Well, I'll get off, Madge, if that's all right."

"You get off," his aunt had said. "They'll be all right. Tough as old boots, you know, are yon."

His mother nodded; she bowed her head briefly as she reached the door, wiped her eyes with her handkerchief, blew her nose, then, thrusting her handkerchief in her pocket, took Colin's hand.

"Well, then, are you ready, love?" she said.

His aunt appeared to be unaware, however, that either of them were leaving: she was stooping to the fire, still talking, poking hot cinders around the kettle, gasping at the heat, then straightening, looking round. "Oh, you're off, then?" she said as she saw them at the door. "You'll be calling in when, then, Ellen?" she added.

"I'll come in tomorrow," his mother said. "It'll be the morning, when Steven's gone to school."

"And how is Steven?" his aunt had said as if anxious now to waylay his mother, coming out to the step, wiping her hands on her apron and calling, "If you could bring in some tea, love, it'd be a help," merely nodding her head at his mother's answer.

"She's so upset, but determined not to show it," his mother said, her eyes glistening again as they left the house. "She's always looked after them, you know, and given them money when they were both without. And she's never had much herself," she added.

They walked through the other rows of houses to catch the bus, his mother still talking, not listening to the answers to any of her questions, her hand, however, clenched tightly round his own, and still gripping it when finally, some time later, they reached the bus.

It was growing dark; they sat downstairs. Fields faded off into the shadows either side; once clear of his grandparents' village, however, his mother grew silent. She sat with her bag on her knee, gazing out, past the driver's figure, to the faint outline of the road ahead. Only when the village came into sight did she suddenly say, "Well, then, I don't think you'll ever see them again," and added, "And neither will I, much more, if God is kind," taking his hand again as they left the bus and not releasing it, nor even slackening her grip, until they reached the house.

PART FOUR

PART FOUR

17

" 'And in the summer,' " Mr. Platt read aloud, " 'when bees haunt flowers, and birds the hedges; when scents and blossoms have been distilled into one heady draught for the reeling senses; then doth my heart shake off the winter's tale of woe and drudgery, and broken pledges, and take on the summer's glow of health and smiles.' "

He put the examination paper down, looking up over the top of his glasses. His eyes moved slowly along the desks until they came to Stephens's, then, with a sullen rage, they moved to Colin's.

"And what is an examiner supposed to make of this, then, Saville? 'Discuss the imagery of the poem below,' and all I can find on your paper is a turgid, unrhythmical and, if I may say so, singularly inept poem of your own construction, entitled . . . ," he glanced quickly at the sheet again, " 'Composed in 4uB classroom while gazing out of the window during the Easter examination.' " He looked round him slowly at the rest of the class. "I can see no sign of any discussion, nor can I trace any reference to the poem in question, unless I take your own creation to be a crude and, in this context, I might add, insulting parody of its finer points. Wordsworth wrote poetry, and if he, in some idle moment, and on the margin of his examination paper, had given me his rendering of 'I wandered lonely as a cloud,' I wouldn't, I venture to suggest, have been altogether displeased. Providing he had kept it to the margin; and providing that he'd answered the question put to him in full. People with a minor talent, or, in this instance, no talent whatsoever, would do better to admire their betters, simply, straightforwardly, and without equivocation, rather than attempt to imitate their creations by constructing verses of an unspeakable banality of their own." He looked at the sheet again. " 'C. Saville.' You might as well have written W. Shakespeare for all the good it's going to do you." A murmur of laughter ran faintly round the room. "Dost think, Bard Colin, that membership of the rugger team entitlest thou to indulgences of this sort?"

The class broke into laughter.

"Dost answer, Master Saville? Hearest thou the question, lad?"

"Yes, sir," he said and nodded his head.

"The eloquent fluctions of his heart are stilled. Sno'ed o'er by the pale cast of thought. Dost think it's a masterpiece, then, young Saville?"

"No, sir," he said. He shook his head.

"May'st we, thy humble admirers, scattered round, take this, thy creation, as a suitable text on which to vent our appreciation, then?"

"Yes, sir," he said. He nodded his head.

" 'And in the summer,' " he read again, 'when bees haunt flowers.' Do bees haunt flowers in summer, Walker?"

"Yes, sir," Walker said, then added, "No, sir."

"They might invade flowers. They might pollinate flowers, Walker. They might enter flowers, Stephens. They might visit flowers. They might hover over flowers or descend towards them; I sincerely doubt that bees could be said, in all their stinging reality, actually to *haunt*." He replaced his glasses, glanced at the paper, and, reading once again, added, " 'When scents and blossoms have been distilled into one heady draught for the reeling senses.' My goodness, Bard Colin, you'll have the breweries after thee if they hear on this. Whence brew'st thou this heady concoction, lad, and more important, hast thou a licence?"

The boys leaned back in their desks to laugh; several at the front turned round; those adjacent to him glanced across, while the expressions of those behind he could readily imagine.

The windows of the room were open; the feet of figures passing in the drive had paused and, from the top of the stone retaining wall, small, inverted heads peered down.

" 'The winter's tale of woe and drudgery, and broken

pledges.' Dare'st we assume, Bard Colin, a broken heart? Dare'st we assume some dalliance with the opposite sex from which thou emergest a little wiser?" He glanced round at the class again, adjusted his glasses and, peering down at the sheet, he added, " 'A summer's glow of health and smiles.' Indeed, now, we've something here to look forward to. That dark and rather sombre expression, habitually worn by our deep-feeling friend, is, if I read his promise rightly, going to be lightened over the summer months by a brighter complexion and even, he actually threatens us, *with a smile*."

The laughter, suddenly, had broken out again; other, larger heads peered down from the top of the window; one or two boys had banged their desks.

Mr. Platt put down the paper.

"As you see, Saville, when I give the papers out, your mark is considerably lower than it might have been had you answered the question with a reasonable degree of modesty and care, not to mention," he added, "with some intelligence."

He began to give the papers out. They were passed from hand to hand across the desks, or, if the boys were sufficiently near, handed impatiently across a ducking row of heads.

"Patterson, Jackson, Swale, Bembridge, Berresford, Clarke . . . Saville."

The paper was handed back along the row of desks; at each one it was glanced at, briefly examined, then, with a ducking motion, handed on.

"Rothery, Gill, Fenchurch, Madeley, Kent."

A faint murmur had erupted round the room; the papers were examined, turned over, examined again. He saw his own mark, the red line drawn down the page at the side of the poem, the corrections made to the other questions, then he put the paper down and folded his arms.

Mr. Platt had waited for several seconds; the last of the papers gone he sat down behind the desk, tapping his teeth, thoughtfully, with a piece of chalk. "Some of us may be bad poets, but even more of you," he added, "are chronic misspellers."

Colin pressed his arms in against his chest; other phrases were read out from other papers, figures standing uncer-

David Storey

tainly then sinking down; words were scrawled across the
blackboard.

"Coming back to you," Platt said, and added, calling,
"Art 'ware I'm talking to thee, lad?"

A burst of laughter rose quickly from the class.

"How spellst thou comprehensive, Bard?"

He stood up, mechanically, to a second burst of laughter;
he heard the question repeated and began to spell it
slowly, getting lost finally in the middle of the word, and
sitting down when Platt had called, "Gill Gill, as a mere
mathematician, can you spell it for him?"

The letters came down, quickly, from the back of the
class.

"Dost yon muse visit thee, then, Bard; in class, I mean,
as well as out?"

He got up slowly from his seat again.

"For homework, Bard, wouldst thou answer the question thou refrainest from answering in the examination,
and bring it to me for marking tomorrow morn. Hast
thou that clear within thine head?"

"Yes," he said, and added, "Sir."

"Not in rhymed couplets, blank verse, or any variation
of the same, I would ask thee, Bard. But in simple English prose for which thou wast requested in the first place,
lad."

"Yes," he said again and, after waiting to see if any
other demand were forthcoming, sank down in his seat
again.

"Methinks I hear the bell, summoning me to my morning cup of coffee, lads." Platt raised a small, thick hand
to one of his ears as the bell clanged out, distantly, in the
corridor above. "Methinks it summoneth thee to break,
and Saville in particular to some clandestine meeting
with his muse, perchance in the cloisters, lads, or, verily,
in the field itself. Dost hear, then, Bard? Or has the light
of common day, the everyday demands of English Lit.,
driven it to some dark and dingy hole from which thou
and thou alone willst rescueth it?"

Colin got up from his desk as the other boys rose. The
laughter, which had died down earlier, had risen again.

"Inclineth thine ear to what thy masters tell thee, lad,"
Platt said as, his books beneath his arm, he moved over

to the door. "Remembereth they liveth many more years than thou, and no doubt strove mightily in their youth to emulate the Bard. Nevertheless, they end up, twenty years later, behind a classroom desk, which, Fate being all-provident, they might have arrived at quicker if they hadn't have wasted their time writing imitations the like of which we have heard today. Verily, verily . . ." He held up his hand, stopping the crowd of boys inside the door. "Thy master hath spoken, lads: pin back thy lug-holes, then, and hear."

Colin wandered out to the cloisters, got his bottle of milk, and stood against the wall; masters passed through, either singly or in groups, to the dining-room where they had their coffee. Gannen went past, his gown pulled tightly round his waist, Miss Woodson, short-sighted, tugging at her glasses, Hodges, stroking down his hair which stood up in two white fangs at the back.

"They always pick on somebody," Stephens said. His back stooping more pronouncedly as he drank from his bottle, he came to stand beside him at the wall.

"I suppose if they don't, there's not much left to teach," he said, finishing his milk and moving to the crates. "I suppose it makes it entertaining."

"Entertaining for some," Stephens said and left his milk unfinished. He followed him out to the field. Figures ran past and for a moment dragged Stephens with them. "I thought it sounded pretty good, in any case," he added as he caught him up. "Better than anything Platt could do."

"Yes," he said, standing at the edge of one of the spaces cleared for a football match. Figures in shirt-sleeves darted to and fro between the piled-up jackets.

"Have you written any more, then?" Stephens said.

"No," he said and shook his head.

"I suppose he gave you a low mark as well," he added.

"Pretty low," he said.

"Would you like to buy a foutain-pen? I can let you have one cheap, then," Stephens said.

He drew open his jacket and showed him the tops of several pens clipped to his inside pocket.

"They're worth two or three pounds in a shop," he said.

"Where did you get them from?" he said.

"In town," Stephens said. "I'll let you have this big 'un,

303

if you like," he added. "You can write any number of poems with that."

"I've already got a pen," he said.

"It won't hold as much as this. And it won't have as good a nib, either." Stephens shielded the row of pens inside the coat, drawing the large one out, then unscrewing the cap.

"I'll make do with the one I've got," he said.

He turned back slowly towards the school.

"I can let you have it for five bob. Four bob. Three and sixpence," Stephens said.

"I've no money, in any case," he said.

"You could pay a bit each week. It'll soon add up, don't worry," Stephens said, and added, "If you come with me, we could start nicking them together. It's easier with two than it is with one."

Walker ran past, then Gill: a tall, thin boy with spectacles, his legs were thrust out at an angle on either side as he ran, in a manner reminiscent of Batty.

"Two are more easily caught than one," he said, watching Stephens now as he put the pen back inside his jacket.

"Not the way I do it," Stephens said, glancing up, sideways, and beginning to smile. Tiny, wedge-shaped teeth showed between his lips. "Come down at dinner-time and I can easily show you."

"Nay, I'll leave it all to you," he said, and laughed, moving back towards the cloisters.

"Any time you want ought special, just let me know, then," Stephens said. "But don't let on to any of the others. I'm only doing it as a favour."

He crossed the yard, re-entered the cloisters, walked down their ill-lit interior and entered the classroom. The fire which heated the room was going out; he put on more coke and sat at his desk, took his paper out again and began to read it. "And in the summer, when bees haunt flowers, and birds the hedges; when scents and blossoms have been distilled into one heady draught for the reeling senses; then doth my heart shake off the winter's tale of woe and drudgery, and broken pledges, and take on the summer's glow of health and smiles."

He crossed out "doth" and wrote in "does," and began to read it through again more slowly.

Stafford swung his bag beneath his arm, leaning up against the window in which his figure and those of the two girls he was talking to were clearly reflected. Traffic passed slowly across the city centre, building up towards the evening rush. Other groups stood around outside the shops and across the front of the large hotel: boys in blazers and the familiar caps, girls with the dark-blue coats, ending just above their ankles, and the small, dark-blue berets.

"You know Audrey, don't you?" Stafford said. "She saw you at the farm where you worked last summer." He indicated the taller of the two girls, slim, fair-haired, her red-cheeked face familiar now that Stafford had pointed her out. "It's her old man's farm," he added, and began to laugh, turning to the girl, who, dark-haired, with dark eyes and a high-bridged nose, had, after glancing at Colin, begun to laugh as well. "This is Marion," Stafford added, leaning up more securely now against the window, and burying both hands inside his pockets.

"He said he worked well," the tall girl said, easing the strap of her satchel across her shoulder. "He worked as hard as a man," she added, at which, his head bowed, Stafford laughed again.

"He *is* a man," he said to the other girl and all three of them began to laugh, more quickly, half-nervous, glancing at Colin to laugh as well.

"Is Jack still there?" he said. "And the man with the bow-legs?"

"Oh, Gordon's still there," she said. "He's been there for years. And Tom's still there. But the other one's gone. He went down the pit, I think," she added.

"Oh, Colin knows something about that, too," Stafford said. "He's a great one for work, and knowing all about it."

"Has the football season finished, then?" the dark-haired girl said, swinging away reflectively, to glance at the other groups along the pavement.

"Over and done with," Stafford said, kicking against the stone covering beneath the window. "We'd been expecting you up to watch, but we never had any fair admirers. If we'd had there's no knowing what we might have done," he added.

"We only watch the First Team," the dark-haired girl said, beginning to giggle and glancing once again, speculatively, towards the other groups. "I think Swallow's got terrific hair," she added. "And Audrey's really keen on Smith."

"Major or Minor?" Stafford said.

"Major, of course." The dark-haired girl laughed, nudging Audrey, who, flushing deeper, began to laugh as well.

"I'll have to be going," Colin said. "The bus goes in a few minutes and there isn't another for nearly an hour."

"Do you go home on the bus?" the dark-haired girl said. "It's so much quicker by train. You don't have to wait in all those queues."

"And we have good fun in the carriages. There aren't any corridors," Stafford said. "Once in, you see, they can't get out."

The dark-haired girl laughed again.

"They'll be reporting Stafford, one day. Just you mark my words," she said, swinging back her satchel.

"There're any amount of tunnels, and you can take out all the lightbulbs," Stafford said.

The light-haired girl had flushed. She glanced at Colin then, vacantly, gazed off across the road.

"Brenda was going to report you, in any case," the dark-haired girl said. "Her skirt was torn when she got to school, and Miss Wilkinson sent her from the room to sew it up." She pushed back her hair, taking her beret off and flicking her head, the dark hair swaying out behind. "I wish Swallow travelled on our train. We'd have a super time," she added.

"You're too young for Swallow," Stafford said.

"I'm not too young for anybody, darling," the girl said and glanced back up the road with another smile.

"Why don't you come through on Saturday, Colin?" Stafford said. "There's a train through your place at one o'clock. Ask for Swinnerton Junction: I can meet you there."

"All right," he said. He bowed his head, hitched up his satchel, and started off across the road.

"Goodbye, handsome," the dark-haired girl said and, as he reached the other side, he saw that all three of them were laughing, the fair-haired girl still gazing across, the shorter, dark-haired girl reaching up to grasp Stafford's shoulder and talking earnestly, half-smiling, into his seemingly indifferent face.

Hedged fields gave way to woodland, then a cutting, with large, orange-coloured rocks jutting down towards the carriage.

A moment later the train drew into a station, a single wooden hut with seats, standing in the centre of a wooden platform.

Colin got down; a woman with a baby, who'd been sitting in the wooden hut, got into the carriage and closed the door. A man with a barrow, weeding a garden at the side of the station, took his ticket.

He set off up a track leading to a fenced-off road that skirted the top of a hill. An old cart stood propped up on wooden boxes in the station yard; a dismembered lorry, wheelless, its engine removed as well as its bonnet, stood mouldering amidst a bed of weeds. From somewhere along the line came the sound of a whistle and immediately ahead, at the top of the track, a man on horseback appeared, riding along the edge of the road. A wooden gate, leaning from its hinges, its bars intertwined with grass and weeds, divided the track from the road itself.

A figure on a bike was pedalling slowly up the hill, its head bowed, its shoulders stooped. Only as it reached the crest of the hill did it begin to straighten, and seeing him standing there beside the gate, it raised its hand and waved. "Hi," Stafford said and pedalled up towards him. "How long have you been waiting, then?"

He pointed to the train: having left the station it was now visible across the fields. A plume of dark smoke drifted back towards the cutting.

"We go this way," Stafford said. He pointed back the way he'd come. The roofs of several houses were visible below. "Jump on."

307

Colin climbed on. Stafford turned the bike.

He pushed off with his foot.

The bike lurched; then, as it gathered speed, it straightened. They careened down the hill towards the houses. "Hold on," Stafford said. As the speed increased he started shrieking; he dragged his feet against the road. "There's a turning at the bottom. Hold on. The brakes aren't working." The bike swung aside; it ran off the road, across a pavement and on to an ashy track the other side. The brakes jarred; they shuddered, locked against the wheels, and, before the bike itself had stopped, Stafford fell. He put out his foot, the bike sliding round, and Colin clung to his arms, to the handlebars, then found himself finally pinned with Stafford against a wall.

"I say, that was pretty good. We've come the wrong way, though," Stafford said. He began to pull Colin upright, laughing. The track led off between tall, clipped hedges: gates opened out on either side, "Do you want to ride it?" Stafford said. "Though if you sit on the crossbar we'll get there much quicker." He wheeled the bike back towards the road.

Finally, having sat on the cross-bar and finding Stafford couldn't pedal, Colin sat on the seat, holding to Stafford's shoulders while Stafford half-crouched on the pedals in front.

They passed the arched entrance to a church; a large stone house stood back beneath a cliff of overhanging trees: small terraces of stone-built houses appeared on either side of the narrow road.

Stafford pedalled slowly; his head moved up and down stiffly, his back straightening as he kept his balance: when they came to a rise in the road he stopped.

"It's not much farther." He pointed up the road.

Colin dropped off.

To one side, as the road levelled out, appeared a large brick house: it was set well back from the road at the end of a narrow, unkempt garden. A pond, surrounded by bare, muddy earth was visible immediately behind the house and, beyond that, a roofless brick-built structure from inside the door of which, as they approached the house, appeared a pig and a flock of geese.

A driveway, rutted and submerged here and there in

pools of water, ran off from the road towards the house; alternative tracks wound through the overgrown vegetation on either side, coming together abruptly in front of the pillared door.

Stafford had got off his bike; he led the way along one of the more circuitous tracks, skirting the pools of water and following a narrow, stone-flagged path which led to a door at the side. He leant the bike against the wall, removing his clips, then, without wiping his feet or attempting to get rid of the mud that clogged his shoes he stepped through the already open door and called, "Mother? Are you back?" beckoning to Colin to follow without waiting for an answer.

A kitchen looked out to the back of the house. The floor was bare. A table, laden with plates containing sandwiches and cakes, stood against the wall. A sink with a single tap and a hot-water geyser was fastened beneath the window. Two doors led off, presumably, to the rest of the house.

"Grab one of these," Stafford said, standing by the table and lifting the tops of the sandwiches, choosing two finally and handing one of them to Colin. "We might as well take one of these as well," he added, picking up a tart from one of the plates and a piece of cake from another. "We'll go out to the back. Or do you want to have a look in here?" He ate the sandwich quickly then picked up another. "We better go out to the back," he said. "There'll be somebody here if we wait too long."

Stone flags led down to an overgrown lawn. Beyond it, where the grass petered out and was replaced by a flattened stretch of mud, stood the pond; the flock of geese were wandering along one side and, by the roofless, brick-built structure, the pig was rooting at the turned-up ground.

The geese honked as Stafford approached; he appeared, to Colin, neither to hear them nor see them, walking round the pond, still eating, glancing uncertainly towards the house, beckoning him to follow to where a fence divided the end of the garden from a clump of trees.

The fence had been broken down at several points, tentatively repaired, and broken down again. Amongst the closely spaced trees, some distance beyond the fence, stood a wooden hut; it was little more than shoulder height and made up from disproportionate bits of timber across the top of which had been thrown a strip of corrugated metal.

Stafford, having climbed the fence, made his way towards it, stooping beneath the branches, hurrying, half-bowed, scarcely glancing back before ducking down inside.

The entrance was shielded by a piece of sacking; a piece of damp carpet covered the floor.

"This is where I come at night," Stafford said. "I get stuff to eat and come out here." Yet he lay back as if disowning it, his head propped on one hand. "It's not much good. I built it about a year ago," he added. "My brother came in once and broke it down."

The dampness, increasing, seeped slowly through Colin's clothes; he could, crouching in the narrow space, see only the vague outline of Stafford's face, the lightness of his hair, and the slow motion of his hand as he ate the cake. Then, when the cake had gone, he lay quite still, the face expressionless, the eyes concealed, a vague darkness around his nose and lips.

"It's not as good as yours," he said, and added, "Lolly's."

"No," he said and shook his head.

" 'Course," Stafford said, "I built it by myself. There's no one round here, you know, to help me much."

He spoke in a whisper now as if, unseen, there were others lurking in the trees outside.

"I get one or two to come up. But we don't have much to do," he said, "with people in the village."

Renewed honking from the geese came waveringly from beyond the fence. A dog had barked.

Stafford pulled back the sacking and looked outside.

Beyond the barrier of the trees the house was visible, the lawn rising up towards it from the muddied pond; a woman's figure had emerged from the door at the side, glancing down towards the pond, then towards the shed, then, shielding its eyes, towards the trees. After a moment's hesitation it went inside.

"I sometimes come here at night. When the others

are asleep. And bring grub in, you know. I have a candle."

A match flared up in Colin's face, but the candle, standing on a punctured tin, was too wet for the match to light: the flame spluttered out and once again they were plunged in darkness. Stafford had let the sacking fall back down.

"That cake was good. What was that tart like?" Stafford said.

"All right," he said.

"What was in your sandwich?"

"Meat paste."

"She makes crab-paste ones, but they're not much good."

The faint murmur of a car engine came from the direction of the drive; Stafford lifted the sack again. A car was approaching the front of the house, bouncing in the ruts and sending up at each bounce a shower of water. It disappeared towards the door.

Stafford let the sacking fall.

"We could go up to my room, if you'd like," he said. "I've one or two things."

He made no move for a moment, kicking his feet against the wooden wall, the corrugated metal roof rattling ominously above their heads.

"Or there's the farm we could go to. At the back of these trees. Or we could cycle over, if you like, to Audrey Smith's. Marion Rayner lives only a mile beyond. There's a path that takes you there across the fields. They've got some horses. We could have a ride."

Yet he continued to lie back with his head propped on his hand, only reaching forward finally when he heard the sound of a second car. He lifted the sacking again, his head stooping, gazing out. Rain had begun to fall: the surface of the pond had been broken up; there was a splatter of drops across the roof.

"I suppose we had better go in," he said. "I thought it might rain but I hoped it wouldn't." He got up slowly, easing himself feet first through the narrow entrance; Colin followed. Rain spattered through the branches overhead, and drummed on the corrugated iron roof. The

311

surface of the pond was ruffled; the geese, however, were swimming up and down.

"We can make a dash for it. We'll go in by the kitchen," Stafford said. He ran ahead, along the edge of the pond, up the paving stones, hesitating slightly as he reached the door, glancing in before he stepped inside. A third car was coming up the drive; pale faces gazed out from behind the windows. A door had opened at the front of the house: a voice called out.

The sandwiches and cakes had gone from the kitchen; Stafford, after glancing at the empty table, had opened a cupboard door; he opened a second door: inside was a narrow pantry, lit by a single window.

"Nothing doing," he said. "We'd better go up."

He smoothed down his hair, straightened his jacket, then opened one of the doors leading from the room. The sound of several voices came from the other side.

"If anybody sees you, just nod your head."

They entered a broad hallway. Bare walls led up to a banistered landing. The front door of the house was standing open: a woman in a blue dress was standing on the steps outside, shielded by the porch, calling to the people who were descending from the car. Through a door leading off the hall came a murmur of voices followed, suddenly, by a burst of laughter. "Irene, for God's sake," someone called.

"That's mother. She's having one or two of her women in." Stafford mounted the stairs in urgent strides, pausing only as he reached the landing and leaning over the banister, gazing down as the woman in the blue dress came back inside the hall, her voice deep, almost like a man's, directing the women who'd just arrived. "We go along here," he added. "My bedroom's at the back."

They passed an open door through which Colin glimpsed two single beds set side by side. At the end of a narrow passage stood a red-painted door to which a notice had been fastened. Stafford, as he reached the door, had felt inside his pocket and a moment later took out a key. "Private. Keep Out," the notice read, with the initials N. K. S. printed underneath.

Having unlocked the door Stafford stepped inside. The room was narrow and lit by two windows on adjoining walls. The floor, like the floor of the hall below, was bare, the walls unpapered. A single bed stood behind the door; adjacent to it stood a chest of drawers, a cupboard and a desk. The floor in the centre of the room was occupied by several cardboard boxes which, the moment they were inside the room and the door closed and locked again, Stafford began to clear away. "Just one or two things," he said, pushing some of the boxes beneath the bed and balancing others on top of the drawers, on the cupboard and the desk. A single dark-blue curtain covered each of the windows, one window looking out to the pond and the roofless shelter, the other to the fields adjoining the sides of the house.

"Sit on the bed if you like. Though usually," Stafford said, "I sit on the floor."

The light pattering of the rain came from the guttering overhead. The sound of voices in the hall had faded. From the driveway, faintly, came the sound of another car.

"What sort of meetings does your mother have?" he said.

"I don't know," Stafford said. "They're always women. They sometimes go on for hours." He lay on the floor, reaching out beneath the bed. He stood up a moment later, red-faced from his exertions, an air-gun in his hand. "We can have pot-shots with that, if you like. We'll try the geese. They're just the distance."

From a drawer in the desk he took out a box of pellets. He loaded the gun, opened the window, and took careful aim towards the pond. There was a soft phut as he fired the gun but the white, stiff-necked birds continued to swim uninterruptedly up and down.

"Aim high to allow for distance," Stafford said. He loaded the gun for him, then handed it across.

Colin aimed vaguely for the flock of birds, where the cluster of shapes was thickest; the rifle kicked against his cheek and one of the geese stood, suddenly, and flapped its wings.

"Oh, good shot," Stafford said. He re-loaded the gun. "Let's try for Snuffler," he added. "You can just see him inside the shed."

The rear of the pig was visible inside the open door

of the shelter. Stafford, his arm propped on the window, took careful aim, his hair falling across his brow, his left eye closed; he stood poised against the window for several seconds, motionless, then squeezed the trigger.

"I say, good shot," he said as the rear of the pig disappeared inside the hut to be replaced a moment later by its head. "It likes being shot at. It's like having a tickle." He loaded the gun again. "Let's try the geese again," he said and, having snapped the barrel to, aimed it once more in the direction of the pond.

A man in a trilby hat appeared a little later on the lawn below; he had evidently dismounted from a bike, for this trousers were clipped at his ankles above a pair of enormous boots. He was tall, with broad shoulders, slightly stooped, with a fringe of grey hair showing beneath the brim of the hat. He wore a sports coat with leather patches on the sleeves, and as he reached the edge of the pond he glanced up suddenly towards the house.

Stafford, who'd been loading the gun, only saw him as he held it to the window, gazing down for a moment surprised to find anyone there at all, lowerng the gun and hiding it beneath the sill.

"Have you been firing that thing, Neville?" the man called, his voice echoing in the space behind the house.

"We've been firing at the pond, Father," Stafford said.

He leaned out of the window to shout his answer.

"You've not been firing at the birds?" the man had called.

"No," Stafford said, and shook his head.

The man gazed back for a moment at the pond; evidently he'd brought something for the geese to eat for they paddled out of the water and on to the bank. He put his hand down amongst them and examined their feathers.

"If I find you have I'll have that gun off you," the man called, staring back finally towards the house.

He went on past the pond, calling for the pig; as he neared the shelter the animal suddenly emerged and ran towards him.

"That's the old man," Stafford said. "He really wanted

to be a farmer, you know. If we'd had more money I suppose he would have been."

He put the gun away beneath the bed, pulling out one of the smaller cardboard boxes and saying, "Have you seen this? I'll take your picture."

He took out a camera with a concertina-shaped front, holding it to his eye and laughing.

"There's not enough light in here. We could go downstairs. You take mine and I'll take yours." He ducked to a mirror fastened to the cupboard and from his jacket pocket took out a comb; he smoothed down his hair, ducking to the mirror once again, then taking out his key and unlocking the door.

The woman in the blue dress was standing in the hall as they came downstairs, talking to several women who were about to leave.

"Have you seen your father, Neville?" the woman said and added, "This is my son," to one of the women at which Stafford bowed his head. "My youngest son, I ought to say," she said, the woman laughing as she turned to the door. "Have you seen him, Neville?" she asked again.

"He's out at the back, Mother," Stafford said, raising his voice as if he were speaking to the other woman as well as his mother.

"Oh well, I'll catch him when he comes back in," Mrs. Stafford said, glancing at Colin then and smiling. "Is this the friend who was coming?"

"We were just going out to take a photograph," Stafford said, already moving off towards the kitchen.

"Try and keep out of the mud," his mother said. "There might be some tea for you when you come back in." She'd already moved out to the porch and called back over her shoulder, Stafford himself already in the kitchen. The table, as before, was bare.

Outside, a larger bike than Stafford's had been leant against the wall, its rear wheel half-enclosed by a canvas hood, a large black canvas bag hanging down behind the saddle.

The rain had stopped. A faint wind was blowing. Stafford, after glancing towards the brick-built shelter, moved off across the back of the house.

"We can go on this side," he said. "There'll be more light."

They passed a pair of windows that opened to the lawn; inside a tiny, square-shaped room a man in a dark suit was reading a paper. He glanced up at the sound of their steps, saw Stafford, and immediately looked back to his paper again.

Several bushes had been planted on the opposite side of the house. A wooden fence, against which a hedge had recently been planted, divided the garden from a field of corn: a green haze showed up across the furrows.

Stafford handed him the camera; he showed him the eye-piece and the small chromium lever he had to press.

"Get it in the middle," Stafford said.

He leant against the fence, half-smiling, smoothing down his hair at one point and calling, "Haven't you got it? Come on, I can't keep smiling here for ever."

He smiled again, his head, with its almost delicate features, angled to one side. Beyond him, in one of the side windows of the house, several women were gazing out. A car was parked outside the door.

Colin pressed the lever and handed back the camera.

"I'll take one of you, then," Stafford said.

"It's all right," he said. "I'm not really bothered."

"No, I'll take one," Stafford said. "Perhaps somebody'll come out and take us both together."

He looked round vaguely for a suitable spot.

"I'll try and get you with the house," he said.

He gazed into the camera for several seconds, swinging it round.

"To your left," he called, and then, "More this way. Come a bit nearer," and then, finally, "Try to smile. Honestly, you look like murder."

The camera clicked and Stafford lowered it, examining it for a while then winding on the film.

"How about taking old Porky? We could get the old man as well," he said.

Several women had come out to the porch; the figure of Mrs. Stafford appeared beyond them. She was a tall, angular woman, with something of the same proportions as her husband, grey-haired, her features thin, the nose pronounced. She glanced across absent-mindedly as they reached the drive, then turned to the women as they stepped down to the car.

At the back of the house Mr. Stafford was carrying a clump of hay on a fork, disappearing into the roofless structure where the hay was still visible above the wall.

The geese had gone back to the pond, some idling in the water, others feeding along the bank. Their heads erect, they moved off as Stafford passed them, his father re-appearing, gazing across, the fork in his hand, the trilby hat pushed to the back of his head.

"What are you up to?" he said, staring at the camera then turning away to a shed at the back of the pen before Stafford could answer.

"We wondered if you'd take our photograph," Stafford said, smoothing down his hair and glancing over at Colin.

"Oh, I'm busy," Mr. Stafford said, disappearing inside the shed then re-emerging a moment later with another clump of straw. "If you want something to do you can clean out the sty."

"You only have to click it," Stafford said, following him across and showing him the camera.

"Has your mother finished her party yet?" he said, glancing up towards the house.

"They're just leaving," Stafford said, and held out the camera.

"Don't come pestering. Do something useful or keep out of the way," Mr. Stafford said. He hoisted the straw above his head, walking briskly over to the roofless building.

His features were large, his nose long, his eyes pale blue and shielded by heavy brows. His mouth, as he glanced across, was drawn back in irritation.

"Isn't Douglas in? Or John?" he added. "Ask one of them. They've nothing else to do."

Stafford, with a shrug, had turned aside.

"Perhaps my mother'll do it," he said. "It doesn't matter. Shall we see if there's anything to eat?" he added.

They went back to the house.

"His brothers have all the money. From the mills, I mean. I suppose if he had more of it we'd have a farm." He shrugged again. "Though I suppose we have enough," he added.

A tall, thick-chested man was stooping over the table

when they went back in the kitchen. Fair-haired, with heavy features, he glanced round as he heard them in the door, then turned back to the table where he was buttering a piece of bread. He was perhaps in his early twenties; a book, opened, was pressed up beneath his arm.

"Is there anything left for us, Dougie?" Stafford said and the man had shaken his head, putting the bread between his teeth, then catching hold of the book and a pot of tea and crossing to the door. He murmured impatiently around the bread, nodding at the door, wildly, and Stafford stepped across and opened it.

"That's Douglas, one of my brothers," Stafford said. "He's home from college. John's here, too. He's home on leave."

"How many brothers do you have?" he said.

"Four," he said. "I'm the youngest, you see, by about eight years."

He pulled back the door to the pantry, looked inside, then crossed over to the door through which the other figure had disappeared.

"Mother? Is there anything in to eat?" he called, waiting for an answer then shaking his head. "She's probably gone out. She often does at this time if she can get a lift." He called again, waited, then came back in the kitchen. "We could boil an egg. Are you keen on eggs?" Yet he stood indecisively by the window, gazing out to the back of the house where his father had once again re-appeared from the shed, a clump of hay above his head, walking over the roofless pen.

"How many pigs do you have?" Colin said.

"There's Porky," Stafford said. "And there's a sow with six or seven young ones. I've never counted them. It might be more."

The figure Colin had glimpsed earlier, through a rear window of the house, came in and seeing only Stafford and himself immediately went back out.

"That's John," Stafford said, fingering the table moodily, then suddenly looking up and adding, "I say, come on up. I've something in my room." He picked up the camera he'd left on the table and stepped out to the hall.

The house was silent. The door to the room where the women had been was standing open; the figure with the book was sitting there, in front of the fire, eating the piece of bread and drinking from the pot. "Can you close the door?" he called as they crossed the hall.

Stafford pulled it to. The front door opened as they reached the stairs and another tall, awkwardly built figure appeared, taking off a peaked Air Force hat and hanging it on a peg, laughing, then calling to the drive from where a moment later came a shout, followed immediately by a burst of women's laughter.

"Is Mother in, Nev?" the figure called, shouting briefly to the drive again, then glancing over half-heartedly towards the stairs. The man was dressed in an Air Force uniform, belted at the waist; a pair of wings was fastened to the breast pocket of the jacket.

"I think she's out," Stafford said, and added, "I say, are you home on leave or what?"

Two women and a second man appeared in the door behind and without answering, the uniformed figure led them off into the room across the hall: the door was closed. A second burst of laughter followed by someone calling a single name came a moment later from the other side.

"That's Geoff," Stafford said, gazing at the door as if half-tempted to step inside. "I bet the old man doesn't know he's back. Though he might have sent a telegram," he added.

They went on up the stairs. Stafford took out his key. He unlocked the door and they went inside. From below, faintly, came another shout then, suddenly, the blaring of a dance tune. After a further shout the tune had faded, followed by a faint murmur from the head of the stairs.

Stafford closed the door; he stood the camera on the desk and from one of its drawers took out a piece of wood to which were fastened several instruments and wires, and attached to the edge of which were a pair of earphones.

"I'll tune it," he said. "You can have a listen."

Stafford manoeuvred a piece of wire against a glass-like piece of rock, scratching its surface with the end of the wire and adjusting the earphones on Colin's head.

A faint voice came through the phones, crackling, fading away then coming louder. It was replaced finally by a piece of music.

David Storey

Stafford sat by the window, gazing out, picking up the earphones whenever he had his turn and holding only one of them against his ear, his eyes fixed below him on the brick-built pen. "I'll get you one made up, if you like," he said. "You can keep it under your bed and listen to it at night. When the crystal wears out you can get another."

At one point he got up and went to the door, listening to the sounds that came from the stairs, glancing back at the room and adding, "I bet they don't know that Geoffrey's back. He keeps coming home on leave and not telling them where he's stationed," leaning by the door, one hand clasped to it, a leg thrust out, as if waiting for some call to join them. "Let's see if I can tune it to anything else," he said finally, leaving the door wide open and sitting at the window gazing out, dreamily, towards the garden.

Later, when the sounds of laughter and shouting came more loudly from the stairs, Stafford had got up and gone to the landing. He'd hung over the banister, gazing down, regarding the figures now who'd gathered in the hall, two men in uniform, three women in coats and headscarves, and the two other brothers, the one with the book, the other with the paper: they were pulling on coats and caps, only the brother with the newspaper evidently remaining, standing in the door and waving as the sound of a car engine revving came from the drive outside.

Finally Stafford came back in the room; he sat on the bed.

"Do you want this?" he said, examining the set. "I can easily get another."

"I can build one of my own," he said.

"It takes ages to build. Why not have this one?" Stafford said. "I'll put it in a box. You can take it home."

He hunted in the cupboard, then beneath the bed. Finally he emptied a cardboard box on to the floor and slotted the piece of wood containing the crystal set inside. The earphones he folded in on top.

"I'd much rather you kept it," Colin said.

"I hardly use it," Stafford said. "I'll be getting a real one, in any case, at Christmas. Then I won't need this," he added, "at all."

He left the house at seven o'clock. A meal was being

320

Saville

laid in the room across the hall, a smell of roast meat and
vegetables coming from the kitchen. The brothers, the two
men in uniform and the three women had now returned.
A bottle of wine was standing on the table, while from an
adjoining room across the hall, where Mr. and Mrs. Stafford, the brother in uniform and several of the other figures
were now gathered, came the sound of a cork being drawn
from a bottle, of glasses clinking, and, as Stafford followed
him out to the porch, a burst of laughter was ended
abruptly by his mother calling from the door.

"You're not going out again, young man?" she said, the
faces in the room peering out from beyond her shoulder.

"It's young Neville," someone said and laughed.

"I was going to the station," Stafford said.

"It's dinner in a few minutes," Mrs. Stafford said.
"There's no rushing out to stations."

Stafford shrugged. He glanced at Colin.

"You know the way to the station, I take it?" Mrs. Stafford said, glancing at Colin across the hall.

"Yes," he said. He nodded.

"It's better that Neville doesn't rush off, otherwise it'll
be hours before we get him back. He's such a terrible
wanderer," she said. "Think on," she added to Stafford
and disappeared.

Stafford shrugged again. He stood in the porch, his hands
in his pockets. The sound of a dance tune came, brokenly,
from inside the house. A car was parked in the drive outside and, as Colin set off towards the gate, a second one
turned in from the road and splashed its way through the
pools of water.

"See you," Stafford said, and raised his arm.

"See you," he called and, the box beneath his arm, went
on towards the road.

A different porter was on the platform when he arrived
at the station; the train when it drew in was almost empty.
He sat in a carriage by himself, gazing out at the darkening fields, glancing finally at the box itself and running his
finger over the smooth black boss of Stafford's earphones.
At one point he lifted them out and put them on, scratching the crystal with the wire inside the box, turned the
dial, heard nothing but a crackling and, seeing a station
approaching and figures on the platform, took them off.

321

He sat nursing the box on his knee until he reached the village, then ran all the way to the house. His father was out when he arrived, his mother at the sink, scarcely glancing round as he came in the door. He went up to his room, where Steven was sleeping, and in the darkness, as if listening to another world, or to some glimmer of the one he'd left, tinkered with the crystal, searching for a sound.

18

They sat upstairs in a small, moon-shaped circle from the back of which you could see into the stalls. Boys in front threw down pieces of paper and occasionally matches, usherettes coming between the seats to flash a torch or call out ineffectually along the rows.

Audrey and Marion sat together, with Stafford on one side and Colin on the other. At one point, near the beginning of the picture, Stafford had leant his arm around the back of Marion's seat and, a little later, placed his hand beneath her arm. Audrey sat rigidly beside Colin. His elbow, which he'd left on the arm of the seat, was touching hers; his knees, which he'd turned towards her, had caught against hers, briefly, before one of them, his or hers, he couldn't be sure, had been drawn away.

The picture droned on, flanked by curtains. At the end the lights came on and Stafford, withdrawing his arm, brought out a cigarette case from his inside pocket.

"Do you fancy a smoke?" he said casually, leaning across and offering one to Colin.

"No thanks," he said and shook his head.

"Marion, darling?" Stafford said.

"Thank you, darling," Marion said.

"Audrey, darling?"

"No thank you, Neville."

They sat in silence for a while. People went in and out to the sweet stall in the foyer. Faintly, through an open door, came the sound of traffic; a glimmer of daylight showed beneath a tasselled curtain.

Stafford lit Marion's cigarette with a lighter and then lit his own. They blew out clouds of smoke past Audrey's face. Their cigarettes alight, Stafford replaced his arm on the back of Marion's seat.

"I don't think much of the picture," Marion said.

"Same here," Stafford said. He stroked Marion's hair casually, almost absent-minded, gazing down to the heads below.

"What's the second one called?" Marion said.

"I don't know," Stafford said. He shook his head, the cigarette slipped in between his lips. Marion held hers between her fingers stiffly, her hand held up against her face, her lips pouting, her head erect.

"Fancy anything to eat, Smithers?" Stafford said.

"No thanks," Audrey said and shook her head. Her elbow, now the lights were on, had been lowered slowly against her side.

"Can I get you anything?" Colin said.

"No thanks," she said again.

"Get you anything, Colin?" Stafford said.

"No thanks," he said.

Stafford looked round at the other couples; there were one or two other boys from the school, and one or two girls from the girls' school sitting in pairs. Most of them Colin scarcely knew; he sat gazing steadily at the folds of the heavy curtain, and the heads, mainly of children, visible in the stalls below.

Stafford had called out to several boys in the rows in front, and one of them came back to lean over the adjoining seats and to take a cigarette.

"Hello, darling," Marion said.

"Hello, Marion," the boy had said, stooping to Stafford's lighter then puffing out, briskly, a massive cloud of smoke.

"Isn't Shirley with you today?" she said.

"I'm with Eileen today, my dear," he said, winking at Stafford who immediately laughed.

"I'd be careful with her, my darling," Marion said, puffing slowly at her cigarette. She held it to her mouth as if she were kissing the palm of her hand As the two boys laughed she crossed her legs and Stafford, who was glancing down, placed his hand across her knee. "None of that, my dear," she added and leaving the cigarette between her lips carefully withdrew it.

The lights went out. The second film began: Marion sank lower in her seat. When Colin glanced across he saw their heads seemingly locked together, their cigarettes glowing as they held them out.

He moved his arm against Audrey's but otherwise gazed vacantly before him at the screen.

Later, outside, Stafford said, "Fancy a walk, or a cup of tea?"

"Can you get tea at this time?" Marion said.

"There's a place in the market I sometimes go to," Stafford said. He put his arm around Marion's waist, but as she straightened her coat she lifted it away.

"Honestly, if we're seen in the streets, we'll never hear the end of it. Not from Miss Wilkinson, at least," she said. "There's going to be a school rule that we can't even talk to boys in school uniform. Isn't that true?" She turned to Audrey.

They walked in pairs, Stafford and Marion in front, the dark-haired girl frequently turning round to pass some comment. They talked mainly about girls at the school, and boys they'd heard about in conversation.

"They take a groundsheet and go out to Bratley Woods. Honestly, if anyone saw them, they'd be expelled."

"I've got a groundsheet," Stafford said.

"You're not getting *me* to share it," Marion said. "Honestly, give them half an inch and they want a mile."

They reached the market; numerous canvas-covered stalls were set out in rows in front of an ancient, brick-built market-hall. Arched entrances led to the gas-illuminated stalls inside. At each corner of the square stood a tiny shop, the windows of which had been drawn up: at one of them women were serving tea. One or two buns were for sale inside.

"What's it to be, then, ladies," Stafford said, and added, "No, no, on me, old man," when Colin began feeling in his pockets. He had no more money anyway, only the torn half of his return ticket.

They stood by the stall, drinking the tea and eating buns.

"How're we fixed for next Saturday, ladies?" Stafford said. He stood in the centre of the footpath to drink his tea so that people passing had to step into the road.

"We're fixed very well, aren't we, Audrey?" Marion said. "I don't know about you and Colin, though," she added, laughing then, her cup standing in its saucer on the counter.

"Heart-breakers, these two, Colin," Stafford said.

"We just don't choose anyone to go out with, do we, Audrey?" Marion said.

Audrey shook her head. She had on a light-coloured coat with a fur collar. The cuffs were also trimmed with fur. Her hair, which normally hung straight down, had been curled up around the edges. Marion wore a jacket with slanted pockets. She'd folded a silk scarf around her hair.

"You don't know what other invitations we might have had, do they, Audrey?" Marion said.

Audrey scarcely drank her tea; the bun which Stafford had bought her she'd left untouched. Colin thought of eating it himself, asking her finally as they turned to leave.

"I'm not feeling very hungry. You have it," she said, pleased that he'd thought to ask.

He ate it as they walked along. They passed through the crowds at the edge of the market, the two girls walking arm in arm, Colin on one side, when the crowds permitted, and Stafford on the other.

"Fancy a stroll in the Park, my darling?" Stafford said.

"We know why *you* want to stroll in the Park. Don't we, Audrey?" Marion said.

Audrey glanced at Colin and began to smile.

"He's only one thought in his mind, has that young man," Marion added.

Audrey laughed and shook her head. She flung out the hair around her collar. Vast crowds were now moving through the town, flooding the pavements and spreading to the road.

"We could observe the trees, not to mention the ducks and the other appurtenances of the natural life," Stafford said.

"Just listen to his language," Marion said. "That's what comes from studying Latin."

"Don't you study Latin?" Stafford said.

"Audrey studies Latin. I study modern languages," Marion said.

They passed through the city centre and turned down a steep, cobbled alleyway leading to the station. The two girls now had walked ahead, the pavement, after the confusion of the street, comparatively deserted.

"We're just watching your legs, Marion," Stafford said as they walked behind.

Marion was wearing stockings with a seam; Audrey wore small white ankle socks.

"I'll ask you to keep your eyes elsewhere," Marion said, only her ankles and the lower half of her calves visible beneath the hem of her skirt.

"Where else would you like me to keep them?" Stafford said.

"If you were a gentlman I'm sure you wouldn't have to ask, my darling," Marion said, walking with something of a swagger.

"I could look a little higher, but then your back's turned to us, darling," Stafford said.

"We've nothing to reveal to *you*, my darling," Marion said, fastening her arm securely now in Audrey's. "Have we, Audrey, dear?" she added.

Ahead of them, at the top of a flight of steps, appeared the station yard.

"In any case, we're expected home for tea. Aren't we, darling?" Marion turned towards the steps. She and Audrey ran up together.

"I say, you ought to go up more discreetly," Stafford said. "You can't imagine how revealing it is to those who follow on behind."

The two girls, however, had started laughing, their arms if anything bound closer, running now across the yard to the black, stone profile of the station. Low, with a steeply angled roof and a tall stone tower surmounted by a clock, the yard was partly covered by a metal canopy. The two girls, darting between the taxis, disappeared inside.

"What time is the train due?" Colin said.

"Usually we get the five o'clock. Though I suppose it's going to be crowded," Stafford said. "If you get the four o'clock it's often empty, and you can get a compartment to yourself." He looked across. "Aren't you coming on the train?"

"I've got no money. Just the return for the bus," he said.

"I'll lend you it. I'm loaded," Stafford said. "You can pay us back whenever you like." He took his arm. "They'll be expecting you to be on the train," he added.

He let Stafford buy the ticket. They went through the wooden barrier and on to the platform. The two girls were waiting at the opposite end. They were standing on a trolley, looking over a railing to the street below. Double-decker buses passed through a tunnel beneath the station.

Beyond the end of the platform the lines curved off towards the river; in the farthest distance a broad vista of wooded hill-land, broken here and there by colliery slag-heaps, stretched away from the fringes of the town.

"See what you can hit, then," Stafford said and gave several copper coins to each of the girls.

"I don't want them," Audrey said. She handed them to Colin.

Marion was already leaning through the railings; she let a coin drop and they watched it bounce then roll, briefly, on the cobbled road below. Stafford dropped his: it bounced on the roof of a bus and then to the road. The girls laughed, quickly, drawing back their heads.

"Honestly, they'll be coming up if you keep on doing that, my darling," Marion said. She dropped another coin herself, laughing then as the crowd, hearing the tinkle of the coin, looked up.

"If it hits anybody's head it's bound to hurt them," Audrey said.

"Oh, we only drop them lightly, don't we, darling?" Stafford said.

The train came in. The engine, slowing, lumbered to the bridge.

Two people got out of the first compartment and Stafford climbed inside. He pulled down the blinds on the windows, then when they'd climbed in, he fastened the door.

"Sit by the windows, girls," he said. "And make it seem we're full inside."

He lowered the window and peered outside.

"Nobody comes in if you lean out looking anxious. They always think it's full," he said, gazing mournfully along the platform. Other doors were slammed. A whistle blew.

The train lurched forward, slowed, then, swaying, crossed the bridge. The pounding of the engine came through the carriage wall.

"Isn't it dark? Who's this, then?" Stafford said. Having raised the window and lowered the blind he groped along the bench-like seat.

The girls had screamed.

"Hey, Colin. Come and help me, then," he said.

The girls had screamed again.

"Whose is this arm, then?" Stafford said. "Hey," he added. "I've found a leg."

Marion screamed.

Colin found Audrey between his arms. He drew her to him, pressed his lips against her, found her cheek, then, when he pressed his lips against her once again he kissed her hair.

He heard her laugh.

She tried to move away. He held her tightly. Briefly, then, their lips had met.

The pounding of the train grew louder, the track enclosed between high walls.

The sound had faded.

"Honestly," Marion said across the carriage. "I can't have that."

A blind went up.

A flood of daylight filled the carriage.

"Honestly, he's terrible," Marion said. She was pressed up now against the wall, Stafford lying full length along the bench.

Colin, releasing Audrey, drew back against the seat, glancing briefly at her face and then at Stafford.

"I'll sit beside you, Audrey," Marion said, easing herself round Stafford's outstretched arm and sinking down on the seat beside her. "Honestly, aren't they terrible?" she said.

Stafford, kneeling, reached over to the blind.

"See what we can find this time, then," he said.

The blind pulled down and fastened, Marion then Audrey screamed again. Colin felt the shape pressed down towards him and put out his arm to hold Audrey once again.

He felt her arm and then her waist. He leant his head towards her, found her lips and for a moment they clung together, jarred by the lurching of Marion on the other side.

"Honestly," Marion said, "he's awful," and gave yet another scream, much louder than the rest.

"Feel there. Honestly, I never knew she wore them," Stafford said.

A blind went up.

"Honestly," Marion said. Her face was red. She tugged down her skirt then fastened her coat. She released another blind and then, stepping quickly across the carriage, released the rest.

Stafford sank back against the bench. He brushed back his hair and began to whistle, gazing out, abstracted, to the fields passing now below the track.

They crossed the river: a dark expanse of water coiled off between low, half-flooded banks.

"Honestly, he's so awful," Marion said. She'd taken a comb from her jacket pocket and standing to look into one of the framed pictures on the compartment wall she combed her hair.

Audrey, her hands clasped in her lap, sat by Colin; she gazed past him to the opposite window where the profile of the town stood up, outlined, like a wall of rock.

"Are you getting off at Saxton?" Stafford said.

"Yes," he said. "I suppose I shall."

"I might get off as well, then," Stafford said.

"Listen to him. Sulking," Marion said. "He's got miles to walk if he gets off there."

"Where do you get off, Audrey?" Colin said.

"I get off at Drayton," she said, naming a village some distance farther on.

"I suppose I'll have to go home with glad-hands," Marion said. "Unless he gets off at Saxton with his *bosom-friend*."

"I might get off. I might not, then," Stafford said.

"Honestly, he's so awful. You never feel safe when he's near you," Marion said.

She sat down now on the other side.

"Don't come near me," she added when Stafford went across.

He sat beside her for a while, his arms folded, gazing at Audrey and then at Colin.

"Honestly, I haven't done a thing. What's she going on about?" he said.

"Not in *daylight*," Marion said.

"Why not try the blinds down. The light's too strong for me," he said.

"Over my dead body, darling," Marion said.

They sat in silence for a while. The train drew into a station. Doors were slammed. A whistle blew.

Smoke billowed down beside the carriage.

The engine lurched. They moved off again between hedged fields.

"Honestly," Marion said again when Stafford raised one arm and, cautiously, put it round her waist. He kissed her cheek.

"There then, my darling. I never meant no harm."

"That's not what it felt like, my darling," Marion said.

"But what's this feel like, my darling," Stafford said and, more slowly, kissed her cheek again.

Marion had turned her head towards him. They kissed silently for a while, their arms finally entwined together.

Colin put his arm round Audrey. He held her lightly, afraid to see her face or glance towards her. As if absorbed by the passing fields and hedges, they gazed out through the window, swaying slightly, jarring, to the movement of the carriage.

Another station came. Stafford, alarmed, leapt up to the door. He leant out of the window until the whistle blew, then fell back in the seat, his arms once again, outstretched, enclosing Marion. They kissed each other silently as the train began to move.

More fields passed; a colliery yard. The train clattered through a cutting, the rock walls hidden by clouds of steam.

Finally the fields around Saxton appeared on either side. Beyond the summit of a hill he could see the colliery mound.

"I'll get out here," he said and waited then while Stafford found the ticket. He got up to the door as the train pulled into the narrow cutting. "I'll see you, then," he said and nodded, flushing, Stafford, his arm round Marion, having scarcely raised his head.

"You're getting off here, darling?" Marion said as if suddenly aware, then, of him standing by the door, lowering the window and reaching the handle. "Aren't you kissing Audrey goodbye?"

He leaned down briefly and brushed her cheek.

"I'll see you, then," he said and stepped down to the platform. He closed the door and glanced inside.

Audrey hadn't moved; red-cheeked, her hair disarranged, she gazed out at him from across the carriage. He glanced back along the platform, wondering when the train might move.

A porter came past and tested the door, then went back along the platform shutting others.

Finally a flag was waved; the engine whistled. The platform trembled as it drew away.

"What're you doing here?" she said.

"I thought I'd come across," he said.

She leant against the gate, glancing back along the track, towards the farm.

"My mother saw you first," she said. " 'Who's that young man?' she asked me. 'Cycling up and down.' "

"I thought I'd just come past," he said.

"Whose bike is it, in any case?" she said.

"A neighbour's." He added, "He lends me it. He lives next door."

The road came over a stretch of heathland on the opposite side of which stood several houses set out like stone blocks across the slope. The farm stood some way back, beneath a clump of trees. A field of rhubarb separated it from the road itself, the hedged track leading to it rutted, and lined here and there with pools of water.

"Do you want to go for a ride?" He waited.

"Where to?"

"Anywhere. I can't go far. I've got to get back in about an hour." He waited once again. "I could leave the bike here. We could go for a walk."

"I don't fancy walking much," she said.

She'd stepped up now on to the rung of the gate, and

swung it to and fro against the post. Over her blouse she wore a coat, her hair fastened back to make a tail above her neck.

A bus came across the heath and stopped at the houses. One or two people got off; she glanced across.

"Have you seen Marion?" he said.

"We went riding yesterday." She gestured back vaguely towards the house. "She came here for tea as well," she added.

A man, wearing jodhpurs, had crossed over the road from the direction of the bus stop and had now approached the gate. Colin recognized her brother.

"Hello, our Audrey," he said, glancing at her but not at Colin, and pushing back the gate. "Not getting into any trouble are you?"

"None that you need mind," she said.

"I shouldn't let the old 'un catch you, then," he said, gesturing off towards the house. He set off up the track towards the farm. Indifferent to where he walked, he splashed slowly through the puddles.

"Jonathan," she said, and gestured back. "He's been riding as well," she added.

"Don't you fancy getting your bike?" he said.

"How do you know I've got one?" she said.

"I don't know," he said. "I thought you might."

"I could meet you tonight," she said, slowly, stooping to the gate.

"Where's that?"

"I go to church," she said. "So does Marion. I could see you after."

"What church is it?"

"St. Olaf's."

"How do you get there?"

"It's over at Brierley. I go by bus."

The church, he calculated, was seven miles away. It would mean an hour on the bike, at least.

"What time does it finish?" he said.

"About half-past seven to eight," she said.

"I might see you there," he said, and turned away.

"I'll walk to the end of the road," she called, suddenly, stepping from the gate. She glanced back, awkwardly, towards the farm. "They'll be watching from the house," she added.

She walked beside him, swinging her coat. He pushed the bike beside him, at the edge of the road.

Finally, when they reached the bus stop, she glanced back once more towards the farm.

"I better go back, I suppose," she said. Her cheeks were flushed; she glanced towards the houses on the opposite slope as if reluctant to be seen talking by anyone she knew.

"I might see you at the church," he said.

"I'll ring Marion," she said. "She might ring Stafford." He turned to the bike.

"See you," she added and waved her arm, yet scarcely glancing as he pedalled off. He looked back from the crest of the hill: she'd already reached the gate and, running, had turned up the track towards the farm.

"I've looked all over the place," his father said, "for nearly an hour."

"I went to Stafford's," he said.

"Tha what?"

"To fetch a book." He'd taken it with him, inside his coat; he brought it out now and dropped it on the table. "I needed it for my holiday work," he said.

His father gazed at the book for several seconds.

"And thy's been right over theer?" he said.

"I came back," he said, "as fast as I could."

His father shook his head. He pointed to the door. "Thy brother's been roaring his head off. He sets some store by thy being with him, tha knows."

"I went as quick as I could," he said.

"There's more important things than books." He added. "Mrs. Shaw's more than enough, you know, with Richard."

His mother was ill; on the second day of her illness she'd been taken off to hospital. Colin was alone in the house with Steven and Richard when his father was at work. On this occasion, however, cycling over to Audrey's, he'd left Richard with Mrs. Shaw and Steven playing in the field; the kitchen itself was already tidy: he'd washed up the pots before he'd left. The floor, too, he'd swept, and had made the beds; he hadn't intended being away for longer than an hour.

"I told Mr. Shaw," he said, "when I borrowed his bike."

"Well, Mr. Shaw isn't in at present," his father said. He stooped to the fire with a lighted match; Steven, who'd been crying on the doorstep, had come inside, sitting on a chair and rubbing his eyes. Richard's cries, loud and prolonged, came from Mrs. Shaw's next door.

Colin picked up the book; his own name, he realized, was inside the cover. "I said, if I was free, I might go over tonight."

"Wheer?" his father said. He swivelled round.

"Stafford's."

"And what's so important about Stafford, then?"

"I said I might go over, if you didn't need me here," he said.

"I need you here. Don't you think I need you here?" his father said.

"I just thought you might be in tonight. It's some work I wanted to check," he said.

"Well, you can check your work in here," he said. He gestured round him at the kitchen; then, attracted by the roaring of the fire, he covered it, briefly, with a sheet of paper.

He stood over it for a while.

"We don't ask much of you, any road," he added.

"I've helped you in the past," he said.

"Aye," he said. "After how much asking?"

He took the paper away; the fire roared up.

"We don't need all that coal on. Not in summer time," he added.

His father went to work that night, Colin saw him off at the door.

"Think on," he told him before he left. "Thy's two young 'uns to look to now. No gallivanting off."

His father took the front-door key, locking it before he went.

When he'd gone he cooked Steven some supper and put him to bed. Richard was already asleep, fastened in his cot.

He tucked Steven up, read him a story, then waited while he fell asleep. It was nearly eight o'clock.

He went next door to Mrs. Shaw's.

"I wondered if you could keep an eye on them," he said. "I've got to go over to a friend's to get a book."

"You've a lot of books to see to suddenly," Mrs. Shaw had said.

"Could I borrow Mr. Shaw's bike again?" he added.

"Nay, you better ask him, love," she said.

"I'll be charging thee mileage on them tyres," Mr. Shaw had said, calling then from inside the kitchen. "First yon farm, and now thy books. Mind how tha go on it," he added.

"Does your father know you're going?" Mrs. Shaw had said as she followed him to the yard.

"I said I might be going. I'll be back as soon as I can," he said.

He set off down the yard, Mrs. Shaw, the key in her hand, watching him from the step.

It took him nearly an hour to reach the church. It stood at a crossroads, some distance from Brierley village. A large manor house, occupied by soldiers, stood immediately behind it, the church itself and the house enclosed by a low stone wall.

Several soldiers were sitting on the wall. The sun had begun to set. Long shadows spread out from the trees beside the road itself. The church was closed. There was no sign of anyone he knew.

He set off up the road, following the bus route back towards the farm. A car came past him and roared off, leaving a cloud of dust. It was long after nine when he crested the hill above the farm. He freewheeled down the heath and cycled slowly past the gate. There was no sign of movement either in the yard or along the track: the wooden gate itself was closed.

He cycled back, dismounted, and gazed up for a while towards the house.

A bus came over the hill and pulled up at the stop. Two or three people got off, laughing, and set off, waving to the bus, across the heath. The bus came past; pale faces gazed out of the darkening windows.

He leant on the gate, sitting now astride the bike and gazing up directly to the house.

It was growing dark; the sun disappeared beyond a line of hills.

He waited by the gate a little longer then, turning on the battery lights, set off slowly up the rise. He waited at the top again, gazing back towards the farm; then, free-wheeling, he set off down the slope the other side.

He thought he saw them, briefly, walking up the road; when he pedalled nearer, however, their three figures turned out to be a man and a woman walking with a child. He set off back, pedalling slowly, drained of all strength as well as feeling.

"So you went out after all," his father said. He'd come into the bedroom to wake him up: Steven's bed, he saw was empty; he'd meant to get up early, cook his father's breakfast, forestalling any inquiry about the night before.

"I went out for a bit," he said.

"It was nearly three hours from what Mrs. Shaw's just said." His eyes were black from where he'd roughly washed; he still had on his pit clothes, his long coat, his cap pushed in his pocket: there was a red line from its neb above his eyes. "I find Steven lakin' with the fire, and Richard crying in his cot. What sort of looking-after is that supposed to be? I can't turn me back without you slipping off. If you weren't supposed to be grown up I'd give you a damn good hiding. Your mother ill and me at work, and you go gallivanting off, after you've been told you're needed here."

"I have to see about this work," he said.

"Work? What work? You can see about schoolwork some other time," he said. "There's another six weeks of holiday yet. Lying on your back i' bed."

"I'd thought of getting a job," he said.

"There's a job here at present, lad. Looking after thy two brothers. I'm off to the hospital as soon as I'm dressed. And what am I going to think when I'm going, then? That you haven't two minutes to help us out."

"I'll help you out," he said.

"Aye, help us into a worse hole than we're already in," his father said.

When he went down his father was washing at the sink; Steven was sitting in a chair, watching him then as he began to get ready: his father pulled on his suit trousers, then his waistcoat. Fluffs of soap from his shaving still clung to his ear.

"You see: he wants to come with me," his father said, indicating Steven. "I've told him children aren't allowed."

"I can wait outside, Dad," Steven said.

"And how shall I know what you're up to?" his father said. "If you're like your brother, it might be ought."

"I'll wait," Steven said and went to his coat. "I'll wait where you tell me," he added, coming back. He tried to pull on his coat, his head thrust down.

"Nay, tha mu'n stay with Colin," his father said. "I've enough to be worrying about without having something else."

Steven, pale-faced, staring at his father, began to cry.

"Nay, tha mu'n cry all tha wants," his father said. "I'm off on my own. They don't make rules for nothing," he added.

Yet, at the door, he'd glanced back at Steven. Richard had already gone next door.

"Sithee, I won't be long," he said as he watched Steven bury his head against a chair. "I might bring summat back with me, if tha behaves thasen," he added. He looked at Colin. "That's both of you I mean. No gallivanting off. Thy get his dinner, and Richard's. Don't leave it all to Mrs. Shaw. You'll find it in the cupboard."

In fact, when his father had gone, he found the potatoes already peeled, standing in a pan. The cabbage had been left, already washed, in a metal colander. Four sausages had been left in the cupboard, with a note pinned on top, "For Sunday Dinner." His father must have got back even earlier than he thought.

He sat with Steven for a while; then he took him out. He called for Richard, sat him in his push-chair, and set off for the Park.

"Your father was cross," Mrs. Shaw said. "About last night. You don't want to go off leaving them," she said.

"Yes," he said and set off down the yard.

"Are you all right for your dinner, love?" she said.

"Yes," he said.

"Nay, if there's anything I can do," she said as she watched them go.

The Park was almost empty; he sat Richard on a swing and pushed him to and fro. The day was bright; the sun came down directly on to the slope of the hill; a faint haze showed here and there across the fields, low down, obscuring at one point the embankment of the railway line running like a rampart towards the distant woods. Corn in one of the nearer fields had recently been cut; men were working at the sheaves and, from farther off, came the dull, grating chatter of a tractor. A huge, ball-shaped cloud of steam rose over the village from the direction of the pit.

There were only children in the park, except on the upper slope where a man with a scythe was cutting grass. Lorries rattled to and fro on the road beyond; from the colliery itself came the dull panting of the engine and across the foot of the slope he could see the headgear, the spoked wheels invisible, spinning round.

Steven had run off across the slope. Colin sat on the swings for a while. He pushed himself slowly with the toe of his foot. He imagined, briefly, what it might be like with his mother dead, with his father at work, or, worse, away from home. He watched Richard on the swing with his tiny fisted hands, his lightish hair, his strangely self-absorbed expression as the swing, still swaying, swung up and down.

A train crossed the embankment, travelling slowly beneath a banner of blackish smoke; in the distance other clouds of smoke rose from the faintly visible heaps and chimneys. At the foot of the slope, where it flattened out towards the railway, a group of boys were playing football. Several girls, at the edge of the fish-pond, were playing round a pram.

He pushed Richard on the swing, then, for a while, he held him on the rocking-horse. The man with the scythe worked rhythmically across the slope, occasionally calling out as the children disturbed the raked-up piles—or standing, sharpening his scythe and gazing off, abstracted, towards the distant woods.

Three figures had appeared at the top of the hill. Two of them were sat on bikes, the third leaning up against a bike; an arm was raised and, faintly, he heard his name being called.

Stafford, stilll waving, re-mounted his bike; a moment later he came coasting down the hill, sitting sideways on the cross-bar, his elbows out.

"We've just been down to your house," he said, dismounting at the foot of the slope. "The woman next door said you might be here."

Steven had come over; he held his hand.

"What happened to you last night, then?" Stafford said.

"I couldn't get out," he said, and shook his head.

"We waited at St. Olaf's. Then went on to Marion's," Stafford said. "Her father drove us home," he added. He gestured behind him to the top of the hill. "They're both here now. We wondered if you could get a bike."

"I've to look after my brothers today," he said.

"Can't you dump them somewhere?" Stafford said.

"I've to cook their dinner as well," he said.

"We've got some sandwiches. We thought we'd have a picnic. We could go over to Brierley Woods. We could really have some fun there," Stafford said.

"Colin," Steven said and pulled at his arm.

"I've got to look after them though," he said.

Behind him Richard, suddenly aware that he was alone, had begun to cry.

"They've come over specially," Stafford said, gesturing once more to the slope behind. "And Audrey's pretty keen. It was her idea to come," he added.

He glanced back up the slope. Marion was calling: she'd begun to wave her arm.

He went back to the rocking-horse and lifted Richard off. He set him in the pram.

"Honestly; do you have to look after them?" Stafford said.

"My mother's in hospital," he said.

"What's matter with her?" Stafford said, looking at his bike, then pulling strands of straw from between the spokes.

"I don't know," he said.

"You could leave them with this woman," Stafford said. "Couldn't she look after them for a day?"

He shook his head. He glanced over at the slope again.

He could hear his name being called. Marion's arm was raised again; Audrey, her slim figure stooping to her bike, stood some distance farther back, almost at the gate.

He pushed the pram towards the slope. Stafford cycled back along the path, standing finally to force the pedals.

The keeper, sitting in his wooden hut, had whistled, waving a stick, wildly, up and down. Stafford got off; he waited for Colin to catch him up.

"She's really keen for you to come. It'll not be much fun with just the three of us," he added.

Steven held on to the pram as he pushed it up. Audrey, as if dismayed, had already turned her bike towards the gate.

"Honestly, who's playing Daddies today, then?" Marion said when he reached the top. She looked at Richard's tear-streaked face and then at Steven: he too, as if sensing danger, had begun to cry.

"I can't get out today," he said, holding now to the handle of the pram.

"Are both of them yours, then?" Marion said, laughing now and bowing her head. Her dark hair was fastened back beneath a ribbon. Audrey, as if reluctant to be seen at all, had wheeled her bike out between the gates.

"I have to look after my brothers," he said and stood for a moment, shaking his head, uncertain whether to follow Audrey.

"Honestly, we'll wait for you," Stafford said. "Haven't you got a relative, or something, you could leave them with?"

"No," he said. He shook his head.

"I suppose we better go back, then," Stafford said. "It was Audrey's idea," he added again.

Marion turned her bike.

"Honestly, you ought to speak to her, at least," she said.

Colin pushed the pram towards the gate. Audrey was at the kerb, getting ready to mount her bike.

"I can't come today," he said. He added, "I came last night. To St. Olaf's, but I got there late, I went over to your place. Stafford said you went to Marion's."

"We went there for a bit," she said.

She glanced at Steven; there were holes in his pullover,

and the sleeves of the pullover had begun to fray. His stockings had slipped down around his ankles; his nose, with his crying, had begun to run. Only Richard had any neatness; yet he was crying now and shaking the pram.

"I've to look after my brothers today," he said, and Stafford called out, "We better get going then, my dear."

"We don't want our sandwiches getting cold, then, do we?" Marion said.

"I'll try and come over one evening," he said.

"My mother doesn't like you coming to the house," she said.

She mounted the bike. Stafford and Marion, freewheeling, had started down the hill.

"She doesn't think it looks very nice," she said.

"Shall I come to the door?" he said.

She shook her head.

"We'll try some other time," she said and, pushing from the kerb, pedalled slowly off, freewheeling finally as she reached the hill.

"I can't make you out," his father said when he came back in. "Here's your mother ill and you don't want to help. Anybody would think you don't want to live here any more."

He stood silently across the room and didn't answer.

"Haven't you got a tongue in your head?" his father added.

"What can I say, in any case?" he said.

"Tha can say I'm wrong in feeling what I do. Tha can say any number of things," his father said. "Here I am: I haven't had a sleep, and I'm off back to work already. You might say summat about that, for a start."

"There's nothing I can say about it." He shrugged.

"And there's nowt thy wants to say about it," his father said. "For it's true."

His mother was away for three weeks. When she came back, at her own insistence, she could scarcely stand. She'd made his father sign her out. "I'm better doing nothing here than nothing there," she said. "Just lying on my back, I might as well be home."

Yet it was some other person now who'd come to the house. Both of her parents had died the previous Easter. Ever since the funeral she had begun to fade: finally, one morning, while he was at school, she had collapsed in the kitchen; his father had taken her to the hospital the following day. Now, returning, she sat silently about the house all day, and at night, sleeplessly, tossed to and fro on the double bed. He did nearly all the housework now: on Mondays he did the washing, under her supervision, standing aside occasionally, as, groaning, she got up from her chair to show him how to wash a particular shirt or blouse; on Wednesdays he cleaned the house upstairs, washing the bedroom floors, on Fridays the front room, the kitchen and the outside toilet. On Saturdays he did the shopping. While she was still in hospital he'd found an opportunity to cycle over to the farm on three occasions; on none had be seen Audrey, though on the last he'd called at the house. A farm dog, barking at the end of a chain, had greeted his arrival, and the door had been opened by a tall, fair-haired woman with bright red cheeks who'd answered his inquiry as to whether Audrey was in with a shake of her head, calling him back as he turned away and saying,"I think she's too young to have boys calling for her. I'd appreciate it very much if you didn't cycle up and down in front of the gate."

He'd thought of writing her a letter; he'd looked up her number in a telephone directory, and had set out on two occasions to ring her up, faltering each time when he reached the phone.

Stafford had called one day when he was out shopping, but hadn't waited until he got back.

"We seem to go from one thing to another, and each one worse than the one afore," his father said one evening, before he set off for work. "If it hadn't have been for this you could have had a job. That's ten or fifteen pounds we might have had. As it is, you're fastened up here and you end up earning nought."

"I offered to get a job," he said.

"I know you offered," his father said. "What's the use of offering if you can't go out and do it? Steven can offer. Richard can offer. But that doesn't add up to much, then, does it?"

"What if I went and got a job?" he said. "What would my mother do on her own in the house?"

"That's what I'm saying. However hard we work we

end up where we were afore. There's no point in doing ought. Whatever we do, whatever we say, we end exactly where we wa' before. I can't see any point in it. I can't. Not any more."

He kicked the table leg. There was something in his father now that was changed from what he'd known before. It was as if some part of him had died: he seemed pinned down; he no longer talked of moving, or changing house. His job was a habit, a kind of bond. He came home on leave like a soldier from a war: his real life, his real worries, were somewhere else, underground, away from them, invisible, even incommunicable. He would talk frustratedly now in front of Colin while his mother, as if sensing herself the cause of it, would get up from her chair, attempt some household task from which, a moment later, he would rescue her, saying, "Leave that to Colin, or we'll have you back inside. You know what the doctor warned. I was a damn fool to let you out."

"How can I sit here," she'd ask him, "and listen to this? If I wasn't poorly none of this would happen."

"If it wasn't you," he'd say condemningly, "it'd be something else. There's been a blight on this family, there always has. We've tried to build up something. And see now where we end." He'd gesture round. "We've got nought, and no hope as I can see of anything better."

His mother would cry; she would hold her apron against her eyes, for she wore her apron though she didn't work, marking out her intention if nothing else. Long after his father had gone to work, or had gone upstairs to sleep, if the argument had broken out in the morning, she would sit in her chair, moaning, sometimes burying her head against her arm, or take Richard to her, and hide her face against his cheek.

She did more work now, however, when his father was out; she would come over to where he was cleaning, or washing-up, and take whatever he was using from him, a scrubbing-brush or a piece of cloth, and say, "You can leave that. I can do that now," almost bitterly, as if the sight of him working was more than she could stand. "You can get the coal," she'd tell him, or, "Wash the windows," or, "Get in the washing," tasks which, despite this, she'd decided with herself she wouldn't do. Each afternoon, after lunch, she went to bed, and whenever his father was around she would sink back in her chair as if determined he should see how placidly she was resting.

Yet, the more determined she appeared in getting better, the more frustrated his father grew. He came home each morning now exhausted, his cheeks drawn, his eyes dark, shadowed, his mouth drawn tight; he would plunge into whatever jobs he could find himself, even digging the garden, mending the fence, washing the windows when, perhaps that week, they'd been washed already. He'd given up his allotment; when he couldn't find anything else to do he'd sink down in a chair himself, sleeping in his clothes, his mouth wide open, snoring, Steven regarding him nervously from across the room, Richard being quietened in case he woke and yet, even when they shook him and told him the time, that he'd only so many hours left to go to bed, he'd refuse to stir, half-opening his eyes, reddened, bleary, and half-snarling with an anger they'd scarcely seen before, "Leave me alone. Get off. I can sleep down here," his mother calling, "Leave him, then, for goodness' sake. He knows when he's resting," his father, his eyes half-closed, turning his head blindly towards the room, then sinking back, his face blank, like a piece of stone, seemingly half-conscious, watching them despite his snoring. His eyes would gleam beneath his half-shut lids.

One morning, after his father had gone to bed and his mother, silently, had begun some cleaning, sweeping the kitchen, she'd suddenly collapsed. She'd sunk down on a chair, holding her chest, half-reclining at the table, and Colin, startled, had stood there for a while, unable to tell how serious it was, unable to decide what he ought to do. His mother had struggled for a while, as if trying to stand or even, perhaps, intending to continue with her job. Calling to her, he'd stood by the table, waiting for some instruction. Her eyes, distorted, rolled slowly in her head.

"Dad," he'd called. "Dad."

His father was upstairs in bed.

He went to the foot of the stairs and called again; then he heard his mother calling out, almost calmly, "Get me a chair, then, Colin," and then, more clearly, "In the front room, Colin."

His mother lay with her head against the table, one arm sprawled out, unable to move. For a moment it seemed to him like an affectation; as if, had she so wished it, she could get up quite easily herself. He hadn't touched her now for years, and could scarcely remember a time when she'd even embraced him.

He took her arm; he tried to lift her. He pulled her to her feet and, her legs dragging, her arms limp, tried to carry her through to the other room. As he turned to the door he saw his father standing there, in his shirt and his underpants, gazing in, bleary-eyed, startled, unable to make sense of what he saw. He thought for a moment he might have leapt across: a look of bewilderment crossed his face; then, as if wakening, with a death-like voice, subdued, he came into the kitchen, calling, "Whatever is it, lad? What's wrong?"

"Harry," his mother said, and called, "Harry."

"I'm here, my love," his father said, taking her then, almost fiercely, roughly, holding her to him.

"She wanted to go to the other room," he said. "To lie down on the sofa."

"Hold on to me, Ellen," his father said, "hold on to me, then, my love," and, trying to lift her, half-carried her through.

He laid her on the sofa.

"Light the fire, then, lad," he said, and added, as he knelt at the grate, "Get a blanket, then, I mu'n get her covered," almost to himself, half-calling.

He went upstairs, saw where his father had been sleeping, and took a blanket.

His father was rubbing her feet when he went back down; his mother was lying stiffly the length of the sofa; her legs had begun to tremble and, as he watched, her arms had begun to shake as well. Her jaw vibrated. Her body was gripped in a huge vibration.

"Sithee, fetch the doctor. Tha mu'n call for him. Tell him it's urgent," his father said. He tucked the blanket round her as if about to go himself. "Go on. Take my bike," he said. His legs were bare, his shirt unbuttoned; Richard, who'd been playing in the kitchen, had come into the room, standing, leaning up against the door. "Mam?" he began to say, "Mam?" his voice trailing off into a sudden wail.

"Go on. Don't wait," his father said.

He rode to the doctor's at the end of the village.

His father was dressed when he got back in: he was in the kitchen, drinking tea. Astonished to see him there at all, he said, "How is she, then? Is my mother all right?"

"Aye. She'll be all right. Is the doctor coming?" his father said.

"They said he'd come as soon as he can," he said.

"And how soon's that going to be? By God, when you want them doctors they're never there."

He went through to the other room. His mother was moaning quietly to herself; her glasses had been taken off; her legs were vibrating beneath the blanket. His father came in with his tea. "Don't touch her, then," he said. He put the pot down. His hands were trembling. He sat on the arm of the sofa, half-crouching, and began, slowly, to rub his mother's feet; then, as she began to moan more loudly, he took out her arms from beneath the blanket and rubbed her hands, half-moaning now it seemed himself, his voice harsh, half-startled. "Nay, you'll be all right, then, love. The doctor's coming. Nay, you'll be all right, then, love. We'll just hang on."

The doctor came an hour later. Colin sat in the kitchen with Richard. He could hear the doctor's voice with its Scottish accent, then his father's murmur, then a fainter inaudible murmur from his mother.

Finally the doctor came out, briskly, screwing back the top of a fountain-pen and clipping it inside his pocket. He went through to the front door, his father following.

The sound of his car, a moment later, came echoing from the street outside.

"You can fetch that from the chemist," his father said, coming in then with a slip of paper.

His mother was in bed when he got back in.

"I've told her she shouldn't do any work," his father said. "She's to do no lifting, and she's not to come downstairs again, except for the toilet until the doctor's seen her. You see what happens when you don't follow instructions."

Her illness frightened his father: it gave him strength; he buckled to the housework now himself, and came home from work with an eye anxious for any job that hadn't been done, ironing his own clothes, washing, scrubbing the floor and washing the windows, but with none of his ear-

347

lier resentment. Now she was fastened upstairs, with the doctor coming every other day, and with the threat of the hospital hanging over them once again, an older, more familiar momentum returned to the place: his father knew what he ought to do, and did it, cooking his mother's meals and carrying them upstairs, sleeping on the sofa now, whistling to himself as he worked in the kitchen, going upstairs to kiss his mother goodbye each evening before he set off for work.

"You take good care of her," he'd tell Colin, coming down, before he left. "Ought she wants you get it. And keep Richard quiet when he goes to bed."

Colin would go in to see her himself before he went to bed; she would be lying back against the pillow, sometimes reading a paper, other times dozing, glancing up, casually, saying, "Have you washed, then, love?" or, "Have you locked the doors? Your father's got his key, then, hasn't he?" half-dazed, almost as if he were some other person, leaning forward suddenly to touch his hair, to push back his fringe, inquiringly, as if unsure for a moment who he was.

In the mornings, if his father wasn't back, he'd take her in a cup of tea, quietly setting it on the chair beside her bed, listening to her breathing, not wakening her or touching the curtains. Then, having got Steven up and Richard, he would tiptoe down the stairs. Sometimes, waking drowsily, she would call to the stairs, "Is that you, Colin? What time is it?" waiting then for him to come back in and adding, "Can you draw the curtains, love?" or, "If you'll hand me the coat I'll have to go downstairs." She crossed the yard on her own to the toilet, white, thin-faced, not glancing up when anyone called so that often Mrs. Shaw or Mrs. Bletchley watched her from their doors, not speaking, their arms folded. "How's your mother, Colin?" Mrs. Shaw would say and shake her head before he answered. "She's not looking well. She ought to be in hospital," she'd tell him.

One Sunday evening, when his father changed shifts, he borrowed his bike and cycled out to St. Olaf's. The service was still on; the soldiers in the old mansion were sitting on the steps below the porch: one or two were playing with a ball between the trees. From several of the ancient, mullioned windows soldiers' heads were hanging out, their voices calling, echoing in the yard beyond the church.

He rode up and down the road opposite the church until he saw a verger hook back the doors. He waited then beneath a tree; several girls and youths came out, the older people standing in groups around the gate. He saw Audrey and Marion with several other girls he recognized; they stood by the stone wall for a while, in a circle, laughing, glancing over at the groups of boys. Finally one or two boys moved off slowly; some of the girls began to follow.

Colin waited for a while beneath the tree; then, as the group of youths rounded the corner towards the village he started after them, cycling slowly. Audrey glanced across, then Marion; perhaps they'd expected Stafford as well for they glanced behind him, but seeing the road empty but for the following line of boys, they continued talking to the girls on either side. Colin paused, not knowing any one of them to speak to, then cycled slowly on until the first of the houses came into sight. He got off the bike, took off his cycle clips, and waited for the youths to pass.

Neither Audrey nor Marion paid him any attention; there was a brief glance across from the dark-haired girl, but it was more a gesture directed at the world in general, half-smirking, the eyes narrowed, the eyebrows raised, the mouth pulled wide in the beginning of a smile.

He got on the bike again after the line of pursuing boys had passed, and cycled slowly in their wake. Finally, when they reached a bus stop in the centre of the village they stood in a large group around a wooden seat, still talking and laughing. Occasionally one figure would chase another, a pursuit egged on by the others and ending in screams—a girl pushed back against a hedge, a boy hanging over her, pinning her arms, helpless suddenly, and grinning.

At one point a boy and girl moved off, along a hedged lane adjoining the stop: two or three of the boys called out and, between the slowly shifting figures, he caught a glimpse of Audrey, sitting on the bench, smiling suddenly and shaking her head.

Some time later the group parted and Marion appeared: she was wearing a reddish hat. She wore high heels. She came over to the hedge where he was leaning on the bike and, glancing back at the boys, who, in turn, were gazing across in her direction, said, "Audrey's given me a message. She doesn't want to see you again. I didn't want to tell you, but there it is." Some comment was made amongst the boys around the stop and a moment later the girls as well as the boys had laughed. Marion, aware of the audience at her back, had shaken her shoulders and tossed her head. "Is there anything you want to tell her, then?"

"I'd like to talk to her," he said. "If she can drag herself away from those grinning idiots."

"Those grinning idiots, as you put it," Marion said, "are some of my friends."

"If she can drag herself away from some of your friends," he said, suddenly gratified by the eloquence his feelings had given him.

"I'm sure she doesn't want to. But I'll ask her all the same," she said.

She walked back to the watching group. His message was passed loudly through the wall of figures to Audrey sitting on the bench.

Audrey, in a slightly subdued voice, had given an answer back.

Marion, her face pale beneath her bell-shaped hat, called over, "She doesn't want to speak to you, my dear. I said she wouldn't."

He picked up a blade of grass from the verge and set it slowly in the corner of his mouth. His hand, he saw, had begun to tremble. His whole body began to shake.

A moment later some of the boys and two of the girls moved off; they disappeared up a road between the houses. A bus appeared at the bend in the road. It rattled down towards the stop.

A man got off; Marion and Audrey, followed by the boys, got on.

He could see them at the rear windows as the bus went past, a hand waving, and behind, a brief glimpse of Audrey's face, half-smiling. The bus disappeared in a cloud of dust.

He mounted the bike and cycled after it for a while, re-passing the church where soldiers now were sitting along the wall, and turning down the road which, from the amount of dust in the air, he assumed the bus had taken.

After half an hour's cycling, and passing several stops, he turned in the road, idly, and, freewheeling, started back, re-passing the church once more, the wall outside deserted, and continuing on towards the village; it was almost dark by the time he got back home.

"And what did Stafford have to say?" his father said when he went in the kitchen. "Not borrowed another book again?"

"I didn't go," he said, and shook his head. It was the notion of cycling to Stafford's that he had used to borrow his father's bike.

"So where have you been till this time? It's long past the time tha mu'n be in bed."

"I just cycled around," he said. "I thought I might go to church."

"Church?" his father said.

"I got there too late," he said, and shook his head.

"And what's thy doing at church?" his father said, as if he connected it in some way with his mother.

"I thought I might go. On Sunday evenings. Instead of the afternoon," he said. "I'm getting a bit old for Sunday School," he added.

"Nay, that mu'n do what thy want about church," his father said. "Tha's not punctured the bike or ought?" he added.

"No," he said, and added, "I'll get up and get you some breakfast if you like."

"Nay, I don't eat ought, when I get up," his father said. He looked at him uneasily as he crossed over to the stairs. "Think on about coming in late," he added.

Later, from his room, he heard his father say, "I think our Colin's been courting. He's come in with as daft a look as I've seen on his face," the door closing then, his mother's voice murmuring from the other side.

He heard a faint laugh from his parents' room, the creaking on their bed; he slowly succumbed to his tiredness, worn out more by cycling than anything else.

19

He started going to church on Sunday evenings with
Bletchley and Reagan. Mrs. Bletchley and Mrs. Reagan,
with their respective sons, but without their respective
husbands, attended church also on Sunday mornings. In
the evenings, however, he and Bletchley and Reagan sat
at the back of the north aisle, on the opposite side to the
pulpit, and behind a row of girls from Bletchley's school.
They passed messages to and fro, fastened in the pages of
a prayer-book, and Bletchley, during the prayers, when
the girls knelt forward from the wooden chairs, would
frequently take a glove, passing it to Reagan, who, with
his eyes closed, red-faced, would put it in his pocket.

Reagan had grown into a pale-cheeked, narrow-faced
youth; he had a prominent brow, a long nose, slightly upturned, which dominated his face. His attempt to conceal
the extraordinary rearward bulge of his head by allowing
his hair to hang down to the nape of his neck was a source
of constant irritation to his father. Frequently on an evening, above the strains of the now somewhat larger violin
on which Reagan practised, could be heard the shouts echoing across the yards: "*You* think it's beautiful: *I* think it
makes him look like a cissy. *You* think he can play a violin: *I* think it's like a cat on hot bricks. *You* think he looks
distinguished: I think he looks like a bloody woman," or,
later, as he came out to the yard, "Don't leave him alone
in that house or I'll have it off him," stalking then across
the backs to sit with his father in the porch, or moving
with an abstracted air towards the foot of his garden
where, standing at the fence, he would call to the miners
playing cricket in the field, "Hit it! Hit it harder," his face
reddening, his neck on the point of bursting from his col-

lar. "Harder, for God's sake. You'll never get anywhere with that."

With Beltchley, Reagan preserved a respectful silence; it was one of Bletchley's mannerisms, when walking, to pause at some relevant point of his conversation waiting for Reagan to turn his head, to pause and, finally, however much in a hurry he was, to incline his body in his direction, even stepping back a pace or two; Reagan's face would be set with a wearied look, contemplating not Bletchley but the space above his head. If, as not infrequently happened, Reagan went on walking, unaware of Bletchley's pause, Bletchley would stand waiting with a patronizing sneer set on his lips until, suddenly aware that he was no longer walking in the company of his friend, Reagan with the same wearied air would walk back down the road to where, with raised eyebrows now, and anxious to continue his narrative, his friend was standing. No word of any sort, during these encounters, passed Reagan's lips; merely his presence and the expression of studied expectancy were sufficient to fire Bletchley into prolonged descriptions of his life at school, of his father's exploits in the war, of the achievements of distant relatives, or into an analysis on recent political events.

The war had ended earlier that year. A party had been held in the field at the back of the house; tables of every description had been lifted over the fences and set with variously colored cloths and miscellaneous plates of food. A gramophone, wound by hand, had been placed on a wooden chair and after the meal was over couples danced in the grass, stumbling over mounds of bricks and bottles, the sounds of their voices echoing between the houses with the dull, almost mournful rhythm of the tune. Children ran wildly between the tables, snatching at the food, gathering in groups to watch the couples, occasionally imitating the dancers' movements, the miners clearing a space finally beyond the tables where they organized races, wives wheeling husbands in garden barrows, or running three-legged, stumbling, to screams and shouts, hopping, husbands carrying wives and wives, later in the day, attempting to carry husbands. Walking slowly amongst all these rushing bodies, his thumbs hooked in his waistcoat pockets, a fresh white handkerchief projecting from the breast-pocket of his suit, his bowler hat on this occasion missing, was Mr. Reagan. Occasionally he would step out from the crowd and producing a second white handkerchief from his trouser pocket insist on starting one of the races, examining each of the contestants first as to their positions on the starting line, the legality of their posture, drawing one back, or thrusting another forward, giving a noticeable advantage to those he judged less likely to show up well, and starting them off, to screams and shouts, with something of a gesture. "When I drop the handkerchief so —before which I shall say, 'Are you ready? Get to your marks,'" waving the handkerchief with a slow, almost derisory gesture above his head, and withholding the signal until that moment when the cries of complaint had risen to a crescendo. Finally, when he had made sure there was nothing left to eat and that the small supply of liquid refreshment had been consumed, he took over this task completely, even following the competitors across the field, calling advice, or running, if the race were one which allowed only intermittent progress, to the finishing-line and indicating to those he favoured most how they might gain advantage over their nearest rivals, getting in the way, if only accidentally, of those whom he judged to have taken an unfair advantage or those whom he thought were too well endowed in any case.

Flags had been draped from several of the houses, and strings of small, triangular flags had been hung across the streets. On some of the houses placards had been mounted, welcoming home a member of the family from service in the forces, and several figures in uniform, khaki, blue and navy-blue, wandered in a desultory fashion about the field, one soldier, his sleeves rolled, tunic-less, competing in several of the races but finally lying in the grass by one of the fences, his mouth open, apparently asleep.

In the evening small groups of miners sat about the field, chewing grass, or collected in dark knots about the doorways, one or two lifting back the tables across the fences, the women standing in the yards, arms folded, or sorting plates and cups and saucers. An air of lethargy had settled on the place, Mrs. Shaw alone, after spending most of her time serving at the tables, stalking from door to door, offering her services for washing-up. Batty and his brothers, who had lingered on the fringe of the activities during the afternoon, now occupied the centre of the field, where, with Stringer's father and two other men, they tossed coins in a half-hearted fashion, their occasional cries echoing back to the open doors, "Nay, Geoff," and, "Toss again," and, "I've won, I've won," while several of the smaller children gathered round.

"They won't have that again for a long time," his father said when he'd finally returned the kitchen table and with Colin's help lifted it inside the room. "That's exhausted neighbourly hopitality for a year or two, you can be sure of that. Did you see Mrs. McCormack complaining that her plates were smashed? And that woman who ate that fruit cake doesn't even live in the street, you know."

"I think they should have it more often," his mother said. "Not wait for a war to end before people get together. It just shows what you can do when you set your mind to it."

"Aye," his father said, sinking down beside the table. "Why, there's half of yon colliers too drunk to go to work."

"Oh, he's exaggerating as usual," his mother said, turning to Colin. "He's enjoyed himself for once, so he's anxious not to show it."

His father, in fact, had taken as prominent a part in the afternoon's activities as Mr. Reagan, only he had done it as a competitor, racing down the field at one point with Mrs. Bletchley, their legs strapped together, on another with Mrs. Shaw, who, screaming, had bundled his father along as a wheelbarrow, while clutching at his legs. It was perhaps his pleasure at these achievements that he was anxious to disown, for his mother had spent most of the afternoon standing at the tables, serving food, or going to and fro between the kitchens collecting sandwiches and attempting to supervise the children who removed the cakes from the plates as fast as they were laid. Now she stood at the sink, flushed, stacking the wet plates beside her and adding, "If you've nothing else to do but grumble you could easily dry these up."

His father took the cloth; he gazed out of the window, wiped a plate, saw someone he recognized in the yard outside and saying, "Hold on, I won't be a minute," dropped the cloth and disappeared through the open door.

Some time later they could hear his laughter across the backs, his voice calling out in protest, followed by Mrs. McCormack's, then Mrs. Bletchley's, then by a screech which they finally identified as Mrs. Shaw's.

"*He* hasn't enjoyed himself, it's easy to see that," his mother said. She handed Colin the cloth. "One war over and another begun as far as he's concerned, and someone else to clear the mess."

His mother had a faded air; ever since he'd known her there'd been some steady diminution of her spirit, first with Steven's birth, then with Richard's, now with this, a slow extraction, leaving her, after each interval of illness, weaker, more disenchanted, half-bemused. It was as if her life had flooded out, secretly, without their knowledge, and she some helpless agent, watching this dissolution with a hidden rage, half-apologetic, half-disowning. "You didn't celebrate much, in any case," she said. "I saw Batty's lad and that Stringer tucking in. They didn't lose much opportunity in taking out more than any of them put in."

"Oh," he said, shrugging. "I mainly stayed in here."

"You and Ian and Michael Reagan, I expect, are above it all," she said.

Yet Bletchley and Reagan had, though taking no part in the activities in the field, played a conspicuous part in the disposal of the food, bringing whole plates back to Bletchley's kitchen, where, since Mrs. Bletchley was busy in the field, they had consumed it unmolested.

"Do you feel above it all?" she said.

He shook his head. "I suppose I feel apart."

"Is that the grammar school," she said, "we shall have to thank for that?"

"You wanted me to go," he said.

"Yes," she said. "Don't worry, love. I'm not complaining."

"I don't feel I'm part of anything there, either," he said, "if it comes to that."

He took another plate and dried it. His mother, still bowed to the sink, took the kettle from beside her and warmed the water. She ran her hand round the pile of plates still there. Then, raising her head, she washed each one and lifted them out.

"I suppose that's a phase you go through." She glanced across at him and smiled. "Aren't there other boys like you?"

"I suppose there are."

"Don't they feel out of it?"

"I've no idea."

"You'll find you'll get no more out of life than what you put into it," she said.

"Yes," he said. "I suppose that's true."

"Couldn't you have joined in today?" she said.

"Yes," he said. He shook his head. "I suppose I could. As it was," he gestured round, "I stayed in here."

His father came back a little later, flushed, bright-eyed, rubbing his hands. "Well, that was a day to remember," he said as if, by the buoyancy of his spirit, he could make some secret of his activities outside. "When you've been through something together it makes a party like that seem well worth while," gazing in surprise then at the pots piled on the table and adding, "What's this, then, love? Have you gone and dried?"

His life had been fragmented into a third and final part. First there'd been his life in the village, then his life at the school; now there was a more formidable portion of his existence which he'd never, consciously, been aware of before, a self-absorption which took him away from the other two. At school he had begun to sense what it might be like to be in the upper forms, the privileges, the association with that part of the hierarchy which enjoyed all the benefits and suffered few of the abuses. His progress through the school had been echoed by his progress through the age-group football teams. He would be taking his first external examinations the following summer, and after that came, if he survived, the Sixth Form. He saw little of Stafford; absorbed into the Classics stream and protected now on sports occasions by a covey of admirers, their brief exchanges were marked more by hostility than any awareness of the companionship they had shared before. Colin spent much of his time at the school on his own, working during the summer on a number of farms, though never as far afield as the first. He saw Audrey on several occasions in the town, and Marion, talking to groups of boys in the city centre; apart from a distant acknowledgment, more evident in Marion than Audrey, they too, like Stafford, gave no sign of their past acquaintanceship at all. For a while he went about with the red-nosed Walker, who seemed good at nothing but avoiding work, then with a boy called Berresford who introduced him to his sister, slightly older than himself, with whom occasionally Colin walked down to the bus stop, a little distance from his own, discussing books he had never read and various aspects of the world situation. She was a dark-haired girl with a large Roman nose, and it was, if anything, her lack of any pretensions as to her appearance which drew him to her. One week-end they had arranged to meet in the town and, after going to the pictures, walked for some time in the local Park. For some reason this encounter brought an end to their acquaintance, as if by mutual agreement, and he even found himself drifting away from Berresford, and once again, but for odd encounters with boys like Connors, whom he saw on the bus as well as in school, he found himself left very much on his own devices.

One evening he had been coming home from the local picture-house with Bletchley when they had seen a girl walking ahead of them, dressed in a dark coat and wearing a dark beret who, as they approached, turned and, seeing Bletchley, said, "Hello, Ian. What're you doing around these parts?"

"I live here, Sheila," Bletchley said, apparently disconcerted by this inquiry, for he added in a belligerent, almost leering tone, "What're you doing round here in any case yourself?"

"Oh, I live round here as well," the girl said simply, removing her beret and suddenly shaking out her hair. On the front of the beret was the single stork motif of Bletchley's school.

Bletchley was smoking; his father had returned home earlier that year from the army, and, as if as a result of his re-appearance, Bletchley had suddenly acquired a number of adult mannerisms. As well as smoking he'd begun, tentatively, since he scarcely shaved, to grow a moustache. The effect, when viewed from the house next door, was that of two men vying for the attention of one woman, and Mrs. Bletchley, far from wilting beneath the weight of these unprecedented demands, had taken on a new life and vigour. She had, as if in acknowledgment, begun to smoke herself. Bletchley, on this occasion, produced the cigarette from the palm of his hand, setting it conspicuously between his lips. He blew out a cloud of smoke and examined her with greater circumspection through it.

"I thought you lived in Shafton," he said.

"We did," she said. "We moved here about a week ago. I'm just coming home from Geraldine Parker's. That's why I'm late." She tossed back her hair. "Where have you been to in any case?" she added.

"We've been to the flicks," Bletchley said, allowing another cloud of smoke to escape, the cigarette propped loosely in the corner of his mouth. He gestured back the way they'd come. The picture-house, built only a few months before the war, stood at the edge of a piece of waste ground opposite the Miners' Institute. It was from that direction that the girl herself was coming.

She had dark eyes; her hair, to which she wished to draw their attention, was dark too, her face pale, almost startlingly white, emphasizing the redness of her lips and a certain gravity, almost gauntness of expression. She had the staidness of an older woman, walking along at Bletchley's side as if they had been together throughout the evening.

"This is Colin," Bletchley said when she finally glanced across and the girl had added, "Not from King Edward's?"

"Why, do you know him?" Bletchley said, removing the cigarette and glancing at Colin himself as if he suspected the casualness of this encounter wasn't all it seemed.

"I've heard about him," the girl had said.

"Sheila's in our form at school," Bletchley said, his tone suggesting that, as a consequence of this, anything she might say could, on his authority, be discounted. "She got a transfer from a county school."

"Oh, we've lived all over," the girl said, nodding her head and indicating a near-by street. "We live down there as a matter of fact. I'll be seeing you around, I suppose. What night do you normally go to the pictures?"

"You never can tell," Bletchley said, the pictures being

but one of a host of activities occupying his attention throughout the week.

"Well, I suppose I'll be seeing you on the bus," the girl had said and nodding to Colin called good night, turning as she reached the corner, and waving, Bletchley raising his cigarette and moving it, airily, in the region of his ear.

"What's her second name?" he said.

"Richmond," Bletchley said. "She came last year and she and this Geraldine Parker spend most of their time together."

He added little else until they reached their respective doors, then said, pausing on the step to light another cigarette, "I think she took a fancy to you. What do you think?"

"I don't know," he said. "I didn't notice."

"I ought to warn you, I suppose," he said. "Her mother's divorced. Some of the boys she goes out with have had her once or twice. Though I suppose it gets exaggerated," he added, "things like that."

"Yes," he said.

"Well," he said. "I suppose I better get inside."

He kicked the door open with the toe of his shoe, pushed it with his shoulder and, his hands in his pockets, stepped inside.

A few moments later through the kitchen wall came the sound of Mr. Bletchley's voice, renewed, if not renovated entirely by his absence during the war. "Will you remove that cigarette or do you want me to remove it for you?"

"You'll remove nothing of mine," came Bletchley's shout, if anything one or two decibels lower.

"I'll remove anything I like. I'll remove one or two other things besides." The words were followed a moment later by something of a cry. "How many more have you got inside that pocket?"

"Mind your own business."

There was the sound of shuffling feet followed, a moment later, by another cry.

"Stop it. Stop it, Arthur," came Mrs. Bletchley's voice.

"I'll stop it. I'll stop him one in the mouth if he answers me back again," came Mr. Bletchley's shout.

"At least, the war's done him some good," his father

said, looking up from where he was reading by the fire. "If it hasn't done much for Ian or his mother."

"Live and let live," his mother said, standing at the sink.

"Don't worry: I've waited long enough to see it as I'm not likely to want to stop it now," his father added, folding up his paper and going to the wall himself. "Go on, go on. Give him another, Arthur," he called in a voice reminiscent of Mr. Reagan's, his shout however, after a brief moment, followed by total silence on the other side.

He saw her stepping off the bus and, by jumping the wall of the pub yard, he came out a few paces ahead of her as she turned down the street towards the village.

"Are you going far?" he said.

She glanced up, casually, as she had on the previous occasion, as if she'd been aware of his presence for some considerable time; as if even, only moments before, they might have been talking on the bus, removing her beret and shaking out her hair in that instinctive, half-engaging manner, then glancing past him to the row of shops standing opposite the pub in the village street. "I was just calling at Benson's," she said. "Then going home."

"Oh, I'll go that way as well," he said.

"I shan't be long," she said. "I've only some medicine to pick up. It's already made."

She went inside the shop and stood, a strangely independent figure, behind several others, calling out finally to one of the assistants, stepping to the counter and, after a moment's conversation, pulling out a purse and setting down some money.

Her face was gaunter than before, the cheeks drawn in. It was like intercepting someone on a journey; as she watched his expression she began to smile herself.

"Aren't you keen on school?" she said.

"No," he said, "I suppose. Not really."

"Why do you go on with it?" she said.

"I suppose I have to."

"No one has to do anything, as far as I'm aware," she said. She smiled again, casually, looking off along the street to where, at its farthest end, the road divided, one arm leading to the Dell, the other to the station. "Where do you live in any case?" she added as if to distract him from this notion altogether.

"Next door to Bletchley. Or, conversely," he added, "Bletchley lives next door to me."

She nodded, walking along then for a while in silence, laughing as if the thought of this had caught her fancy, then saying, "I think people make too much fun of Ian. Just because he's large. He's much brighter, you know, than people think." She drew her brows together, the eyes narrowing as if she had some specific instance of Bletchley's unlooked-for qualities in mind.

"He gets by, I suppose, by being thick-skinned," he said, more to provoke her than anything else.

"Thick skins aren't very much use when it comes down to it," she added.

She added nothing further. They passed the shops with their faintly illuminated panes, the forecourt of a garage, and crossed in front of a row of houses. To their left was the tiny Catholic church with its rectory and, beside it, the converted stone-built house that was occupied by the Conservative and Unionist Club.

"What do you do in the evenings?" he said.

"I usually stay in," she said. "I've a younger sister, and my mother works most evenings. Once or twice a week I go over to a friend at Baildon. Well, my uncle, really. It's where we used to live."

"What does your mother do?" he said.

"She works at a pub. The Stavington Arms. Do you know it?"

He shook his head. It was like one woman talking about another.

"Are you free this evening?" he said.

"I don't know," she said. "I suppose I could be. I could ask the woman next door. She's looked in once or twice when I've had to go out." A sudden concern now had taken possession of her features, the eye drawn down, the frown, an almost habitual expression, suddenly returning, the mouth tightening. "Where do you want to go?"

"We could go to the pictures."

"I don't think I've got long enough to go there," she said.

"We could go for a walk."

"Where do you go for walks round here?" She glanced across.

"Wherever you like."

"I don't know round here at all," she said.

"I could show you one or two places," he said.

"I shouldn't come to the house," she added. "I'll meet you at the corner. Will seven o'clock, do you think, be any good?"

He watched her walk off down the narrow street: it was comprised of tiny brick terraces whose front doors opened directly on to the pavement. She didn't look back. At a door half-way down the street she took out a key, pushed against the door then went inside.

She was already waiting at the corner when he arrived. She'd brushed back her hair and fastened it with a ribbon. She wore a dark-green coat which, he suspected, might have been handed down to her by her mother. It ended half-way down her calves, her ankles enclosed by white socks, folded over, and the flat-heeled shoes he thought she'd worn before.

"I suppose we better not walk back through the village," she said, "in case someone sees me who knows my mother. She's out, you see. So I can't be away for long."

They turned and, their hands in their pockets, walked down to the junction to the south of the village and, after some indecision on his part, turned up towards the Dell.

They passed the gas-lit windows of the Miners' Institute, the front of the Plaza picture-house, and beyond the last houses started down the slope towards the brooding, mist-shrouded hollow round the gas-works and the sewage pens.

"Not very nice air round here," she said and laughed.

"Do you have a bike? We could have gone for a ride," he said.

"No," she said. She shook her head.

"I borrow my father's usually," he said. "Though he's not very keen. He uses it for work."

"What's his job?" she said, casually, looking off now towards the fields the other side.

"He's down the pit."

At the mention of his father her interest had drifted off.

"Where's this road lead to, then?" she said when they reached the foot of the slope and had started up the hill the other side.

"It goes on for miles," he said. "Stokeley. Brierley. Monckton." He gestured to the slopes of the overgrown colliery to their left. "We could go in there if you like," he added.

"All right," she said. "I'm not keen on walking on roads, if it comes to that."

He found a gap in the hedge and held back the branches. He caught a glimpse of her calf, the turn of the white stocking, and the frayed edge at the bottom of her coat.

He led the way between the darkening mounds.

"Is it wet?" she said, stooping, feeling the grass.

"You can sit on my coat." He took off his jacket and put it down, standing in his shirt-sleeves, shivering then at the dampness in the air.

The slope faced back towards the village: below them, partly obscured by trees, were the outlines of the sewage pens, the swamp, and beyond the dark profile of the gas container. The lights of the village spread backwards to the final mound of the colliery with its twin headgears and its faint, whitish stream of smoke. The hill behind it, with the church and manor, was picked out now by a vague, irregular pattern of lights.

He sat beside her.

"I used to play down there." He gestured below. "Years ago. We had a hut and kept food and things, and used to build traps for people who attacked us."

"And who were they?" she said. "The ones who attacked."

"They never came."

She laughed, leaning back. She unfastened her coat. Underneath she wore a blouse and skirt.

"We ought to sit on this," she said. "It's bigger than yours, and you'll get less cold."

"Oh," he said. "I feel all right."

Yet she stood up and took it off, laying it on the ground between them.

"What's school like?" he said.

"Oh," she said. "I suppose I'll leave in a year. I'll have to get a job. My mother's divorced, you see, and my father pays her hardly any money."

She sat with her knees pulled up, her arms folded, her head nodding forward, abstracted, gazing to the mist and shadows in the Dell below.

"What happened to your hut?" she said.

"I don't know," he said. He gazed down now to the Dell himself. "Fell to pieces."

She straightened, leaning back, supported by one elbow, glancing up. Her face was shadowed, the eyes dark, almost hidden, the mouth drawn in. It was like some other person, unrelated to the one he'd seen before.

He leant down beside her and she, withdrawing her elbow, sank back on the coat.

He felt the thinness of her blouse.

She thrust up her head. Their mouths held soundlessly together.

"Have you been out with many girls?" she said, finally, when he drew away.

"Not really, I suppose," he said.

She smiled, her face turned up beneath his arm, only the eyes now, in the darkness, faintly luminous.

"What makes you ask?"

"Oh, the way you do things, I suppose," she said.

She closed her eyes again and, drawn down by the gesture, her face thrust up to his, he kissed her on the mouth.

Her tongue crept out between his lips.

"Does that have any effect?" she said, and added, cautiously, drawing back her head, "Down there, I mean."

Her hand fumbled for a moment by his waist then, coldly, he felt it thrust between his legs.

"Would you?" she said, and added, "Put your hand on me."

He felt the smoothness of her thigh, the softness, then the sudden roughness underneath.

He lay transfixed, as if impaled, her tongue thrust fully now between his lips, moaning quietly in her throat, her body rolled gently from side to side.

Some movements in the bushes above them a moment later made her stiffen. She drew back her head.

365

"I think there's someone watching us," she said. "It doesn't matter. We can just lie here, I suppose."

They lay apart then, gazing up. The movement in the shrubs had stopped.

"I suppose I ought to go," she said. "I ought to be getting back in any case," she added. "I only had an hour, you see."

"Shall I see you again?" he said.

"Whenever you like. Wednesday's usually my best night, and Thursdays. That's usually when I go over to my friend's."

"I could meet you from the bus on the other days," he said.

"Well," she said, and added without much enthusiasm, "I suppose you could."

They picked up their coats. She leant back for a moment against his arm. "We could always find somewhere else," she said and closed her eyes, thrusting up her face to his, moving off finally along the paths that led between the overgrown mounds to the road. A faint shape passed across the slope above them. "I suppose you'll always find someone here," she said. "It's so close to the village."

They reached the road; until they neared the first houses they walked with their arms around each other's waist, she releasing his as they neared the first of the lights, glancing up then, frowning, as they stepped from the darkness and saying, "What do I look like? Do I look all right?" She'd buttoned her coat and straightened her socks. She waited, smiling, while he turned her round. "One or two marks on the back," he said.

"Grass," she said.

"Mud," he said.

"Well," she said, "it'll soon brush off."

She loosened her hair, taking off her ribbon. They passed, blinking, through the light of the cinema entrance, listened to the call from the miners in the Institute door, and reached the corner of her street without, apparently, having been recognized by anyone she knew.

She leant up quickly, kissed his cheek and without adding anything further set off down the street. He waited, watching her pass through the pools of gaslight until, disappearing into a patch of shadow, he finally heard the click as she closed her door.

They went out sometimes twice a week, traversing the fields and copses beyond the manor, lying in the darkness beneath hedges or in some shrub-enclosed alcove in a wood. On some occasions she would remove her skirt, unfastening her blouse, drawing out her arms then gazing up at him, a vague anonymous whiteness against the darkness of the ground, her hands held out, her head thrust up, releasing her breasts, drawing down his head. "No, no further," she would say when he moved against her, drawing out her legs, sometimes crying then and turning away, and saying, "I've seen enough of where that leads to. Honestly, don't you think I want to?" running her hands against him, sinking her lips towards him, drawing him to her mouth with moans and sighs.

One evening, coming back with her through the centre of the village, he met his father setting off for work. He'd already passed them in the road, cycling slowly, his father pausing in the darkness, calling, "Colin, is that you?" drawing his bike against the kerb, waiting for his answer, looking back towards the girl. "Your mother's wondering where you've got to. Do you realize it's nearly ten o'clock?" His voice was muted, as if oppressed, like someone calling from beneath a stone.

"I'm just going back," he said and added, "I'm just seeing Sheila home."

"Well be quick about it," his father said, turning to the bike, setting the pedal. "It's too late for somebody your age to be out like this."

And the following evening, when he got back from school, his father was waiting in the kitchen, Steven and Richard removed, playing in the other room: his mother's voice came from beyond the door.

"Well, who is she, then?" his father said. "What's her name and where's she from?"

"She lives in the village. She's called Sheila." He went to the cupboard in the corner to look for food.

"And what's her second name?" he said.

"Richmond."

367

"I've heard of no Richmond. What street does she live in, then?" His father sat upright at the table, his hands clenched tightly on his knees.

"They've just arrived here," he said and when he mentioned the street his father added, "Not down theer? That's one of the worst districts in the village. Theer's some right people live down there."

"She can't help where she lives," he said.

"Well, somebody can," he said. "What's her father do, in any case?" he added.

"I don't know," he said. He shook his head.

"And that's where you've been all these nights when you said you'd been out with Ian and Michael Reagan?"

"Not every night. Some nights I've been out with them," he said.

"Aye. About one from what I can make out," he said. "What's her mother say to her going off at that time of night?" he added.

"I've no idea."

"They must say summat. They can't all be as daft as we are," his father said.

"Her parents are divorced, and her mother works, so she's to spend a lot of the time looking after the house herself."

"Good God." His father banged his head. "Does she work this girl, then, or is she still at school?"

"Ian knows her," he said. "She goes to the Manor."

"Aye, I bet Ian knows her," his father said. "If she's left on her own like that you can bet quite a few people know her."

"Well, I'm not discussing it any more," he said. "You don't know her, and if you did I doubt if you'd feel it necessary to say things like that."

"And where do you go in the evenings?" his father said as if he hadn't heard this last remark. "Where do you go at that time of night?"

"We go to the Plaza. We go for walks. We sometimes go to the Park," he said.

The door from the passage opened and his mother appeared. His brothers' voices came from the room at the front.

"And what're you going to say to this, then?" his father said. "Did *you* know he was out nearly every night with a girl?"

"I had a good idea of it," his mother said, blinking now behind her glasses.

"Then you kept it a damn good secret," his father said.

His mother closed the door behind her. "There's no need to swear," she said, her eyes if anything growing larger.

"I'm not swearing. Did I say a swear word there?" his father said. He got up from the table; he crossed to the fire, stood there for a moment, then came back to the table. "By God, I could swear, I can tell you that. Where do you think they go, and what do they get up to at that time of the night? Aren't you going to ask him?" He banged the table with his hand, banged it once again then, having sat down, glanced up helplessly towards his mother.

"Why don't you invite her round? Would she mind coming round?" his mother said.

"No," he said. "I think she'd like it."

"There, then. That's settled," his mother said, and added, turning to his father, "Are you satisfied? You'll be able to meet her and see what sort of girl she is."

"A lot that's going to do," his father said, turning once more towards the fire as if there were a great deal he couldn't tell her.

"I think he's forgotten that he was young once," his mother said.

"Nay, I haven't forgotten," his father said. He gazed resolutely towards the flames.

"Oh, well, one man's bitterness mustn't feed another's," his mother said. She picked up Richard as he came into the room, holding his face against her chest.

"I'm not bitter," his father said. "I just know more about the world than some."

"Some things you know about," his mother said. "But about other things, I'm afraid, you know very little."

"Aye. I knew and I know nought about ought," his father said, crossing to the hearth and taking up his woollen socks, his shirt and his faded trousers, and turning

369

to the stairs, since it was nearly work-time, to put them on.

She was strangely disconcerted at being asked. He'd met her from her school bus one evening and had walked with her through the village to the corner of her street.

"Why should I come to the house?" she said.

"They're anxious to see you," he said, trying unsuccessfully to take her hand.

"Anxious since when? We've been going out for weeks," she said. "I suppose it's since your father saw you."

"It's partly to do with that," he said. Yet he was proud of her and would have wished his parents now to see her.

"You'll have to give them my apologies," she said. "It's inconvenient at the weekends. And most weekdays, I'm afraid, are already spoken for. They'll have to do their inspecting another time."

"They're interested in meeting you, that's all," he said.

"Why?" she said. "Do they think we might get married?" Her petulance brought a redness to her cheeks, almost child-like, vulnerable, her eyes darkening.

"It's because I spend so much time with you, and because I'm so interested in you that they thought you might like to meet them," he said. He added, "I mean, I'd like to meet your mother if you'd care to invite me."

She began to laugh, harshly, her eyes narrowing. "I can just imagine you meeting her," she said.

"I wouldn't mind."

"You wouldn't mind. But I would mind. And so would she. As far as I know she's not even aware of your existence."

"Why isn't she?" He gazed boldly down the street as if he intended going down to the house and knocking on the door himself.

"Because she'd beat the living daylights out of me if she knew I spent so much time with anybody. With a boy, I mean. I tell her I'm going out with Geraldine Parker. I'm lucky so far," she added. "She's never checked up."

"What if she saw you now?" he said, still gazing down the street.

"I'd say I was walking back from the bus."

"And if she saw you some other time?"

"I'll meet that when it comes."

Already she was moving off, removing her beret as if anxious to be recognized in the street not as a school-girl but simply as another woman.

"When will I meet you again?" he said, following her to the first of the doors.

"I've no idea," she said. "And don't come down the street. I go to enough trouble, as it is, to see you."

"Perhaps you better not see me at all," he said, pausing now by the first of the houses.

"That's up to you," she said. "You can take it or leave it," turning then with some fresh apprehension as she recognized a voice calling from one of the farthest doors. She started running and, more for her sake than his own, he walked to the corner, glancing round at the last moment to find she'd already disappeared.

"So she's not coming, then. I could have told you that afore," his father said.

"I suppose she's heard about you and didn't want to come," his mother said, yet betraying by her expression that she was secretly dismayed herself.

"Oh, and I remember one or two things about *your* home," his father said, "that'd've kept anybody away, let alone somebody coming courting."

"Well, there was one person it didn't keep away," his mother said.

"Aye, *and* he lived to regret it," his father said, turning away then as he saw the colour rising to her cheeks.

She lifted her glasses and slowly wiped her eyes.

"Nay, damn it all: we all say things we regret," he said. "But one thing I've never regretted, love," he added, "that's marrying you."

"It's at moments like this the truth comes out," she said, drawing up the corner of her apron to dry her eyes.

"Nay, it's this girl, and his going off so often, that's at the root of it," his father said. "If he behaved like any other lad, like Ian next door, we'd have none of this trouble."

"You're always *disparaging* Ian," his mother said.

"Nay. He's good for some things, I suppose," he said.

"Well, let sleeping dogs lie," his mother said.

"There's no smoke without fire," his father added.

"And the way you're going about it you'll have it like a furnace when there's really nothing there at all," his mother said, finally, hitting her fist against the table so that his father turned, sulkily, drawing on his slippers, and went slowly from the room.

"Don't say I didn't warn you, Ellen," he said, stressing her name as if to exclude Colin now entirely. "Don't come to me when you find you've trouble on your back," closing the door behind him and refusing any answer.

"Would she come here? I mean, ever?" his mother said as his father's feet sounded roughly on the stairs above their heads.

"I don't know," he said. "I'm not sure I'd want her. Perhaps I put it badly, making her feel she was to come."

"Perhaps you needn't see her quite so often. And not be out so late," she added. "It's that really that affects your father."

"Maybe I won't see her at all," he said, shrugging, and when she pressed him further he said, "It's really nothing. I think the best thing, Mother, is to leave us both alone."

He avoided those places where he might have met her. He took a later bus home from school. One evening he stood with Stafford outside the hotel in the city centre talking to a group of girls amongst whom were Marion and Audrey. "And how's the farm-labourer, darling?" Marion said. "Still pushing turnips?" at which Stafford had turned, vehemently, and said, "Just cut out all that slangy crap."

"Oh, my darling," Marion said, "just listen to the boy. *Just* because some girls take precautions and aren't prepared to be mauled like cats."

"Some cats throw stones in glass houses too often for their own comfort," Stafford said, drawing out the sentence word by word so that its effect might be admired by virtually everyone around.

"If I didn't think he was such a cad I would have slapped him in the face for that," Marion said, adding,

"Are you coming?" to Audrey, yet making no effort to move herself.

Audrey had grown, if anything, over the previous two years a little thinner, her neck longer, her features more attenuated, still susceptible to fits of blushing for as Colin approached her a faint, familiar redness spread slowly up her neck and cheeks.

A third girl, slim-featured, tall, pale-eyed, was standing behind their animated group, watching their argument with something of a smile.

Audrey hadn't answered, and the tall, slim-featured girl, having watched Marion's final outburst, had touched her arm and though the gesture itself was disregarded had said, "I'll have to be going, Marion. I'll see you tomorrow," glancing at Audrey then at Colin, and turning, a satchel slung across her shoulder, and setting off across the road to an adjoining street.

"Who's that?" Colin said, glancing after her.

Audrey looked up, apparently surprised.

"That's Margaret. She goes on the bus," glancing over once more to Marion and adding, "I suppose really *I* should leave myself."

Yet much later, when he went down to the bus, she and Marion and Stafford were still there, Stafford leaning up casually against the side of the hotel entrance, his hands now in his pockets, his heel tucked up against the stonework, calling, "See you, Col," waving with the same casualness, as if they stood there, or had stood there, each evening of the week.

He'd seen the other girl then standing at an adjoining stop, still waiting there, aloof, tall, with porcelain-like features, when his own bus drew away.

"You've spent long enough avoiding me. How was I to know you were hoping to see me?" Sheila said as, with Bletchley walking behind, along with several other youths, he followed her from the stop. "*I* thought *you* were avoiding me. So did Geraldine," she added, indicating a blonde-haired girl, with round cherubic features, whom he hadn't noticed before and who, as if summoned by some invisible signal, emerged from the group of chanting, laughing youths behind.

"Couldn't I see you on your own?" he said.

"I am on my own," she said.

The blonde-haired girl glanced over at him, cautiously, from Sheila's other side.

"Are you free on Wednesday night?" he said, hoping by the quietness of his voice to insinuate something of their former intimacy.

"I'm going to Geraldine's on Wednesday night."

"How about Thursday?" He ran through the nights of the week. At each one she shook her head, or laughed, or answered, "I thought I'd told you once before. My mother works most evenings."

Finally, seeing his task was hopeless, he dropped behind with Bletchley, who, having left the other youths, was now following him as a chaperon, smiling, taking his arm as he caught him up and saying, "I should leave her alone, old man," and, "I'd call it a day, if I were you."

"I'll hang on for a bit," he said.

Bletchley shrugged. He thrust one hand in his blazer pocket, restrung his satchel across his shoulder and turned back to the village.

After a few minutes Colin set off down the street, glancing at the doors and windows, finally identifying her home from his one previous visit to the street when, late one night, after leaving her, he had followed her, half-curious, to see actually which door she entered, even pausing and putting his ear against it, hearing nothing but silence, however, from the other side. Now when he reached it, the late afternoon light still bright in the street, he noticed the dark, scuffed marks around the loose, ill-fitting wooden handle; it was only a moment's gesture to take the handle, knock, open the door, and step through to the room inside, nodding casually to its occupants as if he had been a visitor many times before. The window beside the door, covered in fine dust and flecked with rain-marks, was shaded by a single curtain, a piece of red cloth, irregularly fastened at the top and bleached, perhaps by the light itself, to a faint whiteness at the centre. No sound emerged from the house as he passed, and he went on walking along the pitted pavement, pausing farther on, and gazing back for a while the way he'd come. Several small children ran from door

to door followed by a barking dog; he went round the end
of the terrace and walked along the narrow backs trying
to work out which of the doors might be her own, gazing
hopefully at several.

Apart from a woman emerging at one point and shaking a piece of cloth, there was no sign of life in the yards
at all. He examined the windows: odd faces and figures
were visible inside. He waited a little longer, then, with
his hands in his pockets, conscious of the stares from several people in the yards of the houses on the other side, he
went on to the road at the opposite end, returned to the
street once more, glanced along it, then, his hands still in
his pockets, walked slowly, with a half-lingering hope that
even now he might be overtaken, back towards the village
and turning to his home.

"The grey seeds of autumn wound my heart with a
languor unknown. I lie down in grasses grey with grief,
and clutch their soft texture to my face, my sorrow fed
with bewilderment and rage, the earth bowed down by
tears. I yearned for touches sure as death, yet all she
gave were wounds that mortified my flesh and drew
what she had hoped for now I see, a cry of anguish from
my breast."

He crossed out "languor" and wrote "an intensity,"
crossed out "an intensity" and put "languor" back again.
He read it through, half murmuring the words, stooping
in the faint light, lifting the pad from his knee and holding
it before him to relieve the pressure on his back. Finally,
when he could think of nothing else to add, he put the
pencil in his jacket pocket and the pad inside the jacket
itself, stood up, unbolted the door, pulled the chain and
stepped out to the yard.

He closed the door behind him and went over to the
house.

"I don't know what you do in there," his mother said.
"I've been waiting to go for half an hour. Didn't you
hear me come to the door?"

"Yes," he said.

"Are you constipated, then?" she said.

"No," he said.

"Well, I don't know what he does," she said to his

father, stepping out then to the yard, her feet sounding briskly across the ashes.

"Are you reading books in there?" his father said. "If you're reading books you can read them just as well in here."

"I didn't know she wanted to go," he said.

"You must have done. Do you think she tries the door for fun?"

"I just forgot she'd been," he said.

"Forgot?" he said. "Do you think it's a palace, or summat, in theer? It's t'on'y lavatory, tha knows, we've got."

"I'm sorry," he said. He went to the stairs.

"And where are you going now?" his father said.

"It's some homework I have to finish," he said.

"Well, finish it and be quick," his father said. "It's getting to be like a monastery this house. You can't go to the lavatory without finding someone theer who has to study."

He closed the door to his room, eased his way between his and Steven's bed, and sank down on the single wooden chair, which, a year previously, his father had made from the dug-out bits of timber from the air-raid shelter. He took out the pad and examined the writing. He read it through again, then, in capital letters, printed "AUTUMN" at the top. Hearing Steven's voice in the kitchen below he stooped beneath the bed, pulled out a wooden box and slid the pad beneath a pile of books and was apparently glancing through these when, a few minutes later, Steven, fair-haired, blue-eyed, opened the door and said, "What're you doing, our Colin? Have you finished? I've got to go to bed."

20

The road bent away to his left. Some distance ahead he could see two cyclists, but by the time he reached the curve of the bend himself they'd disappeared. Reagan was out of sight now, some way behind. He suspected, even, that he might have turned back but, after sinking down on the verge and waiting, leaning on his arm, chewing grass, the tall, awkwardly proportioned figure finally came into view, walking slowly in the centre of the road, his hands in his pockets, looking up when he saw him waiting, evidently with little interest, and saying nothing when eventually he caught him up, merely sinking down on the verge and sighing.

Reagan flung out his legs across the grass, his large head thrust back, his long dark hair lying in loose strands across his face.

"We can wait for a bus at the next stop if you want to," Colin said.

"No. I'm all right." Reagan closed his eyes. He blew upwards, across his face, disturbing the strands of hair. His thin features glowed with a reddish hue, his nostrils distended, a faint bluish patch throbbing at his temple.

For a while, lulled by the quietness, the heat, and the singing of the birds, neither of them spoke. From across the fields came the rattle of a tractor, and Reagan raised himself slightly, thinking he'd heard a vehicle on the road.

Nothing, however, disturbed the vista of fields and woodland.

"I think we ought to be going," Colin said. "It'll be dark in a couple of hours, and to be frank," he added, "I'm not sure where we are."

"Oh, what does it matter?" Reagan said, sinking back

again. "If we get back late we get back late." He closed his eyes, projecting his lower lip and blowing up once more across his face. "What're you going to do when you leave school?" he said a moment later.

"I don't know," he said. "I might go to college."

"I suppose I'll have to do National Service," Reagan said.

"Won't you go to college or university?" Colin said.

"How?" He opened his eyes, gazing at the leaves above his head. "I'll not even get School Certificate," he said. "In any case, I don't really mind. I might not even get in the army. I'm supposed to be anaemic."

"What sort of school is St. Dominic's?" he said. Occasionally he'd seen Reagan in town, wearing the dark cap with the red insignia of his private school, and the red-rimmed blazer, but, away from the village, Reagan had always shown a reluctance to be acknowledged.

"Oh, they work you, if you want to work," he said. "If you don't, they never even bother. In any case," he slowly straightened, "I might join a dance band. Or even form one of my own. I'd rather do that than go to college."

"Where would you have it?" he said.

"In the village. Or at Brierley, or Shafton. Anywhere." He waved his hand, his long, thin-boned fingers thrust stiffly out. "I haven't mentioned it at home. My mother wants me to go to a music college. But I don't think I'd get far there. My dad thinks I ought to go into the County Hall, or work in accountancy, or something."

Colin stood up.

"I suppose we ought to be going," he said.

"You'll be going into the army, in any case," Reagan said. "So will Bletchley. Though I reckon you'll get deferment first. That's one reason, really, why my mother wants me to go on with music. If I'm a student long enough she thinks in a year or two I might miss conscription."

"Will it be over by then?" he said.

"Oh, it's bound to be," Reagan said.

They'd been walking all morning; during the afternoon they'd sat by a lake in which one or two boats were being rowed, then, searching for a quicker route home, they'd set off in a fresh direction. They'd been walking now for over two hours and nothing familiar had appeared to guide them, Reagan himself curiously indifferent as to whether they found their way or not.

"There aren't many dance-halls, you see. And you could give lessons. Or start a club." His long hair thrust back, his feet, which were small and dainty, tapping lightly at the road beneath him, he indicated something of a step. "I've picked it up, you see, from a book. It's pretty easy once you get the rhythm. It's just a question really of one foot following the other." Refreshed by these speculations about his future, if not by the rest at the side of the road, Reagan now walked slightly ahead, his arms held out before him, his eyes half-closed, and, in a fit of unprecedented boldness, danced lightly to and fro, murmuring a rhythm, glancing finally at Colin and adding, "*One*, two, three. *One*, two, three," inviting him to join in.

Colin laughed; he had seldom seen Reagan carried away by anything at all, and a moment later, his arms held out in an identical fashion, he danced beside him, his head stooped as he followed Reagan's steps until, with a blaring of a horn, a car disturbed them and they stepped aside to see a pair of curious faces flying past.

"You see, everyone's interested when it comes down to it," Reagan said, waving through the cloud of dust at the departing vehicle and taking up his stance once more in the centre of the road. "What say thou Lothario? Shall we dance?" laughing then as Colin followed, repeating the steps to Reagan's instructions, Reagan leaning up finally against a post and adding, "Nay, lad, tha s'll be some folk as'll never learn, you can be sure of that," his skeletal figure with its massive, rearward-bulging head stooped over, his long arms flung down, his face flushing, as he tried with much groaning and coughing to restrain his pleasure. "You'll be my first customer, I'm hoping. If there are many more like you I'll make a fortune," his habitual shyness returning as he smoothed back his hair and they set off once more along the road.

The idea of spending the day with Reagan had come from his father. Perhaps, in this way, he had been hoping to ingratiate himself with Mr. Reagan, who reputedly now carried, since the nationalization of the coal-mines, greater weight than ever in the local colliery office. His father, since the ending of the war, had grown increasingly restless. Bread had been rationed for a period. Clothes and food were short. He had tried once again, as he had three years earlier, to get a job in the local pit, applying on this occasion for a job as a deputy, but having, so far as Colin knew, not had an answer. It was on this basis—at least, as a result of his father's prompting—that he'd invited Reagan out for the day. They had wandered initially in the direction of the lake, drawn there by Reagan's information that there was a café on the way whose owner was known to his father and who, on being acquainted with Reagan's identity, would let them have a meal for nothing: information which, in the event, had proved to be if not untrue at least misleading. A café they had come across, set in a green-painted wooden hut at the side of the road: its proprietor, however, on inquiry had turned out to be a swarthy, frizzy-haired woman who, on Reagan's name being mentioned, had looked at Reagan himself over the bridge of her nose and pointed venomously at the blackboard beside her on which were clearly chalked the prices of the food she had to offer. They had come away in the end without purchasing anything at all.

The same aimlessness with which they'd started reasserted itself as the day wore on: a minimum of food they had purchased at a hut by the lake and the notion of finding a shorter way back to the village had been one of expediency more than anything else—to bring the day to an end as quickly as possible, Colin forging ahead as Reagan tired, hoping to identify some familiar landmark before sinking back, disappointed, to wait for him at the side of the road.

Now they walked along quite freshly, Reagan whistling a dance tune, murmuring to himself at odd moments as if anxious to communicate something of which, as yet, he was still uncertain, glancing finally at Colin and saying, "What're your parents hoping you'll turn into, then?"

"They've mentioned teaching. I don't suppose there's anything else."

"They wouldn't want you to go into an office?" Reagan said.

"I shouldn't think so." He shook his head.

"What would you teach, do you think?" he said.

"English. Perhaps geography. They're the best two sub-jects on the whole," he said.

"I've no best subject, really," Reagan said. "They're all about as bad as one another."

They breasted a rise.

Below them stretched an area of plain and woodland, scattered here and there with colliery heaps. To their right, in the farthest distance, appeared the familiar profile of the village pit.

"I think I know where we are," he said.

"And I do," Reagan said, his eyes narrowing as he gazed off in the same direction. "We're miles out of the way. It'll be hours before we get back now."

Yet, a few minutes later, a lorry came down the road behind them and, stopping, the driver offered them a lift. "Oh, Reagan. Bryan Reagan. I know Bryan," he said when, after asking them where they were going, he'd de-manded their names. "I know one or two things about your father," he added to Reagan, "which it'd be wise of me not to mention. Just say Jack Hopcroft gave you a lift and watch his expression." He dropped them half an hour later in a lane leading to the village, sounding his horn as he drove away.

"Well, it's been a good day," Reagan said as they walked into the village, his awkwardness returning with almost every stride. "I hope you won't mention what I told you: about the dancing and the band, and that."

"No," he said.

"It was just a thought," he said. "If my dad got to hear that'd be the end of it."

The lights had come on: faint yellowish pools of gaslight illuminated the pavement and the walls of the houses. A mist had risen in the hollows round the colliery, and had drifted out now across the nearest streets. Their feet ech-oed in the gathering darkness. At Reagan's door a stream of light illuminated the figure of his mother, as angular though not as tall as Reagan himself. Michael almost stopped altogether the moment he saw her, and might even, if she hadn't called, have crossed over the street.

"Is that you?"

"We got lost, Mother," he said, stepping into the light, his manner, the whole droop of his figure, reminding Colin of the night during the war when they had come home from sitting the exam.

"That's all right," his mother said, adding, "Is that you, Colin, love?" stepping down from the door itself and feeling Reagan's clothes. "You haven't got damp, then, have you?"

"No," Reagan said. "We've been walking nearly all the time."

"Would you like to come in, Colin?" Mrs. Reagan said. "I've something in the oven ready for Michael, but we could easily split it up. I don't like him eating too much late at night."

"Is that that cat-gut scraper?" a voice roared suddenly from inside the house, a vast shadow for a moment darkening the doorway before the figure of Mr. Reagan himself appeared. Recognizing Colin, however, his tone and manner changed abruptly. "You two lads got back from your adventures, have you? His mother's been wondering where he's got to, cooking and uncooking, trying to keep his supper hot. We haven't been able to eat till he got back. We never knew he'd be this long."

"Oh, we've had a good day," Reagan said, allowing a certain sense of relief to show. "We got lost coming back. That's why we took so long. We got a lift, you know, in a lorry."

"A lorry?" his mother said, clutching his sleeve again.

"A man called Jack Hopcroft asked us to remember him to you," Reagan said.

"Hopcroft? Hopcroft?" Mr. Reagan said, stroking his chin and glancing at his wife then Reagan as if to see how relevant this might be. "Hopcroft." Evidently no sign of recognition was visible in son or mother and Mr. Reagan added, "Well, we can get in now and have our supper," Colin moving on towards his door.

"And how did it go?" his father said, looking up as he entered as if he had only gone out a moment before.

"All right," he said. "We came back in the end in the cab of a lorry."

"Oh, Bryan'll appreciate it," his father said, as if he hadn't heard this piece of news at all.

The results of the examination came in the post. He'd done

neither worse nor better than had been expected; though his relatively low mark for English surprised his mother. "I thought that was your best subject, love."

"Easiest, I suppose," he said.

"That's all the grounding I gave him," his father said. "Though why he can't come out with it in an examination I've no idea."

"I never feel like it. It all seems pointless when you're examined," he said. " 'Give examples of the use of nature in Wordsworth's poetry,' " he added. "Is that what you read poems for, to give examples?"

"When you can see a damn good job at the end of it you'd be surprised," his father said, "at the number of examples *I* could give. And I've never read a book," he added. "If you were wukking down a pit you'd soon think up summat, don't you worry."

"Well, he's not working down a pit," his mother said.

"He's not at the moment," his father said. "But at the rate he's going he very soon will."

"Well, I don't think there's much truth in that," she said.

"Well there's truth in that there's *somebody* working down yon pit, and to keep him in luxury while he *does* learn one or two examples. That's the point of it all," he added to Colin.

It was arranged he would stay on and go into the Sixth Form. He worked on a farm again that summer, rising early, arriving back each evening late, harvesting the fields where he'd worked before, with the two prisoners of war, earning enough money finally to buy a bike, cycling out to Stafford's one evening, but not finding him at home. He was bronzed and fit by the time he returned to school the following September.

His grandfather had fallen ill that winter. Unknown to his father he had been living in a home run by a local council in a town some distance away. He went with his father one weekend to see him. They travelled there by train, across the unfamiliar flat-land to the east, towards the coast. The town stood at the mouth of an estuary: cranes, and the indications of docks and a port were visible above the roofs of the plain brick houses. They travelled to the home by bus; it stood on the outskirts of the town, a grey brick structure of some antiquity to which

several prefabricated huts had been added. His grandfather's dormitory was at the top of the building, a bare,
barrack-like interior lined on either side with metal beds.
His grandfather and one other man were the sole occupants, though a few moments after they'd entered, following a nurse, several other men came in and sat on the ends
of their beds, bowed, smoking, talking aimlessly amongst
themselves.

His grandfather appeared to be asleep, much aged now
since Colin had last seen him. His large, hooked nose
stood up like a bony armature from the cavernous hollows
around his eyes, his cheeks drawn in, his mouth toothless.
Colin felt the shock go through his father.

"Dad?" he said and the nurse who had come in with
them had added, "Mr. Saville? There's someone here to
see you, love," his grandfather's light eyes slowly opening,
gazing up steadily for a while before him then slowly turning to look at the nurse and, with increasing confusion, at
his father and Colin himself.

"Dad?" his father said. "How are you?"

"Oh, I'm all right," his grandfather said as if his father
had been in the room with him for some considerable time,
then adding, "Harry, is it you?"

"We came to see you," his father said, "as soon as we
heard."

"Who's this, then?" he said, looking up confusedly at
Colin.

"It's thy grandson. Dost remember him?" his father said.

"Colin," his grandfather said, yet with no certainty,
looking back towards the nurse.

"Why didn't you tell us where you were living?" his father said.

"Nay, I didn't want to trouble anybody."

"Nay, Dad, we'd have looked after you," his father said.

"Oh, I'm looked after well enough in here."

"You'd be looked after better, you know, at home."

"Oh, I'm well enough here, don't worry," his grandfather said and added, "And where's our Jack, then? Is he
with you?"

"Oh, he'll be coming in a day or two," his father said.

"I thought he might have been with you." His grandfather closed his eyes.

"I shouldn't tire him too much, Mr. Saville," the nurse had said and, calling to one or two of the other men in the room, went out.

His father found a chair. For a while Colin stood by the bed, gazing down, his father sitting, staring at his grandfather's head. The bag of food he'd brought for him he'd left, on the nurse's instructions, at the desk downstairs.

"Well, he doesn't look too good," his father said and his grandfather, as if prompted by the voice, opened his eyes again.

"Are you still here?" he said.

Colin found another chair. He sat for a while on the opposite side, then his father, his face strained, his eyes reddened, looked up and said, "You can wait outside, if you like, Colin. It's not much fun, you know, in here."

He went out to the stone-flagged corridor, then past several barred windows to the concrete stairs. He waited in the hall for a while, the bag of food his father had brought still on the receptionist's desk. Finally he went out to the street and walked up and down, glancing at the windows at the top of the building, trying to work out behind which one his grandfather was lying.

After something like twenty minutes his father appeared.

He had evidently been weeping and appeared, for a moment, as he came down the steps to the street, like some quaint facsimile of the figure lying on the bed, nodding his head briefly, absently, in his directon, then turning towards the stop.

"He doesn't want to come out," his father said when he caught him up. "And they seem to think he'll be better in there than living at home."

They walked through the intervening streets in silence. The place had a closed-in atmosphere: in the distance they could hear the hooting of ships and, somewhere close at hand, the dull, drumming rhythm of a band.

His father wiped his nose. His wiped his eyes. By the time they'd reached the stop he was more composed.

"Well, it's sad." He looked about him. "To think of the life he's had. I can't stop thinking of him when he was younger. We worked on the same farm, you know. I got him a job when he was out of work, and we used to go in together. I can remember him now. As clear as a bell."

These thoughts, when the bus came, silenced him again. Even later, on the train, he scarcely spoke, and when, some two hours later, they reached the house he sat at the kitchen table shaking his head and saying to his mother's inquiries, "I can't get over it," his eyes reddened, his cheeks and his forehead still inflamed.

A telegram arrived two weeks later. His father came home late from the afternoon shift and stood in the kitchen, dark-eyed, when his mother said, "There's a telegram come for you," his father perhaps unprepared for what it might reveal, or perhaps too tired from his work to think, opening it carelessly, reading it slowly, then, with a child-like cry, turning, as if he would fall, leaning up against the kitchen wall, opposite the door, shielding his face beneath his hand.

"Oh, Harry," his mother said, taking the telegram and reading it herself, his father turning casually aside, going to a chair, taking off his boots, then going to the sink to wash his face. Then, as his mother set out his meal, his father had gone to the door and with the same casualness gone to the stairs. They heard the boards creak in the room at the front. His mother began to busy herself about the kitchen as if nothing had occurred, saying, "Come on, then, Colin, haven't you something you should do? Haven't you finished your homework? There's time, if you look sharp about it, to clean a few shoes," scarcely pausing when a moment later they heard, with a slow chilling, the sound of his father's grief above their heads.

The winter passed. At Easter a party from the school went away on holiday. They stayed in a guest-house at the foot of a mountain. One evening he and Stafford went out to a near-by village. A hump-backed bridge looked out over a lake. From a row of small houses behind them came the sound of singing.

Stafford paused.

Three or four men and women were singing what sounded, from this distance, like a wordless song. No other sound came from the village; columns of smoke drifted up against the lightness of the sky, the dark shapes of the houses strewn out like boulders at the foot of the mountain. At the peak of the mountain, overlooking the village and the bright expanse of lake beyond, snow glistened in the moonlight.

Stafford leant against the parapet of the bridge. He'd lit a cigarette on the way down from the hotel and now, his head back, his arms crooked on the stone parapet behind, he blew out a stream of smoke, half-smiling.

"What do you think?" he said. "They've put me down for Oxford."

"Who?" he said.

"Gannen. I'm going to have special coaching in Latin. They've put me down for an Exhibition."

"Don't you think it's worth it?" he said.

Stafford shook his head. "What do you do with life, do you think?"

Perhaps he hadn't heard the singing, for he stubbed out the cigarette, leaning over the parapet and dropping it into the darkness of the stream below: odd, almost luminescent crests of foam shone up, here and there, from the deepest shadows. Stafford kicked the toe of his shoe against the stone.

"It seems worth going for, I suppose," he said.

Stafford shrugged. He looked up at the cold, cloudless depth of sky, glanced, almost with a look of irritation, towards the moon, and added, "I don't think, really, it's worth all that effort. What really is? Have you any idea?"

"No."

"If you did, in any case, you'd never tell me. You're such an eager beaver. I suppose, with you, getting a job, a house, a car, a wife, and all that sort of stuff, is all that matters."

"No," he said and turned away.

Perhaps Stafford, aware of the singing, had assumed it to come from a wireless. With the same look of irritation he'd given the moon, he glanced up now towards the houses. A door had opened somewhere followed immediately by the barking of a dog.

"What a dead and alive hole this really is. I don't suppose there's a pub or anything," he said, moving slowly from the wall, still kicking his toe and, his hands in his pockets, setting off towards the village. "I mean, what are we when it comes down to it?" he added. "A piece of something whirling through nothing and getting," he went on, "as far as I can see, nowhere at all." He waited for Colin to catch him up. "In a thousand million years the sun'll burn up the earth, and all that everbody's ever done or thought or felt'll go up in a cloud of smoke." He laughed. "Not that we'll be here to see it. Yet metaphorically one sees it. I feel it all the time as a matter of fact." He walked on in the darkness of the road, still kicking his toe, the sound echoing from the walls of the houses on either side. "Everything's so easy for you," he added. "You've come from nowhere: they've put the carrot of education in front of you and you go at it like a maddened bull. I couldn't do half the work you put into it, you know. I can see," he went on more slowly, "what lies the other side."

"What does lie the other side?" Colin said, walking beside him now, his hands in his pockets.

"Nothing, old boy," Stafford said, and laughed. "Take away the carrot, and there really isn't anything at all. It's only someone like you, crawling out of the mud, that really believes in it. Once you've got it, you'll see. You'll sit down and begin to wonder: 'Is that really all it is?'" He laughed again, glancing across at him from the darkness.

They'd come out from between the houses and emerged on a stone embankment which, for a few yards, ran along the edge of the lake.

"I mean, what does Hepworth tell us about these mountains? This lake, you know, and this U-shaped valley. They were formed by ice ten thousand years ago. Here's a few houses put down at the side: a few people live in them, go through God knows what privations, misery, exaltations, and in another ten thousand years another sheet of ice comes down and wipes it away. That, or an atom bomb. So what's the point of suffering or enduring anything at all?"

Colin waited. Beneath them, with a dull, almost leaden sound, the lake lapped against the stone. It washed up in little waves over a bed of pebbles, the white foam glistening in the light.

"I suppose you believe in a Divine Presence and all the

rest of the propaganda," Stafford said. He stooped to gaze down at the water as if, for a moment, he'd suddenly forgotten anyone else was there.

"I don't know what I believe in," Colin said.

"Material progress, backed by a modicum of religious superstition. I can read it in your features," Stafford said. "You even play football as if you meant it. And if there's anything more futile than playing sport I've yet to see it. Honestly, at times I just want to lie down and laugh."

"I suppose it's more touching than anything else."

"Touching?" Stafford glanced across at him and shook his head.

"If everything is meaningless, that, nevertheless, we still ascribe some meaning to it."

Stafford laughed. He flung back his head. His hair, caught by the moon, glistened suddenly in a halo of light. "Touching? I call it pathetic."

He took out another cigarette, lit it, tossed the flaming match into the lake, glanced round him with a shiver and added, "We better get back. There's nowhere to go. That's symptomatic, in a curious way, of everything I've said." Yet later, lying in his bed, Hopkins snoring and Walker half-whining in sleep in their beds across the room, he had added, "Do you see some purpose in it at all, then, Colin?"

He could see Stafford lying on his back, his head couched in his hands. The moonlight penetrated in a faint, cold glow through the thin material of the curtains.

"I've never really looked for one," he said.

"You're an unthinking animal are you?" Stafford half-turned his head, yet more to hear the answer than to look across.

"No," he said.

"Are you frightened of admitting you believe in a Divine Presence?" Stafford said.

"No," he said.

"You do admit it, then?"

Colin paused. He gazed over at Stafford whose head, though not turned fully towards him, was still inclined in his direction.

"It's only when everything has lost its meaning that its meaning finally becomes clear," he said.

"Does it?" Stafford gazed across at him now quite fiercely.

"For instance, I enjoy coming here," he said.

"Oh, I enjoy coming here," Stafford said. "I suppose I enjoy coming here. I haven't really thought about it. Not to the degree that you have." He waited. "If there isn't a Divine Presence don't you think it's all a really terrible joke? I mean, if the world's going to end as all worlds do, as an exploding mass of sunburnt dust, what's the purpose in anything at all? It's like a man taking infinite pains over his own funeral. I can't see the point of it. I mean, if God's going to allow the world to vanish, as all worlds do, what's the point of putting us in it in the first place? To give him a clap, do you think? I mean do you think, really, He's looking for applause? Or that He isn't actually there at all; at least, not in any form that could be defined outside the realms of a chemical reaction?"

Hopkins groaned in his sleep; Walker whined freshly through his congested nose.

"Just look at Hoppy. Just listen to him. Do you think there's a divine purpose then in that?"

Yet, perhaps because of the freshness of the walk, of the air outside, or because of the vague, persuasive murmur of Stafford's voice, he felt himself being drawn downwards into sleep: he opened his eyes briefly, saw Stafford, silent now, with his head couched once more in his hands, gazing with wide eyes towards the ceiling, then remembered nothing more until he heard the calls of Hopkins and Walker across the room, and the sound of a gong from the hall downstairs.

Below them, when they reached the snow-line, lay a vast area of undulating heath and coniferous woodland, interspersed with the cold, metallic sheen of several narrow lakes: a waterfall tumbled immediately below them to the village, and it was here, on the way up, that Stafford had paused and looking round at Colin, still casual, half-smiling, had said, "Do you ascribe to it a divine purpose, or are we ants, mechanistic functions, crawling on an arbitrarily eroded piece of rock?" not waiting for an answer but glancing up, past the head of the corrie lake to where the flattened, cone-shaped peak of the mountain faded away into a mass of swiftly moving cloud. Gannen, booted, plus-foured, with walking-stick and a small haversack on his back, had glanced behind him. "Do I hear a sceptic amongst the ranks?"

Several boys at the front had turned.

"Was that your comment, Stafford," he added, "on the scene below?"

"It was merely a speculation, prompted by the view, sir," Stafford said.

"Far be it from me to ascribe a divine purpose to anything, particularly when I examine the sea of disingenuous faces I see below me at the present," Gannen said. "Nevertheless, examining the terrain beyond, even I, historian that I am, and acquainted with all the more perfidious traits of man, would confess to a feeling of uplift, of exhilaration, and might even ascribe to it an extra-terrestrial significance. After all, we are the end products, as Mr. Macready, a biologist, will tell us, of several million years of evolution, and who is to say, standing at the threshold of human existence, what significance we might ascribe to it? In years to come humanity might stretch out its tentacles to the moon, or, conceivably, beyond the sun, to other galaxies perhaps. We stand today near the summit of a mountain: who can say where a man might stand in, for the sake of argument, another thousand years? God, as the philosopher might say, Stafford, is a state of becoming, and we, as the psychologists might say, are the elements of his consciousness."

Stafford smiled; he looked past Gannen and the boys strung out below him on the path to where the small, grey-haired figure of Hepworth was climbing up the slope towards them with the slower group.

"Stafford, of course, would have no time either for the philosopher or the psychologist," Gannen said. "He is one of the modern school, the sceptics, who see humanity as merely the fortuitous outcome of biological determinism. Like ants, I believe was the phrase, crawling on an arbitrarily eroded piece of rock. Hopkins, of course, doesn't care what we are, nor, no doubt, does Walker, as long as he can get his bottom at the earliest opportunity to the seat of a chair and hands and feet warmed up in front of a fire."

391

David Storey

Macready had taken a small bottle from his haversack and was tasting its contents. He tossed back his head, closed his eyes, then, replacing the bottle, glanced up with blank incomprehension at the peak before them.

It was late in the afternoon by the time they got back to the hotel. Rain was falling. Platt was standing in the doorway with the other boys who had stayed below, waving to Gannen as he appeared in the drive and calling, "We were just thinking of coming to look for you."

"Oh, just a routine climb, Platty," Gannen said, removing his haversack and looking round at the exhausted boys. "Apart from nearly going over the edge on one occasion, the afternoon you might say has passed without incident. Though," he added, "we had to call on Stafford to invoke a divine blessing on our behalf. The fact of the matter was, for half an hour after we left the summit—from which, incidentally, we saw nothing at all—Mac and I were lost. If the sun hadn't have come out, very briefly, in what Stafford might call a fit of arbitrary intervention, I don't think we'd be back at all."

And later, when the corridors of the hotel were full of steam from the baths, Stafford, flushed with the heat of the water, and with a towel around him, had come into the room and said, "I never thought Gannen was a sentimentalist until today. I don't think I'll get through history. It takes credibility from anything he says," lying on the bed, feeling in his jacket for his cigarettes, then adding, "Honestly, with a man like that, what chance have I got of an Exhibition?"

21

His father, finally, with Reagan's help, had got a job at the local pit. The move, however, wasn't a happy one. Now that he found himself working amongst the village men he began to feel uneasy, exposed. Promoted to a deputy, and responsible for an entire face during each of his shifts, he was earning less now than he had, with overtime, as a miner, less even than the men he superintended. He came home from each shift more exhausted than when he'd had a six-mile cycle ride at the end of his work. He would lie in the kitchen, his head sunk down in the corner of a chair, his arms splayed out, his mouth open, his eyes still dark with dust, groaning in his sleep, his mother afraid to disturb him, Steven and Richard creeping cautiously about the house, his mother calling, with a peculiar despair, whenever they made a sound.

The house, too, in some way suffered. It was as if the substance of the pit were brought home each day: some part of it was emptied out, the dust, the darkness, a blackness descending on the house, his father's exhausted figure slumped there as its pivot, his mother and his brothers and himself moving furtively around. There was little communication between them now, the silences broken by his mother's calls, his father's exhausted breathing, deepening finally to a snore, by the odd whisper of his brothers, as, solemnly, their eyes wide, they crept cautiously to the stairs or through the door, their voices, in sudden relief, calling in the yard outside.

"Nay, what do I care what he does?" his father said when, later that year, they discussed his prospects of taking a scholarship. "He's to stay on another year if he wants to go to college."

"He can go to college next year," his mother said. "To train as a teacher. It's for the university that he has to stay on another year," she added.

"Whichever's quickest road to get him working," his father said. "As long as he doesn't go near that pit."

Gannen came one evening to see his parents. He offered to go down to the bus stop to meet him, having worked out the probable time of the master's arrival, but his father had added, "It's not royalty we're expecting. Just let him come like anybody else."

"Nobody ever *does* come," his mother had said. "If people did come more often perhaps it wouldn't seem such a terrible mess."

"Mess? What mess?" his father said, looking round at the bare floor, the chairs from which the springs protruded, the faded cloth on the table, the soot-stained walls. "He's not coming to inspect us, you know. He's coming to give advice."

Yet, when Gannen came, it was his mother who had answered the door, his father standing in the kitchen, his head inclined to catch his introduction, going out finally to the front room where Gannen had been installed. The room, if anything, was barer than the kitchen. After sitting in its draughts and relative coldness for several minutes it was Gannen himself who had suggested they might move through to the kitchen. "Oh, let's sit in the living-room," he said, bestowing on it a title which reassured his mother, for she quickly led the way, holding back the door. "Oh, you needn't turf those out for me," Gannen said when she began to usher Steven and Richard into the room they'd just vacated.

Gannen sat down heavily, his large figure seemingly pinioned in the chair, his arms spread out over the protruding springs. "I didn't know there were two other Savilles at home," he said. "More recruits for the First Team," he added, glancing at Colin.

"Oh, they've plenty of muscle on, if nothing else," his father said, flushing now and sitting on an upright chair beside the table.

His mother made some tea. It was only as Gannen was leaving, however, an hour later, that his father had said, "Well, then, Mr. Gannen. What do you really think?"

"I think Colin should go to university," the master said. He stood in the doorway leading to the street, gazing back into the lighted passage.

"Aye," his father said, his look abstracted, as if in fact the master himself weren't there at all and he was listening to some voice in another room.

"If there's anything I can do," Gannen said, "just let me know." He leant back in the passage to shake his mother's then his father's hand.

"I'll walk down to the stop with you, if you like. I'll show him the way," Colin added to his father.

"If it's no trouble," Gannen said, pausing now on the step outside, and evidently pleased at the thought of having some company. "It took me quite a while to find, in any case," he added.

It was already dark. A yellow moon hung over the colliery, outlining the heap against a bank of cloud. They walked in silence for a while. The air was misty. Their feet echoed between the houses.

"Do you think they'll let you go, then?" Gannen said.

"I don't know," he said. "I've no idea."

"I realize the difficulties, of course," the master said as if, already, he sensed he'd failed. "They've done well getting you as far as they have," he added.

Other figures, shrouded against the sharpness of the air, passed by them beneath the lamps.

"Ideally, what would you like to be?" the master said.

"I don't know," he said. He added, "A poet."

Gannen smiled. A moment later he looked across. "And have you written any poetry?"

"Not much."

"But some."

"A little."

"You don't look like a poet," he said, something of his classroom manner returning. "Poets I always thought were rather delicate chaps. At least, the poets I knew always were. I never had much time for them myself." Then, as if he suspected he might have been too hard, he added, "It seemed to me, and invariably proved to be the case, that it was a stage they went through. Most of them were decent chaps. They soon settled down to teaching, in one form or another, like everyone else." He laughed. His

David Storey

voice rang out clearly in the village street. "In any case, there's not much money attached to that. It's scarcely a profession. What would you do to earn an income?"

"In the end I'd teach," he said.

"Do you compose poetry in the rugger scrum?" he said, pleased with this confession.

"No," he said. "There's not much time for that."

"I've noticed a certain dilatoriness at times, I must confess," the master said, looking up and adding, "Oh, this is the stop is it? I wouldn't have known," pointing down the street the way they'd come. "I got off down there before, I think."

When the bus finally came Gannen put out his hand. "I hope you'll point out the advantages to your parents," he said, *"without* mentioning the poetry. I'd just stick to the professional aspects, if I were you," not looking back as he stepped aboard the bus, making his way to the front downstairs and sitting in his seat as if he had forgotten about his visit already.

He played regularly in the First Fifteen that year, represented the school at athletics, and forwent his Easter on the farm to study for the June examinations. It was one of the happiest periods of his life. Even the football he found absorbing, encouraged by the girls who came to watch, Audrey and Marion, and the quiet-faced Margaret, who invariably stood at the edge of their noisy crowd. Even the two afternoons of training he'd begun to enjoy, Gannen instructing the forwards, and Carter, the physical training master, the backs. The forwards played amongst themselves, scrumming with the Second Fifteen, breaking, practising rushes, line-outs, pushing for what seemed hours against the metal scrum-machine, Gannen calling, "Lower, lower: back straight: thrusting upwards," pushing his muscular arm between the bodies, pressing heads, lifting kicking feet into correct positions, while, from across the field, would come Carter's cries, Stafford distributing the ball or, later, with one other boy, practising place kicks against the distant posts.

In the end it had been decided he would try for college. Gannen had never referred to his visit or his talk with his parents again. When he told him his decision he'd nodded, standing on this occasion at his desk and said, "I'm glad

396

you're not giving it up altogether," collecting his books and adding, "If there's anything I can do just let me know."

He went for an interview. The college was located in a neighbouring town. He travelled there by bus. Miles of furnaces and factories, mills and warehouses, terrace streets and blank walls and advertising signs gave way eventually to a tiny park. At the end of an asphalt drive stood the college buildings, built of brick, a sportsfield stretching away on either side.

The man who gave the interview seemed surprised he was applying. Small, with black hair combed smoothly back, with dark eyebrows and dark eyes, he sat mask-like behind his desk and said, "Frankly, I think you'll be doing yourself no service coming here. I should stay on another year. Take a degree. We'd welcome you here, but I think in all fairness the work is well below the standard you're capable of." He added, "On top of which, of course, there's National Service. In the end, you know, you'll only save two years."

"I'd still like to apply," he said.

"I won't say we'll not be glad to have you. It's your own interests, really, I'm thinking of," the man had added, writing quickly on the sheet before him.

Stafford, his head tilted back, allowed the smoke to drain out of his nostrils: his laughter, light, careless, echoed beneath the trees. He wore evening dress, the black bow knotted immaculately beneath his chin, his fair hair almost luminous against the shadows.

Sitting alone at one of the tables was Margaret. She had on a light-blue dress, her hair fastened beneath a ribbon, and was drinking from a glass which someone had evidently just brought her for a figure was slipping away as he arrived, making directly for Stafford's group.

"Anyone sitting here?" Colin said.

"No," she said. She had light-coloured hair, thin, the ribbon securing it in a horse-tail at the nape of her neck. Her dress, relieved by a large white collar, was secured at the waist with a belt. Her arms were bare. They both sat for a moment gazing to the animated group across the lawn from which, a moment later, came Marion's loud peel of laughter.

"Do you come here often?" he said.

She smiled. "No. Never."

"What's tonight's occasion for?" he said.

"I was invited," she said, "like you."

"Are you leaving this year as well?"

"No." She shook her head. "I'm only in the First Year Sixth. Or was. I'll be in the Second, I suppose, when we start next term." She added, "You're leaving, of course. Marion's told me all about it."

She had light, greyish eyes. Her cheeks were thin, slender, the nose upturned, the face itself so delicate he imagined it, in the fading light, to have been moulded from ice: there was a lightness about her that he'd noticed before, when he'd first glimpsed her in the city centre then later waiting in the queue. Apart from one occasion, at a First Team party the previous Christmas, when he'd danced with her, they'd scarcely exchanged a word.

"And where are you going to now you've left?" she said.

"College." He shrugged.

"You're not going in the army first?"

"I've got deferment."

"Stafford's staying on another year."

"Yes." He waited. "Would you like another drink?"

"I've enough with this, I think," she said.

They sat in silence for a while. Odd couples danced slowly, awkwardly, beneath the trees; a fresh tune started on the gramophone. The house stood on the outskirts of the town, looking out across a valley: a tall, brick-built mansion with gabled roofs into which Marion's parents, who had arranged the party, had recently moved. A lawn at the side of the house and the trees surrounding it had been decked out with lights: Chinese lanterns hung in long rows beneath the branches, swaying in the breeze, white, metal-work tables having been set around the edge of the lawn itself. Marion, wearing an off-the-shoulder gown for the occasion, had greeted him with a kiss when he arrived, affecting surprise that he should have brought a present, although there was a large, unattended pile of them behind, and leaving him quickly, with a quick grasping of his arm, the moment Stafford appeared.

The sun was setting behind the trees, the light scarcely stronger than the glow from the lanterns.

"Do you want to dance?" he said.

"I don't mind."

She got up from the table, stooping, and stepped on to the grass, waiting, her arms raised.

He held her lightly.

They danced slowly round the edge of the lawn. Fresh peals of laughter came from Stafford's group, the smoke from their cigarettes drifting through the pools of light which glowed, almost luminous, against the redness of the setting sun.

They walked round the garden. A path led down beneath the trees to a smaller lawn, a low stone wall and a terrace flanked by roses. Below them were the lights of the town. The sun now had set completely: the light hung high in the sky to the west. Opposite, silhouetted to the north, was the profile of the town, its domes and towers, and the single steeple. He took her hand and then, when she offered no resistance, rested his arm against her waist.

From behind them, muted by the garden and by the darkness, came the voices of the others, and the slow, almost mournful rhythm of a dance tune.

"Do you live in the town?" he said.

She shook her head. "Well, almost in it. About a mile away." She gestured off, vaguely, in the direction of the valley. "My father's a doctor. So we tend to go where the work is."

"I suppose that's true of everyone," he said.

"Is it?"

She glanced across.

"I suppose it is. Though you're not always aware of it," she added.

They stood awkwardly for a moment, gazing out across the garden. Close by, beyond the gardens of several other houses, stood the mound of a castle; some distance below it, silhouetted against the sky, was a line of ruins, and a single vast window set in a jagged wall of stone.

"Do you ever go out at all?" he said. "I mean, does anyone ever take you out?"

"Sometimes," she said. She laughed. "What a question. What if I said no?"

He shook his head.

"Do you know what they call you at the High School?"

"No."

He shook his head again.

"Brooder."

She laughed, flinging back her head.

"I can't see why."

"No," she said. "I don't suppose you can."

Hopkins's voice came from behind them.

"This is where you are. I say, what a super view." He gazed out blankly across the valley.

"Do you want to dance again?" Colin asked her.

"If you like," she said, and added, "I wouldn't mind," turning from his arm and stepping back towards the lawn.

Stafford had come in a car. It was a vehicle he had learned to drive the previous year, his mother's. He'd come to school in it. As Colin was leaving, later, he called across, "Would you like me to drive you home, old man?" standing with his arm round Marion at the side of the lawn where, with her parents' re-appearance, she was wishing her guests good night.

"Oh, you're not going so soon, Nev?" Marion said.

Colin looked to Margaret.

"I was seeing Margaret to the bus," he said.

Marion laughed.

"Aren't you seeing her to the door, Savvers?" Stafford said, glancing at the dark, stocky couple at Marion's side as if to point out the vagaries of this peculiar stranger.

"Our stops are side by side," he said. "If I go now I've just time to get the last bus."

"Oh, we'll drive Colin home as well, won't we?" Stafford said. He bowed to Marion directly.

It was almost dark. The lights in the windows of the house itself flooded out across the lawn, mingling with those suspended beneath the trees.

One or two couples still danced on the grass.

When the car drew up at the front of the house Marion had come out wearing a fur stole. Her parents, after an argument carried out discreetly at the top of the stairs, had been left to dispose of the last of the guests.

Stafford came over to where Margaret and Colin were waiting on the lawn.

"It seems strange we'll never meet here again," he said. From the gate came the voices of the last guests, and the occasional call. Couples and small groups walked off along the road. "All going different ways and that. In twenty years we'll look back at tonight and wonder where all the different people went. The girls married, with children of their own: almost the same age, perhaps. The boys gone off, as Gannen, or is it Platt, so often says, to the four corners of the earth. It's very odd." He smoked a cigarette quietly, looking off across the empty lawn. "It'll seem then, in a way, that we were never here at all."

Marion's voice called from the front of the house.

"I suppose we better get you home, then, Maggie," Stafford said.

The house was located in a small village of old stone houses which had been encroached upon and finally surrounded by the housing estates of the town. Little of the building was to be seen from the road: a gate in a wall, and a path leading off up a narrow garden to a lighted window.

He got out of the car and walked with her to the gate.

"How would I get in touch again?" he said.

"You could telephone," she said. "The name's Dorman. We're in the book."

"Will you be free in the next week or two?" he said.

"We're going away." She stood, her face concealed, in the shadow of the wall. On a post at the side of the gate he could see, faintly, in white, "Dr. R. D. Dorman, M.D.," on a wooden plaque. "For a month. I'll be staying with a friend."

"Where's that?" he said.

"In France."

He waited, kicking his foot against the gate.

"Well, I better say goodnight," he said.

"I could still write to you, if you liked," she said.

"Yes."

"If you write to me here you could send me your address. They'll send the letter on."

"All right," he said.

Stafford hooted in the car behind.

"Thank you for the evening, then," he said.

"Yes," she said and added, her hand on the gate, "I enjoyed the evening. I hope you'll write," and set off up the path towards the house.

When he got back in the car Stafford was sitting with his arm round Marion.

"Where to, old boy?" he said.

"You could drop me at the bus," he said. "It could still be there."

"Oh, we'll drive the warrior home. We might never see him again, might we, darling?" Releasing Marion, he started the car.

The street was in darkness when they arrived. Colin got out of the back seat and stood for a moment by Stafford's open window. Marion's pale face stooped over from the other side.

"Is this really where he lives?" she said.

"Darling, don't be so offensive," Stafford said.

"I'm not being offensive. I'm just being curious," Marion said. "Last time we came you made me wait at the end of the street."

"Ignore her. That's what I do," Stafford said, looking up from the darkness of the car. His hand appeared after a moment at the window. "Pip, pip, old man."

"Yes," he said. He grasped Stafford's hand and slowly shook it.

"Look in some time." He revved the engine.

"Oh, do get started, my darling," Marion said.

"Good night, Marion," Colin said.

"Good night, my darling," Marion said.

The car moved off; it faltered at the corner, then turned, quickly accelerating towards the village.

Reagan left school and got a job in an accountant's office. Of the other boys Colin had know earlier, Batty, after working as a grocer's assistant, and pedalling a bicycle about the village, delivering orders, had gone down the pit like his brothers before him. Stringer had gone there directly after leaving school.

Connors, too, had gone down the pit, to be trained, according to his father, as a manager. Mr. Morrison had taken over the Sunday School. Sheila he had seen often in the village; a year after he knew her she'd married a miner and had had two children by the time she was nineteen.

Of all the people that he'd known before, Reagan was the one he saw most often. His job was in the same city, some eighteen miles away, where Colin was at college: he travelled there and back each day by train, and they frequently met each other at the station.

Over the previous two years Reagan had grown even taller. He was now over six feet, wore suits which were specially made for him by a tailor, and shirts sewn up for him by his mother. On Saturday nights, wearing evening dress, he played in a dance orchestra in town, and on odd evenings gave music lessons to children in the village. Invariably on the train he would sit opposite Colin, his legs crossed, a white handkerchief protruding from his top pocket, and, if he wasn't memorizing a musical score, or reading an accountant's journal, would describe to Colin his plans for the immediate as opposed to the distant future. The names of leading celebrities of the entertainment world were mentioned with increasing frequency: one had almost dropped into the Music Saloon Ballroom where he played; another had written to say he intended to do so in the not too distant future; a third had invited him to an audition which, but for last-minute commitments in the office, he would have attended. A band-leader in a distant town, who had connections with the radio, had said he would see what he could do for him, though the fact that he played the violin, and not a trumpet or a saxophone, "or even a clarinet," he had added nostalgically, invariably limited his scope of operation. His eyes, bright when he described these speculations, invariably darkened when the drab streets of the village came into view.

"I heard from Prendergast," he'd said one day, looking up from a sheet of music, "that your friend Stafford's going into the family business."

"I thought he was going to Oxford," he said.

"After he's been to Oxford," Reagan said. "He has an Exhibition."

"In music?"

"Good Lord, no," Reagan said, affecting something of

an accent that he thought might suit the occasion. "His other subject."

"History."

"Or is it economics?" Reagan said, his interest fading as quickly as it had appeared. "Apparently, you know, he could hardly play the piano."

Over that first summer he'd written to Margaret in France, and had received strange, almost empty letters back, and had been more alarmed by their bad spelling and lack of syntax than anything else. One letter he'd actually sent back with red-ink corrections and for quite some while she hadn't answered. Then came a formal note, every word of which, a footnote stated, had been checked with a dictionary. He wrote back immediately a letter in broad dialect, without punctuation, and the flow of letters, as badly spelt and as badly put together, had recommenced. In his last letter he arranged to meet her the week-end after her return, in town.

He saw her some distance away, waiting outside a shop close to the cathedral. She wore a short, light-coloured coat, her hair brushed back beneath a ribbon. Her skin was tanned. Beneath the coat she wore a light-blue dress. She carried a bag over her arm and wore high-heeled shoes. Only when she turned and he saw the look of recognition did he realize he might, initially, have mistaken her for a woman.

They'd walked about the town, gone to the pictures, where they'd sat rigidly apart, and finally, before catching their respective buses, had walked down to the Chantry Bridge where, leaning against the parapet, they'd watched the dull brown river. He'd taken her hand as they walked; and then, at the bridge, he stood with his arm around her, loosely, uncertain, gazing down at the water without speaking.

Finally he'd turned to her and clumsily kissed her cheek. A moment later she turned to him and he kissed her on the mouth, slowly, still uncertain. Then, not wanting to kiss her again, or have his uncertainty revealed, he turned back to the river.

"Shall I see you again?" he said.

"Yes," she said, and added, "if you like."

"I could see you at the week-end."

"All right," she said, smiling, as if he were making of this more of a decision than he might.

They walked back to the stop. Her bus came. She climbed inside: he saw her stooping beneath the light, waving, then taking her seat as the vehicle moved away.

He saw her most week-ends. There was a casualness about their encounters. At their third meeting she'd asked him if he'd like to meet her parents. "They'd like to meet you," she added, "if you didn't mind. They keep wondering where I'm off to."

"Don't you tell them you're going with me?" he said.

"Yes," she said, surprised. "That's why they'd like you to come."

He arranged to go to the house the following weekend. The light was fading when he arrived. The garden, which he'd glimpsed only once before, from the gate, was broader than he had imagined. The house was set on a slight rise to one side of the original village: beyond it, dipping down to the valley, were the brick houses of the council estates, whilst on the other side, higher up the slope, were the older structures of stone and grey-coloured slate. The house itself was built of brick, with small casement windows and, on the first floor, imitation timber and plaster work. There was an air of spaciousness about it, the front garden, the central feature of which was a sloping lawn, surrounded by thick beds of flowers. Roses, now fading, grew on trellises set against the walls of the house, overhanging the green-painted porch, and along timber-framed walks on either side. The tall stone walls of the older part of the village cut off the edges of the garden beyond.

Before he'd reached the front door it was pulled open and Margaret appeared. She wore a light, greenish dress, her hair, as usual, fastened in a ribbon.

"You made it, then."

"I haven't come too early?" he said.

"Dad's just come in from surgery."

She took his raincoat, which was folded on his arm, and he stepped inside the hall. It was broad and wood-panelled, and ran through to a door at the back of the house. A room opened off on either side, and stairs ran up to the floor above.

She showed him into a lighted room, the door of which

was already open. A light-haired woman with a fresh-coloured face was sitting at a table, sewing. She removed a pair of spectacles, putting down the sewing and coming round the table to shake his hand. "So this is Colin: I'm so glad you could come," she said glancing shyly at his face. "Margaret's father will be down in a minute," turning aside then to indicate a chair.

A fire burnt in a square, metal stove set out from the wall. He sat down in a leather-backed chair beside it.

"Would you like a cup of tea or anything?" Mrs. Dorman said.

"Oh, we're going out in a few minutes," Margaret said.

"Colin might want a cup of tea. He's come a long way," the mother said. "Don't rush him out before he's arrived."

"Do you want a cup of tea, then?" Margaret said.

"I don't mind," he said, looking at the mother.

"Now you put the kettle on, Margaret," Mrs. Dorman said. "And make it for all four of us. I'm sure your father will want one in any case," she added.

Margaret glanced across at him, shook her head, turned her gaze upwards, then went quickly to the door.

"You live quite a long way away, Colin," Mrs. Dorman said. She came over to the fire herself, sitting in a settee directly opposite. She was a small, neat-featured woman, with greyish eyes: it was from her that Margaret took much of her appearance.

"Saxton," he said, describing the village.

"You're starting at college."

"Yes," he said.

"Will you live in a hostel, then, or at home?"

"In a hostel," he said. "I think they prefer it."

"It does young people good to get away from home for a while; after a certain age, I think," she said.

"Yes," he said.

"Does your father work in the village, or does he have a job outside?" she said.

"He works in the village."

"Ah, yes," she said.

"He works down the mine."

"Oh, then we have something in common," she said. "My husband's father worked in a mine. Though that's some years ago now," she added.

Margaret came back in. She stood by the table, her hands clenched loosely before her.

"Honestly, you're not grilling him?" she said.

"I'm afraid Margaret's very much on edge with you coming, Colin," Mrs. Dorman said.

"I'm not on edge at all," Margaret said, sitting at the table and beginning, slowly, to pick at the sewing.

"And where are you going tonight?" the mother said.

"I thought we might walk round. Or we could go to the pictures. We've got one down the road," she added directly to Colin.

"Make sure it's not too late," Mrs. Dorman said.

"Honestly, now who's on edge?" her daughter said.

The door opened a few moments later and the father came in. He was a tall, soldierly man, from whom Margaret evidently got much of her height. He had, like the mother, a red-cheeked face, the eyebrows bushy, beneath them light-blue eyes. His hair was auburn, almost reddish, and brushed down in a fringe across his brow. His skin gleamed, as if he had just washed.

"Oh, there you are, Colin," he said, as if they'd met already, and crossed the room with outstretched hand. "I thought I might have missed you. I'm never quite sure, you see, what time I'll finish," turning to his wife and then Margaret and adding, "Any tea going, is there? Or am I too late for that?"

"You're never too late for tea in this house," Margaret said, going to the door. "I won't be a minute. I'll bring it in."

"Sit down, son. Make yourself at home," the father said, waving Colin back to the chair from which he'd just risen. He sat down at the table, taking out a pipe. "You don't mind if I smoke?" he added.

"No," he said.

"Not smoke yourself?" The father laughed.

"No," he said.

"Wise man. Save yourself thousands." He glanced at his wife. "You don't mind if I smoke, my dear?"

"Not if Colin doesn't mind," she said.

Margaret came in with a wooden tray. She set it on the table, sorting out the cups, pouring one for her father

407

David Storey

and saying, "One for you, I suppose, since you've just been working."

"Oh, give Colin his first, since he's your guest," the father said, blowing out a cloud of smoke. "I come last in any reckoning in this household," he added directly to Colin, winking slowly over the top of his pipe.

"In that case, Colin shall have it," Margaret said, coming over to him and handing the cup to him with scarcely a glance.

"Oh, don't look at me," the mother said, as if some look had passed between the father and her. "She's very much a madman at times. I suppose you'll find that out in due course," she added to Colin.

Later, as they were leaving the house, the mother had come to the door.

"You're not going without a coat?" she called into the darkness.

"It's so hot," Margaret said. "And we're not going far."

"Won't you take a cardigan?" the mother said, stepping back inside the hall and re-appearing with one a moment later. The father too appeared, stepping down to the path, pulling on a hat and carrying a small black case.

"Have a good time. Take care," he called, waving and turning along the path at the side of the house. A moment later came the sound of a car, and lights appeared at the end of the garden.

Margaret went back, taking the cardigan. When they reached the gate she put her arm in his.

"Well, that wasn't so bad, I hope," she said.

"No." He shook his head.

"Let's go for a walk. I'd love some fresh air," she added.

She drew on the cardigan as they walked, returning her arm to his.

The road, which led past the estate and the stone houses, came out on a ridge overlooking the valley: lights were strewn out in vague clusters below. A breeze was blowing. From somewhere farther up the valley, where the faint outline of the hills began, came the soft, exhausted panting of an engine.

"There's a golf-course here," she said. "We could walk on that."

408

They searched in the darkness to find the path. A gate opened out on to an area of darkness, vaguely shrouded by trees and the slope of a hill.

As they reached the nearest tree she paused.

"I'm glad you came," she said. "I think they quite liked you. It's the first time I've brought anyone home, you see."

He put his arm about her.

"I'll come up to your home if you like," she said.

"Yes," he said, and added, "It's a little bit different."

"In what way?"

"A bit poorer," he said.

"What does that matter?" she said.

"Well, not at all," he said, and shook his head.

The path led across the golf-course and came out by the river. The outline of a dyke was visible against the comparative lightness of the sky. They lay down in the grass.

"I've never been down here before," she said.

"Never?"

"Not that I can remember. Though we've only lived in the house about seven years."

"Where were you before that?" he said.

"Oh, all over the place. Though I think we've settled now," she added.

They lay side by side.

He started to name the stars above their heads. Part of the sky was blotted out by the shape of a tree.

"Have you written any more poems?" she said.

Something about his poetry he'd mentioned in a letter.

"Off and on," he said.

"Would you ever show me some?"

"I don't know. It may not be any good," he said.

"I could see if I liked it. And even if I didn't, I wouldn't ever say so." She laughed.

"In that case, I don't think I shall."

"Honestly, I'll tell you what I think," she said.

They got up after a while. Briefly, before they'd risen, he'd caught her hand. Then, as they started walking, he took it again. They walked in silence. When they reached the road again she added, "Shall I come into town and see you off? I can easily get a bus back."

"I'd prefer to leave you here," he said.

"Why?" she said and laughed again.

"It completes things, I suppose," he said. "In any case, your mother'll think you've been out long enough."

"Oh, what does that matter?" she said.

"It matters quite a lot," he said.

"Honestly, I didn't think you were like that at all," she said.

They stood at the gate. A car came past and turned up a drive at the side of the house. He could see the hatted figure of her father silhouetted behind the wheel, then the lights faded off beyond a wall.

"Shall I see you next week?" he said.

"If you don't think my mother will mind," she said.

As before, when he'd left her, he kissed her clumsily on the mouth. She held to him a moment, uncertain, then, when he released her, she added, "We could meet after lunch. And take a picnic. We could go off somewhere, you know. Outside the town."

"Yes, all right," he said. He stated a time.

"You bring something, too," she said.

She stayed at the gate, waving, faintly illuminated by a lamp in the road outside. When he reached the corner he stepped under a lamp himself, waved, and went on towards the stop.

410

22

They walked in the woodland to the south. A stream ran through a tiny valley and ended in a lake. Rhododendron bushes enclosed the lake on one side; on the other willow trees overhung the water and giant beech trees ran up the slope behind. At the head of the valley the stream wandered through small clearings in the wood.

They walked on towards the open land beyond. A large plain stretched out below them: to their left stood a sharp ridge where the edge of the wood began. Its summit was covered in trees and its lower slope with shrubs. They sat down and opened the two bags.

For a while they ate in silence.

Then, almost idly, she talked about the school. She was starting again the following week.

"Most of the girls don't care what they do," she said. "I mean, when they leave. Whether they go on to something else or not. If it's not teaching, then it's nursing. There doesn't seem to be much else." She ran her hand against the grass, leaning back in the shade of a bush. "All they're really concerned about is getting married."

"I suppose that's got its benefits," he said.

"Has it?" The grey eyes had darkened. "I don't think so."

"Why not?"

"There should be more to a woman's life than getting married."

"I know," he said. "But what?"

"Any amount of things. She should be a woman herself, before she even thinks of it."

"But what can a woman do?" he said, lying on his stomach and looking up.

"Why not be a doctor?"

411

"Do you want to be that?"

"I might. I might do languages. I haven't decided."

"But surely you'll have to decide by this week," he said and laughed.

"Don't you take me seriously?" she said.

"Yes," he said. "Of course I do."

"Yet it's really patronizing, isn't it?"

"I don't think so."

She waited.

"But what can a woman do?" he said. "There've been no great women in so many areas of life that it can't simply be explained by a lack of opportunity. Think of the life of leisure so many women led, with time to paint, to play music, to write, to think, to contemplate any number of things. But nothing extraordinary has ever come out of it."

"Because nothing extraordinary was ever expected to come out of it," she said. "You talk like Marion and Audrey. All they think of is a woman's role. Men, men and more men, which in the end comes down to Hopkins or Stafford. It's pathetic."

"Is that why you came out with me?" he said.

"No," she said. "Because I insist on being one thing, it doesn't mean I've to deny being another."

He laughed again. A bird had come down from a near-by tree and after some hesitation hopped on to the grass. It pecked at the crumbs.

"I think you are complacent," she said. "And I thought you might have been something different."

"But no," he said gravely. "I'd like to understand."

"Well, would *you* like to be a woman?" she said.

"No," he said. "But that's not a fair question. I know I never shall."

"Yet so many women I know would like to be men. And it's purely frustration. Not because they want to deny themselves as women, but because they're always treated as women."

"How else should they be treated?" he said.

"As people." She called out the words and the bird, alarmed, flew back with an agitated cry into the near-by tree. "You've really got one of those cloth-cap mentalities," she added.

"I don't know," he said. "I didn't think I had."

"I suppose you're used to your mother always being at home, and waiting on you. And on your father."

"Well, I'm not sure she waits. But she doesn't work, *except* in the home," he said.

She lay back in the grass, her head propped on her hand.

"I was probably being too arrogant," she said.

"Is it just conditioning that there have been no great women poets, or composers, or religious leaders, or painters, or philosophers?" he said.

"What else could it have been?" she said. "You can change anything in a person by changing the conditions, the attitudes they live by. It's a conscious act of will at first. I'm glad I'm a woman. The whole consciousness of a woman lies before her."

He looked away. The figure of a man with a gun appeared at the top of the ridge: he stood there for a moment, looking out across the plain from where, in the distance, came the faint panting of an engine. Then, with a slow gesture, he pulled at the peak of his cap and turned away.

"Yet you could say that someone like Van Gogh, or John Clare, for instance, had more active discouragement from being what they were, or became, than, say, many thousands of emancipated women who were not only supported financially by wealthy husbands, but also had the time and the opportunity to be thinkers or painters or poets."

"I'm afraid you're too set in your ways to understand what I've been saying," she said. "It's the unconscious element in a woman that inhabits or prevents her from doing these things, that *organically* restrains her."

"Yes," he said and with a sigh of something like frustration rolled away.

"Where are you going?" she said.

"Let's go to the top of the slope," he said, "and see the view." He added, calling behind him, "There was a man up there a moment ago. He had a gun," and a moment later, from beyond the ridge, came the sound of a shot.

When he reached the top of the ridge he waited, reaching down to take her hand and draw her up the last few

feet of rock. Beyond the ridge itself lay a narrow field
then, beyond that, the stretch of wood leading down towards the lake. All that was visible, however, were the
summits of the trees, and the deep, v-shaped incision made
by the valley. In the farthest distance, like a smear of
blue against the lightness of the sky, stood the profile of
the city.

"It's like one of those Italian landscapes," he said, indicating the remarkable clarity of the air. Even the woodland faded away in lightening degrees of blue. "The town
must be five miles away at least."

They stood for a while at the summit of the ridge, gazing back the way they'd come. The man with the gun was
visible below them, walking along the edge of the field,
gazing at the trees.

"Wood pigeons. That's probably what he's shooting."

A puff of smoke came from the pointed gun, and seconds later the crack of the shot.

"That's something else that men do, I suppose," he
added.

"What's that?" She glanced across.

"Shoot things. And go to war," he said. "Is that conditioning, too?"

"Yes," she said. "Of course it is."

The faint sound of an axe came floating from the wood
below. Behind them, from the foot of the ridge, stretched
the undulating plain, broken up by collieries and woodland. It too had acquired a patina of blue, as if they were
looking into the bed of a lake.

"In that sense it must be difficult," he said. "I mean
dividing the world in that way," he added.

"How must it be difficult?" she said, her eyes brighten-
ing.

"Even looking at this," he said, indicating the view below. "Fields shaped by men, by economies thought up by
men, the work very largely done by men. Hedges cut by
men, railways designed and built by men, for machines
invented by men. Collieries staffed by men, providing fuel
for industries supervised by men. There seems no end of
it once you divide it into two."

"And how else should you look at it?" she said. "Should
a woman just stand in attendance on all this?"

"She doesn't stand in attendance," he said. "She helps create it."

Margaret laughed.

"It's amazing how deep these prejudices go." She started back to the path that led to the patch of grass below.

He followed her down. When he reached the tiny clearing she was folding the bits of paper away, re-packing the bags. She'd brought a thermos of orange juice which she poured into a cup for him to finish.

"It's so peculiar," he said, half-laughing.

"What's peculiar?" A tone, almost of threat, warning him, had come into her voice.

"Turning the world upside down. It's like seeing people's legs and feet instead of their heads. Surely if women organically had any of the qualities, the *other* qualities you say they have, they would have shown some indication of it before now."

"Of course they've shown some indication of it," she said. "They've never had the economic or moral liberty to do anything about it."

"I can't see why they haven't." He shook his head. "In a way, you, and people like Marion and Audrey, have more liberty than I have."

"To do what?"

"To be yourselves."

"I can't see that."

"Ever since I've known anything I've been fulfilling other people's obligations. I've been educated to fulfil certain obligations; I've worked at manual jobs to fulfil obligations. I've never actually once sat down, or been able to sit down, to decide what I actually want to do. I've been set off like a clockwork mouse, and whenever the spring runs down a parent or someone in authority comes along to wind it up again."

"Perhaps you are oppressed," she said. "But in a different way."

"But I wouldn't belly-ache about it. Not like you. I wouldn't draw a blanket over everything." He gestured vaguely in the air, still holding the cup she had given him. "It's like seeing life out of one eye only. And condemning anyone who sees it out of two. You and girls like you have got much more liberty than I ever had."

She laughed, shaking her head, startled by what she'd roused in him.

"Liberty to be what's already determined for us. Certainly not for anything different. An illusory liberty. Whereas with you: you could be anything you like. You've even got the freedom to work."

"I don't see any freedom in that."

"You would do if work of that nature had been denied you."

"Anyway, I can't see anyone changing it," he said.

"Because you don't want to see anyone changing it," she said. "You're so comfortable with things the way they are."

"Am I comfortable?" he said.

She laughed.

"People are always comfortable. They resist change. It poses too many threats. Even you, if you were honest, would have to admit it."

"Admit what?" he said, frowning.

"What I've just said: it makes you feel frightened."

"I don't mind feeling frightened," he said. He stood up, boldly, to indicate his mood.

"Oh, I don't mean frightened of challenges, of facing the unknown. But of having your view of yourself, as a man, presented to you in a way you can't grasp or understand. You see yourself so much as a man, doing manly things, coming from a manly background; it's what schools and homes like ours instil in us."

"I don't feel manly at all," he said. "In most ways I feel set against what I've been told to become, or felt I ought to become."

"Well, that's the end of one picnic at least," she said, suddenly frightened herself of what she had revealed. She handed him the bag, a small haversack which he took on his shoulder. His own food he'd brought in a paper carrier; she folded it up now and slid it beneath the flap. "Do you want to go on?" she added. "Or shall we go back?"

"I suppose we better go back," he said. The sun was moving down towards the plain. It threw heavy shadows across the slope behind.

They set off slowly around the foot of the ridge.

Where the path became clearer and they could walk abreast, he took her hand.

"It's strange. I feel in a way it's come between us."

"What has?" She swung his hand slowly, to and fro.

"All this." He gestured round. "Even the wood at some time belonged to a man's estate."

"It needn't cloud the future, though," she said. "Things could be clearer between men and women. They could be equals, couldn't they, and still be together."

"Equal in all things?" he said. "It doesn't seem real. Even when women have got freedom they don't do much with it."

"Why go on with it?" she said, as if perniciously she'd pushed some thorn against his flesh, regretting it now, almost wishing to draw it out.

"It doesn't seem real, that's all," he said.

"What's real?" she suddenly said, and laughed. "Real's only what you're used to. Would what you feel, for instance," she added, "be real to your father? Would what *he* feels be real to you? Are you denying that change mightn't come with children? If *they* were brought up to accept nothing else but equality they'd look back on your attitudes as we look back, say, on Viking customs, or some other social paraphernalia that's never stood the test of time."

The path had broadened; it ran through the centre of the wood. A rider on horseback appeared beneath the trees, a figure with a dark bowler hat and jodhpurs who, as the horse galloped past, nodded down in their direction.

"Man or woman?" he said.

"A woman." She laughed. They turned to watch the dark clods of earth flung up by the horse's hoofs.

"There are other inequalities," he said.

"You can draw a line through all of them. They're like a common point on a graph," she said. "All lines of inequality intersect."

The path came out at the side of the lake. A man with a fishing-rod sat beneath the trees. He glanced up as they passed, opened a basket beside him and took out a sandwich. The float rested motionless on the surface of the lake.

"Stafford is a fatalist," he said. "He believes, in the end, it comes to nothing. I feel tempted at times into sharing his view. I sometimes wonder, really, what's the use? You put up a struggle, but what do you struggle for? It's arrogance to assume that things can change, or that you personally can or should be instrumental in effecting them. At times, even to see a wood like this I find exhausting. Any kind of life in a way makes death all the more appalling."

"Or more exhilarating," she said. "It's an invariable sign of an egotism that's been deflated for it to lapse into self-pity. What's Stafford got to be fatalistic about? I've never seen him fatalistic when any of his interests are threatened. It's just that he's had some things too easy. And other things, I suppose," she added, "he's never had at all."

"I sometimes think he's had it harder. Not that it matters, in any case," he said, watching her smile then releasing her hand.

They walked on past the end of the lake and came out finally on a narrow road. Some distance farther down they came to a bus stop, and sat down on a wall to wait.

A boy on a bike cycled slowly past.

"Do you have any brothers or sisters?" she said.

"Two brothers. Younger than me. One's eight," he added. "The other's five. He paused. "I had an older brother though who died."

"What of?"

He shrugged.

"Pneumonia."

"When was that?"

"Before I was born."

"How long before you were born?"

"Six months." He waited.

"Is that what makes you so conservative and gloomy?"

"Oh, no," he said, and laughed. "Its effect," he added uneasily, "is quite the reverse."

When the bus came they sat at the front upstairs, with the window wound down. The wind rushed through their hair. The rest of the bus was empty. It rattled into town. Small buildings in the farthest distance were outlined clearly by the now almost horizontal rays of the sun.

He sat with his arm around her. With the wind in their faces they scarcely spoke, calling out as the bus descended a hill, rushing at the slope, laughing finally when the conductor came upstairs to take their fares. "Where do you think you're at? A fair?" He stood in the gangway a moment, stooping to the air himself, laughing at its force, bracing himself against the swaying of the bus, then, still laughing, going back to the stairs, holding to the seats on either side. "Any more for any more?" he called to them as they got off in the town.

He waited at her stop. "I won't see you for a couple of weeks," she said.

"Why's that?" he asked her.

"My parents think I ought to give school a couple of weeks' attention, without any distractions."

"I suppose, really, it's only sensible," he said.

"Do you think so?" she said.

"No." He shook his head.

"Still, today's been worth it. Despite the argument," she said.

"Yes," he said.

The bus drew up.

"Will you give me a ring?" she said. "We could go out a fortnight today, if you like."

"It hardly fits in, this sudden compliance, with all your arguments," he said.

"Perhaps I'm really looking to my own interests," she said. "After all, education, or certain aspects of it, are a way out of the trap. If you can see the trap waiting, of course," she added.

He watched her mount the bus. Only after it began to move did he remember her bag and, running along the pavement, handed it to her as she leaned from the door. She called and waved. He stood at the corner, by the cathedral, and watched the bus and her silhouetted figure disappear.

They met once, sometimes twice a week if he came over specially from the college to see her. After the first interval of a fortnight something of a regular pattern was set in their meetings. Perhaps her parents resisted it; he was scarcely aware of it. Most week-ends he would go up to her house on the outskirts of the town, talk with her mother as he waited for Margaret to get ready, seldom with her father, who, if he wasn't engaged with a patient, was out on the golf-course at the back of the house where, occasionally, on some of their walks they would see him, in plus-fours, sweeping at the ball or standing, smoking a pipe, talking to other men beneath the trees. He would look up casually and wave, his concentration on the game or the conversation scarcely interrupted.

"And isn't your mother emancipated?" he would ask her. She'd been one of the first women to go up to Oxford after the First World War. On some occasions, in order to inveigle herself into a meeting or some club activity, she'd dressed as a man. Margaret would listen with a spellbound look when her mother described these incidents, not looking at Mrs. Dorman directly, merely adding once she'd left the room, "And what did she do with it all, I wonder?"

"Oh, she's emancipated," she said. "Like all women of her generation. And gave it up at the first opportunity to get married and have children. It's all part of her romantic past. That's why she goes on about it. It's all like puberty: growing-up. A pang you go through at a certain age. Now she puts it all into women's meetings: the Women's Guild, the Voluntary Service, like trying to doctor a sick patient when what's needed is radical surgery."

It was a pose, her militancy, a belief at times she couldn't maintain: at other moments, if he referred to it, she would say, "Oh, don't go on about it, Colin. I have enough to last a lifetime," sucking her finger if they were alone, the knuckle of her forefinger, clenching it between her teeth.

On other occasions her brother would be at home. He'd been away to college and was doing his military service: he'd recently passed a selection board and was now an officer cadet, standing to attention in front of the fire, wearing his uniform with its white flash against the collar, beaming down at Margaret if any of her arguments exploded inside the house. "And what's this? What's this? She was a terrible tyrant when she was a girl. Be-

fore, that is, she became a woman. Turned on the water-
works the first sign of trouble. And didn't the boys who
played with her get it in the neck? Many a hiding I've had
because Margaret flooded at the appropriate moment.
If you think you've seen a woman cry you've seen nothing," he would add, "until you've seen our Mag."

Her brother was a short, compact figure, not unlike
the mother. He would stand beside his sister as if her
height and slimness were somehow a reproach to his
more robust proportions. "Oh, fine *and* dainty," he would
say savagely to some conclusive argument of hers, taken
up, for the sake of peace, by her mother. "Oh, fine *and*
dainty: *two* women in the house," stepping briskly to the
door from where, a moment later, would come his final
remark: "It's the wrong sex they've scheduled for conscription, you've got my word on that."

Her father, if he were present, took no part in the
arguments. He would sit reading a journal or a newspaper, smoking his pipe, pumping clouds of smoke into
the room until Margaret would call out in exasperation,
wafting away with either hand, "Do you *have* to smoke
that beastly stuff? What if women poured out all that
filth?"

"Women pour out the equivalent in words," her brother
would say, invariably defeated by his younger sister.
"Smoke is infinitely preferable if one has a choice," taking out a pipe himself and puffing it vigorously in her
direction.

One week-end Margaret came home to meet his parents.
He'd arranged to meet her at the bus, but whether deliberately or otherwise she came earlier and knocked at the
front door before he'd set off. His mother, mystified, had
gone to answer it. He heard Margaret's voice, then,
inside the passage: "I have got the right house? I'm afraid
I got here sooner than I thought."

His mother came into the kitchen holding a bunch of
flowers.

"Look what Margaret's brought," she said, flushed,
holding them out.

Colin got up. He'd been about to put on his shoes, and
stood there for a moment in his stockinged feet. His two

brothers, who'd been roughly prepared for the occasion, got up from the floor where they were playing.

"See here, Ellen," his father's voice came from the stairs, "have you got a shirt?"

Still holding the flowers, perhaps as a signal, his mother went through to the passage.

"Harry? Margaret's here. You'll find your shirt in one of the drawers," her voice followed by a significant pause then, as if some further message had been passed between them, his father answered, "All right, then. One of the drawers," his feet sounding on the floor above their heads.

"I got here sooner than I thought," Margaret said again, looking across then, and adding, "Are these your brothers?"

"This is Steve," he said, indicating the taller of the two. "And this is Richard."

"Hello, Steven," she said. "Hello, Richard."

"Hello, Miss," Steven said, confused.

"Oh, you needn't call me anything," she said, laughing. "Unless you want to call me Margaret."

His mother came in and started looking for a glass. In the end she found a jug, filled it with water, and put the flowers in that.

"You've met Colin's brothers, then," she said, as if this were a privilege which, but for her acquaintanceship with Colin, Margaret might easily have been denied, calling to Steven then to clear a chair. "Make room, then, love, for Margaret to sit down."

Colin sat down himself. He pulled on his shoes. Margaret was wearing a light-coloured coat which she'd already taken off as she came in the door and now laid on a chair at the back of the room. She sat by the fire, which was heavily stoked.

His father came in a moment later, his face red and freshly shaved; his collar was opened and he wore no tie. He advanced shyly into the room, shaking Margaret's hand as she was introduced, ducking his head, then saying, "I've lost my tie. I wonder if it's down here, Ellen," his mother drawing the tie out finally from the chair where Margaret was sitting. "He leaves everything where he drops it," she said, flushing deeper, then adding,

"Harry, for goodness' sake, put your tie on outside the room."

"Nay, you don't mind me putting my tie on, do you, Margaret?" his father said, glancing directly at her then ducking his head to the fractured glass above the sink. Yet the darkness scarcely left his face, an uncertainty at having someone like this inside the room.

"Would you like some tea, love?" his mother said. "I was going to get a proper tea ready a little later," standing with her hands clasped, gazing at Margaret through her glasses, the lenses of which, reflecting the light, obscured her expression.

"Oh, I'd love a cup of tea," Margaret said and added, "I'll get it, if you like," going to the kettle at the sink where, startled, his father stood back from straightening his tie. She ran the tap, looked round for a stove, saw none, and went directly to the fire. She set the kettle against the flames.

"We're having a gas stove put in shortly," his mother said, more alarmed by this gesture than by anything that had occurred inside that room for some considerable time, standing by the fire, anxious now to re-set the kettle.

"Do you do all your cooking on the fire, Mrs. Saville?" Margaret said.

"I have done, till now. And that's how many years, then, Harry?" his mother said.

"Oh we've been here some time," his father said, refusing to count, gazing in amazement at the bright figure of the girl.

"Twenty years it must be, over," his mother added. She glanced at Colin: he had half-risen from his chair at the incident with the kettle, but now sat back with a resigned air, moving his feet for his brothers who, distracted by Margaret's arrival, had begun to play once again on the floor.

"Aye. Nearly a quarter of a century," his father said. "It seems just like yesterday when we first arrived. We hadn't got much, I can tell you that. We lived down the street, you know. They knocked it down a few year after and built another row."

"Oh, we haven't done so bad," his mother said, sitting

down at the table as if to distract his father. "There's plenty worse off, I can tell you that."

"Oh, plenty," his father said.

"And where do you live, Margaret?" his mother added. "In town, or out of it?"

"Just on its edge, Mrs. Saville," Margaret said, glancing at Colin.

"I suppose in the outskirts, yes," he said.

"And you're at the High School?" his father said.

"Yes," she said, and added, "For what it's worth."

"Oh, it's worth quite a lot," his father said. "Without an education where could you go," he added, "and what could you do? You've come to the right person to tell you that."

"Oh, now, Harry," his mother said. "You've done quite well. You know you have."

"Aye. But with the chances of an education there's no telling where I might have gone," his father said. "That's where people like you and Colin are very lucky."

His father now was almost fifty; his hair was greying. He'd long since removed his moustache. His skin was heavily lined, his figure small, almost shrivelled, his look gaunt; even now, with the liveliness induced in him by the presence of the girl, there was a heaviness in his movements, a slowness in his voice, as if at the back of his mind were some dark dream or vision he couldn't displace.

"Aye we've all done very well," he added as if, finally, to dispel this mood.

They went out walking a little later while his mother prepared the tea. Margaret had offered to help with this as well, but his mother had insisted they should go. "Now, I don't want you prying into *all* my secrets, do I?" she said primly, feeling threatened by the girl.

They walked in silence for a while. Colin turned up the hill towards the Park. There was an air of desolation about the village, the pit silent but for the faint hum of the dynamo. It was autumn and most of the greenery about the place had gone.

"We could look at the church," he said. "It's the only thing of any interest."

He turned up the lane leading to the dark, stone building. Mounds of dead leaves had drifted up against the hedge. The door to the building, however, was locked.

"Do you still go to church?" she said.

"Occasionally." He shrugged.

They went up the overgrown track to the manor. The caretaker, since the end of the war, had left. The place more than ever now was falling into ruin. Great blocks of stone had fallen into the drive itself. They looked in through the empty windows.

"It's strange: but I can't imagine you living here," she said. She gestured to the village below. A faint trail of yellowish fumes drifted off from the colliery heap. The houses, but for odd strands of smoke, were lifeless. The air was still.

"Why not?" He'd climbed up the steps at the front of the manor, suggesting she might look in the now unshuttered windows.

"I don't know," she said, and shook her head. She'd gone on walking around the side of the building; he followed her after a moment. She was standing in the overgrown yard at the back. Vague areas of cobbles and flagstones showed beneath the weeds and grass.

"My father used to drill in the Home Guard here," he said, indicating the now roofless outbuilding where the desk and the chairs and the various pieces of equipment had been stored. A strand of the rope which had fastened the bayoneting targets to the trees was still dangling from a branch. The stairs, however, which had led up to the centre of the main building, from the back, had now collapsed. "I used to come here with Steven in a pram. I'd set him under the trees, then climb up through the building."

"Haven't you ever thought of moving from that house?" she said.

"Often," he said. "We're on the list. They're going to build a new estate, outside the village. They haven't started yet," he added. "In any case, compared to some people, we've more than enough."

They set off back towards the road. He described to her some of the games they'd played, pointing out the Dell across the village. They came out finally opposite the Park. The bare trees stood out starkly across the slope, the apparatus in the playground at the bottom now eroded and, in one or two instances, collapsed entirely.

"Don't you mind it being so poor?" she said.

"I've always minded it," he said. "But living in it, for most of the time you never notice." He added, "We've been better off than most. It's that I've been aware of more than anything else."

They sat on a bench for a while at the top of the slope, disinclined to go any farther. The bare fields stretched away below the Park, in one of which a tractor, ploughing, chugged slowly up and down. A railway engine came coasting along the straight length of track and disappeared into the cutting before the junction.

"I suppose you were lucky even to get out of it," she said. "I mean, into town and to school, and away from this."

"I think I'll get away for good, in any case," he said. "There's nothing to hold me here, you see. Well, not really."

She glanced across.

"I ought really to help out at home, when I start working, you see," he said. "While Steven and Richard get through. There's still quite a bit to go," he added, helplessly now, and looked away.

"One tyranny," she said, "is replaced by another."

"Is it?" he said. "Is it as easy as that?"

"Like teaching a bird to fly, then insisting that it shouldn't." After a moment she added, "Don't you ever want to change it?"

"How?" he said.

"So people like you don't have to live like this."

"I won't have to live like this."

"Won't you?" she said and added, "Somebody will."

"Yes," he said, looking to the trees below. "But things improve."

"Do they?" The irony of their previous conversation had suddenly returned.

"Why do you always lecture me?" he said.

"Because you're so complacent," she said. "So *still*."

"I wouldn't have thought complacent," he said.

"No," she said. She laughed. "It's complacency, I suppose, that makes you think so." And after a moment

426

she added, "Don't you feel any responsibility towards your class?"

"What class?" he said.

"This." she gestured round.

"None."

She was silent for a while.

"Should I?" he said.

"There's no should," she said. "Or ought."

"No," he said. "But you hoped there might be." After a moment he said, "The responsibility I feel I couldn't describe," and a little later, having added nothing further, they got up from the bench and moved away.

As they came down through the village Bletchley, dressed in a pair of shorts and a blazer, cycled slowly past them in the road. He was waiting at the front of the house when they arrived, adjusting something on the bike itself. They still, on Sunday evenings, occasionally went to church together, more out of habit than anything else.

Bletchley's red knees gleamed as he stooped to the bike, his face flushed, bright-eyed, as he looked across. "I thought it was you," he said, glancing at Margaret, sternly, as if her entry to the house would somehow be denied unless it had been sanctioned by an introduction.

"This is Margaret Dorman," Colin said.

Bletchley nodded, saying nothing.

"And this is Ian Bletchley," he added. "He lives next door."

Bletchley nodded again, his flush deepening as if he suspected it were really him she had come to see.

"We're just going in for tea," Colin said and Bletchley had finally said, "I hope you enjoy it," as if his long-held view regarding the Saville household would be vindicated by what they found inside. He rammed his bike against the wall and, his vast figure glowing from his recent exertions, his legs almost luminous beneath the bottom of his shorts, he banged open his own front door and went inside.

His mother had changed her dress. Perhaps this was what had discomposed her from the beginning, that she hadn't had time to prepare herself. She had only two dresses in any case, a brown, faintly speckled one which

427

she wore now, and a dark-grey one which, alternating with a skirt and jumper, she wore about the house.

The jug of flowers had been set in the centre of the table. Around it were arranged the various plates, with one large plate containing meat paste sandwiches immediately beside it. A tin of fruit had been opened by the sink.

His two brothers were already waiting by the table, Steven uncertain where to put himself, while Richard, who had recently been crying, was wiping his face with a flannel. His mother, who was finishing the arranging of the table, looked up, smiling, as they entered. A few moments later his father appeared, smoking, from the yard outside. "So this is where we are," he said, clapping his hands and rubbing them as if some argument had taken place during their absence and he were now energetically trying to remove its atmosphere. "Did you get far round our beautiful village?"

"Far enough, Mr. Saville," Margaret said, her spirits reviving slightly at the sight of his father. "Is there anything I can do, Mrs. Saville?" she added.

"It's all ready, love," she said. "If you'd like to wash your hands, that is."

"Oh, we'd better wash our hands," his father said, going to the sink directly and rolling up his sleeves. He began to sing, cheerily, as he ran the tap.

Colin waited for Margaret to go before him. Then, when he'd washed his own hands and dried them, he held her chair and they sat down at the table. There were only four chairs, so the two younger boys stood at the side, gazing at the sandwiches, waiting impatiently while the plate was handed first to Margaret, then to their mother, their father then handing it to Colin. "No wolfing, now," his father said. "Eat slowly. Give good food," he added, glancing pleasantly at Margaret, "time to digest."

When the sandwiches were consumed and his mother had asked Margaret if she would like any more, the tinned fruit was brought over to the table. His mother served it out, stooping short-sightedly to the bowls, balancing the variety of fruits, lifting one cherry from one bowl, replacing it with a piece of pear, then asking Margaret, "Would you like some cream, love?" which his father also

428

brought over to the table, a small, round tin with two punctured holes. "Oh, do put it in a jug, Harry," she said.

"Nay, it's cream in a tin, and it's cream in a jug," his father said. "So what's the difference?"

"Still, it looks better in a jug," she said severely, flushing, his father going to the cupboard and waiting patiently beside the upturned tin while its contents trickled out. "Or you could have the top of the milk. I've still got a bottle untouched," his mother said.

"Oh, the cream will do fine, Mrs. Saville," Margaret said, watching his father's expression now with fascination and taking the jug from him finally with a smile.

When the last of the fruit had gone, and his two brothers had assiduously cleaned round their plates, Richard standing on tiptoe, his elbow raised, to finish his off completely, slowly licking his spoon and looking over at Margaret as if she herself were responsible for the provision of all this food, a sponge cake was brought out from the cupboard in the wall.

"And where has this been hiding?" his father said. "We've had no news of this, then, have we?" picking up a knife to cut it himself.

"And if you had," his mother said, glancing at Margaret, "there'd be none of it left for tea."

"That's true. That's perfectly correct," his father said, handing the first piece to Margaret on the blade of the knife, his mother adding, "Oh, now, can't you pass it properly? You bring the plate to you, not pass it over."

"Oh we never have much time for etiquette down a coal-mine," his father said, again to Margaret.

"You're not down a coal-mine now, though," his mother said. She added to Margaret, "Though at times, going by their manners, you'd begin to think they were."

"Aye, well," his father said, in a tone of self-pity. "Some of us aren't as well trained as others. I suppose I've to show up my ignorance now and again. I'm sure Margaret will forgive me."

"It's not a question of forgiving, it's just a question of practicality and common sense," his mother said, flushing, her expression invisible behind her glasses.

"Practicality: that's another of those words," his father said. "You can't sit down to a meal in this house without a dictionary ready," returning perhaps to some vestige of the argument they'd had while they were walking round the village.

"Would you like some more tea, love?" his mother said, holding out her hand for Margaret's cup and drawing the episode firmly to a close.

There was a further argument later over the washing-up. "You sit down, love. I'll do it," his mother had said when, the moment the meal was over, Margaret began to clear the table.

"Oh, I can do something for my keep, Mrs. Saville," Margaret said, taking a pile of plates to the sink. The moment she was there, seeing there was no hot-water tap, she filled the kettle and took it to the fire.

"Oh, guests don't have to do housework," his mother said cheerily, taking the kettle from her and setting it quickly in the flames herself.

"Nay, we'll all do it," his father said, removing his jacket and rolling up his sleeves. "I'm damned if I'm going to sit there and watch you wash up, Mother. Steve, go to the yard and fill the bucket," then running the tap noisily to rinse the plates.

"Nay, love, I can do it when Margaret's gone," his mother said fiercely. "There's no reason to make such a fuss of it."

"Fuss? What fuss?" his father said, glancing at Margaret. "We're not going to sit over them mucky pots, now, are we? We'll have us a clean room to sit in."

"Nay, you take Margaret through to the front room," his mother said to Colin. "Your father and I will do the pots."

In the end they went through, sitting in silence in the tiny interior, gazing out to the street, the sounds of his parents' voices coming through the wall, followed a little later by a wail from Steven.

Colin went through to the door.

"You can let him go out and play: he doesn't have to stay in for Margaret," he said.

"Nay, love: they're not going out when we have a guest," his mother said, his brother sitting sulkily by the

430

door, Richard already back on the floor, playing beneath the table.

"Oh, what a commotion. Why does she have to be a martyr to it all?" Margaret said when he went back in the room. She stood by the window, her arms folded, gazing out. Bletchley, as if aware of the commotion, perhaps having even listened to the flood of voices through the wall, was cycling slowly up and down, in loose circles, in front of the house, his large red face intermittently turned towards the door, no doubt aware of Margaret behind the curtains and offering, so his expression and attitude seemed to say, his own presence and personality as a suitable alternative.

"It's just nerves," he said. "She wanted to make a good impression. You're the first girl I've brought back to the house," he added. He waited. She didn't turn from the window. "Her ambitions for the house are so much greater than the things she's got to work with. She really sees this as a sitting-room." He gestured round at the dilapidated furniture and the piece of ill-fitting linoleum on the floor.

"It's so awful. It's so sickening. It's not that I don't feel sorry for her," she said. "I do. But to be driven to live like this."

"Oh, she'll begin to relax," he said, "when you've been here one or two times. She might even be *glad* for you to do the washing-up," he added.

"And do you think that would be an improvement, a step in the right direction?" she said, turning finally from the window.

"It depends what you want to make of it," he said.

He was silent for a while. She returned her gaze to the street outside. Almost like a metronome, Bletchley appeared and disappeared, first in one direction then the other, beyond the window.

"What's his name again?" she said.

"Ian."

"Have you known him long?"

"Almost all my life. Well, certainly all my life," he said. "Though I didn't get to know him really until I went to school."

"Is he still at school?" she said.

431

"He's another year. Then he goes on to university," he said.

"Well, at least one more will have escaped," she said. "Are there any more like you in the village?"

"One or two," he said. "Though in the end they seem to come back to it. Not the village so much as the industry," he added, indicating now a cloud of smoke that was drifting over the street from the direction of the pit.

When the washing-up had been resolved, and his parents had come into the room to sit for a while, they all finally went back to the kitchen to play cards. Richard, at an early hour, was put to bed, and Steven allowed to go out, after a further argument. His voice finally came to them from the field at the back. A further cup of tea was made, the game of cards was played a little longer, his father shuffling and calling out his bid in a loud, raucous voice, his fits of laughter ending in coughing, playing so carelessly that Margaret invariably won her hand. "Oh, she's dazzling me. Intelligence: you can see it at a glance."

"I'm not sure you're really trying, Mr. Saville," Margaret said.

"Trying? I'm trying. But what chance have I got against an intelligence like that?"

Colin, later, in the darkness, walked her to the bus. She took his hand as they neared the stop.

"Are you glad you came?" he said.

"Of course I'm glad. It's you I'm interested in, not your mother and father."

"They're part of it," he said.

"Not the whole of it," she said. "Now the week after next I shall come again. We'll see if there's some improvement."

In the end, she fitted into the house more easily than he'd expected. His mother, even, began to expect certain things from her; not only the regular bunch of flowers and the washing-up, but small services like shopping, ironing, even cleaning-out the kitchen one Saturday afternoon. Colin, arriving home from college, found her there, working alone, a scarf for a dust-cap on her head, sweeping the floor. Steven and Richard were playing down the backs: there was no one, as far as he was aware, in the house at all.

"Your mother's shopping, and your father's in bed," she said. "And Richard and Steven are out somewhere. I haven't seen them for an hour."

He helped her to finish the room and put the furniture back in place.

"How long have you been here?" he said.

"Since this morning," she said. "I thought I'd come over, you see, for lunch. We had some meat at home that no one could eat."

"We're not that poor here," he said.

"No," she said. "But I thought it might help. You don't begrudge it, after all?" she added.

"No," he said. "But I hope you're not letting yourself be used."

"And if I am being used, what does it matter? I wouldn't come unless I wanted."

"But I thought you were against all this," he said.

"I am," she said. "But I wouldn't substitute one tyranny for another: the tyranny of not doing it," she added, "for the obligation that I should."

They went out walking when his mother came back. It was part of the pattern now of their encounters: long, hauling walks, alternating with visits to the pictures, either to the small cinema in the village, or to one of the three in town. They seldom saw anyone at all. He introduced her to Reagan when they met in the street, to Mrs. Shaw when she came in the kitchen one afternoon, to Mrs. Bletchley in the yard outside. Apart from that their walks were conducted in silence, a strange, almost solemn companionship which he looked forward to all week in college, their arguments, whenever they occurred, ending in some embrace beneath a tree or in the depths of some unfrequented wood, their conversations, usually as they waited at stops for buses, or as they rested on some tedious stretch of road, about their respective activities at school and college. Little intruded on them at all.

At the end of that year she applied for and was granted, conditionally on the results of her final examination, a place at a university in a town some forty miles away. He applied for an early medical for his National

433

Service; they talked loosely now of what they would do in the future, of marriage before she went to university. One evening, when he arrived at her house, her father asked him if he'd like to talk about their plans. "Why don't we go over to the surgery?" he said. "There'll be no one there," opening the door for him which led through from the rear of the house into a passage which, when the light was turned on, he found led into the back of the doctor's room. He sat in the patient's chair, immediately in front of the desk, the doctor sitting behind it, smoking his pipe, tapping out the ash at one point, leaning forward, his conversation still about the weather, about certain activities in the sporting world. Glass cabinets flanked them on either side, and in one corner, on a white, metal-covered tray stood a row of empty medicine bottles. A weighing machine with a vertical ruler stood immediately beside the door.

"Margaret tells me," the doctor said, "that you're thinking of getting married."

"We had talked about it, yes," he said.

"I don't want to impose a heavy hand." Dr. Dorman smiled. "I'd just like to talk about it, loosely. As just a general principle in Margaret's life." He took out his pipe again and re-filled it slowly with tobacco. "She'll be nineteen, you see, when she goes up to the *varsity*," he added, stressing the word as if, for him, it were a place of some significance. "Your prospects, well, for two years, will be worth very little indeed. I'm looking, you see, on the practical side." He took out a box of matches, struck one boldly, and applied the flame vigorously to the pipe. A cloud of smoke was blown out steadily across the room. "If, for instance, Margaret gave up the *varsity*, which, if she had a baby, she would be obliged to, she'd have no qualifications of any note to fall back on later in life. As you get older your mind loses the resilience for learning, with the result that, if she did try to pick up where she'd left off, she'd find it very difficult, if not impossible. At the moment, there are no facilities for that sort of thing. And one child might easily lead to another. She'd find herself in middle life suited for what?" He waited, watching him reflectively through the cloud of smoke. "Working in a shop."

434

"That hardly fits in," Colin said, "with Margaret as she is. I think she's determined, in any case, to qualify for what she wants. If we did get married," he added, more earnestly now and leaning forward in the chair, "we wouldn't have a family for several years. Not, at least, until she'd settled, and I'd finished with the army."

"Of that you can't be sure," the doctor said. "And I'm speaking as a professional man as well as a father," he added, smiling. "It would be absurd to put the whole question beyond the realms of human experience. After all, what's the future for? To plan towards, to prepare oneself for. After she has her degree, and once you've got your job settled, as far as I can see there's nothing to stop either you or she getting married. You may, even, by that time, have each found someone else. The human heart is very fickle, and at the age you're both at, as well as over the next few years, you may find it coming up with a few surprises."

Colin waited. Not only was he unprepared for the argument, but it had, he felt, committed him in ways which, if he considered them beforehand, he would have rejected. The whole idea now of working towards some given objective was not only obnoxious in the assumptions it made both about himself as well as Margaret, but, in his own bewildered state, virtually meaningless. He watched the doctor's face for a while, as if he sensed that, given one or two more objections to their getting married, he would get up and go and do it the following day.

"These are just one or two thoughts that came into my head," the doctor said. "Maybe you'd like to think about them. Talk them over with Margaret and we could, perhaps all three of us, have a talk again. Her mother and I, you see, are quite convinced that life at the varsity will be quite tough enough as it is. Without the demands and pressures of marriage. You see my point?"

Colin looked at the empty bottles. There was a chart on the wall beyond the doctor's head, of the human body, a maze of coloured lines and muscles. In a large, thin-necked glass jar a moth or some other insect had begun to flutter.

"After all, how long does a marriage last? Thirty, forty, fifty, sixty years. What are three years waiting, and useful study, at the beginning? If you've both got something to work towards it's an added incentive. You're both sensible. It's not as if I were talking to someone who could only see things, for instance, in terms of immediate gain."

Colin got up. He felt stiff in the chair.

"I'll talk to Margaret about it," he said. "Though we hadn't really thought it out in practice."

"No, I'm sure in practice people at your age seldom do. It's the job of old codgers like us," the doctor added, "to do what we can in that direction."

He got up himself and went over to the door, holding it open as he might for a patient, pausing only to glance round before he put out the light.

When they returned to the house Margaret was sitting in a chair by the fire, sewing, her mother beside her, preparing a sheet of paper, a placard or an announcement, for a meeting she was going to later that evening. "Tea?" Mrs. Dorman said, looking up at her husband's face to see what the outcome of their conversation might have been.

"Oh, tea for me. How about you, Colin?" the doctor said, laughing, puffing out a final cloud of smoke before leaning down casually and knocking his pipe out against the square-shaped stove.

Margaret glanced across at Colin. He gave no sign. The feeling of domesticity in the room was heightened by the quietness of the two women, and the relaxed geniality of the man. As if nothing whatsoever had occurred the doctor picked up a newspaper and sank down in a chair. "Any chance of a biscuit with it?" he called to his wife as she went over to the door. He looked over the top of the paper a moment later at Margaret and added, "You two off out this evening, or staying in?"

"Oh, I suppose we'll go for a walk," Margaret said. She glanced at Colin once again. "Is that all right?"

They went after her mother had brought in the tea.

They walked in the darkness of the golf-course. It was his habit now, whenever they walked, to hold her hand. After a while he took off his coat and they lay down on the grass. He'd told her already of what her father had said.

"I don't mind leaving school and getting married now,"

she said. "I don't feel obliged to do what they want. Though naturally, of course," she added, "I'd listen."

"Even then, it's better that you do qualify for something," he said. She had already, the previous year, decided against medicine, against following her father, and had allotted, largely because it was a shorter course, to go in for languages. Even over that there'd been some disagreement. Now she moved away from him, kneeling in the darkness. "Doesn't it go against everything you've always said? That you ought to be independent? That you should have a separate way of life? Why should you give that up now? What's so different between now and a year ago?" he added.

"I can't see why I can't do both things. If we married in a year I could still take a degree. I can't see marriage being a hindrance. If anything, it would be a settled background to work against."

"What if we did have a child?" he said.

"Couldn't we plan a family?" she said.

"I suppose we could." He waited.

"What's to hold us back?" she said.

"It's all so planned and deliberate," he said. "Like buying a suit, or a house. I've always looked for something spontaneous. It's as if we're laying down our lives, like rolling out a carpet. We know where we'll go before it's begun."

He got up. They moved on after a moment. She took his hand.

"You talk of all this independence," he said. "But you never live it through. You said your mother was like that, but you were different. I don't want you married to me, as a matter of fact. Not on these terms. I'd rather get up and do it tomorrow. Or never do it at all. I'd rather we go on as we are, and let them speculate about the future."

"Then we'll go on as we are," she said.

She came to the stop to see him off. After he'd mounted the bus and it drew away he turned and saw her figure beneath the lamp, poised at the edge of the road, and he almost leapt off the bus and hurried back, she seemed something so slender and vulnerable, scarcely there at all, with her impassioned desire to be something which, in the end, she would never become.

David Storey

He felt her absence through the night, coiled in his
bed. On the Monday morning, instead of returning to the
college, he waited outside the school. He saw her figure
some distance away, unfamiliar now in the uniform of
the school. She looked up in surprise, with a kind of
dread, when she saw him standing by the gate and despite
the other girls' curiosity came quickly across.

"Is anything the matter?" she said.

"No." He shook his head. "I just wanted to see you,
that's all," he said.

Yet even then she gazed at him with dread, her eyes
dark, her hand grasped to the leather case which held
her books.

"I thought something must be wrong," she said, watching his face to see if, in the end, she might be right.

"Not that I'm aware of. No," he said. He added, "And
how are you? Are you all right?"

"Oh, I'm all right," she said, vaguely, looking round
then at the yard, at the other girls, and at a mistress
who, with a querulous look, passed them in the gate.
"They don't like us talking in the vicinity of the school,"
she added.

"We could move away," he said.

"I haven't time." A bell rang somewhere inside the
building. The figures in the yard moved quickly towards
the doors. There were screams and shouts. Someone
called her name. "They asked me what we'd decided, of
course," she said, and added, "I told them we'd go on
as before. Unless something happened. I think they're
frightened more than anything else."

"Or concerned."

"You see, you vacillate," she said, "as much as me.
First on their side and then on ours."

"I'm glad I've seen you, at least," he said. "I couldn't
have got through the week without."

"Me neither. I was going to ring you at college tonight."

"What about?" he said, and smiled.

"Oh, just to talk," she said, and shrugged. "I'll have
to go. I'll call in any case," she added and, after glancing
quickly to the yard, kissed him on the mouth.

438

23

The building was a large, square structure, like a mill or a warehouse built originally of brick, but covered now with a uniform yellowish plaster, darkening and stained with soot, its multitudinous rows of windows framed by peeling greenish paint: the whole edifice appeared to have been roasted inside an oven, seemingly lifeless until he entered the plain, green-painted door at the top of a flight of concrete steps and a man in an army uniform stepped forward.

He gave him his name, showed him the letter he'd been sent, and was directed to a room on the second floor. Here, at the end of a concrete corridor, thirty or forty youths were sitting on benches facing a wooden partition in the centre of which was a small glass panel. This was pulled aside the moment he entered and a man with close-cropped hair thrust his head towards the room and called, "Up to J26 on the third floor, and quick about it."

The youths stood up; some were smoking, some remained standing by their benches, talking, glancing indifferently towards the open door.

A soldier with slightly longer hair and smoking a cigarette came from behind the wooden partition and read off names in a nasal voice.

Colin listened for his own. The last of the youths, with some prompting from the soldier, slowly drifted out. "J26, and quick about it," he said, echoing the words of the man behind the panel. He stood in the corridor outside, still calling, gesturing wildly and adding, "No, no, up the stairs, not down," coming finally into the room, allowing the door to crash to behind, and calling directly to the first of the soldiers who, Colin could now see, as he too came round the partition, was wearing sergeant's stripes: "The bloody fools."

He showed the sergeant the letter he'd been sent and was directed to one of the wooden benches. He waited for twenty minutes. Other youths drifted in, looking round, going to the glass panel, showing slips of paper, coming over to the benches, sitting down, yawning, one or two smoking. Two sooted windows looked out on an empty sky.

After a while, when the benches were full, the soldier with longer hair appeared once more from behind the partition. He read off a list of names and, but for Colin, the youths drifted out.

A third group came in, assembled on the benches, then, after a phone message received by the sergeant, were directed to the room upstairs.

The sergeant came out from the partition and, with the second soldier, sat down on the benches. He took out a cigarette, offered one to the soldier, and for a while stretched there, his head in his hands. The phone rang after a while and he got up, slowly, and went to answer it. His square, bullet-shaped head was visible beyond the glass panel, reddening, nodding up and down. Eventually he came back to the benches, replaced his cigarette in his mouth, and once again lay down.

"What're you doing here?" the soldier with the longer hair said, seeing Colin still waiting in the room.

He showed him the letter. His name was checked on a list.

"You should have gone up three batches ago," the soldier said. He showed the list to the sergeant.

"I was told to wait in here," he said.

"Who told you to wait in here?" the sergeant said.

"You did," he said.

"You couldn't have listened. Half the people that come in here are deaf," he added to the soldier. "Up to J26. That's what I said. You better get up now."

He went out to the corridor. A burst of laughter came from the room behind, cut short a moment later by the ringing of the phone.

He climbed up the steps to the third floor, and walked

440

slowly along the concrete corridor looking at the numerous identically painted doors. Finally he came to a room lettered J29, the six apparently having spun upside down. He knocked on the door loudly, heard no answer from the other side, and pushed it open.

Rows of small wooden desks and chairs were set out inside. At a larger desk, facing the rows, sat a soldier with two stripes on his arm. He was unwrapping a packet of sandwiches, which were held together by a rubber band. As Colin entered he looked up in surprise.

"What is it?" he said. A large thermos flask stood on the desk beside him.

"I've been sent up," he said, "from the room below."

"There must be some mistake. I've just had the last batch through," he said.

He showed him the letter with his name and number and the time of his appointment.

"I was just going to have my lunch," the soldier said. He began to replace the rubber band around the sandwiches. "How many more are there?" he added.

"Just me," he said.

"Just one, is it?" He leant down by the desk, picked up a brief-case and put the sandwiches then the thermos inside and fastened the top. He replaced the case beside the desk. "I can't see why you couldn't have waited. I was just going to have my lunch," he said again.

He handed Colin a printed card.

"Don't look at it," he said, "until I tell you," pointing at the desks and adding, "I should just sit farther back. Not near the front. Have you got a pencil? You'll find one on the desk."

He chose one of the desks, finally, in the centre of the room, looking up to see if the soldier had any objection, saw that he'd returned once more to his brief-case, stooping down, and sitting at the desk set the card down on the top before him.

"Are you ready?" the soldier said. He'd produced a watch from his brief-case and gazed at him with it held significantly in his hand. "When I tell you to go you've got ten minutes to answer the questions on the card before you. I can't answer any inquiries: if you can't understand them just leave a blank."

He pressed the watch down with a significant gesture and nodded his head.

"That means," he added, calling across in irritation, "you may begin."

Colin picked up the pencil on the desk before him, saw that the first question involved a juxtaposition of figures and numbers in sequence, not unlike those he had answered years before in his grammar-school examination, and, deciding it would take a little thought to work it out, moved on to the second. He answered the second question, then the third, writing the brief answers down in a box at the side. When he'd reached the final question at the foot of the card he found that he had still one box empty.

Looking back up the column of answers he saw, as he reached the top, that inadvertently he'd placed the answer to the second question in the box provided for the answer to the first. Similarly the answer to the third question was in the box provided for the answer to the second, the answers, in effect, to all the thirty-two questions, with the sole exception of the first, which had no answer at all, being in boxes once removed from their proper place.

He had just begun, laboriously, to draw an arrow in the margin to indicate the error, when the corporal at the desk called out, "Pencils down. No looking at the card or reading it from now on."

"I was putting in a correction to the placing of the answers," he began to say when the corporal called, "No comments, please. If you wish to make inquiries you may raise your hand."

He lifted his hand. The corporal appeared to take no notice of it for several seconds, his attention on a red pencil which he was sharpening with a knife.

"Yes, what is it?" he said, finally looking up.

"I was about to point out an error I've made in the positioning of the answers," he said.

"No comment may be made upon the examination. Please bring it out."

He got up from the desk and took the card down to the soldier.

"You've left the pencil behind, I take it?"

442

"Yes," he said.

"If you don't watch them the whole roomful can go inside a morning. Please go up to room S27 on the floor above."

"I thought I'd just like to point out," he said, indicating the card over which the red pencil was now sharply poised, "that the positioning of the answers isn't correct. That the answer in effect to number one . . ."

The soldier turned slowly to look at his face.

"Why don't you piss off?" he said.

When he glanced back from the door he could see the soldier placing a neat column of red crosses down the side of the card, checking the answers automatically with a sheet before him, marking a further cross and looking up at him in some surprise before he finally stepped out into the corridor beyond.

S27 was a large room, somewhere near the top of the building. In the centre of it were two or three elderly men in white coats standing by a metal stove. Its metal chimney went up through a large, ill-fashioned hole in the ceiling.

Around three walls of the room were arranged curtained cubicles, large enough to take a table or a bed. Several of the youths from the last group were standing around the entrance to one of the cubicles, most of them undressed, two draped with towels. They went in one by one and as each came out they went on to the adjoining cubicle. In the centre of the fourth wall stood a wooden desk, behind it a uniformed officer and two soldiers.

A third soldier showed him into the first of the cubicles. He was instructed to strip off. Then, naked, he was taken into the second cubicle, was given a glass jar and told to urinate into that and a metal bucket, already full to overflowing. He handed the jar to the soldier when he finally emerged and it was taken off smartly across the room where it was given a label and lined up on a wooden table with several others.

In the third cubicle a white-gowned figure with grey hair and spectacles was reading a book. He looked up in surprise when he came round the curtain.

"I thought they'd all gone through," he said.

"I think I'm the last," he said.

"Sit in the chair and let's have a look in your ears," the man had said.

The canvas on the chair was cold. The man looked in one ear and then the other, shining in a tiny light. Finally he tilted his head to one side, ran liquid inside his ears and plugged them up with cotton wool.

"Come back here when you've finished your eye-sight test," he said, calling now, his mouth close to his head.

His throat and teeth were examined in the adjoining booth. Beyond that his body and legs were examined, finally his chest, the elderly doctor stooping over with a stethoscope. In the booth beyond that he sat in a chair opposite a wall of coloured charts. He read off numbers and figures, had the cotton wool removed from one ear while the doctor, partially deaf himself, called instructions, then returned to the first booth to have his ears re-examined.

"Is anything the matter?" he said.

"It's just dirt, I'm afraid," the doctor said.

"Dirt?"

"You bohemians are all the same," the doctor said, indicating Colin's longish hair.

When he was dressed there was no one left in the room but the group of white-gowned figures, grown larger now, around the stove, and the officer with the two soldiers sitting at the desk.

"Could you tell me my grading?" he asked the officer as he reached the door.

"You'll be informed in due course," the officer said.

"There's no chance of finding out now?" he said. "I asked for an early medical, you see."

"Why did you ask for an early medical?" the officer said.

"So I could go straight in when I leave college at the end of the term," he said. "Otherwise I'll be hanging around for months."

"I'm afraid there's no way I can tell you," the officer said. "You'll have to wait like the rest, and you'll be informed," he added again, "in due course."

As he came down the corridor, several youths, some still dressing in coats and shirts, others pulling on shoes, were gathered round a desk on the landing. Behind the desk sat a soldier with his hat threaded through the lapel on his jacket, calling out names and numbers, and giving out cards.

Colin waited. After several minutes his name was called.

"Grade three," the soldier said, waving the card above his head. He took it from the soldier without the soldier looking up. The knot of youths had almost dispersed. The last cards were given out and he stepped up to the desk.

"I think there's been a mistake," he said.

"What's your name?" the soldier said.

He showed him the card. "The name's correct, and the number, but I think the grade must be wrong."

"Grade three," the soldier said, checking against a sheet before him. "Flat feet. Have you got flat feet?" he said.

"I hadn't noticed them," he said.

"A lot have things they haven't noticed until they come here," the soldier said.

"Does that mean I won't be taken?" he said.

"That's quite correct." The soldier snapped to a file before him. "You've a blighty ticket. No grade threes are taken at present."

Outside he caught a tram which took him to the college. He sat on a wooden bench at the front. He examined the card, his name written out in full and the grade given beside it in roman numerals. The tram rattled on; it screeched at the bends, the wheels grinding at the track, the glass vibrating in the wooden frames, the reversible wooden benches clattering against the metal brackets. He stared down at the street, at the smooth bands of tarmac inset with the shiny rails, the terraces and con-certinaed roofs, the vast furnaces set far beyond the metal coffers, the overhanging pall of smoke, lit by flame, and saw, finally, beyond the farthest roofs, the outlines of the hills to the south beyond which lay the town where he'd gone to school and beyond which, in turn, some twelve miles farther on, lay the village. The tram dipped down; the road ran between high walls and narrow buildings: he glanced at the card and then to the ribbed, ticket-strewn floor between his feet.

"I'll be going in October, I suppose," she said.

She gazed out at him from beneath the brim of the hat, a large, sweeping, straw-coloured shape, fastened round with a pinkish ribbon.

Beyond her, down the track, was visible the crescent of smoke which heralded the train beyond the cutting. Since leaving school that summer she'd taken to travelling on the train, rather than the bus. It had been another cause of tension between them: the cost of things on which they might have saved.

It was Sunday evening. Other groups that had been in the church were now wandering through the fields below the village, the sun's magnified shape, a bulbous, burning red, sinking down in a mist above the pit.

"I suppose I'll see less of you," he said, "if I take this job at Rawcliffe. I can only get away at weekends."

"You could, if you wanted, get a job near the university," she said.

"But then I couldn't help out at home."

"I can't see why not."

"There wouldn't be much left after paying rent. Whereas if I pay rent at home my mother gets it."

"Yes," she said, turning to watch the train herself. Only its sound, however, penetrated to the station. The wedge-shaped mound of smoke slowly grew above the cutting.

"In any case, I don't think much to hanging around: that's what it would amount to," he said. "You'll have your own life to lead."

Already, largely because of this, he'd decided against their getting married.

"Are you going to live for the next three years at home?" she said.

"I don't know." He shrugged. "Anything might happen."

"Not if you stay there," she said.

The train came into sight, a black, cylindrical shape moving through the shadow of the cutting. Its smoke and a white cloud of steam welled up between the grass slopes on either side. A whistle blew as it came beneath the bridge, the smoke ballooning beneath the arch.

The platform shuddered as the engine passed.

"We might find after a year we've no alternative: but

to get married, I mean," he said. "We may find, in the end, it's the best solution."

"Yes."

Her eyes followed the engine as it coasted along the track, the carriages jolting as it came to a halt.

A door opened at the opposite end and Reagan got out. He was carrying his violin case and was dressed in a dark suit, a white handkerchief protruding from the breast pocket. He ducked his head but didn't speak as he hurried past, flushing slightly as he glanced at Margaret, then hurrying to the flight of steps. His tall, angular figure was visible a moment later as he crossed the bridge to the station yard.

Margaret got into an empty carriage. She lowered the window, carefully removed her hat, laid it on the seat, then leant out, gazing along the platform.

"That's all we can do, then," she said. "See how it goes." She glanced at him, briefly, then looked down the platform the other way. Her thin, high-boned cheeks had flushed. A white patch showed at either temple.

Other doors were slammed; a porter came along, testing the handles.

"I'll see you next week-end, then," he said.

She leant to him quickly.

He kissed her mouth.

"Take care," he said. "I'll give you a ring."

A whistle had blown. The train lurched, shuddering; a harsh panting came from the front as the engine moved to the track.

The carriages glided out of the station. Margaret's hand waved, and continued waving until the end of the platform and the signal box had passed.

Reagan was waiting by the bridge when he came out of the station; the smoke and the steam from the train was still visible down the track.

"I thought I'd wait and walk up with you," he said, running his hand slowly across his hair then stooping to pick up the violin case between his feet.

They set off up the slope towards the village. The sun had sunk down behind the shoulder of the hill. Reagan walked with a long, loping stride, his head thrust back as

447

if in some way, unconsciously, he were trying to restrain his body.

"Where have you been this evening?" Colin said.

"Oh, rehearsing." Reagan named a neighbouring village. "They're forming a dance band there. I thought I could play there midweek and in town at week-ends. I give a lesson there as well." He added, "As a matter of fact, actually this evening, I've been playing in a church."

"A church?"

Reagan changed the violin case to his other hand.

"The vicar invited me. It's the saint's day, for the building I mean. There were three other people there. We made a quartet."

They walked in silence for a while. The air was still. The voices of people in the distant fields came clearly to them: a voice calling a name, then a burst of laughter, then several people talking at once. Beyond it all, rising and falling, then finally growing more faint, came the persistent panting of the engine.

"I hear you've failed your medical," Reagan said.

"Yes," he said. "Flat feet."

"I failed too. Weak chest." He tapped it lightly with his hand. "And anaemia apparently. It's probably just as well. It's a terrible waste of time if you've got something you want to do."

A car came down the road, and rattled on, accelerating, towards the station. It covered them for a moment in a cloud of dust.

Reagan brushed down his suit with his one free hand.

"Are you getting married to your fiancée soon?" he said.

"We're not engaged," he said.

"Oh," he said. "I thought you were. My mother mentioned something about it." He scratched his head.

"She goes off to university in a couple of months. For three years."

"I say, that's hard cheese," he said, affecting, momentarily, something of an accent.

The car, which had passed them on the hill, had turned and was now mounting back up the slope towards the village. As it drew abreast the horn was sounded and a moment later a head appeared.

"Hello, old man," someone called, and, as the car

pulled up, the head had turned, backwards. "Hello, there, Savvers."

A moment later a figure in an officer's uniform got out.

It wasn't until it came close to him, its hand extended, that he recognized the sun-burnt features of Stafford half-hidden beneath the neb of the hat.

"I'll be going on, then," Reagan said after they'd shaken hands. "Leave you two to chin-wag about old times." His accent once again was heightened, and without waiting for an ackowledgment he set off up the road.

"Jump in, for God's sake," Stafford called. "I'll drive you up." He added to Colin, "I've just called at your house. Your mother said you were on your way to the station. With old Maggie Dorman, after all this time."

"She's just gone on the train," he said.

"Don't you see her home, then?" Stafford said, holding the door of the car now and beckoning Reagan inside. He took his violin case from him and set it in the back. "In the front, old man. I hate people sitting behind."

They sat abreast, squashed up against the gears, and coasted slowly towards the village.

"I was just passing through," Stafford said. "And thought I'd call. I haven't seen you for how long is it?" not waiting for an answer but blowing his horn vigorously at children playing between the first of the houses.

"Two years," Colin said. "At least."

"How's old Prendergast?" Stafford said, turning to Reagan.

"He's still alive. He hands me on some of his pupils," Reagan said. "We have an understanding in that respect. I do violin and he does piano."

"Poor old Prenny," Stafford said. He added, "Do you mean to say Maggie's gone off on that train alone?" He accelerated quickly now along the street. "What say to nipping into town and meeting her at the station? We could get there, if we hurry, before the train arrives."

"I wouldn't put you to all that trouble," he said.

"No trouble to me, old man," he said. "Did you hear that Marion's gone off nursing? Not available except during bank holidays and that."

Reagan was dropped off at the corner of the street. He

David Storey

ducked his head to the window after taking out his violin from the seat behind.

"That's been very kind of you to give me the lift," he said as if the purpose of Stafford's visit to the village had been this alone. "I'll see you some time. If you're ever near the Assembly Rooms on Saturday drop in for a dance." He nodded quickly and stepped back as the car shot forward, Stafford calling, "See you, Mic, old man. Look out."

They turned out of the village and past the colliery, the car roaring, Stafford leaning casually back, whistling lightly between his teeth, his eyes scarcely visible beneath the brim of the hat.

"How long have you been in the army?" Colin said.

"A year, old man. I thought I'd get it over with. I go up to Oxford a year from now. Get it all cleared up before I go." He glanced across, spinning the wheel wildly when, a moment later, he glanced back at the road.

They turned along the road towards the town.

"Your old lady said you'd got exemption. That was a stroke of luck," he said. "I tried it, you know, but it didn't work. Got a doctor's note about a dicky heart. Couldn't find anything when it came to the medical."

"Is there something the matter with your heart?" he said.

"I shouldn't think so, old man." He whistled once more between his teeth. "I thought I might try it and give it a whirl."

Every vehicle that came into sight on the same side of the road Stafford overtook: within a matter of minutes they were passing through the town. The sun had set. Its light still hung above the valley. When they turned into the station yard a row of gas lamps were being lit beneath the canopy above the station entrance. Stafford, leaving the engine running, ran off quickly up the steps, reappearing moments later as Colin too got out and calling, "It's all right, old man. We've got ten minutes. I told you we'd make it with time to spare."

He leant in the car, turned off the engine, put his hat on the seat behind, then, running his hand across his fair, almost blondish hair, looked round freshly at the yard.

450

"My God: do you remember coming here? That day we went to the flicks with Marion and Audrey?" From somewhere, perhaps the rear of the car itself, he produced a small baton. As they moved to the steps he set it neatly beneath his arm, clenching his gloved hands behind his back.

A soldier, waiting in the station entrance, briskly saluted as they sauntered past.

Stafford flicked up his hand without moving his head.

"Here it comes, old man. What will she say when she sees you again?"

Yet the train rattled through the station and disappeared down the line the other side. A gust of wind swept through the station.

"Must be the express." Stafford snapped up his wrist, examined a silver-coloured watch fastened there, then added, "Another two minutes, I think, old boy."

They went through to the platform. The small knots of people gathered there watched Stafford intently as he paced slowly to and fro: there was an unfamiliar erectness about his figure, the hair cut short, emphasizing the clarity of his features, an almost boyish candour which, strangely, he'd scarcely ever possessed as a youth.

"We're going abroad in a couple of weeks' time," he said, gazing attentively now along the track. "Kenya. Though I don't suppose I'll be there for very long."

"Where else are you likely to go?" he said.

"It could be Malaya. Rumour has it, of course. Though I can't be sure. I've applied for a home posting, in any case. I don't think much to all this travel. I'm representing the army, at rugger, you see, which is one little lever I've got. Apply it in the right place and I've a feeling, you know, it might do the trick."

The dark cylinder of the engine had appeared suddenly down the track. The people on the platform stirred. Stafford began to smile, tapping his stick against his leg.

"I've forgotten, almost, what old Maggie looked like. Does she still go on about women's rights?" He glanced over at Colin and began to laugh. "You weren't in on that, at the time. My God. Some of the ideas she had were out of this world."

When Margaret descended from the train she stared at

451

Colin with such a look of incredulity, pausing by the carriage door as if for a moment she might get back inside, that he began to laugh, going forward to take her hand.

"What on earth are you doing here?" she said, her eyes wide, glancing back at the train itself. "Did you come in another carriage?"

"Stafford brought me," he said, indicating the uniformed figure who, with mock bravura, saluted with his wooden baton and came forward, bowing slightly, to shake her hand.

"My compliments, ma'am. May we escort you to your home?" he said, then added, "Remember me?"

"Good lord." She stepped back a moment and examined his figure. "You've been commissioned as well?" she said.

"That's right," Stafford said and added, "As well as what?"

"Oh, my brother's commissioned. He's in the Tank Corps, as a matter of fact."

"Ah." Stafford paused, his gaze drifting off to the view of the town beyond the station. "Not like us infantry wallahs, I can tell you that." He crooked his arm. "May we escort you to the car?" he added.

Margaret laughed. She placed her arm in Stafford's and, glancing at Colin, started off to the station entrance.

Colin walked along on the other side.

She gave in her ticket and they went through to the yard. Stafford opened the door.

"I don't think, with a lady," he said, "we can squash in, Col, as we did before. Do you mind handing out my hat before you get in the back?"

They drove slowly through the town. The light had faded. The car's headlamps flooded out on the road ahead. Stafford described some of his activities over the previous year.

"Hopkins, by the way, was in my squad at O.C.T.U.," he said. "Went into the Rifle Brigade. Now he *is* in Malaya, as a matter of fact. I heard Walker went in too, but failed to pass. He's a sergeant in the Education Corps. Who else is there?" He went through several more names of boys from the school he'd come across. "You don't know how lucky you've been, old man," he added to Colin. "It's a terrible fag. I mean, all we're fighting at the moment are communists and wogs. Two years out of your life and nothing to show."

They reached the house. Stafford looked over at the green-painted door in the garden wall.

"Remember last time, my dear," he said. "Colin gallantly saw you home?" He added, "I say, you know, I admire that hat."

"Why don't you come in. Say hello to my parents now you're here?" she said.

"Well, that's very kind. I don't think we've any other pressing engagement, have we, Col?"

He stepped down from the car and held the door. On Stafford's arm, Margaret went before him up the path to the house. She knocked on the door, waiting for someone to answer it inside, calling to Colin, "Stay back to one side. See what they say," standing straight-faced, leaning on Stafford's arm, when the door was finally drawn back and her mother appeared.

"What on earth," her mother said, in much the same fashion as Margaret herself at the station.

Stafford saluted smartly.

"Is this your daughter, ma'am?" he said. "We found her wandering in the vicinity of the city railway station. She gave this as her address, though of course we quite anticipate this to be yet one more nefarious tale, a whole bevy of which she regaled us with on our compromising journey here."

"This is Neville Stafford, Mother," Margaret said. "He was a friend of Colin's from school."

"Oh, there you are, Colin," Mrs. Dorman said, gazing out to the darkness of the garden. She stepped aside to let Margaret and Stafford enter, shaking the latter's hand and adding, "Go through to the room, Margaret. Your father's there."

Colin followed them inside. The doctor stood up from his chair by the fire, shaking Stafford's hand, smiling, gazing at him with a look of wonder. "Oh, you're one of these conscripts, are you?" he said, gesturing at the uniform. "Sit down. Sit down. Would you like a drink?"

They stayed an hour. Stafford described to them freshly

some of the incidents of his training, the tests he had passed before being accepted as an officer, a football match he had played in against the Royal Air Force, a night spent with fellow officers when he and several other platoons, on a training exercise, had got lost on a moor. The sound of traffic faded from the road below the house. A clock chimed slowly on a near-by church. "My God, just look at the time," Stafford said, bringing his watch up smartly. "We mustn't keep these good people from their beauty sleep much longer. Maggie especially: it'd be a great pity to see those features fading because Stafford insisted in keeping her from her bed." He turned to Mrs. Dorman. "I was commenting on her hat at the station. She really has the most wonderful clothes. I scarcely recognized her from the girl I knew two years ago. She really has," he added, turning now to glance at Margaret directly, "come on a treat."

Margaret laughed. Flushed already from Stafford's accounts of his life in the army, the redness deepened. "Honestly, you make me sound dreadful. I couldn't have been that bad, could I, Col?"

"Oh, Colin never sees much of what's going on. He's too preoccupied with his thoughts is Colin," Stafford said. "The outward world and all its manifestations he passes by with scarcely a glance."

Margaret's mother, too, had begun to laugh. Almost another half hour, however, had passed before they finally went to the door.

"I must really make a note of this address," Stafford said. "I've rarely spent such a delightful evening. If I'd known it was going to be as pleasant as this, I can assure you," he added with a bow to the mother, "I would have come much sooner. I really think Colin is a secretive fellow, keeping Margaret to himself. Why no one tells me these things," he went on at the door, "I shall never discover. I go from one boring episode to another, while all the really interesting things happen to other people."

The lights were switched on in the drive to see them to the road. The Dormans and Margaret stood in the porch until they'd reached the gate, Stafford calling, waiting for an answer, before he finally stepped through to the car outside.

"I say, you really are a lucky dog," he said as they drove off in the direction of the town. "Talk about the chrysalis. I think it's very sly of you, Savvers, of all the girls available, to have picked out Mag. She really has blossomed, while all the others, if Marion's anything to go by, have begun to fade. They've got 'hausfrau' stamped all over them."

The streets of the town were now deserted. They turned out along the road towards the village. A last bus, its lights blazing, rattled past them in the opposite direction.

"Are you and she engaged, or anything?" Stafford said.

"Not officially." He shook his head.

"Well, unofficially, then?" Stafford glanced quickly from the road ahead.

"I'm not sure what it means," he said. "We've talked of getting married. She's to do three years at university yet. If we haven't married by that time, I suppose we'll marry then."

"You don't sound too sure," he said.

"Oh, I'm sure about marrying her," he said.

"Well, then?" Stafford said.

"It's all that goes with it. The planning, the predetermined life. I thought we might go abroad together."

"What does Margaret think of that?"

"I haven't mentioned it," he said. "But I thought I might teach abroad. There'd be more freedom, and fewer demands." He paused.

"Do you still write poetry?" Stafford said.

"Yes," he said.

"Have you had any published?"

"No." He shook his head.

"Well: good luck to you both, in any case," Stafford said.

When they got to the village and had pulled up in front of the house the light went on in his parents' bedroom. The curtain was pulled aside and a moment later the light went on in the passage and the front door was unlocked. His mother, her nightdress covered by a coat, came on to the step.

"Would you like to come in, Neville? Have a cup of tea or anything?" she said.

"That's very kind, Mrs. Saville," Stafford said. He'd got out of the car with Colin and was standing by the bonnet, kicking loosely at the wheel as he talked. "I was just saying good night to Colin. I better be getting back."

"Well, I've kept a kettle on in case you wanted one," she said. "I thought, since he didn't come back, you must have had a night out together."

"Oh, we've had that, Mrs. Saville," he said and laughed.

His mother glanced up, briefly, at the sky. Odd stars were visible throught the thinning mist.

"It's quite a lovely night," his mother said.

"Oh, it's a grand night," Stafford said, looking up too, his fair hair glinting, almost luminous in the light from the door. "Yes, it's a grand night," he said again, more slowly.

"Well, there's some tea waiting, if you want some," his mother said and, holding her coat more closely to her, stepped inside.

"It's been quite an eventful evening, after all, then," Stafford said, still kicking loosely at the wheel. "I won't come in for the tea. You'll thank your mother for me."

"Sure," he said.

"I'll say goodbye for now, then," Stafford added, and quickly put out his hand. "See you soon. I'll drop you a line. Africa. The Far East. If you've got the odd word, you know, it'll help fill in the time. There's an awful lot of bumf in the army. Damn boring, really. I suppose Oxford'll be the same. I'm not looking forward much to that. Still. Ours not to reason. Ours but to do and try."

He got back in the car. The engine started. The tanned face was visible for a moment in the light from the dashboard, a hand was raised, then the car slid forward. Colin watched it out of sight, then turned to the house.

Bletchley had stayed on at school a further year, won a scholarship, and had gone to university to study chemical engineering. He could be seen occasionally at week-ends or on holiday walking down the street in a university blazer, a large university scarf around his neck, smoking a pipe, a pile of books beneath his arm.

On several evenings that summer, while Margaret was away on holiday, Colin went with his friend to the Assem-

456

bly Rooms in town. The ballroom occupied the entire first floor of the building, a long stone-built structure with tall windows and a pillared entrance, a broad, curving staircase sweeping up to the glass-panelled doors of the room itself. Here, in a small alcove at the side, a man sold tickets.

Reagan, it appeared, had taken over the running of the band. His tall figure, attired in evening dress and holding a baton, was posed in an attitude of studied nonchalance on the edge of a small dais at one end of the room. In front of each of the musicians stood a painted board with the initials MR painted in a single, scroll-like shape from top to bottom. He nodded casually over the heads of the dancers, as they entered, as if there were nothing unusual in their arrival at all, taking up a violin a little later and, stepping forward from the orchestra, playing directly into the microphone.

Bletchley, after some hesitation about coming in his university blazer, had put on his suit. His face was red and beaming, preparing himself before their entry to be amused by if not scornful of what they would find inside, pausing however once they were at the door and gazing with a blank, flushed look of incredulity at the bony elegance of his friend across the room.

Partly discomposed by Reagan's appearance, and partly by the fact that none of the girls they could see in the immediate vicinity of the door were to his liking, Bletchley stood, his hands in his pockets, gazing with an aggrieved expression across the heads of the swaying dancers, turning finally to Colin and saying, "What a terrible lot. He really pulls in the dregs, as we might have imagined if we'd given it a little thought," a sweat already forming on his massive features, his thick red neck protruding in heavy rolls above his collar. As a last concession to his university identity, he'd put on a striped and crested university tie. "I should think most of the people here are colliers. As for the girls, I should think they've brought them in from the mill. Have I told you about the varsity dance? They go on sometimes till one in the morning and some of the girls don't mind where they go on to after that."

Reagan came over during an interval between the tunes, his large head with its long hair greased carefully back to disguise the protrusion at the rear, bobbing disjointedly above those of the now separated dancers, a small, official smile igniting his pallid features, nodding slightly to Bletchley and saying, "It was good of you to come, Ian. I'm glad you could make it," gesturing off across the room and adding, "Come over to the bar and have a drink."

"Only orange juice?" Bletchley said, following Reagan over and examining the glasses of those coming from a table at the opposite end of the room.

"We haven't got a licence yet," Reagan said. "In any case, in my experience, drink and dancing seldom mix. There's bound to be trouble if we started selling beer, for instance," calling then across the heads before him to a woman in a dark dress and white apron, "Three oranges, Madge."

Colin recognized his aunt, now grey-haired and much fatter than when he had last seen her in his grandparents' one-roomed bungalow, years before. He wondered for a moment whether she might acknowledge him, for she handed him his glass without a second look, passing one to Bletchley and saying to Reagan, "Nothing to put in it today, then, Michael?"

"Hello, Aunty," Colin said.

"Aunty. I'll give you Aunty," the woman said, laughing, her look fading a moment later as, with a hand to her cheek, she added, "That's not our Ellen's eldest, is it? It's not Colin, is it, love?" laughing again when he leant across to shake her hand, the crowd milling round on either side. "Well, he was so high when I last saw him," she added to Reagan, measuring off a height level with the table. "And as proud and as protective of his mother as any man. Our Reg, you know, will hardly believe it. Wait till I tell our David. You might see them here: they come in sometimes, later. After they've had one or two in the boozer, you know."

They finally moved away from the table, his aunt's gaze still fixed on him over the heads of the crowd, smiling, nodding, her attention scarcely on the glasses she was selling. "Would you believe it? That's my nephew over there," he could hear her saying. "It's years since I ever set eyes on him. I hope Reg and David come in before he goes."

"It's very hot in here. Don't you find it hot, Michael?" Bletchley said, easing his finger inside his collar.

"They keep the windows shut until they've sold enough refreshments," Reagan said. "Though if you'd like them open, Ian, you've only got to say."

"On no. Don't let me interfere with your normal way of running business," Bletchley said.

"Perhaps you'd like a dance," Reagan said. "There's a couple of our regular ladies who come unattended," he added. "I could introduce you to them. They usually sit on chairs just underneath the orchestra."

The two women were in their late twenties; they wore flared dresses, identical in shape, with a narrow waist, and heavy make-up. One of them wore glasses which, before dancing with Bletchley, she removed. One was named Martha, and the other, Bletchlcy's partner, Joyce. They danced with a professional remoteness. evidently reconciled to and yet at the same time displeased with the incompetence of their respective partners. They circled the room at a steady pace, came under the beaming gaze of Reagan, and passed on with the heavy, swirling crowd.

Coloured lights rotated slowly beneath the ceiling; a window had finally been opened at one end of the room, through which came, along with the roar of the Saturday night traffic outside, a cooling stream of air.

Bletchley, plainly, was having trouble with his feet. He drew his partner's attention to them from time to time, the two of them gazing down, she short-sightedly and apparently seeing nothing, he with a look of irritation as if they'd taken up some independent activity of their own. The huge, bull-shaped head, glistening across its massive brow and cheeks, would be lowered in the direction of the floor, the rouged and powdered face beside it, then, as if some fresh adjustment had been made invisibly to those ponderous shoes, they would set off with a fresh uncertainty, together.

A gentlemen's excuse-me was announced, Reagan's voice enunciating the words carefully through the microphone as if he were placing each one in by hand, Bletchley coming across and bowing slightly to Martha, who, as if it were immaterial to her whom she danced with, immediately took his hand while Colin went over to the short-sighted Joyce, who, having found herself deserted, was gazing around her in consternation. "Oh, there you are," she said. "I thought you'd wandered off."

They left an hour later. It had grown dark outside. All the windows of the room were opened. As they went to the door Reagan, who was playing a violin accompaniment in front of the microphone, had gazed over the heads of the dancers in their direction, questioningly, almost plaintively, nodding with a smile, still playing, when Colin indicated they were going down to the street below.

His aunt came over as they reached the door.

"You're not going yet?" she said. "Our Reg and David haven't come up. They'll be so disappointed, you know, if they find you've gone."

"We'll probably be up next Saturday," he said. "We could see them then."

"I'll hold you to that," she said, laughing, then seizing his hand. "And how is your mother? I heard she'd had an operation a year or two ago."

"Oh, it's more than that," he said. "She's fine. She's keeping well."

"With a son like you I'm not surprised. I hear you've been to college and that. Not like our Reg and David: they've hardly learned to read."

"There might be a virtue in that," he said.

"Well, they're earning more than their father," she said. "But I don't think it makes much difference. Money doesn't make you happy. That's why I come here: to see a bit of life."

A crowd of young men were coming up the stairs when they went outside; for all he knew his two cousins might have been amongst them. He followed Bletchley's perspiring figure down to the door. A great burst of cheering and laughter came from the room above their heads.

Once in the street the music welled out from the open windows.

"How does Reagan get home afterwards?" Bletchley asked, mopping his face.

"He goes on the train, I think. There's one just after twelve," he said.

"Are you waiting till then?" Bletchley said. "I think I'll go on the bus."

"Oh, I think I'll come as well," he said.

"If you ask me," Bletchley said, as they went down to the stop, "I think Michael's heading for trouble."

"He seems to think he's doing well."

"I was talking to that girl we were dancing with." Bletchley ran his handkerchief round beneath his collar. "Apparently he hardly makes anything out of it at all."

"Why's that?"

"Well, there's the regular dance hall, the Emporium. They've got a bar there, and it's twice as big. He only gets people here because he hardly charges them to go in. It's just like Michael. Full of fantasies, you know. He's no idea. Once he's paid for the hire of the hall, and the staff, and he's paid the band, he's lucky if he makes more than two or three pounds a week. And all that talk of going on the radio. He even mentioned films to me."

When the bus finally drew in a tall, wiry, red-haired figure got off, followed by a smaller, stockier, black-haired one. Batty paused as he came along the queue, turning to Stringer, then saying directly to Bletchley, "How do, Belcher. How you been?"

"I've been very well," Bletchley said. "And you?"

"Where're you going at this time of night, then, Belcher?" Stringer said.

"I'm going home, as a matter of fact," Bletchley said.

"We're going to hear the Reagan Orchestra," Batty said. He glanced at Colin. "Fancy coming up for a fling, then, Tonge?"

"We've just been up for one," he said.

The rest of the queue had moved on towards the bus.

"Mic Reagan there, then, is he?" Stringer said. He had recently, to match his hair and eyes, grown a black moustache. It formed a rectangular patch beneath his nose. Both of their faces, in the street light, had the freshness of colliers' faces that had recently been scrubbed.

"Michael's there. He's playing very well, for all that anyone will notice," Bletchey said.

"Oh, we'll notice it, Belcher," Batty said and, digging his elbow against Stringer, laughed.

"Yeh, we'll notice it," Stringer said

"See you sometime, Tongey," Batty said, waiting for

this to be confirmed before he set off up the street after Stringer's departing figure.

They sat upstairs on the bus. Bletchley got out his pipe.

"I don't think those two will ever come to much good," he said.

"I don't know," he said. "They're different."

"Factory fodder. I don't see what hope they have in their lives. I mean," he added, "what prospect do they have before them? A dance hall and a bottle of beer." He blew out a cloud of smoke. Something about the gesture reminded Colin of Dr. Dorman. It was on this same bus, and at the same time on a Saturday evening, that he would ride back to the village after seeing Margaret. He gazed out of the window for a while. "I mean, it's an animal existence when you come down to it. What do you think?"

"Perhaps it's all an animal existence," he said. He had to raise his voice above the rattle of the bus. Below them passed the dark waters of the river.

"Oh, I shouldn't think it's all an animal existence," Bletchley said as if calling now to the rest of the bus. "What's science for, after all? Some men grow out of their environment. Whereas others just seem to sink into it. They make no effort at all, as far as I can see. Take Batty and Stringer. They're prime examples." Another cloud of smoke drifted away from his seat across the rest of the bus. "I mean, they're going to be stuck round here, aren't they, for the rest of their lives."

The bus careered on through the darkness. Odd lights showed up from the darkened fields, from isolated farms or rows of terraces set down arbitrarily on the brow of a hill. Groups of people came into the lights below, waiting at the stops, others drifting off from the bus and disappearing in the dark. Farther off, the sky glowed with the lights of distant villages and, behind them, the dull, sombre redness of the town.

"It's like Darwin's origin of the species," Bletchley said, sweating freshly in the heat of the bus. "Some of the species adapt, others don't. In effect, when coal is acquired by wholly mechanical means or perhaps isn't even needed at all, people like Batty and his brothers, and Stringer, won't have a function. And when the function

ceases so does the species, or those parts of it that can't
recognize or create a further function."

Soon the rattling of the bus grew too loud for Bletchley
to make himself heard; he contented himself with digging
Colin with his arm at some particular man or woman as
they appeared at the top of the stairs or disappeared to
the platform, each one evidently some illustration of his
thesis, his head nodding significantly as he glanced across.

The darkness finally gave way to the lights of the village; they descended towards it with increasing speed,
Bletchley rising and making his way, swaying, to the stairs,
where he waited, clutching the rail on either side while the
bus negotiated the final corner. He was waiting on the
pavement, tapping out his pipe against his heel, by the
time Colin came down himself.

They walked through the streets in silence, Bletchley's
shadow flung bulkily before them as they passed beneath the lights. Mr. Bletchley at one point came cycling
past on an upright bike, with a pannier behind the
saddle. Since his demobilization he'd taken a job in a
shunting yard adjoining a neighbouring village and frequently worked the same shifts as Colin's father. Even
though Colin nodded to him on this occasion Bletchley
himself gave no sign at all, his father cycling on as if
he expected none in any case, dismounting slowly when
he reached the terrace and, without a backward look,
disappearing down the alley at the side.

"Wasn't that your father?" Colin said.

"He's working afternoons," Bletchley said, refusing him
even now any acknowledgment at all. "He's doing overtime. I run up one or two bills at the varisity," he added.
"He's trying to pay them off."

"Aren't you taking a job over the summer?" Colin said.

"I thought I might. The trouble is, I've got so much
work to get through, I don't think I'll have time to take a
job. After all," he added, "there's nothing else the old
man can do. He can't do my work for me, can he? And
I don't feel I'm particularly cut out for doing his. It
gives him a goal to work towards, a motive, you see,
beyond himself."

He'd re-filled his pipe by the time they reached the
house. They stood for a moment by their respective doors,

Bletchley lighting his pipe and puffing out, reflectively, several clouds of smoke.

"Poor old Michael," he said, gazing down the street towards Reagan's door. "I think all his troubles you could trace back to that time when he failed his eleven-plus. Do you remember that? He wrote an essay about being a nurse." He laughed, his heavy figure shaking as he leant up against the wall. "How are things with you, in any case?" he added, the first time he'd inquired at all about Colin's activities over the previous two years. "Is it a worthwhile undertaking, do you think? I thought of teaching, you know, for a while. But you know what they say about teachers? A man amongst children and a child amongst men." He still gazed down, however, towards Reagan's door. Mr. Reagan had appeared beneath a distant lamp, lurching unsteadily from side to side, holding on to the lamp and then, a moment later, to a nearby wall, standing, bowed, his shoulders stooped, then with a final, almost convulsive gesture, moving on towards his door. "I better be getting in. I might get another hour's swotting," Bletchley said, his mother a moment later appearing beside him in the door.

"There you are, Ian," she said, smiling at Colin. "Have you had a nice evening, love?"

"We've been to Michael's dance-hall," Bletchley said, puffing a cloud of smoke directly in her face. "There's his father out here now, staggering home, it seems, from another. Either that or the Miners' Institute. I'm sure he wouldn't know if you could be bothered to ask him" He walked into the open door and called inside from the passage, "Anything for supper, Mum?"

He could hear her voice and Bletchley's, followed by the father's, inside the house after the door had closed.

Down the street itself the Reagan's door had opened and Mrs. Reagan's thin, almost emaciated figure had appeared. "Is that you, Bryan?" she called to the figure standing stooped above the gutter, and a few moments later, having received no reply but a groan, went down the pavement, took his arm beneath her own and guided him in.

"Reagan?" Colin's father said when he mentioned having seen him in the street outside. "There's a wasted talent if ever there was one. He could have got anywhere with a mind like his. He had a sense of style, and taste. And now what is he? Stumbling from one bar to the next. He'll be lucky if he keeps that job. Despite the years he's put in, you know. He's trouble with the pay now almost every week, and he's been at it, you know, for over thirty years."

His father went along the backs a little later; they could hear him tapping at the Reagan's door, then his voice, tentative, light, almost cheery: "Anything I can do, then, missis?" and some fainter, answering voice inside. He came back, frowning in the light. "Nay, they want nowt from us," he added. "He was stretched out there on the kitchen floor, and she bent over him, going through his pockets. I reckon there's nobody could help them now. That's what comes, you know, from marriage. Marriage to the wrong person, I'm talking about," he went on quickly when his mother looked up. "Marry the wrong one and your life is finished. Marry the right one and your life is made."

24

He saw her some distance away and didn't recognize
Stafford at first; accustomed perhaps to seeing him in a
uniform, he thought it might have been her brother.
Then he recognized the build and the fairness of the
hair. Stafford was wearing a dark-coloured blazer and
flannels: a white handkerchief protruded from his breast
pocket.

"I thought you were still on holiday," he said to her
when he'd caught them up; aware of his steps they'd
both turned, glanced away, aimlessly, then waited for
him to draw abreast.

"I've just got back today," she said. "Neville was in
London and drove me up."

Her face was dark, tanned around the cheeks and
brow.

"I've got a forty-eight hour pass," Stafford said. "I
thought I'd do the girl a favour. I was coming up in any
case," he added. He gestured to the car which was parked
across the road. The whirl of traffic around the city centre
hid it a moment later from their view.

It was late evening; lights were coming on across the
street. The spire of the cathedral loomed up against the
sky.

"I was hoping you'd ring this evening," Margaret said.
"I was coming through tomorrow. Did you get the card
I sent?"

"No," he said.

"The post is terrible," Stafford said. "It takes days
just to send a letter across town, never mind from France

to England. As for the south of England to the north."
He waved his hand.

"I suppose I'll see you tomorrow, then," he said.

"Why not come out to the house?" she said. "We just
dropped in for a drink." She gestured now to the hotel
behind. "Or Neville could take on the luggage and we
could go on the bus."

"For goodness' sake, just jump in the car. We'll be
there in no time," Stafford said. He took her arm and
began to guide her through the traffic.

When Colin had crossed to the car himself Stafford
had already started the engine. He glanced in at them
through the open window.

"I'll give you a call tomorrow," he said. There was a
curious similarity between their two figures, the same
delicacy of features, the same light eyes.

"Just leap in the back, Savvers," Stafford said. "We'll
be there in a jiffy," leaning across to release the catch on
the door itself.

"I'm on my way home," he said. "But I'll call you
tomorrow," he added to Margaret. "I'm glad you're back."

She turned to gaze woodenly through the windscreen.

"If you're sure you don't want a lift, Savvers," Stafford
said. "I might pop through the village tomorrow. Give
the odd knock and see if you're home."

The car started forward; Margaret, startled, glanced
out at him sharply, wildly, as if, for a moment, she might
have cried out.

Then the car swept away in the evening traffic; he
could see their two figures silhouetted briefly, then the
profile of the car and the other traffic cut them out.

He rang the following morning but Margaret was out.
Neither she nor Stafford appeared at the house.

He rang again in the evening. Her father answered the
call.

"Oh, it's you, Colin," he said. "I'm afraid Margaret's
out. And so's her mother. I haven't seen them today, as a
matter of fact. I've been standing in, you know, for a
friend and I'm only just back. I'll tell her you called as
soon as she's in."

He walked back through the village from the telephone

booth; it stood, a red-painted box, at the village centre, where the two roads crossed, occupying one corner of the pub yard. Mr. Reagan was coming down the street, setting out for his evening's drinking. He walked slowly, raising his bowler hat with one hand, and saluting him with his cane with the other.

"And how's the intellectual?" he said. "My good lady informs me you're destined for scholastic pursuits. That already there is an insititue of a pedagogical nature opening its portals to the enlightened influence of Harry Saville's eldest son. I shall await the outcome, I might tell you, with the greatest expectations. The *greatest* expectations," he added, his eyes moving on now, past Colin, to the doors of the pub. "Don't forget, now, the ones who formed you when you reach your golden age—the ones who've been swept beneath the carpet, emptied in the trash cans of the world; the waste that has gone to produce the flower of your intellectual emancipation." He replaced his bowler slowly, almost like a runner preparing for a race, judging time and distance, finally waving his stick beside his face and stepping off briskly towards the yard. He gave no further acknowledgment that he'd noticed him at all.

"Why don't you go and see her?" his mother said when he got back home.

"I suppose I shall," he said. In two days' time he was due to start at the school.

"When does she start at the university, in any case?" she said.

"Not for another three weeks." He added, "She said she might come through today. There's still time, I suppose." He glanced at the clock.

It was already growing dark outside.

His mother was ironing. She heated the iron by the fire, stooping to the flames, her glasses reflecting the glow. Her face itself was reddened.

She held the iron with a cloth, dampening her finger on her tongue.

She went back to the table.

The wood creaked. He went to the front door after a

while and waited. Perhaps she and Stafford might come in the car.

He walked slowly to the end of the street. A car went by, its engine moaning a moment later as it ascended the hill to the Park.

He stood on the kerb, his hands in his pockets, his feet tapping at the gutter. A dog crossed the road and disappeared between the houses. Bletchley's father cycled past, dismounted, his head bowed, and went down the alleyway to the backs.

In the distance came the sound of a train drawing out of the station. He went back to the house. She didn't come.

He rang the following morning. Mrs. Dorman answered the phone.

"Oh, it's you, Colin," she said in much the same manner as her husband had done the previous evening. "Margaret's out at the moment. Would you like me to give her a message?"

"I just wondered if she were coming through," he said. "Or whether I should come through to you."

"I don't know her plans, I'm afraid," she said very much as if she were answering some inquiry about her husband. "She didn't say she was going through. Would you like to ring again this evening?"

"All right," he said. "I'll call again."

"She'll be sorry that she's missed you. She went into the town to do some shopping. She's got hardly any of her university things together. And only a few days ago, it seemed, she could hardly think of anything else."

"I'll tell you your trouble," his father said when he got back in the house. "Nothing to occupy you. And when you do get started you'll find you've hardly anything to do. Teaching, you know," he added to his mother, "he can do it out of the back of his hand."

"It's you who wanted me to go in for it," he said.

"I wouldn't want you doing my job," his father said. Small and faded, dressed in his underpants and shirt, he sat smoking, half-crouched on his chair, in front of the fire.

"Why dismiss it, if it's something you wanted me to do?" he said.

"Nay, it *is* something I wanted you to do," his father said again. "But it can't stop me, can it, from saying it's easy."

"But what am I supposed to make of that?" he said, looking to his mother. She was standing at the sink, stooped, her hands slowly plying in the water, washing pots. "The job I end up with you say you despise."

"Nay, I don't despise it," his father said, slowly, looking round. "There's only muck attached to my job," he added. "Muck, and more muck, and sweat, and cursing, the like of which you never heard. We educated you for your job. We got you out of this."

"Why dismiss it?" he said again. "What pride can I have in it if it's something you despise?"

"Nay, I don't despise it. I've said I don't despise it," his father said, getting to his feet and clearing some small, wooden, block-like toys from in front of the fire. "I can't despise anybody who gets out of that colliery, I can tell you that."

They were silent for a while. His mother washed the pots slowly in the corner, setting them on the board to dry. Colin took the cloth.

"I mean, I can't have anything against it, can I?" his father suddenly added, speaking directly to his mother. He was standing over the fire, looking for an ash-tray to stub out his cigarette. Finally he flicked the ash into the fire and put the stub on the mantelpiece. "He'll be earning as much as I do. And that's after thirty years or longer, working down a pit."

His mother didn't answer. Her back bowed, she remained working at the sink.

"I mean, if there's one man that can appreciate a job like that, with two months' holidays or longer, no shifts, no nights, no muck, no sweating out your guts when your over fifty, a nice pension when it's over, writing poetry at week-ends or on an evening, and earning as much as a coal-miner does before he's even started, then I reckon that man, you know, is me. If they want anybody to recommend schoolteaching as a life, they've only

to come to me: I'll have them all schoolteachers before
you can say Jack Robin. By God, if there's one thing
I've learnt in life it's that only a bloody fool would do the
sort of work that I do. Only somebody who's mentally
deficient."

His mother turned from the sink.

"I think I'll go and lie down," she said.

"What?" His father turned from the fire; he'd just
come down from the bed himself.

"I think I'll go up," she said.

Her face was ashen, her eyes dark, shadowed beneath the glasses.

"Is anything the matter?" his father said.

"No. Nothing." She shook her head.

She walked past Colin to the stairs.

"Nay, if there's something the matter," his father said,
"we can send Stevie for the doctor."

"There's nothing," his mother said and a moment later
came the sound of her feet as she mounted slowly to
the landing. A few seconds after that the bed creaked;
his father glanced across.

"I don't know why you've got to get her worked up,"
he said.

"I thought you started it," Colin said.

"Bringing these arguments into the house," his father
said. "And going round with a face as long as this. If
Margaret's gone off with Stafford you've only yourself to
blame."

"How am I to blame?" he said.

"Stuck here. Stuck writing. He gets out and does
things. He doesn't sit still."

"I don't sit still," he said.

"Don't you?" his father said, almost sulkily now.
"What do you call this?"

"I stay here because I have to support you."

"Support me?"

"Support us," he said. "Support the family."

"Why support us?"

"Because you can't manage," he said, "without."

His father glanced away.

"In any case, do you really think Margaret's like that? From what you know of her?" he added.

"Nay, a woman takes no reckoning," his father said, yet quietly now. He looked up slowly towards the ceiling. "I better go up and see how she is."

He heard their voices a little later from the room at the front. When his father came down he'd put on his trousers; he stood fidgeting by the fire for a moment, looking for a cigarette. Finally he picked up the stub he'd left on the mantelshelf. He stooped to the fire for a coal to light it, wincing then as he held it to his face.

"She's going to rest up there," he said. "I think she'll be all right. She takes too much on herself, you know. If you could just do one or two things about the house. Though she's a difficult woman to help, I can tell you that."

His father went to work in the afternoon. After Colin had washed up the dinner pots he took his mother up a cup of tea. She was still sleeping, her round face turned from the curtained window, couched to the pillow, the blankets mounded round her head.

He put the cup down and went to the door; as he pulled it to, however, he heard her stir and a moment later her voice had called.

"Is that you, then, love?"

He put his head back round the door.

"I've just brought up some tea," he said. "Would you like some dinner as well?"

She eased herself slowly from the blanket. "Has your father gone to work?" she said.

"Half an hour ago," he said.

"Did he have some dinner?"

"Yes," he said.

"I had some meat for him. I hope he got it."

"Yes."

He stood waiting by the bed. His mother hadn't touched the tea.

"Is there anything else you want?" he said.

"No," she said. "I'll be all right."

She came down later, when he was clearing the kitchen.

She began looking around the room, about to set to work, going to the sink as if to go back to the washing-up.

"I've cleared everything away," he said.

"There's your dad's pit clothes I've got to wash for to-morrow," she said.

"I'll do them," he said.

"And where's Steven and Richard?" she said, going to the window.

"They're out," he said.

"Did they have their dinner?"

"Yes," he said.

She took the clothes from him.

"I'll wash them. I'll wash them in the sink," she said, setting a pan against the fire. "They need doing thoroughly, otherwise the dirt just clogs. And what you leave in," she added, "you can never get out."

He stood by the fireplace himself, watching her work.

"Has Margaret been at all?" she said.

He shook his head.

"Nay, love, no one's worth suffering over. Not at your age. Not at this time of your life," she said. She looked up slowly from the sink. She was rinsing the clothes in cold water from the tap. "All that your father said you mustn't take to heart. He's just had a hard life, that's all. He's doing work that a young man of thirty should be doing. He's bound to feel embittered."

"Yes," he said.

"He's just grieved that he never had the same chance himself. He doesn't mean to take anything from what you've done."

"I know," he said.

"Ever since you were a baby you've kept things to yourself."

She waited, her hands poised in the bowl, her head bowed to the sink.

"I never thought I'd been secretive," he said.

"Not secretive." She tried to smile, her face shadowed in the corner of the room. "I mean the things you feel you can never express. People can take advantage of that at times."

"Oh, I've never been aware of it."

"No," she said slowly, and looked back to the sink. "It means you'll have to take hard knocks and never be able to show to other people what you feel."

"Oh, I'm not sure of that," he said and added lightly, "Here, let me wash the shirts. You sit down for a bit. You can easily tell me if I'm not doing them right."

She sat at the table. It reminded him of the time they had visited her parents, the same air of exhaustion, some senseless defeat by life, like flies dying in a corner.

"Margaret's still very young, you know. She doesn't know her own mind yet. It's not really fair," she added, "to force her."

"Oh, I haven't forced her to anything, Mother," he said.

"No, but you've been very close to her," she said. "She's never had a chance to look at anyone else. You've made big demands on her in a way she's not aware. She's bound to resist it. And with someone like Neville. Well, he has a lot of glamour, for one thing, I suppose."

"Oh, I don't think things are as black as that," he said.

"No," she said. "I suppose they aren't. Not really."

She came to the house that afternoon. At first he thought she must have come on the bus, then he realized that none could have come to the village from the direction of the town for at least the past half hour, and imagined then she must have been dropped off at the end of the street by Stafford.

His mother, after offering to make a cup of tea, went out of the kitchen, closing the door.

Margaret sat at the table, the bunch of flowers she'd brought before her, her coat folded on a chair. Colin finally took the kettle from the fire, assuming his mother wasn't coming back, and made some tea.

She scarcely drank it, the cup before her, talking lightly now about her holiday, the French coast, the crossing to Dieppe, the friend's house she'd stayed at.

He found a jug for the flowers and put them in.

"Is Stafford still about?" he said as he set the flowers back on the table.

"I think he went back yesterday," she said.

474

"How did you get here?" he said.

"I came on the bus." She glanced across, fingering the cup. "I walked around for a bit as a matter of fact."

"In the village?"

"I went up near the church."

He stood at the table, gazing down at her slight figure, the thin features tanned with the sun, the delicate hands as they traced a pattern now on the edge of the cup.

"Would you like to go for a walk?" she said.

"Yes," he said. "I'll get my coat."

He went through to the passage. His mother was sitting in the room at the front, upright, her shoulders straight, gazing out to the street, the light reflecting from her glasses.

"We're just going out for a walk," he said.

"All right," she said, distantly now, suddenly remote.

"I've made some tea."

"All right," she said again.

"Will you be all right on your own for a bit?"

"Yes," she said. "You go out, love."

Margaret was waiting in the door. They walked across the backs.

"People really are poor here, aren't they?" she said, looking in the open doors.

Only when seeing it with her eyes did he notice the broken doors, the blackened inside walls, the smears of grease and dirt around the switches, the latches, the bare tracts of earth and ash, the crumbling brickwork, the rusted drains and pipes. Periodically, in the past, attempts had been made to renovate the houses, areas of new brick had been inserted, new mortar, a concrete path laid down; in a matter of weeks the soot and smoke had absorbed them within the texture of the old.

"It's good of you to be able to come at all," he said. He took her hand; they went down the alleyway to the street outside.

They walked in silence then, turning along the road that led past the Dell, past the deserted colliery on the slope the other side, then crossing the railway in its cutting. The station was visible at its farthest end.

Behind them, smoke swirled down from the colliery,

David Storey

filtering out in a broad, thin cloud across the fields. The day was grey, the sky heavy.

They turned along a path that led from the road to a tract of woodland. It stretched away to their right, the ground slowly rising, the foot of the slope marked by a broad declivity in the bed of which lay a shallow lake. Odd pine trees grew from the sandy shore, one end of the lake blocked by a stone parapet, its other petering out into marsh and swamp. Cattle stood knee deep along the edge of the water.

They walked along the stone parapet which formed a wall. Shoals of tiny fish weaved amongst the strands of weed and debris floating on the surface. Beyond, the path led up towards the wood.

A fire was burning in a clearing. A thin trail of blue smoke drifted off from a pile of blackened wood. A log, half-hallowed out by an axe, lay beside it.

Colin crouched by the fire. He blew the embers. Soon flames licked up amongst the pieces of wood.

Margaret sat on the log. She gazed off, vacantly, between the trees. The thin, light-grey patch of water showed up between the branches. From some way off, in the cutting, came the panting of an engine and somewhere, closer, at the top of the wood, the barking of a dog.

"Will you be seeing Stafford again?" he said.

"Yes," she said. She still gazed off towards the lake. He put fresh pieces of wood on the fire.

"Is he still going overseas?" he said.

"He doesn't think so now."

"Even then, I suppose it'll be difficult seeing him," he said.

"I suppose it might be." She waited, looking down towards the fire. "He might get a posting near to the university."

"I suppose that would solve the problem, then."

"Yes," she said, gazing now directly at the flames. They flicked up around the pieces of wood, fresh smoke trailing off amongst the trees.

He got up slowly and for a moment stood gazing down at the fire himself.

"I'm sorry it's happened like this," she said.

"You can't help these things happening," he said.

"No," she said, and added, "I wouldn't have believed it though, before."

"If you go back now you'll be in time for the bus," he said.

She got up from the log.

They walked separately between the trees.

"Did you write to Stafford while you were away?" he said.

"Yes," she said, then added, "first of all he wrote to me."

"I suppose I ought to write to him as well," he said.

"I don't think," she said, "there's any need." She added, "He didn't even want me to come today."

"Why not?" he said.

They'd come to the edge of the wood; the path stretched away, past the lake, to the tall hedges lining the road leading to the village.

"He thought I might change my mind. Seeing you again, I mean."

"He doesn't know you very well," he said.

"No. Perhaps he doesn't."

"Do your parents know about it, then?"

"Yes," she said. "In a way I suppose they do. They said for you to come out, to the house, I mean. If you ever felt like it. They'd like to see you."

He walked ahead. He held back the branches when they reached the road so she could climb the fence.

"Perhaps I shouldn't have come," she said.

"No," he said. "I'm glad you did."

They walked back slowly through the village.

"It'll all seem strange, now you won't be coming again." He gestured round. "As if the heart's been taken out of it."

"I think I should have written, after all," she said.

"No," he said. "I couldn't have borne it if you hadn't come."

He waited with her for the bus. She watched his face. When the bus finally came he saw her on to it then walked away, turning finally at the last moment to see it leave. He wasn't sure which was her face at the windows, but he waved, slowly, as it drew out of the village, and went on waiting after it had disappeared, anticipating seeing her coming back, along the road, having got off at the stop beyond.

No one came down the road, however, and after waiting by the pub yard for some time he set off back towards the house.

His mother was in the kitchen with his two brothers when he got back in. Some tea was being set out on the table, the flowers still there in the jug, the plates and the cups arranged around it. A place had been set for Margaret and himself.

He went up to his room.

His mother came up after a little while. She held a cup in a saucer, very much like the one he had brought up to her earlier in the afternoon.

She stood in the doorway of the narrow room, gazing down, blindly, to where he lay on the bed.

"Is she not coming again?" she said.

"No," he said.

"Nay, love," she said. "I shouldn't cry."

"I love her though," he said.

"Nay, love, there are plenty more in the sea," she said. "There's not just one person you can love and no-body else."

"I don't know," he said, and added, "With me, though, I think there is. Just one that I shall ever love," he said.

"Nay, love," she said, setting the cup on the floor and sitting on the bed.

His brothers, a moment later, could be heard quarrelling in the room below.

"You'll be all right in a couple of days," his mother said. "Just think of the future, and hold to that."

"Yes," he said.

"You'll find time heals all wounds, love," she said.

"Yes," he said again and covered his eyes.

"Is there anything else I can get?" she said.

"No." He turned aside.

"Well, then. I'll go and sort those two out," she said.

She got up from the bed. The door was closed.

He lay with his head to the wall, curled up in the narrow space, his arms folded.

His mother's voice came through the floor from the room below.

PART FIVE

they frequently travel." After a moment she added,

"You have ————

She smiled.

The road led upon ————— the river, on the flat ———

25

The school stood on the outskirts of a village, a large, sprawling, one-storeyed building, red-brick, with tall, metal-framed windows and green-painted doors. A playground surrounded it on three sides, the fourth separated from the main road, which led from the village, by a strip of lawn. Flowers grew in a diamond-shaped bed immediately below the headmaster's window.

Behind the school an expanse of heathland led away to rows of small terrace houses set at the crest of a hill. A colliery with three massive headgears occupied a deep hollow, also lined with terrace houses, immediately below the school.

Mr. Corcoran, the headmaster, was a short, squat figure with close-cropped hair and a heavy, bulbous brow, who, on Colin's first morning, had called him to his study and said, "We don't teach poetry here. Just matter-of-fact English. They can pick up poetry on their own. We provide them with the tools: their own inclinations provide the rest. We're like the smithy, if you like, to the pit down there. We provide the means: they've got to dig the coal themselves."

He had no class of his own. On the teachers' rota he was listed as a "supernumerary," and went from class to class as required. The children he taught the most were in the lower end of the school; it was as unlike King Edward's as any school he could imagine.

The boys reminded him of Batty and Stringer; the girls were more docile, cantankerous occasionally, like those he had followed round the Park years before with Bletchley. They had no interest, either boys or girls, in anything he had to tell them, accepting a certain amount of work with an air of resignation, leaning on their desks, writing words they could neither understand nor spell.

He was surprised to find Stephens also teaching at the school, the boy with the misshapen back whom he had invariably sat behind at school, and who had once, perhaps out of sympathy, offered to sell him one of any number of stolen pens. He came to the school each day on a motor-bike with a sidecar, his hunched figure clad in leathers, brown and creased, and cracked in huge weals across his back, his head protected by a leather helmet and his face covered with a scarf and goggles. Occasionally he gave Colin lifts to the bus stop in the village.

"You've got to realize these are the working class," Stephens said as he went with him one evening to the motor-bike parked at the back of the school. "Anything we may have learnt at King Edward's is of no relevance whatsoever here." He waved a leather-clad arm at the sooted windows. One or two boys who had stayed behind were playing football in the yard. Piles of coke were stacked up against the walls. Stephens removed loose pieces from around the wheels of the bike. "What might engage them," he added, "is beyond my comprehension. Nothing we've learnt, however, either at school or college can be related to anything we encounter here."

He checked various parts of the bike itself, stepping vigorously on the starter, then swung his small body across the seat. He clipped the strap of his helmet beneath his chin and waited for Colin to climb on behind. His voice droned on through the roar of the engine. Colin couldn't hear. He held to Stephens's waist as the bike turned across the yard, narrowly avoiding the boys playing there, and into the road outside.

Occasionally Stephens turned his head: he still talking, his scarf, which normally covered his face, lowered round his neck. No word came to Colin at all above the rattle of the engine.

They descended quickly towards the pit, and the bus stops which stood, beside concrete barriers, at the colliery entrance. It was here that his father had worked some four years previously.

He got off the bike and put up the foot-rests. Stephens,

his head bowed, examined them a moment before setting off.

"You have to realize," he added, throttling back the engine and evidently continuing the conversation he'd been engaged with during the descent from the school, "that the working class is a relatively recent phenomenon. Two centuries ago, or even less, the thought of large numbers of men gathered together in towns, or in villages, like this, and vast working places, for instance, like this pit, would have been unthinkable. In my view, the working class, as distinct from the peasant class, will soon disappear, replaced by technicians of one sort or another. And all the revolutionary fervour we at one time associated with the class will have disappeared for good. That's my estimation of the situation." He glanced over to the rows of miners waiting at the stops. "The working class, I'm afraid, is a temporary phenomenon; and our job, unfortunately, is to distract and, if possible, entertain that temporary phenomenon until it, of its own volition, disappears."

He revved the engine. The miners looked across at the strange figure, diminutive and misshapen, sprawled on top of the bike.

"It's what we've been trained to do. And what we're paid to do. But one can't help thinking at the same time that it's a bit of a dead loss. What's it all add up to? A few more colliers down the pit, a few more split skulls, a few more broken arms, a few more bodies carried out."

He nodded his head, anxious now for some reply.

"I don't see them all like that, I suppose," Colin said. "As members of a class."

"But they're members of a class before they're *anything*," Stephens said. "They think, they feel, they diminish, they destroy, they prevaricate, they *breed*, they interject, they do and are everything first and foremost as members of a class. They *are* the working class. I mean," he added, glancing at Colin slyly from beneath the leather helmet, "don't tell me you see them as human beings!" He laughed, revving the engine. "Good God, they're as devoid of sensibility as the coal they'll hew in a few years' time, as thick as the pit-props in that colliery yonder." He laughed again, his teeth showing freshly above the scarf.

Then, with a nod, he pulled the scarf up. "See you," he said through the material and, glancing behind him, turned the bike in the road and set off in the opposite direction.

Colin crossed to the queue of miners and stood there, the only one in clean clothes, waiting for the bus to arrive.

Somebody spat in the road. A man at the front of the queue had laughed. A cloud of cigarette smoke drifted above the heads.

He kept his hands in his pockets and tapped with the toe of his shoe against the piles of dust.

Steven had failed his exam the previous year. It had been his last chance to go to the grammar school. He was now attending the secondary-modern school in the village. All through the previous year, whenever he had been home from college, Colin had coached him for the exam, like his father had coached him, years before. Now his father had been too tired to take any interest, his energy going into persuading Colin to coach his brother, to teach him spelling, maths, the use of words, standing over him whenever he faltered, showed lack of interest or hadn't the time. "He's to have the same chances as you've had," his father said. "You know it better than me, so he's an even better chance than you had. Don't let's miss out on it, not now we've worked so hard for it," he added.

Yet his brother, as he'd known, as they'd all known all along, had failed. He had no aptitude for work; he was not unlike the children Colin taught now: in two years' time it would be Richard's turn. There was a curious disparity between the younger brothers. Steven was large and steady, with heavy shoulders, straight-backed, not unlike Colin in appearance, but with a more open, outward-going, frank-faced nature. He showed no awareness of having failed anything, and went to school with the same imperturbable good grace that he'd always shown; it was Richard who showed a resistance, almost a slowness, half-casual, as if he resented being imposed upon at all. He was more delicately featured than either of his older brothers, with his father's light-blue eyes and something, half-hidden, of his father's nature.

Colin would read with Richard in the evening, the boy crouched against his arm, following the words with his finger, irritated whenever he was corrected; or Richard would write at the table, looking up with a dulled resentment, the end of his pencil slipped between his teeth, protesting, gazing to the window where his friends played in the field.

"You do what Colin tells you," his father would say, yet distantly, remote now from the activities of his children, more clearly exhausted day by day, by the responsibility he had for working an entire face, by his closeness to the men he worked with, some from the houses across the street, maintaining something of his supervisory role even when away from the pit: Shaw was one of the men he worked with, and because he was responsible for measuring off his work each week, the amount he might be paid, they scarcely spoke at all. "You see where Steven's got to," his father would add. "With not paying attention much at school and not doing much work when he got back home either. He's going to be stuck down the pit with me."

"Oh, don't go on with those old arguments," his mother would say, as wearied by this battle now as his father was. "If they want to do it, then it's up to them. If they don't then it's no good forcing them."

Yet Richard, from time to time, would react to his father's demands; though scarcely eight he would sit solidly at the table sometimes for an hour, writing, working out sums, waiting patiently for the work to be corrected, copying out the corrections underneath then looking up at Colin, waiting to be dismissed. "Can I go now? Is that enough, our kid?"

Occasionally too Colin worked with Steven; his father had some vague notion in a year's time of getting him a county transfer to the grammar school; yet Steven would look at the work with a good-natured incomprehension, puzzle over it a while then push it away, shaking his head, glancing at Colin with a smile, and say, "Nay, it beats me. I'll never mek it out." In the end, occasionally, they read together, Steven following the words intently, going over and over each word until he got the pronunciation right, only to stumble over it again when he came across it in the following line. He'd absolved himself, without rancour, from learning anything at all.

Michael Reagan had been attacked one week-end in town and had spent two weeks in hospital. He'd been robbed of over forty pounds, had had his jaw broken and now spoke with a stutter. His father, by a curious coincidence, had been taken to hospital the following week after being found in the road in a collapsed condition. He was in for a slightly longer period than Reagan, having suffered a stroke, and when he was finally released and came home it was rumoured that he would have to finish his job in the colliery office, which he had had for over thirty years, and take on something less arduous which would occupy him for shorter hours.

Reagan, on his mother's insistence, gave up his dance band and returned to full-time work as a clerk in an accountant's office. Occasionally, when Colin passed the house, he could both hear and see Michael giving lessons in the violin to small boys in the front room, but, a few months later, after complaints about his conduct with one of the boys, the lessons stopped altogether. He would be seen, a thin, ghostly figure, walking the streets of the village in a long black coat, a cap pulled down above his eyes, exaggerating if anything the familiar bulbous shape of his head. Occasionally boys followed him, calling names, but on the whole he appeared oblivious of everything around him, scarcely pausing whenever Colin spoke to him, glancing up with haunted eyes, shaking his head or nodding, slowly, to some inquiry, unwilling or unable to speak, his long thin legs carrying him off quickly as if he hadn't recognized anyone he knew at all. His father too, on occasion, would appear at the door, a gaunt, wasted figure, moving with a slow shuffle, his body partially paralysed along one side.

"Oh, they've had it," his father would say. "That family's had a visitation, and no mistake. If trouble doesn't come in bucketloads it doesn't come at all. It'll be the turn of the missis next. There'll be something calamitous happen to her."

Yet Mrs. Reagan, in adversity, appeared to blossom. A thin, shadowy figure herself, invariably dressed in pale clothes, with a ghostly pallor to her skin, she could now be seen talking at her door, or on Mrs. Shaw's step, occasionally even on Mrs. Bletchley's, roaming across the yards to disseminate news of her husband's progress, scarcely mentioning her son at all. It was as if Michael, in a curious way, had never existed: the sound of his violin no longer came from the house, and none of the clothes which, in the past, she had proudly made for him, were ever hung out on the line to dry.

One evening Colin met Michael on the bridge above the station. He was leaning against the parapet, gazing at the line.

"Are you coming up home?" he said.

Reagan didn't answer. His figure, draped in the black coat, the flat cap pulled well down on top of his head, was thrust forward against the stone, almost like a log, thin and angular, propped up against the wall itself.

"Are you coming up home?" he asked again.

Reagan's features were half hidden beneath the shadow of the cap. His hands were clenched together.

"Are you coming up home?" he said again. "If you like," he added, "we could go for a drink."

"I don't drink," Reagan said, so quietly that, for a moment, he doubted what he'd heard. "I don't drink, you know," he added more clearly.

"I'm just walking up home," Colin said.

"I'll walk up with you," Reagan said, looking off to where the road ran past the station, disappearing, beyond a row of houses, amongst the fields.

Colin turned towards the village. Reagan, still leaning against the wall, continued to gaze off in the opposite direction.

"I saw you getting off the train," he said again so quietly that he scarcely heard. The train's faint pounding could still be heard at the far end of the cutting. "Have you been into town?" he added, turning his head to glance at him directly.

His face was lined by tears. He blinked them back, waiting now for Colin to answer.

"I went to the pictures."

"Do you go by yourself?"

"Yes," he said.

"What happened to your girl-friend?"

"She's gone away." He waited.

"Ian said she'd gone off with Stafford."

"Yes," he said.

"Did you mind her going?"

"Yes," he said.

Reagan regarded him with increasing interest. He pulled down quickly at the peak of the cap and for the first time stepped away from the wall.

"Where are you teaching?" he said.

"Rawcliffe," he said. "I believe I mentioned it before."

"Wasn't that where your father used to work?"

"Yes," he said.

More than anything now Michael reminded Colin of Mrs. Reagan, the gaunt figure that he'd known before; there was the same almost mechanical earnestness he'd associated with her in the past.

"Had you thought of moving from the village? Into town, or to some other village perhaps?"

"I had thought of it," he said.

"I've thought of moving," Reagan said. "I've never been happy here, you know."

He stepped into the road, paused a moment, as if even now he were tempted to walk off in the opposite direction, then turned slowly towards the village.

"You've heard that my father's been ill?" he said.

"Yes," he said.

"I don't think he'll ever get out again. Not like he used to in the past."

"I see him sometimes," Colin said.

"He tries to get out. His mind wanders. He keeps asking for his hat and gloves." He measured his strides slowly, as if the closer they got to the village, the more determined he was to turn back. "He sometimes thinks he's in the office and keeps on about the wages. He was always arguing about money with the men. He even argues with my mother sometimes. He thinks she's one of the men, and starts on about the deputies, how they've measured off the coal, and that."

"I haven't heard you playing the violin," Colin said. "Not for some time," he added, "at least."

"No." Reagan shook his head. There was a calculated air of absurdity about him now, as if his coat and the

cap were some disguise he'd deliberately adopted. He
glanced over at Colin and shook his head again. "I've
given it away, you know."

"Who to?" he said.

"Oh." He shrugged. "I don't know. My mother gave it
away, as a matter of fact. I've given up going to the office, as well. They gave me two weeks' notice. I should
have had a month. The doctor said I needed a rest, so I
suppose it's worked out all right in the end."

"Did they ever find out," he said, "who stole the
money?"

"Oh, it was Batty," he said. "Though naturally I
couldn't tell. Batty and Stringer, and two other men.
They'd been at the club, you see, that night. I always had
the takings with me on the Saturday to put in the bank
on Monday morning, then I paid out the staff the following week. They've closed it down, as a matter of fact. I
thought of taking it for classes, you know. In the afternoons, for ole-tyme and modern dancing, for children, you
know. But the fees I don't think would have covered the
cost. I might start the Saturdays up again when I feel a
bit better."

He'd begun to talk more quickly now, as if Colin wasn't
there, his stride lengthening, his gaze, beneath the peak of
his cap, more abstracted. The tears had dried on his face,
leaving dark smears on either cheek.

"Or again, I could always go in for orchestral work.
There's a great demand, at the moment, for orchestral
players. So few were trained, you know, during the war.
There's a whole area I could turn to there. It wouldn't
need much adaptation. Even Prendergast recommended
that, you know, some years ago. He was quite disappointed in his way that I went in for band work. There
seemed more opportunity in that field, of course." He
paused, stopping in the road. The first houses of the village had appeared; lights glowed from the windows, beyond them the vast, dull glow of the pit itself. "The
pendulum seems to have swung the other way."

Colin had paused.

Reagan was undecided which way to turn, his gaze
transfixed, abstracted, his hands clenched loosely together.

Tears appeared once more on either cheek, his eyes half-hidden beneath the shadow of the cap.

"I think I might go back to the bridge. I was thinking of something there. I've forgotten what it was."

Yet he remained, as if suspended, in the middle of the road.

"I'll go back with you," Colin said.

"There's no need to," Reagan said, speaking so quietly again that he scarcely heard.

"I don't mind going back," he said.

"I'd prefer to go on my own," he said, his voice acquiring some of the correctness which characterized his conversations at the ballroom.

"Why not come back home?" Colin said. "You could come in, if you like, and have some tea."

"Oh, I never go in people's houses," Reagan said.

"Why not come up to the house, in any case?" he said, yet already Reagan had turned and set off back along the road, walking with lengthening strides, quickly, as if he had some appointment to keep which he'd suddenly remembered.

Colin watched him go down the hill; he reached a bend in the road and disappeared, in the gathering gloom, towards the station.

For a moment he thought of following him; then, having set off, turned and went on towards the village.

"Isn't your name Saville?" the taller of the two teachers said. He was a well-built, fair-haired man, scarcely older than Colin himself; he had large, bony features, the cheeks red and bronzed slightly by the sun. The other teacher, an older man by the name of Callow, he'd met when he first arrived: he wore a corduroy coat and flannels and a check shirt, his face pallid and square-featured, his mouth broad and thin—he came forward now and said directly to the taller man, "Of course this is Saville. I told you when he came. I've never discovered his first name, though."

"Colin," he said.

They were standing just outside the school where, normally, he waited for Stephens for a lift into the village. Callow also taught English in the school, and though he'd occasionally seen the other, taller man, he'd never discovered his name. Children flooded by on the pavement on either side.

"This is Gerry Thornton," Callow said. "He was telling me he knew you the other day, though in what circumstances he never did explain."

"Aren't you a friend of Neville Stafford?" Thornton said.

"Yes," he said.

"Do you ever remember working on Smith's farm? Oh, years ago now," he added. "I remember seeing you one morning cutting thistles in one of the fields. Then after that, do you remember three boys with one of those collapsible dinghies playing in that pond when you were stooking?" He waited, smiling, for Colin to reply. "There was Neville, my brother, and myself." He laughed simply, watching Colin's expression. "I'm going in the forces in two or three weeks," he added. "I got deferment and seem to have been left on the shelf. I thought I'd put in one or two weeks here." He gestured round, vaguely, at the school. "Not much, but enough to be going on with, I suppose."

He saw Stephens in the distance, emerging from the school. Colin waved him on, and as Stephens pulled up, the scarf wrapped firmly round his face, he said, "I'll walk down today."

Stephens shrugged: he glanced at the other two. "Do you want a lift?" he said to Callow, lowering the scarf.

"Oh, I'll walk down as well," the teacher said, glancing at the pillion seat and adding, "Is it safe?"

"As safe as houses," Stephens said. He rode away, quaint and strangely child-like on the large machine.

"I suppose I should have gone with him," he said, watching the abrupt way Stephens drove off.

"Weren't you both at school together?" Callow said.

"Yes," he said. The bike, seemingly riderless from a distance, disappeared beyond the pit.

The three of them walked on down the hill in silence.

"I suppose you've heard about Neville," Thornton said as they reached the stop at the bottom; he was taking a bus in the opposite direction and had paused at the side of the road before crossing.

"No." Colin looked across at the fair-haired man: he had the same carelessness, almost the same "Glamour," a Stafford himself.

"He's got engaged. His mother and father, I believe, are in a hell of a can. He goes up to Oxford, you see, quite shortly. They believe he's chucking everything away."

"But then, that's just like Stafford," Colin said.

"Is it?" Thornton looked at him again, freshly, then shook his head. "I've never known Neville to be careless," he said. "He's always seemed a schemer to me," and as if this might have sounded too hard, he added, "Not a schemer, but doing things by calculation."

"Who is this Neville?" Callow said. He watched the groups of children who passed them in the road: away from the school there was a strange sense of disowning those to whom, in the school, they might have been close. Only one or two children signalled any acknowledgment.

"Oh, he's quite a card, really," Thornton said, yet casually, as if he knew of no way of communicating his impression of Stafford to the other man. "Excels at everything he does."

"That doesn't sound so cardish," Callow said. He grimaced at the passing children and looked away.

"Well, he *has* excelled, I suppose, at most things," Thornton said. "I don't know who the girl is. Not someone whom his parents are particularly fond of."

"Yes," Callow said and might have added something else only he grimaced once more at the passing children and with much the same expression glanced away.

"Will he give up Oxford?" Colin said.

"Oh, I don't suppose so. Neville gives up most things, but only as a prelude, usually, to his taking them on. He was saying at one time he might stay on in the forces. Had himself marked out as a major by the time he'd finished. I suppose," Thornton added, reflectively, "he'd make a success of it. The thing about Neville, if he puts his mind to it, he can do anything, I reckon." He glanced down the road. "Well, here's my bus." He waved, ran over and joined the queue of children.

"I hear you do writing," Callow said. His pale face had

darkened slightly, as if he'd mentioned something which concerned, or hurt him, very much.

"Not really. No."

"Oh, I heard it," he said, casually, yet relieved. "Thornton mentioned it." He looked round him at the village, the rows of terraces running up the hill, at the dull declivity beneath them, shadowed by the pit. "Relieves the gloom."

"Do you find it gloomy?" Colin said.

"Not really. But then I'm not as hopeful as you."

"Hopeful?" Colin glanced at the other man and laughed.

"Oh, I've had quite a few years. Not just of this." He gestured off up the slope to the low, silhouetted profile of the school. "One or two others. If you didn't have something else I think you'd go quite mad."

"But then, I thought you were reconciled," Colin said. "I mean, to teaching here, or to places like it."

"Do you feel reconciled?" Callow said.

"No."

"I mean," Callow said, returning briefly to his earlier, darker look, "do you envisage staying here for good?"

He shook his head; something of the bleakness of the place, something of the bleakness of Callow, gripped him: he sensed a disillusionment in Callow which hid some profounder discontent. He couldn't be sure in that instant what it was.

"You're young, you're hopeful, you've got it all before you," the older teacher said. He appeared, visibly, to shrink before him: the corduroy coat, even the square-shaped cut of his hair, suggested a hardness, a firmness, even a physical robustness and mental pugnacity which the manner of the man himself denied.

A bus came down towards the stop. Callow flinched as its shadow fell across him.

"Are you getting on?" Colin said as he moved up in the queue.

"No. I walk."

"Do you live close by?"

"I have relations who do. I visit them occasionally."

It sounded like some excuse he'd made up on the spot; as it was, on an evening, Colin had seldom seen him in the queue.

"See you tomorrow," Callow said and, without any further acknowledgment, moved quickly off.

He saw the corduroy-coated teacher frequently over the next few weeks. Though they never caught the same bus—and he never discovered where he lived, or even if he were married—they often walked down the hill together. The evening after their first encounter, when he was waiting for Stephens by the gate, his friend had cruised up on the motor-bike and, his scarf already lowered, said, "I won't, in future, give you a lift, if you don't mind."

"I was wrong to refuse, I know," he said.

"If there are people who interest you more, and you see me merely as a convenience, clearly there's no point in my putting myself out," he added.

"It's entirely up to you," he said.

"I suppose Thornton was talking about Stafford."

"Yes," he said.

"He told me he was. I mean, I asked him," Stephens said. "Apparently he's marrying your former girl."

"He didn't tell me that," he said.

"I made inquiries." He revved the engine; a cloud of blue smoke rose steadily between them. "I'd have nothing to do with those bastards if I were you."

"What bastards?"

"King Edwards bastards. They screwed me up and they've screwed up you."

He said nothing for a moment.

"You can have a lift if you like," he said. "I've had a bad day." He leaned down and lowered the foot-rests for him.

Colin got on: they cruised down the hill. When Colin got off Stephens added, "I'd give it up, only I've nothing else to do."

"Why don't you go abroad?" he said.

"Abroad?" He revved the engine once again, almost as if willing the bike at that moment to take him. "Why don't you?"

"I'm helping out the family," he said.

"I'm helping out the family," Stephens said. "But should families pin you down for ever?"

"I owe them something," he said.

"Oh, debts are never meant to be paid. I owe debts to everybody," Stephens said. "I'd be a damn fool, and *they'd* think I'm a damn fool, if I ever attempted to pay them."

"Isn't there such thing as loyalty?" he said.

"To what?"

Stephens waited for an answer.

"The only loyalty is to oneself," he added.

Colin looked away. Farther up the hill he could see Callow and Thorton descending: the taller man had waved.

"Oh, well, I'll leave you to your friends," Stephens said and without adding anything further drove away.

"Was he cheesed?" Thornton said. "About last night."

"Yes," he said.

"Apparently Neville's fiancée was once your friend."

"Apparently," he said.

"I suppose I'll be seeing him soon. The fact is, when I go in, he's suggested I should join his regiment. I don't know how easily these things are arranged. *If* they can be arranged, I'm sure he'll manage it." He waved his hand without adding anything further and ran across the road as his bus appeared.

26

"Have you ever seen this?" his father said. He held out a square-shaped book of greyish, tinted paper. Inside were a number of chalk drawings, some of fruit, some of flowers, their bright colours imprinted on the sheets of protective tissue. The drawings themselves were done with an adult asssurance, seemingly effortless and uncorrected.

"Whose are they?" he said, gazing in particular at a drawing of three apples, their redness veering into greenness, lying in a bowl.

"They're by your brother." His father laughed. "Andrew." He turned to the front. The name of the village school and his brother's unfamiliar name, "Andrew Saville," were written on the cover. "He was only seven."

"How did he die?" he said, suddenly reminded.

"He died within a few hours. Of pneumonia," his father said. "He was here one minute, and gone the next. I'd give ought to have that lad alive."

"How give ought?" he said.

"Well." His father hesitated then turned aside.

On one occasion, some years previously, he'd gone with his father to put some flowers on his brother's grave: it lay in a small plot of ground at the side of the road leading to the colliery, the whole area invisible, behind high hedges, from the road itself. The grave was marked by a small round-headed stone on which were painted his father's initials, H.R.S., and a number. They cleared brambles from the spot, weeded the oblong bed, set a jam-jar in the ground and in the jam-jar set the flowers. "We ought to come each week and keep it tidy," his father had said, yet as far as Colin was aware neither he nor his mother had been again. Now, looking at the coloured drawings in the book, his father said, "We ought to go and have a look. See how that grave is. We haven't been for some time, you know."

"How did it affect my mother?" he said.

"Well." His father, uncertain, gazed at the book steadily now, his eyes tense. "I think that's been half the trouble."

"What trouble?"

"Nay, Andrew dying," his father said.

The house was silent. His mother had gone off that afternoon to visit her sister, taking, after much complaining from his brothers, Steven and Richard with her.

"Why thy's so silent and morose at times."

"Am I silent and morose?"

"Nay, thy should know," his father said.

"Well, I don't."

"Nay, I can't be the first to mention it." His father flushed.

"I didn't think I was morose," he said.

"Nay, not all the time," he added. "It's just been lately, I suppose." He gazed at the drawings.

A cup stood on a saucer: looking at the picture Colin, with a peculiar sensation, as if someone had touched him, saw how clear and confident the ellipses were, perfectly drawn by his seven-year-old brother, with scarcely an inflection that broke the line, or a faltering in the shading of their blue-painted pattern.

"Your mother was three months gone, tha knows. It must have had an effect, I reckon. She was very down." His father, almost idly, closed the book. "She was very down, I can tell you that." He added nothing further for a while. "It all seemed very strange at the time."

"Strange in what way?"

"It was as if he wa' gone." His father looked up. "And then, you see, came back again."

There was a freshness in his father's face, as if, briefly, he'd gone back to that moment when he was young himself. He gazed up at Colin directly.

"I'm not Andrew, though," he said.

"No."

His gaze drifted back towards the book: only in the writing of the name was there any uncertainty, he thought; as if his brother weren't quite sure, despite the confidence of the drawings, of who he was.

His father too glanced down at the book: it lay between them like a testament, or a tribulation, a strange denial, he couldn't be sure.

His brother's presence, so casually aroused, preoccupied him for several days. He was sleeping now in the tiny room, his two brothers occupying the larger room, and realized in fact he was probably sleeping in Andrew's bed. It was also, he recalled, the bed the soldier had slept in during the war. Certain scenes of his early life came back: he recalled, faintly, the holiday with his mother and father, the journey on the back of the milkman's cart. It had a peculiar familiarity, like the pictures in the book itself.

One evening, when his father was at work, he had asked his mother about his brother, listened to her distant answers, then had asked her specifically about the death itself. "Oh," his mother said, "aren't we getting morbid? What does it matter after all these years?" and had added, "It's the good things, after all, that count."

"Wasn't Andrew good?" he said.

"He *was* good," his mother said. She told him then of the doctor's visit, of the sudden illness, and of the doctor's apologetic statement when he examined his brother on the double bed. "And what brought all this up suddenly?" she added.

"Oh," he said, and mentioned the book.

"And where did your father find it?" she said.

"He must have discovered it," he said.

"He must have been amongst my papers."

"What papers?" he said.

"Oh, I keep things," his mother said, mysteriously, as if this, finally, were something she wouldn't confide. "At any rate, you could say he was going to be an artist. He had the nature as well as the gift."

"What nature?" Colin said.

"Oh, the nature." His mother traced her finger along a chair. "He was very unruly."

"In what way?" he said.

"Questions. Questions!" His mother turned away. Then, as if drawn by the silence, she added. "He was always wandering off."

"Where to?"

"I've no idea. He seemed to have nowhere in mind he was going to."

A blankness in his brother's intentions suddenly faced him, just as presumably it had faced his mother; she gazed steadily before her.

"Away from here, at least," she said.

"Why away?"

"Why all these questions? Honestly, if I could answer any of them don't you think I would?"

She took off her glasses; the light, as it was, had hidden her expression. She dried her eyes on the edge of her apron: it was a contained, almost self-denying gesture.

"I loved him, Colin."

"I know," he said.

"Well," she said. "Wasn't that enough?"

He visited his brother's grave a few days later and found to his surprise it had recently been weeded; fresh flowers had been set in a glass jar which had in turn been buried in the earth. Some image of his brother came to mind, of a wild, anarchic boy, fair-haired, blue-eyed, stocky, square-shouldered, walking along the road from the village. For a moment standing by the grave, hidden by the surrounding shrubs, with the colliery pumping out its smoke and steam, the mountain of the heap above his head, he felt an invisible bond with that figure in the ground, as if they suffered in that moment a peculiar conjunction.

He looked up towards the road: it was past this place that his father walked each day; it was in that school building, adjacent to the colliery, that Andrew, conceivably, had done his drawings. He recalled something then that had been nagging at the back of his mind for several days: it was his recollection of the time when he had first walked. He had been sitting with his parents at the side of a dam—the dam he had visited years before with Reagan on their country walk—and had got to his feet to follow a hen, the bird hurrying before him towards the water's edge, and even as he heard his parents' cries, he recalled vividly the thought that had struck him then, "But I have walked many times like this before: why should they be surprised I am walking now?" And beyond their surprise was this greater conviction that not merely had he walked but lived his life before. It was like glimpsing a headland out of a mist.

He felt a peculiar detachment: some part of his mind had been displaced, fragmented, cast away. He walked out of the cemetery towards the village. The cloud from the pit, with the colliery's clankings and groanings, its peculiar gaspings, followed him: it was as if he were being ejected from the earth himself, disgorged. He glanced back to the cemetery where, unknown, his brother was buried and felt, prompted by that child, a sense of mission, a new containment, a vulnerability which numbed him to the bone.

It affected his relationship with Steven first. There was a peculiar assurance in his younger brother; he questioned nothing: the quietness of his childhood had given way to a robust, undemanding confidence. He played football, but without any intentness; he worked with little concentration. His voice, in the field at the back, would dominate the houses, refusing to be commanded or advised by anyone. "What's up, our kid?" he would say, slumping down in the settee beside him. "Ar't feeling bad?" his shoulder crushing against Colin's almost like an older brother's would. "Has't flighted any sense out of ought, then?" he would add whenever he saw him writing, or marking school books at the table. "Wheer'st the genius in that?" peering mysteriously over his shoulder as if to find in the work some key to Colin's nature which otherwise eluded him. He had grown in build, proportionately, even larger than Colin; his muscles were prematurely developed. There were very few boys in the village who threatened him; and yet, when they did, Steven never fought; rather, he would take their arm and turn them with him. "Nay, wheer'st that gonna' get you?" he would say amicably as if, in fighting, they had more to lose than they could imagine. It was as if his nature had been absolved, cleansed, washed through.

"Why don't you do more with your work?" Colin would ask him.

"Why should I?" Steven would say.

"Well, I've had to."

"Why?"

"To help you," Colin would tell him.

"Why help me?"

"To give you a chance."

"To do what?"

"To get through."

"Nay, I've got through." He would laugh. "What is there to get through, Colin?"

"Don't you feel you ought to get on?" he said.

"Get on wheer?"

"Out of this."

His brother would look round him at the kitchen, he would look at the window and then outside.

"Well, it's not much to look at," he would add. "But we don't have to stay here for good, though, do we?"

"Don't we? The way you're going I think we shall."

"Nay, tha mu'n leave whenever tha wants."

"And leave you and Richard? You should have a chance."

"Nay, I've got a chance. All t'chance I'll need."

His brother's imperturbability disturbed him; it disturbed him as much as his mother's acquiescence to it.

"Don't you want our Steven to get on?" he'd ask her.

"But he's not as bright as you. At least, not as bright in that way."

"But he shows no aptitude, no determination, no need to do anything. He'll just go on like he's always done."

"But he's got an equable nature," his mother said.

"Has he?" The word alone suggested that his mother had thought about this herself. "Acquiescent I should think's more like it."

"Acquiescent to what?"

"To this."

He would gesture hopelessly around him: the pit, the darkness, the perpetual smell of sulphur, the dankness, the soot; it flattened his spirits more than anything; there was no escape.

"Doesn't he want to change it? Is he going to live here all his life?"

"Well, *we*'ve lived here," his mother said.

"But then we've got a chance to change it. We've got a chance of getting out."

"Of leaving."

"Not physically. Spiritually. It does Steven no good to be buried here."

"But why are you so concerned?" she said. "If he's content why should you insist on him being different?"

"I don't know," he said. "I'd just want something better for him."

"But why change his nature when he's always so happy."

"Is he happy?"

"I think so."

"Like a dog is happy. It's bovine. He has no will."

His mother, at these attacks, would draw away: there was a peculiar ambivalence in them. His brother antagonized him; yet there was no enmity, no animosity or resentment in his brother at all. If anything, Steven admired him: when he was younger he would listen to Colin's accounts of school and later of college with fascination. On one occasion, while still at college, Steven had visited him: he had shown him round the buildings, introduced him to the staff and to the students and his brother had admired it all, entranced, without any equivocation. He accepted everything that came before him.

"Why do you get on at Steven?" his father would ask.

"He doesn't do anything," he would tell him.

"He's being himself."

"I can't believe it." He would watch Steven playing in the field with the same irritation: his good nature was apparent from a distance, the lack of guile, of anything considered; his goodness was dishonest.

"He doesn't do anything," he would add.

"Does he have to *do* something?" his father would ask.

"But you insisted that *I* do something," he said.

"How did I insist?"

504

"Everything. There's an insistence. I suppose you'll be content for him to go in the pit."

"I suppose I shall. If he's happy doing it," he added.

"But why should I have had to do things I wasn't happy doing?" he said.

"What weren't you happy doing?" his father said.

"All this." He would gesture at the yards outside.

"I thought it was something you wanted. It was something you were good at," his father said.

"Was it something I wanted? Or something you wanted for me? Like you wanted something for Andrew, too."

"What did we want for Andrew?"

"To make him good. To make him like me."

"Nay," his father said, and looked away. It was as if he'd wounded him too deeply. "Nay," he said again. He shook his head.

"Isn't it true?"

"No. It's not true. And if you said that to your mother I think it would kill her."

"Perhaps it's better that she should know, then."

"You'll say nothing to her," his father said, strangely, turning to him then and standing there as if physically he stood before his mother.

"And what am I supposed to do?" he said. "Why shouldn't I have the freedom that Steven has? Not selfishly, but for *your* good as well?"

"What good? What good? Is there any good in saying this?" his father said. Despite his tiredness he would have beaten him then.

"But why should I have to take the blame?"

"What blame?"

"Why should I be moulded? Why weren't you content with me?" he said. "Why shouldn't I have been allowed to grow like Steve?" It was as if some evil in him had been held in abeyance, while in Steven it had been allowed to flow out, appeased.

"Didn't you want to go to that school?" his father said, yet lightly, anxious to distract him. "When you came home to tell us you'd passed I'd never seen you look so glad."

"It's what I thought you wanted," he said.

"It was."

"Yet why do you want nothing for Steve?"

"I do want something for Steve. But I wouldn't force him to it, not against his nature."

"But why force *me?*"

"I haven't forced you."

"You have."

"I haven't forced you to anything."

"Not through force," he said. "Through love."

"Nay," his father said. "I think it's far too deep for me."

And later, as if he had nursed his wound, and wondered why Colin should have inflicted it, his father added, "We've given you a key. We've given you a key to get out of this."

"I can't get out," he said. "You need the money. And in any case, with what I earn, I couldn't afford to live by myself."

"It's only for two or three years."

"Is it?"

"While Richard and Steven are still at school. It bled us, you know, educating you."

"Why do it, then?"

"Aye," his father said. "I'm beginning to wonder."

And a few weeks later, coming home from school, exhausted, to find his brother playing in the backs, Colin had picked another argument. His brother, listening to his rage, stood smiling, distantly, across the room.

"Nay," his father said. "If you go on like that he'll clobber you."

"Will he?" he said.

His mother, too, had been in the room.

"Steven isn't as docile," she said, "as you sometimes think."

"Isn't he?" he said. "I've never noticed anything different."

"He's got a mind and values of his own." His mother gazed angrily at him through her glasses as if, in his argument, he were attacking her.

"I've never noticed a mind," he said. "As for values, I don't think he even knows the word."

"Oh, I think he knows a lot of things," she said.

"Where from? I've never seen him learning anything."

"He doesn't have to learn," she said, deeply. "He already knows." She glanced at Steven as if she were confessing to something she scarcely knew how to express herself.

"All he knows," Colin said, "is how to eat and drink and take up space, and use the freedom that others have bought him."

"You've bought him nothing," his mother said.

"Haven't I? I'd have thought I'd done quite a lot for him. And Richard."

"Nay, he's done something, Ellen," his father said. "He's looked after those two like a father would."

"Has he?" she said, bitterly, strangely. "He's done what he's wanted. We haven't forced him," she added, "to anything."

"Nay, you mu'n let him get it off his chest," his brother said, confidentially, as if the fault lay entirely now with Colin and their patience alone would have to deal with it. He turned away.

"And if you have something to say to me, it's better you say it to me. Not to my mother and dad," his brother added.

"All I can say," Colin said, "I can say with this." He held up his fist.

"Nay, I don't mind fighting," his brother said as if, by his amiability, he could win him out of this.

"Don't you?"

"I don't at all."

"Nay, Steve," his father said.

"Oh, let them," his mother said. "If Colin thinks he can perhaps he might find Steven more than he bargained for."

And, locked into the logic of a fight, they went out in the backs. Perhaps even then Steven thought he might win him out of his mood, show by his conciliatoriness that he meant no harm. He stood smiling before him, strangely calm, almost acquiescent, putting up his fists as if he suspected the gesture alone would be sufficient to warn him off. Yet there was never any doubt in Colin's mind; with some peculiar rage, drawn from the very depths of his nature, he drove his fist into Steven's face: he saw his brother's look of helplessness, the same guilelessness and acquiescence, as he felt the blow, as if his passivity had at last been shattered. Blood sprang out across Steven's face; a look of anguish came into his eyes; his strength, physically sapped, came out of his body. Almost callously, and with no diminution of his anger, Colin threw him to the ground.

His brother lay still; he appeared quite dazed: when he attempted to rise he fell on his side. Colin had never hated anyone as he hated Steven: he hated his helplessness and he hated his pain. As his father came across the yard to help his brother he turned away. His mother, standing in the door, gazed past him. Her expression was hidden behind the light of her glasses; it was as if, in that moment, she'd been cut in two, unexpectedly, without reason. She attempted to speak, then said, "You bully," yet quietly, unable to express the depth of her rage. "You bully," she said again. "He never hit you."

"You asked him to."

"I didn't ask him." She turned away. "What harm has he ever done to you?"

"More," he said, "than you imagine."

He went out of the house; as he was coming away Steven was being helped into the kitchen.

"No," he was saying. "I'm not really hurt," yet his voice sounded dazed and his movements heavy, uncertain now of what had happened.

Colin walked into the village; he caught a bus. Three-quarters of an hour later he was in the town. He sat in a pub. The blood roared through his head.

It was after midnight when he got back home; he'd taken the last bus in that direction and had had to walk the last four miles.

No lights were showing in the house; the front door was locked. He went round the back.

The back door, too, was locked.

A drainpipe led up to his bedroom window.

After several attempts, hoisting his foot on the kitchen sill, he clambered up: he pulled open the window and climbed inside.

No sound came from the house at all: a movement came finally from the adjoining room, Steven or Richard turning in bed.

He lay down: his clothes were stained from the soot of the pipe, his hands smelled of stagnant water.

A coughing, and then a dog barking came from across the backs.

He lay quite still; he closed his eyes.

The fumes of the beer and the cigarette smoke from the pub obscured the more prevalent odour of the pit.

27

"This is Elizabeth," Callow said, and after a moment's hesitation—stepping away slightly as if being recognized with her were something he disliked—he added, "We were going for a drink."

The woman was somewhat smaller than Callow, with thick dark hair, half-concealed by a flowered scarf, and a broad, thickly featured face.

"Come for a drink as well," she said. She indicated a pub across the city centre. It was early evening: lights flared out across the pavement.

The woman's eyes were dark: they possessed a melancholic light, like those of a doctor examining a patient. She waited for Colin's response with something of a smile. "I hear you teach at the same school," she said when they'd entered the pub and were seated at a table.

"Endeavouring to," he said, bemused by the woman's expression.

"Well that's all Phil does," she said, her attitude to Callow more that of a sister, or a neighbour, than that of a friend. "He daydreams most of the time, so you never really know whether he's there or not."

"I don't daydream. The school we teach in allows no daydreaming at all," Callow said. "Quite the reverse: it drives any poetic inclination clean out of you."

"Nevertheless, you do philosophize occasionally," the woman said. "You do put down your thoughts in the evening and allow your imagination a little licence." There were the seeds here of some old and familiar argument, half-mocking: she glanced across at Colin and smiled.

"Colin writes: he'll tell you how remorseless it is." Callow glanced at him for this to be confirmed.

"Not two in the one building?" the woman said. She was, if anything, older than Callow. There were thin lines at the corners of her eyes: she wore little if any make-up. "That place, despite your protestations, and its prosaic if not depressing appearance, is an incubus of poetic talent."

"I have no pretensions. It's merely therapy for me," Callow said wearily, yet glancing too at Colin as he reached for his drink.

"Do you teach, too?" Colin asked the woman.

"Never." She shook her head. Inside the pub she'd removed the scarf; her hair was swept back from a prominent brow: there was something composed, assured and imperturbable about her expression. "I'm an independent lady," she said with an affected accent and looked at him directly as if to challenge him to make of this whatever he could.

Callow, moodily withdrawn now from the woman's banter, had added nothing further, drinking lengthily from his glass, then, at the woman's suggestion, getting up to order another.

He met the woman again a few days later. It was a Saturday morning: crowds of shoppers flooded the town. Seeing her outside a shop he had, familiarly, caught her arm: he felt her flinch at the touch.

"Oh, it's you," she said and he had the distinct impression that she'd already recognized him: that she'd seen him from a distance and had stopped, as if unconsciously, to wait.

"Are you doing anything special?" he said.

"Nothing," she said, "that couldn't be delayed."

They went into a restaurant in an adjoining alley; it was the same alleyway, he reflected, as they waited at a table, that he had gone up with his mother years before on his first visit to the school.

"So you're familiar with the place as well?" she said when he made some remark describing this.

"I was educated here," he said.

"Educated," she said, looking at him slyly.

Her hair was greying at the temples; she watched him with the same companionable expression which characterized her relationship with Callow.

David Storey

"Don't you lay much store by it?" he said.

"More than most," she said, "and less than some."

"Why do you always make fun of Callow?"

"Do I?" Neither his tone nor accusation had surprised her at all. "He's such a stuffy old bird," she added, and leant across the table to touch his arm. "So are you, but a little bit younger."

She smiled; her eyes were shielded by dark lashes, her eyelids, narrow, almost invisible beneath her brow.

"Are you married?" he asked directly.

"I am," she said. She wore no ring.

"Is your husband here?" He gestured behind him, towards the town.

"I hardly think so. Yet nevertheless," she added, smiling at him still, "you could never be sure."

She wore a dark-green coat; it had a fur collar. The brownness of the collar gave her face, with its broad cheekbones and narrow jaw, a peculiar intensity.

"What does your husband do?"

"He doesn't do anything at present."

"What did he do?"

"Is it important?" she said. "I'd have thought, on the whole, it was impertinent to ask."

There was a certain daintiness about her; her hands were small, her fingers delicate and thin. He watched her pick up her cup: her knuckles were crested white; the veins stood out on the back of her wrist.

"He worked in a company run by his father," she added. "Then he broke away, intending to stand on his own two feet. Unfortunately, he didn't succeed. He'll go back to the firm, I imagine, and take it over when his father dies. We're not living together, you see, at present."

"Are you divorced?"

"Oh, no," she said, casually. "He wants me back."

She watched him for a moment over her cup.

"You're very greedy," she added.

"Am I?"

"Very."

She glanced away: her daintiness, her sudden bouts of petulance, simulated it seemed and in response to some imagined pattern of behaviour, had made him smile. He was smiling still when she glanced towards him.

512

"Is anything the matter?" she said.

"No," he said.

"Philip," she said, "is quite impressed," and after a moment added, "Callow."

"What by?"

"Your rapport with the students."

"I'd hardly call them students," he said.

"He does."

"They're really children."

"Isn't that patronizing," she said, watching him once more through hooded eyes.

"I suppose it is." He smiled again. "I'm not much more than a child myself."

"No," she said. "I believe you're not."

"Does your husband live locally?" he said.

"Fairly locally." She paused. "I use my maiden name." She flushed, then added, "Elizabeth Bennett."

It was as if the name should have had some significance for him. She watched him for a moment then said, "Is anything wrong?"

"Who were you waiting for?" he said.

"No one. I saw you coming. I thought I'd wait for you," she said. There was some declaration of feeling here he thought he couldn't avoid: a moment later when she added, "Do you want another coffee?" he got up from the table and held her chair.

As she preceded him out of the café he took her arm: outside in the street he didn't release it.

"Where are you going now?" he said.

"I'll be going home," she said.

"Is it far?"

"Just out of town. I have a room at my sister's. I usually walk back for the exercise."

"Do you have a job?" he said.

"I work at a chemist's."

"At a shop?"

"Is anything wrong?"

"Why aren't you working today?" he said.

"It's run by my father. I go in," she said, "whenever I please."

Bennett's, a chemist's, stood conspicuously at a corner of the road leading up to the school.

"I'll walk back with you if you like," he said.

"I usually walk through the Park," she said. "It's longer, but it brings me out by my sister's house."

"What does your sister do?"

"Oh, nothing," she said as he led her across the road. "She's married. She and her husband have no children. They frequently travel." After a moment she added, "They're away at present."

"You haven't any children?"

"No," she said.

The road led down towards the river; on the flat land immediately at the foot of the city's central hill a smaller hill stood up from a surrounding mass of trees: the roof of a large old house was visible beyond.

Paths led off through the grounds; a lake glistened amongst the trees. Birds flew up; the day was windy. As if in fear of the wind she held her coat to her, clasped across her chest.

"And you? What do you intend to do?" she said.

"Oh." He gestured round. The trees obscured the view of the town. "I'll teach."

"For ever?"

"For a while." Then, bitterly, he added, "What alternative is there? It's all ordained."

"Is it? You didn't strike me as a fatalist."

Other figures moved off beneath the trees. To their right, as they proceeded in the direction of the river, the ruins of the old house were finally enveloped by the profile of the hill.

"Philip said he'd seen some of your poems."

"Yes."

"In a magazine."

"I don't think anyone reads it," he said.

"Apparently they were reviewed in the national press."

"Three lines at the end of a paragraph," he said.

"Were your family pleased?"

"Yes," he said, though in fact his father's response had been noncommittal. Only his mother had read them with any interest, raising her glasses to gaze at the page. The print was small. She had studied them for quite some time and finally had looked up, flush-faced, as if, in her pleasure, suddenly embarrassed, and said, "Yes," quaintly, strangely, in half a whisper.

"Are you and Callow close friends?" he said.

"Oh, very," she said, and laughed.

On reaching the Park he'd released her arm: they walked along a little distance apart.

"I knew him before he was a teacher," she said.

"When?"

"He was a student. We both grew up in the town together. We perform for one another what I believe you would call a supernumerary role: namely we invariably stand in for someone else."

She didn't explain it further.

They walked along for a while in silence. The path led by a lake; a statue stood in a pillared alcove on a tiny island.

He had walked here quite frequently with Margaret; often they had sat on a seat gazing across at the island and the female statue, draped to its ankles, its breasts clearly outlined beneath its robe, its gaze inclined towards the water: it had seemed, in its calmness, so much a reflection of their own relationship. Now he walked by with another woman and scarcely glanced at it; it was as if a rupture with his past had taken place, tiny, and scarcely to be considered, but perceptible and, to the extent that he discarded so much of what he felt before, disheartening and repulsive.

He added nothing further until they'd reached the gates.

A road led off to a distant housing estate; close by, opposite the Park walls, stood several large houses: their backs looked on to fields running down to the river.

"Well, then," she said. "We're almost there. Do you fancy," she added, "another coffee? Or do you intend on walking farther?"

"I'll come in," he said.

They walked along the road by the bevelled brick wall. Originally the retaining wall to the grounds of the ruined house, which now comprised the grounds of the Park, it had fallen down in one or two places, and they could see the gardens and several covered walks inside.

"It's a pleasant part to live," he said.

"Is it?" She looked back now at the Park herself. "I suppose so. I hadn't noticed."

The house stood away from the road at the end of a drive: bay-windows looked out on to a lawned garden.

Unlocking the front door she revealed a polished hall: a banistered staircase rose immediately ahead; large rooms with carpeted floors opened up on either side.

"Go straight ahead," she said, indicating a door at the rear of the hall. "I'll be with you in a minute."

He heard her feet stamping overhead.

A window looked out to the garden at the back: flower-beds, bare with winter, ran down to a distant hedge; wooden frames provided a covered walk. In the farthest distance were the hills across the valley; immediately beyond the hedge figures ran to and fro in a game of hockey.

She came in wearing a dark-brown dress. Her face, as a result of the walk, had regained some colour. She went directly to the fire, which was blazing behind a wire guard, and warmed her hands.

"It won't be a minute. It's warmer at the back. We're facing south." She indicated the window and the view beyond.

Later, when she brought in the coffee, she said, "I could get you something to eat if you like."

"That's all right," he said.

"What do you normally do at week-ends, in any case?" she said.

"I walk quite a bit."

"Don't you have any friends?"

"Most of them," he said, "have left."

"The ugly duckling."

"Do you think that's right?"

"*I* don't think that's right. I thought you did."

"No," he said.

"It's odd," she said, gazing at him once more across a cup, as she had in the café, "but your mood has changed again. It seems to fluctuate like anything."

He laughed. He looked round him at the house: the furniture was large and set down like boulders around the fire. From outside, faintly, came shouts and the occasional click of sticks against a ball.

516

"Do you play sport?"

"I did."

"Not any longer?"

"No."

"A native of the city. Though, of course, not quite."

"Saxton isn't really anywhere, I suppose," he said.

"Alienated from his class, and with nowhere yet to go."

"Do I seem alienated?" he said.

"I believe that was Philip's word. He's always looking for a champion, you know."

"A champion in what way?" he said.

"Why, someone who's come to the top from the bottom. He, you see, has gone from middle to middle. His father worked in an office in the county hall."

"I don't think," he said after a moment's reflection, "I'd measure progress in terms of class."

"Wouldn't you?" she said. "I mean," she added, "not even as an intellectual?"

"No," he said.

"Well," she said and added after a while, "Wonders of one sort will never cease."

"Why are you always laughing?" he said.

"Laughing?" She smiled.

"Isn't that patronizing in its way as well?"

She didn't answer.

"I didn't think you'd go much by it," he said.

"My boy," she said. "You've a lot to learn."

He left a little later; she came with him to the door.

"You can get a bus back, if you like," she said. She pointed out the stop across the road. It was as if, with his leaving, she'd lost interest in his visit.

"I'll probably walk back, though," he said.

"It was good of you to accompany me," she said.

"Perhaps I can see you next Saturday."

"All right." She shrugged.

"The same place if you like."

"All right." She shrugged again.

He turned at the gate to wave, but found she'd already gone inside the house and closed the door.

"See here," his father said, "it's no good going on at him."

He had been teaching Richard, at the table: a mass of figures on torn pieces of paper lay before them.

His brother's face had wrinkled: it reddened; a moment later, prompted by his father's tone of sympathy, he began to cry.

"See here," his father said again. "It's gone too far." He thumped his hand against the table: pieces of paper drifted to the floor.

His mother, who had been busy in the room upstairs, came down.

"He can't go on at him like that," his father said. "You can hear his voice at the end of the backs. How can he learn anything if he shouts at him?"

"It's better he leaves it," his mother said, looking in despairingly at the crowded table. "I'd rather he worked in the streets than we have all this."

"Nay, he s'll never do that," his father said, indicating Richard. "He's got more brains than all of them despite his shouting and his saying he'll never do it."

"I haven't said he'll never do it," Colin said.

Richard had covered his face in his hands: his head was shaken from side to side; his shoulders shook, some fresh anguish broke from him as his father touched his back.

"Nay, love," his father said. "It's not important."

"It is," his brother said, his voice buried by his moans.

"Nay, just look at it," his father said, stepping back to reveal the situation freshly to his mother. "He's trained as a teacher, he's *trained* as a teacher, but the first thing he does is lose his patience."

"It isn't important," Colin said. "Why should he have to do it?"

"Nay, he'll do it because he *can* do it," his father said. "It's on'y thy shouting now that stops him."

"Do you shout at them at school?" his mother said.

"No," he said.

"Why do you shout at Richard? He's your brother. I would have thought you'd have *cared*, far more than you do for the others. Why can't you show the same patience with him? We showed the same patience with you."

"Nay," his father said. "I s'll teach him myself."

"With a trained teacher in the house?"

"Is he in the house? And is he trained? He's never here on an evening, and if he's trained for ought I'd say it wa' shouting."

Yet the argument on this occasion petered out. It was one of many similar arguments that broke out now almost every night, but particularly at weekends: there was a delicacy about Richard which inspired his mother's protectiveness and brought out a concern in his father which he had seldom shown before. Colin came home each evening from school as he might to a prison: he dreaded the street, he dreaded the houses, he dreaded the pit; the village was like a hole in the ground. In the winter all he was aware of was its greyness, the soot, the perpetual cloud of smoke, the smell of sulphur, the stench which penetrated to every corner of every room, which infected clothes and, seemingly, the brick and stone: no one could escape it. The village was derelict; it was like a wreck, cast up in the wilderness of the fields and on the shores of that ever-growing heap.

Most evenings, if he could, he delayed coming home at all; he would walk with Callow to his relative's house, leaving him at the door, at the end of a tiny terrace street, or ride into town on the back of Stephens's bike. He would walk in the streets, more lost now, amongst such familiar places, than he'd ever been before. There was a wilfulness in his isolation; all the time, despite his longing, he was anchored to the village. On several occasions he walked the twelve miles home, arriving late in the evening or the early hours of the morning, his steps as he approached the village growing increasingly slower, coming over the final rise and gazing down, past the church, at the glow of the pit and the rising eddies of steam and smoke, the bleakness of the lamp-lit streets, and wondering even then, despite the three-hour walk, whether he might not turn round and walk back again. There was nothing to come back to.

"If you feel so fond of the place why go on living here?" his father said. "Tha mu'n find a room. There must be summat, the money thy earns."

"I don't earn all that much," he said.

"Nay, I don't know how much you do earn," his

father would say. "But it's more than I do for doing half as much."

"It's less than you earn."

"Not if you reckon it by the hour."

"In any case," he said, "I've looked."

"Aye," his father said, "and where would we be? It's the first chance we've had to buy summat good."

A new three-piece suite, the deposit paid down as a result of his first month's salary, now occupied the room; a new dining-table had recently followed it; there were plans to put linoleum on the floor. His father was thinking of buying a better wireless. "These are things that we deserve," he said. "We need these things. It's what we've struggled for together."

"It's prostitution," Colin said.

His father balked; he gazed at him with a sudden fury.

"What's prostitution?" His two brothers who'd been listening raised their heads; his mother, too, had turned from the fire.

"Hiring me out."

"Hiring who out?"

"Me out."

"You're not hired out to ought."

"It's supposed to be enlightenment I've acquired, not learning how to make a better living."

"It's both. I thought it would have been both," his mother said.

"But how can it be? The one is in conflict with the other. The one's *opposed* to the other," Colin said.

"Nay," his father said disowningly. "This man is a *mystery* to me."

And later, when his father had gone to work and his two brothers were in bed, his mother had said, "How can it be hiring out? Don't you want us to have any of these things?"

"Of course I do."

"Don't you want your brothers to take advantage of the progress you've been able to make?"

The light, glistening on her spectacles, concealed her expression.

"But it's all shaping us towards an end, it's propaganda,"

he said. "I don't fancy seeing Richard going through all I've gone through. Not to come out of it like this."

"Like what? Like *what?*" she said desperately. "I don't understand."

"To conditioning more people like himself into doing what *he's* had to do," he said.

"But what he's doing, what you've done, is a privilege," she said.

"To who?"

"To you."

"Nay, it takes our best qualities and turns them into something else."

"You've changed," she said, bitterly, "and I suppose I know why."

"I don't see it as a change, I see it more as a realization," he said.

"Nay, you've changed. I hate to see it," and a moment later she added, "I hate to see you taking it out on us."

"I'm taking it out on no one," he said.

"What about Steve? What about Richard? What about your father?"

"I'm doing all I can for you," he said.

"Doing all you can to disillusion us."

"Not to disillusion. To make you see."

"See? See what?" She gazed at him bleakly.

That Easter he had given them money to go away on a holiday, his mother and father together; they'd gone for a week. It was the first time they'd been alone together for over twenty years. He stayed at home to look after Steven and Richard.

"No arguing, and no fighting," his father had said. Colin had seen them off at the station, carrying down their case. There'd been a sudden reconciliation between them: he kissed his mother goodbye and shook his father's hand; it was as if his parents were going off for good.

A few days later he had come home from school to find Steven in the house: he was sitting with a girl in front of the fire; some tea had been made; the pots were on the table; the fire itself was almost out.

"Well, then, our Colin," his brother had said. "This is Claire."

"What's she doing here?" he said.

"Nay, she's visiting," his brother said. His mood was amiable, unconstrained: he'd been sitting in his shirt-sleeves with his arm laid casually around the girl's shoulder.

The girl was small and dark: she stood up quickly when he came in the room.

"Does she realize your mother and father aren't here?"

"Nay, I suppose she does," his brother said. There was no rancour in his voice: he gazed at the girl with a smile. She had flushed and gone to the table as if to clear it.

"And does she reckon it's all right," he added, "coming here alone?"

"Nay, she's not alone," his brother said. "She's here with me. I'm here," he added, "if you hadn't noticed."

The girl had laughed; she glanced away.

"Do her parents know she's here alone?"

"Nay, are you going to dot me one, Colin?" his brother said: he took up a casual pose, as if for a fight.

As it was, since their previous fight, scarcely any mention subsequently had been made of it; to some extent it was as if it had never taken place. Fights in any case frequently occurred in the field or the yards, sometimes between neighbours, sometimes between sons, or sons and fathers; in that sense, he supposed, theirs hadn't been any different.

"I just wondered what her parents would think. Her coming here alone."

"Nay, they'd suppose she was a bit of a flirt. Which you are, then, aren't you, Claire?" his brother said; he ran his hand casually against her cheek.

"Oh, well, I'd better go," the girl had said. She looked round for her coat.

"Nay, I'm damned if thy'll leave," his brother said. "Tha's only just come. We've just had tea."

"Oh, but I'd better go," she said. She had a refined voice: she came from a better home.

"I suppose you realize what you're doing," Colin said.

"Doing?" His brother watched him with a smile.

Yet it was to the girl directly that Colin spoke.

"I suppose you realize this would kill my mother."

"Kill her?" Steven said.

"I suppose," he said, "you've put her up to it."

"You're mad. Whatever's got into you," his brother said.

Colin stood over the girl; he saw her now through a haze of blood.

"Do you know what his mother would think if she came in now?"

"What would she think?" The girl trembled; her face, plaintive, wide-eyed, looked up at his.

"She'd think you were trying to destroy her," he said.

"Destroy her?" His brother's voice came from behind his back; then, urgently, he heard his brother say, "Take no notice of him, love," and thought then for a moment his brother's shadow fell upon him.

"It'd destroy her to see Steven here like this."

"But whatever's the matter?" the girl had said, gazing past him, appealing to Steven behind his back.

"You'd better go. You're trying to kill her. I know you're killing her," he said.

"Whatever's the matter?" the girl had said again, appealing once more to his brother.

"Nay, we're going," Steven said. He'd already pulled on a coat; his face was flushed. "Nay, we're going," he said again, taking the girl's arm. "And I s'll not come back."

"You will come back," he said.

"I shall not," Steven said and, drawing the girl out with him, closed the door.

He could hear their steps across the yard.

He stood for a moment inside the door; finally he opened it.

The air was fresh: it was as if he'd come out from inside a furnace; even the smell of the pit revived him; he stood there for a while, his legs trembling, gazing at the field.

It was only when Richard came in from playing that he felt any different: he stood at the table and got his tea.

"What is it?" she said.

He'd recoiled, broken, rising from the bed.

"Why, what is it?" she said again.

Her breasts were thrust up above the sheet.

"I don't know," he said. "I should be going."

Yet the thing that had driven him back had been her face; as he stooped towards her he saw lying there not the face of another woman but that of his mother, so clear and unmistakable, her features so deeply set, lit then by her smile, that he drew away, pushed back. Only slowly did the broadness of Elizabeth's features re-appear.

"Why? What is it?" She drew herself up. "You needn't go for hours."

"I ought to go," he said.

"But the bus doesn't go for ages yet."

He stood by the bed, gazing to the curtained window. A bus went by in the road outside.

"Is it the bed?"

He shook his head.

"We can go to mine, if you like," she added.

"No," he said.

"They won't be coming in for hours."

"Won't they know you've slept in it?" he said.

"No," she said, yet as if she were familiar with using her sister's bed and had done it frequently before. "Let's go to my room, then," she added. "It's bound to be different."

He began to get dressed; she watched him now without speaking at all.

Finally, she said, "Has anything happened?"

"No," he said.

"I feel something has happened Colin," she said. "I wish you'd tell me." After a moment, she added, "Is it Phil?"

"Why Phil?"

"That you feel you've compromised yourself with him."

"Perhaps you feel that," he said.

"No," she said, and added, "You're the first person I've slept with since my husband."

She began to cry. She turned her face against the pillow.

"I'm sorry," he said. "I think it's me." He sat on the bed. He might then at that moment have lain beside her.

"You shouldn't have come to me in this way," she said.

Her voice was buried against the pillow.

"It's too much," she added. "I want you to go."

Yet he stood by her, helplessly, gazing down.

"I don't know what it is," he said.

"I want you to go." Her voice moaned up at him; he was afraid to touch her. "What is it? Why have I done this?" he thought.

"Please go." She lay quite still, her head turned from him. There was nothing he could do at all.

He closed the door; as he went down the stairs he anticipated her calling him back; yet he knew he had inflicted a defeat, so carelessly, that the thought of what had occurred bemused him entirely.

Outside, in the drive, he looked up at the bedroom window: the curtains were still, there was no sign of life at all.

He walked through the Park; when he reached the town he rang her number. There was no reply.

He got on the bus and went back home.

"I never accused her of anything," he said.

His brother gazed at him astounded.

The previous night he had brought Steven back. Having heard he was staying at a friend's house across the village, he had waited in the road and had seen Steven in the distance talking to the girl then, later, as he approached his friend's door had caught his arm.

"You're coming back home," he told him. "My mother's come back and she's out of her mind that you're not at home."

Yet, strangely, his mother had been careless of the fact that Steven was staying at a friend's. Now she stood gazing at Steven in the door: he had come in suddenly and said, as his father got ready for work, "I left home, Mother, because of Colin."

"Why because of Colin?" His mother had gazed at him half-smiling, unconcerned.

"He threatened the girl I brought."

"What girl?"

"Claire," he said.

"How did he threaten her?"

"He accused her of wanting to kill you, Mother."

His mother glanced at him in some surprise: her face had flushed. His father looked up, intensely, from fastening his boots.

"I don't understand," his mother said.

"It's a lie," Colin said. "I never accused her of anything."

Steven gazed at him in disbelief; his sturdy, open face had darkened.

"Why, he did," he said. "You can ask her mother. I had to take her home, she was so upset."

"But why on earth should he say she wanted to kill me?" his mother said.

"I never said such a thing at all," he said.

"But this is wrong, Mother," Steven said. "He said it here. I heard him. It's why I haven't been home these last two nights."

"I thought you'd been staying with Jimmy," his mother said.

"I have," he said.

"Well." His mother gazed at Colin in disbelief; her face was reddened from the sun: it had an openness, a sudden candour. "I don't understand," she said. "What's going on. It can't be true. He'd never say that."

There were tears now in Steven's eyes.

"But it *is* true, Mother," he said. "Ask him. Ask him to be honest."

"I am being honest. I never said such a thing," he said.

"But he's *lying,* Mother," Steven said. "He's lying now as he lied to the girl."

His mother looked at him in terror; there was some conflict between them she couldn't recognize.

His father had risen.

"Why did you bring her here?" his father said to Steven.

"Why shouldn't I bring her here?" he said.

"You're too young to bring girls into the house," he said. "Particularly on your own."

"*Were* you on your own?" his mother said.

"Colin came in. We were sitting here. You can ask her parents. She's on the phone. I have her number."

"Nay," his father said. "I mu'n not drag other people

in. Particularly if you've been as daft as that. What should I say if he rang her up?"

"Just ask her what Colin said." He gazed at Colin directly.

"She must have misheard him," his father said. "And I don't agree with you bringing her here, in any case. No matter what you think."

"But he's lied about it," Steven said.

"Nay, you mustn't have heard properly," his father said, stubbornly, and wheeling out his bike.

"Well, I s'll never stay here again, in that case," Steven said.

"You will stay," his father said. "You'll stay right now."

"Nay, I shall never," Steven said: he stood over his father, his face flushed. They had never seen him in this mood before.

"Tha should have clattered his lug for him," his father said, suddenly, viciously, and gestured at Colin.

"I don't want to fight him," Steven said.

"Nay, but tha mu'n not come complaining to us, then," his father said. He pulled on his coat; he shouldered his bag. Having wheeled the bike out to the yard he set his lamps.

"I s'll not forgive you," Steven said, turning to Colin. "Having lied about it, you see, as well."

"Tha'll stay, in any road," his father said. "I'll not have you sleeping out at somebody's house."

"I don't want to stay here any longer," Steven said.

"Nay, tha s'll have to," his father said.

He gazed in at them a moment longer; he was darkened from the holiday; his expression was hidden beneath the neb of his cap: it was, with his smallness, like a child gazing in at the door of the house.

"Think on," he said, gazing in a moment longer, staring at his mother, then, mounting his bike, he rode away.

"I don't want to come back to sleep here," Steven said. "I don't want to live here with him in the house."

"Nay, don't go on with it," his mother said. "You'll have forgotten all about it in the morning."

"No, I s'll never forget it," Steven said, quietly, taking off his coat. "I s'll never forget it, Mother. And I s'll never forget," he added, "you giving in to it."

"I haven't given in to it," his mother said.

"Then ring up the Blakeleys and ask them. They live in the village," Steven said.

"I'll do no such thing," his mother said.

"No," he said. "And I know why."

"Oh, and why should that be?" his mother said.

"You know it's true. He's poisoned all of us."

"How can you *say* such a thing?" his mother said.

"How can you let him get away with it, Mother?" Steven said. "He's lied about it and I s'll never forgive him."

He went up to his room where Richard was sleeping.

"*Did* you say something to him?" his mother said as they listened to Steven's movements above their heads.

"No," he said.

"You must have said something."

"I said he shouldn't have been in the house," he said. "Not with a girl alone; not if he respected her."

"And that's all you said to him?"

"Yes," he said.

His mother turned away; there was a strange silence in the house: she stooped to the fire.

"Perhaps you should have left it to him to decide. If that's what in fact you said to him," she said.

"Why? What else could I have said to him?" he asked her.

"I don't know," she said, and added, "But Steven never lies."

"Doesn't he?"

"No," she said. "He never needs to."

"That's all *you* know about it, then."

"Why are you so bitter, Colin?" she said. "You were never bitter before. But I suppose I know the reason," she added.

"There is no reason; and it's not bitterness," he said.

"Isn't it?" she said.

She turned to the door.

"I'm going up," she added. "If you're staying down put out the light."

"Mother," he said, but when she turned to him he added, "Shall I kiss you good night?"

"Good night," she said.

He kissed her cheek.

"Why are things as they are?" he said.

"I don't know what you're trying to turn everything into," she said.

"I'm trying to be good," he said.

"Are you?"

"But not goodness as you would know it. Not goodness in inverted commas."

"What goodness is in inverted commas?" she said.

"Steven's goodness."

"I should leave Steven alone," she said. "He's never meant you any harm."

"I know," he said. "That's what I mean. It can't do him any good at all."

His mother closed her eyes.

"I don't know where I am any more," he said. "I feel that it's something new that I'm living, but I don't understand it any more," he added.

"Oh, I should leave things for a while," she said. "And leave Steven. I can't stand these arguments," she added. "I thought, with a holiday, we'd all have been better."

He heard her going to her bed; he sat by the fire.

A few moments later there was a sound by the stairs. Steven came in: he was in his pyjamas. He picked up his jacket which was lying on a chair, folded it over his arm and went back to the door.

"Why did you lie about it, Colin?" he said.

"I haven't lied," he said.

Steven gazed in at him a moment longer; it was as if some terrible truth had dawned in him. His eyes widened: they took in the reflected glare of the fire.

"Why did you come whining, in any case?" he added.

"No. I can see. I shouldn't have come back at all," he said.

"Why, what are you frightened of?" Colin said.

He gazed directly at his brother who, in his pyjamas, caught in the doorway, appeared now like a little boy.

"I s'll leave as soon as I've got a job," he said. "I'll see about getting one tomorrow." He closed the door.

The sound of his feet came slowly from the stairs,

then his mother's voice calling, then the creaking of the bed.

He dreamt of Andrew; he was first older than him, then suddenly younger; he was standing at a window, gazing in; then he was walking away along a road and he ran calling, "Andrew, Andrew," and when he didn't turn he called, "Steve! Steve!" and saw the figure's face: it was, dreamily, abstracted, that of his younger brother.

28

"Oh, I have come from a promising land
  Which young men love and women can't stand:
  There's whiskey and money both growing on trees,
  And the only policemen come up to your knees."

The children laughed.
"Any more, sir?" a boy had said.

  "Oh, when I am old
   And my feet turn cold,
   And my thoughts have turned to jelly,
   I'll sit by the fire
   And smoke my briar
   And tickle my fat old . . ."

"Belly!" the class had said in a single voice.

  "There's a man in the moon
   With a chocolate spoon
   And eyeballs made of custard,
   When he eats his tea
   He sits like me
   And peppers his rhubarb with mustard."

They laughed again, freshly, gazing at him in admiration.

"Simon Brown was a man with a frown
And eyes as black as charcoal:
He wouldn't have looked bad
If he hadn't have had
A mouth in the shape of his . . . elbow."

"Sir!" the children said. A fresh peal of laughter broke out across the room.

"Though what I have in mind," he said, "is something far different. I thought if we listened to the music you could write down whatever you felt."

He turned on the gramophone.

The class was silent: a faint murmur of voices came from adjoining rooms.

The children gazed, abstracted, towards the front of the room as the music began.

A few moments later the door opened and Corcoran came in.

"What's this?" he said.

"English," he said.

"It sounds more like music to me." The headmaster indicated the gramophone placed on the desk. "And what sort of music is it?" he added.

"Jazz."

"Jazz? What's jazz? What's jazz," he said, "got to do with music?"

"They're writing down," he said, "their various feelings appertaining to the music."

"What feelings?" the headmaster said. His stocky figure swelled with indignation; his eyes protruded; a redness crept up from his neck across his cheeks; as Colin watched the colour deepened: veins stood out on the top of his head.

"I don't know what feelings they are until they express them," he said. "Neither do they, I assume," he added.

The headmaster turned his head to the blackboard so that his voice couldn't be heard by the children, who were gazing at him now in fascination. "I'm not having this in my school: this is a place of education, of enlightenment, not an institution dedicated to the propagation of half-baked drivel."

"Perhaps you'd like to see their essays," he said.

"I'd like to see nothing from this room until that noise has stopped," the headmaster said.

"I'm not turning it off," he said.

"What?"

"If you want it off you'll have to turn it off yourself. I want the children to see you do it."

The headmaster's eyes were dark; the pupils were entirely surrounded by white; light patches showed on either cheek: it was as if the blood had abandoned his face. He gazed at Colin with a sudden, malevolent fascination.

"I'd like to see you in my room at the end of the lesson."

"All right," he said, "if I can fit it in."

"You'll fit it in, all right," he said. "I'll send Mr. Dewsbury to take your lesson."

"I believe he's otherwise occupied."

"Is he? Then I'll send a prefect."

"They can't keep control of a class, I'm afraid," he added.

"Come to my room at break," the headmaster said.

"All right," he said.

"And I want that music off."

"You'll have to turn it off."

"I want it off." The headmaster went directly to the door and closed it behind him.

Some time later the squat, broad-shouldered, bald-headed figure returned along the corridor; Colin turned the music a little louder.

He glimpsed the reddening of the already empurpled headmaster's face, saw the brief falter outside the classroom door then the sudden upsurge of energy as, with a stumble, he hurried on.

When he went into Corcoran's study later in the day the headmaster was seated behind his desk, intent seemingly on a pile of papers.

Colin sat down in a chair and waited.

"Did I ask you to sit down?" the headmaster said without raising his head.

"No," he said. "But since you're rude enough not to acknowledge me I'll be rude enough to go on sitting."

"See here," the headmaster said, rising to his feet and coming round the desk. "I don't know what's got into you, Saville, but this sort of behaviour won't do you or your future any good."

"You'll have to leave me to be the judge of that," he said.

"I'll do no such bloody thing," the headmaster said. "I'll be the judge of that. It's *me* who runs this school, not you."

"And it's me who teaches in it, unfortunately," he added. "I object to you or anyone else coming into my lesson, without permission, and attempting to disrupt it."

"I can come and go when and wherever I please," the headmaster said.

"Not in my lesson, you can't," he said. "Nor in anyone else's, if you had any respect for the staff."

"What staff?"

"Your staff."

"You call this a staff?" Half of them couldn't teach a bag of toffee. Half of them," he added, "couldn't *cobble my shoes*."

"With you standing over them I'm surprised they would even try," he said.

"See here," the headmaster said again but stood gazing down at him in some perplexity. "I'm in charge round here," he added after several seconds.

"If you've any comments to make on how I teach you've plenty of opportunity to make them away from the lesson. What authority do I have with the children if you come waltzing in whenever you please?"

"I didn't waltz in. I walked."

"I thought, on the whole," he said, "you came in more or less in time to the music."

"See here," the headmaster said again, and stood gazing at him once more in consternation.

"There's nothing wrong in playing music. I prefer to approach them from all directions."

"There's only one direction to approach them from. I *know:* I've taught here for over thirty years." He swung out the toe of his laced-up boot. "On the end of that: that's the direction I approach these rough-necks from."

"I disagree."

"Nay, tha's not above giving them a wallop: I've seen you do it myself," he added.

Colin waited.

"What would the Inspector say if he came in a classroom and found you playing that?"

"I'm not particularly interested in what he would say."

"I can *tell* you what he would say," he said. "And what he would say to me," he added.

"Are you frightened of him?" he said.

"I'm frightened of nobody," the headmaster said and returned swiftly to his desk. "N-o-b-o-d-y: nobody." He picked up a pen and gazed down, disconcerted, at the pile of papers.

"I intend to go on using music," he said. "Of any kind. If you don't wish to support me you'll have to fire me."

"See here, Saville." He gazed at him once more across the desk. Then he added, "Have you had your coffee?"

"Yes," he said.

"Even that's not very good round here. I've been in schools where the girls brewed a coffee which made a playtime well worth having. Our girls, I don't think, could cook an egg."

"Maybe you should leave and I should take over here," he said. "I'm not that concerned about the coffee."

"And neither am I," the headmaster said. "What I'm concerned with is running a practical and efficient educational institution, and all this airy-fairy nonsense, all this dissolute and promiscuous-making music, has got no part in it at all, either for me, or anyone else," he added.

He waited once again; he crossed his legs.

"See here, it's my opinion you're a very good teacher," the headmaster said. "You're arrogant and rude, but that's your youth: a few years of what I've been through and you'll have those edges knocked off. I can tell you that for nothing. A few more years, like some of us have been through, you'll toe the line and allow experience to speak instead of ignorance and good intentions. We all had good intentions: *I* had good intentions; Mr. Dewsbury and Mrs. Wallsake had good intentions; unfortunately good intentions don't butter parsnips, they don't redden beetroots and they don't sweeten swedes; the only things that do are practical measures to ensure that they know what four and four add up to and what happens to the water when they boil a kettle. After all," he added, "where are most of these children off to? When they leave here the majority'll go into factories that don't go down the pit: they'll work on the roads, they'll dig holes and clear out ditches; the girls'll do nought but work in a mill, get married and have children: children *we'll* be expected to do summat with. So where's the music come into that? They can listen to music when they get home at night: that's about all they do do, some of them. All thy wants to teach them is how to read a rent book, add up the week's wages, and write a letter of application if they want a job. Apart from that, they'll not thank you, neither will their parents, for teaching them something that doesn't come through on the bread-and-butter line. The bread-and-butter line is the only line of advancement these people understand."

"In that case, you're just confirming them in their roles," he said.

"What rolls? Bread rolls?"

"Encouraging them to submit to a situation which you, if you were in their place, wouldn't tolerate at all."

"Nay, I wasn't a duffer," the headmaster said. "Not that I've ought against duffers, but its no good teaching them the significance of higher mathematics or the beauties of Shakespeare if they can't even spell margarine," he added.

"What are the beauties of Shakespeare?" he said.

"Nay," he said. "I've never had the time. Unlike you, I've been concerned with practicalities." He paused. "You'll be saying next I've done no good."

"I'd like to think you'd done some good," he said.

"Half the children I have here are the children of parents I've taught myself. More than half, three-quarters," he said.

"It doesn't mean you've done them any good," he said.

"Ask them. You ask them. Would they send their children here if it wasn't any good?"

"But they've nowhere else to send them," he said. "I wouldn't say their incomes quite rose to the level of a private education."

"Tha's too clever for your britches," the headmaster said. He got up from his desk once more: he went to the window and gazed out at the flowerless flower-beds. "You'll give me no choice if tha goes on playing music," he added.

"I think I'll get a longer wire and play it in the corridor," he said.

"What are you, Saville? A communist?" He turned from the window and advanced quickly across the room. He stood directly over him so that Colin, as if threatened, slowly got up.

"Yes," he said.

Corcoran gazed at him in disbelief: the redness of his face had faded to a deathly pallor. "Communists don't play music. They're utilitarians like me," he said. "Only, with renegades like you, they put you up against a wall. If you were a communist," he added, "you wouldn't be teaching here."

"Where would I be teaching?" he said.

"Nay, thy'd be in some crack-pot school. Not stuck in a mining village, not stuck in a place where, if they knew you were a communist, they'd kick you up the arse to the village limits."

"There's a communist on the local miners' union," he said.

"Miners' union? Nobody belongs to a union here. There's not one miner you could tell me who's been to a union meeting in twenty-five years. They leave it to all these maniacs like you, communists who think they've got a bit of power without realizing that that conservative, apathetic body of supporters are using *them*: they use people like you, the working classes, to do their canvassing and haranguing for them. Colliery-workers are the most conservative body of people thy can possibly imagine. I ought to know, I've lived here fifty year: my father was a pit-man, and my brother is one, too. I'd have been down there meself, if I hadn't have had the brains, and so would you. I'll tell you: all they're interested in isn't changing society but getting more money, and they'll use a communist trade-union official, or King Kong if they want to, if they think he'll do it for them."

Colin stood back across the room: the headmaster, thumping one fist against his hand, paced up and down: it was as if, for a moment, he'd been forgotten.

"Tha's idealistic, like all of us were. Thy wants to change the world when the world itself doesn't want a change: all it wants is bread and butter, preferably before anybody else, but *with* anybody else so long as it gets it. *Lower* the wages round here and you'd see a difference: put them up a bit each year and you'll keep everything as it is. It's why these communists never cotton on; if they kept the miners' claims lower they'd have a chance: you'd see a revolution tomorrow morning. As it is, the silly buggers are sentimentalists like you, think because they're working-men they live in the same conditions as they do in Russia. Why, a *tramp* is better off here than he is in any other country you mu'n care to mention. We've freedom here, tha knows. Freedom to do nought about ought if nobody wants to, and, if you want to know the truth, thank God that most of them don't."

"You're one of them," he said.

"Aren't you?"

"No."

"You're above it, then?"

"No," he said. "But I know it could be different."

"Different to what?"

"That people could be different. That the children could be different."

"Nay, they'll still have to work down a pit," he said. "They'll still have to work in a mill: they'll still have to get married because they can't control theirse'ns. They'll still have to make do with nearly nought: what difference will music make, or poetry, or these books you're alus on about? Tha'll have 'em so refined they won't want to work in a pit at all."

"Maybe that's all to the good," he said.

"Aye. *Thy*'d say that stuck in front of an empty fire, or teaching in a frozen school. I've seen all thy idealists, you know, before: put a bit of hardship in the way and they're up top screaming before anybody else."

"I think things can be changed," he said. "Maybe we should all take it in turn to work down a pit."

"In turn?"

"Three months down a year wouldn't do you any harm. It wouldn't do anybody any harm, if it comes to that. It'd probably do us all a lot of good."

"I can see thy daftness growing every minute: you'll have us out theer sweeping the bloody street up next."

"Why not?"

"Why not? Because I'm trained and qualified to do something better. These skills don't come out of the air, tha knows."

"It's not difficult, teaching," he said. "You'd probably even do it better after three months sweeping the street." He looked out of the window now himself. "It could do with sweeping, in any case," he added.

"I haven't got the time, even if you have, to hold a philosophical discussion," the headmaster said returning briskly to his desk.

"If you can't hold it in a school where can you hold it?" he said. "And if you can't hold it with the head of a peda-gogical institution, whom can you hold it with?" he added.

"Does that music go, or you?"

"That's for you to decide," he said.

"Then you go, I'm afraid," he added. "Not that I'm not sorry. The football team's improved by leaps and bounds since you came to the school. Unfortunately, life isn't made up of bloody football. You'll have two months' notice from today and leave at the end of the term. I'll notify the divisional office."

"What about a testimonial?" he said.

"For what?"

"For another job."

539

"Art thy intending on remaining in teaching, then?" He gazed up at him directly.

"That's all I've been trained to do," he said.

"Nay, thy'll not get a job with thy ideas," he said. "I'm a liberal headmaster. Wait till thy comes across one with a few ideas of his own. Thy gramophone and record'll be out of the window." He tapped his teeth with the end of a pen. "I'll write you a testimonial," he added. "I'll put 'independence of ideas not normally encountered in our profession' and they can make on that whatever they want."

"I'll be sorry to leave on the whole," he said.

"I'll put it around and they can buy you a present."

"Oh, I don't really want a present," he said.

"Nay, I don't hold any enmity," the headmaster said. "It's just that I've got a job to do. I've done it, one road or another, for forty years. Nobody's complained, as far as I reckon. Based on that experience, I'd say you were wrong."

A bell rang at the end of an adjoining corridor.

"I'll get back to the class."

"That's right." The headmaster returned to the papers on his desk and, as he read them, got out a pipe. "By the way." He raised his head. "Thy'll leave thy coffee money before tha leaves. We've had one or two leave who've forgotten that: it comes out of petty-cash, and the divisional office, I can tell you, have me account for every penny. They shit hot bricks if I'm a halfpenny out."

"Right," he said. "I'll see to that."

"Right," the headmaster said and, flushing at Colin's smile, he lit his pipe.

"How was that?" she said.

"All right."

"You're hard to please."

"Do you think so?"

"*I* think so. Perhaps others wouldn't."

It was a Saturday afternoon: they lay in the double-bed: her sister and brother-in-law were out.

"In any case," she said, "they want me to leave."

"Why?"

"They don't like me bringing a man to the house."

"I'm not a man," he said.

"No," she said. "You're more a boy."

"I mean," he said, "not any man."

"If I want that freedom they think I should take a place of my own."

"Will you?"

"Yes," she said. "I suppose I shall."

A few days previously a man had come up to him in the street.

He had asked him his name, standing directly before him on the pavement; finally, having confirmed who Colin was, he had handed him a letter.

Inside the envelope across which his name had been scrawled in capital letters was a note which said, again in capital letters, "WOULD YOU LEAVE MY WIFE ALONE?"

He'd shown it to her when he'd arrived that afternoon. She'd gazed at it for quite some time.

"I suppose it must be Derek," she said. "It looks like Derek." She'd set the paper down. "Did the man say anything at all?" she added.

"Just asked my name and gave me the letter."

Now she said, as she got up from the bed, "I suppose I ought to, in any case. Derek's not above coming here, if he thinks it suits him."

"Why don't you go back to him?" he said.

"You don't know the Waltons. You don't know *him*. That family is all-consuming. If he couldn't break free, how could I? There are so many of them and their interests are so closely related."

He watched her dress; there was a certain neatness in her movements, self-enclosed, as if she were unaware of dressing in the presence of someone else: she made no attempt to conceal herself.

"You ought to be getting up yourself. They'll probably be back within an hour."

"Do they know you use the bed?" he said.

"I doubt it."

"Haven't you any qualms?"

"Not really."

"Has it some significance? It being your sister's bed?"

"Why?"

"I wondered."

She gazed up at him, surprised.

"We get on very well."

"Is she younger or older?"

"Older."

They went through to her room: it looked out to the fields at the back of the house. As it was, there was a certain strangeness in being in a family house yet having no relationship to the family. When she heard her sister's return, the drone of the car in the drive outside, she went down to meet her.

As she came back up he could hear her voice: "Oh, Colin's here," and, slightly lower, "I thought I'd warn you."

He couldn't hear the sister's response, only the duller tone of the husband.

She brought up some tea; they sat on the single bed.

"Why don't we go down and drink it?" he said.

"Oh, Maureen doesn't approve of this at all," she said. "There's no point in trying to force it."

They went out a little later; they walked in the Park. A certain listlessness came over him now whenever he went out with her. Initially he had liked it: liked it, above all, that she was a married woman. His earlier hallucination had never returned and he'd never attempted to explain it; a fortnight had passed before he'd gone back to see her and it was as if that first abortive attempt to sleep in the sister's bed had never occurred. Callow avoided him at school. Invariably, most evenings, he rode into town on the back of Stephens's bike and either went directly to Elizabeth's sister's house or met her by arrangement at some place close to the city centre or her father's shop.

Frequently they walked in the fields, and lay together beneath the hedges.

"Is Derek looking for evidence, do you think?" he said.

"For what?"

They walked by the pond; they paused opposite the statue. She'd brought some bread: she threw it to the ducks.

"A divorce."

"Don't you want to be cited?" she said.

"I don't know," he said. "I hadn't thought."

"Don't worry. You've arrived on the scene too late."

Yet there was a hardness in her voice: he didn't know whether it was to do with him or her husband.

She had slender arms, her skin pale, glowing, almost luminescent. It was a quality he'd never seen in anyone before. Some days when he met her her cheeks would glow; other days there was a peculiar dullness, or the strange, almost languid luminescence of the skin.

"Since you're an anarchist, I didn't think you'd mind. Flouting convention, I mean," she said.

"Am I an anarchist?" he said. He'd told her already, the day it had happened, that he'd been fired from the school. She'd seemed relieved: she was feeling guilty, he thought, about Callow.

"Well, you're not a communist," she said. "Whatever you told your Mr. Corcoran." And a moment later, she added, "You're more a Calvinist," and when he laughed she said, "Well, aren't you? What allegiance have you got? I'd say you were a medievalist, a feudalist."

She threw the last pieces of bread to the ducks.

"You make it sound," he said, "like a crime."

"I don't know," she said, "it probably is."

"I'd have thought attitudes like that came easily to hand. Aren't you, after all," he added, "much the same."

"I doubt it," she said. "I've had my way, you see, made for me. You've got to make yours." And a moment later, glancing up at him, she added, "In whatever way you can."

A man walked behind them, his hands in his pockets: when they'd paused to feed the ducks he'd paused as well, gazing at the birds, smiling when Elizabeth looked, and nodding his head.

Now, as they continued along the path, he followed them once more.

The mocking, half-affected look came back to her eyes. She watched him closely; her arm in his.

"In the end, what the individual achieves is for the benefit of everyone," he said.

"Is it?" Her smile continued. "That sounds like a credo made *after* the event."

"No," he said. He shook his head. "It's how I would explain most, if not everything, that's happened."

"To you?" she said.

"Yes," he said. "Or anyone like me."

They walked along for a while in silence: a narrow path led up to the central hill.

The man, walking behind, had taken a path divergent to their own.

"You don't really belong to anything," she said. "You're not really a teacher. You're not really anything. You don't belong to any class, since you live with one class, respond like another, and feel attachments to none."

"Do you mind my being so much younger?" he said, harshly, for he felt this lay at the root of her argument.

"I don't know," she said. "I didn't expect it."

"Expect it of whom?"

"Of me. I'm old enough, or almost old enough," she added, "to be your mother."

"Yes," he said. "Perhaps you are."

They continued their walk. The river, shining in the afternoon light, came into view, curving across the valley floor.

"I'm glad you're leaving the school," she said finally, as they reached the summit of the Park.

"Why?"

"I think you should."

And a little later, she had added, "Has Philip ever spoken to you? Recently, I mean."

"Once," he said.

Callow in fact had come up to him one evening, after school, almost in the same manner as, on the one occasion, Stephens had, and had said, with a forced geniality, "You don't have to leave for my sake, chum."

"I'm not," he'd said. "I'm fired."

"By whom?" Callow said. He didn't believe it.

"Corcoran."

"Has he fired you?" he said, searching if anything for qualities of discernment in Corcoran which hitherto he might have overlooked: it was the first direct evidence he had given of his displeasure at Colin's relationship with Elizabeth.

"You could always ask him," Colin said.

"What's it got to do with?" Callow said.

"Playing music."

"Music."

"Poetry. He considers it all alot of waffle."

"Well, I know his views, but they're scarcely enough to fire you," Callow said.

"Mine are," he said.

"You're not," Callow said, "turning into a Bolshie?" His plight, seen now as retribution, had reassured the older man.

Elizabeth had laughed. The daintiness that was always evident in her was never more apparent than when they walked: there was a certain primness in her; anyone glimpsing them from a distance, and seeing their companionability, might have thought they were married. Once, shopping, he'd been taken for her son: "What does your son think?" the shop assistant had said when she was showing her a dress and Elizabeth had laughed, glancing at him however in some alarm. Though she had never told him her age, despite his asking, he'd guessed she was in her middle thirties.

"I still see Phil occasionally," she said.

"How occasionally?" he said.

"Whenever he rings me." She glanced across.

"How often is that?"

"Whenever he feels inclined to." She added, "He has the same attitude to you as he has to my husband."

She was silent for a while: the pressure of her arm had slackened. The path wound in amongst some trees: the view below them was suddenly obscured.

"Are you annoyed?"

"No," he said.

"It's just that at times I feel frightened," she said.

"What of?"

"I don't know," she said. She shook her head.

The man who had been walking in the path below appeared now on the path ahead: the curving track emerged from the trees on to an open area of grass. Below them stretched a view of the valley; the river, sweeping directly away from the Park, appeared now very much as it must have done from the windows of the ruined house behind.

"What you describe as medievalism you described initially as alienation," he said.

"Philip did."

"It amounts to much the same thing," he said.

"How would he describe this?" she said. "Making love to a married woman."

"I'd imagine he'd describe it as symptomatic."

The man too had paused to gaze out across the valley.

"As opposed to forming a relationship, that is, with someone of a proper age."

"What's a proper age?" he said.

"A more compatible age," she said.

"You're not that old, are you, Liz?" he said.

"No, not really, I suppose," she said, yet slowly, as if he'd frightened her.

They descended the hill in the direction of the town; it rose up on its ridge before them.

"Have you anywhere in particular you'd like to go?" he asked.

"Oh," she said. "We'll go to the pictures."

Later that night she saw him on to the bus.

Since the war a bus station had been built on derelict ground adjacent to the city centre: they stood waiting in a draughty concrete shelter; her own bus left from an adjoining stop.

"I'll start looking for a flat," she said. "Do you think you'd like to help?"

"In what way?"

"To help to choose it."

"I don't think I would." The bus station, late at night, was relatively deserted; occasionally an empty bus lumbered in or out; two or three tiny queues were scattered across the concrete spaces.

"I don't think you should rely on me at all," he said.

"No," she said. And as the bus came into the station and its arrving passengers descended she added, "I'll speak to Derek. He's no right in getting in touch with you at all."

"What will you tell him?"

"To mind his own affairs," she said.

"Well, I don't really mind so much about that," he said and, as the empty bus drew up, he stooped down to where her head nestled against his arm and kissed her.

Mr. Reagan had died: he collapsed one afternoon in the garden. His walks had been confined for some time to the yard at the back of the house, and the stretch of narrow garden that ran down to the field. Each day, when the weather was fine, he could be seen shuffling along the overgrown path to the fence where he could gaze over at the children playing in the field, and one tea-time his father, who had been watching him from the kitchen door, had called out, "Bryan's fallen," and had hurried out across the yard.

He and Mr. Shaw had carried him inside.

Two days later, without leaving his house again, he'd died.

"Oh, he was a fine man," his father said. "He was fine in a way that men round here aren't often fine," he added. "It's a tragedy about his son."

Michael now had become a recluse; occasionally he could be seen about the village, invariably in the evenings: he went to the picture house alone, or would walk the road between the village and the station, as if setting out on a journey or coming back.

"He wanted Michael to be a fighter. To take the world by the scruff of the neck."

"You can't force people into what they're not meant to be," his mother said.

"Don't I know that? Aren't I the one *exactly* to know a thing like that?" his father said. On the day of the funeral he had walked with Mrs. Reagan behind the coffin; she had no relative. When he came back, flush-faced from drinking, he said, "Nay, he's got some spirit in him. Did you know what he did at the Rose and Crown? Got up on a table and played his fiddle."

"Who did?" his mother said.

"Michael."

And a few days later Mrs. Reagan came over to the yard and knocked on the door and when Colin answered it had handed him a parcel. It was bound up thickly with string.

"Mr. Reagan wanted you to have this, Colin," she said.

"That was very kind of him," he said.

"He looked on you with special favour," she said, almost formally, her narrow features flushing, her eyes, dark and set closely together, gazing at him over the bridge of her nose. " 'The one nugget out of all this dross,' " she added, imitating vaguely Mr. Reagan's accent.

He watched her go back, round-shouldered, passing with strangely delicate steps across the backs.

"Nay, look at this," his father said, standing at the table, as he unwrapped the parcel. He found him the scissors to cut the string.

Inside was the gold chain Mr. Reagan invariably wore from his waistcoat pocket.

"Well, it wasn't a pebble after all," his father added, looking at the gold disc attached to the end.

It was designed in the shape of a gold star and bore a Latin inscription.

" 'Aut vincere aut mori,' " he read.

"Sithee, he must have thought a lot to give you that," his father said gazing at the chain. "He was a fine sport, was Bryan. In a better world than this he'd have had a grander life."

"So would we all," his mother said.

"Nay," his father said. "But him especially. He could spot a poet. He had an eye. And he always stood up for his opinions."

"Yes, he was a grand neighbour, I suppose," his mother said, getting out her handkerchief to wipe her eyes.

Two weeks later Mrs. Reagan was taken ill herself. She went away to hospital: his mother went to visit her. Mrs. Reagan however had already left the hospital and had been taken into a mental institution.

"I can't understand it, she was standing in that door a few days ago," his father said, more shocked by this than he had been by Reagan's death. "I talked to her in the street a day or two after. Why, I even went to the funeral with her. She was as right as rain I thought after that."

"Nay, but she idolized him," his mother said. "She put him on a pedestal and thought he could do no wrong."

"Well, there's no danger of that happening in this house," his father said. "No danger of that, I should say, at all."

For a few days Michael wasn't seen by anyone; then, one evening, the lights were on in all the rooms: a car stood at the door. The sound of music and laughter came from the house.

The following afternoon, with the curtains still drawn, three men emerged; they stood in the tiny garden, blinking in the sun, then finally climbed over the fence and sat in the field. A little later, white-faced, as if he'd just wakened, Michael joined them; he climbed over the fence with some difficulty and, to the three men's laughter, stumbled in the grass the other side.

"Nay, they look a dissolute lot," his mother said. "Poor Michael. His mother would go mad if she was here to see it."

"She has gone mad," his father said, standing at the door and gazing out with interest at the noisy group: they were wrestling with one another and Michael, his white arms visible, was endeavouring to join in.

The men came again the following week-end; occasionally, too, they came odd weekdays. Sometimes a fourth figure, a woman, joined them. The Shaws complained about the noise: Michael, in his shirt-sleeves, holding a bottle, the laughing group behind him, stood in the yard struggling to apologize.

On odd evenings other groups of two or three men, and occasionally the woman, re-appeared: Michael went away for over a fortnight. Stories came back of him being glimpsed in neighbouring towns, once of being arrested.

Nevertheless, when he finally re-appeared, he was dressed in a suit; he wore a trilby hat; a scarf was knotted loosely round his neck.

"I think his mother must have left him summat," his father said. "Some sort of inheritance she's scraped together. He's got his hands on it, I think, a bit too soon. Do you think I ought to go and talk to him?"

"You'll do no such thing," his mother said.

"Nay, I owe it to Bryan. He was a good friend to me," his father said. And one evening, when he knew Michael was in, he went across.

He came back an hour later.

"Dost know, I don't think I've ever been in their house," he said. "And now I have been I wish I hadn't."

He sat pale-faced, half-trembling, beside the fire.

"He's sold every stick of furniture," his father added. "There's nothing in that house but a chair and a bed. He must have taken it out at night. 'Nay, Michael,' I said, 'dost think your mother's going to like all this?' Do you know what he said? 'My mother'll never see it again.' I said, 'Even if she isn't, and I hope she is, she'd scarce like to think of you living here like this.' 'I like living here like this,' he said. 'You don't have to worry.' Don't have to worry!" His father shook his head. " 'Nay, Michael,' I told him, 'we worry about you because we knew your father, and we've known you,' I told him, 'nearly all your life.' 'Oh, I can take care of myself, Mr. Saville,' he said. 'It's the first time, after all, I've had the chance.' " His father wiped his eyes. "You know how his mother kept that house cleaner even than Mrs. Bletchley's. Cleaner even than Mrs. Shaw's."

"Well, *this* house has never been dirty," his mother said.

"Not dirty, but it's always been lived in," his father said.

"Well, this house is as clean as *anyone*'s," his mother said.

"But not *morbidly* clean, now is it?" his father said, distressed to have to argue with his mother like this.

"Well, I'm sorry to hear he's made such a mess of it," his mother said, yet grieved that her own efforts in this direction had gone unconsidered.

"Nay, I damn well wish I'd never gone," his father said. "I should have kept my nose clean out of it."

Colin met Reagan one evening in the street; he was wearing not only a suit, but a spotted bow-tie, and he carried a cane: his trilby hat was missing. His hair, which was longer now than it had ever been, fell down in a single greased swathe at the back of his neck.

"Hi, Colin," he said, waving the cane casually and having crossed the street to greet him. A smell of scent came from his figure. His eyes were dark; they glared at him with a peculiar intensity; his forehead shone, his cheeks were sallow; a tooth was missing from the front of his mouth. "How have you been?" he added. "I hear you've finished teaching."

"Not quite," he said.

"Come into town one night and have a drink."

"Where do you usually go?" he said.

"Oh, any amount of spots. *Not* the Assembly Rooms, I can tell you that." He tapped the cane casually against his foot: there was some absurd parody evident in his dress, some grotesque misappliance of his father's fastidiousness and style.

"Are you working at present?" he said.

"Oh, I have one or two things," he said. "I've joined a band, on a wholly voluntary basis. I don't do much."

"How do you make a living?" he said.

"Oh," Michael said airily, "there are ways and means," and, as he moved off towards his darkened house, he added, "Remember now: I'll hold you to that drink."

It was in fact several evenings later that he met him again; they were both converging on the city centre. Michael had evidently been upstairs on the bus, and must have been already there when he'd got on himself in the village.

"I say," Reagan said, "are you up here for the night?"

"I'm meeting a friend," he said, and indicated the hunched shape of Stephens waiting by a shop.

Michael took one look at Stephens and glanced away. "Well, see you," he said casually and raised his hand. He carried no cane; he was dressed in a raincoat with a turned-up collar, his head looking even larger than usual beneath his trilby hat. "Do you see Belcher these days?" he added.

"No," he said.

"Maybe one day we should get together." Yet he was already moving across the road and some other remark he made was lost.

"Who was that remarkable-looking object?" Stephens said.

"A friend."

"He looks like an attenuated version of Humphrey Bogart," Stephens added from his own diminutive height and still gazing with amazement at the disappearing figure which, even from a distance, was conspicuous amongst the evening crowds. "What does he do?"

"Nothing at present."

"Good God," he said. "Another like you."

"Oh, I've still got one or two weeks," he said.

"Freewheeling, though. Freewheeling," Stephens said.

And later, as he walked home with Stephens, down the hill towards the river, his friend, who had been in a convival mood all evening, had added, "I'll be leaving soon, of course, myself. Casting myself off from this rotten town: embarking from these shores of oblivion. I've given my notice in from the end of next term. I'll be leaving for London in a couple of months. Why not come with me?"

"We've been through all that," he said, "before."

"You've other tricks up your sleeve, young Saville?"

"None that I'm aware of, no," he said.

"Still bound by convention, piety and a grotesque compliance to the family that hast engendered thou."

"I don't think I'm bound to anyone," he said.

Stephens hummed to himself for several seconds: hunched up, with his head thrust back, he represented, in the darkness of the street, a figure not altogether unlike a tortoise, scenting the air, inquisitive for food.

"You don't deceive me," he said, finally, and adding, "I saw through you from the very start. You're Pilgrim bogged down at the gates of the city. Look southward, Colin: the land is bright."

In fact a moon shone in a clear sky before them. It was early summer.

Numerous other figures drifted through the streets in the fading light: the town looked bright and clean.

"And what are you going to do?" Colin said.

"I shall look around. I shall make inquiries. I have an introduction to a man in television."

Colin laughed.

"Scorn not the medium of the prophets," Stephens said. "Television is the medium of the future."

"Whose future?"

"My future," Stephens said. "I intend to contribute to a programme on which, in visual as well as verbal form, I shall give my views on the topics of the day. The re-emergence, for instance, of Germany as a major power, the confluence of its aims with those of America; the resurgence of Japan; the new philistinism of the post-war intelligentsia; the seduction of the proletariat by a materialism even more hideous than the one that initially engulfed it; the gradual and unconscious debilitation of the west and the coming, inevitable war with Russia."

"It all sounds highly improbable," he said.

"These are the themes of the present," Stephen said. "These are the issues that crowd in upon us every day: the disintegration of the psyche; the communalization of sensibility; the trivialization of human intercourse and reason; the birth, in Russia and elsewhere of a reincarnated bourgeoisie; the plethora of ignorance which, in our generation, after the age of elitism, will rule the world. Where do you place yourself," he added, "in regard to that?"

Colin walked along with his hands in his pockets; Stephens, his face streaming with sweat from the night's drinking, regarded him with a smile.

They came out on the bridge; Stephens's house stood up a narrow street of newly built semi-detached houses almost opposite.

The moon was reflected in the river.

"Well? What *do* you believe in?" Stephens added. He leaned up on the parapet and gazed at the water: the river coiled like a broad, quaintly luminous thoroughfare between the fabric of the mills on either bank.

"I believe in doing good," he said.

"Then you *are* a sentimentalist," Stephens said.

"Not your kind of good. Not at all," he said.

"You're not a religious maniac *as well* as being an idealist?" he said.

"I don't believe I'm an idealist at all," he said.

They parted finally at the end of Stephens's road: he could see his friend's motorbike parked under a tarpaulin cover in one of the gardens.

"I shall look you up when I leave for London," Stephens said. "I shall drench you with letters. 'I come to turn children against their parents,' says Christ in one of the less sensational gospels and I, I can assure you, will do the same."

Colin crossed the road below the bridge and waited for his bus: sitting on the upper deck when it arrived was Michael.

"Well," Reagan said, nodding his head. "I thought it was you. I saw you in the road ahead."

They sat side by side on a long, bench-like seat at the front of the bus.

"Was that your friend you were talking to?"

"Yes," he said.

"What does he do?"

"He teaches at present," he said. "Though shortly, I believe, he's going to London."

"I thought I might go there as well, in the not too distant future," Reagan said. "There are one or two openings for musicians," he added. His collar was undone; because of the low ceiling of the bus he'd removed his hat. "In addition to which I've one or two connections."

"Perhaps the two of you will meet," he said.

"Oh, not in the circles I move in," Michael said. His hands, which were tiny and long-fingered, were clenched and unclenched in his raincoated lap.

The sky had darkened: the lights of the bus lay out in a broad swathe in the moonlit road ahead.

"If I knew I could get some accommodation I'd move out of the village," he added. "I can't tell you how sick I am of living there. You have no privacy with the neighbours. You excepted, of course. Though you, I suppose, have always been different."

Colin waited; Reagan fingered his hat, poised on his raincoated knees before him.

"The fact is the house is a colliery house, and because my father worked at the pit they can't throw me out. I thought at one time of offering to buy it. Then I thought if I did I could never sell it. All these years we've been paying rent: we've paid for that house ten times over. Well, so have you, I suppose," he added.

The bus rattled on. At the summit of a hill they could see, faintly, the glow of the village lights in the sky: it outlined the profile of a wooded ridge between them.

"I can't tell you how sickened I get coming back like this," he said again. He gazed down forlornly, dark-eyed, at the road ahead.

"How is your mother?" Colin said.

"She's mad. She'll never get out." His gaze didn't shift from the road itself. "She never recognizes me when I visit her. Perhaps it's just as well. She blamed me, you know, for my father's death. Not openly, that is."

They sat in silence for a while; at each of the stops more people got off.

Soon they were sitting alone on the upper deck.

A peculiar desolation gripped Colin. It was as if all his past had come together, that some final account had been submitted: his future suddenly seemed as desolate and as empty as the road ahead.

"Well, here it comes, then," Michael said and squeezing past him made quickly for the stairs.

They walked through the darkened streets together.

A man was waiting at the end of the road; he moved away from beneath a lighted lamp as they passed.

"Do you want to come in for a drink, Colin?" Michael said.

"I don't mind," he said.

"Don't if you don't want to."

"I'd like to, if you didn't mind," he said.

"Oh, company's company," he said and glanced up, as if unconsciously, towards Bletchley's house.

It was the first time he'd been inside Reagan's home. There was a pungent odour of stale food.

As his father had described, the rooms were bare: in the kitchen a mat stood before an empty fire; a wooden chair, with its back broken, stood directly opposite. On the floor in the corner, was propped a violin case.

The wallpaper, meticulously shaped and patterned, and which Mrs. Reagan had kept scrupulously clean, was now stained and greased. The unblemished lino had vanished from the floor.

"Sit down," Michael said, indicating the chair. "I'll get you a glass."

He opened a cupboard and lifted out a bottle.

He set two cups on the floor and proceeded to fill them.

"You've never been in here before?" he said.

"No," he said.

"Your father came out one night. It was kind of him to bother. Mrs. Bletchley came as well. She's been two or three times. She was fond of my mother. She's even been to see her, though my mother didn't recognize her. She's got something the matter with her leg as well."

"What?" he said.

"I don't know," he said. "It might be cancer. None of them give her much chance." He added, after drinking from the cup, "I've never heard of cancer in the leg before."

From outside came the quiet panting of the pit. The light was dim, there was no shade around the bulb.

"Do you want to sit on the chair?" Colin said.

"No, no," Michael said, and sat on the floor. "I don't light a fire," he added. "I'm not often in."

"When do you propose to go to London?" he said.

"Oh, I've one or two opportunities I want to look at first," he said. "The whole style of music, you see, has changed. The one I was brought up in has gone for ever.

The story of my life." He finished the cup and half-filled it once again.

Colin, less quickly, drank from his.

"Have you noticed how there are no young people living here," he added. "There are hardly any young ones at the pit. They don't even play cricket in the field any more: Batty, Stringer, your father, Shaw—they're all too old. And there's no one, as far as I can see, has taken their place. They're even talking of shutting up the pit."

"Yes," he said, for his father had mentioned this some time before.

"It's too old-fashioned, and its resources are too limited," Michael said. "Just think: my father worked there all his life. And Shaw. And your father's worked there a year or two himself." He raised his head. "Do you remember that time we walked to Brierley, and a man gave us a lift in the cab of a lorry? Oh, how I'd like to go back to then. Everything seemed certain and safe, though I don't suppose it was, or didn't seem so at the time. I never did know what relevance that name was supposed to have: the one the man told me to mention to my father. I suppose now we'll never know," he added.

He began to moan to himself a little later: his head dropped. He hadn't taken off his coat; his hat, which he'd hung on a hook, had dropped to the floor.

Finally, when Colin called to him, he shook his head: he'd been drinking heavily, he'd assumed, throughout the evening. As Colin stood up, Michael slumped to the floor.

He lifted him, astonished at his lightness; with considerable difficulty because of the length of his body he carried him upstairs.

The main bedroom at the front was empty; so was the second bedroom at the back.

In the tiny remaining bedroom was a single bed.

Colin laid Michael down and took off his coat.

"Is that you, Maurice?" he said and put up his arms, speculatively, reaching out.

"It's Colin," he said. "I'll cover you up."

"Oh, Colin," Michael said, as if he had trouble remembering who he was.

He took off the raincoat, removed Reagan's shoes and drew the blanket over him. His socks were in holes; his feet stuck out at the end of the bed; the shirt, too, he noticed, was black at the collar.

He turned off the light.

Michael made no sound.

Colin took out the key from the lock downstairs, let himself out of the front door, then posted the key back through the letter-box.

Then, his hands in his pockets, he went up the street towards his home.

29

"What do you think of it?" she said. The room looked down into a tiny yard. From the open window at the opposite end came the bustle of traffic in the street outside.

"Do you mind living here?" he asked.

"Mind?" She watched him with a smile. She seemed content.

"You've always had a house before. Even your sister's house," he said.

"Haven't you ever lived on your own?" she said.

"No," he told her.

"You ought to try."

She moved across the room; there was a faded carpet on the floor; the furniture was old. The wallpaper was faintly marked: it sprawled in a dull pattern of sepia flowers across the walls.

"I've never been able to afford it," he said.

"Oh, you always go on about money."

"It's all there is to go on about," he said, "or very nearly."

"Where *you* come from," she said. "But not where I come from."

Yet she was disconcerted by his dislike of the room; it might have been the first time she'd lived on her own herself. The flat was in no way like the stolid elegance of her sister's house, with its polished floors, thick rugs, and heavy, chintz-covered chairs and mahogany furniture.

"Where did you live with your husband?" he said.

"We had a house. Near one of the shops. His family bought it. It stood in a little park, a stone affair, with an asphalt drive. It had eight bedrooms."

"Did you sleep in separate rooms?" he said.

"No." She laughed; the inquiry, suddenly, lightened her mood. "We had a nephew staying with us. He was going to one of the local schools."

She was small and serious; some reflection on the past, or her home, brought back a darkening of her expression. She glanced away towards the window: perhaps the desolation of living in a flat, alone, with no connections, had suddenly occurred to her. He was surprised she'd chosen such a neglected place: the house, one of a row of old Victorian terraces, occupied a street opening off the city centre; many times he'd walked past it on his way to school.

"What was your husband like?" he said.

"I believe I told you."

She stood now with her back to him; it was as if he'd cast her off entirely.

"I prefer a small place, actually," she said. "For one thing, I never liked the Snainton house. It was dark and huge and damp and cold and there never seemed to be anyone in it."

"Were you in it alone all day?"

"I worked at the shop."

"What sort of work?"

"I supervised the office. We manufactured carpets, and sold them retail, you see, as well."

He grasped her arm, she was very light and slim: he could almost have lifted her in one hand. Yet, in other moods, she seemed heavy and unwieldy, as if she wouldn't be moved, physically, by anything at all. He had never known anyone whose physique, seemingly, changed with every feeling; even the texture of her skin varied from soft to hard—it appeared to be something over which she had no control herself.

She'd turned now and looked up at him directly.

"Why won't you commit yourself?" she said.

"To what?"

"Anything."

She released herself and moved away.

"In any case, I shouldn't ask. I've nothing to reproach you for."

Once, when they were walking round the town, she had shown him her parents' house. It stood in a tree-lined road beyond the grammar school, a large, detached, brick-built house in the garden of which a man not unlike his father was working, overalled, stooped with age, grey-haired.

He could never understand why she hadn't gone back there to live.

"What do your parents think?" he said now, gesturing at the room.

"About this?" she said. "They haven't seen it," and, a moment later, half-amused, she'd added, "Why do you relate everything to parents? Are you so inextricably bound up with yours?"

"No," he said. "It's economics."

"Is it?" she said, and added, still smiling, "I'm beginning to wonder." And a moment later, still watching him, she went on freshly, "In any case they haven't seen it. Nor, I'm glad to say, are they likely to."

"Won't they want to come here, then?" he said.

"Only if I ask them."

"Won't you ask them?"

"Not for the present. No," she said.

On two occasions, when he knew she would be working in the shop, he'd gone to Bennett's and surprised her behind the counter; she'd trained as a pharmacist as a girl and had frequently, during periods of her parents' illness, or during holidays, taken over the shop completely. It stood, an old brick building, at the junction of a narrow sidestreet: the windows were tall, and bevelled outwards, and contained the old jars and coloured liquids and large, black ebony cabinets of a century before.

On the first occasion he thought she'd been embarrassed: she was standing in a white smock, immediately inside the counter, serving a customer. Her father, a small, delicately featured man, with white hair and a virulent red face, had been turned to one of the cabinets, removing packets. Evidently surprised by the change of tone in her voice as she greeted Colin, her father had gazed at him with some curiosity over the top of a pair of spectacles.

On that occasion she had made some apology and come out of the shop, walking down the street towards the city centre with her arm in his as if to reassure herself that nothing untoward had happened, that she hadn't lost him or been diminished by this sudden revelation of her working life and to confirm to her father, who was undoubtedly watching from the window, that this was no ordinary encounter: in such a way she had drawn Colin closer to her.

On the second occasion she had refused to come out at all. It was an hour to closing-time: he came in after school, driven into town on the back of Stephens's motorbike, and he had had to go away and wait in the bar of a pub until an hour later she came in and greeted him, as she did always, with a formal kiss on the cheek. It was as if, in a curious way, they'd been married several years: she had this peculiar intimacy and directness, a self-assurance which came from her curious bouts of introspection, a self-preoccupation which diminished her, in his eyes, in no way at all; out of them she invariably came to him more strongly.

"What did your father say?" he'd asked her after his first visit to the shop.

"Nothing," she'd said, then had added, after some moments' reflection, "He thinks you're very young."

Now he said, "Do they know you've taken a flat? I suppose they do."

"I told them I was looking for one," she said. "In any case, they'll have heard from Maureen. That I've stopped living there, I mean."

"Do you ever go home?"

"Occasionally," she said.

She watched him with a frown: he was trying to unknot a puzzle, one she herself couldn't recognize, or—if she could recognize it—understand.

"They're very much preoccupied," she added, and when he said, "With what?" she said, "With one another. They always have been. They married young: I don't think, really, they wanted any children. Apart from the shop, I don't think my father's thought about anything except my

562

mother. And she's never thought about anything except him. They're totally absorbed in one another. And that, mind you, after almost forty years."

"What were they like when you were young?" he said.

"They kept us very much in attendance. Maureen went off and got herself engaged when she was only nineteen. It didn't work out. But she married, however, very soon after. My parents, finally, have never really been interested in either of us; they never neglected us; we went away to schools; they were pleased to see us whenever we came back, but it was always, I had the feeling, as an adjunct of their lives."

In the shop he had sensed a peculiar amiability between the father and his daughter: they worked casually together, without any tenseness, with a great deal of fondness. They might have been friends, or brother and sister; there was nothing of the obsessiveness he experienced at home.

He had told her about his family: she was very much interested by his parents and at one point he had been tempted to take her to meet them, then, for some reason, he'd resisted and merely talked about them, and Richard and Steven.

"Why are you so jealous of Steve?" she'd said. "He sounds so fine and unprejudiced."

"But, then, what's made him so fine and unprejudiced?" he'd said. "He's had chances of a freedom I've never had myself."

"Haven't you?" she said, smiling. "I'd have thought you had. Isn't it his nature, not just his circumstances, you're envious of?"

"No," he said. "It's the circumstance, it's *been* the circumstance, all along."

"It's very odd."

"I don't know," he said. "It happens in most families, I imagine."

"Does it?" She'd watched him with a smile. "I've never been jealous of Maureen, nor, as far as I'm aware, has she ever been jealous of me. We've quarrelled, but not as rivals, always more or less as equals."

"But then your parents threw you out," he said.

"They didn't throw us out."

"But you felt *disengaged* from them, disengaged *by* them, to a mutual degree. Whereas Steven always had more of my mother than I have."

"Yet you're very involved with your mother," she said.

"Am I?"

"I think so."

He'd been very surly: he hated to have elements of his behaviour pointed out, even if, absurdly, he'd pointed them out himself only a moment before. It was because he'd pointed them out that he hated her to refer to them: his having referred to them, he imagined, made them invalid.

"I think you're very naïve," she said. "It stands out a mile what you're jealous of."

Now, in the faded flat, he looked at her with a sense of defeat: both their pasts had caught up with them, she with her strange abstractness, her separateness not only from her parents but from her husband, he with his strange absorption in his family which, now that he needed it, refused to release him.

They sat in silence for a while. The room had a musty smell: he had brought some flowers; even they failed to dispel either by their brightness or their scent the drabness of the room; it was as if it were something she'd deliberately chosen.

"You being so depressed about it, depresses me," she said.

"Am I depressed?" he said.

"Not really by the room. I can have it decorated. I'll get some different furniture. It'll look like new in a week or two. The room itself is not important."

"Then what am I depressed by?" he said, for his spirits, the longer he was in the room, with the bustle of the town outside, sank lower and lower.

"It's because it's faced us," she said, "with one another, and there's no Phil, no Maureen or her husband, and no *mother*," she added, "to hide behind."

"I suppose that's something you wanted," he said. "I suppose that's what you mean by commitment."

She stroked her skirt around her knees: her figure, in

the vastness of the chair, looked tiny and vulnerable once again. He'd begun to hate her, and to be frightened of her; she represented more than he could imagine, some sticking to the past, some conformation of his past which he didn't like, some determination to secure him. He was wanting to hurt her all the time.

And as if she sensed his preoccupation she said, "What about you? Do your parents know about me?"

"No," he said, then added, for no reason he could think of, "I shouldn't think so."

"Do you want to tell them?"

"I see no point." He added, "They know I see someone. I'm out every night."

"But not with me."

"No," he said.

"Do I complicate your life?"

"No," he said again, stubbornly. He shook his head.

"You complicate mine. But in a way I like," she said, anxious to appease him.

They went out a little later; they had a meal in a café: there was scarcely anywhere to eat in the town.

When they went back, later in the evening, to the flat, he felt his resistance, a slow, half-hesitant rancour, rising. He'd become peculiarly brutal: it was he who was frightened, and he was frightened more by himself, he thought, than by anything outside. He had left her after midnight, when the last bus had gone, and had hitched a lift part of the way to the village in a lorry. It was two o'clock in the morning by the time he got back home.

His mother was quiet the following morning.

"Is anything the matter?" he said, bitterly, constrained himself by her silence and the gravity of the house. Steven and Richard had already gone to school.

"What time did you come in?" she said.

"I don't know," he said.

His mother was completing dressing herself behind a chair. It was something that he hated: she would come down with her worn skirt and jumper, or her faded dress, and stand behind a chair to put on her stockings. It was some habit from her childhood, for she always took off her

565

stockings in the evening, by the fire, and laid them on a chair; they were invariably in holes. It tormented him to watch her: it tormented him to ignore it. He never knew why she persisted, and she went on with it mechanically, finally flinging down the hem of her dress with an absurd gesture of propriety.

"Your dad said it was two o'clock."

"So what?" he said.

After he'd gone to bed, locking the back door to which he had a key, he'd heard his father rise and go downstairs, ostentatiously, to make some tea. Only three hours later he'd got up again to go to work.

Now his mother said, re-emerging from behind the chair, "It means none of us, particularly your father, gets any rest."

"I can't see why."

"Because we lie awake wondering where you are. Then, if we do fall asleep, we're woken up when you do come in. Then your dad has to get up at half-past five."

"He could get up later. It doesn't take him half an hour to walk to the pit." He went on eating his breakfast.

"He gets up earlier so he can light the fire. To help *me,* when I get up," she said.

"I'll get up and light it, then," he said. "Or Richard can. Or Steve."

"And who gets up to make sure they have?"

He didn't answer.

"If you're so little in the house I don't know why you go on living here," she said, turning away now to the sink and occupying herself with washing-up.

"I come here because I can't afford to live anywhere else. Not do that and go on paying something here," he added.

"You should apply yourself more to teaching," she said. "No wonder you were asked to leave. If you're out half the night how can you teach? You can't," she added, "have the concentration."

"It wasn't lack of concentration I was fired for," he said.

"No," she said, "but it might just as well have been."

He was caught in a dilemma which, a few years before, he could scarcely have imagined. He even began to look enviously at Reagan, and wondered, wildly, if he might not move in with him. Yet Michael's house was increasingly deserted: it was rumoured, when he didn't appear for a week, that he'd left the place for good, but late one night the light went on in the upstairs room and the next morning his figure could be seen across the backs.

New houses were being built across the village: his father had put down his name for one. People were moving in from neighbouring villages. A factory employing women sewing garments was set up in a prefabricated building in a yard adjacent to the pit. A new shop was opened; a corner of the village street was widened; a bus shelter had been built; the Miners' Institute hired entertainers whose names were heard on the radio. The Shaws had a television; shortly after, the Bletchleys bought a set as well.

Bletchley himself had been taken on, during his final term at university, by a large firm of cloth manufacturers in a neighbouring town: he worked in the laboratories. A few months later he was sent to America on a training course. He came back with a light-grey suit, a small, neat, metal-stemmed pipe and a slight American accent. A photograph of him appeared in the local paper. Mr. Bletchley, who had been promoted from his local job on the railway to a divisional office, bought a second-hand car. It stood in the road outside, the first car to be owned by anyone in that part of the village.

His father would gaze out at it in fury; he would listen with the same dull rage to the sound of the television set through the wall. "Ian looks after his parents," he would say, although Ian himself was scarcely ever to be seen in the village and only came home occasionally at weekends, staying half a day and only rarely a night. His father would drive him back to the station.

The village had a worn-out look; from the centre it looked like the suburb of a town: new houses sprawled across the slope of the adjoining hill, and reached up to the overgrown grounds of the manor. Over half a century of soot appeared to draw the buildings, the people, the roads, the entire village into the ground, the worn patches of ashes between the terraces gashed by children digging and worn into deep troughs by the passage of lorries. Very little of the brightness that he remembered as a child remained: so much had been absorbed, dragged down, denuded. Occasionally, on an evening, when he walked out of the place he would gaze back at if from an adjoining hill and see, in the deepening haze, the faint configuration of the village as it might have been—the smooth sweep of the hill with the manor, the church, the cluster of houses at the base. The light would deepen: the simple, elemental lines of the place would be confirmed; then lights sprang up, and across the slopes and in the deep declivities would be outlined once more the amorphous shape of buildings and the careless assemblage of factory, pit and sheds and the image, almost in a breath, would be wiped away.

He taught for three years in a variety of schools; in none did he stay for very long: he was preoccupied by a peculiar restlessness. His relationship with Elizabeth fluctuated from one extreme to another. For a time he gave up seeing her altogether, long after the flat had been redecorated and looked, superficially at least, not unlike a room in her sister's house. Then, of his own volition, he had gone back to her; they both struggled to escape, yet from what in their relationship he had no idea—his youth tormented her, her age preoccupied him; she tried to pretend at times she would soon re-marry.

Shortly after her decoration of the flat had been completed he was visited by her husband at home.

The man arrived one evening; his mother answered the door.

She showed him into the room at the front. She came in, flush-faced, her gaze hidden, however, behind the glare on her glasses.

"There's a Mr. Walton to see you," she said and he recoiled instantly, knowing it was him.

The man was short and fair-haired: he might have

been a schoolteacher like himself, or a clerk in a local office.

His embarrassment was even greater than Colin's. He refused a cup of tea and stood awkwardly before the empty fire; finally, at Colin's insistence, he sat in a chair.

"I came to see you about Elizabeth," he said, his hands clenched together. "I suppose she's mentioned me," he added.

"Yes," he said.

"We're not divorced yet."

"No," he had said. The man had stated it hopefully, as if suspecting Elizabeth might have told him something different.

He wondered what she'd seen in him, interpreting his extreme nervousness perhaps as sensitivity, and sensing in him someone she might mould: some image, hopefully, of her enterprising father.

"I sent a message once," Walton said.

"Yes," he said. He felt there was very little he could tell him.

"And I had a man, I don't know why, collecting evidence."

"Yes," he said again. "I thought you had."

"The fact is, I think it's only a temporary break. I think she got very frustrated, being at home. I'm trying to make plans to leave," he added.

"She said you already had. And that you'd decided, finally, not to."

"No, no," he said, suddenly. "She's twisting it there." Yet he gazed at him hopefully, as if the solution of his problem might come from him.

"What do you want me to do?" he said.

His mother had opened the door.

"Do you want a cup of tea?" she said, looking in intently, flushing at her concern.

"Mr. Walton says he wouldn't like one," he said.

"Oh, in that case." She looked at the man for this to be confirmed, but he said nothing, sitting stiffly in the chair, anxious for her to leave. "In case you do just let me know," she added.

Her footsteps sounded remotely from the other room, then the sound of Richard's voice inquiring.

"I thought, if you didn't see her, and recognized the reality of the situation, it might do some good," the man had said waiting a moment for the sound of the kitchen door to close. He added, "You see, from my point of view, you're just exploiting it."

It was as if someone else had persuaded him to come; that he were listening to some other voice, but faintly now, and which he could scarcely catch, struggling to decipher the message, the urgent things he'd been asked to say.

"I can't refuse to see her," Colin said. "I can't agree to that," he added.

"But to you," the man said quickly, "this is nothing. It's my life you're playing with, my marriage."

"But surely Elizabeth has something to say in that."

"Liz?" His voice thickened; the colour deepened in his face. His hands were vigorously entwined together: the pressure of some other place, and some other person, drove him on. "Elizabeth has a responsibility. It's something she's run away from. She has her problem, just like me, but you're preventing us from working it out," he added.

"She can see you if she wants to," he said. "You can see her. I'm not preventing that."

"You *are* preventing that. You've become a distraction." Yet the word wasn't precisely what he wanted. "You've become an obstacle to us getting closer, or resolving what is, after all, the problem of our marriage and which has nothing to do with you."

"It has now," he said. "I've been included." It was as if he suspected that Elizabeth had sent him herself: this was her latest attempt to "commit" him; yet the thought had no sooner arisen than he began to dismiss it.

"I want you to leave my wife alone. I want you to leave her alone," the man had said, almost chanting, his small face flushing even deeper, the eyes starting, his lips drawn back. He thrust himself forward from the chair: he appeared no longer to be in control of himself, to care what he said. "I want you to leave my wife alone."

He knew from the silence in the adjoining room that the man's words had carried through to the kitchen.

"I don't want any promises. I don't want any conditions. I'm telling you," he said, "to leave her alone. She is *my* wife. I married her. We have a right to decide this thing together."

"But she left you over a year ago," he said.

"I don't care when she left me. She's coming back. She'll see it's the only way in the end. Meanwhile," he raised his fist: he pushed it wildly in front of his face, "I'll kill you if you as much as see her again."

"But you can't kill *me*," he said, absurdly, wanting to laugh; to intimidate the man, he stood up himself.

"I don't mind what I do, or what punishment I get. She'll see how much I love her. She'll see how much I care," he said.

He turned to the door. Colin moved as if to open it for him, but the man flinched: he grasped the handle himself and stepped out quickly to the passage. For a moment he fumbled with the door to the street.

"I've told you. I've warned you. I can't do anything else."

He opened the door. When Colin followed him he could see a car parked some distance down the street, opposite Reagan's: its lights came on; its engine started. As it swept past a face peered out; its lights disappeared in the direction of the station.

"Who was that?" his mother said. Both she and Richard were standing in the kitchen, unable to sit down.

"His name is Walton."

"Yes," his mother said. "I gathered that."

"It's just something he wanted me to do," he said.

"He mentioned his wife." His mother gazed at him in angry surprise.

"Yes," he said.

"Have you been seeing his wife?"

"Yes," he said, and added, "They're getting divorced."

"They're *getting* divorced, or they *are* divorced?"

"Getting. They've been separated," he added, "for over a year."

Nothing had ever alarmed his mother as much.

She gazed at him for several seconds: Richard sat down and looked at a book.

"So this is your way," she said, "of getting back."

"But there's no getting back," he said. "It's someone I met by accident."

"Yes," she said, and added, "That's what you might well believe, my lad."

She sat down at the table; she was worn and thin; so much of the life that might have been in her now had gone, torn out with each of the children, torn out by the struggle to make ends meet. He even saw the kitchen as might Walton himself, if he'd come inside, its worn patches, its bare floor: only its furniture was new, yet its design was poor. The place was like some cave they'd lived inside, worn, eroded, hollowed out by the vehemence of their use.

His brother's slender face looked up at him, the eyes fresh, alert, still startled from Walton's shouting, his cheeks flushed.

"It's bad," his mother said. "It's something bad when you take a man's wife."

"I haven't taken her," he said. "She's no intention of going back."

"Hasn't she?"

Yet it was as if his mother had cut some final cord: the last attachment between them slipped away. She saw something bitter and remorseless in him, first with Steven, now with this, then with his job; the triumph they had looked for in his life had never occurred.

"It's bad," she said again, "it's bad," almost in the same way the man himself had chanted "I want you to leave my wife alone." She clung to the table as she might at one time, in some affliction or illness, or some quarrel with his father, have clung to him. "It's bad," she said again, remorselessly now, unable to leave go of her rancour, or of herself.

"There's nothing bad in it. Why should someone be tied to what they've done in the past? Particularly if they've let go of it themselves."

"*He* hasn't let go of it," she said. "And he's her husband."

572

"But what's a marriage count if she's dropped out of it?" he said.

"Oh," she said, "Colin, you don't know what marriage is."

"Don't I?"

"You've no idea." Some part of her own life had been disrupted: the man had left a conflagration in the house that neither of them could put out. "You've no idea what a marriage entails, and if one partner falters it's no man, no decent man, who comes along and takes advantage."

"I'll bring her," he said. "And you'll see where the advantage lies."

"I don't want her here," she said, so violently, so immediately, it was as if Elizabeth had come in the room with him. She got up quickly and turned to the fire: she poked it vigorously, her figure, its shoulders rounded, stooped to the flames. She put on more coal and dampened the blaze.

Smoke rose in thick clouds across the chimney.

And it was as if he had fought his last fight in the house: he could feel it slip away from him, his younger brother sitting there, his mother standing, turned away, then carrying the bucket out to the yard.

"I'll get it, Mother," Richard said.

He thought he might have left it then, gone for good: yet he stood gazing down at the smoke-filled hearth.

Outside his brother rooted at the coal. His mother came inside.

"I hope you're going to break with her," she said.

"No," he said. "I don't believe I shall."

She said nothing for a while.

"And what shall you do," she said finally, "when he comes again? Half the street must have heard his shouts. What will Richard think? What effect will it have on him?"

"I shouldn't think it'll have any effect at all," he said.

"He looks up to you," she said. "So does Steven."

"Does he?"

"I think he still does, despite how badly you've treated him." And strangely, as if to prove her point, they could hear Steven whistling cheerily across the backs, then his voice, "How are you, Dick?" as he called to his brother bringing in the coal.

Then, standing in the door, looking in at the lighted room, he gazed brightly from one to the other of them, and added, still cheerily, "Well, Mother, then. What's up?"

30

When he told Elizabeth about her husband's visit she'd been alarmed—as much by his own reaction, he thought, as anything else. "But aren't you *worried?*" she said, and added after a moment, "And what your mother must have thought."

He burst out laughing at this speculation.

"Why this sudden concern about my mother?" he said. "That's the last thing, I'd have thought, you'd have worried about."

"I don't know," she said. "She seems a remarkable woman. I can't imagine what her life is like—what her life has been like. It's a pity now I'll never know her."

"You can still come and see her. I won't take her injunction at its face value," he said.

"No," she said. "I'm not going to push it down her throat."

Yet what the "it" was to push down his mother's throat she didn't mention.

"Oh, I'm not worried about him coming," he said. He felt in fact, on reflection, more relieved. He liked to see strong feeling in others, it reassured him: it was the lack of feeling, in himself and others, that disconcerted him. He would even, as with Corcoran on his dismissal from the school, provoke someone deliberately in order to find out where he was; he could no longer accept the sobriety of life, he wanted to be an exception. The thought of Walton feeling anything violently was a consolation in the weeks

575

that followed; he even hoped he might come again, even angrier, more violent.

Yet her husband didn't come back. Each evening when he arrived home he looked for the car or for a figure waiting: neither was ever there. Several weeks had passed before he discovered the reason—Elizabeth had gone herself to see him.

"What did he say?" he asked her later.

"I think it was what he was really wanting all along," she said. "For me to see how much I'd hurt him. He was very cold. But then," she added, "you don't really know him, do you?"

He wondered if he did. The man was insignificant: she diminished herself in seeing him; he was beginning to see how ordinary she really was, despite her independence, her determination, if only for a while, to live alone. Perhaps, he speculated, it was some fault in her: her incapacities made her humourless. Perhaps there would never be anyone she trusted, or whom she allowed to live up to her expectations: she was always looking for a reason in everything.

"We're two such egotists," she said on one occasion. "I don't think anything will ever come of it."

Now she said, "He'd been instructed by his father to offer me a stake. In the firm, I mean. He thought I might be tempted."

"He must really be desperate," he said.

"I don't think he is. Not with me. I think it's his family that put him up to it: I think he's desperate because of them. It wasn't really at you he was shouting: I think he'd be relieved not to be married at all. I offered to divorce him, by putting the onus on to me. *They* wanted him to get me back or, if not, to get a divorce and cite you as co-respondent."

She'd had difficulty in telling him this: it was the thing she was most afraid of. All along she had told him, "It's quite safe, you know," and when he had asked, "Safe for what?" she had said, "Safe with me. You're not likely to be exploited." Now she said, "It's the one threat they've always held over me: that anyone I went with would be involved. I think, in the end, it's what kept Phil away. But even Derek drew back at that: it's done some good, I imagine. He's insisted that you shouldn't be used."

"Nevertheless, it won't stop them if they wanted to."

"No."

"Perhaps their solicitor might prefer it."

"Yes."

She watched him gravely.

"It's like being engaged. I'll have to marry you after all."

"But it's absurd," she said. "You occurred much later."

"Not that much later."

"Oh, far too late," she said, "for them."

Yet perhaps it was what the husband, and the family, had been attempting all along—to cool his ardour, to inhibit his relationship, her freedom, in this particular way. There was a sudden halt to their openness: he became evasive. He started seeing other women, particularly a teacher at one of the schools. She was younger, closer to his own age, yet empty, he found, and finally silly. Beside the gravity of Elizabeth she had no presence. The relationship ended as suddenly as it began: he found himself back in the flat in Catherine Street.

"Well, my boy," she had said, when he'd told her about the woman, "I feel more sorry for them than I do for you."

"Why?"

"You go from strength to strength. You suck the meat out. You drain these women. Like you drain your mother with your abuse."

"I don't drain her," he said.

"Don't you?" she said as if she knew his mother intimately, better than he knew her himself.

Yet there was a shallowness in her, a desperation: she was afraid he might leave her now for good.

For he did feel a strength. As the world faded all about him, as the people faded, as the bonds faded with his family he felt a new vigour growing inside.

"You'll leave me soon," she said one evening as they lay in bed. Yet she stated it not sadly, but as if relieved she too might be moving on.

577

They were like prisoners; he wondered where their new assertiveness had come from; he could see, secretly, no hope for her at all. She still worked at her father's shop, though she had mentioned, since she had trained as a pharmacist, she might move to a larger firm and take charge of a department. "I've had experience of administration: I'm not as stupid as I look."

"I never thought you were," he said.

"Oh, yes." She appeared quite confident of his assessment of her. "You're an opportunist, Colin. You'll move on from one advantage to another."

"It sounds awful," he said.

"You don't know what power is," she said. "Nor," she added, "what power you've got. I don't think anything will arrest you. The fact of the matter is you've been cut loose. Much to your chagrin, and perhaps to your loss. But from what I can see, you've no alternative. Once you are free, well," she paused, "I hope to hear of it but I don't hope I'll be around to see it."

Yet her view of him was never clear. It was one of her ways of fencing him off, threatening him with a future he couldn't see himself; his instinct was to cling to her more closely.

"Oh, you'll go, my boy," she said on another occasion when, provoked by her certainty, he'd attacked her. "You'll go, my boy. But *I*'ll not do it for you."

They were constantly battling with one another; chiefly him with her. There was a calmness in her: she had a strength, a humourless and unperceiving certainty which he felt he had to thrust against; he tested himself continuously against her.

"Oh, leave me, my boy," she would cry at times when his anger became too much, and the thrill of her challenge, the way she condescended to him, knowingly, in that phrase, "my boy," only drove him on.

"I want you to know you can rely on me," he said. "I want you to trust me. I love you. I'll do anything you want." Finally, in order to make himself feel real, he had said, "I'll marry you, if you want."

"Is that a proposal, or a threat?" she said.

"It's a proposal."

"It sounds like a challenge. I refuse to take it up. I refuse for your sake to take it up. You're not in love."

"But I am," he told her. "Tell me something I haven't done."

"You haven't loved me," she said. "*You* can't see it, but *I* know."

He tormented himself with this accusation.

"Show me," he would say. "*How* haven't I loved you?"

He proposed to her that they go away.

"Where?" she said.

"On holiday."

"Oh," she said, suddenly mocking. "But not for good?"

He hadn't answered: she was marking out areas in him he didn't like. His cantankerousness spread back towards his brother.

"Why won't you live, Steve?" he would say when he saw his brother, dumbly, getting on with his work. "Why won't you *live?*"

"I am living," his brother said, unruffled by these charges.

"You're going to end up down the pit, like my father. Something they threatened they'd never let me do."

"Nay, he'll end up as a manager," his father had said. He was wearied now almost to extinction by the pit himself. Each time he came home he seemed physically smaller: he shrank before them, lying prostrated by the fire, too tired to go to bed, too sick from exhaustion even to eat; his presence was a constant reproach, one he deliberately cultivated, flaunting himself before them, his tiredness, his diminution. "He'll not be like I am," he had added, indicating Steven's robust figure and the set good nature of his looks. As it was his brother was popular: he had left school and was apprenticed as a mining mechanic, attending, for part of his time, a local college. Yet he never thrust himself forward in anything; he had an incalculable strength which Colin envied.

"I can't understand why you let him give in to it," he would tell his father, indicating his father's own exhausted condition. "You were convinced at one time he would never go down."

"He's gone down," his father said, "because he wants to. He's gone down with a skill. I started with nothing. I was fresh from the land when I first went in. *He*'s been educated, he's been trained for it," he added.

The familiar arguments began again: but only Steven himself antagonized him, his docility. He could see so much more in his brother than Steven could see himself.

"Nay, I'm not complaining," Steven would say, shaking his massive head; muscles were hunched now around his shoulders. He had started playing football; he was in much demand: youths his own age as well as girls were constantly coming to the house. Steven would keep them at the door in deference to his mother, or only show them into the kitchen if he knew she was out. "I can't see what you're getting at," he added on another occasion when he and Colin were alone in the house.

"But what are you going to get out of all this?" he asked him.

"Nay, I'll get a living. Like thy gets a living out of teaching," his brother said.

"But it's slavery," he said. "My dad's a slave. You're a slave. They pay people enough to work down a mine, but never enough for them not to. It's like a carrot: put it up a bit each year. Like good-natured donkeys they go on turning it out."

His brother shook his head; he ran his hand through his tousled hair.

"You develop a slave mentality to live with these slaves. In acquiescing to it you're reinforcing it."

"But the mines have been nationalized," his brother said.

"So what difference does that make?" Colin said. He waited.

His brother rubbed his head again.

"Nay, I'm content with what I'm doing." He glanced up at him and smiled, but shyly, as if he were embarrassed by his concern. "If *I'm* content, I can't see why thy can't be content as well."

"Well, I'm not content," he said, bitterly.

"If tha's not content," his brother said, broadening his accent, "tha mu'n start to change it."

"I am starting," he said. "I'm starting with you."

"Nay, tha's starting with the wrong end. It's the head tha hast to get hold on."

"You're closest; I love you; you're the nearest. You're young, you're flexible, you're amenable to new ideas. You haven't been conditioned like my father has."

"Somebody's got to work down," he said. "I reckon I can do it better than most. I can improve conditions. I can do a better job. We're making changes all the time. What dost tha want me to do? Become a communist?"

"No," he said. "I want you to get out."

"Nay, I'm in," his brother said simply. "I can't get out. I like what I'm doing."

"It'll not bring you anything at all," he said, "except a dumb acceptance."

"And supposing I did get out: what'll happen to all the other slaves?"

"You'll leave them."

"And my dad?"

"My dad as well. *He's* accepted. Look where he is. Look where all of them are," he added, indicating with a sweep of his arm the whole of the village.

"My dad's too old to be down, that's why."

"You're too old to be down. You can set an example by getting out."

"Nay, I'm damned if I know what you're after," Steven said, sitting so sturdily there and looking so confused that Colin smiled, dazed by the strength and the obtuseness of his brother. "I think thy's got thyself into a muddle. You lie and cheat; you lied about Claire: you say no one should accept responsibility for ought."

"Except themselves."

"Accepting responsibility for yourself is accepting it on behalf of other people," his brother said with difficulty, thinking it out.

"It is," he said, "precisely. And not the other way about."

He laughed, looking at Steven now in triumph.

"You should experience everything about you, Steve. You should go out and live."

"Nay, thy's a hypocrite. Thy's a treacherous hypocrite," Steven said; he flushed deeply, looking away.

"But I'm other things," he said, "as well. Good things. I can help you. I'm not only bad. There are things about me you might accept. There are things about me you *should* accept. I know them."

"What things?" Steven said.

"Things you'd never experience yourself: things you'd never experience by accepting."

"It's like Jesus in the wilderness," his brother said.

"Is it?"

"When he was offered all the kingdoms of the world. I believe in what I'm doing. It does some good."

"Good. What good is that? That's Jesus's good. It's not the good of understanding; it's not the good of embracing evil—it's only the goodness, the primness, of cutting evil off."

"Nay," his brother said, gazing at him slowly. "I believe you are evil, Colin."

"So are you," he said. "I'm trying to get you to admit it."

Yet his brother continued to look at him in his heavy way, his brows furrowed, his gaze confused, his eyes troubled. He shook his head.

"Well," he said. "You're a mystery to me."

"But do you feel, Steven," he said, "that I want your good? Not your 'Jesus' good, but your fundamental good: the good that makes you real."

"Well," his brother said.

"You're after the 'good' that my parents want for you, out of fear. You've to disabuse them of that fear. You've got to break out."

"Aye." Yet he'd stopped listening to him. Richard came in from playing outside. He was at the grammar school now himself: he was at the top of his year. "You'd better ask Dick. He's the one with ideas."

"Oh, Richard's got brains, but he hasn't any ideas. Brains beget slavery as much as anything else. He'll go to university and be lost for good. He'll be cleaned out: 'brains' will become his panacea."

"Will they?" Richard said, his thin face pale, yet as if, almost perkily, he accepted his challenge.

"It takes all sorts," Steven said. "We don't all want to end up, tha knows, like you."

"Not like me, but *for* me," Colin said.

"Nor for you, for I think all thy's after is grabbing for thysen."

"Oh, Steve," he said, morosely, looking at his two younger brothers as if he would never really talk to them again.

It was but one of many quarrels that he had with his brother; they upset Steve: his lethargy drove Colin on. He watched him playing football: he had the same robustness, the same stubbornness, the same now almost conscious amiability as he was pushed up against the first deep waves of life. He hoped he would rise above them, not insist on breaking through, but on floating, on rising, not standing immobile, like a rock, moving nowhere, accepting his imperturbability as a gift rather than a handicap.

Coming away from one such match he had said, "I hear they've asked you to sign professional. There was a man there from the City."

"Yes," Steven said, his face reddened from the game, his nose, which had been damaged, fastened with plaster.

"Will you go?" he said.

"Well," he said, "it's quite a bit of brass."

"Won't they turn you into a sausage?"

"What sort of sausage?" he said, beginning to laugh. "Doing it for money."

"And what's wrong with money, all of a sudden? Dost mean tha doesn't want it when tha does a job of work?"

"But not for doing that," he said. "Doing it for the money becomes the end."

"Oh, I don't think so," Steven said.

A few days later two men came to the house: a chauffeur-driven car was parked at the door.

The two men went with his father into the front room: Steven was called in a little later.

"Do you want me to come in with you?" Colin said.

"Nay, I'm bigger than all three on 'em," his brother said. "I mu'n think I can look after it mesen."

A few days later the car came again; his father and Steven were taken off to town. Steven had put on his suit; his father, too, had put on a suit, but taken it off again and said, "I'm not kow-towing to them lot," and had gone finally in a sports coat of Richard's.

They came back almost four hours later.

His father's face was flushed. He clapped his hands as he came in the house.

"It's done," he said.

Steven followed him in more slowly, smiling, looking round. His head, strangely, was stooped as if in fear of the ceiling: it was as if he suspected he was much bigger than he was.

His father, feeling in the inner pocket of the sports coat, produced a cheque.

He unfolded it on the table.

"Two hundred pounds," he said slowly, following the writing with his fingers then stabbing at the figures. "And all due," he added, "to my powers of persuasion."

"Well," his mother said. She looked at Steve—it was as if all she'd suspected of him had now come true. There was some gift, some peculiar power, unspoken, in her son: he'd brought it in at the door, casually, neither dazzled nor even surprised by it himself.

"Nay, but it fastens him up more firmly," Colin said. "Why did you sell him for as much as that?"

"Oh, take no notice," his mother said. "You can have no doubt he would have a comment."

Half of it was put in the bank for his parents; half of it was put in the bank for Steve. His parents bought a television set; a carpet was bought for the stairs; an electric fire was fitted into the fireplace in the other room.

The following spring the Shaws left the house next door and went to live in one across the village. A family with two young children moved into the empty house. At first the strangeness was acute: the sound of crying came through the walls each morning, and of the man shouting impatiently at night.

Beyond, too, in the Reagan house, Michael finally had disappeared: he was reported being seen in a seaside town, serving as a waiter, then as a doorman at a cinema. Workmen came and carried out refuse from the front room of the house. An elderly couple moved in, a miner who was still working at the pit, his wife and, a few weeks later, an older parent, a woman with white hair and a reddened face who, strangely, would come and stand in the garden as, years before, Mr. Reagan himself had done. She would gaze over at the children playing in the field and occasionally, calling to them, pass them sweets across the wooden fence.

"When you think of the war, and all we've lived through here together," his father said. "There's only us and the Bletchleys left." The Battys, too, a year previously, had left the village, the father with a chest complaint which had made him leave the pit; the various brothers and sisters had moved to the town. "How long are we going to be here?" he added. "No inside lavatory, no bath: there's people who came here long after us have been rehoused."

Once the impetus of Steven's football had faded, his father went back into his previous decline. From going to watch every match he now, on occasion, made excuses, and though he would wait eagerly for Steven to come home each Saturday evening, the significance of Steven playing slowly died. He would sit with a fixed smile on his face as he listened to details of the game which, genially, Steven was always pleased to describe. When he did go to the match he came back invariably disgruntled, complaining bitterly about the cold, or the way Steven himself had been cheated or let down by the other players. The impetus of his children's lives had passed him by, leaving him stranded. He would examine Richard's books and question the marks, look at the remarkable results and favourable comments Richard brought home in his school reports, and give some acknowledgment which both disappointed Richard and yet drove him on to greater efforts. A master came from the school to talk of Richard's university chances.

"Fancy," his father said when the man had gone, "who'd have thought it: to come so far from where we began."

One week-end Bletchley came home. Colin called at his house. "Oh, come in," his mother said brightly when she opened the door. "He's in the front room."

Ian was now huge: his neck had tightened; a heavy jowl concealed his chin; his waist was scarcely concealed by a reddish waistcoat. He was sitting in his shirt-sleeves when Colin came in but quickly stood up and pulled on a jacket. He'd been watching television and didn't turn it off. He appeared to be in no good humour, as if he resented being home.

"I'll leave you two together," Mrs. Bletchley said, closing the door with a smile at Colin.

Bletchley almost filled the room; he indicated the only other chair to Colin and they sat down together, Bletchley's gaze turned resentfully to the television screen. "How have you been?" he said, watching the picture. "I hear your brother's signed up for the City."

He described his present teaching; he was, as a supernumerary, being moved on from school to school.

"Don't you fancy getting anything steady?" Bletchley said. "Not that there's much scope in any case in teaching." He took out a pipe and quickly lit it. "I'm on a management course at present. That's why I'm home. No work but lectures for the next three weeks. After that I start in the office. I'll have a department of my own inside three years: after that, the sky's the limit."

"I'll be leaving soon," he said.

"Where to?"

"I don't know," he said. "I'll go abroad."

"Teaching?"

"Whatever comes to hand."

Bletchley said nothing for a while: clearly, he'd cast him off in his mind. As if prompted by this thought, he said finally, "What happened to Reagan?"

"He was working in a cinema, the last I heard."

"His mother died. Did he tell you that?"

"No," he said.

"My mother got a message from the hospital."

"Poor old Michael," he said.

"Oh, I don't know. I reckon he'll be better off without. Do you remember that violin? And going to Sunday School? It seems funny to think of it." Bletchley gazed out at the street as he might at an unknown town. There was nothing to connect him with the place at all.

Mrs. Bletchley brought in some tea.

"Are you two going out?" she said.

"Where to?" Bletchley said.

"Oh, anywhere. Anywhere young men are likely to go," she said.

She set down the tea on a tiny table; the room was even cleaner than Mrs. Shaw's had been.

"There's nowhere to go to," Ian said. "Not round here." He turned, with renewed discontent, towards the television.

"Well," Mrs. Bletchley said, handing Colin the tea, "I'll leave the two of you to it, then."

"It's a terrible place. I don't know why they go on living here," Bletchley said. Through the wall Colin could hear Richard's voice calling to his mother: he wondered how much of their life had been heard through the wall, and what impression it had made on Bletchley. "I tell them to move, but they never do. Do you remember that Sheila you used to go with? She has seven children. *Seven*." He picked up his cup blindly, still gazing at the screen.

He was still gazing at it an hour later when Colin got up to leave. "Oh, are you going?" Bletchley said, standing up himself and thrusting out his hand. "Where did you say you were going?"

"Abroad," he said, grasping the podgy hand.

"What are you going to do?"

"I've no idea." Bletchley gazed at him blindly, nodding his head.

"It doesn't sound very promising."

"No," he said.

"What happened to that Stafford?"

"I don't know," he said. "I never heard."

"Give my regards to your mother, in case I don't see her before I leave," he said.

He'd already turned back to the screen before he'd reached the door.

"How *is* your mother?" Mrs. Bletchley said and as he reached the door she added, "I'm sorry you're not going out. I get so worried about Ian at times."

"Why?" he said.

"He's progressing so well, but he ought to be married."

"Oh, he's bound to be married soon," he said.

"Do you think so? He never goes out with *girls*."

"Who does he go out with?" he said.

"Well," she said, "he drinks a lot, on top of which he studies. His work, too," she added, "is very demanding. His boss thinks he'll be in charge of the works when he retires. And that, Ian's told us, is in less than *ten* years!" She gestured back to the kitchen where Mr. Bletchley sat reading a paper. "We sit here at times and think of when you and Ian were boys and wonder how all these incredible things have happened. You'll be leaving soon yourself."

"Yes," he said.

"Well," she said, gazing at him. "Give my love to your mother."

One evening he was coming down the street and a figure came out of a ginnel at the end of the terrace and called his name, speculatively, as if unsure he'd identified him correctly.

At first he thought it was Reagan; then, in the light, he recognized the red hair.

"Hi, Tongey," Batty said. "How ya' keeping?"

"All right," he said, and added, "What're you doing down here?"

"I came to see Stringer. I've just discovered he's left." He gazed about him aimlessly, almost like Bletchley might have done, at the empty street.

"They left two or three years ago," he said, and added, "Where have you been?"

"I've been in the nick."

"What for?"

"For nicking." Batty looked at him with a great deal of

irritation; his tall figure was stooped, his head turned from the light.

"Come and have a drink," Colin said.

"Where?" Batty said.

"Wherever you like."

They walked back together towards the centre of the village.

"You can't lend us any money?" Batty said.

"Yes," he said. "How much do you want?"

"How much have you got?"

"Two or three pounds."

"Do you have a cheque book?"

"Yes," he said.

Batty said nothing for a while. When they reached the public house at the centre of the village he went quickly ahead as if anxious to get inside: once in he went directly to a table.

Colin went to the bar and ordered the drinks, calling back to Batty to find out what he wanted.

"Whisky," Batty said, and added, "A double," looking round slowly at the bar then shielding his face.

When he carried the drinks over he said, "How much would you like?"

"As much as you want."

"How much have you got already?"

"To tell you the truth," Batty said, avoiding looking at him directly, "I'm skint. I came out today. I've got the clothes on my back and nothing else."

"What were you had up for stealing?" he said.

"You name it," Batty said, emptying the glass at a single swallow.

Colin bought him another: the extraordinary pallor of Batty's face was relieved by bright red patches on either cheek.

"Stringer was my last bet."

"I can let you have ten pounds," he said.

Batty glanced away. "We'll, it's better than nothing, I reckon," he said.

When he'd written the cheque Batty examined it before putting it away.

"I could change this, you know, and make it a hundred."

"Why don't you?" he said.

"Are you tempting me?" he said.

"It's up to you. If you can get away with it I reckon it's worth it. There's not that in the account," he added.

"What you been doing with yourself?" Batty said as if he had misjudged the success of Colin's life entirely.

"I'm teaching."

"Mug's game."

"Like being in prison."

"I was in the nick because I was framed. I'll never be framed again." He looked at his glass, which he'd emptied a second time at a single swallow.

"Fancy another?"

"I wouldn't mind."

"Have you been back home?" he asked him when he brought the drink across.

"What for?"

"Where are you going to sleep tonight?"

"I'll find somewhere," Batty said. "They live in town. My dad. I called today. They wouldn't see me. Go with open arms: what do you get?"

"What about your brothers?"

"Two of 'em are inside already: their wives don't reckon much to having me around."

He gave him a pound when they went outside. He waited at the bus stop with him for a bus to take him back to town.

"Do you remember that hut we had?" Batty said. He looked about him at the deserted, lamp-lit street. "What a dump," he added. When the bus came he got on without adding anything further, climbed the stairs and disappeared.

One evening, visiting the town, he came out of a pub in something of a daze and gazed around. It was early evening: the sky was clear; sunlight lit up the roofs above his head; an evening bustle came from the city centre; farther along the road was the dark, pillared building of the Assembly Rooms; a faint sound of music drifted down the street.

He walked back slowly to the bus.

When, a little later, the bus crossed the river, the sun was setting beyond the mills.

"It could be Italy," a voice said behind him and when he turned a man gestured off towards the river. "Italy," he said again, indicating the yellow light.

31

She had known the break was coming and said nothing when he told her.

He had told her he was leaving on two occasions before: both times, however, he'd finally come back.

Now, he could see, she knew it was different.

"I'll have to go," he said. "I have no choice."

Still she didn't answer.

He'd been sitting across the room; he got up and went to her chair. There was a peculiar immunity about her. Beyond her he could see directly into the street, the parked cars, the bustle of the town from the opposite end.

"Will you stay here yourself?" he said.

"No."

"Where will you go?"

"I've no idea."

She sat with her back straight; she was wearing a light-blue dress; her hands were clenched in her lap, her head erect. Her gaze was abstracted: it was as if she'd removed herself from the room entirely.

"Well," she said, putting up her hand. "We'd better say goodbye."

He drew her up: almost formally, as whenever they met, they kissed each other on the cheek.

"It's very strange," she said. "This town. I wonder if I'll ever leave it. In the old days children stayed in the same community. When we discover everywhere is very much the same, when we find that everyone is very much like us, when we realize the world is smaller than we thought, do you think we'll all drift back? I used to despise Maureen for staying here; it is sterile in one sense, but does it have to be? Doesn't the change of renewal come wherever you live?"

"No," he said.

"You make it sound so clear. But all you do is take the destitution with you: of belonging nowhere; of belonging to no one; of knowing that nowhere you stay is very real."

"Why shouldn't it be real?" he said.

"Don't the dead, doesn't the past only make it real?"

"No," he said again. "The dead just hold it back."

"But what is there?" she asked him. "Doesn't everything finish the way it began? Won't I end up working with my father? Despite all I might do in order to avoid it. I might even," she added "take over the shop."

"And marry a pharmacist," he added, "to go with it?"

"Why not?"

"I don't know," he said. "Although it would be terrible if it turned out you were right."

"Shakespeare never travelled farther than London; Michelangelo never went farther from Florence than Rome; Rembrandt stayed virtually where he was. It's an illusion to think you've to break the mould. The mould may be the most precious thing you have."

"Yes," he said. "But I wouldn't believe it. Travelling is only one way of breaking it."

"Why not stay?"

"Would you want us to get married, then?" he said.

She laughed: she was driving him in circles, yet it was an argument she couldn't conclude.

"My chances of victory are so much less than yours," she said.

"In being older?" he said.

"In being a woman."

"But then, that should be more of a challenge."

"Yet I'm a woman formed," she said, "by old conceptions. I believe, at the end of it, there is only one man. Just as for a man there is only one woman. Not any man, or any woman, but one man. And one woman. Despite the circumstance."

"In any case," he said, freshly, "I don't believe it."

"Perhaps you'll learn that later," she said.

"No," he said. "I refuse to believe it."

"You may refuse, my boy," she said. "But you'll come to it in the end. One man: one woman. The unity of that is irrefutable; growth is impossible without it."

It sounded so much like her older self that he laughed. He took her hand.

"It's been a friendship of a kind," he said.

"Oh, I wouldn't wish to make it sound decent," she said. "There's a lot of bitterness here you'll never see. I'm the senior partner. I've had my chance: I feel it's my duty not to show it."

"But you try to diminish yourself so much," he said. "You make the mould yourself instead of allowing life to do it for you. I believe that life is limitless, that experience is limitless: yet it can't be conceived by standing still."

"Go out and experience it, in that case, then," she said. "Perhaps when you come back, *if* you come back, you'll see you may have been mistaken. What, after all, is a community if it isn't formed by people who are committed, who commit their lives, and have their lives committed for them?"

"But a community isn't anything," he said. "It exists," he went on, "of its own volition. When the volition goes, the community goes with it. It's no good hanging on."

"Oh," she said bleakly, gazing at him as if there were a great deal she might have told him. It was like a child crying to be let outside a door.

"I can see now," he said, "the difference between us. You have no faith. Whereas everything that happens to me, even the worst things, merely strengthens mine. Because things are bad, because they only get worse, faith is all the stronger."

"Faith in what?"

"Impossibility. Everything is allowable; everything is permissible; anything can happen. It's arrogance," he added, "to assume it can't. Not an arrogance to assume it should."

"Well," she said quietly, sitting once more, gazing at her hands, the fingers intertwined, lying in her lap. "Well," she said, tired, as if he were a force that couldn't be countered.

"But I can do so much," he said. "I don't know what makes me feel it: but I know it must be true." And when she looked up he said, "I was a pessimist like you. Now I'm diffcrent. I wish you'd take this assurance from me. For I haven't just taken: I've given something back."

"Yes," she said, then added, "It's only youth. You can't give that back, however much you wanted."

So they parted with a certain bitterness, she couldn't help it. Perhaps even she thought, or hoped, one part of her, at this last moment too he would finally come back: that there was something intangible between them that only temporarily he resisted. Yet he never went again: his last glimpse of her was of her standing in the room, for she left him to close the door. He glanced back, frowning, as he might at a shadow he couldn't make out, and feeling guilty, as he did now about almost everything.

Once in the street, however, he felt the certainty return; a cloud had lifted: the town, even the village when he finally arrived there, no longer held him. There was nothing to detain him. The shell had cracked.

His mother came to the station: it was a Sunday afternoon. The place was quiet; there was the one train that stopped on its way to London.

"We shall miss you," his mother said. Yet it was as if he had left her a long time ago. They stood in silence waiting for the train.

The air was still: from farther up the line came the haze of the other villages, with just the blankness of the cutting in the other direction.

He had saved, over the previous four years, nearly fifty pounds. He had little luggage: a bag he carried easily in one hand.

"Well," his mother said with relief when the train came into sight.

The large engine thundered by the platform.

He found a seat near the front.

His mother came to the door: he stooped and kissed her.

There was a dull pallor in her skin.

"And you haven't any lodgings," she said, "or anything."

"I don't need lodgings," he said. "I can always sleep on the street."

"No. Not in the street," she told him, and added, almost aimlessly, "Think of the people who love you, Colin."

She had begun to cry.

She got out a handkerchief and glanced away.

He waited impatiently then for the engine to start. Everything was quiet in the station; only two other people had got on the train.

"Nay, I shall come back," he said. "I'm not going off for ever."

"No," she said. Yet it was as if she sensed she would never see him again, or he the village, or the family: the ugliness of the engine would take him away.

The whistle sounded.

"Well," he said. "Don't wait."

"Oh," she said. "I'll wait," and raised her hand, vaguely, as the engine started.

The carriage jolted: a moment later it was gliding away beneath the bridge. He leaned out and glimpsed her figure; then, in a cloud of steam, she disappeared.

The cutting obscured the village. Finally, as the embankment sank he saw the church, the ruin of the manor on the distant hill, the idling of the smoke above the pit.

The side of the cutting rose again and when, a little later, the train ran out across the fields all signs of the village had disappeared. Above a distant line of trees a smear of blackish smoke appeared.

THE BIG BESTSELLERS
ARE AVON BOOKS

☐	**The Thorn Birds** Colleen McCullough	35741	$2.50
☐	**Lancelot** Walker Percy	36582	$2.25
☐	**Oliver's Story** Erich Segal	36343	$1.95
☐	**Snowblind** Robert Sabbag	36947	$1.95
☐	**A Capitol Crime** Lawrence Meyer	37150	$1.95
☐	**Voyage** Sterling Hayden	37200	$2.50
☐	**Lady Oracle** Margaret Atwood	35444	$1.95
☐	**Humboldt's Gift** Saul Bellow	38810	$2.25
☐	**Mindbridge** Joe Haldeman	33605	$1.95
☐	**Polonaise** Piers Paul Read	33894	$1.95
☐	**A Fringe of Leaves** Patrick White	36160	$1.95
☐	**Founder's Praise** Joanne Greenberg	34702	$1.95
☐	**To Jerusalem and Back** Saul Bellow	33472	$1.95
☐	**A Sea-Change** Lois Gould	33704	$1.95
☐	**The Moon Lamp** Mark Smith	32698	$1.75
☐	**The Surface of Earth** Reynolds Price	29306	$1.95
☐	**The Monkey Wrench Gang** Edward Abbey	30114	$1.95
☐	**Beyond the Bedroom Wall** Larry Woiwode	29454	$1.95
☐	**Jonathan Livingston Seagull** Richard Bach	34777	$1.75
☐	**Working** Studs Terkel	34660	$2.50
☐	**Shardik** Richard Adams	27359	$1.95
☐	**Anya** Susan Fromberg Schaeffer	25262	$1.95
☐	**The Bermuda Triangle** Charles Berlitz	25254	$1.95
☐	**Watership Down** Richard Adams	19810	$2.25

Available at better bookstores everywhere, or order direct from the publisher.

AVON BOOKS, Mail Order Dept., 250 West 55th St., New York, N.Y. 10019

Please send me the books checked above. I enclose $_____(please Include 25¢ per copy for postage and handling). Please use check or money order—sorry, no cash or COD's. Allow 4-6 weeks for delivery.

Mr/Mrs/Miss_____

Address_____

City_____State/Zip_____

BB 6-78

AVON ◭ THE BEST IN
BESTSELLING ENTERTAINMENT

- [ ] **Your Erroneous Zones**
  Dr. Wayne W. Dyer — 33373 $2.25
- [ ] **Monty: A Biography of Montgomery Clift**
  Robert LaGuardia — 37143 $2.25
- [ ] **Majesty** Robert Lacey — 36327 $2.25
- [ ] **Death Sails the Bay** John R. Feegel — 38570 $1.95
- [ ] **Q&A** Edwin Torres — 36590 $1.95
- [ ] **Love and War** Patricia Hagan — 37960 $2.25
- [ ] **If the Reaper Ride** Elizabeth Norman — 37135 $1.95
- [ ] **This Other Eden** Marilyn Harris — 36301 $2.25
- [ ] **Berlin Tunnel 21** Donald Lindquist — 36335 $2.25
- [ ] **Ghost Fox** James Houston — 35733 $1.95
- [ ] **Ambassador** Stephen Longstreet — 31997 $1.95
- [ ] **The Boomerang Conspiracy**
  Michael Stanley — 35535 $1.95
- [ ] **Gypsy Lady** Shirlee Busbee — 36145 $1.95
- [ ] **Good Evening Everybody**
  Lowell Thomas — 35105 $2.25
- [ ] **The Mists of Manitoo**
  Lois Swann — 33613 $1.95
- [ ] **Flynn** Gregory Mcdonald — 34975 $1.95
- [ ] **Lovefire** Julia Grice — 34538 $1.95
- [ ] **The Search for Joseph Tully**
  William H. Hallahan — 33712 $1.95
- [ ] **Delta Blood** Barbara Ferry Johnson — 32664 $1.95
- [ ] **Wicked Loving Lies** Rosemary Rogers — 40378 $2.25
- [ ] **Moonstruck Madness** Laurie McBain — 31385 $1.95
- [ ] **ALIVE: The Story of the Andes Survivors**
  Piers Paul Read — 39164 $2.25
- [ ] **Sweet Savage Love** Rosemary Rogers — 38869 $2.25
- [ ] **The Flame and the Flower**
  Kathleen E. Woodiwiss — 35485 $2.25
- [ ] **I'm OK—You're OK**
  Thomas A. Harris, M.D. — 28282 $2.25

Available at better bookstores everywhere, or order direct from the publisher.

THE HISTORY-MAKING
#1 BESTSELLER
ONE YEAR ON
THE NEW YORK TIMES LIST!

THE THORN BIRDS

COLLEEN McCULLOUGH

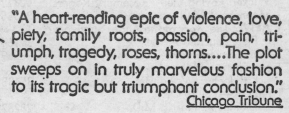

"A heart-rending epic of violence, love, piety, family roots, passion, pain, triumph, tragedy, roses, thorns....The plot sweeps on in truly marvelous fashion to its tragic but triumphant conclusion."
<u>Chicago Tribune</u>

"A perfect read...the kind of book the word blockbuster was made for."
<u>Boston Globe</u>

 35741 $2.50

TTB   6–78